Valkyrie Knight

Also by Tyler Weaver

The Griffon and the Dragon series
The Maiden's War

VALKYRIE KNIGHT
Tyler Weaver

First edition (all versions) December 2022

Cover art and illustrations by Bekarys Zhabagin

ISBN 978-1-7330341-4-2 (Hardcover)
ISBN 978-1-7330341-5-9 (Trade Paperback)
ISBN 978-1-7330341-7-3 (KDP Trade Paperback)
ISBN 978-1-7330341-6-6 (eBook)

Published by the Royal War Ministry Press
Email: rwmpress@gmail.com

The book is published with print-on-demand technology and that little line of numbers used to track printings within a single edition is unnecessary. The more you know!

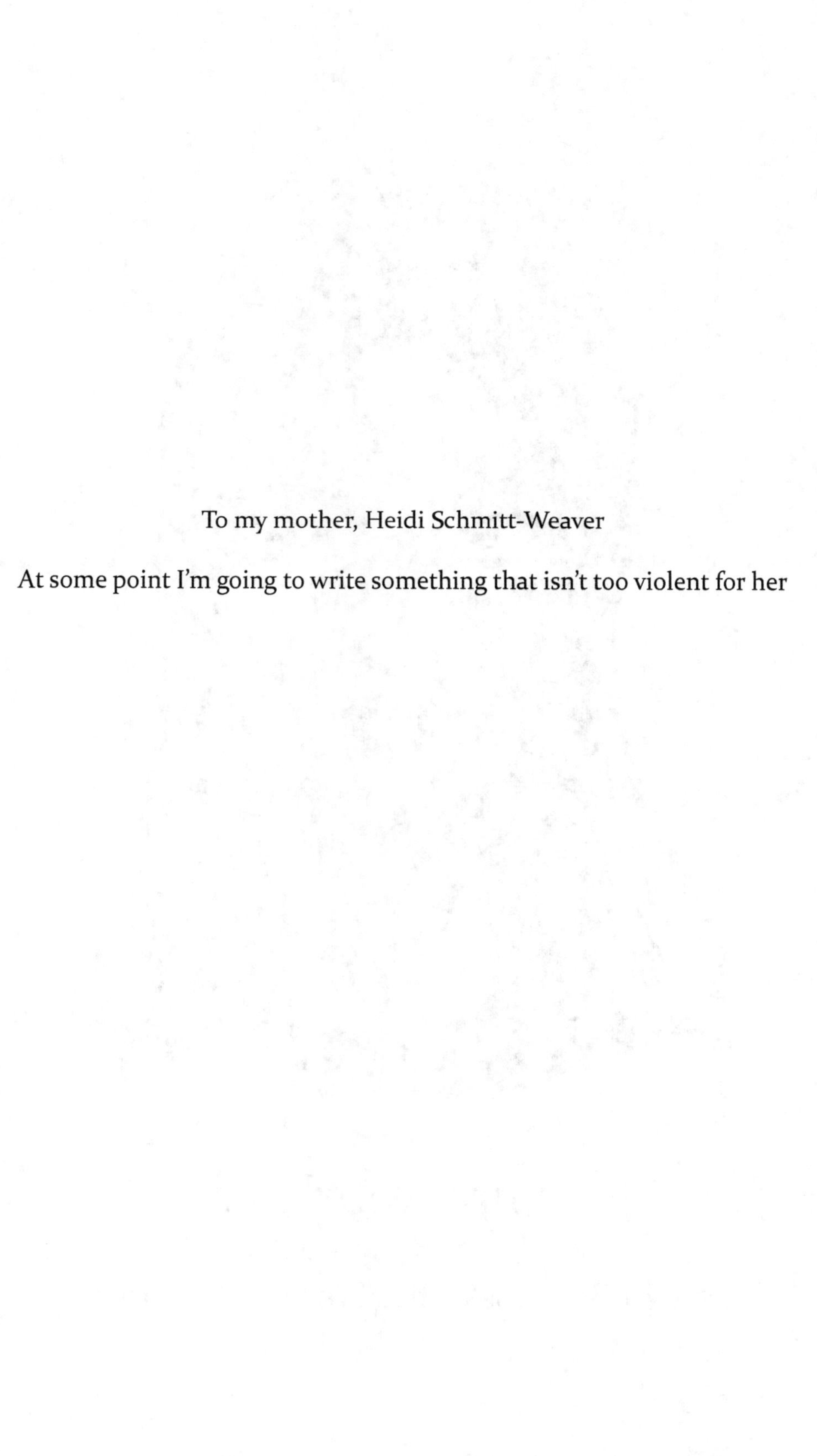

To my mother, Heidi Schmitt-Weaver

At some point I'm going to write something that isn't too violent for her

Arilin Wehrherz

Crown Princess of the Western Kingdom

Sophia Rose

Private First Class, 24th Infantry Regiment

Table of Contents

Chapter 1
Vigil of the Princess

Every church bell in the Capital was ringing. They seemed to reverberate in her soul, ringing around the great, dark void her brother had left behind. She supposed it was as true for the Kingdom as it was for her.

Prince Adrian had been many things to many people. He had been her father's son, a strong and handsome heir untouched by the family's scandals. He had been a friend to her mother and had made it clear he preferred her to his own. He had been a leader to his men and a hero to the people, *his* people one and all. He could have walked into the grimiest slum in the Capital and been greeted with roses. He had been someone's lover, she was sure. Probably a lot more than one someone, yet he was so discreet nobody had ever breathed a word. He was her brother. She loved him so much it hurt. And he had been cut down in his prime and left the weight of the Kingdom on her shoulders.

It was suffocating. Princess Arilin's eyes blurred with tears again as her horse rocked gently under her, the soft clatter of Midnight's hooves on the cobblestones sounding under the all-encompassing pealing of the bells. She had thought she was out of tears to cry after she had watched them take her brother's body off the ship that morning in the harbor, a big liner-turned hospital ship painted with the Red Cross and draped black in mourning. They had loaded his coffin onto an artillery caisson for the long ride up to the High City and she had managed to keep it together long enough to get back into the carriage with her mother. She had wept for *hours* and thought she was done. Clearly she had been wrong.

A concerned voice slowly worked its way through her misery, "...lady... milady, are you all right?" She shook her head quickly and looked over at the source of the voice, a red-headed Valkyrie Knight in the regiment's summer dress uniform, pink jacket, powder-blue riding breeches and snow-white boots all swathed in gold lace. A second jacket hung gallantly over her shoulder on a strap. As the woman leaned in towards her concernedly the High City's harsh streetlights managed to turn even her sunburned complexion pale. She didn't even want to think what she herself looked like as Captain Helbrecht went on, her brow knitting in concern, "You're crying." Reining her horse to a stop, she held up a hand to halt their escorts and went on, "Milady, we do *not* have to do this. Nobody is going to think less of you."

Arilin quickly wiped her eyes and shook her head. Midnight had stopped with the other horses, and she self-consciously straightened up and looked back at her companion. Trying to keep her voice from cracking, she replied, "No, I do." She shook her head and tried to smile, "Sorry... I'll keep it together." She nudged Midnight forward and went on, "Come on, we're late as is."

She didn't have to look back at the red-haired hussar to feel the dubious look she was getting. After a couple seconds the hoofbeats started up behind her again, and she heard the woman pull her horse alongside her and reply dubiously, "If you say so, milady." She went on, "I can't say I understand why."

Arilin sighed heavily, "You will when we get there."

"Just give me a minute with you when we get there." Captain Helbrecht snorted, "You're a mess."

"Thanks, I guess." Arilin looked over and gave her a half-smile, "What's your *first* name, by the way?"

The woman gave her a surprised look. In a happier time Arilin was sure she would have burst out laughing. She managed to compose herself and said, "Alyssa, milady." She snickered, clearly at herself, "I apologize. I should have introduced myself properly earlier."

"It's fine." A well-dressed man on the sidewalk recognized her and tipped his hat, and Arilin waved back politely and went on, "I should be thanking you for coming up on short notice."

Alyssa chuckled, "Milady, if you'd asked we would have sent every trooper we have in the Capital. These two," She nodded at the pink-jacketed hussars riding alongside them through the growing crowd of mourners, "Both volunteered."

"Well, thank you regardless." Arilin replied, smiling sadly, "You're just back from the front yourself, aren't you?"

The captain raised an eyebrow, "Yes, actually." She went on, "The colonel wanted me to come back to help stand up the Fourth Squadron." She snorted and went on, "Your little appeal for volunteers really paid off, milady. We're swimming in girls right now with nobody to train them properly."

Arilin was opening her mouth to ask what she had meant when she spotted the lights of Saint Valeria's bell tower rising above the buildings nearby and the crowd suddenly thickened, black-clad mourners spilling out of the Cathedral Square ahead. With the High City's clubs and theaters closed for the occasion there was really nowhere else to go for the evening. Arilin wondered darkly how many of the people starting to crowd around them were resenting her brother for cancelling their nightly fun.

"Hey, it's the princess!" Someone shouted, and a loud murmur ran through the crowd as people pressed forward to get a look at her. Arilin self-consciously straightened herself on Midnight's back and waved to the onlookers as Alyssa kicked her horse ahead, shouting for people to make way. Her other two escorts fell in alongside her protectively and they pressed forward against the tide towards the square.

They made their way around the last corner and the bells grew suddenly louder, the ringing echoing from the buildings around them and submerging the crowd as the Cathedral of Saint Valeria rose above them in all its fiery splendor. Every surface of the building burned with light, stained glass windows a hundred feet high painting the history of the Faith and the Kingdom across the night through a filigree of flying buttresses. Even from the distance Arilin could make out Maximilian beheading the Faceless King, the tyrant's dark robes and blood-red aura an ugly smudge in the glory of the light.

One of her escorts nudged her and she looked over to see a group of Foot Guards at the entrance to the square standing stiffly to attention, their rifles upright in salute. Arilin saluted back a little self-consciously and the men relaxed and went back to watching the crowd, she supposed for any unsavory types who would like to see another member of the Royal Family lying in state. Their sergeant pushed his way forward and shouted over the crowd at Alyssa, "Ma'am! What's the princess here for?"

The red-haired hussar yelled back, "Vigil party!" She gestured at the cathedral ahead, "Where are they staging?"

"For vigil?" The man asked, as a murmur went through the crowd around them. Alyssa nodded and he replied, "Go in the front doors, they're using the atrium."

"Thanks!" Giving the man a nod, Alyssa twisted in her saddle to look back at the three of them and said, "Come on, we're going in the front."

Arilin nodded and nudged Midnight forward after the woman, her two escorts following a moment later. The crowd parted respectfully before them, faces flat and pale as they looked up at her under the arc lamps lighting the cathedral square. Men removed their hats as they rode by, and Arilin swallowed hard and waved weakly in acknowledgement as her stomach churned and she tasted bile in the back of her throat. It occurred to her dimly that she hadn't eaten all day.

Looking out over the square as they rode around the cathedral she made out a long line of mourners stretching around the far side of the square, shuffling into the cathedral's side entrance. Saint Valeria's was laid out like a gigantic cross facing east, and people were spilling from the near side's great double doors, catching sight of them and hurrying over to get a look as they made their way around the square. Arilin understood at once. Adrian, her brother, was lying in state at the very center of the great cross underneath the cathedral's great bell tower, where he would remain until they lowered him into his space in the Royal Family's burial vaults beneath.

Arilin felt her world spin at the thought. The harsh streetlights and the cathedral's warm stained glass blurred together for a second, until a strong hand on her shoulder snapped her back to reality. Looking over, she saw one of her escorts had reached and grabbed hold of her. The woman gave her a hard look and said, "You're looking a little wobbly, milady."

"I'm fi…" Arilin trailed off. She wasn't fine and she knew it. Finally shaking her head, she gave the woman's hand a reassuring squeeze and said, "Thanks… I haven't eaten much today, I'm sorry."

The hussar snorted and took her hand back, "Don't you *dare* faint on us, milady." She turned and gave her another glare, "I'm assuming you know not to lock your knees when we're standing up there. That *will* make you faint."

"Ah… yes!" Arilin lied.

The woman, who she saw was a hard-bitten sergeant now that she had gotten a look at her, chuckled and said, "Don't lie, milady. It doesn't suit you."

Arilin swallowed and said nothing. They rode on around the square for a little longer, gradually coming around in front of the cathedral as they wound their way through the crowd. Light spilled from the vast double doors and painted a streak of warm light down the long staircase leading up to the front entrance, turning the backs of the white tunics of the Foot Guards arrayed across the steps to a warm yellow-cream. The men turned to dark silhouettes against the bright light inside as they came around before them, and Alyssa reined her horse in beside their commander as he stepped forward. They exchanged words and the man waved for soldiers to take their horses as they dismounted.

Arilin shook her head to clear it and walked up to the pair as they kept talking. She made out the guards officer say, "…on my list, ma'am."

Alyssa snorted, "I don't think we need to be, lieutenant." She stepped aside for Arilin to join the conversation, "Milady here brings her own list."

The man stiffened to attention and saluted as she approached, and Arilin returned it. Relaxing, he looked between them and said, "I'm certainly not going to stand in your way, milady. Go on in."

The princess nodded, "Thanks." She paused for a moment, then asked,

"Is my uncle inside?"

The lieutenant raised an eyebrow, "Yes... let me see." He pulled a long list from his tunic's hip pocket, turned a little to get it into the light coming out of the doorway and went on, "He's actually on vigil right now, milady. Went on five minutes ago."

"Thank you," Arilin gave the man a nod and they started up the long stairs. Turning to look at Alyssa, she remarked, "I guess it can't be helped."

The lady hussar gave her an even look, "I don't suppose you planned this, milady?"

Arilin sighed, "Yes, but..." She grit her teeth and went on, "I was hoping he wouldn't be here."

Alyssa raised an eyebrow and grunted, but said nothing as they mounted the steps and walked into the light of the cathedral's atrium. The sanctuary beyond was hidden from view by another pair of massive doors carved into monumental reliefs of King Maximilian and Queen Angelique looking down upon them. She got the distinct feeling she was being judged and found wanting.

The hum of soft conversation among the knots of soldiers scattered around the soaring stone chamber died suddenly as they walked inside, every man turning to look at them. At her. Arilin cast her eyes around the room as they strode in, looking at each group in turn. Most just looked surprised. Some were sympathetic, men nodding or even bowing. She recognized a few of them. A few others shot them poorly-disguised looks of contempt, or worse.

Glancing down at her own uniform, of a lieutenant in the Valkyrie Knights, Arilin hoped their distaste was for her *regiment* and not her *person*. The 14th Hussars was not universally loved, and distaste for the Finishing School was a lot more benign than for the Legitimation that had now made her the Crown Princess. Once upon a time, a couple of weeks ago, her and her sister's status in the family had been an *abstract* matter, frowned upon in certain circles but something that could be seen as a good man doing right by a good woman that had been his mistress long before she became his second queen.

Nobody was going to die over the succession while Prince Adrian lived. Now he was lying in state on the other side of those giant doors and her uncle, the man who would be Crown Prince, who she was sure wished he would be King, was standing vigil over his body. The thought made her shiver.

Alyssa's voice snapped her out of her reverie, "Milady, come on." She looked over to see the woman giving her a sympathetic look as she gestured towards the bathrooms off to one side of the atrium, "You look like hell. I need to fix your makeup before we go out there." Before she could protest Alyssa turned to her sergeant and went on, "Go find whoever's in charge here and tell him we're going up next. Don't take 'no' for an answer. And come get us when we're five minutes out."

Their sergeant leaned in close to Alyssa and said something Arilin couldn't make out. She opened her mouth to interject, thought better of it and quietly followed after the hussar captain as their escorts looked around quickly and set off towards an important-looking major standing by the double doors with a clipboard. The powder room was abandoned and Alyssa quickly backed her up against a wall, produced a makeup compact from her uniform and set to work getting her presentable. Arilin knew better than to protest and Alyssa spoke first as she pressed a cold, wet washcloth against her swollen eyes, "Here, just let this cool for a moment." She went on, "Milady, are you sure you want to do this?"

The princess sighed, feeling the cold cloth soaking into her face, "No. But it's not like we have a choice now."

Alyssa sighed heavily in return, "I was worried you'd say that. Just don't faint on me, milady." Arilin opened her mouth to protest, but the woman pressed a finger against her lips and went on, "Shush. Your brother just died, I understand you haven't eaten and you're about to stand at attention for half an hour in front of his body. *That makes people faint*, and you look like you're about to collapse as is."

"Thanks for the vote of confidence." Arilin said bitterly. The woman pulled the compress off her eyes, and she looked at the floor and went on, "I'm sorry I-"

Alyssa slapped her hard enough she tasted blood. Arilin's eyes widened in shock as she looked up at the woman, her cheek stinging from the impact. The red-haired hussar jabbed a finger into her chest hard enough to push her back against the wall and snarled, "*Shut up. I am not* going to listen to you moaning about how sorry for yourself you are, *lieutenant*." She pierced her with a glare and went on, "We are going to march out there, you are going to relieve your uncle and look oh-so dutiful and capable in front of the public, and you are going to keep it together until someone comes out to relieve *you*. If you want to faint, cry, whatever, you're welcome to *after* we leave." She poked her in the chest again, "Do you understand?"

Arilin swallowed and managed, "...yes."

Alyssa snorted contemptuously, "Yes, ma'am to you."

Arilin shook her head and glared back at her, "*Milady.*"

The woman's eye twitched and for a moment Arilin was worried she was going to try to slap her again. Then she chuckled and said, "There's my princess. Come on, milady, I need to finish up with you."

"You'd better fix my cheek." Arilin remarked, then added sourly, "Ma'am."

"Any more out of you, *milady*, and I'll balance it out." Alyssa shot back.

Arilin gave her a dirty look but held her tongue as Alyssa leaned in to work on her. After a few minutes she leaned back out again to check her work and was opening her mouth to say something when the door opened behind her. They both turned to look as their sergeant stepped inside gingerly and announced, "Ma'am, we're up." She looked between the two of them for a moment and sighed with relief, "She looks just fine, ma'am. I was getting worried."

Alyssa turned back to Arilin and raised an eyebrow, "You think?"

The sergeant walked up and studied her for a moment before turning to Alyssa, "I've seen worse lieutenants on parade, ma'am." She paused and went on, "And they hadn't just lost brothers."

The red-haired hussar shrugged, "Fair enough." She jerked her chin at the mirror mounted over the sink nearby, "What do you think, milady?"

Arilin stepped away from the wall and turned to look in the mirror. In a lot of ways she looked like the same little girl who had ridden out with the Army a couple short months ago. She had the same golden hair spilling over her shoulders and well down her back and she hadn't spent enough time in the saddle out on that unexpected battlefield far to the west of Fire Ridge to get more than the faintest hint of a tan. She still looked like a kid with no business wearing a hussar's uniform, her features still a ways from sharpening into adulthood. Alyssa had fixed her makeup with the skill of a virtuoso socialite and she couldn't even notice what she knew must be an ugly red mark on her cheek where she had slapped her.

Only her eyes were different. They were red as two burning rubies from the family curse and bloodshot and redder still from her tears, it almost made her shudder to look into them. But it wasn't just the startling color that made a chill run down her back. Those red eyes had once been as soft and innocent as any girl's, wide and eager for adventure. Now they had *depth*, and deep down in those bloody wells something stirred that was a little hard and a little sharp.

Arilin closed her eyes, shook her head slowly and took a deep breath, feeling the anxiety drain from her body. She had made it through the last, horrible weeks since her brother died. She had made it to the cathedral to stand vigil over his body, and she was *going* to make it through the night. No matter what. Opening her eyes again she saw a determined young woman looking back at her in the mirror, and she saw herself crack the faintest hint of a smile. Turning to her companions, she nodded and said, "It's good." She gestured to the door and said, "Let's go."

Moments later they were standing before the great doors to the sanctuary. Beside her Alyssa adjusted her uniform self-consciously before turning slightly to mutter, "I'll call the cadence. Just stay in step with me, milady."

Arilin nodded wordlessly and the red-haired hussar gestured to the guardsmen standing by to pull the doors open. The ancient latch popped open with a clank that echoed through the room as the soldiers hauled the doors open, the massive slabs of carved wood rotating smoothly outwards to reveal the cathedral's true glory within. The ceiling vaulted off impossibly high overhead and though it was darkest night outside the sanctuary blazed with light, electric chandeliers burning almost as bright as day. Massive stained glass windows marched down the walls, turned to shining frescoes against the darkness beyond as they drew her eye far, far down the central aisle to see Christ on His cross towering above the grand altar. Under His gaze lay her brother, resting on a plinth at the center of the huge cross formed by the cathedral's wings. Arilin felt her vision cloud and her knees wobble for a moment before the thud of the great doors hitting their stops brought her back to reality.

Four big men in cuirassier armor stood vigil over Prince Adrian, heads bowed as an endless line of mourners shuffled past. She saw a few pale faces already turning towards them curiously as Alyssa muttered, "On your left, milady. Forward, march."

The princess stepped forward. Arilin felt like she was floating as they stepped slowly down the aisle, Alyssa's slow murmur of, "left, left, left," keeping her upright as though the woman was pulling her with a rope. It seemed to take hours to walk down the aisle, their slow footsteps on the smooth stone floor lost in the immense space as they approached the casket and the throng of mourners shuffling through began to murmur and jostle forward against the ropes set up beyond the plinth to get a better look. Not at her brother, whose golden hair she thought she could barely see above the rim of the coffin. At her.

As they approached and the murmur of the crowd grew the cuirassier on their side of the plinth looked up to study them for a second, his eyes sweeping across their group before settling on and boring into hers. Arilin's blood ran cold as she recognized him. The big man with a brigadier general's star on his blue cuirassier's collar patches was someone who she had perhaps naively hoped to never deal with again. She had played no small role in seeing him relieved of command a few short weeks ago and reassigned to the obscurity of directing the Remount Service. From an office which she realized was probably located in the War Ministry across the street from her own home.

After too many seconds Brigadier General Chapman turned his head slightly and murmured something inaudibly over his shoulder. The tall, ice-blonde man on the far side of her brother's coffin straightened up from his pose of mournful contemplation, spun on his heel and strode across the plinth to stand beside him. Eyes as red as blood glared back at her as she saw her uncle's jaw clench and set, his silvered breastplate shifting slowly on his chest as he took a slow, deep breath.

Alyssa murmured for them to halt as they reached the base of the plinth and Arilin heard Prince Alphonse's breath hiss softly as he slowly exhaled. His flaming eyes stabbed down onto her and Arilin felt her head spin and her knees start to buckle as she craned her head back to meet his gaze. Catching herself at the last second, she took a deep breath of her own to steady herself. She was opening her mouth to speak when her uncle said, very quietly, "You are not needed here, dear. You should be resting." He glanced over at Chapman and went on, "Don't you agree, David?"

The general looked them over contemptuously and said, "Yes, we'll-"

Arilin cut him off, "Yet here we are." She looked between the two of them and nodded as respectfully as she could manage, "Uncle, sir, you are relieved."

Neither man moved for a couple seconds. Finally Chapman snorted and replied, "You are not a proper relief, *milady.*"

The general was turning to say something more to Alphonse when Alyssa cut in, barely-contained anger hardening her voice, "You'll have to take that up with the commander of the guard, *sir.*" Chapman's eyes narrowed with anger as the crowd took notice of the scene and started to jostle and buzz behind him. The red-haired captain went on, "We have his approval and," She gestured at the three of them, "My troopers are fully prepared."

"You do not have *my* approval, *young lady.*" Chapman hissed over the growing murmur of the crowd.

"David, please." Alphonse gave him a reproachful look, then looked down at them apologetically, "Ladies, look, I'm sorry. It's been a long day for all of us." He stepped down and patted her on the shoulder affectionately, then looked at Alyssa, "Take Arilin here home and put her to bed, alright? We'll stand an extra shift."

"I appreciate it, uncle, but," Arilin said as she brushed his hand away, "I'm still standing vigil." Before he could turn back to her she stepped up onto the plinth and strode past Chapman. Her head swam as she walked around her brother's coffin, carefully avoiding looking inside. She would faint if she did, she knew that much. Alighting on the far side of the plinth facing the jostling crowd, she unclipped her sword from her belt, rested the tip of the scabbard on the floor in front of her and folded her hands atop the pommel, bowing her head slightly and looking down at the mourners.

Agonizing seconds dragged by as Chapman and Alphonse exchanged quiet words behind her. Finally she heard the general grate out the order for his men to fall in and the other two cuirassiers on the platform stepped down with heavy footfalls against the flagstones. A moment later she heard Valkyrie Knights step up lightly to replace them. The crowd murmured uneasily as the men made their way back down the aisle before slowly starting to file past again.

After that it was just a matter of waiting. Adrian's presence behind her seemed to put strength in her legs as though he was physically holding her upright. She was too tired to cry any more, and she watched the mourners filing past through a dreamlike haze. Almost all of them gave her a sympathetic look as they passed, and she noticed more than a few of them furtively producing pocket cameras as they passed. Arilin sighed. It was all the better, she supposed.

A shape stirred in the corner of her eye and Arilin looked over to see a handsome lieutenant in the red jacket of the 1st Hussars, tall enough to look her square in the eyes despite her position atop the plinth. Stepping in front of her, he gave her a gracious nod and said, "Milady, you are relieved."

Arilin nodded back and replied, "Thank you." Stepping aside to give the man space, she clipped her sword back to her belt and turned to see her companions stepping down as they were replaced. It was quite the contrast seeing the feminine rose-pink of the Valkyries next to the bright, swaggering red of the Winged Knights. She realized absently there was probably a bitter rivalry between the two Guards hussar regiments, although if there was one it didn't seem to be on display tonight. She supposed it would be amazingly petty if it were.

She risked a glance at her brother as she walked back over the plinth, and her steps slowed to a halt as her eyes fell on him. Adrian looked like he was sleeping peacefully in his immaculate blue cuirassier's uniform, eyes closed with his blonde hair spread out on the pillow beneath his head. There wasn't a mark on his face, and apparently barely a mark on his body. They had told her the lethal wound was deceptively small, a deep stab into his armpit as he had raised his sword-arm to strike. They said he had died in seconds from half a dozen severed arteries. And none of them knew what had happened to her ribbon, the one he had promised to get back to her.

Looking down at him from beside the casket, he really did just look like he was sleeping. Sighing heavily, Arilin bent down and kissed him gently on the forehead. His skin was cool and smooth under her lips and tasted like chemicals. Straightening up, she brushed her hair back over her shoulders and strode over to where Alyssa and the others were waiting, ignoring the excited murmur that ran through the crowd behind her.

The hussar captain made her sit down as soon as the sanctuary doors closed behind them and sent her troopers to get a carriage to take her back to the Palace. Arilin knew better than to protest.

Chapter 2

Firelight and Fireflies

Sophia Rose stared into the fire crackling cheerily in front of her and slowly exhaled, feeling the knot of tension deep in her chest loosen just a tiny little bit. For the first time in too long she felt alive again. She thought for a minute and chuckled to herself. The last time she'd felt alright had been when she'd gotten a hot shower and four hours of sleep at that estate west of Fire Ridge, and gotten to meet Prince Adrian for a minute on top of it.

The thought of the battle and the Crown Prince sent a spike of ice straight through her chest again. She remembered, far too clearly, Prince Adrian and his cuirassiers charging into battle. They had leapt over them as they crouched in what was left of the last Imperial trench atop Fire Ridge and spurred into battle, flags flying and swords burning overhead. And they had *died*. Sophia shivered as she remembered wave after wave of Imperial dragoons pouring over the distant rise, their black and red battle flag leading the assault. Not long after the cuirassiers' own colors had gone back up that hill in the enemy's hands.

The survivors had been gunned down trying to rally in front of their trench. Massacred, more like it, leaving a hellish windrow of dead men and horses they and the dragoons had traded fire over and *through* for hours. Eventually the enemy had demanded their surrender. Sophia could still see that long-haired dragoon standing in front of her, snarling that Prince Adrian was dead and none of them were getting off the ridge alive. June Anjanou, son of the enemy's supreme commander. It hadn't been their first encounter. The sight of his sword burning in the moonlight flashed through her mind, bodies strewn across the floor and blood sprayed across the ceiling.

"Sophia?" A friendly voice snapped her back to reality. She'd known Tony Gravesend her whole life. They'd played together, gone to school together and a year ago had joined the Army together. And just a couple months ago they had marched off to war together. The fire popped and crackled warmly as he went on, "Are you okay? You were shaking there."

Sophia shook her head, "Yeah... I mean, as much as anyone is around here."

"Right?" Edward Bellamy cut in on her other side. She'd barely known the tall, gangly ferryman before they had marched out of Jade Falls that fine spring day so long ago, but his biting sense of humor had kept all of them on their feet at some point recently. He tapped the livid scar on his forehead and joked, "Look on the bright side, Sophie. *You* didn't get shot in the head."

Sophia shot back, "I kind of wish I *had* been." She snorted and went on, "I bet I wouldn't remember things as well."

Edward chuckled, "Yeah, most of Fire Ridge is one big blur for me."

Across the fire from her, Robert Hargrave leaned forward and tapped out his pipe into the fire. The old man just seemed happy to be able to smoke in peace for once and not have to worry about his glowing pipe coals drawing half the Imperial Army down on their heads. Producing a tin of tobacco from his jacket, he started packing another pinch into his pipe and commented, "You're damn lucky to be alive, Ed." Striking a match, he lit his pipe and took a contemplative puff. Blowing a long cloud of acrid smoke out over the fire, he chuckled and went on, "The Lord protects fools and children."

Edward shrugged, "I'm not complaining, old man."

Tony cut in, "I still can't believe we made it through that." He shivered, "God, was that bad."

It *had* been terrible. The battle didn't bear thinking about, their escape through the mountains afterwards even less so. The cold, the rain, the endless march with hunger gnawing a hole in her belly and the echo of their pursuers' gunfire chasing them through the endless spires of the Dragonspines. Pushing the thought from her mind, Sophia snorted and leaned back to look up at the night sky far above.

Two of the Moons were out, swift Courage shining silver among the stars far overhead and Hope's great disk growing in the east. In another week it would be bright enough to read by the moonlight. Courage and Hope. Sophia supposed it was appropriate as she remarked, "*Someone* was looking out for us." Looking back down to her friends, she changed the subject, "Any guesses when we'll get mail?"

Hargrave chuckled, "Probably when the Army Post figures out that we still exist as a unit."

"Good luck on that one." Edward remarked bitterly, "With our luck we're probably all listed as missing in action right now."

Tony sat up and gave him a nervous look, "You don't think they...?"

Sophia felt her stomach clench at the thought. If they *had* been declared missing people would have been notified. Her *mother* would have been told her husband and her only daughter had disappeared at Fire Ridge, along with half a million other Royal soldiers. She didn't even want to think about the hell she was going through. Finally she ventured, "I hope not."

Tony sighed heavily, "Yeah." Picking up a twig lying in the grass, he sullenly threw it into the fire. It caught fire and flared brightly for a moment as he said, "I can't wait to get home." He looked around the group and went on, "When this war's over, I'm *done*. I'm never leaving Jade Falls again."

Edward raised an eyebrow, "Yeah? Hm... I'll get my own boat, I guess." He snorted, "I'm getting *real* tired of working for other people." He looked over at Hargrave, "What about you, old man?"

Hargrave puffed at his pipe contemplatively for a moment before he replied, "I'm getting a safer hobby." He gave Sophia a look, "That's the last time I ever let your father convince me to do *anything*, young lady."

Sophia blinked, then burst out laughing. It was a little hysterical, but it felt good and after a second the others joined in. Feeling the tension and worry drain out of her body, she gradually calmed down and leaned back to look up at the night sky again as she replied, "Well, I don't know about you guys, but," She looked back down and smiled sheepishly, tugging at her trousers' wool fabric, "After this is over I'm *never* wearing pants again."

That got them all going again. They had just about calmed down when she heard footsteps in the grass behind them and she turned to see a very familiar figure. Her father smiled down at her, "Well, I can see you're doing alright, Sophie." Another man stepped out from behind him and Sophia's eyes widened as he went on cheerily, "Look who I just found."

They all jumped to their feet, Sophia saying, "*Kelly?*"

Kelly Hager raised his arm a little stiffly as she rushed over, saying, "Hey-" Sophia threw her arms around him and he grunted, "Oof, Sophia, good to see you..." He looked up as the others hurried up behind her, "You guys too, really."

Sophia disentangled herself and asked, "Where have you been? How'd you get out?"

Kelly chuckled, "They had me patched up and on a train back to Grenville by that night. I didn't even *hear* about what happened until a couple days later." Sophia set her jaw and was about to speak when he rushed on, "First Sergeant... er, Sergeant Major told me about Jack."

Jack Mulligan. The *other* student-reservist in the company besides herself and Tony, who had gotten up from class that beautiful spring day so long ago and marched to war. He had only joined the Royal Army in the first place to put a feather in his cap to brag about to girls. He had never liked her in the first place and had bitterly resented her being put in charge of their squad. And he had died behind his machine gun in that last trench on Fire Ridge, shredded by a hail of Imperial grenades following an order she'd given him. Sophia sighed heavily and looked at the ground, "Yeah... I'm sorry."

"You're sorry?" Kelly clapped her on the shoulder, "*I'm* sorry. I should have been there."

Hargrave snorted and cut in, "Not with your arm the way it was. How're you doing now?"

Kelly flexed his arm and winced, "I've been better. At least it went clean through." He went on, "But when I heard about you guys there was no way I was going to hang around that hospital any longer. I snuck out and hitched a ride up."

Her father cut in, "I ran into him bothering the duty sergeant at Corps trying to figure out where we were." He went on, jokingly angry, "Had to call back to Grenville and tell them he hadn't deserted."

Kelly looked over at him apologetically, "Thanks for that, by the way, Sergeant Major."

He chuckled, "It's a problem I like having."

Her friends took Kelly back over to sit by their campfire and fill him in. Sophia's father turned to leave and she quickly retrieved her rifle and hurried after him, asking, "Dad, you just got back from Corps? Any word on what's going on?"

"Priming the rumor mill, Sophie?" He chuckled, "Yes, actually. Might as well tell you and save myself the trouble of putting it out myself."

Sophia laughed, "Come on, Dad."

"It's *true.*" The Sergeant Major snorted and went on, "Kellerman doesn't want to admit it, but he's happy to have us. The Corps is spread thin as is."

They had staggered down out of the mountains a week ago and almost immediately run into cavalry. Miraculously they had been Royal Army lancers. A few flashes with a shaving mirror later and they had walked out of the forest to run straight into a certain old friend of her father's and then, a couple hours later, gotten a *heavenly* truck ride back to the newly-established First Cavalry Corps' main supply depot. What was left of the 24th Infantry Regiment had been there ever since, gradually spreading out as the Corps ordered them to guard the spreading network of depots, command posts and bits and pieces of important infrastructure the cavalry couldn't function without and which they didn't have the troopers to guard. Having seen some of their support troops on sentry duty themselves, Sophia could see why the Corps wasn't in any hurry to get rid of their adopted infantrymen.

Speaking of that old friend of her father's, Sophia asked hopefully, "You didn't happen to see, ah... General MacMahon, did you?"

"No, unfortunately." She deflated and her father went on, "I can't believe that girl is a *general* now. When I first met her she was about five minutes older than you, you know." He chuckled, "She was a *real* piece of work."

Sophia smiled over at him, "In a good way or a bad way?"

"Both." He conceded, "She's the real thing, though. I can see how it happened."

They were walking through the regiment's camp, set in the patchy woods a little ways off from the supply depot itself. Campfires burned through the darkness all around them, a luxury among soldiers when the enemy was distant and they could take the time to create a few creature comforts for themselves. Now and then a man would give them a friendly wave or shout out a greeting to the Sergeant Major, and her father nodded and waved back. It felt as peaceful as the end of one of their little training exercises back at Jade Falls, men unwinding before the march back home. As she took a deep breath of the smoky forest air Sophia could barely believe the Empire was out there, somewhere, coiling in the dark. Finally she asked, "Any word about the Empire?"

She could hear her father exhale softly as he grimaced, "Yes. They're starting to move." He looked over at her and went on, "The Ninth Division, MacMahon's actually, got into a couple fights with Pathfinders today. They won of course, but God knows how many got past them."

Sophia raised an eyebrow at the unfamiliar term, "Pathfinders?"

Her father nodded, "Something new the Empire cooked up for this war." He snorted, "Well, not really. They've always had irregular scouts and spies on top of their dragoons. I don't think the higher-ups expected them to be able to do that outside of the Empire, though."

"They were wrong?" She asked.

"Yes." He explained, "They've been sending out soldiers by ones and twos to try to infiltrate through our lines before their big push. Very tough, very well-trained, none of them wearing a mask or any kind of Imperial uniform."

"You don't think...?" Sophia trailed off questioningly.

Her father nodded, "They might be poking around here soon. Get your guys back on their toes."

Sophia nodded, "Will do." They had left the infantry camp behind and come up on the edge of the support troops' camp, with its big squad tents laid out in careful rows. An infantryman standing guard near the first row peered at them carefully as they approached before relaxing and waving them through. Noticing a the silver wheels of a Transportation Corps guidon in front of a tent a little ways back, a thought occurred to her and she asked, "By the way, Dad, are we still officially a regiment?"

"Funny you should ask," He grunted, "That's actually what the boss and I were over at Corps to talk about."

"Oh, really?" She asked.

He nodded. There was a bitter note in his voice as he went on, "No, we're not." He went on, "I can't say I blame the man. Right now we've got a battalion's worth of soldiers, no headquarters to speak of, no supply train and our heaviest weapon is a machine gun. It's a stretch to call ourselves a regiment right now. And I'm not even mentioning the colors."

"Damn." Sophia commented, "So what now?"

"We're the 224th Independent Infantry Battalion now." Her father went on, "The boss and I are going to sit down tomorrow and figure out how we're going to look from now on." Seeing the look she was giving him, he chuckled and patted her on the shoulder affectionately, "Don't worry. Charlie Company is *not* going away. And you'll keep your team."

She smiled, "Thanks, Dad." Thinking for a moment, she went on, "Did you ever figure out what happened to them, by the way?"

He raised an eyebrow, "The colors?" Her father shrugged, "Not really." He paused and went on, "Colonel Paget wasn't stupid. He took about half the headquarters with him when he went to go have his meeting with Division. They must have taken the colors with them. And, well..." He didn't need to finish the thought. The regiment's old commander had disappeared that night on Fire Ridge. He hadn't been the only one. By the time they pried open the jaws of the enemy's trap and escaped almost all of the regiment's senior leaders were dead, dying or had simply vanished in the swirling battle. Major Matheson, the regiment's old logistics officer, had found himself in command by default. As the senior NCO still alive her father had taken over as the regimental Sergeant Major.

Sophia sighed, "That's a shame." For a unit to lose their battle flag was the ultimate disgrace. It was a failure before the King himself, who had trusted them to carry one of his banners into battle. Given the circumstances, though, Sophia barely felt more than mild disappointment. The colors she *really* cared about, Charlie Company's, were safe and sound. Looking back over at her father in the dark night, she perked up and added, "I've still got *ours*."

Her father looked over at her for a moment, then threw his head back and laughed. Calming down a little, he quickly looked around to make sure nobody could see them and, still smirking, reached over, pulled her hat off and started ruffling her hair. "Yes, you do, Sophie," he chuckled warmly, "you sure do."

"Oh, Dad, come on," Sophia felt herself blushing as he petted her. He hadn't done that since she was a little kid. Still, she didn't try to brush him off like she would have a couple months ago.

Eventually he let her go and warmly pushed her hat back down onto her head. A ways off she could hear a faint clatter of hooves and creaking wheels as a wagon convoy rolled out for the front, and he said, "Anyways, Sophie, I'm going to go walk around and check on the guards. *You* need to head on back."

Straightening her hat, Sophia smiled back at him as he turned to leave, "Sure thing. See you, Dad."

"You too." Her father raised his hand over his shoulder in a wave good-bye as he walked away towards the commotion.

Sophia turned herself and started walking back through the camp, the long grass rustling underfoot where it had been trampled down into a trail by hundreds of soldiers going back and forth every day. The sentry waved to her as she came back by, and great dark trees rose around the trail to blot out the night sky as she left the transportation troops' camp behind and the flickering light of her friends' campfires began appearing through the forest.

A warm wind stirred the trees overhead as she walked, bringing with it the earthy scent of the summer forest. As she emerged into their camp she looked around at the spreading campfires amid the dark trees and long grass, and something caught her eye. A spark of green light in the distance. Sophia felt a flash of fear in her chest, her eyes widening at the thought of enemy Pathfinders stalking through the woods.

Then she saw another spark, and another and another. Dozens, no... hundreds, *thousands* of them danced all through the glade and the forest beyond as a spreading cloud of cool light rose from the grass and flared among the trees and campfires. Fireflies dancing in the summer night.

It was at times like this she could barely believe the war was real.

Chapter 3
The Lord in Shadow

Birds were singing in Lindestadt, cheering the battered town's tree-lined streets in the cool morning. The clatter of their horses' hooves on the cobblestones echoed off the buildings all around them in a steel-shod river of sound as they rode along, burbling, rushing and falling off as gaps appeared in the trees and side streets branched off. Closing his eyes for a moment, June Anjanou felt Lucky gently rock beneath him as the horse stepped along with his usual surefooted gait. The town's air smelled of trees and stone with a hint of acrid smoke, and he slowly took a deep breath just to soak it in.

"Enjoying the weather, lieutenant?" He opened his eyes and looked over at Colonel Vann where she was riding beside him. Her mask's jaw plate was cocked up a little in what he supposed was probably a wry smile. The Fifth Dragoons' commander went on, "I've certainly seen worse."

June chuckled and replied, "Yes, ma'am." Running a hand through his long hair and feeling its soft mass shift off his neck and back for a moment, he went on, "I don't think we could ask for better."

"Well," she said, "If we're meeting who I *think* we are a thunderstorm would be more appropriate, but I'm not complaining."

He raised an eyebrow enough to shift his mask on his face and asked, "My father?" The exact location of the Imperial Western Area Army's headquarters was not something the line regiments needed to know and that went double for the Lord General himself. Still, Lorenvale sat right on the rail line where it turned around the tip of Fire Ridge, square in the center of gravity of what was rapidly turning into the greatest army the Empire of Masks had ever sent to war. It made sense that he would be here.

Just two weeks ago the Royal Army's Field Marshal White had seen fit to establish his own headquarters in Lorenvale as he sent half of his Army of Drakenburg lunging into the hundred-kilometer jaws of an Imperial trap. He could still see the scars of battle pocking the town, here and there an arc of cobblestones plowed up by a tank's treads or the jagged flower of a mortar shell's blast. A few windows were boarded up where they had been shot out and when he looked closely he could see the tracks of bullets where they had ricocheted across the street and torn at the buildings' brick walls. There wasn't really much damage. The battle had been short and resistance in the town itself looked like it had been light.

Colonel Vann chuckled and brushed her own icy hair back over her shoulders, "Maybe. We'll see."

"Well, ma'am, we've certainly got enough presents for anyone." June hefted the set of colors he was carrying across his lap in a gesture, the blue flag rolled and tied back against its pole, "I think whoever it is will be satisfied."

His commander nodded, her satisfaction clear even through the hard steel of her mask as she said, "I think you're right." Looking past her June could see the rest of their companions following them up the street, about fifty dragoons from their regiment. Most of them had a flag of some kind in hand. Newly-promoted Sergeant Marin gave him a friendly nod from just behind him, and June smiled a little under his mask and turned back to his front. He couldn't think of a group of people he'd rather ride to war with.

They quickly made their way through the town's mostly-deserted streets, a few groups of Imperial soldiers stopping to gawk at the procession. Curtains twitched behind windows as they rode by, and June saw a few civilians skitter into alleys or doorways as they caught sight of them. Clearly the locals were taking no chances with their conquerors. June smirked to himself with satisfaction, sat up a little straighter in his saddle and let Lucky carry him onwards.

Soon enough they made their way to the center of town and turned onto its shaded central boulevard, the dragoons weaving their way through the trees along the street onto the sidewalk as a convoy of trucks rumbled along in the opposite direction. Spilling back onto the street in their wake, June wrinkled his nose at the foul smell of the exhaust and looked around to pick out their destination among the official-looking buildings, fancy hotels and fine houses lining the street. Most of them were draped in black-and-red Imperial flags by now.

Spotting a group of cavalry horses hitched up outside what looked like a particularly nice hotel, June gave Colonel Vann a look and pointed, "I think that's it."

The woman's mask shifted on her face a little as she raised her eyebrows, and she looked down the street after his finger. Looking closer himself, he noticed more than few dragoons standing guard in the street outside. Some of them had machine guns. The colonel gave him a satisfied nod as she nudged her horse into a trot and agreed, "Yep. Let's get moving."

June prodded at Lucky's flank and the horse obligingly picked up into a trot. They quickly arrived out front of the building in a clatter of steel-shod hooves on the cobblestones and pulled up outside. June dismounted with his flag, handed Lucky off to a trooper to hitch up and watch and turned to go inside, giving the horse an affectionate pat on the nose for his efforts as he left. He glanced at the hotel's sign as he walked up to the front entrance, carefully lowering his flag's spearhead under the covered walkway's canvas roof as he went. The Royal Eastern Hotel. June allowed himself an extremely satisfied smirk at the irony as a sweating doorman pulled the front door open for him and he strode inside.

The lobby looked even better inside than the building had outside, full of opulent furniture and fine crystal. June's boots thudded solidly on the rich hardwood floor as he turned to see an older man in a fine gray suit waiting near the door, his bare face pale and set as rigid as any Imperial mask. Giving him an even look, June said, "We're here for the ceremony."

The man looked down at the flag June was carrying and took a very slow, deep breath. Finally he looked back up at him and said flatly, "So you are." June raised an eyebrow enough to obviously shift his mask on his face and the man jerked his head slightly down the long central hallway leading off the lobby, "Main ballroom, on the left."

"Thanks." June nodded. Pegging the man as the owner, he chuckled and added, "By the way, you might want to change your sign. I was thinking the 'Imperial Western' has a ring to it."

The man's eye *twitched*, and he hissed, "Go to hell."

June laughed, "Welcome to the Empire." Stepping aside as Colonel Vann came in behind him, he turned to her and said, "We're in the main ballroom, ma'am."

The colonel snorted and gave him a look, "Don't antagonize the civilians, June." She turned to the man and gestured down the hallway, "After you." The man nodded coolly, turned on his heel and strode off down the hall with the colonel in tow. June shrugged and followed them.

They headed down the hall for a ways before stopping by an impressive set of double doors with a dragoon standing guard outside. The hotel's owner stepped aside and gestured for them to go inside as the guard nodded and pulled the doors open for them. Maneuvering his flag inside, June looked around the cavernous room and spotted a group of Imperial soldiers silhouetted against the light streaming in from the tall windows on the far wall. His eyes widened as a tall soldier in a dragoon's uniform with an unmistakable mane of long black hair turned from his conversation to look at the newcomers. At him.

June hurried forward to meet him as he stepped forward, saying, "Father?"

Lord General Slade Anjanou gave him a level look as he stopped in front of him, then looked down to slow cast his eyes over the flag June was carrying. Finally looking back up, his father nodded slowly and June saw his mask shift a little in a smile as he said, "Good to see you, June. I can see you've been keeping busy."

June laughed, "You could say that." Giving his father a look, he went on, "How about you?"

"About the same thing." The Lord General chuckled unpleasantly as he tugged at the strap of a satchel he had slung over his shoulder, "I've found a couple souvenirs too, you know."

June raised an eyebrow, "So... wait." He thought for a moment and went on, "You got the same message we did?"

His father nodded, "Yes." He turned a little to look at Colonel Vann as she walked up beside June and went on, "Ilya, good to see you again. I'd ask if you'd been keeping my son out of trouble, but, well..."

The colonel chuckled, "I've clearly been a failure at that, sir."

"No worries, colonel." His father nodded and went on, "You've both done well. Now," he reached out and gave June an affectionate pat on the shoulder as he went on, "It's time for you to meet someone."

June had noticed a few other Imperial soldiers and what looked like a couple of masked civilians filtering into the room after their group and had thought nothing of it. His eyes widened as he realized he had *not* noticed the man that was standing not ten feet away from them, tall and stately in a fine black suit and mask yet somehow so utterly nondescript he seemed to just blend into the background. Looking closer and willing his attention not to skitter off the man and onto something more interesting, June saw the telltale wrinkles of old age around the man's neck and how his expertly-tailored suit hung off his body ever so slightly.

The old man's mask shifted a little as he smiled and took a step closer, leaning on a heavy cane that June realized almost certainly concealed a sword's blade. He was opening his mouth to greet the man when something moved in the corner of his eye and looked over to see his father, the Lord General of the Western Area Army and one of the most powerful men in the Empire, settling onto one knee on the floor beside him.

"My lord," his father said, "We are honored by your presence."

The Emperor chuckled drily, "Sharp as ever, Slade." His eyes swung over to stab into June like spears the color of congealed blood, "And who is this?"

June shut his hanging jaw with an audible click and knelt next to his father, feeling the Emperor's eyes bore into him as the rest of their group dropped to their knees in a chorus of dull thuds and clattering flagstaffs on the wooden floor. When the racket had died down his father replied for him, "My son, June." He nodded to the colonel beside him, "As well as his commander, Colonel Vann of the Fifth Dragoons and their soldiers."

June felt a weight lift off his shoulders as Emperor Sai's gaze shifted away, back to his father. He finally gave them a satisfied grunt and said, "It's always a pleasure to see a new Anjanou. And, colonel," June felt those eyes burn across him as he looked over at the woman, "I can see that my Black Knights are in good hands."

He could hear the smile in her voice as she replied, "Thank you, my lord."

"Well, now." The Emperor said, "You may rise." They all climbed to their feet, June feeling a little light-headed as Lord Sai turned and walked a little farther out into the cleared center of the ballroom to create some space around himself before turning and going on, "I think it's time to see what you have for me."

June heard his father smiling as he said, "Of course, my lord." He turned to look at him and gestured him forward, "I think you should go first, June."

Nodding, June replied, "Yes, sir." Stripping the ties off the flag he was carrying with a couple quick motions, he unrolled the massive blue and gold banner. The Royal griffon and the crossed swords of the cuirassiers surrounded by dozens of battle honors unfurled before him and he heard his companions gasp softly despite themselves. This was the standard of the knights that had fought the Faceless King. They had battled Lady Vai and the Emperors and Empresses after her, and they had shattered the Masked Army under that standard on a hundred battlefields from the Shield Mountains to the heart of the Empire itself. Two weeks ago he had wrenched that standard from the dying hands of the First Cuirassiers' color sergeant.

June marched up to the Emperor and threw their colors on the floor at his feet. The clatter of the staff bouncing on the hard wood echoed through the room like a king's death rattle as June announced, "My lord, the standard of the First Cuirassier Guards Regiment. I seized it person-ally, but..." June turned and gestured for his soldiers to come up, the seven he still had left from the twenty he had made that insane charge with, "My soldiers got me there."

Sergeant Marin approached with his own flag, Tarai, Sagara and the other survivors with him. The Western Kingdom's national flag was a golden cross stretched across a blue field, with a second, smaller gold-en cross stretching across from the canton and overlapping the first. It brought to mind the True and False Suns. However, in the presence of the Royal Family the Kingdom flew a different flag, with a white field instead of blue.

Marin hurled the white Royal Standard to the ground at the Emperor's feet, saying, "We had to fight for this, my lord."

Lord Sai replied, clearly amused, "I'm sure you did."

June looked over to where Colonel Vann was waiting and nodded. She gave him a satisfied nod back and gestured for the rest of her troopers to advance with their own flags as he turned back to the Emperor and said, "And, my lord, our *regiment* got us out."

Falling in beside him to form a wide semicircle around the Emperor, his comrades threw every single guidon, color and flag the First Cuirassiers had carried to their doom on Fire Ridge to the floor at his feet. There were almost two dozen of them piled in disgrace by the time they finished. Somewhere at that very moment in the High City, he was sure, a statue was crying blood.

Finally Colonel Vann stepped past him and presented a long, straight sword in its scabbard to the Emperor. With its swept, gilded guard and rich leather mountings it looked like nothing so much as a knight's longsword rendered in a smooth modernist style instead of medieval gothic. The Royal Army's cuirassiers had replaced their clumsy straight sabers with swords much like it for the current war, and June's comrades had been paying the price ever since. With a satisfied note in her voice his commander said, "My lord, I give you the sword of Prince Adrian."

That sword had mowed down dragoons like wheat before the scythe. For a moment June could see Adrian before him as he had been that day, helmet gone, blonde hair flying, red eyes burning with rage as dragoons died with every stroke of his sword, almost as fast as they could press forward at him. He had *screamed* his battle cry, a mighty griffon fighting utterly alone against a thousand enemies. If the rest of his regiment had shown that much courage, June knew he wouldn't have been standing there. The Emperor took it, hefted it for a second and seemed to understand as much himself. The old man's mask tilted a little as he smiled, saying, "Excellent."

Colonel Vann nodded and stepped back as he handed the weapon off to an aide, who vanished as quickly as he appeared. Looking around at the wreckage, the Emperor chuckled and said, "Well. I need to reward you properly for your efforts." Turning to June, he reached into his pocket and strode forward over the First Cuirassiers' colors, pulling out a medal and unfolding its unmistakable red-and-black ribbon as he stopped in front of him. Every Imperial citizen knew that red-and-gold dagger-pointed cross, and June's breath caught in his throat as he bowed his head. An instant later Emperor Sai hung the Imperial Cross around his neck.

June looked up to see the Emperor standing quite close to him, his mask tilted a little in a smile. The old man patted him on the shoulder and said quietly, "Keep it up. The war's not over yet."

June nodded and replied, "Yes, sir."

"Good." Lord Sai turned to look at Marin and his other soldiers, then back to June, "Now for your soldiers. Young Miss Lai has already received her medal, by the way."

"Thank you, my lord." June said gratefully as the old man turned to Sergeant Marin and produced another medal from his pocket on the silver-and-red ribbon of the Emperor's Medal for Heroism. A rank below the Imperial Cross, but still a supreme honor. The soldiers who had ridden at his back deserved nothing less. Marin bowed his head gratefully and the Emperor hung it around his neck, then leaned in and said something too low for June to make out. The sergeant laughed, and the old man slapped him affectionately on the arm and moved down the line.

Anastasia Lai had been his communications trooper and his constant shadow during those months they had spent on campaign before the battle, riding deep into the Kingdom and back again as they drew out the Army of Drakenburg into the great trap at Fire Ridge. The girl had never been any good with a sword, and from what the others had told him she had survived the charge by riding as close in his wake as she could. There hadn't been many cuirassiers left able to take a swing at her by the time he'd gone by, but she had taken a nasty slash to the face regardless that had cost her an eye. Without her steel mask it would have been her head. She was back recovering in the Empire now, her war over.

Having finished with his troopers the Emperor walked across in front of him again, saying, "And now for you, Colonel Vann." June turned to see the woman brush her hair back over her shoulders and bow her head as the Emperor produced another medal from his pocket on a gold-and-black ribbon. The Imperial Star Second Class, an award for skillful command instead of valor. She straightened up and Lord Sai gave her a satisfied nod and went on, "Your regiment will receive a heroic battle honor."

The woman bowed her head again, "Thank you, my lord."

The Emperor chuckled, "No, thank *you*, colonel." Leaning on his cane, he stepped back a little and looked past June, saying, "And what do you have for me, Slade?"

"Well," His father started forward behind him, saying gruffly, "I'm afraid I can't quite match their *theatrics*, my lord, but I think you'll like this regardless."

"Oh?" Sai's mask shifted a little upward on his face as he raised his eyebrows.

Hearing his father approach behind them, June and Colonel Vann stepped aside to let him through. Reaching into his satchel, the Lord General produced a blue baton encrusted with spiraling gold filigree, and June felt his eyes widen as he realized what it was. His father went on, clearly enjoying himself, "Courtesy of Field Marshal White."

The Emperor took the Royal Field Marshal's baton and hefted it, chuckling, "Well. You don't get one of these every century." His mask tilted as he looked back at the Lord General and raised an eyebrow, "I heard he shot himself?"

Slade nodded, "Yes."

"I *weep*." Sai said, his voice dripping sarcasm. Reaching inside his jacket, he said drily, "Usually I don't give these out before the war's won, but I'm making an exception today." The general bowed his head as the Emperor produced an Imperial Star, First Class and hung it around his neck, its red and gold ribbon standing out brightly against his green uniform. Slade straightened and the old man went on, "I'll give you another one at Drakenburg."

The general nodded, "I'll see you there, my lord."

The Emperor snorted, "I hope to see you all there." He went on, asking, "I understand the King himself has taken the field?"

"Yes, my lord." June's father went on gravely, "General Haas has assumed command of the Army of Drakenburg."

The old man remarked, "Somehow I'm not surprised."

Slade growled, "If not for him they wouldn't *exist* right now."

"Well," The Emperor said, "You'll just have to make sure of that going forward." Stepping back, he looked around the group and said, "I don't need to tell you all this war isn't over yet. The Empire will not be *safe* until Drakenburg is ours. And I will not be *satisfied* until the High City *burns*."

"Yes, my lord!" They shouted as one.

"Make it so." With that the Emperor turned and walked away, almost seeming to deflate in on himself as he leaned heavily on his cane. His aides rushed in to clear away the battle flags piled on the floor, and despite the man being in plain sight June still struggled to keep his eye on him as he went. As the Emperor approached one of the ballroom's side doors June saw another dark-suited man push himself off from where he had been leaning against the wall and go to put an arm around him for support. Sai gave him a look and he stepped aside, pulling the door open for him instead.

The newcomer was skinny, gangly even, moving with an ever-so-slight awkwardness. And, June realized as he stepped into the door behind the Emperor and was silhouetted for a moment with his back to him, he was wearing *two swords*, one on each hip. The door swung shut behind him and June turned to his father, raising an eyebrow as he asked, "Who's the kid with the two swords?"

"Well," His father sounded genuinely surprised, "I almost didn't believe he existed myself."

"What do you mean?" June asked.

His father's mask shifted as he smiled broadly, "I think that's the Crown Prince."

Chapter 4

Brother and Sister

The entire cathedral was filled with light. It flooded in from the great stained-glass windows arrayed along the walls until it seemed the whole building was floating in a sea of shining glass, supported by the holy light itself. Arilin felt the sick knot of anguish in her heart ease ever so slightly at the sight. The architects of Saint Valeria's might have, she thought wryly, designed it with exactly her needs in mind. Her brother was far from the first prince to lie in its light and she was far from the first princess come to mourn.

Every pew in the grand nave was filled, *packed* with mourners, every one of them softly shuffling to get a look at them as they walked down the aisle and making a sort of feathery grinding that filled the still air and hung heavily behind them with every step they took. Everywhere she looked Arilin saw mourners, shining military uniforms standing out against the sea of black-clad civilians like stars in the night sky. Every face was turned towards them, every pair of eyes not hidden behind a veil watching the princesses and the Queen as they slowly made their way towards her brother's plinth. It felt like an electrical charge slowly crackling away at the base of her skull, and Arilin was thankful her mother had insisted on veils themselves. They kept the stares off. For now at least.

After walking for what seemed like forever they finally approached the front row of pews just feet from where her brother lay in state. The final group of guards stood vigil around Prince Adrian's casket, heads bowed in mourning as they waited stoically for their next duty. Arilin knew what was coming herself, and she felt her heart twist at the thought.

Her uncle stepped out from where he had been waiting for them in the very first row and Arilin felt her jaw set as he loomed between her and her brother. Resplendent in his gleaming cuirassier's uniform, Alphonse either didn't notice or ignored her glare, and after looking them over for a moment he stepped aside and gestured for them to take their seats, his face set in an air of gracious sadness. Beatrice darted through without looking at him, but her mother paused to give him an appreciative nod and say, "Alphonse, thank you again for everything you've done for us. I... don't know what we'd do without you."

Sleep better, Arilin thought caustically as her uncle took her mother's hand and kissed it gallantly, replying, "Milady, it's my pleasure to do whatever I can." He smiled sadly and went on, "I wish I could do more."

The Queen smiled back through her veil as their audience murmured appreciatively, "I appreciate it regardless." Taking her hand back, she turned to Arilin and went on, "Come on, dear."

Arilin followed her mother into the pew, giving Alphonse a sidelong glare as she passed. He looked down at her levelly, and she thought she saw the muscles at the sides of his jaw clench ever so slightly as she walked by. Smoothing her skirt, she sank quietly into the pew's padded seat beside her mother as Alphonse sat down heavily on her other side, his heavy jacket rubbing unpleasantly against her arm through the light, tight fabric of her dress' sleeve. Her skin crawled, and she fought to keep from shivering as a sudden silence fell inside the cathedral.

Arilin looked up to see a figure in red had stepped onto her brother's funeral plinth and was slowly making his way towards a lectern standing at its corner. Cardinal Grayson's footsteps sounded slow and soft on the smooth stone as the old man advanced and grasped the lectern with both hands as though to steady himself. Straightening up with an immense dignity, the cardinal announced, "Friends, it is time to bring our vigil upon our dearly departed Prince Adrian to a close." His soft, gravelly voice resounded through the hall from cleverly-concealed speakers, a new installation to ensure the High City's congregation could actually hear the services. Arilin realized that what she had taken for a decorative protrusion on the lectern probably held a microphone as he went on, "Before we begin the Requiem, I think it is appropriate to call upon two people gathered here with us today to speak in his memory." He paused and went on gravely, "These would be his uncle and his sister, Prince Alphonse and Princess Arilin. I cannot think of two better people to speak on his behalf, given our present circumstances." Casting his eye over to the two of them, he nodded and said, "Lord Alphonse, if you please."

Alphonse rose to his feet with a heavy rustle as the weight of his silvered armor settled onto his shoulders, swept his sword into its place at his hip and stepped into the aisle. Striding forward, he mounted her brother's plinth in a single quick motion, giving the cardinal a dignified nod as the old man stepped aside and gestured for him to go on. Wasting no time and without producing so much as a notecard her uncle stepped before the lectern, straightened himself in his armor and thundered, "Friends and comrades! Today is a dark day indeed for our Kingdom!" Arilin winced as the speakers rattled the stained glass, and Alphonse turned and glared daggers off to the side at what she supposed was some poor functionary controlling the volume concealed back in the transept.

After impatiently waiting a couple seconds Alphonse went on, the sound a little less deafening this time, "When I learned my dear nephew Adrian had fallen in battle I felt darkness in my soul, fear and... regret." He paused to let it sink in and went on, "Darkness, for the light of Adrian's life was so cruelly snuffed out, long before he had the chance to accomplish all that had been set before him. I do not think I am alone among us here today that I remember the day of his birth so clearly. My heart *soared* at the news, at seeing the look on my brother's face. At holding our future King in my arms. At seeing him grow to become a man." Alphonse paused, seeming to fight back emotion. Arilin felt her eyes narrowing skeptically as he went on, "And what a man he was. Prince Adrian was our hope for the future. He would have made a new, shining Royal century. Lasting peace and prosperity alongside our good friends in the Dominion. Victory, lasting victory, over the Empire of Masks!" He finished with a snarl and forged ahead, "Alas, my friends... it was not to be."

Alphonse let that one sink in for a while as he collected himself. Sobs echoed out of the audience, and the gentle murmur of men comforting women. He drew a breath, pinched the bridge of his nose theatrically and went on, "My friends, I must be honest. I fear for the future of our great nation. Even now my brother the King is at the front attempting to stem the enemy's advance." He paused for a moment, his eyes sweeping across the mourners, "Who could have known the Empire had become so strong? Who would have expected they were prepared to strike such a devastating blow?" *Probably Father*, Arilin thought, feeling her teeth grind as her uncle continued, "Ours is not the only family to suffer from Field Marshal White's folly. Too many of you here lost your own sons, fathers, brothers on that black day. And that man... no, that *coward*," Alphonse snarled as her mother gasped, "Couldn't be so much as *bothered* to face us to explain his *failure*."

The Field Marshal had shot himself rather than surrender as the Imperial Army closed in on his headquarters north of Fire Ridge. His body had come back on the same ship as her brother's, and Arilin could still see his widow's ashen face far too clearly. She felt a pang of sympathy for the poor woman, distracting her for a moment from the implied rebuke of her father's judgment. All else aside, Lady White was a lovely woman and her husband had come back from the war dead, disgraced and reviled by the Kingdom. It was certainly not something she had deserved.

Prince Alphonse was going on, "Too many of our great Army's leaders have been revealed to be *donkeys* in this present war. It is my dearest hope my brother the King can find a few lions among them. We certainly lost one when Prince Adrian fell." This was hardly eulogy material. An unsettled murmur traveled around the cathedral, and Arilin's mother reached over and grasped her hand reassuringly. She must have felt her stiffening beside her on the pew.

Alphonse plowed ahead, "And as for the Assembly..." He let it hang for a moment, his mouth twisted with a contemptuous smirk. Arilin got the distinct impression that if he hadn't been stuck talking into a microphone he would have started strutting around the stage. Her brother's funeral plinth, which he was using as a *stage*. The princess felt herself *tremble* with anger as he went on, "The less said about the Government, the better. Our nation deserves representation equal to the sacrifice of my dear nephew."

"Speaking of *sacrifice*," Her uncle went on, wiping at his eye theatrically. Arilin doubted he was actually crying, "It is my deepest regret, and I am sure this is felt by all of us here today, that I, or indeed any of us, were not there with Prince Adrian on that fateful day." She sarcastically thought that she absolutely agreed with the first part of the sentiment as he continued, "I know it is, perhaps, a little optimistic of me to think that my sword alone could have turned the tables on that battlefield, but I know I would have tried. I know anyone here with us today would have done the same."

The audience murmured warmly as Alphonse paused for a moment to collect himself. Running a hand through his hair dramatically, he straightened himself at the podium and went on, "Unfortunately none of us had the chance, no, the *opportunity* to lay down our lives for our future King. His regiment did, and they fought to the last at his side. There is no stain of dishonor on the First Cuirassiers. Maximilian's Knights did their duty on that battlefield with strength and honor against an overwhelming foe, and they did their forebears proud. We would all do well to remember their example."

Arilin felt her eyes narrow uneasily. The simple fact of the matter was that they didn't *know* that. Her brother's regiment had been wiped out in their last charge. Few men had made it back to Royal lines alive to tell the tale, and they had *fled*. For their part the enemy had said little about the battle itself.

For an instant the scene from just a couple weeks ago, of Lieutenant Bettancourt and his platoon wheeling and charging into certain death so she could escape, danced before her eyes. She knew a couple of his men had survived to be taken prisoner, horribly wounded and unable to so much as lift their swords to strike at the enemy. Those were heroes right there. Adrian's men... she didn't want to think too hard about.

Her uncle was wrapping up, "In the end my nephew, Prince Adrian, died as he lived. He was a hero and an inspiration to us all, and he will be sorely missed. I pray we have the strength to carry on without him."

Alphonse gathered himself, stepped back from the podium and nodded to the Cardinal. The old man gave him a short, shaky bow and stepped forward as her uncle stepped down from the plinth to stand beside their pew, ever-so respectfully keeping the path open for her to go up herself. Arilin looked over to see him gesturing for her to go ahead as the Cardinal said, "Thank you, Prince Alphonse, for your kind and, ah... stirring words." His voice softened as he went on, "Princess Arilin, please, come up."

Smoothing the black fabric of her dress, Arilin stood and stepped past her uncle into the aisle, feeling his heavy presence shift behind her and the soft thud as he sat back down. The soft murmur that had filled the cathedral while Alphonse spoke died instantly as she stood there alone, a slender figure in black before her brother's immense coffin, looming over her on its stone plinth. The future Queen.

Arilin closed her eyes and took a deep breath, feeling her corset tighten around her chest as she slowly filled her lungs. She held it for a moment, feeling the garment's reassuring grip around her, the soft fabric of her dress as it fell around her legs, the tight, thin leather of her gloves. The soft weight of her veil on her hair as it shaded the light seeping through her eyelids just a touch darker. Finally she exhaled, reaching up to grab hold of her veil as she strode forward.

Stepping up onto the platform, Arilin pulled off her veil and shook out her hair theatrically, a soft murmur running around the hall at the gesture. The Cardinal stepped aside, eyebrows raised in surprise. She gave him a respectful nod, and he smiled back sadly as she turned to the lectern. The princess took a moment to meditatively wrap her veil around her hand as she stood there facing the assembly. Her brother's mourners, and her future subjects. The fine lace was almost unnoticeable against her gloved palm as she grasped the podium.

"I remember the first time I met Adrian," Arilin began, "I was seven years old, playing with Beatrice in our living room when we got a knock on the door. Our maid went to answer it." The silence in the cathedral seemed to deepen, as though everyone present had slowly drawn breath in shock. As far as polite society was concerned, at least in public, the two princesses had sprung into being fully-formed with the Legitimation. She smiled sadly and forged ahead, "She walked back in with him a minute later, white as a sheet." Arilin went on, "She ran off to get Mother and left the three of us alone together. I'd gotten up to say hello, and he crouched down, got on one knee actually, and looked me straight in the eye."

The sight of Adrian's eyes welled up in her memories, startlingly, vividly red as they bored into hers from just a few inches away. Her greeting had died in her throat as she stood there, her mouth seeming to glue itself together as his gaze fixed her in place like a spiked butterfly. She had practically *seen* the gears turning behind his eyes, and even at the time she had known his thoughts were dark indeed. Knowing what she knew *now* the thought was enough to make her shiver despite the cathedral's stuffy warmth. Steeling herself, Arilin left out that terrifying moment and went on, "He smiled and ruffled my hair, and said, 'How are you doing, Princess?'" Despite everything she smiled at the memory and went on, "And just like that I had an older brother. The next thing I knew I was a princess for real."

Someone gasped, and with good reason. She'd left out a couple things. Adrian's little visit had turned into the Affair of the Hanged Queen and her eyes hurt just thinking about the Legitimation. She and Beatrice had cried blood in screaming agony for a week while the Faceless King's curse turned their eyes blood-red. Arilin pressed forward, "What I didn't know at the time was that there was a great deal more to being a princess than my... childish fantasies, I guess you could call them. Adrian taught me that. Adrian *showed* me that, every day."

The crowd murmured softly as Arilin paused. She thought she felt a hint of warmth in it as she went on, "As the Crown Prince, my brother worked every day to prepare himself for the day when he would carry the Kingdom on his shoulders. He worked every day to do everything he could to help my father and to fulfill his duty as a soldier, and to be a father to his men in turn. And..." Arilin felt her throat tighten as warm memories of her brother welled up. Biting her lip for a second, she closed her eyes and took another deep breath, her corset tightening around her and holding her upright like a suit of armor.

After a long moment her throat loosened and she opened her eyes, casting them around the cathedral's light-flooded great hall. When Alphonse had spoken the crowd had *hummed* as it reacted to his fiery words, people shifting and murmuring to their neighbors despite the solemn occasion. Now they were silent, thousands of eyes staring intently at her in the still air. It was unnerving. Looking down at the first pew just below her, Arilin recognized her mother and Beatrice smiling behind their thick veils and she felt a warm glow spark in her heart for the first time in far too long.

Next to them Alphonse was giving her an unreadable look, his red eyes narrowed ever so slightly as he stared up at her. Arilin felt the corner of her mouth twitch up just as slightly as she looked back to the wider audience and went on, "Adrian somehow found time on top of all of that to teach *me* how to be a princess. I think... well, I think he was worried he would never be King himself. I think he knew, somehow." She let her words hang for a moment, echoing through the cathedral's still air. Finally she went on, "He always seemed... relieved, I guess, knowing I was there. I must have taken some of the burden from him, even if I didn't know it at the time."

The weight of the Kingdom that had landed on her shoulders as she sat beside General Haas that dark night just a couple weeks ago, when he told her of Adrian's death, was still there. At the time it had felt as though it would crush the air from her lungs. Now it was just a weight sitting in the back of her mind, the terrible knowledge that one day she would be Queen. Answerable to nobody and responsible for a nation. She had imagined it would be empowering, as though she was about to spread her wings and fly from a castle's walls. It did feel as though she was standing atop the battlements to be sure, just with no wings and the stones crumbling beneath her feet. Not to mention that *she* had Beatrice. Arilin could barely imagine what it had felt like to her brother to bear it alone for so long. No wonder he had been so happy to have her as a sister.

"I wish I could have been there, too. I've... fantasized about going into battle beside Adrian for almost as long as I've known him." *I probably could have accounted for at least one dragoon*, she thought grimly as images of steel on steel, sparks flying from her saber as she parried the man's blows, danced through her mind. She'd stabbed him through the chest and almost been dragged from Midnight's back as her sword stuck fast. She could still see the masked soldier reining his horse about with her sword sticking clean through him. She went on, "But I also know that Adrian was exactly where he wanted to be. My brother would have given his life for *any* of his men, and he would have given it gladly."

"My brother died a hero. I'm sure..." Arilin's eyes burned, and as she blinked she felt hot tears running down her cheeks. Her throat tightened and she barely kept herself from sobbing as she fought her way onwards, feeling her voice crack, "I'm sure... God had need for a knight among the angels that day." The tears were pouring down her face now, pattering onto the fine-grained wood of the podium as she grasped it with both hands, fighting to steady herself as her corset's steady grip tightened into a crushing vise and stars danced before her eyes. Taking the deepest breath she could she finished, sobbing, "Adrian, I know you're watching... I love you."

Her knees were starting to buckle when she felt a steady arm wrap around her waist. Arilin looked over to see Cardinal Grayson smiling back at her kindly. "You did very well, milady," he murmured as he helped her away from the podium. Alphonse leapt to his feet and rushed forward as they neared the edge of the platform, his much stronger arm tightening around her back as he stepped up and took her from the Cardinal. Her blood flashed cold and her vision clouded over at his touch, and she felt bile well up in the back of her throat as he half-carried her blindly forward, her feet barely touching the ground. A few too-long seconds later she felt a much lighter touch on her arm and smooth wood behind her knees, and she collapsed into her seat on the pew.

"...ght, Arilin?" Her mother was saying something, the outlines of her face starting to resolve through the fog covering her eyes. Arilin closed her eyes and rubbed at them for a moment, shaking her head. When she opened them back up she saw her mother's face right in front of her own, concern written over her features. She was still talking, "...lin? Are you okay?"

Arilin felt another presence glowering to her side. She looked over to see Alphonse staring down at her with what she supposed was his try at a sympathetic expression. He looked too smug by far, she thought, looking down at the biggest obstacle between him and the throne after she had just about fainted in front of half the High City. Very commanding of her. He looked over at her mother and was opening his mouth to say something when she turned back herself and cut him off, "Yes, Mom, I'm fine. Sorry... I haven't been eating much lately." Her mother exhaled with relief and she gave her a half-smile, "I think it caught up with me up there."

Her mother patted her warmly on the shoulder and half-heartedly scolded her, "I think it did. Do you need to go home? We can have the carriage brought around..."

Alphonse added, "Yes, I think that would be an excellent idea."

He was straightening up to call for a servant when Arilin gave him a hard look, "*No.* I will not miss my own brother's *funeral* because I got a little *light-headed.*" She added, "And you're not dragging me out of here."

Her uncle gave her mother a pointed look and the Queen reproached her, "Arilin, it's for-"

Arilin glared back at her and cut her off, "No, Mom. It *isn't.* I'm fine."

Her mother looked back at Alphonse and shrugged helplessly, "She's got her father's personality." He rolled his eyes angrily as she looked back at her and went on, "You're *sure* you're fine, dear?"

Arilin looked back at her mother levelly, then sighed and shook her head, "No, but I'll hold up."

Her mother chuckled sadly and sat back down next to her, patting her thigh warmly, "That's my girl." She dug in her purse for a moment and pulled out a vial, handing it to her as she said softly, "Here's some smelling salts in case you get light-headed again."

"Thanks, Mom." Arilin looked over at her and smiled. On her other side she felt Alphonse reluctantly sink back into his seat as the cathedral's bells began to toll the start of the ceremony. As the sound washed down over them from high above Arilin looked down at the little vial in her hand. She had the feeling she was going to need it more than a few times before the ceremony was over and her brother, Prince Adrian, was laid to rest in his burial vault.

Arilin wasn't wrong about that. But she got into the carriage with her mother and Beatrice on her own two legs at the end of that long, terrible day, and the whole High City saw her do it. Her uncle saw her do it. None of them saw, or knew, that she spent the whole ride back to the Palace sobbing inconsolably in her mother's arms.

Chapter 5

Ghosts and Shadows

Crickets chirped and fireflies danced in the damp summer night, almost making Sophia forget about the cold dew starting to soak through her boots. She was probably in desperate need of a new pair now that she thought about it, and she had left her spare set in a rucksack at the bottom of Fire Ridge. Self-consciously stepping out of the wet roadside grass and back onto the road's dry gravel, she looked over at Tony and asked, "How're you holding up?"

Her friend had been silent ever since they had waved through the last convoy about an hour ago, a dozen mostly-empty wagons heading back to the Corps depot with a few wounded troopers and some mail. Heavy clouds had rolled in earlier, blotting the moons from the sky and plunging them into the kind of deep darkness that made masks swim out from behind every tree and killed conversations before they began. Her question seemed to snap him out of something, and he glanced back at her quickly before shaking his head, "Okay, I guess." He yawned, "Bored."

"Better than the..." Sophia trailed off as she yawned herself. She gave him a look, "Great, now you've got *me* doing it."

Tony chuckled and was about to reply when something caught his attention, eyes narrowing as he looked off down the road to where it cut into the forest and curved out of sight of their checkpoint. Sophia followed his gaze to see a faint light flickering through the trees in the distance. As they watched it come closer he asked, "A car? Is there anything on the list?"

Sophia had memorized the convoy schedule for the night. "No." She replied, looking back at Tony and waving him towards the foxhole the day shift had left for them, "Get into cover. I'll talk to them."

Tony nodded, unslinging his rifle as he stepped into the shadow of the trees and disappeared down the rough-cut steps into their fighting position. Sophia heard the faint rustle of his rifle on the sandbagged rim of the foxhole as she reached down and picked up an innocuous piece of cord laying on the side of the road, the other end lost in the darkness far off to the side of the checkpoint. She gave it a couple tugs, and a few seconds later it tugged back. Chuckling to herself at their little system, Sophia unslung her own rifle and waited.

A small river, more of a stream really, had cut a tree-lined gully across the fields and pastures a couple kilometers west of the peaceful little town of Allenby, now home to the First Cavalry Corps headquarters. It wasn't going to stop soldiers on foot and wouldn't be much of an obstacle for cavalry, but nothing with wheels going to or from Grenville, forty kilometers further down the road, was going to pass without going over the little bridge they had set their checkpoint in front of. They weren't exactly in a position to be holding off the entire Imperial Army, but they could absolutely keep unwanted visitors from bothering General Kellerman.

Like whoever was in this car that was emerging from the trees, headlights painfully bright in the dark as they spread a constellation of reflections across the dewy fields. Sophia heard the engine's pitch change faintly as the driver saw their checkpoint's lantern hung on its picket a little ways in front of her and eased off the gas. Stepping through the gap between the coil of barbed wire they had pulled across the road and the wire they had strung to keep any enemies from simply running up to their foxhole under the trees nearby, Sophia pulled the flashlight from her harness, thumbed it on and waved it from side to side in the sign for 'halt'.

The driver obligingly rolled to a stop next to the lantern and mercifully shut off the headlights to reveal a long, low staff car in its dim light. Sophia raised an eyebrow as her eyes readjusted to the darkness and she noticed a long whip antenna protruding from the car's rear fender, bouncing back and forth slightly from its momentum as the passenger-side window cranked down. This clearly wasn't the vehicle of some lost country squire trying to get back to his estate on a dark night.

Sophia clipped her flashlight back onto her harness and walked forward, bringing her bayoneted rifle to the ready as she said over the low purr of the idling engine, "Dismount one to be recognized!"

The passenger-side door swung open and a stocky man in what looked like a gray jaeger's uniform got out, his face set in an unreadable expression as he looked her up and down. By the lantern's light she saw... crossed cannons on his red Artillery collar patches? That was new, his rank should have been there. And the collar was wrong, it was a stand-and-fall design, not the old straight-up model. Uneasiness tingled in the back of her head as she quickly cast her eyes over the man, finally noticing that he was wearing shoulder boards, something else new. Three silver bars gleamed dully in the light of their lantern, set against what looked like a pale gray background. A captain.

The man's eyes had narrowed as she looked him over. His hand slowly shifted onto the butt of his holstered pistol as he said, "Not a lot of women in the infantry... what's your unit?"

Sophia ignored the question and shot back, fingers tightening on her rifle, "Moon."

The man gave her a flat look for a second before he realized she was asking for the countersign. Relaxing a little, he chuckled and replied, "Witchcraft. There, happy now, Miss...?"

Exhaling, Sophia lowered her rifle and held up her hand to tell Tony to relax. Walking up to the man, she said, "Rose. Ah, sir." She snorted and apologized, "Sorry, you're not on the list and we've heard of the Empire doing crazier things."

The captain shook his head, "No need for that. I'm sure you have your orders." He looked around into the darkness and asked, "Where's your sergeant? I need to speak to him."

Sophia laughed, "I'm it."

"Really, Miss..." He looked down at the rank on her shoulders skepti-cally, "Private First Class Rose?"

"Yep." She grimaced, "We're... short right now."

The man glanced around into the darkness, "I was meaning to ask where everyone else was." Looking back at her, he raised an eyebrow and went on, "*Please* don't tell me it's just you out here."

Sophia shook her head, "No." Stepping aside a little, she looked back at where their foxhole was hidden under the trees and said, "Tony, you can come out now. And, uh..." She glanced back at the captain, then back into the darkness, "Bring the phone."

Tony quickly emerged from the darkness trailing a wire reel, their field telephone in hand. Setting it on the car's hood, he looked between the two of them and said, "Here you go, Sophie... and, uh, sir."

"Thanks," Sophia turned back to the officer, "Do you want to just talk to our command, sir? I can't let you through without clearance anyways." The man nodded, and she cranked the phone and spoke to the operator back at Charlie Company's headquarters in Allenby, who quickly sum-moned the duty officer.

Lieutenant Thorn's voice buzzed over the handset, "Sophie, what's going on?" For a while the unassuming young banker from Jade Falls had been their company commander, a job he had gotten by being the only officer in Charlie Company who hadn't been wounded or killed going up Fire Ridge. With the regiment reorganized down into a battalion he was back leading her platoon.

"We've got a guy up here, a captain." She replied, "He just drove up in a car, I think he's got..." She glanced into the darkened vehicle for a moment before setting the phone back against her head and going on, "Yeah, he's got two guys with him. Driver and I think a radio operator." She finished, "He knew the password."

She imagined Thorn checking his own copy of the convoy list for a few seconds before his voice came back on the line, "What's he doing out here?"

"I don't know, sir." She chuckled, "I figured I'd let him tell you himself."

Sophia handed the phone to the captain and the man started off, "Hello, this is Captain Beck." She heard her lieutenant's voice buzz over the line faintly and the man replied, "I'm an advance party. Griffon and Monocle are visiting Wildfire Six." After a very long pause Thorn's voice buzzed again faintly and the man said, "Very soon... thank you, yes."

He handed the phone back to her and Thorn's voice immediately came over the line. Even through the tinny field telephone his voice sounded strained, "Miss Rose?"

"Yes, sir?" She replied.

"I want you to listen to me very carefully." She raised her eyebrows in surprise as he went on, "Make sure you keep a couple men at the checkpoint, but otherwise you and your team are to do *anything* that Captain Beck requires of you. Do you understand?"

Sophia nodded and immediately felt stupid for doing it to someone talking to her over a *phone*. Getting herself back together, she managed, "Yes, sir. I understand."

"Thanks." The faint hiss of the line died abruptly as her lieutenant hung up on her.

Sophia swallowed and handed the phone back to Tony. Turning to the captain nervously, she started, "Ah, sir... do you need anything? My boss just told me to help you out with whatever you need."

Captain Beck looked her up and down for a second, then chuckled to himself. Sophia was pretty sure she knew what he had thought of before he glanced off into the darkness at the other end of the bridge and said, "I could use a guide. After the rest of my convoy gets here we'll be moving on to the Cavalry Corps headquarters... I'm assuming you know where that is in town?"

Sophia nodded, "Yes, sir." She shared a glance with Tony and went on, "We'll both go with you."

The captain raised an eyebrow skeptically, "Wouldn't that leave your post unmanned?"

She laughed, "No, sir. I have more guys." Stepping into the lantern's pool of blue light, she waved into the darkness off in the direction the string had run earlier. Sophia raised one finger, held it for a second and then waved her hand towards herself as though she was beckoning something out of the darkness.

After a minute a faint shape appeared in the gloom and Sophia heard soft footfalls out in the field over the low purr of the car's engine. A moment later Hargrave emerged from the darkness, the lantern painting his craggy face with its unearthly light. The old man looked between the three of them and asked her, "What's going on, Sophie?"

"I need you to take over here for a while." She nodded at the captain, "Once the rest of his convoy gets in we're going to guide them in to the headquarters..." Trailing off, she looked back at Beck and asked, "Do you know when that'll be, sir?"

The man glanced at his watch in the dim light, "Any minute now I'd think." Looking off back down the road, he nodded and said, "Actually, I think that's them right now." Sophia followed his gaze and saw faint lights bobbing through the trees as Beck turned back to her and asked, "Where'd he come from?"

She chuckled and pointed off into the darkness Hargrave had come out of, "We have a machine gun dug in out that way, sir. If you'd been Imperial, well..."

Beck raised an eyebrow and remarked, "Right." Looking at Tony, he went on, "You're coming with me. I'm assuming you know the way?" Her friend nodded and he turned back to her, "As for you, miss, there's someone I think would like to meet you."

"Oh?" Sophia raised an eyebrow as the rest of the convoy began emerging from the trees. It was only four cars, one of them sporting a long radio antenna like the captain's. Beck waved for them to halt and they slowed, pulling to a stop behind his car.

Gesturing for Tony to get into his own vehicle, the captain began walking back down the line of waiting cars. Sophia followed him wordlessly, pulling the bayonet off her rifle and sheathing it at her belt as she went. She noticed the middle two cars of the group were longer than the front and rear vehicles. *Limousines*, not just staff cars, she thought as Beck reached down to open a rear door. Faint light spilled out as he pulled it open and said, "My lord, I've think I found someone you might want to meet." A deep voice from inside said something she couldn't quite make out and Beck replied, "Well, there's not many women in the infantry, my lord."

"Oh, really? Now I *am* curious." The voice drifted out again. Coming around Beck's side, Sophia saw a man's lower body inside the car where he was sitting with his back to the car's front, the limousine's seating area having been set up to put its passengers face-to-face with each other. He seemed to be wearing that same gray jaeger uniform as Beck. The man shifted a little as he took notice of her and raised a black-gloved hand from his lap to gesture for her to get in. Sophia felt her breath catch in her throat.

Heart hammering in her ears, Sophia swung herself into the car and settled onto the rich leather seat across from the man, setting her rifle between her legs. She looked up timidly to see someone any Royal subject would recognize. His face was on the money, after all.

"Well, what do we have here?" King William IV looked back at her, smiling ever so slightly. His deep voice reminded her of Prince Adrian, a lot, but it was somehow... she couldn't quite put her finger on it. Stronger, harder, but gentler somehow. Like her own father. Unlike Prince Adrian, the King had nothing to prove to anyone.

Sophia swallowed hard and managed, "Sophia Rose, my lord. Two, ah..." Her mind went blank for a moment as she tried to remember their new unit designation, "Charlie Company, Two-Twenty-Fourth Infantry."

"Oh?" The King leaned back and folded his hands in his lap as he looked over at the man sitting beside her. The car started rolling forward gently, bumping over the bridge's planks as he went on, "I don't recall there *being* a 224th Regiment, Walter. One of your new units?"

The man chuckled and shifted to look over at her, reaching up to stroke his goatee. In a dreamlike haze Sophia counted four stars on his collar as he studied her for a moment before turning back to the King, "Not exactly, but you could say that." He chuckled, "It's a battalion, actually. They're what's left of the 24th Infantry." General Haas turned back to her and said, "You know, I couldn't believe my ears when I heard you'd turned up. How on *Gaia* did you get off Fire Ridge?"

For a second Sophia wondered if she was going to run into every single important person in the Royal Army before this war was over. She'd met Prince Adrian three times, General Kunst, General MacMahon, and now General Haas and the King. Not to mention June Anjanou. She felt like she was playing *bingo*. Who was next, the Emperor? Quickly pushing the thought out of her head, she replied, "We walked out, sir. Through the Dragonspines." She shivered at the thought of jagged black mountains in the darkness, like the jaws of a great beast eating her and her friends alive. Pushing *that* thought out of her head too, something occurred to her and she turned to the King, "My lord, we were on top of Fire Ridge when Prince Adrian... well..."

Sophia trailed off as the King's eyes narrowed, his face hardening into an unreadable expression. His voice was flat and hard as he said, "Go on."

She cursed herself for a moment. Why had she decided to bring *that* up? What was she even going to say? That Prince Adrian's men had abandoned him and fled? That she and her friends had huddled under an artillery barrage that *hadn't been that bad* instead of charging out to help them? They could have done something. She *should* have done something. But she hadn't, and the King's son was *dead*. Sophia felt tears well up in her eyes suddenly as she looked down at her lap, "I'm sorry, my lord." She repeated herself, sobbing, "I'm sorry... we should have..."

"Hush, young lady." Sophia felt a strong hand on her shoulder and looked over through blurred eyes to see General Haas offering her a handkerchief. She took it wordlessly and started wiping at her eyes, feeling like she wanted to die as he shifted in his seat to face back towards the King and went on, "My lord, I was waiting for a better time to bring this up, but I finally got a chance to talk to Leon in private a couple days ago."

"Oh?" William IV's voice was unreadable, "Do tell."

General Haas went on without so much as a pause, "He sent the First Regiment forward, but he told me, and I don't think he'd lie to me about this, that he gave Eighth Division *explicit* orders that they were not to be committed unless the situation was near-perfect." Sophia thought that he was clearly used to being the bearer of bad news as he went on, "Nothing I've heard about that battle, my lord, sounds *perfect* to me. I know their horse artillery was stuck in traffic halfway down the ridge."

The King snapped back, "What are you getting at, Walter?"

Sophia heard the leather seat creak softly as General Haas leaned back slightly to look over at the King, "I think Adrian made his own decision that day." She looked up blearily to see him glance at her, then back to the King, "I certainly wouldn't blame the infantry."

"The only people I blame for my son's death, *general*," The King snapped back, "Are the Imperials. And even they," He added bitterly, "Gave him the honors he deserved."

General Haas diplomatically said nothing. Sophia thought absently that she was probably one of the few people in the Royal Army to have heard a full general's rank used as a curse. After a few hour-long minutes of icy silence she heard the seat beside her creak again and the general said, "You said your name was *Sophia Rose*, miss?"

She looked over quickly, surprised, "Yes, it is... sir?"

"Any relation to John Rose?" General Haas asked, raising a snowy eyebrow.

Surprised, Sophia blinked and replied, "Yes, sir, he's my father."

The general grunted. She supposed it was about as close to a laugh as he got these days as he went on, "It's a small world, dear. I suppose you don't remember me, though, you were just a baby at the time." He gave her a thin smile, "How *are* your parents these days? I haven't seen either of them since the Dragon's Jaw."

"They're fine." She chuckled nervously and elaborated, "Dad took over as Sergeant Major after the battle and Mom's running the bakery back in Jade Falls." Her lips tightened as she thought for a second before she went on boldly, "Uh, sir, I'm *really* worried she was told we'd both been killed. We've both sent letters, but we haven't gotten anything back."

"Well, you're not alone. My own chief of staff has been complaining about the mail, and he's a *general*." General Haas frowned and looked over at the King, "One more thing for me to fix, my lord."

Clearly happy to be off the subject of his son, William IV replied, "If it keeps Ziggy happy it'll be worth it."

Both men chuckled. The car began bumping along cobblestones as darkened buildings rose around them, and after a couple minutes Sophia felt the slight tug on her body as the car braked to a halt. Looking out the window she could see the outline of the block of offices the Cavalry Corps staff had taken over in the darkness. They had previously belonged to a crop insurance company that was, she thought idly, probably about to go out of business given the war.

Shapes moved in the darkness outside and someone popped the door's latch, swinging it open to reveal the headquarters' entryway. The Charlie Company sentries on guard outside were already saluting, their bayonets gleaming dimly in the gloom as they held their rifles rigidly up-right. Sophia looked over at the King, and he smiled and gestured for her to get out, saying, "Ladies first."

General Haas added, "Tell your father I said hello, by the way."

"Will do, sir," Sophia nodded and looked back to the King, "Ah, thank you, my lord."

She picked up her rifle and climbed out, giving the sentries an apol-ogetic smile as she went. They managed to keep the surprise mostly off their faces as the King and General Haas climbed out a moment after her. She stepped aside as the door swung open, Lieutenant Thorn silhouetted for a moment holding it open as light poured out of the entryway. The two men quickly disappeared inside and Sophia faintly heard Thorn call-ing the headquarters to attention as the door swung closed.

Sophia turned to see who had pulled the door open and found herself face to face with Captain Beck. Even in the darkness she could see his smirk as he remarked, "I trust you behaved yourself, Miss Rose?"

She sighed and looked away. All she really wanted to do was go crawl in a deep hole somewhere and sleep for a while. "Yeah." Glancing back, she added, "Sir."

The burly captain chuckled, a little unpleasantly. Sophia got the feeling he didn't laugh a lot. "If I hear about this later I'll have only myself to blame." Stepping back a little, he looked between her and the other side of the car. Following his gaze Sophia saw Tony standing there, looking a little dazed himself. Raising his eyebrows questioningly, Beck asked, "Can you two make it back to your post by yourselves?"

Sophia shared a look with Tony. His eyes pleaded, *get me out of here.* Nodding at him, she turned back to the captain and replied, "We'll walk. It's not that far."

"Alright then." He gave them each a nod and went on, "Thanks for your assistance, Miss Rose, Mister Gravesend."

"No problem, sir." Tony chimed in, "Come on, Sophie, let's go."

Glancing over at Tony, she said, "Alright." Sophia turned back to Captain Beck and nodded, "G'night, sir."

Tony had already started walking and she hurried to catch up to him, the cars' softly idling engines fading quickly into the night behind them as they went. Darkened buildings turned the cobbled street into a black, jagged canyon rising against the night sky, their tops lost in a thickening blanket of fog that had rolled into the town in the wet night. Ever since the Cavalry Corps had moved in Allenby had apparently been under blackout and the few remaining civilians confined to their homes after dark by a strict curfew.

Heavy, muffled footsteps sounded on the street ahead of them, and Sophia reached back to rest a hand on the butt of her slung rifle as shapes swam out of the darkness. After a tense moment she made out the silhouettes of Royal soldiers, with their field caps and equipment slung around their waists. Pale faces stood ever-so slightly out of the murk as they turned to look at her and Tony, and she saw the group tense and relax just as she had as they made out they were friendly.

"Hey," The lead man raised a hand to greet them. Sophia recognized him as Corporal Stennis with the rest of his team from her platoon's Second Squad. He went on, "Sophie, Tony, what are you two doing out here? I thought you two were on checkpoint duty."

Sophia chuckled, "We *were,* the two of us got pulled to guide in some visitors." Leaning in close to him, she murmured in his ear, "I wouldn't go back to headquarters right now if I were you, the King and General Haas are in there."

Stennis gave her a look, "Seriously?" She nodded and he laughed nervously, "I'll keep that in mind... are you two heading back?"

"Yeah." She replied, "Seen anything we should be worried about?"

He shook his head, "No. It's a ghost town." He looked from side to side warily, then back to her, "Honestly this place has been giving me the creeps tonight. I don't know why."

"I don't blame you." Sophia said, "I can barely see the hand in front of my face in this."

"Tell me about it. Anyways," Stennis gestured back towards the headquarters with his chin, "King or no King, I've gotta go check in. You two take care heading back."

Sophia smiled and replied, "Will do, thanks." The patrol went on their way, the soldiers' equipment creaking slightly as they walked past. The men were quickly lost in the darkness behind them, and Sophia and Tony were once again alone in the dark, wet street.

A light, misting rain began to fall as they started walking again, slickening the cobblestones and dampening their uniforms. Sophia was opening her mouth to complain about it when she froze, the words dying in her throat. Tony walked on for a couple steps before he realized she had stopped. Turning around, he was opening his own mouth to say something when she held up a hand to stop him. Looking perplexed, he stepped closer and whispered, "*What's going on?*"

She shook her head and replied softly, "I thought I heard something... like a door closing." She closed her eyes, opened her mouth slightly and listened for a moment. Tony considerately shuffled back a little to give her some room. After a couple seconds she opened her eyes and looked at him, "And footsteps, I think." She pointed off down a side street they had stopped just short of, "Down there."

"Want to check it out?" Tony asked, unslinging his rifle.

"Yeah." She pulled her own rifle off her shoulder, drew her bayonet and slowly pushed it onto the locking lug under the weapon's barrel, holding the release button down until it was fully seated so it wouldn't make a loud click in the darkness. Tony quickly followed her example and fixed his own bayonet, and she stalked off down the side street with him at her heels.

After a few seconds Sophia stopped and listened again. She heard the same soft footsteps, now seeming to come from up ahead, down the street and towards the far side. A row of picturesque townhouses sat along that side of the street, and she motioned for Tony to cover her as she crossed over. He dropped to a knee at her side and patted her leg, and Sophia darted over to the far side and tucked herself behind a row of brickwork steps leading up to one of the front doors. Tony joined her a moment later and she climbed to her feet and crept off down the sidewalk, rifle at the ready.

The residents of the townhouses had planted hydrangeas in the gaps between their front walkways, their sweet smell and sprays of white flowers against the darkness giving Sophia a surreal feeling as she advanced, the mist beading on them soaking cold against her shoulder as she brushed by. Pushing the thought from her mind, she listened closely and heard the soft footsteps again, now seeming to come from the end of the building where it looked like it split off into an alley. After thinking for a moment Sophia realized the buildings themselves were shaping the pattern of sound, and whoever was making the footsteps was down the alley or even behind the townhouses.

Stopping just short of the alley entrance, Sophia listened for a moment and heard the footsteps again, now quite noticeable. Whoever was making them sounded like they were moving down the other side of the row of townhouses in the same direction as she and Tony, away from the main street. And they probably didn't know they were being followed. Sophia thought for a second and looked further down the street. Past the alley there was a little glass-fronted corner store, then a side street. Shifting back a little, she turned and whispered to Tony, "Move up to the corner and cover left down the street."

"Sure," He murmured back, "What's your plan?"

"I'll call them out from here. They might bolt." She went on, "If they look Imperial, shoot them."

"Got it." Tony padded past her and ducked under the shop's windows, quickly making his way to the corner and crouching behind it, leaning out slightly to stick his rifle down the street beyond. Anyone who wanted to take a shot at him would only have his weapon and the very side of his head to draw a bead on, if they noticed him at all.

Pushing down the sick feeling in her stomach, Sophia tucked herself into the side of the alley and shouted, "*Royal Army!* Come out where I can see you!" The footsteps stopped suddenly. Sophia waited for a moment, then another moment. Several seconds went by as she thought she heard murmurs in the darkness. Feeling faintly ridiculous, she went on, "I can hear you! Don't make me come in there!"

"Alright, alright, you caught me." A deep voice floated out of the alley. She stepped back as a dim silhouette floated out of the darkness, pale hands open and half-raised at the level of his head. She felt her breath go out a little as she saw the pale face between them. No mask, and he was wearing what looked like workman's clothes, ordinary pants and a patched jacket. Sophia was tall for a woman, taller even than a lot of men, but this man towered over her easily as he stopped at the end of the alley and looked her up and down, "It's awful late, young lady. Where are your friends?"

"I'm doing the talking here," She snapped, gesturing pointedly with her bayonet, "And where are *yours?* I know it wasn't just you back there."

The man smirked, but it didn't reach his eyes. Sophia felt a finger of ice work its way down her spine as he replied, "Just me. I was going to vi-"

The gunshot smashed through the dark air, Tony's muzzle flash catching the man for an instant as he lunged at her like a viper, an arm sweeping down to knock her bayonet aside. Sophia dipped her rifle a little and his arm sailed through empty air, her bayonet circling back over it as she stepped forward and slammed it though his chest hard enough she felt his feet leave the ground.

This was where most people collapsed. Sophia felt her eyes widen as his feet came back down and *planted*. His hand snaked back to clamp down on her rifle's muzzle, locking it in place like a steel vise while he reached for a weapon behind his back with his other arm, snarling with animal fury. She shifted her weight forward and kicked him viciously under the ribs, driving him back as her bayonet came free with a sick squelch, his hand still locked around her rifle.

The man was almost inhumanly strong, but Sophia was pretty strong herself and she had three feet of leverage. Yanking her rifle around in a short, vicious circle, she bent his wrist back on itself and lunged again as his pistol came out from behind his back. The bones in his wrist *broke* with a ripping pop as she stabbed her bayonet through his throat, smashing him backwards again. He collapsed like a rag doll in the alley and Sophia spun towards Tony as a volley of shrill, hammering automatic gunfire tore through the night.

The shop's windows shattered and small, fast, evil things cracked through the air in front of her, Tony silhouetted for a moment in the enemy's muzzle flash as he popped the safety cap off one of his stick grenades. Through the falling glass she saw a dark shape rush forward in the street past him, and Sophia flicked off her safety and leveled her rifle as another one of these *demons* appeared around the corner, his submachine gun swinging down at her best friend as she pulled the trigger. Gunfire erupt-ed just past Tony, the strobing muzzle flash catching flying brickwork as the man staggered back from the impact, spraying the storefront with bullets as his finger tightened on the trigger. Sophia racked her weapon's bolt and fired again as he steadied himself, driving him to his knees, then again and again and again as the man slowly fell to the cobblestones.

Tony looked at the man for a second, then grimly pulled the igniter on his grenade and waited for two more of the longest seconds in Sophia's life before throwing it down the street. It exploded a moment later with an ear-splitting crack, filling the gloom past him with light and fire. Duck-ing carefully beneath the shattered storefront and feeling her feet crunch over broken glass, Sophia carefully crept up behind Tony and shouted over the ringing in her ears, *"Is that all of them?"*

Picking his rifle back up and peering out into the street carefully, Tony said, "Yeah, looks like it. I counted three, plus yours..." He glanced back at her for a moment, "I'm assuming you handled him?"

Sophia sighed heavily, feeling the tension drain out of her body, "Yeah. Yeah, I did." Shaking her head, she risked a peek over the store's shattered glass window. All she could see were the buildings on the far side of the street, and she quickly ducked back down and asked Tony, "How can you tell?"

Tony replied, "I hit one coming out of the alley, plus your two... and it looks like the last one tried to throw my grenade back." He chuckled, a little unpleasantly. Going on, he asked, "Do you want to push down the street?"

Taking another deep breath, Sophia shook her head. The fight couldn't have lasted more than fifteen or twenty seconds. The Imperial who had tried to flank them was still gargling and twitching on the cob-blestones not ten feet away. If she and Tony had done *anything* wrong, if she had been distracted for even an instant and hadn't been so quick with her bayonet, they would be the ones dying in the street right now. Whoever these guys were, they had been *good*. Pathfinders, her father had called them. Feeling like she was about to start shaking, Sophia grit her teeth, settled her nerves and replied, "No. We don't know if that was all of them. We're staying right here and waiting for reinforcements."

"Alright." Tony added sarcastically, "Of course we have to deal with *this* when all the brass in the world's in town."

Heavy, running footsteps started echoing through the buildings be-hind them, and Sophia turned to see what looked like Stennis' patrol emerging into the street behind them. Hoping they didn't get mistaken for the enemy themselves, Sophia shouted, "*Royal Army!* Hold your fire!" She went on, "We've got four dead Imperials over here!"

Stennis rushed up, glancing at the dead man in the alley as he went by. After calling out where he wanted his soldiers to place themselves he crouched next to the two of them and remarked, "Jesus, Sophia. We really can't leave you alone, can we? Was that a *grenade* I heard?"

"Yeah." Tony replied, a little smugly.

Sophia gave him a look, which he ignored. Turning back to Stennis, she gestured down the street and said, "There's two more down there. We counted four, there might be more still around."

"*Great.* Just what we need right now." Giving her a hard look, the corporal said, "Alright, Sophie, I've got this here. I need you two to run back to headquarters and report to Lieutenant Thorn and whoever else cares to know about our pathfinder problem. The Ki-" He caught himself, probably well aware they could be being overheard, "*That guy*, if he's interested. They're probably going to want to get the rest of the company out here."

Sophia nodded, "Sure thing." She tapped Tony on the shoulder, "You heard him, Tony. Let's go."

The two of them got up and ran back to the headquarters, rifles in hand. A few minutes later they were talking to a very perturbed Lieutenant Thorn, who probably would have been much calmer about the entire situation if he hadn't had nine stars' worth of generals and the King standing around his duty desk listening to them.

Chapter 6
En Garde

Unseasonal rain beat at the palace windows, the storm turning the day outside the Privy Council's meeting room a menacing gray. Looking over her shoulder, Arilin saw the storm lashing Sapphire Bay far below, dark water turning white as the wind whipped it into frothing whitecaps. The islands at the bay's mouth had already been blotted from view by the low clouds that were now threatening to engulf the High City itself. Down in the Low City, she thought, people were probably running for cover.

"Princess?" Alphonse's deep voice broke her out of her reverie. She sighed and turned to him, and he went on, "I understand if we're boring you... you shouldn't feel any need to be here, you know."

Yet here I am, Arilin thought. Smiling politely, she replied, "I'd be lying if I said this was the most *interesting* discussion I've ever heard." It was actually one of the *least*. Looking around at where the rest of the Privy Council sat around the massive conference table, she went on, "Gentlemen, I'm afraid I don't see how what you've been talking about relates to me or my father in the slightest."

"Neither do I, milady." From the opposite end of the table the Prime Minister looked between his coalition partners angrily and went on, "This is something we should be discussing back at the *Assembly*. I did not come here to waste their graces' time."

"Oh, I agree with you." The Labor Minister's sharp voice dripped sarcasm, "It would be nice if you would give us the time of day to discuss it at the Assembly, and thus, well..." He glanced between Arilin and her uncle before chuckling unpleasantly, "Their graces' time is going to get wasted."

The Commerce Minister harrumphed nervously, buttons straining tight against his shirt at the gesture. The man reminded Arilin of an over-stuffed sausage. His name was Mr. Henriks, if she recalled correctly. Giving the two of them an apologetic glance, he turned back to the Prime Minister, "I do not often agree with Mister Meyer, sir, but he is correct in this case. The Dissenting Union has stood loyally by the government in this crisis and we believe that we are entitled to a greater share of the ministries." He nodded graciously across the table at his temporary ally, "As are they, for that matter."

"We agree then. Thanks, Jurgen." The Labor Minister, Mr. Meyer said, chuckling again as he leaned back in his chair. Arilin had to think for a second before she realized that he had called the Commerce Minister by his first name.

The Prime Minister looked between the two politicians helplessly, then at Alphonse. Arilin saw her uncle's jaw tighten as he started, "Well, if we can do this quickly, I suppose-"

"*Enough!*" Arilin jumped in her seat as Alphonse slammed his hand down on the table with a crack like a gunshot, "We did not come here to listen to you negotiate with *communists* over who gets to run the Forest Service." Her uncle speared the Prime Minister with a glare, "I do not care in the slightest about the difficulties of your current position, Mr. Gainsborough. You will resolve them, or we will find someone else who can." Alphonse glanced over at her, "Don't you agree, Arilin?"

The princess thought for a moment, then sighed. Politics in the Western Kingdom wasn't really that complicated. There were six political parties, six and a half if she counted the Anti-Legitimist schism in the Royalist party that nobody wanted to admit existed. Most of them hated each other, but because none of them could hope to get a clear majority in the Assembly some of them had to put aside their differences after every election to form a government. With the recent military disasters the current Socialist-Liberal-Union coalition was on thin ice although, she noted wryly, they still all still seemed happy to meet with the Crown together.

Which brought her to Alphonse's question. There were a number of possible alternative governments, most of which would be more supportive of the war effort and, by extension, the monarchy. And it probably wouldn't be hard to collapse the current coalition without even showing the Crown's hand by officially dismissing them. Her uncle had suggested as much himself before the meeting. Something as basic as a crackdown on union organizers would humiliate the Socialists and drive them into the opposition, and without their support the Liberals would lose their majority. The Dissenting Union would predictably defect to the Conservatives and they would have a supportive new government to wage the war. It was all very simple.

What was not simple at all was Alphonse's angle in this. In fact, Arilin had yet to figure out the slightest hint of what, if anything, her uncle was plotting. He had been nothing but helpful and supportive ever since she had returned from her time with the Army. Her father had told her he didn't completely trust him, and for good reason, but what did that really mean? Maybe *she* was the crazy one, jumping at shadows and imagining conspiracies. Maybe Alphonse was simply doing his duty as a member of the Royal Family and pitching in at the nation's hour of need. Logically, even if he was running some kind of scheme against her his actions wouldn't all be in service to it.

Arilin was trying to unravel one plot in a town full of them and she felt like she was deaf and blind. If she had been in a room full of other teenagers, students at the Royal Academy, then this would have been simple. She would know who her friends and enemies were and how to leverage the others into doing her bidding. Here, in this group of adults... she didn't even know where to start. She needed a clearer picture.

In the meantime one of Patricia's lessons popped into her mind. The Lady General had told her, more than once, that people would try to pressure her into making decisions without having all the information she actually needed. Too-clever subordinates jumping to conclusions, impatient superiors demanding results, the enemy painting exactly the picture they wanted her to see. The government seemed to be in the process of patching things up, so why did she need to join Alphonse in threatening them? A couple days of backroom bickering among the politicians wasn't going to lose the war.

"Arilin?" Her uncle asked. She had been thinking for more than a long moment.

His voice broke her out of her thoughts, and she smiled politely and looked back at him, "I don't think that's *quite* necessary right now, Uncle." Turning to the politicians, she went on, "I'm sure you'll be able to work things out among yourselves, gentlemen. Just..." She chuckled, "Please not now. It's all very *boring* to me."

The Prime Minister visibly deflated, the dim light catching the sweat on his bald head as his head moved. She realized that Gainsborough had been sweating bullets, waiting for the Royal hammer to fall and shatter his political career into a thousand pieces. He might feel like he owed her something later. Straightening up quickly, he replied, "Of course, milady."

Feeling the heat of her uncle's gaze boring into the side of her head, Arilin moved along before he could object, "Now, sir, if we could move on to the Service Law...?" She trailed off hopefully.

The Prime Minster blanched, most of the other Liberal Assemblymen looked at their hands and the Commerce Minister harrumphed again, inflating rather alarmingly. Meyer, the Socialist, snorted and replied, "Out of the question." He looked around the table and back to her dismissively, "We're not interested in giving you our children to kill this time around, *princess*."

Arilin snorted and looked over at her uncle. The muscles at the corner of Alphonse's jaw bulged dangerously as he glared at the smirking Labor Minister. For a moment she was worried he was going to get up and give the man an honestly well-deserved beating when Henriks cut in harshly, "Enough, *Curtis*. She doesn't deserve that." He went on, "I apologize for my, ahem, colleague milady, but from what I understand the needs of the Army are being quite well supplied with volunteers for the moment."

"I don't apologize for myself." Meyer added snidely.

"*Get out.*" Her uncle said, in a cold, flat tone she had never heard before. The cocky half-smile drained from Meyer's face as Alphonse went on icily, "Don't make me call the guards. We're on the fifth floor and communists take the *stairs*."

The Labor Minister sat for a second, pale-faced as he stared back at her uncle. Just as she heard him open his mouth to keep going Meyer quickly pushed his seat back and fled with as much dignity as he could muster. As the heavy door swung shut behind him thunder crashed outside and Arilin jumped in her seat, icy fingers clenching around her heart. For an instant she had been back at Fire Ridge, cuirassiers falling from their horses all around her as the enemy's swords reached out.

Arilin shook her head quickly and came back to reality. It wasn't much better. She could *see* Alphonse's murderous gaze working its way across the seated Assemblymen, the men collapsing in on themselves one by one. Despite the humming radiators along the walls the room felt so cold she half-expected to see her own breath hanging in the air as she slowly exhaled. Her uncle went on, quite conversationally, "Does anyone else feel like insulting the Crown?" His basilisk glare landed on the Prime Minister, "How about you, Gainsborough?"

The old man replied unsteadily, eyes wide, "N-no, milord."

"Is that communist weasel representative of your government?" Alphonse asked, his voice like a dagger of ice, "Or are you just incompetent when it comes to picking your ministers?"

Gainsborough sat up in his seat, reddening as Arilin's thoughts raced. What did her uncle think he was doing? This was the second time in almost as many minutes that he had picked a fight with the Assembly, shouting and pounding the table and... she didn't know what he had meant by Communists taking the stairs but she assumed it was some kind of threat. Was he *trying* to collapse the government? To just be so rude to the Prime Minister that the poor man was forced to resign?

Arilin grabbed hold of that thread in her mind and pulled on it. To be fair Meyer's comment had been inexcusable, but Alphonse had just exploded at him as though he didn't care about the political situation at all. And he had done this *after* she had thrown Gainsborough a lifeline once already. Why he was doing this was beyond her, but she could assume it was nothing good.

The Prime Minister was pushing his chair back to stand when she spoke up, "Please, sir, hold on a second." He froze and looked back at her, palms splayed against the table ready to heave himself up. Smiling apologetically, Arilin went on, "I'm sure you understand my uncle is very protective of me, and with Adrian's..." Her throat, barely recovered from too much crying, swelled shut at the thought of her brother. The men around the table looked back at her sympathetically as she swallowed hard and managed, "It's been an awful week for us. Please, can we just get back to business?"

"I don't see how we really can, dear." Arilin looked over to see her uncle looking at her with the kind of fake sympathy adults have for well-meaning but annoying children. It made her skin crawl. He went on, "I will not sit here and be insulted in my own palace."

There we go, Arilin thought. *His* own palace? That was either an unfortunate choice of words or his mask was slipping. Pushing the thought to the back of her head, she gestured at the still-frozen Prime Minister and replied, "I wouldn't ask you to, Uncle. But he deserves to be treated better than that."

Alphonse crossed his arms and settled back in his seat angrily, saying, "Perhaps."

Looking back at the parliamentarians, Arilin smiled and said, "Please, gentlemen. Let's pick up where we left off... I believe it was the Service Law?"

Gainsborough opened his mouth, thought better of it, closed his mouth and settled back into his chair. Thinking for a moment, he finally turned to the War Minister, who had been doing his level best up until then to blend into the background and asked, "Well, how is recruitment going?"

The man made a show of shuffling through some papers before finally replying, "Perfectly fine, sir. We've had over a million volunteers."

That wasn't a real answer. For a moment Arilin remembered how, standing on her balcony on that warm spring night a lifetime ago, the War Minister had wilted when she suggested he go over to the actual War Ministry and bring his concerns about... whatever it was he had concerns with at the time to Field Marshal White himself. She had imagined the old Field Marshal throwing him bodily out of a window. He certainly didn't seem to have improved much in the interim.

Alphonse jumped in before she could reply, snapping dismissively, "Of whom a quarter are not fit for service." He went on, "Not to mention this doesn't even get us back to square one." Her uncle looked across the table at the Army's representative, a rather stout colonel that Arilin vaguely recognized. She had been trying to remember where she had seen him before since he had arrived from the War Ministry an hour ago.

The man chimed in, a little bit shakily but with the confidence of someone who dealt with the figures every day, "Ah... yes, sir. We've inducted a little over seven hundred and thirty thousand men and," He gave her a look and smiled, "Eighteen thousand women thus far. Unfortunately," He went on, "Even if every single one of them was to appear at the front fully trained and equipped tomorrow that wouldn't replace our losses so far, particularly given Fire Ridge."

The War Minister sputtered, "Well, we couldn't equip more than that regardless."

The colonel furrowed his eyebrows and seemed to genuinely think about it for a moment. Something stirred in the back of her mind as she looked at him. Arilin had *definitely* seen him before somewhere. Finally, he replied, "No, sir, we could. The major bottleneck at this point is training. It'll be another month before any additional corps are prepared to deploy, but they're either fully equipped or on track to be right now."

The War Minister opened his mouth, then shut it again. He was opening it again when Arilin asked the colonel, "How many soldiers do we *actually* need, sir?"

"I thought you might ask that." The colonel chuckled, "I don't suppose Lady MacMahon ever told you about that little study she did?"

"She may have." Arilin replied slyly. Before she had convinced Patricia to chaperone her off to the front lines the Lady General had been in charge of an obscure division of the Royal Army's war planning office dealing with strategic analysis. Her work had been almost entirely ignored, but among other things she had foreseen the vulnerability of Raven Wing Fortress' outlying coastal batteries to long-range railway guns fired from the Imperial side of Night Bay. This oversight had left the main fortress vulnerable to bombardment from the Black Fleet's full battle line after its coastal defenses were destroyed by precise, methodical siege artillery. Plowed under by a volcano of naval gunfire, the mightiest fortress in the Kingdom had fallen in a matter of hours and opened the way for the Imperial invasion. Arilin had been sitting between Lady MacMahon and General Haas in the War Room when the terrible news had come, borne by a harried, overweight colonel who had broken down halfway through the announcement.

The same colonel who was looking back at her right now, smiling slightly. Looking down at his name tag for the first time, she saw that it read 'Goeben'. He went on, "Well, if her work on the subject is to be believed, and I don't see any reason why it *shouldn't* be given how manifestly wrong our assessment of the Imperial Army has been, we probably need another three million men immediately." Someone gasped, and for good reason. The Kingdom was a large country, but that was a *huge* figure regardless. The colonel kept talking matter-of-factly about the approaching apocalypse, "That's just an initial goal, by the way. If this turns into a long war we could need considerably more."

The War Minister stammered, "W-what's driving this?"

The colonel looked back at him and replied, "It's really quite simple, sir. We know the Empire conscripts both men and women and they have been doing so for some time, so their reserve of trained soldiers is made up of most of their population." He chuckled drily, clearly in his element now, "Of course they can't field that many, but we think we've identified five separate field armies in the East so far, made up of fifteen to twenty corps in total. This is likely only their first echelon."

That was an unfamiliar term. Arilin asked, "Echelon? What do you mean by that?"

"Well, milady, I'm glad you asked." Colonel Goeben explained, clearly enjoying himself, "Logistical factors at this scale, mobilization and railway scheduling and so on, will tend to separate the Imperial Army into what are effectively separate waves as they attack." He paused and thought for a moment, then went on, "It's really a little more complicated than that, but you can think of it that way."

"So even if we defeat these twenty corps..." Arilin raised an eyebrow questioningly, "There could be another twenty behind them?"

The fat colonel nodded, "Yes, milady. And another twenty behind *them* if Lady MacMahon's worst-case scenario is correct." His air of mild amusement was, she had to admit, a little infuriating. No wonder White had been using him as a verbal punching bag that day.

"God in heaven. And we have, what, fourteen corps in the East right now? And that by stripping out the Dominion border? How did we get here?" Alphonse remarked sourly. The colonel opened his mouth to reply and he cut him off, "Don't answer that. Rhetorical question." He glared as the Assemblymen again, "We got here because people like you thought if there was no more conscription there wouldn't be another Marchlands War." He paused to let it sink in, then went on coldly, "I was in the Marchlands. I've fought the Empire, and that's a decision *they* get to make."

"There will be riots." Gainsborough replied matter-of-factly.

Alphonse leaned forward intently, "Better another Red December than we lose this war." Resting his elbows on the table, he laced his fingers together in front of his face and went on, "Get the law passed. I don't care how many communists we have to shoot afterwards."

The Prime Minister raised his eyebrows and looked around the table at the rest of his government. Arilin could see the uneasiness written on all of their faces, but he finally nodded and said, "We... we will start discussions on it, my lord." He recoiled a little as Alphonse gave him a venomous look and added quickly, "*Serious* discussions. We'll have it up within the week."

"Thank you." Her uncle turned to her. Something she couldn't quite place was sitting just under his polite tone as he asked, "Princess, I think that's it for this meeting. Do you have anything else you'd like to bring up with the council?"

Arilin shook her head. She had enough to think about for one day. Smiling, she looked across the table and said, "Thank you for your time, gentlemen. That's all I have."

Alphonse pushed his chair back on the heavy carpeting beside her and stood, pushing his way through most of the ministers as he walked out. Goeben wasn't far behind him, the colonel sliding through the jostling huddle with an ease that belied his generous size. Arilin waited for a moment, leaned back in her seat and watched the Assemblymen. A few made to talk to Gainsborough as they got up, but he shooed them out the door quickly and made his way down the long conference table towards her. Stopping beside her in the suddenly-empty room, he wordlessly looked her up and down.

It was a little unnerving. Smiling nervously and crossing her legs, Arilin asked, "Anything I can do for you, sir?"

The man guffawed, "There's an awful lot, young lady, but nothing right now, no." He leaned in towards her and went on, "I was just wondering if you and Prince Alphonse rehearsed that little good-cop bad-cop routine or if you came up with it on the spur of the moment."

Arilin looked at him for a moment, then giggled despite herself. He actually thought that had been an *act?* He was giving them far too much credit. Calming down a little, she replied, "Oh, no, we didn't." Still smiling, she went on, "I don't suppose you'd know why my uncle wants you out of power, though?"

Gainsborough chuckled, "I can think of a few reasons, milady."

"Care to name them?" She asked innocently.

"Well, I think he might be a Conservative. A Royalist, even." The Prime Minister joked, avoiding the question.

Arilin raised her eyebrows in mock astonishment, going along, "You wouldn't say. You know," She went on conspiratorially, "I'm really starting to like them myself. I think they might be on to something."

"That's funny, milady." He replied, chuckling, "I had you pegged for a Socialist."

Arilin smirked, "After a while you get used to being called 'milady.' I don't think I'd do so well with 'comrade.'"

"You are much too cute, milady." The Prime Minister quickly leaned in close to her and murmured, "It takes a lot more than that to survive in this town, dear."

An icy finger worked its way up her spine as the man straightened up and, nodding politely, turned on his heel and walked out. The heavy, paneled door swung closed behind him with a solid thud, leaving Arilin alone with her thoughts and the rain beating on the windows. After a couple minutes of going around in circles in her mind she finally sighed and got up. Padding to the door, she pulled it open with a little effort and stepped out into the hallway beyond. A familiar figure in white was standing there, clearly waiting for her.

Rebecca Stone curtsied as she emerged. Dressed in an immaculate white dress and apron that declared her a servant of the Royal Family itself and not some Royal Household Agency employee, she looked every inch the perfect lady's maid. It was still a little jarring after she'd gotten used to seeing her in her Army uniform.

"I trust your meeting went well, milady?" Becky greeted her.

Arilin shrugged and shook her head, "Not really, no." Looking at her maid, she raised an eyebrow, "Were you here when the Labor Minister ran out?"

She furrowed her brow, "I passed him coming over... at least I think it was him. Short, dark hair, bad suit?" Becky gave her a questioning look, "He looked like he'd seen a ghost."

"I'd imagine." Arilin started walking back towards the Residence, as they called the part of the Palace the Royal Family actually lived in. Becky fell in alongside, the maid's footsteps on the corridor's hardwood floor inaudible beneath the drumming rain on the windows. The Royal Palace was shaped like a gigantic letter 'H' oriented north to south, with its northern opening containing the palace gardens and the southern enclosing a grand plaza. Looking outside, she could see clear across to the east wing through the garden treetops, now swaying violently in the storm. Turning back to her maid, she went on, "Alphonse had him thrown out. He threatened to call the guards."

"I can't say I blame him, milady." Becky replied, "He's a Socialist, isn't he?"

"Yes," Arilin said, "But what I'm more concerned about is *why*..." She trailed off, giving Becky a questioning look. Finally, she asked, "Can I trust you?"

"Against your uncle, I'm assuming?" Becky asked. She went on before Arilin could answer, "Of course, milady. *You're* the crown princess, not him. I know what your father would want."

"Thanks." Arilin replied. They passed a couple RHA maids in the hallway who stood aside and curtsied respectfully. With their black dresses and white aprons they were a little more inconspicuous than her own companion. Waiting until they were well past, she went on, "Uncle Alphonse spent the entire meeting yelling at the government. I'd calm things down and he'd go at them again. It was bad enough that Gainsborough almost walked out."

Becky laughed, "I think I heard him a couple times. Those walls aren't completely soundproof, you know."

Arilin snorted and went on, "What I don't understand is what he's trying to accomplish."

Her maid didn't reply. Turning, a sentry from the Foot Guards snapped to attention and hauled open the heavy door to the Residence for them. Her home took up the fourth and, raised above the rest of the Palace itself, fifth floors of the massive structure's central rung. Walking through the reception rooms and servants' quarters of the fourth floor in silence, they reached the grand staircase leading up to the Royal quarters themselves and started climbing. Arilin trailed her hand along the worn banister, feeling a spark of unease dancing in the back of her head. Once upon a time, about three months ago, the Palace had seemed like the most inviting, comfortable place in the world to her. Now she could barely relax in her own home.

After much too long, her maid finally replied, "What is it you're worried he's trying to accomplish, milady?" Arilin stopped on the stairs suddenly at her words, and Becky, noticing, turned around and walked back down to her. Giving the princess a reassuring look, she went on, "You can tell me anything, milady. I know you're afraid."

Arilin looked across at her levelly, then replied, "I think he wants to overthrow my father."

"Why?" Becky asked.

"Because with me around he'll never be King." She answered bluntly.

Her maid furrowed her eyebrows for a second, then nodded and said, "I can believe that. And a lot of people would go along with him, you know." The princess nodded grimly, and she went on, "Maybe some of them are Conservatives or Royalists, and he wants them in power."

Arilin sighed, "I was thinking it was something like that." Turning, she started up the stairs again, shaking her head, "I feel deaf and blind. If this was school and I was dealing with some plot with my friends, people would *tell* me things. Here, I don't even know where to start."

Becky reached out and patted her on the back reassuringly, "All these people have servants, milady. I'll start asking around. It shouldn't be too hard to figure out who Alphonse is visiting, or if he's sending messages around."

The princess looked over and gave her a shaky smile, "Thanks, Becky."

"Think nothing of it." Chuckling, she went on, "Speaking of school, milady, I need some time with you tonight. You *do* know that it's starting back up tomorrow, right?"

Raising her eyebrows, Arilin looked over at her, "Uh... I do now?"

Her maid chuckled, "Yes, and you haven't tried on your new uniform yet. I need time to adjust it if it doesn't fit right."

The Royal Academy's old uniforms had been frumpy, old-fashioned disasters and she had pestered her father endlessly to have them updated. If the war hadn't happened she would have probably thought it was the greatest accomplishment of her life. Her friends would probably think it was regardless. And now it just seemed so stupid and petty it made her head spin. Laughing, Arilin replied, "Sure, come get me after dinner."

The welcoming scent of her mother's cooking hit her as she emerged from the stairs, her feet sinking into the thick carpeting. Feeling a hand on her shoulder, Arilin turned to see Becky smiling at her, "Now go laugh at your mother some, I haven't heard *that* for a while and I'm sure she'd love to hear it too."

Chapter 7

Stand and Fight

The hot sun beat down across the endless, rolling fields of what they had started to call the New Empire. Lucky rolled gently beneath him, hooves crunching the hard stalks of recently-cut wheat into the moist ground with every step. At least with the rain earlier they weren't raising dust clouds.

June Anjanou turned in his saddle to look over his command, dragoons on horseback shrunken to distant specks all around him. The forty troopers of his platoon were spread across the better part of a square kilometer as they made their way across the countryside in search of the enemy, the better to actually find what they were looking for and not die in the process. With the casualties his platoon had taken on Fire Ridge most of them were fresh replacements from the Empire, still wide-eyed and eager to prove themselves. Beyond his troops were other companies, battalions, regiments of dragoons sweeping across the western plains like the bristles of a brush hundreds of kilometers long, sweeping away the Royal cavalry and clearing the way for the Empire's great offensive.

That was the idea anyways. It was all well and good to talk about crushing the huddled remnants of the Royal Army and marching onwards to Drakenburg and the High City, but despite the summer heat June felt ice crawling up his spine at the thought of the battles to come. It wasn't even from the low conversation he'd had with his father after their audience with the Emperor where the man, normally as harsh as he was confident, had told him it was going to get bloody and to take care of himself. It wasn't from the intelligence reports saying Royal morale was through the roof now that the King was at the front himself, or the fact the whole Western Area Army hadn't pulled in a Royal deserter for days. It was the look in *that girl's* eyes.

June's mind flew back to the top of Fire Ridge, as he faced down that girl and her lieutenant and demanded their surrender. He'd had good reason to after they had gunned down what was left of the 1ˢᵗ Cuirassiers in front of them and with an Imperial corps crashing its way down the back side of the ridge. He'd seen it in that lieutenant's eyes. The man had been ready to give up and was working his way through a long list of rationalizations to justify it. That Royal regiment had *broken through* after all, had smashed their way through line after Imperial line like a sledgehammer. If they ended up surrounded because the Royal Army had lost the battle elsewhere it was hardly their fault. Of course *he* didn't have the authority to actually surrender the unit, but he would have fetched someone who did and a few hours later Colonel Vann would have gotten someone's sword and the enemy would have stacked arms.

Then *that girl* called him a long-haired bastard and told him to go to hell. Her name was Sophia Rose. He could still see her eyes flaming in the moonlight as she cursed him out, the only girl he or anyone else had ever heard of in the Royal infantry. Instead of surrendering, a few hours later that regiment had turned around, steamrolled their way back down the ridge, shaken their pursuers and disappeared into the Dragonspines. If rumors were to be believed they had somehow gotten back to Royal lines afterwards and were hanging around their new cavalry corps' rear area for lack of anything better to do. Which meant they were going to have to deal with them again sooner rather than later, and if the rest of the Royal Army had learned from their example they were about to have a *real* fight on their hands.

Distant banging snapped June out of his thoughts. One, two, and then a few more sharp cracks from far off to his right. Looking over he saw Second Squad galloping forward in the distance. Here and there dragoons reined in their horses and raised their rifles to fire, their dark outlines clear against the rolling fields beyond. Looking back in the direction they were firing, June noticed two riders briefly appear up and over a rise maybe a kilometer away, whipping their mounts to get away from the Imperial bullets snapping after them. He reached for his binoculars to get a better look, but they had crested the rise and disappeared beyond by the time he had freed them from their belt pouch.

Second Squad's gunfire quickly died down, and June thought he could see Sergeant Tarai in the distance waving for her troops to slow down and push forward gradually. Looking to Third Squad on his other side, he waved to catch Sergeant Fang's attention and gestured for the man to bring his squad up on line with First, now pushing forward themselves up a long rise a couple hundred meters ahead of him. June was about to put spurs to Lucky and ride forward himself when a voice interrupted him, "Sir, do you want me to call this in?"

June looked over to see Genjiro Sagara looking at him, his radio's handset in hand. The thing occupied most of his horse's cavernous dragoon saddlebags, the long antenna bobbing overhead like a poorly-stowed fishing rod. They had gotten it barely two weeks ago and June was already starting to hate the thing. It was perfectly useless for actually directing his platoon around, but it sure let his superiors intrude on his business like never before now that they could talk to him with the push of a button. And for all his good points Gen was infinitely more annoying than Anastasia had been. Gritting his teeth, June replied, "Go ahead. Two enemies and probably more soon, we're engaging. No need for support now."
He looked beyond Sagara as the man brought the handset to the side of

his head and shouted, "*Carsten!* Bring your guys up with me!"

The stocky machine-gunner, twenty or thirty meters past Sagara, nodded and waved for his heavy weapons squad to come up. Growling to himself, June finally kicked Lucky forward as more gunfire rang out from First Squad and something small and angry whistled in and sent dirt flying ahead of him. Cresting the ridge, he found his dragoons firing on a small group of Royal cavalry milling in the distance, maybe six or seven hundred meters away down the rise, just short of a winding line of trees that told of a stream. June counted nine or ten horsemen, gray-jacketed hussars, swinging around on line towards them. They had probably been caught watering their horses when Second Squad had engaged their picket, had mounted up to charge the intruders and were now getting their bearings on this new group of enemies.

The lead hussar drew his sword dramatically and spurred his horse forward as Imperial bullets snapped around him, the blade glinting coldly in the sunlight as he waved it overhead. Nudging Lucky forward into line with First Squad, June rested a hand on his sword's hilt as the dragoons kept up their fire, Sergeant Marin calmly calling out the range to his troopers as they shot from the saddle. A few seconds later one of the rear hussars toppled from the saddle, followed a moment later as another man's horse swung out of line and collapsed, the hussar barely jumping clear of the dying animal.

Marin called three hundred meters and June drew his sword. He was opening his mouth to call for his troops to draw swords and countercharge when the lead hussar's horse pitched forward sickly, dead on its feet at the gallop. The man flew off, bounced like a rag doll and tumbled to a stop as the hussars behind him seemed to shiver in their tracks, men starting to rein in their horses. Their leader sat up in the dirt, shook himself and was turning to encourage his troops onwards when Marin's rifle cracked. June saw a faint puff of blood even at the distance, and the man dropped like a marionette with its strings cut.

The other hussars turned about and galloped back down the slope, Imperial bullets slapping down all around them. Sheathing his sword, June looked over at Sergeant Marin and shouted over the gunfire, "Where'd we get shot at from?"

The lanky sergeant racked his rifle's lever with a grimly satisfied air before looking over at him, "They took a few shots at us before they charged." He chuckled darkly, "Probably should have kept it up!"

June snorted and looked back at the fleeing hussars. Even as he watched one of them slumped forward limply over his horse's mane, but the animal kept running with its herd as they splashed across the stream and disappeared behind the trees for a moment, eventually emerging again heading up the long, grassy slope beyond leading up to a stately manor house perched on the far hill amid a cluster of stables and outbuildings. June chuckled to himself. This was the Royal Army all right. No matter how serious things got, they just couldn't help setting themselves up in the biggest house in the county.

By now the hussars were well out of range and Marin called for his troops to cease fire. He was turning to June to say something when June held up a hand to stop him. Something had just flashed quickly in the house's third-floor window, and June didn't bother reaching for his binoculars to figure out what it was. Looking back at the sergeant, he said, "We need to get off this hill, *now*." Pointing at the stream below, he went on as machine-gun bullets began whistling overhead, "Ride down there *quick*, dismount and get your horses under cover. There's our attack position."

"Yes, sir!" Marin whistled to get his troopers' attention and waved them forward after him as they galloped downslope.

Turning on his horse, June looked back at the machine-gunners and his radioman. They had enough good sense to have dismounted behind the cover of the hill, and June kicked Lucky back around to join them. He spotted Sergeant Fang riding over from wherever Third Squad had gotten off to as he came around and sighed inwardly with relief. That was one group of soldiers he wasn't going to have to go find, at least. Turning back to Carsten's troops, he called out, "Set up here! You'll be supporting our attack!"

The stocky machine-gunner nodded and yelled for his troops to unload their heavy weapons. Turning to Fang as the man pulled his horse to a halt, June remarked, "Good timing." Smiling beneath his mask, he went on, "Move your squad up alongside First, they're setting up along the stream downhill. We're attacking the manor house, the machine-gunners will support us from here."

"Will do, sir." Fang turned his horse about and rode off just as quickly as he had come. More bullets whistled overhead, much lower this time, and for what it was worth June swung himself off Lucky in case the Royal gunner's aim got any better. At this range they weren't so much whipping across as falling in like hail.

"What do you want me to do, sir?" Sagara asked.

June sighed. Anastasia would have probably been halfway through setting up by now. Turning to his new radioman, he said, "Stay here and dismount the radio, there's no way it'll work from that hole up ahead.

When that's done get a line run down to First Squad so I can talk back here... were you able to get ahold of command?"

"Yes, sir!" Sagara replied enthusiastically, "And they want an update!"

June rolled his eyes, then froze as he had an idea. His own machine-gunners hammered out their first burst, drowning out his words as he reached his hand out to Sagara. The private got his idea anyways and handed him the handset. Keying the handset, he said, "Aegis six, this is one-six. I need a fire mission."

After a moment Captain Marsten's voice buzzed back out, sarcastically chipper through the howling static, "Why am I not surprised. Go ahead."

June pulled out his map. The manor house was prominent enough of a terrain feature to have been marked on it ahead of time. Chuckling to himself, he went on, "It's a mansion and some stables at Romeo Yankee, uh..." He squinted at the map for a moment and made out the grid lines, "Five four seven one five five. It's on my map. I need it suppressed *now*. Enemy is type one-three, bullseye fifteen, I'll lift." Code for a cavalry platoon, that he would be attacking in fifteen minutes and that he would make another call to lift the artillery fire.

Marsten replied good-naturedly, "At your service. Anything else you need?"

"Yeah." June said, "Their four element is out here somewhere. Or more. Can you try to keep them off me?"

He heard the man chuckle darkly through the line, "No guarantees. Let me know how it goes."

"Thanks," June said, "One-six out." Tossing the handset back to Sagara, he swung himself back up onto Lucky and galloped off to go find Tarai's squad. He didn't have far to go. The stream curved around to the northeast and he spotted them dismounting in the trees out of easy sight from the manor. Spurring Lucky on, he met the dragoon leading their horses back to the rear, grabbed his rifle out of its scabbard, hopped off and threw his reins to the surprised trooper. Hurrying onwards on foot, he found the dragoons watching the growing exchange of machine-gun fire.

"Good to see you, sir." Katya Tarai greeted him as he crouched beside her, "What's the plan?"

June gave her a wry smile, feeling his mask's jaw-plate cocking up at the side as he replied, "Nothing complicated. Advance on my signal, your squad has the stables there." He pointed the long, low outbuilding out to her, "The rest of us are going to clear that house. We've got artillery on the way... speak of the devil." June remarked as wet earth sprayed into the air near the manor house. An instant later they heard the sharp crack of the exploding round and its low rumble overhead.

The woman looked back at him. He saw her mask move as she raised an eyebrow and asked, "Do you want us to attack from here?"

June thought for a moment, then nodded, "Yeah, this is fine." He started to get up, then paused for a moment and added, "Same signal as usual, one whistle and a green flare."

Tarai chuckled, "I'll watch for you guys going forward."

June snorted, "That works." Climbing the rest of the way to his feet, he rushed off down the stream back towards the other squads as bullets whipped overhead and shells slapped down around the manor. Dodging trees and leaping roots, it took him a couple minutes to make his way back, and a few heavy Royal bullets thwacked into the trees nearby as he went. Either those were stray rounds or he was starting to draw fire.

Spotting Marin's troops ensconced among the spreading roots and occasional boulders on the far bank of the stream, June splashed across and quickly found his man. The sergeant handed him the field telephone handset as he slid into a convenient hollow in the riverbank alongside him, greeting him, "Good to see you, sir! I was starting to get worried!"

"Not relieved? I'm honored." June joked, "Second's up, they'll step off when we do. How's it going here?"

Marin nodded, "Just fine, we're ready when you are. The artillery's dialed in, and I had them mix in some phosphorous." Sticking his head out of cover for a moment, June saw the manor was shrouded in brilliant white phosphorous smoke. It wasn't having much of an effect on the main house's heavy stonework, but ugly gray smoke was already starting to waft out of the stables. June hoped the hussars hadn't been keeping their horses there, but he had a dark suspicion they had been. The thought of terrified animals, probably already wounded from shrapnel and splinters, penned into stalls in a burning, collapsing barn was enough to make his stomach turn.

Still, they had a job to do. With any luck the smoke would mask their advance and keep the enemy's fire off them until it was too late. Raising the handset to his head, he spoke into it, "Sagara, are you there?"

The private came back distractedly, as though he was holding the phone to one side of his head and the radio to the other. Which he probably was, "I'm here. How much longer before the attack, sir? Bronze only has so many rounds they can give us."

He was pretty cheeky when he had someone else yelling in his other ear. Snorting, June replied, "About a minute. Listen, I need you guys up there to lift the fire when we get too close. You should be able to see us attacking."

"Yes, sir..." Sagara came back nervously.

"If not," June went on, "I'll shoot a red flare if I need it shifted earlier. Understand?"

"Got it." He came back, a little more confidently. Maybe he was getting used to the pressure.

"Good," June shot back, "I'll see you later. Out." Sticking the field telephone back into the carrier Marin had set between them, he looked over at the other man and said, "Looks like it's time."

The sergeant nodded grimly, then drew his bayonet from its scabbard on his harness' shoulder-strap and ceremoniously locked it to his rifle, saying, "Yes, it does." Turning, he shouted to the rest of the squad, "*Fix bayonets!*"

June drew his own and pressed it down onto the locking lug under his rifle's muzzle. The spring catch locked with an evil click, a sound that spread along the stream like a chorus of steel crickets as the rest of his dragoons followed suit. Drawing his flare pistol from its home on his harness, he pulled out a green flare shell, dropped it in and locked the barrel closed. Pointing it up into the gap in the trees over the stream, he pulled the trigger and sent a green flare blazing into the warm summer sky. Dropping the shell free on the ground and sliding in a red one to replace it, June re-holstered his flare pistol, pulled his whistle on its lanyard out of his breast pocket, set it between his lips and blew,

The shrill sound rang out across the battlefield, and June tucked it back into his pocket, snatched up his rifle and charged into the open, shouting, "*Let's go!*" His dragoons ran at his heels as he darted through the thick, deep grass for a few seconds before throwing himself down. June pushed his rifle forward, seated it onto his shoulder, flicked off the safety and fired at the upper floors of the manor house, visible over the shallow curve of the hill. Dragoons threw themselves down all around him, rifles and machine-guns cracking and spitting as he racked his weapon's action and fired again. Working the lever one more time, he flipped on the safety, hurled himself to his feet and dashed forward again as enemy bullets started humming by like lead bumblebees.

The hussars had chosen their position well. June felt like he was naked, lying exposed in the grass leading up to the manor as Royal bullets buzzed overhead and slapped down around him from what he was pretty sure were two or three machine guns set up just right to skim their fire along the slope of the hill. More were roaring back at them, though, and the smoke and hammering shells must have been rattling the gunners. June heard one of his soldiers scream and call out for a medic, then another, and then they were sliding into the cover of what was left of a low stone wall that some enterprising groundskeeper had thrown up in years past to separate the gardens from the lawns. The hussars had knocked it down to improve their fields of fire, but they had left the rubble in place and there was still more than enough for a suitably terrified dragoon to hide behind.

Shells were slapping down in front of them, terrifyingly close, and the stench of phosphorous and burning shrubbery filled the air. June felt someone dive into the wall's cover behind him and turned to see Sergeant Marin, breathing hard from the dash and wide-eyed behind his mask. "Sir!" he said, "I'm starting to think you're a little crazy."

The ruins of the wall were barely knee-high and June was laying on his side to get under its cover, twisted around to get a good look at the sergeant. Of course it was crazy. It was a miracle any of them had made it this far. It was a miracle the hussars hadn't strung up barbed wire to slow them down. But here they were, only a hundred meters from the manor house with more than a few fallen trees littering the gardens that they could hide behind during their final assault, felled by hussars that had neglected to skid them off. June could feel the tide of battle turning already. Smiling crazily, he sat up a little and replied to Marin, "*You're crazy for following me then! Now get the grenade launchers up!*"

One of the deadly little weapons thudded behind June and Marin shot back, "Way ahead of you, sir!" The shell tore a chunk out of the house's heavy masonry and the thudding Royal bullets swept off down the line towards the launcher.

June rolled up onto a knee and flopped into a convenient slot in the rubble, pushing his rifle ahead of him as he scanned the house's upper floors in the sudden respite. *There* and... *there*, he saw bright flashes and smoke pouring from upper-floor windows. Rolling onto his side, he shouted, "Second window from the right and first window from the left, this side! *Take them down!*"

His machine-gunners had also taken the opportunity to push their heavy weapons up into the rubble pile. Moments later the line was alive with cracking, snarling Imperial machine guns, shredding into the mansion's façade like some kind of gigantic grinder as they zeroed in on the enemy's gun positions on the upper floors. The enemy's gunfire faltered, then died off as more grenade launchers thudded and bombs started punching through windows, filling rooms beyond with fire and death. Seating his rifle on his shoulder, he fired off a round at a fleeting shadow in a window and racked his rifle's lever. The action stuck open, and June glanced in through his weapon's ejection port to see his magazine was empty.

June flattened himself into the rubble pile, turned his rifle on its side and thumbed the magazine free, stuffing it into a pocket. The rush of battle had numbed his fingers, but he managed to get another one out of his chest harness and nose it into the magazine well. It locked into place with a solid click as he rocked it back, and a moment later he had slammed the action closed and was back in the fight.

Tunnel vision was a curse in battle. It was too easy to focus *only* on what was in front of him, on his own private little war, on his own rifle and the occasional muzzle flashes in the windows that sent sullen rounds snapping across the gardens. Reminding himself that he had forty other dragoons who were counting on him, June grit his teeth and forced himself to look from side to side and take stock of the situation. By now his troops seemed to be well established along the ruined wall, with machine guns and grenade launchers raking the manor house's façade. June heard cracking Imperial gunfire far off to his right and looked over to see dragoons firing from the part of the stables that *wasn't* on fire. Clearly Tarai had done her job.

That being said, they weren't moving *forward* any more. Battle ebbed and flowed according to its own logic. Right now they had a decent position and had suppressed the enemy, but they needed to close in for the kill *now* or their advantage would slide through their fingers like sand. As another artillery shell smashed into the building in a shower of masonry and hot, sharp steel scything overhead, June rolled over, ignored the sharp pain as a brick speared him in the kidneys, drew his flare gun and sent a burning red star arcing into the sky.

Now it was up to them alone. Stowing his flare gun and flipping back over, June threw himself up onto a knee and shouted, *"Attack! Follow me!"* Clearing the ruined wall with a bound, he darted into the garden and slid in behind a piece of decorative stonework as bullets snapped all around him. Turning, he spotted a soldier rushing forward with a small, tubular grenade launcher in hand, locked eyes with him and shouted, "You, with the launcher! Blow the main doors down!"

The man nodded and gave him a thumbs-up as he dropped into the cover of a felled tree, and as June darted forward again he saw the first shell streak overhead towards the manor's sturdy main doors. His aim was good, and the first shell smashed in just beside the doors with a crash of shattering stone. By the time June leapt forward again the doors were smashed in crazily, and his third shell filled the entryway with fire and death, blowing the doors clean off their hinges. June ducked behind a tree felled across the manor's gravel drive, barely fifty feet from the doors and thought he heard someone screaming through the smoke inside.

One of Marin's machine-gunners dropped in beside him, braced his heavy weapon across the top of the fallen trunk and emptied the magazine into the open entryway. As the gun's cracking shriek tore at his ears and burning shell casings plinked off his mask, June saw the house's dark interior illuminated for a moment in the green fire of tracers, saw rushing gray uniforms as they plunged through open doors at the far side of the entry hall. A few toppled in the hail of gunfire, silhouetted against the daylight beyond as they rushed for the horses June saw through the clearing smoke. Horses and hussars trying to make good their escape.

There was a correct way to clear a building, carefully, room by room and hall by hall. The Imperial Army generally frowned upon crazed bayonet assaults as an alternate solution to that tactical problem. The thought filtered through June's mind quite clearly as he vaulted the tree and sprinted for the entryway bayonet-first, screaming, "*Come on!*" He'd have to apologize to his tactics instructor later, he supposed. Darkness swallowed him as he leapt into the grand entryway, feet pounding on the stone floor as he accelerated. A silhouette blotted out the daylight streaming through the far door, the hussar raising his carbine to shoot back at his machine-gunner.

June saw the man notice him, saw his eyes widen as he leapt, burying his bayonet through the man's throat and slamming him back out of the door. June ran straight over him as he pitched backwards, let go of his rifle as it stuck fast, seized his sword, pivoted and *drew* into the group of recoiling hussars he had exploded into. His first, rising stroke cleaved through a hussar's chest and he pivoted again to slash under a carbine desperately raised to block. His next step took him forward, sword reaping in a brutal horizontal arc that smashed aside another rifle and bit into a man's neck. Bringing his sword back for a moment, he lunged to stab another hussar through the chest, yanked his sword free and angled it down, deflecting a saber slash from his other side.

Whipping his sword back over his head, he brought it down at the stunned hussar as the man reeled backwards to escape, slipping on the courtyard's flagstones as he fell backwards. He landed on the ground with a heavy thud and June walked forward and stomped on his chest, slamming him back down as he tried to rise. Laying his sword's tip on the man's throat to keep him there, June turned to see his dragoons corralling the rest of the hussars, seven or eight of them, against the courtyard's far wall at bayonet-point. Most of the horses the hussars had brought into the open-ended courtyard to make their escape on were disappearing across the grounds into the distance.

Those that had survived the gun battle, anyways. Three Royal cavalry horses, beautifully taken care-of animals, were lying dead on the cobblestones, still twitching as they expired. Worse, one was still thrashing on the ground, *screaming* inhumanly with what looked like a hideously shattered leg. June grimaced as one of his soldiers stepped forward with a pistol and put it out of its misery.

The gunshot died away and stunned silence descended. Breaking away from his soldiers and their group of prisoners, Sergeant Marin made his way over to June, carefully stepping around the bodies scattered in his wake. The sergeant gave him a wary look and said, "Sir, you... scare the hell out of me sometimes."

June gave him a hard look, then shrugged and changed the subject, "How's your squad?"

Marin's mask shifted a little as he grimaced, "I'm missing Razo... I think he's fine though, I heard him yelling for a medic earlier."

June chuckled grimly, "Good." He glanced down at the hussar he was using for a footstool, absently noticing the man was still holding his saber, fingers locked with fear, "Can you, uh, deal with this guy?"

The sergeant nodded, "Can do, sir."

"Thanks." June gave him as much of a smile as he could in the circumstances and took his foot off the man's chest. Marin crouched down as he did it, grabbed the man by the collar, twisted his arm behind his back to force him to drop his sword and started roughly dragging him back to the group of prisoners now kneeling against the far wall. The hussar looked almost *grateful* to get away from him. Looking down at himself, June supposed he couldn't blame the man. He was covered in blood.

June snorted as he stalked back into the manor house, now alive with dragoons rushing about clearing the place. Off in a corner of the great hall the wounded moaned, attended by his medic. Most of them looked like hussars. A couple months ago being covered in blood was shocking to him. It had made his knees weak and his stomach churn. Now it was depressingly, disgustingly routine. Some of his soldiers, the new ones, gave him shocked looks as he stalked by and he ignored them. They'd get used to it soon enough.

Sergeant Tarai called out to him as he stood in the middle of the great hall, cleaning his sword meditatively with a handkerchief, "Sir! You need to get up here!"

June turned and looked up at her. The great hall's ceiling soared to the second floor for the first half of the room, embraced by grand staircases along the walls that swept up to a sort of second-floor landing stretching across the width of the room. Tarai was leaning over the railing, and even through her mask June could tell she was worried. Sheathing his sword, he hurried up the stairs to her and asked, "What's going on?"

"It's easier to show you." Tarai led him down the second-floor hallway to a room standing open at the end. It looked like it had been someone's private sitting room once, probably a middle-aged lady who had filled it with questionably-tasteful knick-knacks and lace drapery. Despite the battle it was almost completely intact. June supposed the hussars had probably stayed out of the place.

His idle speculation about the house's owners and prior occupants fluttered and died as he followed Sergeant Tarai's pointed finger out the window. Masses of dark horsemen moved in the distant fields, some of them towing stubby, angular devices that were probably horse artillery. June sighed and shook his head. They had gone out looking for the Royal Army, and it looked like they had just found it.

It was going to be a *very* long day.

Chapter 8

Special Delivery

Sophia leaned back in her seat, stretching out her feet and wiggling her bare toes in the cafeteria's cool air. It felt wonderful as her feet slowly decompressed, a simple little pleasure after she had spent the morning rushing around the Cavalry Corps' headquarters with urgent messages from increasingly irritable colonels to increasingly sleep-deprived majors about how this or that detail of the operation needed to be worked out *sometime last week* or they would lose the war. She'd never seen this many officers before in her *life*, and as much as it pained her to admit it she was honestly starting to feel sorry for some of them. At least in the infantry they got to shoot back at the enemy occasionally. Around here the enemy was the red tidal wave of doom stretching across the map, and their efforts at stopping it so far had been about as effective as spitting into a hurricane.

Subtle strategies and elaborate maneuvering were for battles between equals. When one side had a crushing advantage there was such a thing as being too clever by half, and the Empire's battle plan showed that merciless logic. The enemy's dragoons were steamrolling forward on a five-hundred kilometer front and drowning the Cavalry Corps' thin screen of squadrons with sheer numbers. Behind the impenetrable shield of their own cavalry the Empire's infantry was presumably marching for Grenville and the Great Steel River in endless columns stretching across the dusty plains of the New Kingdom, totally unmolested by the Royal Army. They would smash across the river, annihilate the remnants of the Army of Drakenburg and the conquest of the Kingdom would become largely a matter of marching. At least that was what the intelligence officers were saying the enemy's plan was.

Of course, *planning* to do something and actually doing it were entirely different things. Looking around at her friends sitting scattered around the little cafeteria they had staked out for themselves in the headquarters, Sophia chuckled to herself. They'd have to get through Charlie Company first.

"What's so funny, Miss Rose?" Sophia looked over to see Lieutenant Thorn had glanced up from his pile of papers on the other side of the table. The platoon out on patrol duty had caught a couple of Transportation Corps soldiers breaking into houses in town late last night, and she suspected he was dealing with the aftermath.

"Nothing in particular, sir." She replied. Explaining the joke wasn't worth the time, and it wasn't funny anyways. Changing the subject, she went on, "Dealing with those two clowns from last night?"

Her platoon leader nodded, "Yeah. Can you believe their commander actually complained?"

Surprised, she snorted, "Really?"

He went on, "He claimed we roughed them up for no reason. *How exactly our guys were supposed to know they were petty criminals instead of Pathfinders is beyond me, but he seemed to have it all figured out."

Sophia rolled her eyes, "He sounds like a piece of work."

"Tell me about it." Thorn sighed, then gave her a serious look, "You know, after your little run-in the other day I'm honestly surprised they weren't *shot*. I mean, they'd deserve it, but I'd have twice as much paperwork to do."

A chill ran up her back at the thought of that desperate fight, her and Tony against four Imperial spies in the darkness. If either of them had made the slightest wrong move they would have been killed. She could still see that man's face in front of her, lips drawn back in a snarl as he clamped her bayonet *into* his chest, his pistol a dark little shape in his other hand as it snaked towards her. The room was warm, it should have been warm, but Sophia shivered in the cold, wet night as gunfire crashed in her ears.

"Sophia? Are you alright?" Concern was written over Lieutenant Thorn's face.

She shook her head, "Sorry, sir, you just... reminded me." She sighed heavily and looked away, "It's easier when you *know* they're there."

Thorn gave her a hard look, then slowly cracked a sympathetic smile as she looked back at him, "Nothing to be ashamed of, Miss Rose." He snorted, "We're all going a little crazy these days. Just let me know if it gets worse."

Sophia smiled half-heartedly, "Sure thing, sir. Thanks."

Her lieutenant turned back to his papers, and Sophia was pulling on a fresh pair of socks from her haversack when the door swung open. Despite herself, she smiled as she recognized the figure striding through the door with a bulging satchel slung over his shoulder.

"Hey, First Platoon!" Her father called out, "Mail call!"

Every soldier in the room including *Lieutenant Thorn* leapt to their feet and rushed the Sergeant Major. Her father quickly swiveled his back against the wall to keep from getting totally mobbed, pulled off his mail bag and held it protectively over his head to keep anyone from getting ahold of it. Mindful of getting her feet stepped on in the press, Sophia quickly pulled her boots on and joined them. Her father shouted over the clamor as warmly as he could manage, "Alright, alright everyone, back off, one at a time!" He chuckled as they backed off a little and went on, "Most of your girlfriends haven't found someone new yet, and if they did they were probably cheating on you beforehand. And no, the Army never told anyone we were dead, just missing."

Amid the kind of nervous grumbling that told her nobody really believed him, the Sergeant Major pulled out a thick bundle of letters and a small, paper-wrapped package and announced, "Private Gravesend!" Her friend pushed his way forward, and her father remarked as he handed him his mail, "Most of these are from your sister."

Her friend's face reddened and he quickly retreated with his bundle. Her father laughed and remarked, "Sometimes Beth worries me a little bit." He fished another couple letters out of his bag, "Private Hargrave!" The platoon's old man stepped forward, and her father said, "Two from your wife and one from your son in Gyrburg."

Hargrave raised an eyebrow, "Huh. He never writes." He snorted, "Maybe he's gotten a damn fool idea to volunteer. I *hope* for the Navy."

Her much-older friend tucked the letters into his jacket and her father replied, "No accounting for good sense." The Sergeant Major dug into his bag and produced another stack of letters, "These have all been forwarded three of four times and only one of us has the Post confused *that* badly... Kelly Hager! You need to have a talk with the mail room."

Laughing, Kelly took his mail and remarked, "Will do, boss."

Her father snickered, then pulled out another set of letters. And another. Everyone had something from *someone*, wives, sweethearts, children, parents or friends. The Dissenting Church in Jade Falls had sent out letters to their members in the service, as had the Rifle Club and the Chamber of Commerce. Edward got a letter from the Ferryman's Association. Finally only Sophia and Lieutenant Thorn were left standing in front of the Sergeant Major.

Rather than fishing around in his satchel, which still looked like it contained a fairly large package, her father popped open one of his jacket pockets and fished out a couple letters. Looking at the lieutenant grimly, he said, "I've got one here from your mother, sir... and one from your boss at the bank, I think."

Thorn sighed heavily and took them, "Just great... she couldn't even write me herself?"

"Doesn't look like it, sir." Her father said, "I'm sorry."

"Not your fault, Sergeant Major. Mine for giving that girl a ring."

Thorn replied coldly.

Sophia looked over him and raised an eyebrow. Now that she thought about it, she'd never heard the lieutenant talk about his personal life before. Maybe that had been for a good reason. Her father reached out and patted him on the shoulder warmly, "Look at it this way, sir. Better now than later." He went on, "And don't let that jerk you work for try to twist this around like somehow it's *your* fault. If his worthless daughter gets restless because her man is out of town for a couple months, that's on her and then it's on him for raising a brat."

Thorn chuckled sadly, "Thanks." Taking his letters, he walked past them and out of the room to have some privacy.

Sophia watched him go, then turned back to her father and said, "Ah... did Mom...?"

Her father smiled and pulled another letter out of his jacket, "Of course she did." He handed her the letter, then opened his satchel and pulled out the package, "She made cookies, too."

Sophia grinned as she took it from him, "Oh, did she? Wait..." Looking the package over, she noticed the end rolled over as though it had originally been larger, and the strings had been cut and re-tied to secure it. Glancing back up at her smirking father, she said, "You ate some, didn't you!"

He shrugged, "They wouldn't fit in my bag otherwise. What was I supposed to do?"

"*Dad!*" Sophia exclaimed in mostly-mock outrage, "Come on..."

Her father reached out and ruffled her hair warmly, "Postal fee, Sophie." He winked and went on, "Anyways, I need to go talk to General Kellerman." He stepped in close to her and murmured, "If he likes having us so much he needs to start supporting us like he does all his precious cavalry."

Sophia hugged him, "Thanks, Dad."

Patting her on the back warmly, he replied quietly, "Take care of yourself, Sophie." Disentangling himself, he turned and strode out the door.

Sophia turned to see most of the platoon staring at her. Well, actually at the package in her hands. Edward piped up, "Hey, Sophie! Are those your mom's cookies?" She glared at him, and he plowed ahead undisturbed, "You know those are too many to eat by yourself."

Corporal Stennis joined in from across the room, "Yeah, you'll get fat!"

Walking back to her seat, Sophia shot back, "Why are you complaining about my breasts getting bigger, Stan?"

That shut them up for about a minute before she got mobbed anyways. Sophia was tucking a few she'd managed to save for later into a pocket when the door burst open and Lieutenant Thorn strode back in, looking grim. Looking over the scene with a raised eyebrow, he raised his voice and announced, "Guys! I have good news and bad news!"

Someone replied, "Don't keep us waiting, sir!"

"The bad news," Their lieutenant said sarcastically, "Is that I'm now single! It's not as though I'd made commitments for this girl only for her to cheat on me the instant I walk out the door! And her father's just *fine* with it!"

The room made sympathetic noises and Thorn went on, "The good news is that while I was going to the telegraph room to send one to that *deadbeat* that the twenty-two hundred and five mark ring I gave her-" Sophia whistled under her breath. That was a *lot* of money, "-is going to be in my safety deposit box when I get back or she'll be facing a lawsuit, I ran into the Chief of Staff. We're being committed and we've got thirty minutes to get to the rail station." Thorn finished, "Strap up, I'll fill everyone in on the train!"

Everyone stared at him for a moment in shock, then sprang into action. Sophia quickly wrapped her puttees around her calves, the motions so natural to her now she could do it almost unconsciously, and picked up her harness and her rifle. They had both worn in since she left Jade Falls, the black canvas of her infantryman's rig worn and scuffed and her rifle's once-immaculate stock scarred and gouged from battle. The thin layer of bluing had started to wear off the weapon's exposed metal and she could see spots of rust beginning to form, doubtless helped along by the summer rains and the damp they never really seemed able to get rid of.

Thinking she'd have to take a wire bush and some oil to it later, Sophia shrugged into the harness and exhaled as its familiar weight settled on her shoulders. Ammunition, water, food in her haversack, a compass and a first aid kit, a little pair of wire cutters, her bayonet, her entrenching tool and gas mask in its bag. A long, solid weight settled against her kidneys, the blanket and poncho that had saved her life in the Dragonspines and, broken down and rolled securely inside them, her father's spear and Charlie Company's battle flag. By now it was all as familiar to her as her own skin. Buckling the belt, she hefted her rifle, caught her friends' eyes and called out, "You guys good?"

Having gotten a head start on her, they had been waiting on her to finish up. Hargrave, Edward and Kelly all gave her thumbs-up. Tony felt all over himself quickly, then apologetically pulled out what looked like a very light canteen and said, "I need to fill this up."

Sophia chuckled and said, "Sure, go ahead." Tony rushed off for the nearest faucet, and she thought that a couple months ago she would have insisted on patting them all down. After Fire Ridge and the Dragonspines, they knew what they needed and she trusted them to have it. Although, now that she thought about it, she could almost *feel* her father's disappointed look. *Why, Sophia, are your men unprepared for combat? This is unacceptable. It's your duty to check them.*

Rolling her eyes, Sophia turned around and ordered, "Alright everyone, open up your pouches. I'm checking *everything*."

It seemed like a complete waste of time, and it was until she found out Edward was worse on water than Tony had been. She sent him packing, and he managed to make it back by the time Corporal Stennis walked over and looked them up and down. Turning to her, their new squad leader asked, "Your team's ready to go, Sophia?" He chuckled and went on, "You're sure?"

He had come over with what was left of his guys from Second Squad when they had reorganized a while ago. She laughed and replied, "I am now."

Stennis patted her on the shoulder affectionately and pointed at a couple soldiers breaking open ammo crates on one of the tables, "Make sure you all take a bandolier coming out. It's all belts."

Sophia nodded, "Will do." Glancing over her shoulder, she said to her team, "You heard the man."

A couple minutes later they were all sporting cloth bandoliers loaded with belts of machine-gun ammunition over their shoulders as they filed out of the headquarters into the street and the bright noontime sun. Sergeant Cross called for them to fall in, sling arms, right face and forward march. Lieutenant Thorn hurried to the head of the column as they stepped off, and they had barely taken a few steps when she saw him salute and call out, "Eyes right!"

Sophia snapped her head to the right and noticed a tall, hard-bitten man in a gray-and-red hussar's uniform grimly returning the lieutenant's salute. General Kellerman. A couple staff officers curious and brave enough to have followed him out quickly saluted behind him. They marched past him a moment later and Thorn dropped his hand and called out, "Ready, front!" Waiting until they were out of easy sight of the headquarters, he turned in his tracks and walked backwards to say, "Route step and spread out, you're making me nervous!"

Cross barked a couple commands and they spread out onto the sidewalks on either side of the road as they made their way to the train station. Allenby was a small town, half-deserted from the war and they made good time. The station was empty when they arrived except for a couple other Charlie Company soldiers standing guard, and after they climbed onto the platform Lieutenant Thorn looked around, clearly came to some kind of decision and called out, "Alright, everyone! I think our ride's late, so we'll do this now. Gather around and get your maps out."

Every single soldier in the platoon produced a map from a pocket or haversack, Sophia fishing hers from inside her service coat's deep cuffs. The Corps headquarters had a print shop and Major Matheson had prevailed on them a few days earlier to run off a few hundred pocket-size maps of the Allenby area, which had been gradually filtering through the battalion since. They'd all learned their lesson about getting lost between Fire Ridge and the Dragonspines. Thorn was going on, "We're heading about twenty kilometers east of here, our guys guarding that rail bridge you see on the map there were attacked by dragoons, *lots* of them, a couple hours ago." The group murmured uneasily at the thought, and he went on quickly, "Fortunately they held them off long enough for Ninth Division to send some troops back to help them out and hold the position, but General Kellerman thinks this only the tip of the iceberg."

"Why's that, sir?" Someone in one of the other squads asked.

Thorn looked at the man, then around the group as he went on, "The Tenth Hussars got beaten to hell earlier today. I don't have much information on what happened, but from what I've gathered they got pulled into a fight with a *lot* of dragoons and there's not much left right now. Without them there's a hole in the line just north of Ninth Division and, the Masks being good at their jobs, they're probably pouring through it right now." He finished grimly, "Hence our guys getting hit just now."

Sophia spoke up, "So what's our plan, sir?"

"The Ninth is pulling out. We're going to go forward, link up with Second Squadron, Eighth Cuirassiers at that bridge and keep their line of retreat open." Thorn pulled out his notebook and checked it before going on, "We'll be working for a Colonel Jenssen." He chuckled, "Show respect, guys. And, unless my eyes deceive me, I think our ride is here."

Turning, Sophia saw a plume of thick black smoke rising over the houses down the tracks. A few moments later their train came around the final bend and braked into the station in a cloud of blown-off steam as it squealed to a halt alongside the platform. Sophia had seen a lot of things so far during the war, but she gasped despite herself. She had been expecting an ordinary military train with its line of depressing boxcars, forty men or eight horses each. Glancing over at Lieutenant Thorn, she saw him smirk as he introduced the armored monstrosity that had appeared instead, shouting over the growl of its idling engine, "Gentlemen, we're taking the *Bad News Express!*"

Apparently someone in the Rail Service had a sense of humor, as shocking as the idea was. As far as trains went it wasn't very long, only five cars, but with the amount of armor plating it was sporting Sophia suspected it was as heavy as a normal train two or three times its length. A massively-armored locomotive pulled the usual fuel car piled with coal, behind which what looked like an armor-plated boxcar was sandwiched between two double-turreted artillery wagons.

As Sophia watched a hatch popped open in the side of the locomotive and a rather soot-stained captain swung himself halfway out with the ease of someone who was very much at home in his rolling fortress. Squinting out under the brim of his cap with bloodshot eyes, the main speared Lieutenant Thorn with his gaze and said, "You're our infantry?" Thorn started to salute and he waved it off tiredly, pointing back towards the rear of the train, "Get your guys in the infantry car, I'll come back once we're going again."

The train's commander swung himself back inside and slammed the hatch shut. Thorn gestured for them to get moving and they hurried down the platform to the armored boxcar, which Sophia could now see was covered with firing slits and armored shutters. Massive, steel plated doors were set at each side of the car, with 'ASSAULT RAMP, STAND CLEAR WHEN OPENING' helpfully stenciled on them. They stood aside nervously as particularly brave soldiers pulled the external releases and the ramps slammed open. Sophia was pretty sure they had left gouges in the platform's concrete surface as she hiked her rifle up on her shoulder and walked into the darkness inside.

The stale air inside the infantry car smelled of steel and oil, with the lingering varnish scent of ammunition. As her eyes adjusted Sophia made out a small platform built up in the middle of the car, and what looked like hatches in the roof above it. She stepped up onto it and popped one of them open as soldiers began to crowd in behind her. As bad as the air was in there, they were all going to die if they didn't open every hatch and firing slit they could. Her friends clearly thought the same way, and light and fresh air were pouring into the carriage by the time they hauled the assault ramps up on their chains. An instant later the train shifted under them, and Sophia stuck her head out the hatch to see they were beginning to move, the train accelerating out of the station hard enough she had to brace herself against the coaming to keep from falling. She heard someone not as fortunate crash to the floor and curse loudly below.

They were clear of the station almost immediately and kept accelerating out of Allenby until they were whipping down the tracks about as fast as Sophia had ever gone before in her life. The stiff wind in her face, buffeted into eddies by the artillery car's turrets, was refreshing until she realized that at this rate they'd be in the battle zone in *minutes*. It was an unsettling thought, and she nervously dropped back down into the car to see the front-end door slide open and the tired-looking Rail Service captain from earlier stride in.

The man picked out Thorn and the two of them stepped into a corner and started comparing notes. Sophia was about to sidle over and see what she could overhear when her lieutenant produced his copy of their orders from inside his jacket and she realized that she had a letter from her *mother* tucked inside her own and she hadn't read it yet. Forgetting her curiosity, Sophia sat down on the fighting platform and pulled the letter out of her jacket. Slitting open the envelope with her knife, Sophia quickly pulled out the paper inside and unfolded it to read, squinting to make out her mother's cursive in the dappled light from the car's firing slits.

> *Sophia,*
>
> *Thank God you two are alright. I can't even describe how the town's been since we heard the whole regiment had just gone missing at Fire Ridge and then no word for weeks. People were going crazy. Just about the only reason I kept myself together was remembering how we all got out of the Dragon's Jaw, and if anyone was going to pull a disappearing act like that and turn up unharmed later it was you and your father. Of course, try telling that to some of the people around here and you won't get very far. Now that you've all turned up again I've gone from the most hated to most loved woman in Jade Falls and people think I'm some kind of prophetess.*
>
> *The bakery's still doing fine. Beth has been coming over to help out lately, I think her parents are a little much for her with Tony being gone. Such a gloomy girl, but she's fine with customers. Not as good as you, of course! She mentioned she was going to send him a voodoo doll, I hope she doesn't end up getting you all cursed.*

Sophia looked up at where Tony was leaning against the wall, looking out at the countryside going by through a firing port. An evil-looking little rag doll was dangling from the side of his belt by a string tied around its neck like a hangman's noose, soulless black bead-eyes and a smile crudely stitched in red thread leering back at her. Shivering despite the heat, Sophia quickly looked back to the letter.

> *I baked you some cookies. I know they're in high de-mand, but they're for <u>you</u> so try to keep some for yourself. If the guys want some for themselves I expect them to pay. Prices have gone up about half with the war, so I expect you to drive a hard bargain.*

> *Take care of your father for me, for a little while there I was starting to worry I'd lost you both.*

> *Your loving mother,*

> *Maria*

Reading the last sentence, Sophia felt her throat tighten as her vision blurred. Setting the letter down in her lap, she wiped at her eyes and took deep, ragged breaths until her head stopped spinning and her throat loosened again. Sometime later, when she wasn't going to be getting shot at in a matter of minutes, she'd read it again and sob her heart out, pref-erably into her father's chest. Until then she needed to keep it together. Folding the letter back up, she carefully slid it back into her jacket and climbed back up onto the fighting platform, sticking her head into the stream of mercifully-cool air outside and letting it dry her off.

After a couple minutes she felt someone step onto the platform be-hind her. Turning, she saw Lieutenant Thorn leaning his elbows on the hatch coaming behind her, raising his binoculars to his eyes. Noticing her, he paused for a moment and asked, "Seen anything, Sophie?"

She'd barely been looking, but there wasn't much point explaining it. Sophia shook her head, "No, sir, nothing so far."

Smiling, he finished raising his binoculars and said, looking off to the right of the train, "Alright. Well, I'll look this way, you take the other side."

"Yes, sir." Sophia turned and looked out as the countryside unfurling off to their left. They sped through a small forest, the trees dappling the sunlight green overhead for a minute before they emerged from the other side. Sophia blinked as her eyes readjusted to the bright sunshine and raised her hand to shade her eyes. She wasn't used to observing from a moving platform, let along one moving this fast, and she almost missed the dot out in the fields maybe a mile or so away. Without taking her eyes off it, she shouted over the rushing air, "*Sir! I've got something!*"

Feeling Lieutenant Thorn turn behind her, she pointed and just as quickly saw another dot even farther in the distance behind the first one, coming over a low rise in the fields. After a few moments Thorn said grimly, "Yep, that looks like our friends."

Still looking out over the countryside, Sophia saw the second dot turn and disappear back down the rise. Just to make sure, she asked, "Dragoons, sir?"

"Green jackets." He paused for a second, then Sophia saw him holding something out to her in the corner of her eye. She reached out and felt his binoculars in her hand as he went on, "Keep looking, I'll call it in."

Sophia looked over to see him holding up a field telephone handset to his head. Thorn started talking into the handset, too low for her to hear over the rushing wind, as they rushed through another patch of woods. Sophia looked out over the countryside as they emerged from the latest tunnel of trees and quickly raised the binoculars to her eyes as she saw a puff of smoke in the distance. She searched for a second, then two, three, four, five before she finally picked it out, a long, spindly shape in the distance. Green-jacketed shapes scurried around it, one of them slamming a shell into the cannon's breech as she called out, "Sir! Imperial artillery, ten o' clock, they're firing!"

"At us? What's the distance?" Thorn asked, a little nervously.

"No, looks like two and a half kilometers..." Sophia trailed off as the piece fired again with a puff of smoke, "Looks like they're shooting *ahead* of us."

"Great," Her lieutenant remarked, "Looks like we're already flanked to hell. At least we know they're still fighting up ahead now. Keep looking."

Sophia set the binoculars back to her eyes as Thorn started barking commands into the telephone. A few moments later she was startled by a shuddering whine and looked over to see the artillery car's turrets swinging to bear. A few seconds later they came all the way over, the guns elevating a little as they laid on target. Quickly hanging Thorn's binoculars around her neck, Sophia managed to get her hands over her ears an instant before the guns fired with a crash that drove the train over on its suspension, sending the whole war machine rocking as they flew down the rails.

Sophia flexed her legs and held on as the train accelerated even further, the whistle bursting to life as they charged into battle. Feeling Thorn's hand on her shoulder, she turned as he shouted, "Get below! We've got to be close now, and we'll dismount as soon as we find a good spot!"

Nodding, she swung herself down into the car below, deep in darkness now that they were sliding most of the firing slits shut. Gathering her friends together in the gloom, they crouched on the hard steel floor as the train heaved and bucked beneath them and the cannons hammered overhead. After a couple minutes in the pitching, shrieking darkness, Sophia heard something small and hard ping off the car's armor.

One Imperial bullet. She knew it wouldn't be the last.

Chapter 9
Flanking Maneuver

"I wasn't so sure about the new uniform, milady." Becky said as she finished tying off the bow at Arilin's waist, tightening her skirt's fabric around her body, "But you look wonderful."

Arilin smiled, "Thanks." Before she had any inkling that she would be spending her whole summer at the front with the Army, Arilin had begged her father to get the Royal Academy Middle School's frumpy uniforms updated. She had even suggested some designs herself. And it seemed as though before *he* had any inkling that *he* would be going to the front with the Army, her father had agreed with her and given the Academy Board their marching orders.

The princess looked herself up and down in the mirror as her maid took a last moment to fuss with the back of her sailor collar and make sure her schoolgirl's scarf was lying correctly under it. The new summer uniform had a red, high-waisted skirt that fell to her mid-thighs, something that would have been scandalous a few years ago and probably still would be if people didn't have more to worry about with the war on. The skirt's snug upper section covered her stomach and, just above it, slid smoothly under the hem of her short white sailor jacket with its puffed sleeves, red collar and gold scarf. White gloves, black stockings, and a little makeup completed her outfit.

"There we go." Becky finished smoothing something out and stepped back.

Turning, Arilin looked over at her and asked, "Planning on coming with me today, Becky?"

Her maid had come to get her up earlier wearing her blue 'downstairs' uniform instead of her white house uniform. The woman nodded, "Yes, milady. I'll wait for you."

No point in arguing with the war on and probably no point in arguing even if it hadn't been on. Arilin smiled and replied, "Thanks. I'll see you."

Becky opened the door to the Residence's grand central hall for her and Arilin walked out to almost run into Beatrice, wearing the same uniform as her and followed by a couple nervous-looking maids. The sour look on her face dissipated a little as she saw her, and Arilin chuckled as she stepped out of her little sister's way and fell in alongside her. Leaning in close so the maids wouldn't overhear, Arilin whispered, "Ill girl act getting old, BB?"

Her sister whispered back, "*Today*, yes. Ugh."

Arilin laughed and replied, "Come on, let's see what's for breakfast." They stepped into the dining room and Beatrice pulled out a chair and sat while Arilin followed the smell of crisp ham and eggy hollandaise sauce and stuck her head into the Residence's kitchen. Her eyes fell on a very familiar figure, and she guessed, "Eggs benedict, Mom?"

"Yes, dear..." Her mother replied absently as she finished drizzling the sauce over what looked like a set of flawlessly poached eggs. Then she froze for a second before, ever the chef, self-consciously leveling off the pot to keep it from spilling everywhere as she turned, eyes wide, "*Arilin?*"

"Mom?" Arilin raised an eyebrow, "Need a hand or something?"

Her mother shook her head, "No, well... yes, actually. I was just surprised to see you." She snorted, "I've been worried about you is all. It's good to see you up and about again."

Arilin smiled, "What do you need?"

"It's good to see you smiling again, too, light." Her mother smiled, then nodded at the plates on the counter and said, "Can you take yours and Beatrice's plates out?"

"Sure thing." Arilin collected the plates as her mother turned and set the hot pot back on the stove. Walking back out into the dining room, she set one down in front of her sister, pulled out her own seat and sat down as her mother came out with her own plate, her apron making her look a little like one of the maids as she walked into the bright light of the dining room.

Setting her own place across from her girls, Queen Catherine shooed out the maids and settled down without bothering to take off her apron. As she picked up her utensils Arilin said, "Thanks for making breakfast, Mom... and sorry for not helping out."

Her mother chuckled, "Don't be, light. It's your first day back at school, I need to spoil you a little." She gave her a stern look for a moment, "Not to mention, you may think you're feeling better but I still wouldn't trust you around an oven right now."

Arilin blushed and looked down at her plate, "Well, thanks anyways." Picking up her own fork and knife, she set to and quickly cleaned her plate. Her mother's cooking was, as usual, perfect. Before she had become Queen, when she was just her father's long-time mistress, Lady Catherine had owned and run the Orient Restaurant down by the Royal Opera House on the other side of the High City and had earned her share of stars for fine dining. And while she would occasionally eat something the Palace kitchens had prepared outside of her supervision, say, for a state dinner where she was expected to entertain the guests ahead of time instead of spending all evening shouting at the kitchen brigade, there was no way under the Five Moons she was going to let someone else cook breakfast for her family. Although Arilin got the feeling she was going to give her a shot eventually.

Probably well after the war was over with at this point. Arilin and Beatrice got up, thanking her again as she rang for the maids to come in and clean up. Meeting them at the door with their school bags, Becky smiled and asked, "Ready to go, your ladyships?"

Arilin nodded politely and took her bag from the woman, the polished red leather of the straps smooth and supple in her hand. Beatrice gave Becky an unconvincing blank look for a moment before Arilin glared at her and, pouting, she reached out to take her own bag.

"Come on, BB, let's go." Arilin told her as she turned to leave. Still pouting, Beatrice followed her. Arilin could feel Becky's bemused, ever-so-slight smirk behind them as they walked down through the Palace, Royal Household Authority maids working on their morning cleaning pausing to curtsey respectfully as they passed. The Sergeant of the Guard at the Palace's side entrance had the great wooden doors already open as they descended into the entry hall, and he called his men to attention and saluted as they approached. Arilin returned it with practiced ease as she walked past, the warm summer air washing over her as she strode outside.

Arilin smelled dark, earthy trees and the neutral tang of damp stone as she stepped into the narrow strip of flagstones, just wide enough to maneuver a carriage about in, between the Palace itself and the low wall along the east side of the grounds. More guards at the wrought-iron side gate sprang to attention and hauled it open for them, and they stepped out under the picturesque trees lining Malheur Avenue. Turning left, Arilin started walking. After a couple steps she heard Beatrice's feet on the sidewalk behind her, and her sister demanded, "Where's the carriage?"

Arilin chuckled and gave her sister a sidelong look, "We're walking today." Talking loudly enough for Becky to hear, she chided Beatrice, "You need more fresh air and exercise anyways. I told them not to bother with a carriage this morning." Beatrice gave her a look as though she had just sentenced her to hard labor. Arilin chuckled and kept walking and her sister hurried after her to keep up, pouting harder than ever. She thought she might have heard Becky stifle a chortle behind them.

It was difficult to even comprehend just how large the Palace was from the inside. Even looking at it from the outside it was a mind-boggling structure, tall enough that their half of the street was still deep in shadow from its bulk looming overhead. It took them a couple minutes of walking to get past its projecting wings to the base of the Grand Plaza, where the bright morning sunlight finally washed over them and burned through the pleasant cool of the shade. Arilin realized it would be unpleasantly hot by midday as the stone buildings and streets slowly turned the High City into an oven under the summer sun.

Stepping over a puddle and glancing both ways to make sure there weren't any out-of-control carriages flying around, Arilin crossed Crown Avenue in front of the Palace and kept walking down towards the Royal Academy, waving and smiling as bureaucrats making their way to the Finance Ministry and a few soldiers reporting in late to the War Ministry for whatever reason lifted their caps and stepped out of the way respectfully. A few minutes of walking later they emerged from the government district and started seeing red and white Royal Academy uniforms going their direction, first by ones and twos and then in a steady, ever-thickening stream of students.

Arilin was giving a perfunctory glare to a couple green-uniformed Holy Cross students cutting across the stream when her eyes fell on a familiar pair of brown-haired girls emerging from a side street, both of them practically indistinguishable from each other. One of the twins looked their way and froze for a moment, eyes widening with surprise before she grabbed her sister's hand to rush over. Smiling, Arilin called out as they approached, "Liri! Miri! Good to see you!"

"Arilin!" Liriel called out as they approached, "You too! How are you?"

"We were worried about you, with, well... everything." Miriel added. Glancing over at Beatrice, she went on, "You too, Milady."

Arilin sighed, "I've been better, I guess. But," She smiled sadly, "I can't sit around moping all day."

"I guess..." Liriel replied doubtfully, "By the way, uh, we'd been meaning to come over and ask but, uh, with everything it didn't really seem–"

Miriel cut her sister off bluntly, "How's Dad?"

General Siegfried Reinhardt, formerly Walter Haas' chief of staff at IX Corps. Now left in charge of the corps after Walter had moved up to command the entire Army of Drakenburg. The last she had seen of him, he had been trying to extricate what was left of V Corps off Fire Ridge fast enough to avoid getting steamrolled back into the Dragonspine Mountains as the jaws of the Empire's trap slammed shut. From what she'd gathered since then he'd managed it somehow.

That was the same black night Walter had taken her out on the front porch of the manor house IX Corps was using for a headquarters and told her Adrian was dead. Shaking off the memory as it clawed at her throat,

Arilin smiled weakly and managed, "He was doing fine, last I saw... I know he misses you two."

The Reinhardt twins instantly brightened up, "Oh, really?" They exclaimed simultaneously.

Arilin managed a chuckle, "Yeah, he won't shut up about you two, actually. I know he reads all your letters."

"Oh?" Liriel started, "We, ah, we didn't..."

Miriel finished, "He doesn't write back much... at least as much as we'd like."

Liriel pouted, "He always says he's busy."

Arilin started walking again, and the Reinhardts fell in alongside her as she looked over at the two of them and replied, "He really is... it's hard to even *explain*. He's just working *all the time*."

Which was an understatement. Almost every day she had been with them the IX Corps staff had gotten up early in the morning and worked until late at night trying to decipher the Empire's moves and adjust their own accordingly. It had felt like watching people trying to build a grandfather clock out of cookie dough and somehow make it work. And Siegfried had been the ringmaster in charge of the circus, keeping the gears of war turning so when Walter steepled his hands and adjusted his monocle and ordered IX Corps to deploy north into the teeth of the Empire's flanking maneuver the better part of a hundred thousand soldiers had jumped off of trains at the exact right stations at the exact right times with the exact right supplies to hold the jaws of the trap open for twenty-four hours and save most of V Corps.

Something in her tone of voice got that across, and the twins nodded understandingly and let it well enough alone. They walked on in silence for a little while until they saw the high brick wall around the Royal Academy's grounds rise on the right side of the street ahead, and Arilin smiled despite herself as she saw the school's majestic buildings towering beyond. Its sprawling grounds butting up against the west side of the High City's plateau, the Royal Academy had to be the most beautiful school in the Western Kingdom. It certainly had the best view, out over Sapphire Bay and the Lower City.

As they crossed the street and joined the stream of students flowing down the sidewalk towards the front gates Arilin noticed another girl, very short and petite with pretty golden-blonde hair, being dropped off by her maid at the front gates. The older woman looked a little rough for the High City's usual polished servants, with a wariness about her that

Arilin hadn't seen since she'd come back from the front. She patted the girl on the shoulder and turned to leave, and the girl slowly shouldered her bag and nervously turned to look in the front gates. Just from her profile, Arilin got the feeling she'd seen her before somewhere.

The muscles of the girl's jaw clenched, and she started inside as their group arrived. Hurrying a little, Arilin quickly caught up with her, put on a smile and asked, "New here? I don't think I recognize..." She trailed off as the girl turned and looked up at her, and she felt her eyes widen as she finally managed, "...*you.*"

The photographs all over that manor house had been in black-and-white, but she knew now the girl in them had blue eyes. They were widening in something close to sheer terror as the girl jumped away from her. They stood there staring at each other for a second before the girl managed, "M-milady...?"

She had a nervous one. Smiling reassuringly, Arilin said, "Yes, I'm Princess Arilin." Try as she might, though, she had no idea what the girl's name was. The house hadn't had a name tag on it or anything. She forged ahead, "You have me at a disadvantage, miss...?"

The girl visibly collected herself, curtsied and replied, "Charlotte Espinay, milady."

Arilin nodded politely and replied, "No need for that, Charlotte. We're all students here." The rest of the group had caught up, and she turned to introduce them, "This is my sister, Princess Beatrice, and Liriel and Miriel Reinhardt."

"Pleased to... meet all of you." Charlotte managed, clearly surprised.

"New here, I presume?" Arilin asked, gesturing for her to come with them.

Charlotte nodded anxiously as she fell in alongside her, "Yes... it's my first day here." She sighed, "My family has an apartment in the High City, so I moved here after our estate in the East was overrun." She gave a forced chuckle, "It's a little bigger than the school in Sharp's Mill, I'll give it that."

"I expect." Arilin replied, "You know, I think I owe you one. I spent a night in your bed after the Army took over your estate. I recognized you from the pictures."

Charlotte looked up at her, eyes wide with surprise, "Really? But you're..."

Arilin laughed, "It's a long story, I'll tell you sometime." The way Charlotte had phrased her reply earlier was odd, though. Arilin changed the subject and pressed back in on it, "You said that you moved out here?

Where're your parents?"

"Dad's in the Army." Charlotte said proudly, puffing herself up a little before she went on, deflating, "Mom's... around. She left for here ahead of me and I ended up stuck at the estate for *weeks* thanks to the Empire." She looked up at her angrily, "There were Royal troops still in *town*, we were packing up and in comes Alice with this very nice hussar who supposedly had a wounded man that needed taking care of."

"Oh...?" Arilin asked.

"Yeah. Guy had a green uniform, a two-handed saber and thigh gaiters. And hair down to his butt." Charlotte scratched at her cheek nervously, "I might have fainted." She went on, "So we got stuck playing host to the Empire for a month before they pulled out. The Army showed up that night, thank God... and your brother, actually, the morning after."

"Oh? Really?" *The girl's full of surprises*, Arilin thought as she raised her eyebrows and looked over at her.

Charlotte nodded, "Yes... we left while his regiment was still using the place." She sighed and looked up at her sympathetically, "I'm sorry about him. He... seemed really nice."

Arilin sighed, "He was... thanks."

By now they had passed the Royal Academy High School's complex and separated out into the stream of younger students heading for the middle school. As the main hall started to loom overhead in all its Gothic splendor, Becky spoke up, "Alright, your ladyships, I think you're safe enough here." She went on, "I'll pick you up at... three, here? Neither of you are staying after?"

Turning, Arilin nodded, "Yes, Becky, that's fine. We'll see you then." She chuckled, "I need to join a club this year like I need a hole in my head."

"Don't joke about that, milady." Her maid told her sternly, "That's what I'm here to prevent."

Arilin swallowed and nodded politely, and Becky turned on her heel and left. They watched her go for a moment before Arilin turned to her friends and put some fake cheer into her voice, "Well. Let's go to school, then!"

They had a desperately boring school assembly to start the academic year, where the vice principal hectored the students to make sure they maintained their dignity with the new uniforms. Arilin supposed this was code for them to make sure the boys weren't trying to look up their skirts, which she supposed was a fair point but very unlikely barring some sort of foul play. She absently wondered if it would be possible to prove the point using trigonometry so the adults would stop worrying about it. Then they had class, which were boringly informative. Arilin paid attention dutifully.

By the time lunch rolled around Arilin had gotten more than her fill of other people for the day, particularly other people giving her their most sincere condolences for her brother, and turned right out of the classroom instead of left to go down to lunch. She hadn't gotten more than a few feet down the hall when she hear Liriel behind her, "Going somewhere, Arilin?"

Arilin turned, "Yes, actually." She went on bluntly, "This is all a little much right now for me, I was going up to the roof."

"You're not eating?" Liriel asked, a note of concern in her voice.

"I wasn't really planning to, no." Arilin replied.

"Well that won't do." Liriel scolded her, before turning back into the classroom, "Miri, can you keep Arilin company? She's going to go brood about serious things on the roof over lunch, I'll get you both something and come up."

Miri's voice drifted out, "Can I take Charlotte? I like her."

Liriel turned and gave Arilin a look. God save her from her busybody friends. Sighing heavily, Arilin replied, "Sure, do whatever you want."

Liriel immediately brightened and rushed off, and a few minutes later Arilin and her two companions emerged from the school's central bell tower onto the middle school's "roof". Granted, it was really an arcaded, open-air floor at the top of the building underneath the actual, steeply-pitched roof that kept the snow off in the winter, but that was beside the point. Everyone called it the roof. The wind off the sea stirred her hair and ruffled her skirt as they emerged, and Charlotte exclaimed, "Wow, look at *that!*"

She wasn't wrong. The view was *incredible*. Walking to the railing, they looked out over the vast sweep of the Capital and Sapphire Bay sparkling like its namesake far below, the wind in her hair seeming to lift the cares from her shoulders. The Lower City spread far to the west around the bay in a vast stretch of color, the grimy red brick and gray concrete of the tenements and factories along the waterfront giving way to the business district's skyscrapers, majestic white stone and glass glimmering under the sun. Along the distant bay and off to the south the buildings shrank into houses and dropped under the canopies of the trees lining the suburban streets, and she could barely make out a few of the magnificent mansions set in their estates along the western bay far from the bustling city. Squinting, she was pretty sure she could spot one belonging to the Royal Family, far out along the headlands.

With the war and the weekday the bay itself was devoid of its usual speckling of sailing yachts, but the dark shapes of steamships and tugs going about their business dotted the bay under rapidly-dispersing plumes of boiler smoke. Anchored out in the roadstead like spiders in a web of anti-torpedo nets Arilin could see the Northern Fleet's warships, tiny destroyers, lean cruisers and gigantic, menacing battleships, white mastheads standing out among the great spread of blue hulls and red decking. There weren't nearly as many of them as there had been before Diamond Shoals, and the Navy Yard was packed with warships under repair. The most prominent among them were the long, lean shapes of the *Griffon* and *Gorgon*, the battlecruisers staggeringly huge even at the distance. From what she'd heard it was a miracle either of them had made it back.

Sapphire Bay itself was dotted with islands, most of them implausibly green and lush in the sunlight. Some of them, the ones that didn't have good fields of fire, sported a few extremely expensive vacation homes. On the ones that did she could make out the low, grim shapes of coastal gun batteries. Moving along the bay, her eyes fell on an island completely cleared of trees and dominated by a squat, ugly compound, and she shuddered despite herself. The Labyrinth Prison, home to the Western Kingdom's worst criminals, perched on its bare rock like a particularly ugly lizard in full view of the Capital. The message was clear, she supposed. Stay in line or you know where you'll be going.

An icy finger of unease worked its way down her neck, and Arilin looked over to see they weren't alone on the roof. An ice-blonde girl about her age had stepped out from behind one of the roof pillars and was staring at her, pale blue eyes narrowed in... anger? Arilin had never seen her before in her life, but she supposed that didn't rule out her having a problem with the monarchy.

Pushing herself back from the railing, Arilin turned to glare back at the new girl and asked, "Do I know you?"

The girl snorted unpleasantly, "Probably not."

"It's rude to stare, you know." Arilin shot back.

The girl chuckled, more energetically than Arilin would have expected from someone so pale, "I suppose you'd know a lot about that, *milady*." Her lip curled in a sneer, "What about throwing people down the stairs? Have you asked your etiquette teacher about that one?"

Arilin blinked. *What in the world is her problem... oh,* she thought as Liriel stepped ahead of her protectively, snapping, "You'd better watch your mouth."

Miriel stepped forward on her other side, saying coldly, "Apologize."

The girl threw her head back and laughed theatrically before she suddenly stopped and snapped her head back down, mocking, *"Make me, rich girls."*

The twins snarled and were about to step forward when Arilin laid her hands on their shoulders, "Calm down, you two. I know what she's on about."

"Milady!" Liriel protested, "You can't just-"

"Oh, do you now?" The girl shot back, cutting her off.

Arilin crossed her arms and asked, "I don't suppose you know Curtis Meyer?"

"Yeah." The girl smirked, "He's my father."

She must really take after her mother, Arilin thought. The Labor Minister had black hair and a dark complexion. How his daughter had turned out almost as pale as Beatrice was beyond her. Raising an eyebrow, she went on, "I don't suppose you have a name, miss...?"

"Lily." The girl went on snidely, "Don't worry, I know yours already."

Sighing, Arilin smiled apologetically and approached her, "You must have heard about that meeting then."

Lily crossed her arms defensively, "Me and half the city by now. I don't know where you get off on this kind of thing."

"You know that was my uncle's doing." Arilin replied.

"Like I care!" Lily shot back, "All you red-eyes are the same, and you all hate *us*."

"Oh, really?" Arilin snapped, "I barely even know who *you* are. And maybe you should ask your father about how I *obviously* didn't care for what Alphonse was doing."

Lily tossed her hair sullenly, "You didn't *do* anything about it."

"Yes I did!" Arilin demanded, "What more was I supposed to do, get into a fight with my uncle in front of the whole government? How do you think *that* would have gone, little miss know it all?"

Lily rolled her eyes angrily, "Poorly for you, I expect. Anyways, it's not going to be my problem much longer." She went on, "My, uh... father's pulling us out of the government. I'll be back at Tidewater next week." Lily snorted, "I'm gonna miss the food, I admit."

Arilin felt her eyes narrow, "So he's just going to cut off his nose to spite his face, huh?"

A puzzled look spread over Lily's face, "What do you mean?"

"Who do you think benefits from that?" Arilin shot back.

"You?" Lily replied sullenly, shaking her head, "I'm sure you'd love not having to look us in the face before you send us off to *die*."

Arilin fought off the urge to slap her and spat, "*My uncle*, that's who. I'm sure he'd love having a conservative government, and I'm sure his first order of business would be to start having your little communist friends arrested." She snorted, "Your father's probably first on the list."

Lily raised an eyebrow, "I'm supposed to believe you're different?"

"*Yes!*" Arilin shouted, before going on, "You realize there's Royalists that don't like me, right? That want to see him on the throne? Do you *seriously* not realize that?"

Lily looked at her for a second, eyebrow furrowed in thought. Finally she replied, choosing her words carefully, "I... don't know what they'd think." She chuckled, "And I wouldn't mind staying here this year, but you're going to have to tell my father that. He's pretty worked up right now."

Stepping back a little, Arilin thought out loud, "Well, I can't exactly go waltzing in the front door of the Socialist Party offices."

"No, but you *can* go to the Palace." Charlotte interjected, having worked her way up beside them. They both looked over, surprised, as she went on, "Just throw a tea party after school or something and invite her." Charlotte looked over at Lily, "Have your dad pick you up afterwards. Piece of cake."

Lily shook her head, "I guarantee he's being watched. He can't just go to the Palace, it'd be obvious."

Charlotte smiled slyly and looked at the twins, "What about *their* house?"

Lily raised an eyebrow as she looked at them, "Your dad's a general, right?" They both nodded, and Lily shrugged, "Well, nothing's saying I can't make some friends while I'm here." She curtsied, smirking, "In that event, I'd love to have tea with you, your ladyships."

"It's decided then," Arilin said, "We'll meet up at the front gate and walk over after school." She thought for a minute, then went on, "Do you two mind if Beatrice comes?"

The twins shook their heads. That afternoon Arilin explained her plan to an increasingly-enthusiastic Becky, who had arrived to pick them up for the walk home and didn't object at all to their change of plans. She promptly recruited Charlotte's no-nonsense maid, Alice, for her own little intelligence-gathering network as they headed over to the Reinhardts'.

Lady Reinhardt was a little surprised to host a sudden invasion of schoolgirls, but she seemed grateful for the distraction and warmed up immediately. She was a clearly little *more* surprised when Arilin ambushed the Labor Minister and yanked him into her husband's office after he showed up to retrieve his daughter. Arilin spent the next ten minutes explaining the situation and why he absolutely needed to ignore Alphonse's provocations and keep the Socialists in the government, some of it at the top of her lungs. He finally agreed to discuss it with his comrades, collected Lily and left. Apparently the Assembly was having some kind of special session later that night and he needed to get back to work.

Arilin opened the newspaper the next morning to find the government had survived a vote of no confidence.

Chapter 10
The Winds of Battle

Lieutenant Thorn swung himself down into the car as the train's guns fired again with an ear-splitting crash, rocking their carriage on its suspension nauseatingly despite its armored weight. Hanging his intercom telephone back on its hook by the overhead hatches, he shouted over the ringing in all of their ears, *"Change of plans! We're dismounting here!"* The train's brakes squealed and Sophia staggered from the deceleration, half-falling into Tony. He wrapped an arm around her waist to steady her as Thorn went on, "We'll dismount out the right ramp, they're dropping us in a little forest so we shouldn't, *shouldn't*, take fire right away! Once the train moves off we'll push left, to the north!"

Even without an open window in the armored box, Sophia could tell they were slowing quickly. The sharp pings of incoming bullets cut off suddenly as the light coming in from the open hatches overhead turned to a dappled green. They were in the forest. She recognized Corporal Stennis as he spoke up, "What then, sir?"

Their lieutenant laughed, a little crazily, "We fight like hell!" Calming down a little, he went on, "We'll set up a strongpoint once we've pushed out far enough. There should be a farm on the north side of the woods we can use. Cross!"

Their platoon sergeant spoke up, "Yes, sir?"

Thorn replied, "Start getting wire run as soon as we get off. I'm not getting us left out here."

"Will do!" Sergeant Cross replied, "Miller, have one of your teams grab wire and come with me. We'll unload last."

Third Squad's leader, Corporal Miller, started barking orders to his men as the train finally squealed to a lurching halt. Someone pulled the release on the right-side assault ramp and it slammed open, digging into the soft earth beyond the railroad embankment with a heavy thud as Lieutenant Thorn shouted, "Let's go!"

The lieutenant sprang out the door and the rest of the platoon started pouring out after him, feet drumming on the ramp's steel. Sophia made to follow them only to realize that Tony was still holding on to her, and she twisted to look at him. Smiling sheepishly, Tony let her go, hefted his rifle and gestured towards the door, "After you."

Now that she thought about it, she didn't particularly mind him holding onto her. That being said, they had a train to get off of and probably about a thousand dragoons trying to murder them afterwards. Making a mental note to figure out how to get some time alone with Tony later, Sophia pulled her own rifle off her shoulder and said, "Come on."

Sophia emerged from the infantry car into dappled sunlight, Tony and the rest of her team moments behind her. Turning to make sure she had everyone, she saw Sergeant Cross emerge behind a couple soldiers carrying heavy wire reels, shouting for someone to help get the ramp back up. Sophia and her friends rushed over to haul on the lifting chains and the massive ramp went up with stomach-churning slowness as the *Bad News Express* kicked back into gear and slowly started to grind forward. Sophia let go of the chain and let Tony and Kelly finish yanking it the last little way as they walked alongside the accelerating train, the door finally clanking shut as the spring-loaded latch slammed home.

Sophia looked forward to see the train's commander hanging halfway out of the locomotive, giving them a worried look as the armored behemoth crept forward. Her two friends let go and backed away from the train, and he saluted them with his free hand and ducked back inside. An instant later the locomotive roared as he *seriously* applied power and the *Bad News Express* leapt forward on the tracks, quickly building speed as it rounded a curve down the tracks and disappeared from view. A few seconds later they heard its guns roar again as it emerged from the forest.

"Alright, form up and move out!" Lieutenant Thorn shouted, pointing, "Wedge formation, first in front with me." He pointed left and then right, "Second left, Third right. And spread out!"

They quickly rushed into position, Sophia walking forward to her usual place at the front of the platoon. Tony and Edward fell in angled off to the right beside her with a couple paces between them, and Kelly stepped into position with the heavy, reassuring weight of his machine gun on her left, with Mr. Hargrave on his other side. Behind her she could hear Corporal Stennis and the second team positioning themselves, and Thorn having a hushed conversation with Sergeant Cross. Apparently satisfied that everything was in order, she heard him approach behind her and say, "Alright, Sophia. Let's get going."

"Yes, sir." Raising her left arm, Sophia waved forward in the signal to move out. They walked through the forest for a few minutes, feet rustling through the loamy carpet underfoot as the wind stirred the trees overhead pleasantly. If she ignored the cracking salvos from the *Bad News Express* as it receded in the distance and the dull thudding of Imperial shells starting to rain down in response, it was downright pleasant. And it actually *smelled* like a forest. Fire Ridge had stank of matches, turpentine and death by the time that battle was over.

Sophia's wandering thoughts came back to the present as she carefully looked around the forest, the hair on the back of her neck starting to stand up. Motioning for a halt, she ducked behind the nearest tree and cautiously peered around the trunk, searching through the forest for something, *anything* out of place. A moment later she felt Thorn crouch down on her other side, asking, "What's going on? Notice something?"

She shook her head, "Nothing so far... but I don't think we're alone."

"I'd be surprised if we were." Thorn replied, a little sarcastically.

He let her sit and ruminate for a few moments, though. What had it been? *Something* was off in this forest, she just needed to figure out *what*. There weren't any Imperial helmets poking out from over logs or around trees in front of her, or gleaming tripwires betraying booby-traps. She was about to give up and wave the platoon forward again before Thorn told her to when she *heard* it. Clopping, stamping hooves, barely audible through the hammering battle in the distance. Turning to Thorn, she whispered, "Someone's riding a horse up ahead."

Her lieutenant raised an eyebrow, "Dragoons?"

She shrugged, "Maybe."

Thorn jerked his chin forward, "Let's go find out."

Sophia motioned for the platoon to advance again, and they cautiously picked their way forward as the forest began to thin ahead. First crouching and then creeping forward on their hands and knees, they made the edge of the forest and Sophia slowly slid forward on her stomach to look through the tangle of brush along its edge.

The farm they had been aiming for was a wreck, the barn little more than a pile of charred lumber and the farmhouse half caved-in from what she recognized as shellfire. It had clearly been fought over some time ago, probably when the Empire first attacked Grenville a couple months back. And nervously sheltering behind the near side of the building were two cuirassiers in their gray-and-red uniforms, one holding a pair of horses and the other peering around the side of the building with what looked like a pair of binoculars.

It was all she could do not to laugh. Rolling over, Sophia gestured for Thorn to come over, and he obligingly crept over and dropped down next to her. He took one look, shook his head and looked over at her incredulously, "Are these guys serious?" Sophia shrugged and he rolled his eyes, "Might as well go say hello."

Tony butted in mischievously, "There's a hole in the bushes over there if we want to do it quietly."

Lieutenant Thorn gave him a look, then snorted softly, "No pranks, if they're as nervous as they look they'll probably think we're dragoons and start shooting."

"I doubt they'd hit," Tony replied sarcastically.

Thorn chuckled before he rolled up to one knee and whistled. The cavalry horses shuffled nervously and looked at them, and a moment later their handler turned and peered towards them. Sophia saw the look on his face change from puzzlement to shocked surprise as Thorn waved slowly, the man taking a step backwards in shock as he noticed his pale hand moving. The man quickly turned and said something to his companion, who made a dismissive gesture with his free hand as he kept peering around the wall. The horse-holder repeated himself, and his superior pulled himself back behind the wall and turned with a skeptical expression. Thorn whistled again, and the man quickly put his binoculars to his eyes. Sophia saw his jaw swing free for a moment as he noticed them.

"Looks like they know we're here." Thorn commented to nobody in particular. Looking at Sophia, he went on, "Want to go say hello, Miss Rose?"

She nodded, "Sure thing, sir."

Thorn motioned for the platoon to stay where they were and climbed to his feet, Sophia with him. Pushing their way through the brush at the edge of the forest, Sophia held a hand up and saw the cuirassiers visible deflate as they were clearly able to make out that they weren't Imperials. It was a fifty-yard walk or so to the ruins of the farmhouse, and on the way she was able to look out over the little farm's impressive view. No wonder the cavalrymen had been scouting from there.

The farm looked out over a shallow valley, the fields rolling away for three or four hundred meters to the north before the ground rose again and the forest reappeared. A hard-beaten dirt road across the fields in front of them through the valley, and looking to her left Sophia could see more farms dotted up and down the road where it meandered back towards Allenby, a branch splitting off to the north through a wide gap in the trees maybe a kilometer away.

As they cleared the forest Sophia looked to the right to see the fields rolling away in that direction as the railroad ran down and out of sight towards the bridge. She spotted a couple dark blots on horseback amid the rolling fields and what she thought was the *Bad News Express'* black boiler smoke merging into an ugly haze building in the distance. Now that they were in the open she could clearly hear artillery echoing through the countryside, not the grumbling roar of the guns at Fire Ridge but more of an incessant popping, like a bucket of evil popcorn over a weak fire. And dead in front of them, a little washed out from the distance and the intervening forest, a steady, high-pitched cracking like the biggest Imperial rifles she'd ever heard.

The cuirassier with the binoculars walked out to meet them, looking around a little nervously. He was a big man, taller than her and Thorn and clean-shaven, with a layer of fat around his neck she found vaguely infuriating. Now that she was close enough to get a look at his collar where it peeked over the lip of his gray-painted breastplate Sophia saw that he was a lieutenant from the second battalion... squadron, she supposed, of the Eighth Cuirassiers. Not quite Colonel Jenssen, she supposed, but he probably knew the man. The cuirassier spoke first, "Where'd you come from?"

Thorn gestured with his thumb over his shoulder, "The armored train just dropped us off at the tracks, we're going to dig in here to protect the division's left flank as they fall back." He added, "We were originally supposed to go to the bridge, but I guess they didn't need us there any more."

As if to punctuate the thought another wave of ugly pops boiled up from the direction of the bridge. Sophia thought she heard the armored train's guns roar back in response. The thick-set cuirassier replied, "Well, I'm out here trying to find that damn Imperial battery that's been hitting us from over here for the last half an hour."

Thorn raised an eyebrow and jerked his chin at the far woods, "I think you succeeded, they're on the other side of that. We saw them coming in." Looking around, he gestured at the ruined farmhouse, "Let's get under some cover first, though."

They quickly walked back towards the inviting shelter of the shambles of half-destroyed brick walls, the cuirassier asking, "Aren't you worried? About being seen?"

"Trust me," Lieutenant Thorn replied, "If there's a Mask in those woods, they've noticed *you* already."

The man gave him an indignant look as they ducked into the wall's cover, but he looked them up and down and clearly thought better of pushing it. He changed the subject, "You're sure they're on the far side of that?"

Thorn looked at her, and she nodded. Looking back to the cuirassier, he said, "Yeah. We can probably walk rounds onto them from sound at this point." He went on, "Honestly, you guys should head further west along the tracks. We were taking small arms fire on the run in on the train, and we saw more than a few dragoons. They might be working around us already."

The cuirassier lieutenant shrugged. It made him look fatter than he actually was as his tight collar pushed his neck fat up against the line of his jaw, "I've got my orders. Find the guns, take them out."

Sophia and Thorn exchanged a skeptical look. Turning back to the cavalryman, she jumped in, "Sir, that's... not a good idea." The man gave Thorn a dirty look and he shrugged cavalierly in reply as she went on, "It's not just going to be those guns over there. There's dragoons too, probably a lot of them. You'll get shot to hell."

The big man rolled his eyes, "Thanks for your advice, *private*."

Thorn cut in bluntly, "She's right, you know." The man glared at him as he made a conciliatory gesture, "Is your squadron on the phone network?"

"Why?" The man demanded, "It's not like we have one ourselves."

Her lieutenant chuckled, "*Had.*" Looking to the woods, Thorn made a handset gesture, then waved his hand back towards himself. Sergeant Cross emerged a moment later, trailed by a couple of obviously-tired soldiers unrolling a spool of telephone wire behind him. A few moments later they'd made it to them and Thorn took the field telephone set from him, asking, "Does this thing work?"

Cross chuckled, "Yeah, we're plugged into Two-Eight right now."

Thorn looked at the cuirassier lieutenant and smirked, "Well, let's ask your boss for his opinion." The man rolled his eyes, but he gestured towards a half-ruined doorway leading into the farmhouse and made to step inside. Thorn turned to follow him, then paused and glanced at Cross, "Sergeant, get the platoon set up here and have them start digging in. This place might get hot."

The officers disappeared inside and started having a hushed conversation over the phone as Cross turned to the woods and started making hand signals. First squad, come forward and dig in at the farm. Second squad, dig in along the edge of the woods facing east. Third squad, along the edge of the woods facing west. Getting a better look at the section of forest they had come out of she could see that it fell off back towards the railroad tracks on both sides, giving both of those squads a field of fire up and down the valley on either side. No wonder Thorn had picked the place out for their position.

The other cuirassier sidled over with his horses as the rest of her squad emerged from the trees and started making the walk over. He was as tall as his boss, but an awful lot better looking. Sophia thought he couldn't have been more than two or three years older than her as he started, "I haven't seen a lot of girls in the infantry... *our* infantry, anyways." He chuckled self-consciously, "What's your story?"

Sophia patted the less stuck-up looking horse's nose while she thought about how to respond. By the way he smiled while she did it, it was probably his. It was a good question, really. She'd always liked her father, it hadn't taken a lot of convincing when she was younger to get him to teach her how to fight and it hadn't taken a lot more to get him to convince Captain Jaeger to swear her in when she was old enough. Now *there* was someone she hadn't thought about for a while. Basic training at Wolf Rock last summer, with a bunch of would-be infantrymen who stopped giving her trouble after it became obvious she could pull her own weight. Honestly, Tony had gone through a much rougher time than she had.

Then back to Jade Falls and Charlie Company, and the fellow soldiers that had become her friends. Soldiering had been something fun to do on the side, exciting and a little dangerous, and a welcome distraction from tiring high school drama and the constant drumbeat of work at the bakery. It had been something exciting in a boring, peaceful life.

Then the war had come, and she'd seen too many of those friends die. Jack had mistaken her for his own *mother* as he lay there, bleeding to death in her arms in that last trench on Fire Ridge. Slaughter and Falcon, urging them forward one minute and gone the next, lost in the screaming hell of battle. Allen Janssen, the big lumberjack's shredded body being laid out by the medics in that cursed house alongside the rest of what had once been Second Squad. June Anjanou's sword, burning white in the moonlight, her friends' lives streaked in dark spiderwebs across the flashing blade.

She didn't want to talk about it. Shaking her head, Sophia gave the horse another pat and changed the subject, "Is he yours?"

"Yeah. He's named Chestnut." The cuirassier smiled, "I think he likes you."

"Oh? Well, he's a cute horse." Sophia smiled back at him and realized absently that he was flirting with her.

The man laughed skeptically, "That's one way of looking at it." He had a point, Chestnut was close to the size of a draft horse and despite his dopey, good-natured attitude probably did not get called cute a lot. He ventured, pretending he couldn't see her name tag, "What's your name, miss...?"

She chuckled and replied, "Sophia Rose."

He smiled back, pleasantly enough, "Hans Vogel."

Sergeant Cross cut in, "Alright, *Hans*, stop hitting on my soldier." Sophia turned to look at him and he gave her a perfunctory glare, "And as for you, Sophia, get your guys and get to work. This house isn't going to get that machine gun set up for you." He gestured at the ruined barn, "The other team's setting up in there."

Sophia sighed, then nodded gamely, "Sure thing, sarge." Waving for her team to hurry up, she ducked into the house, noticing Tony giving Hans a death glare just as she turned, when he thought she wasn't looking. She... still didn't really know what to think about that. Shaking her head in frustration, she walked past the two crouched officers, who sounded like they were finishing up their phone conversation, and waved Kelly towards a ragged hole blown in the far wall at a convenient level to accommodate a machine gun set up on the floor. It was way too large for a proper firing port, but they quickly set to plugging the gap with piled bricks and debris.

They had gotten to piling up rubble in that corner of the house to make it more-or-less, and hopefully more, bulletproof when Sophia heard a whinny outside and the clatter of hooves receding in the distance. A moment later Thorn called, "Sophia! Need you for something!"

Letting Hargrave and Edward argue over the ballistic value of broken crockery, and hoping they wouldn't decide to *test* it, Sophia stood up and walked over to the lieutenant, asking, "What do you need, sir?"

Thorn nodded in the direction of the Imperial guns as they fired again, "I talked the cavalry out of their suicide mission, but now it's our problem. Your hearing's better than mine, do you think you can spot for the artillery?" He gestured with the field telephone handset, "I've got Morningstar on the phone."

"Sure," she nodded, "Who's Morningstar?"

"The artillery," Thorn explained, "I'll call the mission, just listen for the rounds and tell me what needs to be done to bring it on line with those Imperial guns."

Sophia nodded again, "Sure thing, sir." She paused for a moment, then gave him a quizzical look, "I don't really understand what's going on."

Thorn shrugged, "Apparently they're triangulating this Imperial battery, and if we bring their rounds on line with it they'll hit." He added, "They were *real* happy to hear from us, I think they were at their wits' end about these guys." He shooed her out the door, "Get outside and listen, I'll call the mission now."

She hurried outside into the sunlight and crouched in the overgrown grass, feeling frankly ridiculous as she waited. An Imperial gun cracked again beyond the forest, then a long pause, then another slightly offset from it to the left. She counted to thirty and another cannon thudded in the distance, a little further to the left again. Slow and deliberate fire, moving down the line, conserving ammunition, just pinning the enemy down. Thorn called out to her before the fourth gun could fire, "They're firing now, stand by!"

Rounds thudded down, popping softly through the trees a way off to the enemy's left as the fourth Imperial gun fired. Sophia opened her mouth, thought for a second, then closed it and pulled out her compass to check the bearing. Ten... no, twelve degrees left. Turning, she yelled back to Lieutenant Thorn, "Have them bring it twelve degrees right!"

The fifth Imperial gun fired, right on schedule. If the enemy gunners had been shaken they weren't showing it. Thorn called out a moment later, "Firing, stand by!"

Rounds cracked down through the trees a few seconds later, just a little right of where she could hear the enemy guns. The sixth gun fired a moment later, ahead of schedule. Sophia called back, "Left maybe one or two! That was close!"

"Alright-" The rest of Thorn's reply was blotted out as Second Squad's machine guns hammered to life off in the woods behind her, joined a moment later by the other team's gun from the ruined barn. Sophia threw herself flat on the ground instinctively and twisted to get a look at what was going on. Seeing what looked like Sergeant Cross standing full in the open with his back to her beside the barn, looking at something out beyond the valley to their east, she rather sheepishly climbed to her feet and rushed back inside.

Thorn was getting up himself as she got inside. He looked up at her, a look of alarm written over his face as he asked, "What's happening? Did you see anything?"

Sophia shook her head, then added, "We're not under attack." The lieutenant was opening his mouth to tell her to take over talking to the artillery so he could go sort it out, and she beat him to it, "I'll go ask the other team what they're shooting at."

He thought for a moment, then motioned for her to go ahead, "Sure, come right back. Thanks."

Sophia rushed over to the half-collapsed barn as the machine gun inside cracked off another long burst, finding Sergeant Cross standing by the front corner of the building staring intently at something off in the fields to their west through his binoculars. She heard Stennis call out from inside, "How's that?"

Cross snorted and called back, "No idea!" Noticing her, he turned and greeted her cheerfully, "Oh, hey, Sophia. Did Thorn send you?"

"Yeah," she replied, "He's still dealing with the artillery. What're we shooting at?"

"There was a whole platoon or so of Masks moving past the base of that little rise out there, the one with the three trees on top." The sergeant pointed, and Sophia followed his finger out through the fields and pastures, past where the valley opened up to a scenic little rise with three big trees spreading out above it. It must have been a kilometer away at least. Cross went on, "They're all down on the ground now... oh, there's one."

Sophia noticed a tiny speck appear, run for a ways and throw itself down, disappearing out of view as one of the machine guns out in the woods squeezed off a few shots. Much farther away down the long slope to the west, Sophia heard a couple more Royal machine guns open up at the Imperials. Raising an eyebrow, she asked, "Who's that?"

"Our friends from earlier, I think. Those two rode off that way." Cross replied. A moment later something hit high up on the barn next to them with a dull thud, like someone had thrown a rock. The machine gun inside let off another burst with a sound like she was standing next to the world's biggest set of pots and pans being slammed together by a toddler the size of a horse, and as the ringing in her ears subsided it happened again, twice in fact. One of them was quite close to her and Cross.

A couple more little things pocked to the ground behind them, and Sophia tapped him on the arm and said, "Hey, uh, sarge, they're shooting back." Cross looked over at her questioningly and she volunteered, "I'll tell Thorn."

Sophia turned and ran back towards the house, any reply Cross had lost in the noise as another one of their machine guns fired. She heard artillery shells beginning to slap down on the far side of the trees as she skidded inside, the distant, dull pops barely audible under the hammering gunfire nearby. Thorn was standing as she came in, and he raised an eyebrow and asked, "What's the story?"

"Dismounted dragoons, probably fifteen hundred meters east or so. Cross thought a platoon." Something small and evil popped through the roof and buried itself in the far wall, and Sophia added, "They're shooting back."

Thorn nodded, "Right." He jerked his chin at the rest of her team, busily smashing open a hole in the east wall's bricks with their rifle butts, "Your guys have been hard at work, get your gun into action when you can."

Sophia nodded, "Yes, sir!" Thorn picked up the field telephone and cable reel and ran out past her, and she rushed over to her team, carefully navigating around a couple gaping holes in the floor as the boards creaked unpleasantly. She arrived just as they managed to smash out an acceptable-looking hole, and the group stepped back as Kelly nosed the gun in and slid down behind it. She told him, "You're looking for Imperials near the little hill with the three trees, maybe fifteen hundred meters."

Kelly looked for a second, then calmly adjusted the gun's sight and squeezed off a burst. Fortunately he'd pushed the muzzle outside and the sound wasn't quite deafening. Dropping her ammunition bandolier next to him, Sophia said, "Easy on the ammunition, we might be here for a while." Looking around, she gestured at the debris lying around the half-burned house as another bullet gouged into the far wall, "Come on, let's reinforce this wall. They probably have something bigger to shoot at us."

About two minutes later the first mortar bomb whistled in and cracked in the woods behind them. Then another, and another, the drizzle turning into a steady rain of explosives falling around the farm. Sophia and her friends barely paused their work as they tore up boards and piled up debris around Kelly as he methodically worked away at the machine gun, firing short, calm bursts like he was on the range.

By the time the first oncoming-train whistle split the sky and the first *real* artillery shell shrieked in *way* too close and sent loose boards and roofing tiles raining down on them, they'd built a pretty good ring of debris around him, and Hargrave and Edward had just finished pushing a table over top. They got up, used the new debris to finish roofing their bunker and crammed in with Kelly as more heavy rounds swept in, the earth-shaking thuds gradually working off to their right and into the forest around where Second Squad was positioned. Sophia absently hoped that they'd been digging in.

Kelly twisted around behind the gun and glared at her and Tony where they had squeezed in on top of his legs and back, and snapped, "Can you two cuddle somewhere else?"

Sophia looked at him, then at Tony, then realized that was literally what they were going to have to do. She was opening her mouth to say something when Tony boldly dragged her off Kelly and tucked himself close in behind her, his arms wrapped securely around her waist. It would have been romantic if they hadn't been sharing the space with three other people and she hadn't been staring straight into a machine gun's belt feeder.

Blushing a little despite everything, Sophia managed, "What can you see?"

Kelly looked at her blearily, "Not a whole lot. I think they're mostly in the woods by now, on the left."

"Wanna switch?" Edward asked from his far side.

"Yeah, sure." Kelly replied. He rolled aside, and Edward climbed over him to take his place on the gun. He had barely squeezed off his first burst when Sophia heard more shells shrieking in, louder and louder, straight on top of them.

Sophia felt herself lifted into the air and slammed back down hard enough to punch the air from her lungs. She tasted blood as her ears *rang* from the blast. Shaking her head, she tried to sit up, straining against the pressure around her midsection as she blinked at the sunlight that was now streaming into their little rubble bunker, painting solid bars of light into the dust-filled air. Looking down, she met Edward's eyes as he looked up from the machine gun, a ribbon of blood beginning to drip from his nose. He must have bashed it against the gun when they were hit.

Kelly and Hargrave stirred on his far side, getting up on their elbows and giving her concerned looks. Twisting around as well as she could, she noticed what the pressure on her midsection was. Tony was hanging onto her for dear life. She patted him reassuringly and he loosened up a little. A *little*.

As for the house, well, a lot of debris seemed to have fallen onto their shelter and daylight was shining in cheerily. They must have taken a direct hit that caved the roof in and, Sophia noted with a sick feeling in her stomach, probably blown most of the floor behind them out. The floor was *definitely* not at the same angle it had been. They were probably going to have to dig themselves out somehow after this was over. As it stood, if they hadn't built their little bunker they all would have died. They all seemed to be alright, though, and Sophia slapped Edward's shoulder and shouted over the ringing in her ears, "*Keep shooting!*"

Her friend gamely pushed the machine gun forward on its bipod and cranked off another burst. After having an *artillery shell* go off maybe fifteen feet away from her it didn't sound nearly so loud as before. They kept on shooting for a few more minutes until Sophia realized she couldn't hear the other teams' guns and tapped Edward again, gesturing for him to cease fire. Shouting seemed like a wasted effort, and her mouth was coated in dust anyways. Hopefully they hadn't been abandoned.

They lay there quietly for a couple minutes, Sophia wondering when and if the ringing in her ears was ever going to subside. She was about to say something about digging themselves out when she saw a shadow move in front of their firing port as someone bravely waved their hand in front of it. Sergeant Cross' voice drifted in faintly, "You guys all alive in there? Anyone wounded?"

"Yeah, we're fine." Sophia said, "Edward's got a bloody nose, anyone else hurt?" The others gave her exasperated looks and she went on, "Okay, yeah, we're all fine. Did we win?"

"I think so, looks like the dragoons pulled out. At least they stopped shooting at us." Cross laughed outside, "Probably decided to go find an easier nut to crack. Now hold still in there, we're going to have to get you out and I think the easiest way's going to be taking the rest of this wall down."

The world was spinning a little. Sophia closed her eyes as the chinking and hammering outside faded away, and a moment later someone was shaking her as hot sunlight poured down on her face. She started awake to see Stennis and Cross looking down at her, concern written over their faces. Starting to sit up, she managed, "Wha... what happened? How lo..."

A wave of irresistible nausea hit rolled over her and she twisted and vomited on the ground, harder than she ever had before. It finally passed... mostly, and she managed to push herself back and sit up, Sergeant Cross patting her reassuringly on the back as the world spun around her. Stennis pushed an open canteen into her hand as Cross said, "We were getting worried about you, Sophie. You were out like a *light*." He chuckled with more than a hint of relief and went on, "Although you were all in pretty bad shape when we got you out of there. Must have been the fumes. Honestly, I was worried you were all *dead* until you kept on shooting like nothing had happened."

Sophia twisted around blearily and took a look at the house. It had looked bad earlier, but still vaguely like a house. Now it was nothing more than a pile of rubble and wreckage. Their portion of the brick wall was still standing somehow, and she could see where Cross and the others had opened up their firing port to pull them out. They must have taken a direct hit from an artillery shell, a *big* one. And if the Imperials had their range, it occurred to her as she sat there staring at the destroyed house, they could absolutely hit them again.

She took a heavenly swig of water, then looked up at Stennis and asked, "Can we use the barn? I'm scared right now."

The corporal laughed and pointed at the pile of burning lumber and hay that had once been the barn, "You're welcome to it, but you'll have to put it out first. We all had to run out after it caught on fire."

Sophia snorted, feeling her stomach settle a little, "How about your team, how're they?"

He gave her a sour look, "Not as good as yours, Massey got a big piece of shrapnel through his arm and Montour had the damn side of his head opened up, although I think that looks worse than it really is. God knows he felt good enough to complain about it." He jerked his head off towards the forest, "Doc's working on them now. Hopefully we can get them out on the train, I think it's heading back this way now."

Sophia faintly heard someone blowing the assembly signal on a whistle back in the forest, probably Lieutenant Thorn. Stennis gave her a look, "Looks like it's time to go."

She nodded, then looked around at the rest of her team where they were sitting or lying around her. They all looked about like she felt, maybe a little better. She was pretty sure she was the only one who had emptied her guts all over the grass. Picking up her rifle and climbing to her feet a little unsteadily, she looked between them and said, "Alright guys, get up. Time to go."

They all groaned as they got up, but soon they were on their feet and following along behind her as she hurried back into the forest. She quickly located Lieutenant Thorn with his field telephone, sitting on a convenient log that she was pretty sure hadn't been there when they came in. The air smelled pleasantly of fresh pine sap with an undercurrent of TNT and looking at the tree standing next to it she could see the trunk ended abruptly in a splintered stump thirty or so feet up.

Someone groaned nearby, and she looked over to see their medic working on a soldier laid out on the ground nearby, wrapping a bandage around his head. It looked like Montour, a man she barely knew if she was going to be honest about it. Three others were sitting or lying nearby. Looking back to the lieutenant, she saw Thorn smile at her with excessive cheer and pat the log next to him invitingly, and she obligingly sank down next to him as the rest of the platoon filtered in.

Thorn called out, "Leaders only, the rest of you all face out!" The junior soldiers spread out into a protective circle around them, and he went on, "Alright everyone, I just got off the phone with Guardian. The division's across the river and we're pulling out." He went on, "We'll head back to the tracks first to drop off the wounded, then we're walking back to Allenby." Everyone groaned at the news, but he pushed on, "Stennis, they're mostly your guys. Can you have someone flag down the *Bad News Express* and get them on? I don't want to wait."

The corporal shrugged, "I'll do it myself with the rest of my team." He looked at her, "Rose, you'll take your guys and go with the rest of the platoon."

Thorn nodded, "Sounds good. Let's go." They quickly shuffled back into a tactical formation and made for the tracks, Stennis, the rest of his team and the other wounded dropping out beside the tracks. The *Bad News Express* fired a salvo reassuringly on the far side of the woods as they pressed on to the south, eventually pushing their way out of the forest. The sight as they stood there in the golden late-afternoon sunlight took her breath away.

The vast plain opening up in front of them was *covered* with Royal cavalry, troop upon troop and squadron upon squadron streaming back towards Allenby. Here and there she could see the stubby shapes of Horse Artillery cannons and boxy supply wagons snaking along the farm roads and paths through the fields. Volleys of Imperial artillery whistled down occasionally, sending a few men and horses crashing to the ground, and off in the distance Sophia saw massive muzzle flashes as one of their own batteries paused to return fire. It wasn't that reassuring.

Lieutenant Thorn shouted for them to head down to the nearest road, spread out and hurry up, and they were soon marching single-file down the nearest road south of the railroad tracks, all of them casting nervous glances over their shoulders as the *Bad News Express* emerged from the trees and paced them maybe five hundred meters back. The armored train fired occasionally, and a couple times accelerated and reversed down the track as Imperial shells whistled in and burst around it.

As the sun began setting in front of them Sophia heard hoofbeats off to their left and looked to see a group of riders approaching. The one in the lead, wearing a hussar's uniform, looked very familiar and despite everything Sophia smiled as she recognized General MacMahon. The 9th Cavalry Division's commander trotted her horse up the length of their column and reined back to a walk as she reached its head and picked out Lieutenant Thorn in his usual position behind her. The Lady General chuckled and remarked, "Usually it's easier to pick out cavalry officers. These are your troopers, lieutenant?"

"Yes, ma'am," Thorn replied tiredly, "At your service. Err, milady, sorry," he added.

"Don't be, I've been called much worse." She went on, "As much as I hate being indebted to the infantry and the Rail Service, between you guys and that train you let us get most of our vehicles and the Horse Artillery across that bridge. Eric was losing that fight pretty badly before you showed up." Sophia guessed that was Colonel Janssen's first name as Lady MacMahon went on, "Thanks."

"I'm not sure what exactly we *did*, milady." Lieutenant Thorn replied, "We shot up some Imperials, I'm glad we helped out regardless."

"The way he told it to me, one minute his cuirassiers were getting shelled and had dragoons working around their left flank, and you guys showed up and turned the tables on them." The woman snorted, "Of course we're going to have a rematch in Allenby. If what I'm hearing is correct, if it wasn't for the rest of you guys there the Empire would own the town already and then we'd be in *real* trouble."

"They've attacked Allenby?" Thorn asked worriedly.

"Not in force." Lady MacMahon replied, "I think they saw infantry and decided to wait, thank God."

"So, milady," Thorn ventured, "What's the plan now?"

She laughed, "Good question! We're falling back to Grenville, Kellerman wants to reform the screen closer to the river and the rest of the army for support. We're not going to fight this many Imperials this far out." The Lady General thought for a moment and went on, "We might end up getting withdrawn completely, we've done our job out here. But that's not my call. *You* need to link back up with your company."

"Thanks, milady." Thorn replied.

"Oh, by the way, Sophia! How are you these days?" Lady MacMahon asked, nudging her horse up beside her.

Sophia looked up at her and smiled, "I've had worse days, milady." She chuckled, "Had a nice train ride."

The Lady General laughed again, "I bet it was very exciting! Say hi to your father for me, and take care of yourself!"

"Sure thing, milady." The Lady General gestured to her followers, nudged her horse and started to canter off, and Sophia shouted after her, "Thanks!"

A few minutes later they came over the last rise before Allenby and looked down into the town under the flaming sunset. As she watched dirty, orange light rippled across the north side of town around the train station, and a few seconds later the dull cracking of Imperial artillery washed over them. Sighing heavily, Sophia pulled her rifle off her shoulder and patted her bayonet's hilt where it sat at her hip. This was going to be a long, *long* night.

Chapter 11
A Waltz with Daggers

"There we go, milady." Rebecca said, as Arilin felt her corset's firm grip around her waist tighten into an extremely secure squeeze. Her maid's fingers tugged and fussed at the small of her back as she knotted the laces and tucked them away securely, and the woman patted her on her now-extremely slender waist as she finished, "You can sit down now if you'd like, milady."

Arilin turned and gave her a half-smile, "I'm not much of a fainting type, Becky. I'll be fine."

Her lady's maid raised an eyebrow and snorted, "Could have fooled me. But," she shrugged, "If you're good I'll finish getting you dressed."

The princess pouted, "Well, I'm eating properly now."

"Yes, you are, milady." Becky made a dismissive motion, "Now turn back around, I need to get your bustle on."

Her maid was finishing with her petticoats when someone knocked gingerly on her bedroom door. Calling for them to wait, Becky did up the last few closures and walked over to the door. Opening it a crack, she had a short, low exchange with the person on the other side before she turned, "Milady, did you ask for an... intelligence report? There's a Lieutenant Remarque here to see you."

"Oh, good!" Arilin replied, "Please, let her in. I don't think you two have met."

"No, we haven't." Becky stepped back enough to let the young lieutenant, resplendent in her white dress uniform, squeeze inside. The confused look on her face disappeared when she noticed Arilin was half-undressed, and Becky chuckled and soothed her as the girl started blushing and stammering, "Don't be embarrassed, dear, you're the one with all your clothes on."

Arilin laughed as the brown-haired lieutenant nervously walked further in, Becky closing the door silently behind her with a smug look. "Thanks for working late, Maria." The princess smiled, "What do you have for me?"

The girl produced a couple sheets of typewritten paper out of her purse, "Well, ah, milady, it took me a while but I managed to get something readable out of the Intelligence section." Arilin gave her a look and she quickly added, "That wasn't dumbed down beyond recognition." Maria rolled her eyes at the thought, "No wonder nobody pays them any attention."

Becky chortled, covering her mouth with her hand politely. She quickly busied herself retrieving Arilin's dress, and the princess smiled and remarked, "Please, go ahead."

Maria cleared her throat, quickly leafed through her papers and started, "Well, ah, milady, it's all very confusing and none of it sounds good." Arilin gave her a half-hearted glare and she sighed, "We know the Dominion has declared what they're calling a 'national emergency' and conducted a partial mobilization to their east to defend against a possible Imperial attack. This included recalling most of their regular garrisons from their colonies."

"Nothing new here." Arilin remarked as Becky reappeared with her ball gown, a beautiful piece in sapphire-blue silk with a little bit more of an adult cut than the one she had last worn in Drakenburg. Her maid had told her earlier that red was out of the question, not least because she was ostensibly supposed to be mourning her brother. Arilin sniffed a little at the thought. She missed Adrian. If he'd been around her only concern for the evening would have been her dress, and she probably would have had a furious fight with Becky over it and spent the rest of the night sulking. It would have been *wonderful*.

The lieutenant was talking again, "...they've continued to mobilize troops since Fire Ridge, although they seem to be keeping them in their home stations. They've also begun to, quite openly, modernize their fortresses along our border with them and upgrade their rail infrastructure in the area."

"How so?" Arilin asked as she raised her arms for Becky to slip the dress onto her, the fine silk gliding across her long gloves with just the faintest brush through the fine leather.

Her maid got the dress settled and started to button it up behind her back as Maria replied, "Mostly expanding platforms, milady, they've got plenty of lines in the area already. There's only one thing you use a big, long platform with no roof for." *Troops*, she left unsaid. The lieutenant frowned and went on, "More concerning, one of the Dominion's eastern battle squadrons put to sea last week with colliers and has yet to return to port, at least anywhere we're getting reports from. They may be redeploying to the west."

Against the Kingdom. Due to the Dominion's geography, facing Imperial Arastrea to their east and the Western Kingdom to their north, with the great mass of their colonies in what had once been the Caliphate to their southwest, they were forced to maintain two separate battle fleets. Sailing between their separate coasts would take a week or more, even in a fast liner. And with the Royal Navy maimed after the Battle of the Diamond Shoals, it didn't require a lot of imagination for Arilin to think of a few reasons for the Dominion to want to mass their fleet facing north.

Becky finished buttoning up her dress behind her back, and Arilin turned away from the lieutenant to look at herself in her vanity mirror. She looked fine, wonderful even. A beautiful young woman dressed up for a ball she wasn't terribly interested in attending. Her maid hung a necklace beaded with sapphires, a fine piece pulled out of the Crown Jewels, around her neck and she looked even better. Giving her a smile she didn't feel, the princess said, "Thanks, Becky." Looking at the lieutenant in the mirror, she went on, "How about our troops in the south? How many do we still have there?"

Maria frowned, "Not many, milady. South of the Storm Range we've got the Fortress Corps, of course, Thirtieth Corps, they're brand-new... and they're just starting to stand up the Thirty-First and Thirty-Second. Some gendarmes and border guards, I'm sure." *They wouldn't last a week*, Arilin thought sourly as the girl went on, "Everything fit for combat's been sent east." She added, a little hesitantly, "I, uh, asked if they'd done any digging in and they looked at me like I was crazy."

Arilin sighed as heavily as she could in her corset, then turned and smiled warmly at the lieutenant, "Thanks, Maria. I couldn't have asked for better, at least on your part." She chuckled, "I do have to say, I was surprised to see you again this morning. You know I just *mentioned* to my father in a letter I could use a military aide?"

The girl nodded quickly and stepped aside for Arilin to sweep past her towards the door, replying as she followed along behind, "Really, milady? General Reinhardt came down himself and pulled me out of the office just... three days ago now?" She laughed, "I barely had time to pack."

Becky had somehow maneuvered around both of them and pulled the door open for her. Arilin stepped out into the hall, replying, "Then thanks for hurrying, you've been a great help so far." She turned and looked the girl up and down before smiling again and asking, "Now, how would you like to go to a ball with us?" She snorted, "Ambassador Carrera seems to have decided to kick off the social season all by himself, war or not."

Maria raised an eyebrow, "He's from the Dominion, right?" Arilin nodded and she went on, "I don't suppose this has anything at all to do with what I just told you?" The princess smirked at her, and she smoothed her uniform's skirt embarrassedly, "I feel a little *underdressed*, milady."

Arilin giggled, "You'll be *fine*."

"Yes, dear." Queen Catherine added, as she appeared from down the hall in an elegant purple gown with her own maid, Abigail, in tow. She went on, smiling, "It's all confidence anyways." She turned to Arilin and said, "You look wonderful yourself, dear..." She trailed off, then chuckled, "God, have you grown up."

"Thanks, Mom." Arilin said, reddening, "I don't *feel* older."

The Queen laughed, "You never do, my love. Now come on, let's go be good neighbors."

They started to head downstairs, Beatrice sticking her head out of the parlor's heavy, wood-paneled door as they passed to wish them farewell. Arilin thought she looked a little jealous. Putting on their evening cloaks, they made their way down to the palace's grand hall to find her uncle waiting for them, dazzling in his starched cuirassier's uniform. Not content to pull their carriages up into the plaza, Alphonse had backed them up to the foot of the grand staircase in the hall itself, the horses shuffling about on a cloth the guards had rolled out to protect the floor.

Her uncle gave them a courtly bow as they descended the stairs. Arilin somehow managed to keep the distaste off her face as he straightened up to greet them, "Your ladyships, so good to see you!" He took her mother's hand and kissed it as they alighted in front of him. Arilin rolled her eyes behind his back as he stepped between them and went on, "You look brilliant tonight, Catherine, although I must confess I'm surprised to see Arilin here."

Her mother laughed, "She's certainly old enough for this kind of thing, Alphonse. I think she'll enjoy it."

Her uncle shrugged and went to open the carriage's door for them, "I hope so, milady. At her age I would have been bored stiff."

Her mother shrugged and took his hand to climb inside. Arilin hesitated for a moment, then put her hand out herself. Her uncle took it firmly, his massive hand enveloping her own in a vise of strong muscle and hard flesh barely softened by their gloves. Arilin's skin crawled as she realized he was strong enough to break her hand with just a sufficiently vicious squeeze. She avoided his eyes, and an instant later he released her as she turned to sit down next to her mother. Her mother gave her a concerned look as she smoothed out her skirts and settled down next to her, but said nothing as Alphonse climbed up behind her and sat down across from them, closing the door as he went. Behind them Arilin heard the other carriage's door close as Maria and the two maids settled in, and Alphonse rapped hard on the ceiling to signal the driver to go.

The foot guards by the door saluted, rifles upright as they rolled out the front doors into the night. Looking out the window, Arilin saw a detachment of cuirassiers that had been waiting outside in the plaza break formation and fall in around them. Judging by the golden knotwork on their sleeves they were from the 2nd Cuirassier Guards. Her uncle's old regiment, whose uniform he wore constantly. Now was no exception, although his gala dress uniform put the troopers to shame.

Alphonse noticed her look and smiled thinly, "Something bothering you, little lady?"

Arilin raised her eyebrows innocently and asked, "I was just wondering when you served last."

He leaned back in his seat and smirked, steepling his fingers across his stomach, "The Jihadist War. I was your father's liaison with Dominion Supreme Headquarters." He chuckled, "Probably most of the reason why we didn't start shooting each other instead of the *enemy*."

"What about before then?" Arilin replied as the carriage made a couple small turns and the smooth flagstones of the Palace plaza turned to rougher street cobblestones under the carriage's wheels, bouncing them gently on the suspension.

"I commanded the Guards Heavy Cavalry Brigade in the Marchlands War." Alphonse made a distasteful look for a moment, "Not the *best* time I've ever had in my life, young lady. I decided to hang up my spurs afterwards, until your father asked for my help with the Jihadists."

Arilin supposed that explanation was literally correct but probably not totally accurate. She remarked, "And now you're here."

Alphonse smiled, his eyes colder than they should have been in the darkness, "That I am." He turned to her mother and brightened, "I'm sorry I've been such a stranger for the last few years, Catherine. Clearly I've been missing out on something special."

Her smiled and replied politely, "Arilin and Beatrice? They're a handful every day, that's for sure." Noticing Arilin's dirty look, she laughed, "Don't think I can't see you just because it's dark in here." She patted the seat right next to her, "Come over here, young lady. I don't get to hold onto you enough these days."

Arilin was halfway through sighing and rolling her eyes when something occurred to her. Their invitations, the original ones they had received a few days back, *had not had her on them*. Her mother had *wanted* to take her along with them, and had told the Embassy as much. Of course they had passed it off as a mistake, they had been concerned about her emotional state with her brother's death and so on and they were very sorry for being so presumptuous. But that... no, that wasn't it. It wasn't all of it at least. Ever since he had reappeared, and particularly since her father had gone to the front, Prince Alphonse had been as supportive of her mother as he could *possibly* be.

Of course the Queen had appreciated it, or at least *seemed* to, to Arilin... and then an icy, slimy tentacle worked its way up her back and spread nauseatingly across her body in a slick, clammy wave, her sigh turning into more of a strangled gasp as she realized what was going on. Only her corset's tight grip kept her from shuddering outright as she sat there. She knew *exactly* what Alphonse was after, and so did her mother, and that was why her mother *did not want to be alone with him.*

Her mother was opening her mouth to scold her when Arilin meekly slid over next to her, took her hands in her own and wanted to do nothing else beyond talk about the most vapid teenaged gossip for the entire rest of the ride to the Embassy. As it turned out, her mother had an entire stockpile of juicy *adult* gossip to respond with. After a few minutes of this Alphonse rolled his eyes and turned to look out the window with a soft snort, and Arilin felt herself let her breath out just a tiny bit.

Maybe ten minutes and a few turns later Arilin heard their cuirassier escorts slow to a walk, a couple of the horses whinnying softly as the troopers reined them back. A moment later the carriage slowed as orange torchlight flickered through the windows, and Arilin let go of her mother and turned as the door popped and swung open, letting the warm night air pour in smelling of smoke and sweet flowers, with an earthy undercurrent of the lush, green trees that shaded the walk up to the Embassy's front steps.

They had the red carpet laid out for them lined with a torch-bearing honor guard, huge ambassadorial guardsmen resplendent in their red-jacketed uniforms. Every one of their shined brass buttons and silver-plated parade helmets was a constellation of dancing reflections in the torchlight. Her uncle gestured for them to go ahead and Arilin carefully climbed out, one of their footmen taking her hand to help her. She alighted on the carpet, close enough to feel the heat from the torches on her face. The whole street in front of the Embassy was filled with carriages and the sidewalks with well-dressed partygoers who didn't merit Royal treatment, and an audible murmur rose as she straightened up and looked around. The other carriage had disappeared, presumably around the back to the servants' entrance. A couple flashbulbs popped out beyond the guards, and Arilin supposed she'd be seeing her picture in the newspapers tomorrow.

Her mother and Alphonse climbed out a moment after her and the crowd's buzzing grew louder as an Embassy footman hurried out to them and bowed courteously. They nodded back politely as he greeted them,

"Your Royal Highnesses, welcome! Please, come in!" He stepped aside and gestured towards the entryway, "The Ambassador is waiting."

Alphonse offered them his arms and Arilin reluctantly set her hand on his sleeve, feeling her skin crawl a little. They swept down the red carpet and Arilin hitched up her skirt with her free hand to ascend the stairs. Embassy servants appeared in the foyer to take her and her mother's cloaks, and they were quickly ushered into the Embassy's grand ballroom. A servant by the door puffed himself up and announced them as they entered, "*Ladies and gentlemen!* I am pleased to announce the arrival of Princess Arilin, Prince Alphonse and..." he paused for effect, a little obnoxiously, "Her Royal Majesty, Queen Catherine."

The murmuring conversation in the hall died down for a moment, then started back up again almost immediately. This was, Arilin thought, a harder town to impress than Drakenburg. In fact, she noted as she saw Ambassador Rosenheim and his wife, the Archduchess Bianca, swooping towards them, they weren't even the only royalty in the room. Letting go of Alphonse with more than a little relief, Arilin curtsied politely to the two of them. They returned the gesture politely enough, and Arilin felt a little knot of tension she hadn't realized was there ease inside her chest. They were acting polite, at least.

The Archduchess smiled at her warmly, "Arilin! So good to see you again!" She looked her up and down, then raised her eyebrows in what seemed like genuine surprise, "And my, have you grown!" She glanced across at the Queen quizzically, "When did I see her last? I think it was at the ball for, oh, what was that ship?"

Her mother offered, "The *Gorgon*, I think?"

"Oh, yes." The woman pursed her lips prettily, thinking. Bianca was a beautiful woman, a little younger than her mother, with hair like dark chocolate and eyes like dark honey, wearing a rather adventurous dress the color of dark fire. She colored a little and ventured, "It, ah... it survived the battle, I hope?"

Arilin snorted grimly and replied, "Yes, barely."

Bianca brightened vapidly, "Oh, good!"

The Ambassador cut in, smiling, "Well, it seems like you three have a lot to catch up on." Taking Alphonse by the shoulders, he turned him around and led him off deeper into the ballroom, saying, "Come on, Alphonse, there's some people I want you to meet."

Arilin watched them go for a moment with a vague sense of relief, until it occurred to her that the *last* thing in the world she wanted was for her uncle, who was *probably* actively plotting to usurp the throne, to be having deep, detailed conversations with the official representative of a country that was *probably* preparing to invade. *Probably* to advance his claim, given how friendly he was with them. On the plus side, given the amount of people that were starting to gather around the two men, she didn't need to have any worries about them plotting anything for a while yet. Smiling, she turned back to the Queen and the Archduchess, saying, "So, have you heard..."

A few minutes later the orchestra switched from chamber music to a waltz, and Arilin realized they were surrounded by a crowd of handsome men who had infiltrated into their general vicinity of the ballroom and were busily pretending to have some reason to be there beyond waiting for the three of them to look up from talking. Arilin raised an eyebrow and remarked, "We seem to have attracted a crowd."

Bianca laughed, and her mother replied, "No, dear, they're all here for *you*. We're married."

The Archduchess added, "Oh my." Giggling like a schoolgirl, she took Arilin by the shoulders, spun her around and gently pushed her towards the suitors, "You shouldn't spend all night gossiping with us old hens. Go have some fun!"

The men all exchanged calculating looks and started subtly converging on her, jockeying for advantage as politely as possible. A foot placed here, an sword's scabbard ostentatiously swept in the way there, a couple of discreet elbows in the ribs that they thought she wouldn't see... and then a boy she vaguely recognized from school, dressed in a Guards Infantry cadet's uniform, shouldered his way through them and stopped in front of her. They murmured as he took Arilin's hand, kissed it and asked her bluntly, "Milady, would you like to dance?"

Arilin felt herself blushing a little as she smiled and replied, "I'd love to." Her new friend turned and made a gesture with his head at the wall of disappointed suitors, and they reluctantly stood aside to let him lead her out onto the floor. She noted with a sly smile that Maria was already among the couples dancing, whirling about in the arms of a very good-looking man in a naval uniform. Her partner confidently slid an arm around her waist, took her hand and stepped them into the line of dancers. He was quite good at it, and she barely needed to think about dancing at all as she spun about in his embrace. Looking up at him, she ventured, "Thanks back there."

He chuckled, "I'm surprised they didn't give you *some* cover."

Arilin laughed, "I think they're both from the old school of hard knocks."

"Law of the jungle, huh?" He smiled, "You looked like you needed a rescue."

"Well." She smiled back, "To whom do I owe it?"

"Thomas Strathclyde, milady." He replied.

That rang a bell, although she had to think about it for a moment. Arilin raised an eyebrow and asked, "I don't suppose you have a sister?"

"Yes, actually." Her partner chuckled and nodded at an older girl dancing on the other side of the room, "She's the one in the yellow dress. Why do you ask?"

Arilin laughed again, "Long story."

"I hope this doesn't have to do with her last birthday party." He replied, frowning.

The princess smiled apologetically, "It might?"

He sighed, "I'll have you know, milady, that was *entirely* our mother's idea."

She replied, "I'm not saying I blame you, I was just curious."

"Anyways, milady." Thomas let go of her waist and lifted her hand in his as he spun her around. Arilin expertly twirled about and stepped back in to be caught by him, feeling a little shorter of breath than she had any right to be as he went on, "Liri and Miri talked to me earlier."

"Oh, really?" She asked, blushing a little, "About what?"

"Your little problem." He chuckled, "My dad's the commander of the 1st Guards Infantry Regiment, they thought I could help out."

Her friends clearly had amazing judgement. Arilin asked, "Well, can you?"

Thomas chuckled, "Of course, milady. I know what side my bread is buttered on." He added, "I'll sound out my father and let you know."

"Thanks," she replied gratefully. A moment later the song wound down and Thomas let her go. Stepping back a little reluctantly, she gave him a deeper curtsey than he was strictly entitled to and, straightening up, looked around for a new partner. As things happened they had stopped next to Maria and her dreamy blonde Navy lieutenant. Thomas and the older man exchanged looks, gave each other almost imperceptible nods and smoothly switched partners.

This new guy's name was Felix, and his dancing made Thomas look like a stumbling, lead-footed oaf. After a few minutes of floating around the ballroom lost in his sea-blue eyes he deposited her with the Union's ambassador, an old man in understated evening dress who turned out to be remarkably light on his feet. The only things he was concerned about were how well she was holding up now that she was Crown Princess, and whether he could get some time later in the week to talk to her about a fisheries treaty she'd never heard of before. Apparently his government was breathing down his neck. He passed her off to Mr. Jacob Masters, owner of Masters Heavy Industries and one of the wealthiest men in the Kingdom. *He* was concerned about Royal prisoners of war in the Empire, and wanted to know if she would put in an appearance on behalf of the Red Cross, which of course she would. And on and on it went. At least, Arilin thought as she noticed her uncle dancing with a succession of good-looking women, she didn't need to worry about him cooking up any conspiracies with the Dominion's ambassador while the orchestra was playing.

Finally, however, the orchestra wound down and a servant announced that dinner was about to be served. The room was still spinning a little for Arilin, but fortunately Becky appeared with a glass of water in hand to lead her to her seat. In between gulps, Arilin managed to tell her maid to keep an eye on Alphonse, and the woman replied that she was way ahead of her and that her uncle hadn't so much as gone to the bathroom since he'd arrived.

Arriving at her seat, Arilin discovered that she had been seated with Lady Bianca and her mother at the ladies' high table, a distinctly Dominion-style arrangement but one that, she supposed, she was entirely alright with given the circumstances. She managed to make it through the toast to the ladies before half-collapsing into her chair, grateful that she at least wouldn't have to match wits with Alphonse over dinner.

Her mother and Bianca fussed over her through all eight courses, which given the circumstances she appreciated. The room stopped spinning midway through her bowl of consommé, and by the time she had polished off her cannoli and the after-dinner coffee came around Arilin felt fully refreshed. Which was just as well, because she had just started on it when she felt a familiar presence behind her and twisted in her seat to see Becky standing there. Her maid bent down and whispered in her ear, "Milady, Alphonse and Ambassador Rosenheim just excused themselves and went upstairs."

Arilin nodded, took another sip of her coffee like it was the most natural thing in the world, smoothed her skirts and stood. Bowing her head politely, she said, "I'm sorry, mother, milady, please excuse me for a minute." Straightening up, she gave the Archduchess an apologetic smile, "I actually have something to speak to your husband about before we head back for the night."

Bianca raised her eyebrows in surprise, "Oh, certainly. I suppose you would, actually, now that I think about it." The woman shared a glance with her mother and teased her, "You really have grown up fast, haven't you, dear?"

Her sword had gone into that dragoon's chest and stuck there like it had been set in concrete, almost dragging her out of her saddle as she stupidly tried to hang on. *Much too fast*, Arilin thought grimly, *and now I need to find out if your husband is plotting to overthrow me.* Giving Bianca a smile she didn't feel, she replied noncommittally, "I guess I have."

Turning, Arilin followed Becky through the Embassy's grand hall, into a side gallery and up a long staircase to the second floor. A guard who had been stationed discreetly in the hallway beyond stepped into the door to block their way as they finished climbing the stairs. Smiling down on them through a magnificent moustache, the big man started gently, "I'm sorry... milady, but the ball is *downstairs*." He chuckled, "Nothing but offices up here. Are you lost?"

Arilin smiled back, "A little, but I think you can help me. I need to speak to the Ambassador."

The man's face hardened, "He has retired for the night, milady, and he gave strict orders that he was not to be disturbed." He went on, "I suggest that you please return downstairs."

"Oh, my, that is a problem." Arilin pouted, "I'm sure he wouldn't like to be summoned to the Palace later tonight to speak to me, it's late enough as is." The man's expression sharpened, and Arilin dropped the act and glared back, "*Your choice, corporal.*"

The man looked at her for a second, eyes narrowing. He finally said, "Very well then." Stepping back, he pressed a button on his side of the wall and they heard a distant buzzer sound. Another guard showed up to relieve him an awkward minute of waiting later, and he turned and said, "Come with me."

They followed him down the darkened corridor towards a room with bright, warm light spilling out from under the door, their footsteps swallowed by the upstairs carpet. The guard knocked on the heavy door and the dull sound of conversation within died down. After a too-long moment she heard the Ambassador call out faintly, "I'm indisposed, so unless it's *Charles* on the phone for me I suggest you leave."

"It's Princess Arilin here to see you, sir." The guard replied, "She says it can't wait."

"Well, it will..." Ambassador Rosenheim trailed off as Arilin brushed past the guard and popped the door open, bright light and a cloud of acrid cigar smoke blinding her for a second. Stepping inside regardless, she closed the door behind her in what she supposed was the guard's shocked face and blinked the tears from her eyes to see Prince Alphonse and the Ambassador staring at her from overstuffed seats on either side of the little smoking lounge. Rosenheim gave her a murderous look and cursed, "*Damn it*, girl. Do they not teach manners any more these days?"

Arilin shrugged, "I go to public school."

She was opening her mouth to go on when her uncle cut in snidely, "Clearly the Royal Academy has gone downhill recently."

Shrugging again, she smoothed her skirts and sank into the closest chair to the door, the seat practically exhaling smoke as the cushion gave way under her weight. She was going to *stink* later. With her corset on she frankly would have preferred something with a little more back support, but it was comfortable enough once she worked herself into it a little. Finally settling herself, she crossed her legs demurely and looked between the two men before settling her gaze on Rosenheim, "I *do* have something I need to speak to you about, though."

"Oh?" The Ambassador said, rudely, "Out with it, then."

"Three things, actually." Arilin said, "First, back in April my father sent your uncle-in-law a letter requesting troops, weapons, *money*, really anything he could spare to help us fight the Empire. We have yet to receive your reply."

Alphonse rolled his eyes and snapped back, "Arilin. We've talked about this. *I've* talked to *you* about this." He waved his fingers at her angrily, "Why, under the Five Moons, did you think I wanted to talk to the Ambassador privately? This is *extremely* sensitive, and it needs a delicate touch!" Piercing her with a glare, he went on, "What do you *think* I was doing for your father before now? I handle issues with the Dominion for him, *privately!*"

Gritting her teeth, Arilin exhaled slowly to calm herself and then theatrically raised an eyebrow, "Why?" Alphonse scowled at her, and she went on before he could cut her off, "Is it sensitive, I mean? Last time I checked we're allies, and I'm assuming they'd like a chance to settle scores with the Empire as much as we would."

Alphonse snorted contemptuously, but the Ambassador cut in before he could speak, "You assume wrong, milady. Very wrong." He glared at her contemptuously, "Have they taught you about the Disaster of the Tai Shan yet?" They had not. Arilin supposed that it was probably scheduled for later in the eighth-grade History curriculum. Regardless, she read plenty of books on her own time, and she knowingly rolled her eyes as he went on with the theatrical outrage of a schoolteacher denouncing an outrage a hundred years late, "*Fifty thousand men* marched to relieve Tai Shan Fortress. Do you know how many made it back *alive* after the Masks were through with them, princess?"

"Less than fifty, if I recall." Arilin replied coldly. The Tai Shan Campaign had been fought in the summer of 1880, weeks after Emperor Sai had sent out his bone-chilling declaration of war from his stronghold in the Arastrean Highlands. It would be decades before Patricia MacMahon's little mission convinced him to amend his Rescript to his soldiers and change the line about showing no mercy. The Imperial Army had happily used their prisoners as human shields afterwards.

"Yes, milady." Rosenheim spat, "My country is *never* going to go through that again, not unless we have no choice at all."

"Do you, though?" Arilin asked.

Rosenheim shrugged theatrically, "My government seems to think so."

"Judging by the precautions you're taking, you seem to think the whole Kingdom will fall soon." Arilin observed, "I'd think you'd want to help us out sooner rather than fight the Empire yourselves later." She snorted, "But what do I know? I'm just a kid."

"Arilin. Enough of this." Her uncle reproached her sternly.

She ignored him and raised an eyebrow at the Ambassador. Finally the man responded, "What do you mean, *precautions?*"

The princess shrugged, "Fortresses, railways on your northern border?" She gave him a smile that was as fake as it was cute, "You know, I *did* learn something today, actually. If you want to unload a whole infantry regiment at once you have to build this *big, long* rail platform, and it's *really* obvious. I mean, the Intelligence Office would have to be *blind* not to notice."

The Ambassador gave her a hateful look. A moment later his contemptuous act dropped back down over his face like an Imperial mask, and he rolled his eyes, "We build rail stations all the time, milady."

"Fortresses too, I guess. Oh, and that mobilization you're trying to hide." Arilin replied sarcastically, "Why are you so worried that the Empire is going to attack you from the *north...*" She trailed off to let the thought settle before shrugging helplessly, "Unless you're planning on *betraying* us or something."

"*Arilin!*" Her uncle leapt to his feet, face turning red as he thundered, "How *dare* you accuse them of that! Are you out of your *mind*, you *stupid little girl?*"

Alphonse advanced on her, face contorted in rage, boots thudding heavily even on the room's soft carpet. Arilin fought to stand as he loomed overhead, feet tangling in her skirts as the deeply-padded seat itself seemed to hold onto her like quicksand. She finally managed to heave herself to her feet and reel backwards as he lunged for her, pulling her arm away from his grasp a moment before his bone-crushing grip could close on her wrist. Backpedaling, she tripped on her skirts and half-fell into the door, getting the doorknob under her hand and twisting it desperately as he lunged for her again.

The latch popped under her weight and Arilin fell backwards into the corridor outside. Something hard hit the back her of head as she landed, and she tasted blood in her mouth for a moment as her vision clouded over, her corset like an iron vise around her chest. A gigantic shadow loomed over her, blotting out the hazy light pouring out of the smoking room as it started to stoop down and reach for her.

The shadow paused after a second, then straightened back up. People were shouting all around her. As her senses cleared Arilin recognized Becky's voice, "...not lay hands on my lady, I don't care *who* you are."

Shaking her head quickly, Arilin kicked her legs free of her skirts and quickly scooted back beside her maid, who was staring death at Prince Alphonse. Beside her the guardsman was looking between the three of them nervously, as though he was unsure of what to do. Arilin supposed he probably didn't deal with disputes between Wehrherz family members every day. Spreading her skirts, the princess got her legs under her and shakily climbed to her feet as her uncle snarled, "The *meaning* of this is Arilin making a perfect fool out of herself in front of Emperor Charles' representative." His eyes were blood-red knives fixed in her soul, his teeth white and sharp as he hissed, "You will *never* speak to Ambassador Rosen-heim in that way again, do you understand?"

Arilin slowly took a breath, held it for a moment and exhaled. Then, very deliberately, she rolled her eyes at him. Alphonse stiffened with rage as she replied, "Go to hell."

"Foul-mouthed *and* petulant." He shot back icily, looming above her, "Your father *will* hear of this. And it will not be pretty."

Arilin shrugged, "Go ahead. You'll still *never* be King."

Alphonse flexed his arm as though to strike her, and the guardsman unexpectedly stepped between them and set a hand against the man's chest, saying, "Hold on, my lord. It's not worth your trouble. I'll escort the ladies out."

Her uncle glared back at the man for a few seconds before he snorted, shook himself and retreated back into the smoking room, slamming the door shut behind him. Arilin let out a breath she hadn't realized she'd been holding as Becky relaxed beside her and said, "Thanks, corporal."

The big man shrugged, "This isn't the first date I've seen go bad around here." He gave Becky a hard look, "And I don't think anyone wants to see someone *shot* tonight, miss."

Her maid pulled her hand out of a convenient slit in her skirt's waist and replied innocently, "I have no idea what you're talking about."

He chuckled, "I'm sure you don't. Now come on, I think you two have worn out your welcome."

The guard walked them downstairs, sent one of the Embassy servants to bring one of their carriages around and politely but very firmly ensured Arilin, Maria, the two maids and the slightly miffed Queen were loaded inside and heading back to the Palace in record time. As they rolled back down the street, the carriage bouncing a little over the cobblestones on its suspension, Arilin's mother raised an eyebrow at her in the darkness and remarked, "You know dear, if I didn't know better I could have sworn we were just thrown out."

The princess sighed, "We... kind of were?"

"I figured. Not the first time I've been thrown out of a party, trust me." Her mother chuckled, then smiled at her from across the carriage, "First time on your account, I think. Your talk with the Ambassador didn't go so well?"

Arilin rolled her eyes, "Really, it was Alphonse." She gave her mother a look and came out with it, "I think he's plotting to overthrow Father and he's in bed with the Dominion."

The Queen raised her eyebrows, "My. Here I thought he was just trying to get in bed with *me*."

"That too." Arilin replied levelly.

"Ugh." Her mother wrinkled her nose, which was about as much of a scowl as she could manage, "I wish your father was here. Although, I don't know *what* he sees in that man." She paused, thought for a moment and went on, "It might have had to do with them both having to deal with your *grandfather*."

The princess raised an eyebrow, "You know, Mother, neither of you have told me much about him."

"King Alexander?" Her mother shook her head, "Your father overthrew him on your account, you know."

"Mine? How?" Arilin asked, "I wasn't born yet..." She trailed off, thinking, then gave her mother a questioning look. The older woman nodded, and Arilin swallowed hard, "Oh, wait, you mean...?"

The Queen smiled grimly, "Yes."

They rode in silence the rest of the way back to the Palace, the ugly implication hanging in the air the whole way. Finally arriving, they headed upstairs to the Residence and Queen Catherine and Abigail quickly disappeared into the Royal chambers. It was past midnight and the rest of the Palace was dark and silent, the heavy walls and deep carpeting seeming to suck the sound out of the air. Stepping into her own champers, Arilin walked into her little sitting room and out onto the balcony facing out into the gardens instead of turning into her bedroom, the other two women following her a little hesitantly.

"Milady? Are you alright?" Becky chuckled, "It's well past your bedtime, we need to get you undressed."

"Not really." Arilin replied, letting the scent of the trees and the faint, distant flowers below waft up around her in the darkness. Looking up at the clear night sky she could see little Truth and the even smaller Wisdom, tiny disks bobbing in the great river of stars above. It was calming, even if only just a little. The princess finally looked down from the sky and said, "Maria, I hate to ask you to do more for me tonight but this needs to be done. Take as much time tomorrow as you need."

"Milady?" Her aide asked, her white uniform shining faintly in the darkness.

"Go back to the War Ministry and tell them to arm the fortresses south of the Storm Range." Arilin said, "Orders direct from me. Based on my conversation with their ambassador, we can no longer trust the Dominion, and we need to prepare for an attack."

Modern fortresses required an immense amount of work to prepare for combat. Supplies and ammunition had to be stockpiled. Fields of fire had to be cleared for the cannons with callous military efficiency, razing everything that could provide cover for the enemy. Those weapons had to be test-fired and registered on known points out in the potential battlefield. Miles upon miles of trenches had to be dug between the widely-spaced outer forts and interval blockhouses, and the whole complex had to be practically wrapped in barbed wire. The infrastructure nearby, bridges and tunnels, had to be wired with explosives for immediate destruction. And the whole area had to be garrisoned, with troops that the Kingdom couldn't spare. The whole process was known as 'arming' a fortress.

The fortresses along the Night River had been maintained in constant wartime readiness and all of this had been done there simply as a matter of course, the simple facts of a border with the Empire that had been little more than a front line across a wide river. The Marchlands had been sparsely populated, a backwater whose only importance to the Kingdom was as a buffer before the Empire could strike somewhere more economically important.

The peaceful border with the Dominion south of the Storm Range, bustling with commerce and dotted with busy cities, growing towns and lush farms, was another matter altogether. Families, *lots* of them, were going to be turned out of their homes tomorrow and watch their property mercilessly destroyed in the name of military necessity, all because she had a *bad feeling* and wanted to make a point about it. Sighing, as Maria turned to go she held up a hand and added, "No demolitions for now. Homes, bridges, whatever. Not based on what we have."

"Yes, milady. I think that's a good call." Maria curtsied and withdrew.

Arilin was left there looking at Becky. "Time for bed?" The princess ventured.

"Just one thing, milady." Her maid said, "I was waiting for her to leave. She doesn't need to know about this."

"Oh?" Arilin asked.

Rebecca reached into her skirts and produced a thin object. Pressing it into Arilin's hands, she said, "I'd like you to have this, milady. Please, keep it on you from now on... tonight scared me, and I'd like you to at least have *something*." She paused and went on, "And, milady, the fewer people know about this the better. I'd appreciate it if you didn't tell... well, anyone, really."

Arilin turned the small, flat dagger over in her hands. Popping it loose in its sheath, she pulled the blade free to see it was double-edged and barely longer than the width of her palm, and she didn't need to test it to know it was razor-sharp. The weapon gleamed coldly in the night, and despite the summer warmth Arilin shivered.

Chapter 12

Fangs of the Dragon

Allenby was easy to find in the darkness. The town was on fire. June kept the orange glow and occasional flare of a star shell through the trees to his right as he led his platoon south, the dragoons walking closer together than he would have liked in the darkness. He frowned under his mask at the sight, but there was nothing to be done about it. It wasn't every day they got the chance to kill a division, and they were going to have to take a few risks.

Stalking over the railroad tracks, June held up a hand to halt his platoon and pushed through a final, scrubby barrier at the edge of the woods. He crouched there for a minute, letting his eyes play over the battlefield. Farms spread out in the darkness east of the town, the fields shot through with streams and ditches and crinkled up just enough to give them cover as they moved in. Looking off to his right he could see about half the town past a finger of the woods, the outer buildings jagged silhouettes against the ruddy glow of fires within. As he watched another volley crashed down on the north side of town, dull flashes through the trees followed by the familiar sharp snapping of Imperial shells one... two... three seconds later. They had about a kilometer to move.

The bushes rustled behind him, and June turned to see two familiar shapes emerging from the forest's murk to crouch down on either side of him. Both of them had a strip of white cloth tied over their shoulders, just as he did. Leaders during a night attack. Captain Marsten started, "I was wondering why we'd stopped."

June pointed towards the burning town as a couple of green Imperial tracers flickered over the buildings like fireflies in the distance. Gunfire was already starting to build off towards the town as the rest of the battalion began their attack, cracking distantly like popcorn in a hot skillet. Occasionally a deeper thud would cut through the patter of noise as the Royal Army shot back. He was opening his mouth to reply when a string of blue tracers flickered through the trees to his right and a string of heavy bangs rang out in the night, closer than the rest of the gunfire. Smirking beneath his mask, June said, "We just found one of their machine guns. Probably right at the corner of town."

His commander replied after a moment, "Yeah, looks like it was north of the tracks." He paused, then went on, "Did you see that, Catalina?"

Lieutenant Rudenko, on his other side, nodded as she peered out across the battlefield, "Yes, sir."

"Good." Marsten went on, "June, your platoon is going to have to deal with that position. Catalina, you're going to go in echeloned left of June, understand?" He pointed out towards the left side of the Allenby, past the spur of trees, "There's probably another machine-gun nest on the southeast side of town, and you'll need to suppress it while June's troops go in. After he breaks through I'll follow with Third Platoon, and then you follow after me, Catalina. We fight from there. Got it?"

Catalina nodded and asked, a note of worry in her voice, "How's the weapons platoon doing?"

His commander snorted, "Just fine. They're setting up on the other side of those trees. By the time we go in they'll be ready to support."

"Any word on that armored train?" June chimed in. That damn thing had been shooting at them all afternoon, and it was *starting* to piss him off. If it hadn't been for it, well it and those machine-gun nests the Royals had set up to cover their retreat, they would have cut this damn cavalry division off at the river and he'd be sleeping in a peaceful bivouac somewhere instead of thrashing through every farmers' ditch in the Kingdom trying to catch them.

"It hasn't shown its head yet. If it does, well..." Marsten snorted, "We'll be ready. Now come on." He slapped him on the back as the gunfire off to their right noticeably built, and June noticed some green tracers dancing in the sky well beyond the town. From the looks of things the rest of the regiment was beginning to engage, "We're late enough for the party as is."

They got up and plunged back into the woods, June producing a little "cricket" noisemaker from his pocket as he went. One of the Imperial Army's many good ideas, it was a whole lot more convenient than hooting like an owl whenever he was trying to get someone's attention at night, and June clicked it three times to gather his squad leaders. Marin, Tarai and Fang quickly appeared, and June got them up to speed quickly.

They would push out of the woods, deploy right with First and Second squads on line to the front and Third Squad behind, advance with their right flank passing by the spur in the woods, breach any wire the enemy had laid, and finally deal with that machine-gun nest and the armored train if it showed itself. If it pulled out to engage them the heavy weapons platoon would destroy it with their heavy antitank rifles. If it stayed tucked into the buildings, well, June had sent a couple dragoons over to the regimental sappers earlier. More than a few of his soldiers had demolition charges slung over their shoulders.

Dismissing his sergeants, June watched them melt back into the darkness. Soon the forest around him murmured with low conversation as they briefed their troops. June gave them a couple minutes, then turned and blinked his flashlight back into the woods behind him, the trees in front of him looming up in the red light for a second. A few seconds later a red light blinked back through the trees, and a couple hour-long minutes later the light blinked again, twice. June flashed his own light twice in confirmation and clicked his noisemaker twice, then drew his bayonet from its scabbard on his shoulder-strap and locked it to his rifle, the click ringing through the woods over the hammering gunfire in the distance. A moment later the forest around him rang with clicks, like it was alive with evil crickets as his soldiers locked the blackened blades to their weapons. Hefting his rifle, June raised his hand, held it there for a second and let it drop, waving his platoon forward into battle.

They pushed out of the forest into the starlit fields east of Allenby, Truth and Wisdom tiny, bright diamonds in the waterfall of jewels overhead pouring into the burning hell of the town. The dew had set heavily over the unharvested farmland and the recent rains had filled every ditch and gully in the fields with standing water, and June's boots and pants quickly soaked through as they stalked along. Marin and Tarai's squads spread out on line ahead of him as they went, soldiers beginning to instinctively crouch in silhouette against the guttering fires as the flurry of tracers built into a storm before them, the air over Allenby seething with angry blue and green sparks. The individual gunshots meshed into a grinding roar as they approached, now and then shot through with the cracks of artillery and mortars like some infernal engine had run out of oil and was beginning to throw its tie rods.

They finally cleared the last arm of the forest and June grimaced as he saw the town spread out before him, the entire north side alive with blue tracers flying out and green tracers and the occasional heavy shell thudding back in. The buildings had to be disintegrating under the onslaught, but the Royal defenders didn't seem fazed in the slightest. Even their own little machine gun nest, which he now saw was on the top couple floors of a townhouse at the northeast corner of town, had joined in the action, shooting back over its shoulder to the north. He tried counting the enemy's machine guns for a moment, then quickly gave up when he realized there were *way* more there than there should have been. Either that entire enemy division was making a stand in the town or their rear guard had more firepower than any Royal unit he'd ever seen. Either way it wasn't a good sign, he thought, a bad feeling that got worse as first one, then another ricocheting green tracer arced overhead.

A blinding light flared off to his left and June looked over to see a searchlight's ghostly beam in the air overhead. Throwing himself flat in the standing wheat, he shouted, *"Get down! Hold fire!"* He heard his platoon thud to the ground all around him, an instant before the searchlight panned down and across them. It played across his position for a second,

June holding his breath as the light seemed to pin him down before finally moving slowly off to his rear as the operator scoured the fields. Exhaling a little, June pushed himself to his knees and turned to wave his troops forward.

He looked back over his shoulder just in time to see the field behind him come alive with green tracers as the spotlight swept over Second Platoon, a wave of cracking gunfire sweeping over him a moment later. *Great,* he thought as blue tracers started sparking back from a blocky-looking building on the left-hand corner of the town, *there goes our operation... wait.* June looked around quickly. The spotlight was pinned on the other platoon, with a hail of Imperial gunfire going the other way. Right now those Royal troops were hunkered down behind their machine guns, firing through tiny little loopholes in the walls while bullets tore at their cover. What they were absolutely *not* doing was looking at *his troops.* Leaping to his feet, June shouted, "Hold fire! Hold fire!" The fields shook around him as dragoons looked up from their weapons to look at him as he went on, "They haven't seen us! *Keep pushing! Go!*"

The realization hit his troops like a lightning bolt, and they leapt to their feet and hurried for the town, dragoons splashing through ditches and across the soaking fields as the buildings loomed ahead in the firelight like misshapen teeth in a giant's jaw. On his right a muzzle flash danced in the upper floor of a building and blue tracers snapped overhead, probably aimed at Second Platoon. *Probably.* June skidded under a split-rail fence, got up and kept running. A moment later he saw one of his soldiers raise a hand in front of him, the man faintly silhouetted as he skidded to a halt. A moment later June heard Marin's voice drift back over the cracking gunfire, "Sir, we've hit wi-"

June lost the rest of his squad leader's words as a flood of green sparks poured out of the forest and tore at the right-hand strongpoint, a crackling wave washing over him a moment later as the sound of their machine guns carried through. A green-sparking ricochet hissed by about three feet from his head and slapped down somewhere behind him, and June sensibly threw himself down and shouted over the gunfire, "Cut through it! *Keep going!*"

Dark shapes worked ahead of him with wire cutters as the seconds dragged by, bullets snapping overhead. After what felt like several hours Tarai's voice drifted out of the darkness to his right, "*Sir!* We're through!"

"Got it!" June called back. Turning, he yelled, "*Fang!* Breach on the right, move!"

"Yes sir!" Fang called back, rolling up to his feet to wave his squad forward, shouting, "On me!"

Pushing himself up to his knees, June looked back to his front, past the dim silhouettes of dragoons starting to rush through a gap in invisible barbed wire to the strongpoint itself. It looked like a sturdy three-story building maybe two hundred, a hundred and fifty meters away, slowly eroding under a flood of green sparks from their machine guns. Judging by the gap in the buildings to its left the double railroad tracks ran right by it. A machine gun flared in one of the upper windows, blue tracers snapping by overhead as it lit up the back side of the building for just a second. June felt a steel claw close around his heart as he made out the massive, black shape nosing forward in the faint, strobing light. The armored train, the enemy's trump card to an attack on the west side of town.

Nothing to be done about it. Leaping to his feet, June ran to his right and ducked in behind a soldier making their way through the wire. There wasn't much, and he was through it in an instant and in among Second Squad as they fanned back out. Skidding to a stop next to a diminutive figure that looked like Sergeant Tarai, he pointed at the train, "*Tarai!* See that?"

She looked at him for a moment, her mask an indistinct blur in the darkness, then followed his finger. After a second of puzzled silence she cursed and went on, "Yeah."

"That's yours." June went on, "I'll bring First and Third around on your left to support."

After a long moment, Tarai replied tensely, "Yes, sir." Standing, she started forward and called out, "Train's coming out, we've got it! Hold fire until my signal! Bravo team, you'll assault, use the demo charges! Get on line! Move!"

Sergeant Fang dropped to a knee next to him and remarked, "I think I heard most of that, sir."

Sapphire-blue tracers whipped by, big as jeweled bumblebees and close enough overhead to touch. Hopefully the gunner was low and not high. Hopefully he hadn't seen them in the light they gave off. June chuckled a little crazily and replied, "Good. Move up on Tarai's left and support her. She starts shooting, light 'em up." Fang made to stand, and June remembered something and slapped the man's side, "You shoot *right*. Marin will be on your left. Understand?"

"Got it." Fang waved his men forward and dashed off into the darkness, "Come on!"

Picking himself up, June rushed off to his left to *find* Sergeant Marin. After a few nervous seconds of running down the line he saw silhouettes pulling apart a tangle of barbed wire on his left, and he shouted, "*Marin!*"

"That you, sir?" A voice floated back out of the darkness.

"Yes! The train's coming out! Move up to our left, and if we start shooting engage the strongpoint on the left, understand!"

"Move on your left and shoot left, I understand!" Sergeant Marin's voice came back, "Now get through this damn wire! Come on!"

June turned and rushed off to find his troops, ricocheting bullets whistling through the air all around him as he closed in on the strongpoint, the stream of tracers from their machine guns in the forest skittering off the sturdy building like sparks from an unholy angle grinder. Someone cried out nearby and June saw a silhouette tumble. Gritting his teeth, he rushed on as the steel monster rumbled out past the edge of the buildings, grinding forward cautiously in the firefly-light of burning Imperial bullets, the dim shapes of gun barrels turning towards them. Seventy-five meters. Sixty. Fifty. *Forty*, Tarai urging her soldiers on as the steel monster loomed before them.

A searchlight flared to life atop the train's armored locomotive, the beam burning a hole through the wet night over June's head from a little armored cupola atop the machine's great bulk. For an instant June and Tarai's squad were lit up, seemingly clear as day in the dark night even in the searchlight's coronal beam before the dark ring of June's rifle sight swam through the light, the hooded post of his front sight a stark silhouette against the blazing light. The searchlight swung down onto him, blindingly bright as June thumbed off the safety and squeezed the trigger.

The light went out and all hell broke loose. June threw himself to the ground as the air filled with tracers and hissing lead, his soldiers' machine guns screaming to life around him. Propping himself upright with an arm, he looked into the hailstorm of lead and saw a car on the armored train, the squat one slung between the two dual-turreted artillery wagons, lit up clear as day with strobing muzzle flashes. An infantry wagon, with machine guns lashing at them from its firing slits. They'd need to deal with it first. Leaping to his feet, June sprinted towards what he supposed was Fang's squad and threw himself into a ditch next to a shape that looked like his short, new squad leader, yelling over the gunfire, "*Hit the middle car!*"

He could barely hear himself over the shrieking gunfire. Fang rolled halfway over and gave him a dumb look in the blue tracer-light, and June hissed deep in his throat, slapped the man's shoulder and rolled to a knee, bringing his rifle to his shoulder. The machine guns flared again beyond his front sight, lead whistling all around him as he fired. His green tracer whipped into the side of the infantry car and ricocheted off into the town as he worked his rifle's action and fired again, and again, tracers bouncing off the train's armor as it slowly ground forward. A moment later his sergeant got the idea and joined in. Then their machine gunners realized they were trying to tell them something and the waterfall of Imperial tracers coming out of their position converged on the infantry car, painting it an infernal green in the darkness as they tore at the steel armor like an enraged animal.

The Royal machine guns sputtered and went out under the onslaught as the gunners flinched away from the firing slits, and June saw dark shapes rushing forward on his right. Two dragoons, one of them with the unmistakable shape of a satchel charge in his hand. In an instant they dashed past the train's locomotive and threw themselves down, disappearing from view. A moment later June saw the satchel charge silhouetted in the unearthly light of their tracers as it flew towards the first artillery wagon, which, he noticed, had swiveled its guns about and was starting to swing them down onto them. He absently thought that the thing probably mounted fortress guns that could be depressed well beyond the normal range of an artillery piece to sweep defensive ditches or, in this case, deal with assaulting infantry.

Then night turned to day for an instant as the blast punched him in the face, shrapnel scything overhead as dirt and debris rained down onto them. The armored train rocked on the tracks as it ground forward, seemingly undamaged, and for an instant June thought the charge had failed. Then he saw a door swing open at the front of the car and a couple dark shapes leapt out, shrouded in a mass of glowing smoke like refugees from the mouth of Hell. A moment later the ruddy glow spiked, building inexorably to an unholy, flaring white that shone for an instant through every tiny crack and gap in the car's armor, flame erupting from the open door into the back of the coal car like a rocket engine as the artillery propellant inside ignited.

June ducked into the ditch as the artillery car exploded, the shockwave tearing at the back of his helmet as the air filled with flying metal. His ears rang like a bell as something heavy gouged into the ditch next to him, and he looked over to see a smoking artillery shell dug into the far wall. Cautiously sticking his head back up, he saw the armored train was torn in half, the cars on either side of the mass of murky smoke that had once been the artillery car twisted and crumpled, the locomotive still grinding forward stubbornly dragging the burning, derailed coal car behind it. As he watched it twisted off the tracks and skidded to a halt, still stubbornly upright. As the smoke cleared from the mass of skeletal, twisted metal that had once been the forward artillery car, he saw the strongpoint building on the train's other side was caved in as though it had been struck with a massive fist, the whole building leaning crazily on its foundation.

A blue tracer whipped by overhead from behind him, and June turned to see a muzzle flash strobing defiantly from the *other* strongpoint despite its halo of green tracers. Clearly they still had a job to do. Slapping Fang on the shoulder, June pointed him at the nearest street leading into town, hopped out of the ditch and went to go find Sergeant Tarai further down the line. A few blue tracers whipped down from the other strongpoint, but as he went the stream of fire from their support position in the forest shifted overhead, and he looked over his shoulder to see the renewed stream of sparks eating into the offending position. Every couple of seconds a particularly massive, glowing ball whipped overhead as their antitank rifles fired, and the enemy fire quickly started to taper off.

June found Tarai over by what was left of the armored locomotive, holding a couple of dazed-looking Royal soldiers at gunpoint. The ringing in his ears had died down enough for him to hear himself think, and he shouted, "Tarai! How's your squad?"

She glanced over at him, "Alive. A couple bleeding out their ears." She went on, "What now, sir?"

"We'll get them medals." He chuckled grimly, "I'll take the other two squads in. Can you clean up here and walk the rest of the company in?" He gestured over as the silhouettes of a few Royal soldiers with their hands raised appeared over by the rear of the train, a dragoon from Third Squad shoving one of them along, "I saw someone get hit as we came in, this side of the wire, too."

"Prisoners, wounded and traffic control, yes, sir." She glanced at him again, "Anything else, sir?"

"Link back up with me when you get off." June finished.

"Yes, sir!" Tarai called out behind him, as he turned to leave. A moment later she shouted at the prisoners, "Hey! What the hell are you looking at!"

A few dragoons had gathered just inside the shelter of the town's buildings, and June hurried up to find Fang's squad spread into a defensive position, the dragoons tucked behind curbs and into the gaps and chinks in the buildings. He found the stocky little sergeant looking over the group of twenty or so prisoners they had sitting against a storefront, a pretty even mix of weedy types in dark uniforms, probably from the

Rail Service, and beefy cuirassiers. They all looked more beaten-up than scared, like they'd been punched in the head a few too many times.

June was about to blow his whistle to bring in Marin and First Squad when he heard a noise behind him and turned to see them running up. As the lanky man waved his troops into cover, June asked Fang, "What's the story with these guys?"

The sergeant looked over at him, the rough green paint of his mask a deep, bloody brown in the red firelight. Shaking his head, he replied, "These ones here were milling around when we moved up, and the cuirassiers started coming out of that house right after. We shot one and the rest surrendered."

June chuckled unpleasantly, "Hard to blame them. Now... oh." He turned to see a couple soldiers from Second Squad hurry up, and asked, "You're here for the prisoners?" They nodded, and June yelled for Marin to come over. The man hurried up and June laid out his plan, "We're *in*, and we're going to keep pushing. We should be able to roll up their line. Fang, we're going straight down this street." He looked over at his other sergeant, "Marin, take your guys down to the next street on our left and push there. And watch *your* left, there may be guys falling back from that other strongpoint. Got it?"

Marin gave him a predatory half-smile, his mask's jaw-piece cocking up unpleasantly, "Yes, sir." Turning, he yelled to his squad as he rushed off, "First Squad, on me!"

Looking over at Fang, June theatrically popped his rifle's magazine free, fished a replacement out of his chest harness and locked it in. Tucking the half-empty one into its place on is rig, he asked the man, "Well, sergeant?"

The shorter man nodded, "Got it, sir." A moment later he had the squad on their feet and stalking forward through the murk. The dragoons were shapes in the smoky darkness as they padded forward down either side of the street, the stars overhead quickly disappearing under the pall from the fires now burning all across the north side of the town. Every few seconds another Imperial shell would whistle in and crack off to their right, punctuating the constant back-and-forth chatter of the Royal and Imperial gunfire.

They pushed forward one block, then another, the dragoons winding their way cautiously around the debris now littering the streets. June was picking his way around a wagon that had been abandoned and shoved onto the sidewalk when the jackhammer thud of a Royal machine gun tore through the darkness off to his left, followed a moment later by one, then another Imperial weapon hammering back sharply in response. He smiled under his mask, just a little. First Squad had found the enemy. Raising his voice, he called out, "Keep pushing! We'll flank them!"

Fang called out in response, "Come on! Keep moving!" The dragoons hurried forward as one, June straining his eyes to pick something, *anything* out of the murk as they neared the end of the third block. By the sound of the gunfire off to their left they were about halfway there... *wait. There.* Something small and dark shifted in the darkness down the street as June ducked into the entryway of a shop, raised his rifle and fired. The green tracer skipped off the sidewalk down at the end of the next block and ricocheted, just barely illuminating a dark figure that had risen up to a crouch there.

The Royal machine gun roared back in reply a second later, bullets whistling by as June ducked back into cover. One of their own guns shrieked across the street as someone flopped down right behind him, and June turned to see a dragoon trying to politely angle his own machine gun around his own hiding place at the corner of the entryway's wall. June snorted and backed out of the way to let the man slide up to the corner on his belly, and a moment later he was firing back down the street towards the enemy.

Well, great. So much for that maneuver, June thought. They'd have a hard enough time even moving forward as things were, at least down the street. The buildings were another matter, he thought as he took a look at the shop door. Another Third Squad dragoon had ducked in with them when the shooting started, a shorter woman whose name he hadn't picked up yet. Looking across at her, he gestured at the door and said, "We're going through to the next cross street. You and me." He looked down at the machine-gunner and went on, "After we clear through, you follow us!"

The man gave him a thumbs-up, and June turned and kicked the door open, the mechanism giving way and swinging open after the second blow. He stepped inside with his rifle up, followed a moment later by his companion. They found themselves in what looked to have been a general store, shelves carefully emptied and ghostly in the strobing muzzle-flashes drifting in through the plate-glass windows fronting on the street. The wall fronting on the cross-street was blank, and June hurried to the back of the store to look for a side exit.

Spotting an open doorway into the rear of the store, June jumped the counter and carefully crept up to it. It was dark enough inside that his eyes could barely pick up the outlines of boxes piled up in the murk, and he paused for a moment while his companion negotiated the counter herself. Motioning to her to check the left side, June switched his rifle over to his left shoulder and rotated himself into the storeroom, feeling the dragoon behind him turn herself into the room bayonet-first a moment later. Nothing leapt out of the gloom at them, and June noticed the barest outline of a door in the wall in front of him as his eyes adjusted.

"I've got the door here. Come on." June said. He heard the girl turn behind him, and he felt forward in the darkness for the handle. Finding a heavy deadbolt, he hauled it open and dropped his hand onto a handle, then said, "I'm going to pop this and kick it open. If there's anyone out there, I've got left, you take right."

"Yes, sir." The girl replied nervously. She sounded scared half out of her wits. He'd probably be smart to sit down and talk to her later, or have Fang do it. Pushing the thought to the back of his head, June hauled down on the latch and kicked the door open. The street beyond was lit at a harsh angle by a fire raging further up the street, the red glare turning the blue uniforms of the Royal soldiers running across the street towards him an inky black. The lead one stopped short and looked up at him, pale face red in the guttering light as June pulled his rifle into his shoulder and fired. Once, staggering the man, twice, poleaxing him backwards, three, four times as he furiously worked his rifle's lever and sent the man behind him crashing to the ground.

June slammed his lever forward again as he swung his sights onto the third man, who was being dragged back into an alley on the other side of the street by an unusually long-haired Royal soldier giving him a look that, even through the darkness and the smoke, he recognized instantly.

Sophia Rose, angry as hell. He racked his rifle's action back just as she disappeared back into the alley, yanking the man after her so hard he was practically airborne. Glancing over at his companion, who was staring at the carnage, he slapped her on the shoulder and pointed at the alleyway, "Put a grenade in there!"

A few seconds later the alleyway filled with fire and shrapnel. It didn't ease the icy claw around June's heart in the slightest. That girl wasn't going to go down that easy.

Chapter 13

The Coiling Serpent

Corporal Stennis darted out into the street, Merrill only a couple steps behind him and Montour pushing past her to step out of the alley into the dim firelight as Sophia raised her hand to wave her team after her. She was about to lunge forward herself when a door on the far side popped open and a rifle's barrel reached out of the inky darkness within like the Grim Reaper's skeletal finger reaching out of the Black Gate, the faintest hint of a mask floating behind it like Death itself made real. She lunged and got her fingers around one of the back straps of Montour's harness as the street rang with gunfire, one, two, three, four gunshots as she desperately threw her weight against Montour's bulk and yanked him back into the alley. The Imperial soldier's long hair caught the firelight, flowing out past his waist as he shifted into the door to swing his rifle down onto her, his bayonet's dark silhouette shrinking to nothing.

God damn it, June Anjanou, Sophia thought absently. Then they tumbled back into the alley, the big machine-gunner falling heavily on top of her. Quickly rolling back to his feet, he grabbed her arm and pulled her back upright as someone yelled from behind them, "Come on! In here!" It sounded like Tony, she thought. Montour practically picked her up and threw her inside as the rest of the squad ducked into a building's rear door opening off the side of the alley, Tony sidling in behind them to crouch with his rifle sticking back up the alley as the door slowly swung shut.

They found themselves in a pitch-black little room, and Sophia heard some of her friends moving around on what sounded like a staircase. Somebody turned on a flashlight, lighting up the room to reveal it as a little ground-floor landing beneath a staircase leading further up into the building, presumably serving as an entryway for the upper-floor tenants. She looked over at Montour and saw him open his mouth to say something when Tony jerked back into the building and slammed the door behind him, yelling, "Shit!"

They all looked at him for a second before the building shook and plaster rained from the ceiling as a grenade went off in the alleyway outside. Shaking herself, Sophia stepped away from Montour into the clearest part of the little room and yelled, "Everyone, upstairs! We'll find an apartment facing the street and set up there." Looking down at her childhood friend as he pulled himself upright, she went on, "Tony, Edward, watch the door."

Tony grunted, "Got it. Edward, you got a grenade?"

"Yeah," Her lanky friend replied, extracting one from his harness and snapping off its igniter cap.

"Good," Sophia heard Tony reply as she rushed upstairs after the others. As she reached the upstairs hallway another sharp crack from outside shook the building. This one sounded Royal. Smiling a little, she pushed her way to the front of the hall, boots crackling over the broken glass littering the floor as Hargrave kicked the last door in. Whoever had the flashlight wisely turned it off and they cautiously spread out into a generously-furnished flat, lit only by the demonic firelight guttering in through the windows. It would have been positively homey if it hadn't stank of rotting food and garbage.

Sophia took stock of the situation. Tony and Edward were downstairs watching the entrance. Stennis and Merrill were probably dead. She'd barely known Merrill, but she had to swallow the lump out of her throat and grit her teeth to push the thought of her friendly old squad leader of the last month to the back of her mind. That left Hargrave, Kelly, Montour and herself. Fortunately their little group had two machine guns. Looking around, she called out, "Kelly, you set up on the left and try to get an angle on that fight going on down the street. Montour, you've got the right. Cover the cross street and the building across from us." The two men ducked low and padded into what looked to have once been the living and dining rooms. Looking over at Hargrave, she went on, "Mr. Hargrave, uh, care to help me with the furniture?"

"Same as before, Sophie?" The older man asked.

"I don't think we've got the time." She replied, "Let's just get them something to shoot off of for starters."

They quickly had tables pushed up against the machine-gunners' respective windows. Not ten seconds later Kelly fired a long burst at something down the street, the weapon's jackhammer song beating at her in the confined space. Hargrave went over to another window facing on the street to spot targets as Imperial bullets started to pop back into the building's brick façade and snap through the windows into the ceiling, and Kelly fired back again and again.

When she cared to stick her head up enough to look, Sophia could see blue and green tracers whipping past down the streets on either side of them. For a few minutes the fight seemed fairly even, each side's guns singing against each other at about even volume, a deep Royal growl versus the high Imperial shriek as tracers danced through the night. Then, slowly but inexorably, the enemy's chorus got louder. And louder and louder still, rising with a cloud of firefly tracers to spread out around them as Montour swung his gun around far to the right and started firing down the cross street. Something thumped out in the street and a moment later a blast shook the building overhead, plaster raining from the ceiling as bricks tumbled outside the window. Sophia grit her teeth as her stomach sank. This wasn't looking good.

She was about to order her gunners to move farther back into the building when she felt movement behind her and turned to see the dim silhouette of a Royal soldier coming through the door. It was someone she didn't immediately recognize, and she asked, "What's going on?"

The man replied, "We're pulling out. Rally point's at the square."

"The whole company?" Sophia asked.

"Yeah." The man replied. "Thorn sent me to find you guys and tell you."

Sophia nodded, "You came in by the alleyway? It's still safe?" The man nodded, and she turned and yelled, "We're pulling out! Down the alley and then back to the square, where we'll meet the company!"

The messenger asked as she finished, "Is there anyone forward of you, Rose?"

Sophia shook her head, "Not that I know of. Tell Thorn that..." She hesitated for a second, then pushed on, "Stennis and Merrill didn't make it."

"Where are they?" He demanded, as the others pulled their weapons back from the windows and began making their way around them.

She gestured at the street outside, "Down in the street, they got caught crossing. No way are we risking that."

"Damn it." The man swore, "I'll tell him."

Sophia made it down the stairs to see Hargrave slap Tony on the shoulder where he was crouching by the door, and a moment later her old friend sprang up and disappeared into the alley's darkness. Sophia heard his running footsteps disappear into the night as Hargrave stepped just behind the doorway to cover down the alley. The old man raised his rifle a little and waved Montour out the door, then Kelly, and Sophia pushed the messenger towards the door after him. The man darted into the alley, and she gave Hargrave a look, "Your turn, old man."

He chuckled, "You run faster than me. Go ahead, Sophie."

She chuckled, "Thanks. See you later."

Praying the enemy hadn't taken advantage of the situation to get a machine gun in position to sweep the alley, Sophia ducked out the door and sprinted towards safety, her lonely footsteps echoing from the narrow walls as she ran. After a few heart-stopping seconds she burst into the next street, nearly bowling over Lieutenant Thorn as she emerged. The rest of her squad had gathered around the alley's exit with him, and he turned and smiled grimly at her as she skidded to a stop, "Sophia, good to see you." She was opening her mouth when he held up a hand to stop her, "Sorry to hear about those two." He pointed across the street, past a piece of frankly tasteless municipal statuary at a churchyard that dark shapes were even now starting to filter back through, "We're heading back to the square. Stay out of the streets if you can."

As if to make his point a swarm of green tracers flickered past through the intersection. Sophia nodded and replied, "Got it." The lieutenant turned and hurried across the street towards the church, and Sophia barely had time to turn back towards her own squad when Hargrave emerged from the alleyway, running at his usual deliberate pace. Stepping out of the way, Sophia took stock of the situation and said, "Tony, you and Kelly come with me. We'll lead. Mr. Hargrave, you take Ed and, uh, Montour." She thought for a moment, then turned to the burly man and asked, "By the way, what's your, ah, first name?"

He her for a second, head cocked to the side quizzically, then chuckled, "James."

Sophia nodded, "Good to hear, James. You guys trail." Looking around, she hefted her rifle and went on, "Let's go!"

They darted across the street and made their way through the church's wrought-iron gate, now wrenched open and standing askew in the warm night. Making their way across the flagstones through the small churchyard, they leapt the short flight of stairs up to the main doors and ducked inside. The darkness within was broken only by a few candles, gigantic shadows darting along the walls as soldiers rushed through the church and carved swathes through the feeble light. Aloof from the soldiers hurrying through his sanctuary, an old priest stood by the altar, his white vestments standing out starkly amid the rushing shadows.

Sophia slowed as she approached the altar, and the old man motioned her forward, saying, "Go ahead, child. There's a door through the back."

"Thanks, father." Sophia climbed up onto the apse, crossing herself reflexively.

A moment later she felt cold water on her face, and she looked over to see the man shaking a holy water sprinkler over her squad. The old priest smiled and went on, "Bless you, child. Now go!"

Sophia took his advice and hurried into the back of the church, through the priest's small, darkened offices and out the back door. They made their way across the street, through more buildings and down a couple more alleys until they emerged into Allenby's central square. She could see dark shapes hurrying out the other side of the square, and someone on the far side blinked a flashlight at them as they emerged amidst the rest of the platoon. Lieutenant Thorn shouted out of the darkness, "Sophia, are you here?"

"Yes, sir!" She shouted back.

"Good!" He went on, "You're leading us out! Head to the flashing light and hurry until you catch the rest of the company!"

"Will do!" Sophia replied, then encouraged her friends as she took off running across the open space, "Come on!"

She pounded across the cobblestones for a few heart-stopping seconds, hoping the enemy hadn't gotten close enough to start firing into the square itself. The clouds of green tracers rising above the town had died down as they had made their way back to the square, and it didn't take much effort for her to imagine masks in the dancing shadows as she ran along. And then she plunged back into the half-imagined safety of the buildings, noticing Captain Martin's imposing silhouette next to the man with the flashlight. She was pretty sure that was Corporal Ferguson separated for once from his switchboard. Charlie Company's new commander waved her through, shouting, "Keep moving! We need to break contact!" He turned and yelled after her as she went by, "Rally on the first bridge!"

"Got it, sir!" She replied over her shoulder. Sophia hurried down the darkened streets, her friends running along behind her. Every now and then a shell whistled in and cracked behind them, and for a minute the street was bathed with a flickering, unearthly light as a star shell burned to life overhead. After a bit they passed the side street where she and Tony had fought the Pathfinders, and she shook herself a little as her stomach clenched. They had a lot more pressing concerns right now than shadowy infiltrators.

After a little while they caught up with what looked like a group of infantrymen marching quickly along ahead of them, and Sophia held up her hand to slow her squad down from their jogging pace and called out, "Charlie Company?"

"Yeah!" Someone up ahead called out, "Third Platoon!"

"I'm with First!" Sophia replied, before turning and calling over her shoulder, "We're caught up! Spread out!"

Her friends fanned out on either side of the road, and for the first time in a while Sophia had time to hear herself think. Looking back over her shoulder, she could see an occasional green tracer flit across the sky like a shooting star under the pall of smoke hanging over the town. She was about to turn back around when she saw a blue flare rise into the sky from farther down the street, then a second one a few seconds later as it arced away into the night. Moments later the sky whistled overhead as though it was filled with wasps the size of her arm and a wave of cracking blasts unrolled across the city. Turning back to her front she could see massive muzzle flashes out in the countryside west of town. The horse artillery, firing to cover their retreat. They looked to have pulled into battery near their checkpoint on the second bridge.

They marched along quickly for a few minutes, as the town thinned out and the houses spread apart and then gave way to farmland. As her body cooled off and the haze of adrenaline lifted from her mind Sophia felt fatigue descend to replace it, like a heavy blanket draped around her shoulders. They hadn't really even moved around that much since they had gotten the order to move out and counterattack towards the east side of town, less than an hour that felt like a week ago, but her uniform was soaked with cold, clammy sweat despite the warm night. And two of her friends were dead. There was that.

Shaking herself, Sophia turned and almost stopped in her tracks at the sight. The smoke had cleared overhead and the stars had broken back through as they climbed away from Allenby to the west. The darkened town was swathed in a hellish orange haze, here and there pocked with the ruddy, guttering light of burning buildings. Over it all, burning through the smoke like the gaze of the Faceless King himself, Faith and Hope hung blood-red over the carnage. The names of the two big moons had never been less appropriate. Tearing her eyes away with a force of will, she looked down to see the rest of her squad stumbling along as badly as she had been. Raising her voice, she called out, "Heads up, guys! I don't think we're done tonight!"

Tony called back angrily, "I *know* we're not, if those tracers are anything to go by."

Sophia turned back around and looked out through the dark night, her heart sinking as she looked around. Tony was right. The entire sky off to the north was alive with green tracers, and dimly, in the distance, a few blue ones as well. Off to the north, past the artillery and the second bridge, the forest looked like it was *haunted*. It was practically *glowing*. She could see a traffic jam of wagons backed up out of the forest beyond the second bridge, drivers struggling with their horses in the dim moonlight. Here and there riders rushed back and forth over the dark fields, probably messengers going to and fro. She grit her teeth and marched on, the gravel crunching under her boots as the ringing in her ears died off. Eventually Captain Martin hurried past, heading up to the front of the company, and Lieutenant Thorn took his usual positon just behind her.

The little bit of normalcy calmed her heart for a moment.

They reached the first bridge after a few more minutes and tramped across. Looking to the side as she went across herself Sophia noticed dark figures hunkered down in the cover of the riverbank behind a bulky shape that looked like a heavy machine gun, the smooth silhouettes of the cuirassiers' breastplates obvious even in the darkness. Soldiers repeated a hand signal from the front of the column to move along, and they kept going past the bridge for a ways as the road wound gently through the fields and the tracers got closer and closer. With a sick finger of unease twisting in her stomach, Sophia noted that green tracers were starting to come *out* of the forest.

They had about drawn level with the artillery, most of it still pounding away steadily at the town with another battery drawn up and firing off to the north, when Sophia noticed a party of riders moving back through the column ahead of her in the growing moonlight. The riders reined up around where she figured Captain Martin had positioned himself in the column, and she noticed a signal coming back to assemble around the commander. She led her squad forward as the company spilled off the road ahead of her.

Noticing them coming up, Captain Martin called out, "Lieutenant Thorn, come up here! And bring Miss Rose!"

"Yes, sir!" Thorn replied from behind her. Stepping up beside her, he gave her a look and said, "Come on, Sophia. Just like old times."

Sophia called for Hargrave to take care of the squad for a moment and walked forward with Thorn, to finally get a good look at the riders that had pulled up in front of Captain Martin. Her eyes widened as she recognized General MacMahon's slender silhouette, and as they drew nearer she made out the Lady General's voice, "...those woods, we're going to be in *real* trouble. Your company is my last reserve right now."

Their commander nodded, "Yes, milady. We'll do it." He chuckled darkly, then added, "Or die trying." Noticing them approaching, he called out, "Miss Rose? You have the guidon?"

Why would he want it now? Sophia thought as she felt behind herself instinctively. Feeling the spear's familiar bulk strapped across the back of her harness, she replied, "Yes, sir?"

"Good," he shot back, "Get it out, we're going to need it soon." Sophia exchanged glances with Thorn. He shrugged and gestured for her to go ahead, and Sophia started unstrapping the weapon as he went on, "Alright, Charlie Company! Listen up! We've got a job to do!"

The artillery fired another salvo off towards the town as though to emphasize their commander's point as he went on, "The Lady General has just told me that we're about to be cut off! Right now most of the 20th Lancers are in *that* forest," He pointed towards the glowing, hellish woods further up the hill, maybe a kilometer away, "And they're losing!"

He didn't need to explain further. Even in the darkness they could see the division's wagons slowly snaking their way forward along the road into the forest, drivers struggling with horses on the verge of bolting. God only knew how they were making any progress at all once they were inside, with stray bullets hissing through the air and the trees echoing with gunfire. The road was probably lined with wrecked wagons and dying horses. If the enemy pushed to the woodline they'd have most of what was left of the division blocked in on three sides, with the only escape over the open fields to the south. With five moons in the sky they might as well be targets on a shooting range. Gritting her teeth at the thought, Sophia got her spear out of its carrying bag and started locking the segments together as Martin went on, "We *cannot* let that happen! We will attack, drive the enemy out of the forest and keep the road open until the division can move through!"

"Yeah!" Someone shouted off to the side. Despite everything, Sophia smiled to herself as she locked her spear's head to its body and pulled the scabbard off the lethal blade. They'd been running for long enough. It felt good to have a chance to *attack* someone for once.

"We will approach in column, order of march first, second, third, then deploy on line and attack on my signal." Martin went on, "Second, you're on the left. Third, you're right. Remember, we will have friendlies in *front* of us to start, so watch your fire." He finished dramatically, "Company! Fix bayonets and move out!"

Sophia unrolled their flag and held it aloft, the white flag with its crossed rifles practically glowing against the night sky. Someone shouted back in the ranks, then another and another until the whole company was cheering. They were going to do this. They were doing to *God-damn* do this, no matter the odds, and then enemy didn't stand a *God-damn* chance. Feeling a hand on her shoulder, Sophia turned to see Lieutenant Thorn smiling at her in the darkness. "Come on," he said, grinning, "Let's go."

Sophia waved her squad forward and led the company out, guidon blazing overhead as she walked across the bridge and stepped off the road towards the haunted forest. As she passed General MacMahon she heard her saying something to her staff about it not being every day that you got to launch a charge. The Lady General's warm voice was quickly swallowed by the sound of dozens of footsteps tramping and crunching and thudding behind her as the company deployed in column, one platoon falling in behind the next as they moved to the attack.

Out of the town and its pall of smoke and the paint-thinner stench of explosives the air was warm and moist, thick with the sweet smell of growing plants with an undercurrent of turned earth. They advanced in silence across the fields for a few minutes, the sounds of the battlefield washing over them. The swishing, shuffling sound of the company trampling the crops underfoot, the ghostly crackle of the enemy's rifles all around them, here and there washed out by the thud of a cavalry carbine or the low growl of a Royal machine gun in the distance. The crack of their artillery as it fired behind them, and the low whistling and popping of Imperial shells in the distance. A few whistled in and plunged into the fields around them, sending fragments whistling through the air and raining into the fields nearby. They ignored them and marched on.

The horizon burned all around them. Green Imperial tracers flashed and skipped overhead like shooting stars, and Royal ones danced faintly in the distance like blue fireflies above the rising ground all around them. A star shell popped faintly and blazed to life off to the north, then another, as the enemy sought their comrades' positions. And to their front as they marched along, growing closer with ever step, the forest burned with tracers flashing through the trees. Every few seconds a flash and an ugly crunch rolled out of the woods as a grenade went off, and Sophia felt an ugly dread stirring in the pit of her stomach as small, angry things began to hiss overhead.

She was thinking of saying something to Lieutenant Thorn when the commander's voice rang out behind her, "*Company! On line!*" He added, a little more privately, "You can take down the guidon, Miss Rose. See to your men."

She nodded and replied, "Will do, sir." A few hundred meters out from a bayonet assault was hardly the best time to take the guidon apart, but she got it torn down, cased and strapped securely back down onto her harness in record time. Unslinging her rifle, she drew her bayonet and locked it to her rifle, smiling a little at the satisfying click, then turned to look over her friends. Tony and Kelly had come up on her left, Kelly easily handling his machine gun's spindly bulk over the furrowed ground. Just over her shoulder she could see Lieutenant Thorn and Captain Martin, and a couple silhouettes wearing swords that she supposed were cavalry officers. And beyond them, far beyond them, bayonets gleaming in the moonlight, bobbing and working like the spines of a great beast, was half the company as they spread out on line. She looked to her right to see Edward's spindly form, Hargrave, and Montour with his own machine gun. Beyond them was another forest of bayonets, borne aloft by the grim-faced men of Charlie Company, most of them just silhouettes in the moonlight. Despite everything, the tracers and the shells and the bullets hissing overhead, it took her breath away.

They were close enough now to see the edge of the forest was alive with motion, dark shapes running and staggering among the trees. Not far beyond them Sophia could make out the muzzle flashes of the lancers' carbines, broken up by the occasional roar of a machine gun and a spurt of blue light through the distant trees as they tried to hold back the steel-masked tide. Beyond them, barely visible even now through the trees, the forest *danced* with gunfire as that tide came in. A little green firefly zipped out of the woods and passed not three feet to her right, and she heard Thorn say behind her, "Sir, I think we need to get in there."

"You're right." Captain Martin replied conversationally, then went on, apparently to the cavalry officers on his other side, "You folks can make yourselves useful by getting the lancers back together and coming in behind us. I know a breaking unit when I see one, and we're about to run over *plenty* of men that can still fight."

"Uh, sure." Someone she didn't recognize replied faintly.

"Alright." Martin said, to no one in particular, "Let's get this over with." He paused for a long moment, and Sophia heard him crack his knuckles behind her, her heart pounding in her ears as she waited for the command. Finally she heard him draw his breath in and roar, "*Charlie Company! Attack!*"

They surged forward as one, Sophia breaking into a run after a few steps. Men were shouting all around her as they charged, Tony letting out a whoop as they leapt an irrigation ditch at the edge of the field in the darkness, pounded across a farmer's dirt track and into the last field short of the woods. Dark shapes were everywhere, sitting, lying, rushing about aimlessly. Wounded lancers, men helping their friends. And men who had simply fled the enemy's assault. The leering masks in the darkness, the Emperor's rage incarnated in fire and burning steel. Back before Fire Ridge she would have called them cowards. Now she wasn't so sure.

Sophia heard someone shouting behind her, demanding the lancers assemble, and then she plunged into the forest and the battle. The forest *hissed* with bullets, tracers whipping out of the darkness and splinters raining from the trees. As she dodged through the trees she saw the lancers' ragged line ahead of them, written out in their carbines' fireball muzzle flashes, and then, *there*, a blaze of light in the darkness and a murky silhouette through the distant trees. The enemy, pressing ever closer.

The hot, angry wasps hissing through the trees built to a swarm of killer bees, and Sophia skidded behind the cover of a sturdy-looking tree as someone screamed off to her side. Someone flopped down prone next to her, and she saw shapes moving in the darkness on either side as the company went to ground. She grit her teeth in frustration. They hadn't reached the lancers' line yet. If they opened fire now they'd probably kill a lot more of their own friends than Imperials. Which meant they were going to have to do this the hard way.

Rolling over, Sophia shouted, "*Come on! Keep pushing!*" With that she sprung to her feet and dashed to the next tree, then the next, and the next, then dropped forward and slithered on her belly as bullets whistled over her head. Reaching forward in the darkness, she felt someone's boot and drove forward to find herself face to face with a lancer who had rolled over onto his back behind a mossy pile of rocks half-sunk into the ground, probably marking some ancient farmer's field. It did a wonderful job keeping the bullets off.

The man had been frantically patting himself down as though he was looking for something in his pockets, and he gave her a look as she appeared, "Hey... got any ammo? I'm out."

"Yeah," she answered, popping open a pocket on her harness and handing him a stack of clips, "There."

"Thanks," he replied. She heard him strip one into his carbine and slam the bolt home as she half-rose up to get her knee under her. All around her in the unearthly glow of the enemy's tracers she could see dark shapes pushing themselves up into position alongside the lancers, infantrymen thrusting their rifles around cover and machine-gunners settling their heavy weapons onto their bipods. It looked like Charlie Company had made it forward.

Sophia figured she might as well get things started. Leaning out into the hissing storm of bullets, she tightened her rifle into her shoulder, leveled it on a spot in the darkness that seemed to have a lot of muzzle flashes coming out of it and pulled the trigger. Her rifle bucked in her hands, and she quickly worked the bolt and fired again as the darkness danced with light and enemy bullets started cutting the air around her. Something sprayed on her face and she tasted dirt on her lips as she worked the bolt again and heard the rolling, ripping crackle of Charlie Company's riflemen opening up.

The Imperial gunfire built in the darkness against them, poison-green tracers flooding out of the seething forest as the enemy kept pushing forward. Something exploded off to her side with a sickening crunch, and a moment later she heard a sickening *whack* and her new lancer friend toppled onto her like a rag doll, something hot and wet pouring onto the back of her neck as his dead weight pinned her to the ground. Her stomach lurched as he twitched and gargled on top of her, and she was about to roll over and push him off when the forest turned *blue*.

Charlie Company was made up of the remnants of the better part of an infantry battalion that had gone up Fire Ridge, and they had managed to keep most of that battalion's machine guns during their long retreat through the Dragonspines. This meant that while an ordinary Royal Army infantry squad had one machine gun, every squad in *their* company now had two or three. And every single one of them had just erupted into fire, painting the trees an unholy blue and cutting down dragoons like the sword of Maximilian himself.

The hail of enemy gunfire instantly thinned, and Sophia elbowed the dead man off of her, rolled to her knee and screamed, *"Come on!"* Springing to her feet, she rushed through the firefly light to her next piece of cover, a sturdy-looking tree. She dove behind it and fired a couple shots as the apocalyptic blast of their machine guns tamped down to a steady, volcanic roar and the silhouettes of her friends came up all around her. And then they did it again, and again, and again as the enemy fire fell away to a drizzle, then a trickle, then nothing as the darkness cleared ahead of them.

They hadn't gotten that far before Sophia, through the ringing in her ears, heard someone blowing a whistle to signal them to halt. Rolling over onto her back, she made out Lieutenant Thorn's silhouette from his map case in the darkness, standing against a moonlit patch in the forest with his whistle raised to his lips. Shaking her head slowly, she called out, "Hey, guys! You all okay?"

Mr. Hargrave called back in his rough voice, "Yeah, I've got Ed and Jim over here!"

Kelly called out of the darkness, "Yeah, I'm alive." He swore loudly a moment later, "Christ, that's hot!" Sophia chuckled as she made him out in the moonlight, waving his burned hand in the air to cool it.

Where's Tony? She thought. A sick feeling twisted in her stomach as she called, "Tony? You around here?"

She was about to get up and go look for him when a shape detached itself from the forest floor quite close to her, walked over and sat down heavily next to her. Looking over at her, her old friend smiled and remarked, "Hey, Sophie." She shook her head and smiled, and he slid an arm around her waist and remarked, "Hell of a night, eh?"

Chuckling, she slowly took her hat off and set it on her lap, letting the cool forest air wash over her. Tony seemed to have gotten stronger lately, all ropy muscle and hard sinew. Once upon a time she had been able to overpower him easily, but these days it would probably be entirely the other way around. In any event it felt good sitting there with his arm around her, and she probably would have been happy to for a lot longer when Lieutenant Thorn, operating on some officer's instinct that she didn't understand in the slightest, started calling for them to assemble and fall back.

They got back to the road in time to load the wounded and the dead onto the tail end of the wagon column as it trundled by. Most of both of those were lancers, although Sophia saw seven or eight men she knew with them. The dragoons left them more-or-less alone as they marched through the night, strung out along the road with the artillery, although they had to scramble into the ditch and return fire a few times as tracers whistled out of the distant fields. Finally the False Sun rose behind them, brightening the moonlit world into a sort of magical dawn-light, followed about half an hour later by a beautiful summer sunrise.

They met the rest of the battalion on the road shortly afterwards, marching out to walk them the rest of the way into Grenville. After a minute in his bear-hug with her feet barely touching the ground, Sophia was pretty sure her father was never going to let go of her.

Chapter 14

The Lady and the General

Before Grenville grew into a bustling little city, a center of industry and a hub of transport on the eastern plains, it had been a fortress. Hundreds of years ago, as the tide of the Thousand Years' War ebbed back across the plains from the Shield Mountains, Imperial engineers had carved a hulking stronghold across both sides of the old river crossing. Grenville had been an ugly, geometric spider in masonry, moats and cannon at the center of the Empire's web of roads across the plains, and it had taken Steinwitz a year with explosive shells and half the Royal Army's siege train to capture the place. The accounts said the river had run red with blood after the final assault.

Even now, riding over the Old Bridge, Patricia got the distinct feeling the stones *hated* her. Maybe they did, actually. God only knew what kind of dark magic the Imperial sorcerers had put into the original construction, and now the old bridge probably felt its masters returning. She shivered at the thought despite the late-afternoon heat.

Feeling eyes on her, Patricia turned to see General Kellerman giving her a concerned look. Seeing she had broken out of her reverie, he shrugged and turned back to the road ahead. Shaking her head to clear out the cobwebs, she nudged her horse after him and ventured, "Sorry... it's been a long day."

"I'll say." Kellerman replied tersely.

Walter would have asked how she was doing. Her heart fluttered at the thought. She'd barely seen him since she'd gone a little crazy and kissed him goodbye at the Wolf Rock rail station, in front of half the Army with the Black Cloaks lurking in the bushes if the rumors and, lately, the Imperial propaganda was anything to go by. She'd gone a little crazier a few days later and had written him a letter that bleak day, not so long ago, when Walter's hunch about the enemy's plan at Fire Ridge had paid off. Patricia hadn't wanted to go into battle without getting her feelings off her chest, and carrying that and the rest of her dispatches had given Princess Arilin a perfect excuse to exit the battle with her dignity intact. Unfortunately though, the Empire hadn't done her the favor of a quick death and she was going to have to confront the man she had written an anguished love letter to when she was supposed to be fighting a battle.

She felt herself turning red and wished she could sink into the bridge herself. Here she was, a major general, commander of a *division*, going to report to the King himself and she was blushing like a giddy school-girl. Kellerman gave her a disappointed look, grunted skeptically and kicked his horse on ahead. Unlike her, he presumably had more import-ant things to worry about. At least he gave her the small mercy of not pressing the matter.

They passed a couple of soldiers slowly laying out wire the same way they were riding. Grateful for the distraction, Patricia looked them over and was about to dismiss them as particularly lazy signal wiremen when she realized their roll of wire was black and much thicker than the normal copper telephone wire. Following the line with her eyes, she saw it snaked back down the bridge to disappear up and over the side, and she felt a chill run up her spine as she realized what it was. They weren't being *lazy*, they were being *careful*, because that was a spool of detonating cord and probably connected to hundreds of pounds of explosives attached to the bridge's pilings. Turning away, she nervously kicked her horse after Kellerman.

The eastern city had been abandoned as they rode through ahead of the division, a few nervous sentries skulking in the alleys watching for Imperial infiltrators. As the guards at the end of the bridge recognized them and leapt to attention, she could see that Western Grenville was a hive of activity in comparison. Every street fronting on the river sported a fresh rubble barricade, and she saw more than a few loopholes knocked into the waterfront buildings now that she was looking. From her perch on horseback she could see soldiers rushing about on the far side of the barricades, tearing Grenville's old main boulevard apart with unsentimental military efficiency.

The sergeant in charge of the guard post stepped forward as they reined up. By his gray uniform she had him pegged as a jaeger until she noticed the white tabs on his collar. It looked like someone had finally made a decision on the new uniforms, after the jaegers had spent the last ten years kicking and screaming about it. The smartly-dressed man smiled and asked, "Milord! Milady! Looking for headquarters?"

Someone must have called ahead. Kellerman didn't advertise his title. Her boss gave the man an archly raised eyebrow, "Is that the challenge these days?"

The man shrugged, "We can check your papers if you'd like, milord."

Kellerman snorted, "No need. And no need for directions either, I've been to the Ravelin before."

The man nodded and saluted, "Very well, milord!"

Kellerman returned the gesture smartly and nudged his horse down the street. Patricia gave the man a salute that, she was sure, looked about like she felt and followed after him. They had set up the barricade on the main street as a series of shorter piles projecting from the buildings on either side, creating a winding path for traffic while still providing a barrier to enemy fire, and they quickly navigated through it. Passing out the other side and carefully guiding her horse around a group of soldiers carrying vicious-looking coils of barbed wire forward, Patricia reined up next to her boss and ventured, "Ah, Gustav." As a fellow general she was entitled to use his first name, but the look of barely-concealed annoyance he gave her made her skin crawl regardless. A couple years ago he'd been 'sir' to her, and don't-you-ever-forget-it, "I don't suppose you have any idea what's in store for us?"

The man shrugged, "Probably into the operational reserve."

It would be a break for a couple weeks at least. God knew the Cavalry Corps wasn't in any shape for more combat right now, after the mauling they'd taken. Their orders had been to cover the army's deployment to defend along the Great Steel River, and given how quickly they'd been swept aside by the Empire she wasn't entirely certain how well they'd done that. She wasn't entirely certain what *Walter's* opinion on the subject would be, either. And he hid it well, but she was pretty sure that Gustav was thinking the same thing. She chuckled in reply, "I wouldn't complain."

Dodging soldiers and the occasional truck and wagon, they rode down the main street for a few blocks and passed by a scenic park that she supposed had once served as a parade ground for the garrison. Fortunately the Army hadn't gotten around to chopping down the sturdy old trees for barricade material yet, but she supposed that was probably only a matter of time. It had, however, been pressed back into service as a parade ground, and a surprised-looking First Sergeant recognized them and shouted at his company to put their eyes right as they rode past. Patricia smiled and returned his salute.

Grenville had long since sprawled over and beyond the walls of its fortifications, but the jagged bastions had burned themselves into its fabric like a hot brand, a star with way too many points wrapped around the narrow streets of the old city center. The Ravelin Hotel had been built right on top of a decommissioned outwork, although, she thought sourly as she laid eyes on it, 'Ravelin' was inaccurate. It *did* sound a lot better than 'Half of a Hornwork,' though. Chuckling to herself that she still remembered her star-fortress architecture from the Academy, Patricia dismounted alongside Kellerman by the grand entryway, handed her horse to a liveried groom who stepped out to greet them and walked in.

Patricia MacMahon was a duchess, a general and the daughter of a Field Marshal. She was an extraordinarily wealthy woman, had traveled all over the continent and stayed in some of the finest hotels, and more than a few palaces, across the Kingdom, Dominion and Union. She had hung her saber in the Harem Gardens in the Jihadist War, and her hunting rifle in the Griffonspire Lodge. She'd even spent some time in the Empire, which hadn't been *that* awful given the circumstances. And the Ravelin, she thought, was wasted out on the plains. It could have been dropped whole into the High City and made a killing there. No wonder the King had chosen it for his headquarters, although, she thought wryly, it was probably a little much for Walter.

The grand lobby was three stories of gold, crystal and light pouring in from high overhead. Massive landscape paintings unfurled across the walls above subtly-veined marble floors, and even the gray-uniformed soldiers hurrying about with boxes and armfuls of paperwork seemed to be taking the time to appreciate the place as they went through. Patricia supposed they were probably packing up the headquarters to move further west before the Empire's artillery got in range.

Which *did* beg the question a little as to why the hotel's owners hadn't evacuated some of their expensive artwork and décor. They were probably expecting a bustling trade soon from the Imperial Army, she thought sourly as another one of the hotel's liveried servants approached and asked, "Milord, milady. Are you looking for someone?"

"The King." Kellerman replied brusquely.

Patricia chuckled, "And a room sometime after the war's over.'"

The servant gave her a blank look for a second before he realized she was joking and turned back to her companion, "Of course, sir. I'll take you back." Kellerman gave her a weary look as the man went on, "No guarantees that you'll be admitted to see him, I'm afraid."

"We're not worried." Patricia remarked. They followed the man up the grand staircase at the far end of the room and turned out of the lobby and down a long, richly-decorated corridor, their footsteps echoing softly off the smooth stone floor. The crowd of soldiers died down immediately to a couple nervous-looking messengers rushing past. The main headquarters with its maze of staff shops and conference rooms was elsewhere in the building, probably below them on the ground floor. The people that worked *here* got their updates when they asked for them, and they had more important things to worry about than the crisis of the hour.

The corridor finally ended at an impressive wood-paneled door with a sign reading 'Stag's Club' overhead and two burly military policemen posted on guard outside. As they looked them over and saluted, Patricia thought wryly that with that kind of name they probably wouldn't have let her in had it been peacetime. The two generals returned the salute, and one of the soldiers quickly pulled the door open and motioned for them to proceed.

The Stag's Club was the second most-exclusive place on the grounds, a place for tired millionaires and noblemen fed up with their wives' company to drink and tell ever-more impressive stories without the risk of getting side-eye from a female companion. She didn't particularly blame them for it given what she knew perfectly well went on at the *most* exclusive spot in the hotel, the ladies' club. The walls were covered with taxidermy, the carpets were dark, the seats were overstuffed and the whole place smelled like they issued you a cigar at the door and expected you to finish it before the wait staff would so much as look at you.

A secretary Patricia recognized from her time with the IX Corps staff looked up from what seemed to have once been the reception desk as they entered, but anything she would have said was forestalled as a tall, stocky man in a gray uniform stepped into the room. She smiled as she recognized him, "Captain Beck!"

"Milady." Walter's aide nodded politely, then turned, "Come with me please. They're ready for you."

"I hope we haven't kept them waiting." Kellerman muttered, to no one in particular.

Beck replied anyways, "Of course not," as he led them through a couple of very nice sitting rooms that had been recently plastered with maps and lightly dusted with military paperwork. If it was this bad up here they were probably using shovels on the first floor. He went on, "You're early, in fact. We weren't expecting you until tonight."

"If we'd moved that slowly we'd all be dead by now." Kellerman replied bluntly. A few staff officers she recognized from her time doing strategic planning at the War Ministry looked up as they went by. At least it seemed that White hadn't taken the Army's *entire* strategy shop with him to go get captured on Fire Ridge.

Beck grunted noncommittally as he ushered them along to a particularly imposing door, turned the latch with a quick, noiseless motion and pulled it open for them. He probably motioned for them to go inside, but Patricia didn't notice or particularly care. Her attention was fixed on the two men inside, just now standing up from a table covered with the kind of outrageously large-scale map that soldiers only got to use if were either teaching geography to particularly thick cadets or responsible for an entire war. Those two fell very firmly into the latter category.

General Walter Haas, commander of the Army of Drakenburg, smiled slightly as they came in, the movement twitching up the corner of his frosty moustache. She got the feeling it was the first occasion he'd had to smile in a long while. Removing his monocle and stowing it in his breast pocket with a smooth gesture, he turned to his companion and remarked, "Well, sire, looks like the cavalry's here."

"My lord." They both said, bowing slightly.

King William IV grunted what she supposed would be a chuckle in better times. Gesturing for them to raise their heads, he replied, "Enough of that." They straightened up and he went on, "Come here. I want to hear how this battle went, and there's no reason for you two to stand over there to do it."

They walked up to the table, Walter giving her an encouraging look that she was pretty sure neither of the other men noticed. Patricia was a tall woman, taller than many male troopers, but the two other general were both almost a head above than her. The King, taller still and broad-shouldered, made her look like a child. She'd thought she'd gotten used to it after years of dealing with big men in the Army, but the sheer weight of his presence seemed to suck the air from her lungs. She'd been *terrified* talking to him about Arilin, just a few short months ago. God only knew how Walter handled it.

At least he didn't seem to expect her to do the talking. Kellerman smiled thinly and asked, "Where would you like me to start, my lord?"

"How is your corps holding up?" The King asked.

"We're in bad shape." Kellerman replied bluntly, pointing at the line of the Great Steel River snaking north along the map for emphasis. "We've fallen back onto the line of the river, and we're at about seventy-five percent strength after this recent fighting. That's on top of the casualties during the recent battle, most of which, my lord, haven't been replaced."

"But some units have been harder hit?" King William pressed him.

"Unfortunately, yes, my lord." Her commander said, parsing his words out carefully, "The enemy broke through Fifth Division and then turned south to fall on Lady MacMahon here's Ninth Division."

"That's *one* way to put it, Gus. I'm not White, you don't have to sugar-coat it for me." Walter said what they were all thinking, "We're had patrols east of Stahlkirk scooping up what's left of the Fifth all day." That was the next major crossing downstream of Grenville, "That unit disintegrated. And Patricia was lucky to get out in one piece with her own."

He had turned to look at her, clearly expecting a response. "You're not wrong." Patricia replied, "We were almost surrounded. If it hadn't been for our infantry..." She didn't want to think about it, honestly, "We wouldn't be having this conversation. They cut us out."

The King smiled thinly. It was the happiest she'd seen him so far, as he remarked, "Oh, I remember them!" He went on, "That was the night we had that infiltrator scare. I'm happy to hear they've worked out."

Patricia had only heard about *that* incident after the fact, courtesy of a few hair-raising phone calls with the Corps about Imperial pathfinders. Kellerman blanched and replied, "Yes, they're really excellent troops, milord. We'd like to keep them if we can, and get some more."

"Of course." Walter replied, "I'll try to find more for you, but no guarantees. I've got a couple mangled corps right now that need every soldier I can spare." Narrowing his eyes, he went on, "How much damage do you think you did to the Empire?"

Kellerman furrowed his eyebrows and tapped his finger on the map slowly, thinking. The truth was that they didn't know, and anything he said would be an educated guess. That being said, some educated guesses were better than others. Finally, he managed, "We were substantially outnumbered, and per our orders most of the units did not decisively engage. We probably took ten percent off the enemy's leading cavalry divisions, if that." He added, "Some got it worse than others."

Patricia ventured, "We know the Fifth Dragoon Regiment got hit pretty hard."

"You identified them?" Walter raised an eyebrow.

She nodded, "Yeah. We think they got through the Fifth Division first and then turned south to try to envelop us. We must have chewed them up pretty badly as we broke out." She explained, "That's June Anjanou's regiment. We had a sighting."

Kellerman remarked drily, "Clearly doing his father proud." The King snorted angrily, and her boss hurried on, "Right now the corps is still east of the river. Do you want us to continue to cover the bridgeheads or are we going to pull back across?"

Walter shook his head, tapping Grenville and the little circle of Royal unit markers spread out protectively around it on the map, "At this point I think I have a pretty good idea what Slade is trying to do, and our trying to keep a presence east of the river is playing right into his hands."

Patricia gave him a questioning look, "You think he's trying to bounce a bridge?"

Walter nodded, "No other reason to throw that many dragoons forward. He's counting on us maintaining an offensive posture out of sheer pride." He looked at Kellerman, "Get your corps back across, Gus. As soon as you give me the word we're blowing the bridges. All of them."

The King frowned at this, but remained silent. She guessed he and

Walter had had it out on this subject prior to their arrival. He would not have wanted to effectively abandon the Kingdom east of Grenville to the enemy, no matter what the odds seemed to be. Given how the war had gone so far, as soon as those bridges fell the right bank of the Great Steel River might as well be in Sylvania for all the chance they had of reconquering it. An attitude, she thought wryly, that she could very well see Slade Anjanou counting on them to adopt.

General Kellerman nodded, "Very well. What are our follow-on orders?"

The map had been oriented so Walter and the King could read it easily, with north on the far side of the table from them. He pointed across it at the Northern Ocean, and, as she followed his finger, the stretch of coastline from the mouth of the Great Steel River, across to maybe a third of the way back to the great Ellarian Bay, fed by the Serpent River and not far short of the Shield Mountains themselves. For a moment the true gravity of the situation struck her, and Patricia inhaled sharply despite herself. They'd already lost half the New Kingdom.

Walter gave her a curious look as she shook her head to clear it, and said, "I also think we may have figured out one of Slade's backup plans. The assault on Raven Wing, you recall, wasn't any normal river crossing." At that point the Night River was more than a mile wide and practically an arm of the ocean. He went on, "It was an amphibious assault. Their first wave launched from assault transports out in Night Bay."

She finished the thought, "You think they're aiming for a repeat?"

He nodded, "Yes. The Empire's made several runs along the coast so far, at first with light ships, probing the defenses. Yesterday Tarasburg Fortress engaged two *battleships*. The Navy thinks they might try a landing."

"Or at least that's what they want us to think." Kellerman countered, "But you want us up there anyways?"

Walter nodded, "You're my most mobile troops, and I don't know where they'll land if at all. If they do, delay them until I can move to seal the breach and keep them from breaking out to the west. We'll deal with them if they try to move south." He went on, "You'll serve as my deep operational reserve in the north in the meantime."

Her boss raised an eyebrow and asked, "I understand we're losing some regiments?"

"Yes, unfortunately. The corps need *some* of their cavalry back, now that they're back on the front line." Walter replied.

"Very well." Kellerman nodded decisively, "We'll move north and prepare to hold back the tide." He raised his eyebrows questioningly, "Do you need anything else from us?"

"Not from you, no. Good work out there, Gus." Walter looked at her, then back at Kellerman, "His Majesty and I do, however, have a few things to discuss with Lady MacMahon."

Her commander raised an eyebrow, "About *what*, exactly, if you don't mind?"

"About whatever the King wants to talk about." Walter replied flatly.

Kellerman opened his mouth, thought better of whatever he was going to say, shut it, clicked his heels sharply and swept out. The door swung shut behind him with a thud, and the King snorted with the closest thing she'd heard to amusement so far, "Is it just me, or is he angrier than usual?"

Walter shrugged, "He'll get over it."

They both turned to her, as a hard knot grew in the pit of her stomach over what she was certain was about to come. It was an unwritten Article of War for female soldiers: *Never get romantically involved with your commander if you want to keep your job.* After eighteen years in the Army, she'd been certain she was far too professional to ever fall afoul of it. As it turned out, she just hadn't met the right guy yet.

The King spoke first, "Lady MacMahon... about my daughter." The knot dissipated suddenly. *Arilin?* What was going on with her now? He went on, "I've been receiving information lately that's very concerning to me, and I need your opinion on it."

"My lord?" She asked, a note of concern in her voice.

"I get a pile of telegrams every day." He said tiredly, stepping back from the table and crossing his arms, "Most of them are from people outraged that Arilin told them something I would have told them myself, and I ignore them. This is a bit more serious." Patricia thought that was, barring White's intelligence estimate at Fire Ridge, probably the understatement of the year as he looked her straight in her eyes and demanded, "Milady, did Arilin ever strike you as paranoid?"

Patricia shook her head, "Not without good reason, milord."

The King sighed heavily, "I'm afraid that I made a mistake." He went on, "When I flew here, I had just a minute with Arilin to talk to her in person, and, well... Walter knows what I was like at the time. And I decided, for God knows what reason, to tell her that I didn't trust my own brother just then."

Those were the kind of words that would stick in an impressionable young girl's head. That being said, without the Legitimation, Alphonse *would* be next in line for the throne with an incumbent who had just presided over what was shaping up as a particularly disastrous war. The man certainly had a motive. Patricia ventured, "I'm guessing she's taken it to heart?"

"She's convinced that my brother is conspiring with the Dominion to overthrow me. Among other things." He replied bluntly, "Alphonse is telling me she's cracked under the stress."

"Arilin..." She replied carefully, "Is not the kind of person who would *crack*."

Walter ventured, "Your brother is known to be very friendly with the Stahlbergs, my lord. And not just on a personal level, my understanding is that includes *policy* as well." He went on, "Arilin might be *mistaken*, certainly, but I got to know her recently as well. She's not crazy."

King William sighed heavily and shook his head, "God, I hope not." He cracked a half-smile, "I'll leave you two lovebirds to it, I need to think about this some more."

Patricia's heart skipped a couple beats and she felt her face burn as he walked out past her. The door swung shut behind him with the heavy thud of something built to be completely soundproof so important men could have important discussions inside, and she looked up to meet Walter's eyes. It was a mistake. Her ears were turning red. Seeing her blushing, Walter gave her a sly smile and remarked, "I thought that was brilliant, by the way."

"What... do you mean?" If she'd been wearing a corset she would have been flat out on the floor and he would have been calling for smelling salts. As things stood she felt her knees wobbling.

He chuckled, "Sending that letter of yours with Arilin. Either she'd deliver it personally or she'd be captured and we'd have much bigger problems to deal with."

"Oh..." Patricia managed in reply.

Stepping back from the table, Walter turned and walked back across the room to look out the magnificent bay windows stretching across the far wall, most of them open to let the summer's warm air circulate. Unbidden, she followed and ended up beside him, looking out onto the Ravelin's gardens. In a more peaceful time they'd probably be full of strolling lovers instead of soldiers trying to catch a few minutes off. Finally, he said, "You know, Patricia, ever since I first met you I've cared about you...

quite deeply, in fact. But, well…" He chuckled, half to himself, "I don't suppose you've ever heard of the Iron Law?"

"Don't ever get involved with your commander?" She ventured.

Walter looked at her, then laughed, "No, no. I've heard that one, too, and it's rubbish. If a man can order his own son into battle he can sure as hell do the same to his lover. No, young lady," he gave her that sly smile again, "It's about the youngest person you can see romantically."

What was he even talking about… wait. She *did* know that. "Isn't that half your age plus seven?" Patricia asked.

"Very good," he chuckled, "I'm sixty-three, you're thirty-eight, and as an artilleryman I am entitled to round down to the nearest even number." His math was dead on, and it was *infuriating*. Clearly this was *exactly* what she had to look forward to with him. She gave him a look, and he laughed, turned and sat down in one of the overstuffed chairs scattered around the room. Steepling his fingers, he went on a little more seriously, "I'll confess I was a little surprised."

"Why's that?" She asked.

Walter shrugged, "Honestly, I thought you were out of my league."

"Well, here I am." Patricia said as she walked over and sat in his lap, "And *I* confess that I've been fantasizing about this for a *long* time." Then she kissed him.

Walter must have spent most of the morning brushing his teeth and gargling mouthwash, because he barely tasted like cigars. Clearly a man who had his priorities straight. She closed her eyes and felt the tension drain out of her body as his arms wrapped around her, pulling her into his embrace. Eventually he let her come up for air, and she pulled back a little as she felt one of his arms unwind from her to gently drop something heavy and solid to the floor by the chair. Twisting around a little, she realized he had relieved her of her sword while they were kissing. Clearly it would be an impediment to whatever he had in mind.

He was giving her that sly look again. After a long moment, he said, "You're not the only one who's been fantasizing about this, although…" He chuckled, "I had you in a little bit of a different *position*, young lady."

"Oh?" She asked, giving him her best naughty schoolgirl smile as she teased him, "Is that why you took my sword, you old goat?"

Walter's smile broadened to something positively *wicked*. "Here," he said, like a cat who had just eaten a particularly impressive canary, "Let me show you."

And he flipped her over on his lap.

Chapter 15

War Tide

The Royal Academy's botanical gardens were a haven of peace and quiet on the ordinarily-bustling grounds, a place for students to catch a few moments alone or, depending on their inclinations, together. With their lovers or their friends although, all things considered, Arilin would rather have been left alone.

"...us what's wrong at some point?" Liriel was saying something, probably to her. Arilin looked over at her bleakly, and her friend went on, "Arilin, you've been moping and snapping at us all day. What's wrong?"

The princess rolled her eyes and shook her head slowly, "I don't want to talk about it."

Across from her, Miriel rolled her eyes and finished her twin sister's thought, "Clearly you need to though."

Arilin glared at her, "I *said*, I don't want to talk about it."

"We know you don't want to!" Both girls exclaimed simultaneously. Arilin wondered idly if those two shared a hive mind, as they went on, "But we think you need to!"

"*I don't!*" Arilin shouted back, heaving herself up from the blanket her friends had very considerately brought for them to sit on, "God, you two need to learn to leave well enough alone."

The twins leapt to their own feet and glared at her, Miriel snapping back, "We wouldn't be your friends if we did that, now would we?"

Liriel added, "Yeah, milady, you're not an easy person to hang out with."

Arilin sighed heavily, "It's nothing you two don't know about already. And I need to *think* about what I'm doing next about it." She added, peevishly, "And you two aren't helping."

"We can, though!" Miriel shot back.

"Yeah!" Liriel chimed in.

Arilin shook her head and changed the subject, "Where is Charlotte, anyways? She said she'd meet us here... is she lost?"

The twins looked around quickly. Miri was opening her mouth to say something when Liri caught sight of something and pointed through the trees, "Oh, I think that's her... and who's that?"

Miri tittered excitedly, "Wait, wait, is that *Tom?*" She shared a knowing glance with her sister and went on, "No wonder she took her time."

Thomas Strathclyde emerged into the clearing with her diminutive friend, looked her up and down and remarked, "Oh. Now I know why you wanted me to bring equipment." Looking back at him, she noticed that he was carrying a bulky bag and a long case over his shoulder, as though he was going to a fencing match. Which, she supposed, was probably *exactly* what he was going to. He smiled at her and dropped his fencing equipment on the ground, "Afternoon, milady."

"Oh. Hey, Tom." Arilin smiled back reflexively. Liri and Miri exchanged sniggers as she glanced at Charlotte accusatorially, "Was this your idea, Charlotte?"

The girl blushed a little, "It might have been... I thought you needed to fight someone."

The girl hadn't been *wrong*. Giving Tom a half-hearted grin, she asked, "What'd you bring?"

Opening up his bags, Tom produced a fencing saber and helmet and tossed them over to her. She noticed him looking at her legs as she tied the helmet on, and he asked, "Going riding later, milady?"

She was wearing jodhpurs and riding boots instead of her usual skirt. So was Tom, for that matter, given they were both members of the Equestrian Club and they'd been riding that morning, but usually the girls would change afterwards. Finishing with her helmet, Arilin replied, "Yeah. There's some kind of trouble with the fleet, I'm going down to the dockyards later."

"Oh?" Finishing with his own helmet, Tom gave his saber a couple experimental swings to warm up, "That's pretty vague."

"Right?" Arilin chuckled grimly, flexing her own wrist around. The fencing saber was a little lighter than a real one, but it wasn't that different all things considered. She went on, "The fleet was supposed to leave early this morning, but they're still there and Admiral Brooke gave me a runaround when I called him about it." Brooke had stepped in to replace the fallen Admiral Kensington after the Battle of the Diamond Shoals. The man wasn't easy to deal with at the best of times, and he'd only gotten worse lately.

Tom squared up to her and saluted with his sword. She returned the gesture and dropped her weapon on line, watching him carefully as he brought his sword around into a hanging guard. She'd fought him before a few times, and knew that he was a good, no, an *excellent* swordsman. Still, this wasn't the Academy fencing hall, and she'd learned a few things in her time with the Army. She absently wondered if that dragoon she had run through had actually ended up dying afterwards as Tom's rear foot crept forward to give him a longer lunge. Sneaky.

Tom shuffled forward quickly, snapping his sword up and around to beat hers aside. Dropping her point quickly to let his sword whip by harmlessly, she shuffled back half a step and brought her sword around in a short, vicious circle to cut at his wrist. Tom pulled his hand back quickly, and her saber's blade bit into his with a sharp crack that turned into a short, sharp hiss as he swept her blade aside with his handguard and lunged back at her, snapping his sword down at her head. Bringing her own sword up, she parried his blade aside as her sword rose and cracked him square on the forehead on the downstroke.

Backing off, Tom nodded politely, "Your point, milady... I can see you've been training."

She chuckled, "Of course." Feeling herself smile for the first time in too long, she taunted him, "Is that all you've got?"

"Not if you're going to put it that way, milady." He laughed, squaring back up to her with his same hanging guard, "I can see what Charlotte was getting at now. On guard!"

Arilin snapped her sword's point back up as he lunged at her, driving her sword out of the way with a long, spiraling thrust. Backing off, Arilin disengaged and slapped his blade aside with a small, circular motion, then stepped back in with a short thrust to his face. Tom smashed it aside with his handguard, but Arilin went with the momentum of the blow and brought her sword around and up into his ribs, probably harder than she needed to. Tom hopped backwards a little, and his mask moved as he winced, "Ouch... I wasn't kidding, you know. You've gotten better."

"Sorry," Arilin apologized, "I've been angry all day."

"I'll say," He remarked, "Why's that?"

She chuckled, "My uncle's a terrible person and plotting to overthrow me?"

Tom shrugged, "Sounds pretty normal to me, what's new?"

"My father doesn't believe me." Arilin replied bitterly, "You should have *seen* the telegram he sent me."

"Wants you two to get along, huh?" He asked.

Arilin shook her head, "And then some." She gestured with her sword, "I'm going to have to deal with Alphonse *myself* at this rate."

Tom laughed, "God help us when you become Queen, milady."

"Big words for my future *subject*." Arilin shot back, bringing her sword back on line, "I'll remember that. On guard!"

Tom had barely brought his sword up into his usual hanging guard when she lunged at him, her saber whipping in a sharp little circle to slap his weapon further under his arm and break his grip on his hilt. Dropping his hand, he blocked the blow and drove himself forward, saber whipping up and around his head in a vicious circular cut aimed square at her head. Arilin jumped back, the shock of the blow crashing through her hand as she blocked. She was about to clear his blade aside and riposte when she realized Tom was still pushing forward, his left hand coming off his hip and up in a very ungentlemanly maneuver to catch the chin of her fencing mask and rip it clean off her head.

Arilin hopped away awkwardly as Tom smiled and waggled her mask at her, "I believe, milady, that this is my point." He laughed, "At least under Army rules."

She conceded, pouting, "You're not wrong." Evidently she still had a few things to learn about fighting.

He tossed the mask back to her, asking, "So what's this about the battle fleet? Think they've had a mutiny?"

Catching it and tucking it under her arm, she replied levelly, "They say they have steam up."

Tom asked, "Think they're having a Stahlberg Charge?"

Arilin raised an eyebrow, "What's that?"

He snorted, "I've heard when Dominion troops don't want to do something they'll all start screaming, 'Attack! Attack!' and none of them will actually *move*. Maybe the sailors got the boilers going and then refused to actually engage the engines."

Arilin shrugged, "Could be." The school bell started bonging noon in the distance, the signal that they needed to get back to class, and she tossed his equipment back to him and remarked, "Guess I'll find out, I'm riding down there after class."

Catching his sword and facemask, Tom smiled, "Well, then you'll have to let me know how it goes." He bent to start packing up and Liri and Miri ostentatiously rushed forward from where they had been watching to help. Although to her it looked like they were mostly just getting in his way in the most pleasant way possible. Tom left with the twins in tow, and Arilin turned to see Charlotte holding out her bag to her. She must have picked it up from where she had left it over on their blanket, which also seemed to have been her idea given that she had it tucked up under her arm.

"Oh, thanks..." Arilin said, slipping her arms through the straps.

"Ah, milady...." Charlotte started hesitantly. She still seemed to be working her way around to treating her like a normal person sometimes. She could hardly blame her, considering her father was a country baron from the back of beyond.

Arilin raised an eyebrow and looked over as she started walking back towards the Academy's main cluster of buildings, her petite friend trailing along beside her, "Yes, Charlotte?"

"I was meaning to tell you, milady... Alice also came by looking for me, I ran into her while I was off hunting down Tom." Which explained why she'd taken so long, "And, well, what she told me makes sense now."

"Oh?" Arilin asked, "What's that?"

"She heard a rumor this morning, apparently Alphonse trashed his suite at the Royal Sapphire." Charlotte told her conspiratorially. Only the best hotel in the High City, and he'd been staying in the penthouse. Why he hadn't chosen to stay in one of the Palace's many guest rooms was beyond her although, now that she thought about it, it probably had something to do with his trying to avoid being spied on.

His mistake. She replied, "Really? Throwing a party, or...?"

Charlotte shook her head, "Not that kind of trashed, he did it himself."

"Oh really?" Arilin raised an eyebrow, "Maybe..." She trailed off. Her father hadn't told her what he'd told *Alphonse*. Maybe his solution to their dispute had been more even-handed than she'd thought. Or maybe Alphonse just had a horrific temper.

"Maybe, milady?" Her diminutive friend asked.

"Maybe I shouldn't have been so angry all day." Arilin laughed, changing the subject, "How's your father these days, anyways?"

Charlotte smiled happily, "He wrote me just the other day, apparently they're giving him a unit."

"Somebody misplaced their colonel?" Arilin joked.

"Pretty much." Charlotte replied.

* * *

Arilin walked out the school's grant front entrance later that afternoon to find the crowd of departing students backing up practically to the front doors. Why wasn't hard to tell. It wasn't every day that twenty Valkyrie Knights trotted up to the Royal Academy Middle School's front door. The girls were admiring the horses, the boys were admiring the riders, and for the end of the school day nobody seemed to be quite interested in going home just yet.

A waterfall of fiery red hair caught the sunlight as it swished back and forth, Alyssa Helbrecht turning her head to scan the crowd back and forth for her. Midnight was already waiting in hand, eyeing the crowd and shuffling nervously. An instant later the woman caught sight of her and waved, and Arilin started forcing her way forward through the press of students towards the hussars. After a few seconds the redheaded captain started shouting at her classmates to give her some room and the crowd parted enough to let her make her way through. Ignoring the hundred or so jealous glares boring into her back, Arilin swung herself up onto Midnight's back and took her reins back from Alyssa, patting her horse's neck gently to calm her.

Arilin smiled as they wheeled their horses about and started on their way out of the Academy grounds, the crowd of admiring students trailing behind like a comet's tail as they went, "Thanks for the pickup, Captain."

Alyssa nodded back, clearly extremely pleased with herself, "My pleasure, milady." She laughed, "If I'd taken all the troopers who volunteered we'd have the whole squadron lined up here to the last girl. These ones here are my best."

Looking around, Arilin could see why. The hussars escorting them were a bunch of tall, serious-looking young women, comfortable and elegant in the saddle and turned out in immaculate gray and red service uniforms. A couple of older sergeants quickly divided them into two columns to either side of them as they turned into the street and finished shedding their tail of spectators. Raising her eyebrows in appreciation, the princess remarked, "They look great. When are they going forward?"

"Next week, actually." Alyssa grimaced, "I wish we weren't having to send so many replacements, though. Third Squadron is barely more half built right now, and if we make a Fourth Squadron it'll be out of recovered wounded at this rate."

The Fourteenth Hussar Regiment, the Kingdom's famous Valkyrie Knights, had gone to war at less than half the strength it was supposed to have in wartime and the fighting since has scythed down its ranks with terrifying speed. It was all Alyssa and the rest of the regiment's training cadre could do to get volunteer girls trained into hussars and sent to the front to keep the unit from collapsing altogether, let alone build out the entire new squadrons the regiment needed to get properly up to strength. The one upside to their current situation, Arilin had gathered, was that unlike the recruiting situation in most of the Army there was no shortage of adventurous girls volunteering to fill out the ranks so far.

Arilin raised an eyebrow, "Isn't the First Regiment helping you out with training now?"

The redheaded captain shot back, "Yeah, and now half my problems are with *them*. More than half! And I thought *girls* were a handful." Chuckling, she went on, "Now I know why the Masks are so angry all the time, if that's how they do things."

The princess laughed, "You might be on to something."

"Oh," Alyssa remarked, leaning over to unbuckle something from her saddle, "I brought this for you, milady."

Arilin looked over to see Alyssa holding out a hussar's saber to her, sword belt already attached. Feeling her eyebrows rise in surprise as she reached out to take it, Arilin said, "Thanks..." Buckling it on, she felt the blade's familiar, solid weight settle against her thigh, and she went on skeptically, "Do you know something I don't, Alyssa?"

Her companion raised an eyebrow, "What, about the trip, milady?" Snorting, she made a dismissive gesture, "No, no, of course not. I thought you needed *something* to impress the admirals."

Arilin chuckled, "Thanks."

"And *Alyssa?*" Her companion remarked, "That's new."

"I'm the Crown Princess, Captain." Arilin teased her, "You're lucky that you're not Aly yet."

Alyssa rolled her eyes, "We're doomed."

It was a long ride from the High City down to the dockyards, about five miles. Passing through the High City's immaculately-kept streets, they rode out the Cardinal Gate in the southeast corner of the old city walls and began to descend through the broad, leafy streets of the Middle City, the homes of the Capital's wealthy and noble citizens passing by on either side. The Guards Cavalry Division garrison was in the area for lack of space in the High City and nobody batted an eye at the hussars, but Arilin drew more than a few onlookers herself. As they rode further down from the High City's promontory the buildings grew closer together and turned into townhouses, then apartments and commercial districts. The citizens' suits got rougher and their dresses plainer, the liveried maids and manservants disappeared, and the raised hats and curtsies became rough and exaggerated with surprise as they made their way through the streetcars and midafternoon crowds of the Lower City. It wasn't every day a member of the Royal Family took a ride through the Capital.

They were three miles in when Arilin saw the first Red Star, a rough pentagram hastily daubed onto an alley wall in a middle-class neighborhood, between a butcher's shop and a ladies' clothing store. It stuck out like an ugly pimple beside the display window full of corseted manne-quins sporting the latest fashions. Noticing her looking, Alyssa snorted and remarked, "Probably stupid kids, milady. Don't worry, we're not go-ing anywhere near Tidewater."

"Thanks," Arilin replied drily. Not parading her through that par-ticular communist fever swamp was about the least she could ask of her bodyguards. Even so, the communist graffiti got more and more common as they made their way further down through increasingly working-class districts and the warm, dry scents of the more prosperous parts of the city turned to the acrid smoke and sea-salt tang of the harbor. Arilin was about to say something about it when her companion called out to the hussars to make a turn up ahead, and they rounded the corner to see the towers of the Financial District soaring above the streets ahead.

The pedestrians rapidly got better-dressed, the dour housewives and curious schoolchildren from earlier quickly replaced by hurrying busi-nessmen, sleek secretaries and the occasional businesswoman trying too hard not to look like one. People stopped staring and started giving their respects again. Evidently having heard a rumor, Mr. Masters stepped out the imposing front entrance of the Masters Heavy Industries Building and walked alongside them for a while to chat. Arilin promised to drop by and visit him at the office sometime so he could show off. MHI was only the largest industrial concern in the country, after all.

Passing through the Financial District's shadowed midafternoon streets quickly, they rode on into the Theater District, fancy restaurants and all kinds of entertainment establishments starting to open up for the night. The Sunset Pearl Opera House was just opening its doors to get ready for the evening as they rode past, attendants hurrying about get-ting ready for the guests that would be along in a couple hours. Noticing the hussars riding by, most of the younger-looking ushers quickly disap-peared back into the building, refusing to meet her eyes. The nation was at war, the conscription law had just passed and those particular young men didn't seem to have been eager to volunteer ahead of time. Arilin frowned and turned to the road ahead.

After the Theater District the Low City's streets coarsened again as they approached the Royal Dockyards, seedy bars and cheap restaurants interspersed with workshops, warehouses and the occasional factory humming with activity, smokestacks belching ugly plumes into the clear afternoon sky. The streets were speckled with sailors in their blue uni-forms, and Arilin felt her throat tighten a little as she noticed more than a few Red Stars painted covertly here and there. The Shore Patrol, she suspected, had bigger fish to fry at this point than casual vandals.

They made another turn and emerged onto the waterfront. The sight took her breath away, seemingly-endless rows of warships under repair tied up along the Dockyard's piers in a mile-long blanket of steel, most of them thick with sailors standing about on deck. Looking out to sea, Arilin realized what had brought them all topside. The whole horizon as a mass of moving steel and black smoke, squadron after squadron turning out towards the mouth of the bay and the open ocean. In the distance Arilin made out the *Champion*, the fleet's flagship, as it pushed forward in the water. The harbor flag at its stern disappeared and was quickly replaced by a battle flag run up the rigging behind the latticework of its main fire-control mast. It was a small, businesslike flag, but it sent an unmistakable signal. The Northern Fleet was back in business, and they intended to get revenge for Diamond Shoals.

Now if only they'd told her ahead of time. Some of the sailors gathered out on the ships began cheering at the sight of the flagship heading out, and Arilin groused over the noise, "It would have been nice if they'd told us!" She pouted theatrically, "I've got homework, you know."

Alyssa shrugged, "Maybe they heard we were coming."

Arilin raised her eyebrows, "And, what, they just decided to get going?"

Her companion laughed and teased her, "I don't know, milady, I'd rather fight off a horde of mutineers than have to deal with you."

The princess gave her an extremely level look, "I will take that as a compliment, as I am sure you intended it."

"Of course, milady." Alyssa smiled back at her pleasantly.

"Well." Arilin mused, "I wonder if anyone around here knows what happened." Looking down the pierside street, she spied a crowd of sailors a ways down that looked like they were walking back to their ships, the men dispersing into small, familiar groups. She nudged Midnight forward towards them, and the hussars quickly fell in around her as she went.

Someone shouted as they noticed them, and Arilin quickly found herself returning salutes as the sailors surrounded them. The men seemed friendly enough, but rather than gathering around as she had expected they kept walking quickly back towards the docks. Looking against the flow she realized why. Twenty or thirty naval policemen had fanned out on line and were shooing the sailors back to their posts, occasionally waving a baton at the most recalcitrant ones. Past them she saw a small knot of men gathered around, what she guessed was the shore patrol's duty officer and a few policemen talking to some scruffy-looking sailors and a petty officer who looked like he spent most of his time working on machinery that was covered in oil and occasionally on fire. Nobody looked like they were being arrested, so Arilin nudged Lucky over in their direction.

The police parted to let them through, and the men noticed them approaching and saluted. The ragged sailors were noticeably slower on it than the crisp-looking military police. Saluting in return, Arilin greeted them, "Hello there! I don't suppose any of you know what's been going on?"

The officer laughed, "Now that the fleet's off it's just a surprise visit by you, milady!"

"I'll say," she remarked, "I was coming down here to ask the Admiralty about the holdup. They were supposed to have the fleet out this morning."

The grimy petty officer cut in, "They were, aye." He chuckled, "Good thing they got that pay issue worked out. I was just telling the lieutenant here how this should have been resolved months ago."

The other man rolled his eyes, "Me and half the fleet just now. I should take you in for inciting mutiny, chief."

"How?" The machinist asked sarcastically, "The only thing I was doing was *informing* them of the fact that Admiral Brooke went back on his damn sea pay policy. Hell, I bet most of your officer friends are happy about it themselves."

"I'm pretty sure the orders aren't going to have anything in them about the triumph of the proletariat." The officer shot back, although there wasn't any particular venom in it.

"Anyways, your ladyship," the greasy petty officer went on, turning to her with a flourish. She noticed his nametag read 'Sikorsky,' as he went on, "There's been a bit of a disagreement going around the fleet recently about sea pay, and things sort of... boiled over when the order to sail came down last night." A mutiny then. Right. The man went on, "Then about an hour ago it came down that we'd all be getting the full sea rate, with back pay since Diamond Shoals."

The officer explained, "Look, milady, did you ever hear about the riot when the fleet got back to port after the battle?"

She had in fact, although it seemed like half a lifetime ago. Raising an eyebrow, she replied, "Yes...?"

Chief Sikorsky cut back in, "That was *hardly* a riot, sir."

"Someone threw a bottle at me." The man replied drily, "Counts in my book." Sikorsky gave him a look that suggested he had bottles thrown at him with good reason four or five times a week, which he ignored and plowed on, "Long story short, the Admiral decided to deal with it by confining the men to their ships indefinitely, and without sea pay while they were in harbor."

"All this while working twelve, fourteen hour shifts fixing battle damage." Sikorsky added bitterly.

Alyssa, who had been listening in, remarked, "God, I'm sure that raised morale."

"Ha!" Sikorsky laughed, "Hey boys, even the Blood Valkyries agree with us! I like you, miss, want to go get a drink later?"

Her companion narrowed her eyes, "I don't socialize with communists."

"Oh, but I'm not one!" The chief chuckled again. Arilin began to suspect that he might be a little drunk, "Tried and found innocent, and no thanks to your friends trying to crack my damn skull open."

Alyssa was opening her mouth angrily when Arilin raised a hand to cut her off, "Alright, enough of that." The woman gave her a venomous glare, then looked away deliberately. The princess went on, "Thanks for your ti-"

"*Look out!*" Alyssa shouted next to her, kicking her horse forward viciously. Arilin looked over to see men jumping out of her way as she charged, her saber flashing up out of her scabbard and down viciously. Wheeling Midnight about and ducking low to her mane, Arilin dodged back through the group of hussars behind her, the girls scattering as she went through, most of them turning to chase after her as men shouted and gunfire split the air. Midnight leapt forward like a rocket, and Arilin was easily a hundred meters back down the street when the first explosion ripped through the air. A couple seconds later another one thudded dully, and she looked back to see a gout of water rising from the docks nearby.

No more gunshots or explosions rang out, and after a bit Arilin reined in and let her escorts catch up. Pulling Midnight back around, she demanded of the first girl to gallop up, "*What was that?*"

Red-faced with the excitement, the hussar stammered, "I-I think someone just tried to kill you, milady!"

"No kidding!" Arilin replied angrily. Back down the street it looked like most of the men were on their feet and rushing around angrily. Alyssa was galloping about, pointing her sword here and there as she ordered around the couple of hussars who had stayed with her. Arilin's breath caught in her throat as she noticed two dark shapes crumpled on the pavement, men prodding at them carefully. Whatever had happened, it looked like it was safe enough now. Setting her jaw, Arilin nudged Midnight back down the street towards the scene.

Alyssa noticed her coming and cantered back to meet them, sword flashing in the afternoon sunlight where she had it sloped against her shoulder. Arilin's stomach clenched a little as she pulled up in front of her and she saw the spiderweb of blood across the blade, startlingly red against the bright steel. Alyssa shifted in the saddle as she spoke, revealing a dark line across her gray jacket where the blood had soaked in, "Milady! We need to get you out of here, *now*."

That was a good idea. Even so, she wasn't one to flee that easily. Arilin replied, "What happened? Is anyone hurt?"

Alyssa snorted angrily, "Two men with grenades. They're both dead, nobody else hurt. Now come on or I'll *make* you."

Her companion was giving her a look that said she'd be leaving hogtied over the front of a saddle if she objected. Knowing when to pick her battles, Arilin gave in, "Back to the Palace?"

The hussar captain shook her head, "No, there could be more assassins waiting." She thought for a minute, then swore, "Damn it. This is going to be a *mess*. Let's go to the Admiralty, we can arrange a proper escort back." She went on as they started cantering back up the street, towards the Admiralty complex at the far side of the Dockyards, "We'll probably have the whole damn division out tonight. I'm *never* going to hear the end of this."

Arilin waved at the police and sailors as they clattered past. The shore patrol officer looked away from ordering his men about to salute her smartly. Sikorsky looked up from cutting one of the dead men's bags loose from where it was still strapped around his... Arilin felt her stomach heave as she realized the man's body had been torn open, blood and bits of flesh sprayed across the pavement around it. Sikorsky waved politely with a hand stained bright red and then went back to his grim task, Arilin looking away quickly as they went by. Once they were a little further down the street she asked, "That man... ugh, what, what happened?"

Alyssa replied coldly, "I hit him after he'd lit his grenade but before he could throw it. That chief managed to get to him and flip his body over on top of it before it went off." She went on, "The other one threw his, but he didn't cook it off and someone picked it up and threw it in the water. The gunfire was from the police shooting him afterwards." She chuckled coldly, "Maybe I *do* owe that guy a date."

Arilin looked over at Alyssa incredulously to see her calmly pinching her saber's blade in the fold of her elbow and running it through to wipe the blood off. It left an ugly black stain on her uniform, but it let her sheathe the weapon quickly and get back to controlling her horse with both hands. The sailors, who had disappeared from the street when the gunfire and explosions rang out, were starting to rush back out in droves. Fortunately they were smart enough to stay out of their way, although after a little while Alyssa rode forward and started shouting for the men to get out of their way.

The Admiralty's red-brick buildings quickly came into view as they cantered down the street, and the guards recognized her and pulled the gate open for them to turn into the grounds without challenging them. Safe for the time being, they pulled up on the front walkway. Some of the other girls' horses were already huffing and a few of the hussars dismounted to let them rest, but Midnight wasn't even breathing hard and Arilin just settled back in the saddle for a moment, letting her breath out slowly through her nose as she closed her eyes.

Someone had just tried to have her *murdered*. Granted she'd been shot at before, chased by dragoons, lost a sword after it stuck in one of their chests even, but that had been a chance encounter. This was different. Someone, earlier that day, had coldly given the order to kill her. Men had prepared grenades, followed them or learned where they were, stealthily approached, struck and been foiled at the last second by bystanders and her quick-thinking bodyguards. It made her skin crawl. It made her want to go home and hide under her covers and never come out again. And, maddeningly, she knew that was *precisely* what whoever ordered this would want even if the attack itself failed. The Crown Princess, crippled by fear and afraid to so much as set foot outside of the Palace.

The officer on duty had rushed out to meet them, and Arilin was rocking herself forward in her saddle to get off when she heard something in the distance and froze. It sounded like something was *grinding* faintly on the cobblestones down the street, quickly growing louder as it came towards them. It took until she heard a faint whinny that she realized exactly what it was, dozens or hundreds of cavalrymen riding down the street, their horses' shod hooves crashing on the cobblestones like a steel waterfall. The cavalry quickly approached the Admiralty buildings, hidden from view by the wall around the headquarters until finally the guards at the gate snapped to attention again and hauled the elaborate wrought-iron barrier open for the newcomers.

Cuirassiers thundered into the grounds, silvered breastplates gleaming beneath their squadron's colors. At least the colonel at their head had the good grace to only bring a platoon in with him instead of crowding the whole squadron onto the Admiralty lawn just to impress her. Quickly surrounding their little group, the big men on their bigger horses glowered down at them sternly for a moment. In Arilin's admittedly limited experience, cuirassiers usually thought the Valkyrie Knights were cute girls playing soldier who deserved a sort of amused benevolence. Clearly playtime was over, and there was nothing at all cute about the current situation.

Finally a particularly imposing man with lieutenant colonel insignia on the collar poking out above his breastplate growled, "You're all coming back with us."

Arilin and Alyssa shared a glance before the princess replied, "When did you leave the High City? We just got here ourselves."

"About an hour ago. Prince Alphonse ordered us to retrieve you." He narrowed his eyes, "Clearly none too soon. Now come along."

Clearly they didn't have much choice in the matter, either. Arilin, Alyssa and the rest of the hussars glumly fell in behind the colonel and made their way back up to the High City in the middle of a phalanx of silvered steel. The cuirassiers didn't let her go until she had dropped Midnight off at the Palace stables, and even then they insisted on walking her inside and firmly handing her off to the Foot Guards for the night. Alyssa had told her troopers to take off when they passed the 14th Regiment's barracks on the way up, but she insisted on accompanying her all the way back to the Palace herself.

The doorway between the stables and the Palace proper swung shut with a solid thud and the cuirassiers moved off outside like a thunderstorm passing over the High City. The Foot Guards, clearly bemused at their situation, nodded politely and turned to leave the two of them alone, and Arilin sighed as the men departed. Noticing her distress, Alyssa remarked, "Chin up, milady. We all made it back in one piece today."

Arilin rolled her eyes, "I'd like to have higher ambitions in life, Allie."

Her companion, well, she supposed more of a friend now, chuckled benevolently, "You take what you can get in war, milady."

"I know, I know." Arilin changed the subject, looking back at her hopefully, "Want to stay for dinner?"

"With you?" Alyssa looked down at her dirty, blood-spattered uniform, "Got a dress I can borrow?"

Arilin smiled, "We'll figure something out."

Chapter 16

A Rose in the Sun

In his infinite wisdom her father had decided to form the battalion up on the grass in Garrison Park, and he had told them to do it in shirtsleeves. Even so, Sophia thought as she felt the slow river of sweat flow down her spine and gradually seep into the waistband of her new gray uniform pants, he should have done it at *night*. This was miserable.

Looking to her left a little from where she was standing with her spear, Captain Martin looked like he was slowly wilting himself. She could see the sweat glistening in the sunlight on the back of his thick, muscular neck as he stood there at parade rest, and the wet patch across his shoulder blades seemed to be growing by the second. As tall as she was, the man had to have a hundred pounds on her. God knew how he didn't just burn up in the heat.

Feeling her eyes on him, the commander turned his head a little and smiled back at her, and she felt a tension in her heart she hadn't known was there ease a little. The last time they'd done something like this, a few months and a lifetime ago at the regiment's Southbend barracks, their commander at the time, Captain Jaeger, had rolled his eyes up in his head and passed out right next to her. It hadn't even been that hot of morning, he'd just locked up like a steel beam while Prince Adrian was talking to her. Martin was made of much sterner stuff. He could probably stand there for hours and barely blink, the blazing sun and the steaming river air be damned.

Just thinking about Captain Jaeger made her head spin. Never mind what he'd gotten off to since he was ignominiously disappeared out of command right after their first battle, not that far away to the south. Martin was their *fifth* commander in the last four months. Two of them had come off Fire Ridge on stretchers. *Fire Ridge...* for an instant she thought about Jack, her old friend lying there dying with a chest full of shrapnel, because she'd told him to go right while she went left. Her skin crawled, the blazing sun cold as ice on her skin as she shoved the thought from her mind.

Taking a deep breath, Sophia flexed her legs a little and shook her head slowly, feeling the tendrils of ice slowly unwrap their blood-curdling grip on her body. She'd be flat on her back soon herself if this kept up. She looked back up to see the battalion's colors swinging upright at the front of the formation, Jenny anticipating Major Matheson's command as he spun on his heel. Lacking a rifle as a personnel clerk and not having bothered with her typewriter, Jennifer Musgrave had ended up with the 2nd Battalion's battle flag on the march out of Fire Ridge. She'd been carrying it ever since, and Sophia thought it was pretty amusing that both women in the 224th were now standard-bearers. A moment later, the commander called out, "Battalion!"

Martin and Sophia both came to attention, Sophia raising her spear with its battle-scarred flag vertical as he called over his shoulder, "Company!"

Major Matheson finished, "Attention!" Spinning on his heel again, he came to attention and waited. After a few seconds Sophia noticed movement off to her side, and she discreetly moved her eyes over to see her father walking across the front of the formation accompanied by a *much* shorter man. He barely came up to her father's shoulder. He'd probably barely make it to *her* chin. And, as she got a closer look at him, everything from his expressive blonde beard to the very way he walked seemed incredibly familiar. She wondered where she had seen him before as he walked up to the front of the formation with her father, Matheson saluting as they approached. The man returned the gesture and stepped into his place as Matheson turned and walked off around the other side of the formation with her father in tow.

Giving them a familiar-feeling smile, their new commander called out jovially, "Rattlesnakes, at ease!" Even his *voice* rang bells, casually imperious and a little self-important, but very indulgent. He probably had a house full of servants somewhere that all loved him. They relaxed with a shuffle of feet and shifting rifle butts on the grass, and he called out, "Major Matheson! Sergeant Major! Come back up here, let's inspect the troops!"

Then he walked off to the side he had come in from. Turning, Sophia saw the two men walking back up to him at the far end of the formation, and together they started working their way across the front of Delta Company. Occasionally the new commander would stop, speak to a man, look at a rifle, laugh at a comment. The mood, which Sophia hadn't even realized was dark, eased. After a few minutes he worked his way over to Charlie Company, and she heard him talking with someone she knew from Third Platoon behind her. Then Second Platoon. And then, finally, she heard footsteps in the grass behind her and the man himself ducked under her flag and stepped square in front of her.

As their new little colonel looked up at her, Sophia realized *exactly* where she knew him from. She didn't even need to see his nametag to be sure, although a glance at it confirmed what she thought. Pictures of him had been all over that house, and the manor's young lady had clearly taken after her father. Lieutenant Colonel Espinay chortled, looked over at her father where he had stepped in beside him and remarked, "Oho! Is this your Sophia I've heard so much about?"

Her father chuckled proudly, "She certainly is."

Charlotte's father turned back to her, "My God, you're like one of those big masked girls the Imperials keep around." He chuckled, "I thought my daughter was making up stories when she mentioned you... oh! Sergeant Major, you mentioned you had something for her? Might as well do it now."

Her father raised his eyebrows, then shrugged, "You're right." He turned to her with an extremely serious look, "Sophia."

Swallowing hard, she looked back at him, "Dad?"

Reaching into a pocket, her father pulled out what looked like a couple scraps of cloth and handed them to her. Taking them from him with her left hand, she looked at them for a moment, then another moment as her heart climbed her throat. He'd given her a pair of shoulder boards, the new style for the new uniform. *Corporal's* shoulder boards, the gray fabric edged with white piping and set with two black chevrons. Sophia glanced back up at her father to see him smiling as broadly as she'd ever seen him before as he said, "We had a sergeants' meeting this morning, and we all figured it was time." He chuckled, "I've got another set for Bob."

Screw Army decorum. She hugged him, spear in hand and all, and managed, "Thanks... thanks, Dad."

Her father chuckled and gently pushed her back into position, "There, there, Sophia. Don't go crying on me now. Chin up."

The colonel, standing next to them, chortled, "Oho! Congratulations, young lady!"

Damnit. Her eyes *were* tearing up. "Ah... yes, sir." she managed in reply.

The men moved on, speaking to Captain Martin for a moment before walking back behind them to continue reviewing the troops. It took them another twenty or so minutes, a short eternity in the sun, to finish reviewing the battalion before Colonel Espinay made his way back up to the front of the formation. He looked like he was melting a little himself, she thought as he puffed himself up and announced, "Rattlesnakes! I am very pleased with what I have seen today!" He went on, "We will move out tomorrow morning, and your leaders will brief you tonight. In the meantime..." He chuckled, "Take the rest of the day off! I expect you all to report to your companies by sundown to prepare for movement tomorrow." Remembering something, chuckled and went on, "And the Sergeant Major told me to pass on that if any of you damage your bicycles today, you'll be walking!" He finished, "Commanders, take charge of your troops!"

They'd been issued more than just their new gray uniforms that morning. As part of their new, permanent assignment to Lady MacMahon's 9th Cavalry Division, the 224th Independent Infantry Battalion had also been issued a new, wonderful piece of equipment to let them keep up with the fast-moving hussars. Down at the Cavalry Corps' supply depot, every one of them had been handed a bicycle that looked like it had been recently requisitioned from an unfortunate local citizen and had it duly recorded in their pay book. Sophia wondered why nobody had thought of doing that earlier. She also realized, with a little amazement, that the last time they'd gotten time off had been at Wolf Rock Fortress.

Captain Martin wasted no time telling them to get lost, and the formation quickly dispersed. Heading back towards First Platoon and her squad, Sophia saw most of her friends quickly walking off with the crowd of soldiers. Furrowing her eyebrows in confusion, she was about to hurry after them when she noticed one very familiar face that *wasn't* walking away in a hurry. Tony grinned at her, "Hey, Corporal."

She gave him a stern look for a second before they both broke down laughing. "Hey, Tony," she replied, "Where's everyone else going?"

He chuckled, "I told them not to wait up for us." Tony went on, "Want to take a ride?"

Sophia smiled, "Sure thing, where to?"

Something started buzzing in the distance, rapidly growing louder. Sophia and Tony both looked up as a couple Royal Army aircraft appeared overhead, the little gray-and-yellow biplanes climbing out away from the town and banking to fly downriver to the north. After a minute they disappeared into the distance, and Tony ventured, "I asked around and found out they've got an airfield a couple miles west of town, want to go check it out?"

That actually sounded like an excellent idea. She'd never seen an airplane up close before. Overzealous Airship Corps guards had kept them away from the airfield at Wolf Rock when they'd tried to go take a look then, and they'd barely seen them since. Smiling eagerly, she agreed, "Of course!"

"Then come on!" Tony reached out to take her by the hand, and she felt her face reddening a little as they went to go retrieve their bikes. She didn't pull away, though. Soon they were riding west through Grenville, bicycles jostling uncomfortably over the old town's cobblestones until they made it through the old fortress gate. They waved to the bemused guards from the saddle as the road turned to smooth asphalt under their wheels and they accelerated out into the suburbs.

The dense commercial district just outside the old fortress quickly thinned out to townhouses, then single homes, most of them by now abandoned with once-manicured lawns going wild and the occasional broken window or door hanging off its hinges. If it hadn't been for the constant stream of traffic on the road, Army trucks, wagons and riders, the ride would have given her the creeps. An infantry company marching into town gave them jealous looks as they rode by, and they picked up the pace before the tired men got any ideas.

Finding the airfield was easy, although Tony had been a little optimistic when he'd said two miles earlier. All they had to do was head towards the occasional circling aircraft in the distance. After half an hour of peddling they turned off onto a road helpfully marked as going to the Grenville Fairgrounds, and a minute later they braked to a stop in front of a swinging-arm barrier set across the road. A bored-looking guard with overlapping-wheel Transportation Corps collar patches on his collar greeted them skeptically, "Hey... this is a restricted area. No getting through unless you've got a pass or you want to pull rank on the boss." Getting a better look at them, he raised an eyebrow, "Are you two on a date or something?"

Sophia and Tony looked at each other for a moment, then away quickly as they both stammered, "Ah..."

Beating her to it, Tony boldly announced, "Yes! Yes, we are."

Well, it was official now. Surprised, the guard looked between them for a long moment, then laughed, "Eh, what the hell. No way you two are Black Cloaks." He swung the gate open, "Just don't go around bothering anyone."

Sophia blinked. She had *not* been expecting that. Blushing as she settled back onto her bike, she managed, "Thanks."

"No problem." The man replied, clearly amused at them, "You kids are cute together."

They quickly left the guard behind as they pedaled onwards, keeping their thoughts to themselves. The airfield itself was maybe half a mile further down the road, just a cluster of temporary-looking clapboard buildings and tents beside a long row of Royal Army aircraft. A biplane returning from its mission buzzed in on final approach along the road as they went along, seeming to float for a moment as it flared short of the closely-trimmed landing field and gently settled back to earth. A puff of dust rose around its landing gear as it made contact and rocked back onto its tail-wheel, and the pilot quickly steered it off towards the flight line as a few crewmen rushed out to meet it. Seeing it next to the other planes,

Sophia realized it was substantially larger, with two seats and a swiveling machine-gun mount at the rear.

Braking to a halt next to the closest of the little buildings, Sophia and Tony got off their bikes and spent a few minutes just marveling at the airfield, as another heavy two-seater swooped in to land and a couple of the little single-seaters cranked up, pulled out of line and slowly made their way over to their end of the field. They had swung around into the wind, cranked their engines up to a thundering roar and were starting to accelerate back down the field to take off when Sophia saw movement out of the corner of her eye and turned to see an Army Air Corps captain had stepped out of the building and was approaching them. Nudging Tony, she turned and saluted as the roar of the two planes' engines quickly receded to a droning buzz and they hopped up into the air.

The man returned the gesture with a casual air and asked, "You two here with a message?"

"Ah, no, sir." Sophia smiled innocently, "We got a few hours off and figured we'd come take a look."

The captain raised an eyebrow suspiciously, "What, you're on a date?" He snorted, "We get tourists ten times a day and they *all* outrank you two. You tell that to Morris?"

That had been on the guard's nametag. Tony chimed in, "Ah... yes, we did, actually."

"And he let you in anyways?" He rolled his eyes, "I can't believe it. We should start selling ice cream at this rate." He narrowed his eyes as he looked them over, "Are you two jaegers or something?"

Sophia thought for a moment, then ventured, "Uh, I mean, I guess we are now that I think about it, sir." The captain raised an eyebrow skeptically and she explained, "We're with the Ninth Cavalry Division."

"You were in that mess east of here?" He asked. They both nodded, and he went on, "Good job getting out of that. Every flight we sent up over that told us the same damn thing, the whole area's *crawling* with Masks." He snorted again, "Just dragoons though, they're being cagey with their infantry again. God knows where they're planning on hitting us next."

"Heard about anything up north, sir?" Sophia asked hopefully.

"Yeah, they're fixing the northern rail lines and they never busted up the lateral ones to begin with." The captain shot back, "You guys heading up there soon?"

"Yeah," Tony replied, "It's why they gave us some time off."

The officer thought for a moment, "Rumor is they're going to try a landing up there because we're dug in along the river right now." He shrugged, "I wouldn't be surprised. Watch out overhead when you're up along the coast, I know they've got a carrier running around and if they try to land they'll be using it."

"A... carrier, sir?" Sophia asked, "What's that?"

"A ship that carries airplanes." He chuckled, "I know, the Navy was looking about like you two are when they found out at Diamond Shoals. They *shouldn't* have been, but what the hell, I'm in the Army for a reason. Anyways," he made a shooing motion, "This is a restricted area, so you two lovebirds run along before someone less indulgent than me comes along."

Sophia swallowed, "Ah, sure... sir." Turning to Tony, she added, "Come on, let's get out of here."

Getting back on their bikes they pedaled down the road out of the airfield, a smiling Morris waving them through the gate as they left. As they approached the turn-off back onto the main road into Grenville, Tony slowed and braked to a halt in the shade of a particularly large maple tree spreading its leaves over the road. Stopping herself, Sophia hopped off her bike and walked the few feet back to him, asking, "Tony, what's up?"

He gave her a very level look, dappled sunlight falling on his face through the tree's spreading branches. Tony had changed since they'd marched out of Jade Falls, not all that long ago now that she thought about it, and it wasn't just the hardening of his freckled features with the sun and wind and dust. Back then he'd been a boy following his longtime crush around like a puppy dog, and she'd been the girl happy to let him do it. War had a way of sharpening things, she supposed. Finally, Tony spoke quietly, "You think we're going back into it, Sophie?"

"Yeah," she replied simply. The wind puffed up as she said it, ruffling her hair and sending the light dancing across his face.

He shook his head slowly, "God... I hope they don't get us all killed." Tony looked back at her, "I don't want to lose you, Sophie."

"Me either," Sophia said.

Her old friend raised an eyebrow, "You or me?"

Sophia snorted, "You, dummy."

Tony chuckled. Then he stepped in close, put his hands around her waist and kissed her. After a couple seconds she relaxed, closed her eyes and starting kissing him back. After a while they came up for air, and she teased him, "Took you long enough."

Tony snorted, "You're hard to get through to."

"I like direct guys." Sophia shot back.

"Oh? Then how's this?" He asked. Sophia was opening her mouth to reply when he kissed her again.

After a while they heard a motor coming down the road and decided to move around the back side of the big maple tree. Making out with Tony was, she supposed, a hell of a way to pass the time. They sure looked a lot better than everyone who had spent the afternoon drinking when they got back to their billets around sundown, and they were chuckling together as the hung-over battalion pedaled out onto the road north the next morning. They were heading for a little place called Pine Harbor, set right at the mouth of the Great Steel River where it flowed into the sea.

Chapter 17

Declaration of War

Some wonderful person had decided to put a verandah out on the northeast corner of the Palace roof, where it overlooked the gardens and the gorgeous scenery of Sapphire Bay. As the shoreline curved away to the north the massive trees of the Seyam Royal Forest replaced the Capital's suburbs as sharply as though it had been cut with a knife, only a scattered few church spires poking out of the lush blanket of green running off towards the coast and the Shield Mountains. Even the looming bulk of the War Ministry below didn't completely spoil the view over the rest of the bay to the west, although Arilin made a note in the back of her head to have it torn down as an eyesore when she became Queen. It was, she supposed, probably the least of the problems her grandfather had left her. If she didn't figure out how to deal with his second son, she thought bitterly, she'd probably never get a chance to deal with the tastelessly grandiose architecture he'd left all over the High City.

Sighing at the thought, Arilin turned back to her friends, "Thanks again for coming over... I didn't realize how much I needed to see you."

"How could we not have?" Liriel exclaimed, "It's the *least* we can do for you."

"At least the guards let us through." Miriel added wryly, "I was worried for a minute."

Arilin snorted, "With the parade I was seeing this morning, it's the least they can do." She added, smiling, "Everyone who's anyone in the High City was coming up to make sure I was still alive. I even got a note from the *Empire*."

The girls' eyes widened. Charlotte asked, "Really?"

"Yeah." Arilin reached into her pocket and produced a small piece of paper, "Ambassador Stromsburg gave it to me when he came up this morning. I guess their embassy up in the Union sent him a telegram."

It read, cryptically, 'RESTRICTIONS ON POLITICAL ASSASSI-NATIONS IN LONG RESCRIPT TO SPIES REMAIN IN EFFECT STOP PLEASE CONVEY TO ROYAL AUTHORITIES STOP'. Just looking at it made a chill walk up her spine despite the ostensibly reassuring message. Handing it to Charlotte, she couldn't help but notice the girl's fingers shaking a little as she took it, and all three of her friends paled a little as they read it. Handing it back to her a little shakily, Liriel swallowed hard and changed the subject, "Well, *we* were worried when you didn't show up this morning."

"At school?" Arilin thought for a moment, then snorted, "Mom told me to take the day off last night. I thought I was fine, but..." She chuckled,

"I don't think she was worried about *me*."

"Here you go, milady." Becky, who had appeared at their table in her white maid's uniform as if by magic, set down a plate of tea cakes and macaroons for them. She gave her friends a nod, "Girls."

"Thank you, Miss Stone." Charlotte replied from her seat on Arilin's other side.

Becky smiled, "My pleasure, dear." Noticing her diminutive friend barely holding back her urge to reach out and grab one or several of the sweets, she chuckled politely and went on, "Please, help yourselves. They're meant to be eaten." By that point she had somehow gotten all of their teacups refilled, and she disappeared as quickly as she had come.

Arilin raised an eyebrow, "I *really* want to know how she does that."

"Oh?" Liriel asked, "What?"

"Just appear like that. It's spooky sometimes." Shaking her head incredulously, Arilin took a macaroon and changed the subject, "I'm surprised you didn't bring Tom along."

Liriel and Miriel exchanged knowing glances while Charlotte pouted. Clearly she'd been outvoted. Miriel lied to her, "He... needed to help out the regiment!"

"And he told you that?" Arilin raised an eyebrow as she popped the treat into her mouth. It tasted like strawberries from a particularly decadent Elven garden and cream made from unicorn milk. Getting the delight off her face with an effort, she tried bitter sarcasm, "They must be *really* hard up for troops."

"Anyways, he couldn't make it." Liriel covered for her sister, "But he *did* mention that he'd talked to his father, after he heard about the... well, he spoke to him."

"Oh?" Arilin asked, "How'd he say it went?"

The three girls glanced around the table at each other before Charlotte finally piped up, "He... I don't even know. Tom told us that he said he supports you, but he didn't exactly sound like he *believed* you were in danger from Alphonse."

Arilin sighed heavily. *Adults.* And as smooth as Tom was with girls, he'd probably taken the matter up with his father with the subtlety of a bayonet charge. She finally replied, "But he's not going to go running to Alphonse, at least?" Charlotte shook her head emphatically, and the princess went on, "Well, that's a relief."

Seeing the impression it had made on her, Liri and Miri had filched their own macaroons and were both swimming in their own little pools of sugary heaven. Charlotte had taken a whole collection of sweets practically as soon as Becky gave her the go-ahead, but she seemed to be in no hurry to actually eat them for the time being. After thinking for a couple seconds, the girl replied, "I bet Colonel Strathclyde is in the palace right now, actually, with all the guards around. You can probably talk to him yourself if you want to."

And she could cover it as an inspection of the troops. Arilin smiled happily, "That's brilliant! Charlotte, you're a born schemer."

The girl blushed and covered for it by quickly stuffing a tea cake into her mouth. It had the expected effect, and Arilin was chuckling happily when Miri recovered enough to speak and asked, "Do they have an idea who... well, who did it yet?"

Arilin felt the temperature drop about twenty degrees at the thought. By the expression on Miri's face when she looked back at her, she'd returned the favor with interest. Grimacing, the princess replied, "Yes, actually." Neither of the twins had the courage to ask her to elaborate, so she went on, "A couple of known anarchists. The police told me they thought they were harmless." Arilin rolled her eyes, "Clearly they were mistaken."

"Clearly." Charlotte agreed with her, "Could your uncle be involved somehow?"

Arilin shook her head in frustration, "I'm *sure* he is. I just have no idea-" Feeling an unfriendly stare on the back of her head, she shut her mouth abruptly and twisted in her chair to see a newcomer approaching across the colonnaded rooftop. Most of the servants didn't walk around seething with anger and glaring at members of the Royal Family. This girl was no maid, despite her immaculate white uniform.

"Lily!" Arilin smiled as the girl approached, "I can see you found your way in! Please," she gestured to the table, "Pull up a chair."

"I don't know about that, princess," her socialist classmate hissed, propping her hands on her hips angrily, "Wouldn't it be *beneath* you to eat with your servants?"

Arilin chuckled, "It's not like you're working for the RHA, we don't even let them come up here."

Lily snorted angrily and opened her mouth to say something when Arilin saw her eyes dart over to their plate of sweets. Shutting her mouth abruptly, she leaned forward a little to get a closer look at them, then turned back to her, "Are those... what are those things even? I didn't think those were real."

They all looked at her for a moment before the twins started giggling. Charlotte quickly joined in, then Arilin. It was at Lily's expense, but it felt good regardless. Recovering quickly, Arilin explained, "Those are macaroons, they're really very good."

Lily reached in to take one and popped it into her mouth. Chewing meditatively for a few seconds, she finally swallowed, then turned to go retrieve a chair. Smoothing her skirts, she sat down beside her and gave Arilin a look that, while sour, was remarkably less murderous than she'd been just a minute ago. "Consider me bribed," she quipped.

Charlotte asked, "Did you have any problems getting in?"

Lily sighed, "No, your maid passed me off to *her* maids," she looked at Arilin meaningfully, "Who got me dressed, and nobody even looked sideways at me coming in. You should probably have words with the guards." She changed the subject, "Now why did you want to see me?"

"I'm trying to figure out who tried to kill me yesterday, and why." Arilin replied bluntly.

"And you think I might know?" Arilin nodded, and Lily shrugged, "I can *guess*... I'm not sure if you'd like my guesses, though."

"Go ahead." Arilin snorted, "It won't be any worse than anything I've thought of myself by this point."

"Who're they saying was behind it now?" Lily asked.

Arilin replied, "I'm getting *told* a couple anarchists saw me riding down to the harbor and decided to take their chance."

Lily rolled her eyes, "Jeez, you think they'd at least try to be *plausible*." She went on, "Which *kind* of anarchist are they talking about, green, red or black?" Hesitating for a second, she added nervously, "Or the... *weird* ones?"

"I'm afraid I don't follow you." Arilin replied, taking a sip of her tea. It tasted heavenly, but the subject of the conversation was like ashes in her mouth.

"Ah. *Those*, then." Lily replied bitterly, "The nonexistent ones the police blame any time they're at a loss." She gave her a look and added, "I guarantee you they're provocateurs under someone's control. Especially after so many people got thrown in jail three years ago, anyone who needed a hitman and had the right connections could practically take their pick. Might be working for the police, even."

Arilin chuckled nervously and looked out at the city for a moment, "Well, I know *that* isn't the case."

"The police?   Why?" Her classmate demanded, "Wait... wait, I've heard *rumors* about that, but are you seriously saying...?"

That Red December was 'accidentally' kicked off by someone working for the police, and Dad made sure it would never happen again afterwards? Yes, actually. Some of these people do a lot more harm than good... and I probably shouldn't have let that one slip out. Arilin thought. Smiling demurely, she replied, "I have no idea what you're talking about, I just very much doubt they'd do something like that."

"Sure..." Lily replied skeptically, "It could be anyone else wealthy and connected."

Arilin looked back at her skeptically, "Or your communist friends wanting revenge for Red December."

"If it had been, I wouldn't have come." Lily snapped, as the twins gasped. They probably hadn't been expecting quite this level of strife at a tea party. The girl grimaced, "Anyways, trust me, it wasn't the communists. No way, no how."

Arilin leaned back in her seat and replied, "Why should I?"

Lily gave her a particularly snide smirk, "For the same reasons I'm trusting you about the *police*."

That made a few dots line up. The sailors she had been talking to at the time had certainly been sympathizers. It occurred to her that their leader, Sikorsky, was probably a lot more than that. Any communist assassins might have known him. Filing that information in the back of her head, Arilin made a dismissive gesture, "I understand. The question is what to do now."

"Why's that?" Liriel cut in across from them.

"Yeah, I mean, you're alright now, so...?" Miriel joined in.

Arilin shook her head, "It's not that simple." She gave Lily another look, "I heard there's going to be another no-confidence vote tonight."

The girl sputtered, "My, ah... father hasn't mentioned anything."

Arilin felt her eyes narrow almost-imperceptibly at the verbal hiccup. This wasn't the first time Lily had sputtered talking about her father... not to mention that, now that she thought about it, she looked nothing like him. Although maybe she took after her mother. With an effort, the princess chuckled, "That's because it's going to be a surprise. With the anarchist rumors going around, some... sensitive people are getting very nervous about continuing to cooperate with your father and his friends." She gave her a sly smile, "Care to guess who?"

Lily rolled her eyes, "I'm guessing it starts with a 'D' and ends with 'issenters.'

"We have a winner." Arilin chuckled drily, then looked around the table, "I don't suppose anyone knows anything we can do to convince them otherwise? This is the second attempt on the government in two months, and, well..." She shook her head, "This *stinks* of my uncle."

They all looked between each other glumly for a few seconds. Arilin was about to give up on it as an offhand request when she practically *saw* the lightbulbs go off over Liri and Miri's heads at the same time. The two girls looked at each other, smirked, turned back to the rest of them and exclaimed, "Let's start a rumor!"

Charlotte gave them a quizzical look, "I... guess? How? I don't think our usual methods are going to work here."

Liriel tossed her head in frustration, "Well, where are they getting their information? We'll start one there."

Lily pursed her lips, "All the workers' newspapers are already screaming that this was a provocateur, nobody up here pays them any attention."

Arilin thought for a moment, then smiled slowly, "What about the Star?"

The twins' eyes widened as they all shook their heads in unison. Miriel spoke first, "Milady, that's a *gossip rag!*"

The princess shrugged, "Yeah, but they'd print anything we told them, not to mention it'd be confirming what the workers' papers are already saying. I bet they'd have a special edition out tonight with this kind of news." She smiled predatorily, "And trust me, everyone in the Assembly will see it. If they don't read it themselves, their wives will and they'll tell them."

"Well, yes, milady," Liriel objected, "But *you* can't be going around talking to them!"

Smiling, Arilin sipped at her tea demurely, "Exactly."

"Wait... you don't mean...?" Miriel said incredulously. Arilin continued sipping at her tea, and she sighed heavily, "You do, don't you... at least they keep their sources private. This *better* not get out."

Arilin looked at Lily pointedly, and the girl shook her head, "Your secret is safe with me."

"Very good." Arilin smiled, "Becky can get you all a phone downstairs. Even if it gets investigated, they'll think it was a servant."

"Oh, milady." Charlotte asked, "Have you asked Beatrice about this?

She might have an idea, too."

Arilin pursed her lips, "No, actually… I was expecting her to be up here. She probably got wrapped up in something down in the library again and lost track of time." Thinking for a second, she finished off her tea with a determined swig and said, "Now that you mention it, I need to go check on her. And I need to go find Colonel Strathclyde if he's downstairs." Pushing her seat back, she stood, "I'm assuming you four can finish up here?"

"Of course, milady!" Her three friends chorused happily.

After a pointed look, Lily added sullenly, "I… don't want the food to go to waste."

"Of course you don't." Pushing her seat back in, Arilin curtsied and took her leave, enjoying the quiet of the Palace's rooftop gardens for a moment as she walked back inside. Becky, who had been waiting at a respectful distance with another one of their maids, curtsied and fell in beside her as she approached, leaving the other girl to wait on her friends. The woman thought of everything.

"Leaving early, milady?" Arilin nodded, and her maid went on, asking, "Where to?"

"The library, I think." The princess replied, "I haven't seen Beatrice for hours. Then I need to find Colonel Strathclyde, assuming he's in the building."

Becky gave her a concerned look, "If you're worried about her, milady, I can get more people to search…" She bit her lip, then went on, "I haven't seen her myself, actually."

"I mean, she does have her own maids." Arilin remarked, as Rebecca opened the door to the Residence for her and she stepped inside, "I doubt it's anything more than her hiding out in the back of the library."

"Of course, milady." Becky replied, a little hesitantly as she dropped back in beside her, "Even so, these days we can't be too careful… I'll have people look for her, you deal with the colonel."

Arilin hesitated for a moment, then nodded, "Okay." She waited for a moment inside as Becky flagged down one of the other maids and sent her rushing off to organize a search party, before they continued downstairs. After taking one of the side staircases down, she was in the middle of nodding at the guard standing outside the door when she noticed the 1st Regiment number on his collar patches and stopped, asking, "By the way, have you seen your colonel around? I'm looking for him…" She trailed off as the man swallowed hard in mid-salute, clearly unsure of what to do upon being confronted by a member of the Royal Family, "You can relax, by the way."

"She doesn't bite." Becky added, chuckling warmly.

The man dropped his rifle's butt back down to the floor next to him with an audible thud on the carpeting. Swallowing again, he managed, "Er, yes, milady. He just came by, actually." He pointed down the hall towards the main stairway up to the Residence, "He headed off that direction, I think he's still on this floor."

"Thanks." Arilin said. They caught up with Colonel Strathclyde at the staircase on the other end of the Palace. The guard he was inspecting glanced over at them as they approached, and he turned and raised his eyebrows in surprise as he saw them. Arilin curtsied politely, followed a second later by her maid, and greeted him, "Good afternoon, sir. Thanks for everything you've done for us lately."

Smiling, he bowed politely, "It's my honor, milady. Although..." He paused for a second, then went on, "I *am* surprised to see you up and about so soon. You should be resting."

Rising, Arilin smiled back as cheerfully as she could manage, "I'm harder to put down than that." She went on, "Do you have a minute? I do have something I wanted to speak to you about."

He gave her a forced chuckle, "I don't suppose this has anything to do with my son, does it?" He pressed on, "That boy can get the strangest ideas sometimes, I'm sorry if he's been bothering you."

"Not at all." She replied, "Let's go upstairs, I don't want to do this in the hall."

They took the side staircase up, Arilin racking her brain for a place to talk as they went. As they emerged in the Residence proper it occurred to her that the solution to her problem was literally staring her in the face, and she smiled and said, "We'll use my father's office. Becky, can you please make sure nobody bothers us?"

Her maid nodded and stepped forward to open the door for them, "Of course, milady."

She'd rarely ever been into her father's sanctum, and something washed over as her with the scent of books, wood and taxidermy as she stepped into the King's private office, running like an electrical charge up her spine to spark at the back of her neck. The room was, like most of those in the Residence, large and airy, but most of her home was decorated to her mother's domestic tastes. This was her father's domain, and the Queen clearly had no influence here. Even the *floor* was different, the light tapping of her own footsteps on the rich hardwood mixing with the colonel's heavy, thudding tread as they walked inside. And the décor, well... it occurred to her that her parents might have a private disagreement about the tastefulness of plastering the walls with hunting trophies. Her father even had a *griffon's* head mounted on the wall, the animal's glass eyes somehow still baleful in death.

The effect was mildly terrifying. It occurred to her that the feeling she'd gotten when she walked in was *power*, strong and solid as the High City's promontory. This was a room where an immensely powerful man made decisions that changed the course of history. She felt tiny, walking in here in her tea dress and ribbons. She felt like an *intruder*. The room was deserted, yet somehow it felt worse than her barging into the War Room in front of the military's whole high command. Maybe it was, she thought. A few months ago she would never have *dreamed* of so much as sneaking in here.

And yet now here she was, walking in to borrow a cup of her father's power. She hoped the room succeeded in impressing her guest of the seriousness of her situation, at least. Shying away from her father's massive desk, which looked like it had been carved out of an impossibly ancient and possibly magical tree, and the imposing tooled-leather chair behind it, Arilin led the colonel over to a set of slightly less-intimidating seats in the corner of the room that looked meant for informal visits and, smoothing her skirt, sank into one. Clearly bemused, Colonel Strathclyde joined her a moment later.

"Now..." She started, settling her elbows on the chair's padded leather armrests and steepling her fingers in front of her chest, "Sir, what... exactly did Tom tell you?"

Leaning back in his seat, he smiled and replied, "Well, milady, he seemed to think you were in some sort of trouble." He chuckled, "He wanted to know if you had my loyalty."

"Well..." Arilin replied, raising her eyebrows questioningly, "Do I?"

The colonel gave her an incredulous look, "Of course you do! I've served in the Army since *well* before you were born, young lady. I did not take my oath with my fingers crossed." He shook his head, then looked back at her sympathetically, "God, and I thought Tom was imagining things. I owe the boy an apology. Princess... what's troubling you?"

"Beyond the hand grenades?" Arilin asked wryly. Strathclyde looked taken aback for a moment before she pressed on, "Colonel, are you a Legitimist?"

The man looked at her for a moment, hard, as though he was thinking something over. He finally answered, choosing his worse carefully, "As a matter of principle, no. Your father undermined the stability of every noble house in the Kingdom when he legitimized you two girls. This includes *my own*." He snorted and went on, "Pragmatically speaking, though, absolutely." He looked her square in the eyes, "I'd rather see you on the throne than your uncle."

Arilin let out a breath she hadn't realized she'd been holding. Finally, she managed, "Thanks."

Strathclyde's brow furrowed in concern, "You still haven't told me what you're worried about, milady."

"I think Alphonse is plotting to usurp the throne." She replied bluntly, "He's got the motive to do it, and the opportunity, with Adrian…" Tears welled up in her eyes suddenly at the thought of her brother, and she rushed on quickly, "And my father at the front, and him back here trying to put me in a… in a…" Her mind raced, trying to fit the words to the dread she had felt gnawing at the back of her mind since she came back, "In a *cage* that he can just control however he likes!"

She was crying. Clearly an old hand with women and children, Strathclyde produced a handkerchief and leaned forward to dab them away, muttering, "Now, now, princess." After a moment she took it from him, and he patted her on the shoulder and went on reassuringly, "I don't know what's going on, if anything. But, milady, if it comes down to fighting, you'll be able to count on my men." He smiled at her warmly, "Now enough of that. You may be putting on a brave face, young lady, but you're on your last legs. I'm going to give you back to your maid, and she is going to put you to *bed*."

Arilin opened her mouth to object before she got a look at his eyes and realized it would be useless. Meekly, she submitted, "…sure."

The colonel stood and offered her a hand, "There we go, milady. Come on n-"

Someone knocked on the door, hard, and Becky's voice drifted through faintly, "Milady! Sorry to interrupt, but-" A flower of dread blossomed in Arilin's stomach, petals razor-sharp and cutting a hole through the middle of her heart at her maid went on, "We've found Beatrice! She's not well!"

Strathclyde gave her a worried look. She had probably turned white as a sheet. Even so, he helped her up as she stood and strode to the door, quickly pulling it open for her to rush out. She almost ran into her mother as she rushed out, who had emerged from her own sitting-room across the hall trailing a cloud of horrified-looking society ladies she didn't recognize in the slightest. Coming down the hall towards them, Arilin spotted Mr. Drake cradling her sister in his arms, her silvery hair a shining streak across his dark suit. Their butler was walking gingerly, trying not to disturb the girl. Trailing behind him gingerly she spotted an older woman she recognized as the Palace librarian. The woman *flinched* as Arilin's gaze fell across her.

Arilin's head spun, but the last thing the Kingdom needed right now was *both* of its princesses passed out on the floor. Taking hold of herself sternly and ignoring the dozen or so people who seemed to all be talking at once, Arilin raised a hand for quiet, then glared at her mother's guests and snarled, "*You. Out.*"

They hesitated for a moment, looking at her mother. The Queen gave them exact same look, and pointed to the exit for emphasis. They fled as one, and in the moment of calm that followed her mother asked, "What happened?"

Mr. Drake replied, "We found her fainted down in the library... she's breathing alright, but she's burning up." Her sister whimpered in his arms as he spoke, and he stepped aside and gave the librarian an iron glare, "I could *feel* that book she'd been reading *twenty feet away*. Probably the only reason she isn't *dead* is she managed to close it, somehow." He looked between Arilin and her mother, then went on, "It's still down there where we left it. I didn't want to touch it."

The librarian protested, "That book was *safe!* I went through it myself, like every other grimoire we let people handle! Hell-" The woman swore, "*She'd* read it before!"

Her mother waved her off, "That's quite enough, Helen, I believe you. Go see to things in the library." Looking at the butler, she ordered, "Get Beatrice into bed and go get the doctor."

"Mom," Arilin cut in, "We need someone who knows how to deal with magic."

Her mother glared at her, much harder than was necessary. Arilin felt herself wilting as she demanded, "Like *who*, in this day and age?" Noticing her discomfort, the Queen softened a little, "It's not like we've got mages at our beck and call."

Arilin shook her head, "There's a Department of Arcanology at the University. They might be able to help." She'd taken Beatrice down there a few times, in fact.

Her mother looked at her for a long moment, then acquiesced, "Miss Stone... you used to work with Beatrice, do you know how to get down there?"

Her maid nodded, "Yes, milady. And I have someone in mind already."

"Good." Arilin opened her mouth to volunteer to go with, and her mother cut her off, "You're staying here, young lady." She turned to Colonel Strathclyde and asked, "Can you get Miss Stone a car and an escort?" He nodded, and she finished, "Well, what are you all waiting for? Go to it!"

Everyone scattered. Arilin's head was starting to spin again, but she managed, "Mom, I can, uh..." She trailed off, feeling perfectly useless. Now that she thought about it, she had very little to contribute in this situation. She could pray, she supposed.

Her mother gave her a smile, "Go send your friends home. I'll put you to bed right afterwards."

What *was* it with people wanting to stuff her into bed constantly? Arilin pouted, "Mom, it's *five*. I just need to sit down for a little."

"It's not *you* I'm worried about, Arilin." Her mother gave her a sly look, "Your sister probably needs rest more than she needs doctors, and if you're sleeping *next* to her I can keep them from spending all night fussing over her, at least until your mage gets here."

Chapter 18

The Scarecrow Army

Bright moonlight sifted through the canopy of leaves overhead, dappling the road beneath an unearthly white. All the moons were up in a cloudless sky tonight, blazing a swath through the stars and casting a million lights and shadows beneath the trees like a ghostly kaleidoscope. The dragoons rode through it like swimmers in an ocean of stars, troopers swaying gently as their horses walked along. If he had been riding alone, June supposed he would have heard the peaceful sounds of a summer night on the northern plains and smelled the forest moss in the cool air. Surrounded by dragoons, it sounded like a grinding mill and it smelled like horses and soldiers in desperate need of a bath. Chuckling to himself, June patted Lucky's neck affectionately. At this point it was a miracle the horses put up with them.

The trees opened ahead and they found themselves back surrounded by pastureland, the farm road twisting ahead gently into the distance in a sea of long grass, the cattle that would have normally grazed it down long-since driven off. In the blazing moonlight June could easily make out another string of dark shapes ahead of them, bunches of bulky figures just ahead of long, low silhouettes strung out along the road in the distance. Artillery grinding along ahead of them, the cannons throwing up a thin skein of dust that shone silver in the moonlight. Looking across the fields, he could see it again and again, on every dirt track and country road that came into view, and he knew it was happening across a hundred-mile stretch of the countryside east of Grenville. Imperial soldiers, moving north.

The Imperial Army was a nocturnal animal. It trained at night. It moved at night. When it could, it fought at night. One of the stock jokes of life in the Empire was conscripts struggling to get back into a normal daily cycle after their time in the Army. Darkness was safety, one of many shields protecting the Emperor's soldiers, and even the light of five moons was preferable to the sun. Now it was protecting them as they wheeled to their next point of attack, stalking like a panther across the moonlit plains. A million soldiers were on the roads tonight, and June thought he could almost hear the earth tremble.

June's eyes caught a plume of smoke off in the distance to the east, a train trundling north along a lateral line. Maybe tanks, he supposed, but more probably the infantry. It was a lot easier to cram men into boxcars than horses, and the footsoldiers simply couldn't be expected to march the distances required for this operation and be remotely fresh to fight when they finally ran into the enemy. They would be shipped to the fight. The dragoons, on the other hand, had a long and proud tradition of getting themselves anywhere they were needed, one which the Army's logisticians were more than happy to oblige. Which meant that the 5th Dragoon Regiment, and his platoon with it, was in for a very long ride.

Artillery popped faintly off towards the Great Steel River. The front line, some thirty kilometers away to the west by now, was either at the river or feeling out the few bridgeheads the Royal Army still seemed interested in maintaining. Those probably wouldn't last long. Word that morning had been that the enemy was starting to blow the bridges and retreat west of the river. So as far as anything mattered, they were back in the Empire now.

A familiar voice broke him out of his thoughts, "How're you holding up, sir?'

June looked over to see Sergeant Tarai, friendly as always, had pulled her horse alongside him. Smiling under his mask, he replied, "Just thinking."

"Oh?" She asked innocently, "About what?"

"Well." June replied, rolling the thought around in his head a little before he went on, "I was thinking that if they've blown the bridges, we're back in the Empire now."

Tarai cocked her head for a moment, then laughed and replied, "You're not wrong, sir." He chuckled in response, and she thought for a moment before asking, "So, wait. If we're as good as back in the Empire, and I'm pretty sure we're not trying to be too quiet tonight... ah..."

June looked over at her and raised an eyebrow, feeling his mask cock a little over to the side, "If we were worried about the Royal Army, sergeant, we'd be doing this *entirely* differently."

She swallowed and came out with it, "Can we sing? I'm getting bored."

June thought for a moment, then shrugged, "Sure." She kept looking at him, though, and after a moment he glanced back, "Is that all?"

"Ah, well..." Her mask moved a little as she smiled nervously, "You know sir, we've never heard *you* sing before."

I see where this is going, June thought sarcastically. Teasing her, he shot back coldly, "No, you haven't."

"Well, uh..." Mustering up her courage like a true Black Knight, she managed, "Can you?"

"I do know how to sing." He replied.

Persistent, Tarai tried again, "Ahm... will you, though, sir? For us?" She added hopefully.

Chuckling, June relented, "Sure." He added, sternly, "I expect you all to do the chorus, though."

"Hey!" Tarai turned in her saddle and shouted to the platoon, most of whom were behind them, "He said he'd do it!"

They all started cheering. Clearly there was more to this than he'd thought at first. Chuckling, June raised an arm and motioned for them to quiet down. Eventually they did, and he cleared his throat theatrically and started, his voice ringing clearly through the night.

> *The Royal Army, blood on its sword;*
>
> *They dare to call their king our lord;*
>
> *But from the Islands to Sapphire Bay;*
>
> *The Scarecrow Army fights today![1]*

The story went that some unfortunate military governor, either from the Kingdom or the Dominion, had made the mistake of mocking the then-ragged Imperial Army as nothing but a bunch of scarecrows at some point during the Liberation War. To say the insult had backfired was something of an understatement. June chuckled at the thought as his troopers joined in.

> *We are the Scarecrows!*
>
> *We are the demons!*
>
> *We will cut them down in rows!*
>
> *And relentless;*
>
> *Pushing onward;*
>
> *Now into the war we go!*

Before the Marchlands War the line 'and relentless' had been 'without mercy.' His father had told him once he preferred the old version, but given that they took prisoners these days it was a bad example for the troops. June raised his voice to sing the second verse.

> *Scarecrow Army, march, march onward!*
>
> *Now is the time to draw your sword!*
>
> *And from the Islands to Sapphire Bay;*
>
> *The Scarecrow Army kills today!*

Some of the dragoons had been reluctant to sing earlier. They seemed to have found their voices as they roared the chorus back at him.

---

[1]   *The Scarecrow Army* is sung to the tune of *The Red Army is the Strongest*, also known as *White Army, Black Baron*

We are the Scarecrows!

We are the demons!

We will cut them down in rows!

And relentless;

Pushing onward;

Now into the war we go!

We are the Scarecrows!

We are the demons!

We will cut them down in rows!

And relentless;

Pushing onward;

Now into the war we go!

Smiling beneath his mask, June sang the last verse, letting the first lines hang a little in the air for impact.

Peace we will bring with all we have done;

Our enemy falls and the war is won;

For from the Islands to Sapphire Bay;

The Emperor's Army wins today!

Then he joined the troops to sing the chorus and close the song, because it was a fine night and he was entitled to.

We are the Scarecrows!

We are the demons!

We will cut them down in rows!

And relentless;

Pushing onward;

Now into the war we go!

We are the Scarecrows!

We are the demons!

We will cut them down in rows!

And relentless;

Pushing onward;

Now into the war we go!

Their voices rolled around the countryside as they rode, Imperial dragoons at war with a thousand miles in the saddle and a thousand yet to go. Their deeds so far were the stuff of legends. His platoon alone had taken hundreds of Royal prisoners. He had taken Prince Adrian's colors with his own hands, and seen the Prince himself slain a moment later. He had heard the man's dying words, and he still had his sister's ribbon in his pocket. God knew what he was going to do with it.

For all that, he thought grimly, there had been a terrible price in blood. Two-thirds of the dragoons he had met when he first reined Lucky in at the company's bivouac that morning east of Fire Ridge were gone. Dead, like Sergeant Itogawa, shot through the head during their charge in the fog, or Ghaznavi, who had bled out unnoticed in that brutal fight at the base of Fire Ridge. Permanently mangled, like Anastasia Lai, who would need an eyepatch from now on. Some less-permanently injured, like Sergeant Khan, who had told him what she *really* thought of him as they loaded her into the field ambulance with her broken leg. If he knew anything at all about the woman, the medal he knew she'd gotten afterwards hadn't changed her opinion of him in the slightest.

It was easy to tell himself he needed to do better. The hard part was *how*. At the end of the day they had a job to do and a war to win, and the fastest way to bring everyone home again was probably to get down to doing exactly that. He wasn't going to be able to save everyone. He didn't even know, June thought coldly, if he was going to be able to save himself. With that cheery thought in mind, he looked over at Sergeant Tarai and said, "Alright, sergeant, my turn. I don't suppose you know *Katrina?*"

As it turned out, she did.

Chapter 19
Shadow Out of Hell

Someone was talking and shaking her awake, strong fingers digging into her shoulder as they jostled her to and fro. Totally disoriented, she jerked upright in her chair and awkwardly batted at the offending arm, forcing her eyes open from their hard rime of salt and gummed tears. That took a few blinks to deal with, but at least her attacker let go for a moment to let her rub her eyes clear.

"Miss Carmen Sykes?" Her assailant was talking again. Finally getting a good look at her, she saw that she was dealing with a tall woman with light brown hair and a striking if hard-edged air. She was wearing a blue dress that she vaguely recognized as important, although she wasn't entirely sure *why*. The woman looked at her sternly for a couple seconds, and she realized that she'd been asking a question earlier.

"Ah... yes, that's me." Carmen managed, glancing around quickly to see that the window nearby was pitch-black with the darkness outside, the two of them reflecting clearly in the glass. The last thing she remembered, the sun had been going down and they had just turned on the overhead lights in the library. She must have fallen asleep. She noted bleakly that she looked like a complete mess compared to the polished woman standing over her at her little reading table, spread with old books that she really hoped she hadn't been drooling on. At least this woman didn't seem to be in any hurry to throw her out of the library. Straightening her glasses, Carmen tried to push her uncooperative hair back over her shoulders, going on apologetically, "Sorry, I... I don't think we've met?"

"No, we haven't." The woman replied, with a tone that implied she didn't particularly care about the omission. There were other chairs at the table, but she remained standing as she went on, "I got your name from Professor Greyhawke. He said you're the closest thing he knows to a practicing mage."

Carmen blinked at her blearily, "That doesn't sound like him."

The woman chuckled drily, "He said you were a pity project who leached money out of the department doing research that's unreadable nonsense."

"That sounds about right." Carmen sighed. He wasn't wrong that her thesis amounted to a filing cabinet full of handwritten notes that were probably never going to be published. Shaking the rest of the cobwebs out of her head, she looked up at the woman and asked nervously, "Ah... I'm not in trouble, am I?"

Her interrogator smiled thinly. Now that she had a better look at the woman, she realized that she was probably both under an incredible amount of stress and extremely good at hiding the fact. "No, you're not." Carmen let out a breath she didn't know she'd been holding as the woman went on, "I'm here because I think we have a need for your services."

Carmen raised her eyebrows questioningly, "'We,' ah... do you work for the Army?" She'd heard things were bad, but the military must really be getting desperate to take an interest in her research.

"Sometimes, but not in this capacity." The woman smiled, "I work for the Palace."

Carmen's blood flashed cold, and she felt herself turn white as a sheet at the thought. Finally she managed, "I... I... this isn't about...?"

The woman chuckled, a little more warmly this time, "No, no, of course not. In fact, given our current situation your... record with the Palace Library is actually a positive thing."

Starting to breathe again, Carmen slumped forward in her seat, "Whew." Raising an eyebrow, she looked back up and asked, "Then, wait, what's happening? Has something gone wrong?"

"Yes." The woman said, bluntly, "It's faster if I explain on the way." She stuck out a gloved hand, "I'm Rebecca Stone, by the way. Lady's maid to Princess Arilin."

Jumping to her feet, Carmen quickly took her hand, "Oh, ah, pleased to meet you, ma'am!"

"Likewise." The princess' maid glanced at the books covering the table and asked, "Are those yours?" Carmen shook her head, and she went on, "Good. Leave them for the staff, we need to get going." Letting go of her hand, the woman turned and walked off briskly, Carmen hurrying after her. She practically had to run to catch up, the librarian looking up from a newspaper with a headline shouting 'ROYALIST SHOCK VOTE, GOVERNMENT LIVES' to give her a dirty look for making a commotion as they passed the circulation desk. Her companion, meanwhile, made as much sound and attracted about as much notice as a ghost.

The woman remained silent as they walked into the University Library's lobby, the Gothic vaulting and stained glass as glorious as any church in the Kingdom. Normally the whole place blazed with lights after dark, but with the war on someone in the administration had gotten the bright idea to do their part by conserving electricity, so it was as gloomy as an abandoned church at night to boot. Most of the students that had once thronged the hall, even after dark, were gone now. Many had volunteered a few months ago, even some of the girls. More recently the rest had begun disappearing to conscription, or finding reasons to make themselves less visible so close to the War Ministry.

Carmen followed her companion out the heavy front doors to find a running automobile parked at the base of the steps, a uniformed driver already pulling the rear door open for them. Rebecca motioned for her to climb in first and clambered in behind as she settled into the luxuriantly-padded leather seat. Seeing what must have been the expression on her face, her host remarked, "It's to your liking?"

"Oh, yes," Carmen replied. Just the seat was incredible, the leather luxuriant and smooth to the touch. The driver swung himself in ahead of them and wordlessly put the car in gear, pulling smoothly out into the road. Finally, she looked over at the maid and ventured, "So, ah... what's going on?"

"There's been an... *incident* with a grimoire." Carmen looked over at her seriously, "I'm a nurse myself, and I'll be the first to tell you that we've been dealing with something out of our league."

Her eyes widened, "Is anyone hurt?"

The woman grimaced, in her usual restrained way, "Princess Beatrice was reading it when it... *fired*, for lack of a better word. She's..." The maid shook her head, "Well, there's nothing *medically* wrong with her that we can find, but she's barely responsive. At least she's breathing..." She trailed off before muttering, half to herself, "I was worried we'd have to put her in an iron lung."

Carmen felt her hair standing on end, a chill running down her back as the car bumped over the High City cobblestones towards the Palace. Whether it was fear or excitement she couldn't tell. Her eyes narrowed as she looked over at her companion, asking, "Has she woken up at all?"

"Yes, barely." The maid replied, grimacing, "Only for a few seconds, and then she just falls asleep again. It's like something just sucked the life out of her and she's trying to recover."

"Yes and no." Carmen chewed her thumbnail reflexively, thinking, "Sounds like severe mana drain, like if a mage *really* overexerted themselves... but I've never heard of that as a curse on a grimoire before. Let alone that it could fire that powerfully these days."

"What do you mean?" Miss Stone demanded.

Carmen shook her head, "Most mages put curses on their spellbooks. Some of it was trade secrets, some of it them trying to keep dangerous spells out of the wrong hands. But most of them are safe these days regardless because there's not enough magic around for the spell to activate. Unless you're looking at some Elven doomsday scroll you'll be fine."

She went on, eyes widening, "Did Beatrice *cast?* Successfully?"

The woman shook her head, "No, she didn't. She was just reading. And trust me, we've caught her trying before and we know what it looks like."

"*By the eternal gods themselves, a maiden after my own soul and spirit.*" Carmen remarked to herself, in Royal Elven. Stone gave her a dubious look, and she pushed on quickly, "What'd you do with the book?"

"Very little, so far." She shrugged, "Beatrice managed to close it before she passed out, at least. We've been keeping people away from it. Last I checked it had frosted the table over and you could feel it from across the library."

"So you haven't moved it? Good." Carmen nodded, "What you're seeing isn't the curse itself, it's just an aura. I'm going to need to take a look at it first. After that I *think* I can do something about Beatrice. I think. If you have the right stuff in the Palace, which you should. But I think I need to neutralize the book first. Do you have a containment box?"

The woman raised an eyebrow at her rambling, but she gave her a reassuring smile and replied, "You can ask yourself, we're here." Carmen blushed as she realized she had been so focused on the problem she had completely forgotten where she even was. The car braked smoothly to a stop in the plaza, and Stone climbed out without waiting for the driver. Carmen scrambled after her a moment later, and the maid went on, "There might be some fairly intimidating people around the Palace right now, Miss Sykes. Let me handle them, you do what you've been brought here to do."

Swallowing hard, Carmen replied, "Yes, ma'am."

The Palace loomed overhead in the darkness as they walked towards the grand doorway, their footsteps echoing eerily on the smooth flagstones. It was late at night and most of the great building's windows were dark, reflecting the cut-glass moons overhead. Looking further up, she could see them all floating across the sky like a string of glowing pearls. Quite the witches' night.

Following the line of moons back down to earth on her right, she noticed there was one part of the Palace that was still working. The Palace library was dimly lit, as though some lights on the other side of the building were on and shining across the library's cavernous central hall. Some of the windows betrayed silhouettes with slung rifles. And now that she was able to focus on it, that disquieting feeling she'd gotten stepping out of the car didn't seem to *entirely* come from the abandoned, late-night Palace square.

The guards at the main door recognized her companion. One of them snapped his rifle vertical in what she supposed was a salute as the other pulled the door open for them. Miss Stone returned the gesture crisply leaving Carmen to walk into the darkened Great Hall behind her, doing nothing and feeling immensely awkward. As the door swung closed behind them she ventured, "Ah... should I have done something there?"

"Of course not." Stone chuckled, "You're a civilian. Now come on."

They turned right, passing out of the Great Hall itself and into a succession of magnificent rooms that she wished she'd had several days to admire, every one of them exquisitely designed to overawe any visitor. In the moonlight with a dark presence growing ever nearer as they walked, she realized more than a few of them were probably haunted. The second time she noticed an inky silhouette disappearing out of the corner of her eye she remarked, "I don't suppose you've named the ghosts around here? That's the second one I've seen so far."

Her companion laughed darkly, "Amelia usually stays in her room in the Residence. The Duelists haunt the Gardens, but maybe they're curious tonight." She snorted, "The Lady in Black had terrible taste, they've *both* grabbed my ass before. Although I've heard she bothers the male staff, so maybe they all deserved each other."

Carmen looked at her for a moment, eyebrows raised in surprise, then chuckled weakly, "And they call me crazy for thinking the University's haunted."

Miss Stone chuckled, "Most of that place is about a hundred times worse than here. This building's actually pretty new." They stepped into a short hallway, and Carmen noticed an ornate door with more guards in front of it at the end. She'd never been down this particular corridor before, but that was clearly one of the doors into the library, the private ones the Royal Family would use. The woman slowed when they got halfway down it, looking over at her with her jaw set seriously, "Are you ready?"

Carmen shrugged, "I'm not getting any readier."

"Good enough," the maid replied, a hint of sarcasm in her voice. A few more steps took them to the door, the guards saluting and opening the door the same way they had before. They probably rehearsed the routine, Carmen thought absently as they stepped into the Palace Library itself. The thought slipped from her mind as the room's air washed over her, the familiar scent of a million old books mixed with something... *else*, like someone had decided to make a perfume out of varnish and brass and something dead far too long and not yet buried. It slipped and slithered around and over her, vulgar and far too familiar as it forced its way up her nostrils. Carmen gasped, fought back the urge to retch and only then realized the air was about ten degrees colder.

Shaking it off, Carmen realized that her earlier observation about the lighting had been correct. The Palace Library occupied half the southeast wing of the grand building and substantially more of the basement, rising in a series of tiers around a central open space from the ground floor all the way to the roof, where she glimpsed Faith's massive disk occupying most of a skylight. Even with a few lights burning on the second floor off to their left the moonlight painted the enormous space with crazy shadows, and she wasn't entirely sure that some of them weren't twisting about unnaturally.

Setting her jaw grimly, she was about to start marching over to where it looked like they'd left the grimoire over on the second floor when a too-familiar voice cut through the darkness, "Hey! Miss Stone, what *exactly* do you think you're doing, bringing *her* in here?"

Carmen spun to find the Chief Librarian had been waiting for them. Helen Etheridge, her old nemesis, was opening her mouth again when her companion cut her off, "Solving your grimoire problem, actually."

The older woman snorted, "She's banned for life. You don't have the authority to bring her in."

Stone rolled her eyes and spat, "Would you like me to go get someone who does? Maybe Princess Arilin would like to hear about how you're in a hole and demanding to be allowed to *keep digging*."

"She's a dirty, sneaking *thief*." The librarian glared at her venomously.

"Don't care, let's go." The maid grabbed her arm and hustled her along, Mrs. Etheridge seemingly reluctant to follow them. Given the... *presence* she could feel growing up ahead, Carmen wasn't entirely sure she blamed her. Finally, the woman asked her, "What was that over?"

Carmen sighed, "I might have borrowed some stuff out of the, ah... restricted reference collection." The original 1705 folio printing of Mulhouse's *Wyches & Their Haunts & Magicks: A Scientifical Treatise,* to be precise. The one with the proper illustrations and all the details, not the sanitized version after the mages got through with it. Considering it still gave her nightmares occasionally, it was no wonder Dr. Mulhouse had gone insane. Stone gave her a dubious look and she defended herself, "She caught me *returning* it!"

"Very public-minded of you." Stone remarked. Anything more she cared to say died in her throat as they walked up the stairs to the second floor and the already-chill air turned to ice, that cloying, evil smell blotting out the pleasant scent of the library entirely. Passing a miserable-looking guard shivering at the top of the stairs they crept forward cautiously, damp carpeting squishing slightly underfoot. By the next bookshelf down it was positively *soaking*, condensation running down the dark wood of the shelving and beading on the books' leather spines as their breath fogged from their mouths. Her feet crunched on frost as the corner of a table came into view around the next set of shelves, rimed with a crazy spiderweb of ice.

Carmen took another step and it struck her like a blow across the face, dark shapes dancing in the corners of her eyes as that hideous scent wrapped itself around her, *caressing* her, almost gleeful. Her stomach heaved and bile acid burned in the back of her throat as her knees wobbled and she realized those dark shapes weren't just dancing in the corners of her eyes, they were busily bobbing all around the table. Some of them, she was pretty sure, had eyes and teeth. *Christ above*, what on Earth had Beatrice gotten into?

Calm down, Carmen. Breathe. It's not active, this is all residual. If it was active, you'd know by now, she thought, a little unconvincingly. Steeling her nerves by pure force of will, she reached out an arm and pushed everything else out of her mind, *feeling* the scar in reality in front of her, like a barely-clotted stab wound. The book itself was mostly dead, although she guessed that had been the case when Beatrice had opened it earlier. She could still feel weak skeins and drops of magic in the air, slowly dissipating into the great magical void of the world. And then the *hole*, where *something* had reached through and then fled, covering its tracks as it went. It felt like a shadow in an endless abyss, two flaming red eyes slowly opening to gaze down upon her...

Gasping, Carmen jerked backwards, swatting at the shadows where they had begun to gather around her. Retreating a little, she turned to see that Stone had stopped *well* short, and she retreated some more until she was next to her. The shadows with teeth stopped following after a few feet. Still breathing a little hard, she managed, "I think that book has a hook on it." The woman gave her a dubious look and she explained, "Like a, uh, a magic string almost. Whoever put it there would be able to sense if someone was reading it."

The maid raised an eyebrow, "And attack?"

"If they had the magic to do it, and power the tracker in the first place... yeah. Which this one definitely does. And remotely, too, it's much more difficult than just a booby-trap spell." Carmen shuddered involuntarily, "Definitely, definitely. This is... I don't even know what it is, but it's got *power*."

"Great." Stone remarked sarcastically, "One more problem around here." She gave her a hard look, "Can you deal with the book?"

Carmen nodded, "Sure, although we'll want a *serious* box, not one of those little lockers they use here. Gold's best, although I understand if you don't just have that lying around."

The older woman chuckled and asked, "Does lead work?"

"Yeah, it works fine." Carmen nodded. Lead was never *fashionable* among mages, but it had been in use as magical shielding since Elven times.

"Give me a few minutes. I'll get you a box." The woman turned and walked back the way they had come, leaving her alone with the damp and the shadows. After a while she heard her faintly calling for a couple guards to assist her. The wet air was starting to soak through her blouse and the shadows had mostly lost interest in her when Stone returned with a couple soldiers in tow, with what looked like an *extremely* heavy box strapped to the stretcher they were carrying. Handing her an extremely long set of tongs, she said, "Show them were you want the box and it's all yours."

Swallowing hard, Carmen ventured back towards the book and pointed to the base of the table. The soldiers bravely maneuvered the stretcher into position before jumping back like they'd been scalded, and she bent over and hauled on the lid, *hard*, to open it. The inside was mostly fitted lead blocks, with barely enough space for the book. Gasping a little from the exertion, Carmen hefted the tongs and steeled herself again as she prodded the grimoire enough to break it free of the ice that had formed on it, carefully slid it to the edge of the table, got a grip on it with the tongs and maneuvered it down into the box. The shadows gave her disappointed looks as she straddled the stretcher and lifted the box's lid with an effort, got it over vertical and let it fall on the book with a satisfying clang.

The air started warming almost immediately as the echoes faded, the shadows slowly dissipating from around her. Miss Stone and the two soldiers gingerly approached, and Carmen turned to them and said, "This probably needs to be welded shut and buried in the vault. I wouldn't take any chances with it."

"You heard her." Stone gestured at the stretcher and its contents, and the soldiers nervously picked it up and departed. She looked around the little reading space, a table with some comfortable chairs sandwiched between bookshelves now running with condensation, next to a window that probably looked out over the gardens. No wonder Beatrice liked the spot, Carmen thought as the woman went on, "Is all of... *this*..." She waved her hand through one of the toothy shadows, breaking it apart into shards that rapidly faded from view, "Going to dissipate properly?"

Carmen shrugged, "Probably. You might want to have a priest go through here. Those things *really* don't like Jesus. Now," she went on, "Let me see the princess."

The maid nodded and led her back out of the library, Carmen taking the time to smirk at the librarian on the way. The gray-haired woman rolled her eyes at her and turned to go inspect the damage herself. Leaving the library, Stone navigated them back through the Palace, winding through the corridors to a nondescript corridor that she guessed was near the kitchens and not far from the Great Hall itself. Pulling aside a wrought-iron screen set into the wall, she ushered her into the elevator and, closing the internal screen behind them, punched the button for the fourth floor. The machine rumbled to life, and Carmen remarked, "I didn't know you had one of these in the Palace."

The maid chuckled, "Best-kept secret in the place. Alexander had it installed for the dining service, so I've heard. And it goes straight to the basement."

Carmen raised an eyebrow, "Isn't the Residence on the fifth floor?"

"There's a separate one on the fourth floor for the last leg, but we'll use the stairs." Stone explained, "Security. Old Alex was paranoid. Not that it helped him any in the end," she finished, chuckling.

"I still don't know how William's his son." Carmen mused.

"There wasn't any love lost, that's for sure." Her companion replied noncommittally. Now that they were talking about the current King, she got the feeling that she wasn't going to get a lot out of the woman. The elevator slowed to a stop in a dimly-lit corridor with a dull thud, and the maid pulled the door open and said, "We're here."

Carmen followed the woman out of the elevator and into a warmly-decorated corridor, most of the lights dimmed for the evening. With the *presence* no longer scratching at the back of her skull it was practically homey. They quickly turned to walk up a magnificently-appointed staircase, enough moonlight pouring in through the windows and skylights above that her companion didn't even feel the need to turn on a light. Finally they alighted before a massive door that looked to have been carved out of a solid piece of some kind of wood that she expected was imported and *felt* was a little magical.

The guards did their familiar routine and they stepped into the nicest home she'd ever seen in her life. And it was, she realized, a *home*, unlike the rest of the Palace. Someone had decorated to satisfy their own personal tastes instead of to make visitors feel desperately inadequate. Those tastes tended towards rich wood paneling, thick carpets and breezy Impressionism that took on a ghostly air in the moonlight pouring in from the skylights overhead. Her snappy remark died in her throat, and Miss Stone gestured to follow her. They moved a couple doors down the wide central hallway, and the maid soundlessly opened a door and ushered her inside.

She found herself in what looked like a lady's sitting room, a place where the occupant could easily hold court with friends and admirers. Then she looked around, she felt her heart skip a beat. *Everything* in the room was Elven, or done after their exquisite High Imperial style. The furniture was probably 18th or 19th-century reproductions, although she wasn't entirely sure about some of the end tables. And the *walls*... God in Heaven, no wonder they had taken down those two smaller Altemesion frescoes at the Royal Museum. Princesses got first pick, apparently. Her ears were feeling pointier by the second although, she supposed, maybe she should have been feeling like a human slave brought in to minister to her immensely superior Elven mistress. Either way she was going to find out soon.

Miss Stone opened a final door in the side of the room, and Carmen followed her into the princess' bedchamber. The room was pitch-dark and quiet, just the faintest hint of night noises drifting up with the night air from the gardens through a cracked window. The maid padded through the darkness adeptly to pull back the curtains, letting bright moonlight flood into the room. It was almost blinding, and Carmen blinked a couple times as her eyes adjusted. She found herself standing quite close to a massive canopy bed with heavy curtains drawn and shut tight, just the kind of thing a princess would sleep in. Something shifted behind her, and she turned to see a woman stirring in a chair by the door, now behind her after she had walked in.

Rubbing her eyes tiredly, the woman looked up at her and asked, "Becky? Is that you?"

The maid walked back past her and curtsied to the woman, crisp and elegant despite the fact it was well past midnight, "Yes, milady. I've brought an arcanologist... a proper mage, actually. We've already disposed of the book down in the library."

Carmen got the sense that she should probably be curtseying as the woman shook herself and leaned forward in her seat, raising elegant eyebrows, "Already, you say? It's taken care of?"

"Yes," Carmen volunteered, "They should be welding the containment box shut as we speak. The book itself wasn't dangerous, but... *something* was able to reach through it. Something bad. Best not to take any chances with it."

The seated woman looked at her, a little nonplussed. Finally she smiled, "That's good to hear. And you are...?"

"Carmen Sykes." She snorted, "I guess I'm a mage." Catching herself, she belatedly added, "Milady."

They had been talking quietly, but apparently not quietly enough. Carmen felt a shiver of unease in her chest as someone stirred in the bed behind her, and she turned to see a lithe hand pulling the curtains aside. A moment later the girl inside had swiveled herself out of the covers to perch on the edge of the bed. Either Princess Beatrice had made a miraculous recovery, or... no, there was another shape in the darkness behind this newcomer, hair pale as snow gleaming softly spread out across the pillows. Even in the darkness she knew this new girl's eyes, quick and gleaming in the moonlight, were red as blood. Chuckling softly at the appearance, the older woman said, "I'm Catherine. This is my daughter, Arilin. And, well..." She stood, and the older princess obligingly leaned back to give her a better view as she gestured deep into the canopied bed, "That's Beatrice there. She's been... out for hours now." The Queen gave her a questioning look, "I don't suppose you know of anything that could help my daughter, Miss Sykes?"

She hadn't realized until then just how *tall* the Queen was. The woman had to have four or five inches on her. Even from her seat, she could tell that Arilin was probably just as tall, even at her young age. It was frankly intimidating. Taking a deep breath, Carmen screwed up her courage and managed, "Yes, ah, milady. There's a mage's brazier in the other room that we can use, if you have something magical you don't mind me burning. And which will *burn* and not explode." She went on quickly, "I think Beatrice was mana-drained, pretty badly actually. If we can get magic loose into the environment here, she should absorb it and recover... well, fairly quickly anyways."

Princess Arilin gave her a look and asked, "Would griffon feathers work?" She glanced at her mother, "There's a head in Dad's office."

Queen Catherine sighed, "Might as well." She looked at her, "How many do you think you'll need?"

Carmen shook her head, "I don't know. Ten or twenty for starters, assuming they haven't degraded."

"Okay." Princess Arilin interjected, hopping out of bed nimbly. Becky curtsied and followed her out of the room, leaving her standing there awkwardly with the Queen. After a couple seconds under the woman's gaze Carmen muttered an excuse and ducked into the other room, quickly retrieving the mage brazier from where she had spotted it on top of one of the princess' bookshelves. The other two had yet to return, and Carmen busied herself pulling back the bed's curtains and examining her hapless princess.

Beatrice was certainly striking, with delicate features and hair so pale it shone like silver in the moonlight. In a few years men would be walking clean into light poles whenever she walked down the street, and probably a few women too. For a girl that was clearly obsessed with the Elves, she certainly looked the part. Her chest rose and fell gently, her breath warm on her fingers. Feeling her throat, Carmen felt the girl's heartbeat for a few seconds, then snorted. Beatrice was probably healthier than she was. Grabbing the princess' shoulder, she shook her, gently at first, then harder as the girl stubbornly kept on sleeping. Still nothing, but there were *ways* to get someone's attention. Grunting, Carmen pulled back the covers a little to expose the girl's chest, clenched her hand into a fist and coldly dragged her knuckles down her sternum, hard enough that she probably left an ugly bruise.

Carmen felt the Queen's hand on her shoulder as the older woman demanded, "What are you-"

"Hold on," Carmen shot back. The princess' eyes flashed open for a second and focused on her, unearthly red in the bright moonlight. Just as quickly they started to flutter closed, and Carmen raked her hand down her chest again, harder. Beatrice let out a pained moan and looked at her again, slowly shaking her head. "Wake up!" Carmen demanded, "Stay with us, Beatrice."

"I... what... I... where am...?" The girl asked, confusion written all over her face.

"You're safe." The Queen said, reaching under the covers to take the girl's hand.

"Mom..." Beatrice looked at her mother for a minute, then sort of shrugged back into her pillow and instantly fell back asleep.

The Queen gave her a look, and Carmen smiled apologetically and said, "I'll... I'll get your chair." Quickly retrieving it, she positioned it so the woman could sit down and volunteered, "Definitely mage's collapse, pretty bad too. Helps that she's so young. Some older mages, it'd just kill them outright." The woman gave her a poisonous look, and she coughed and went on, "If we get some mana back into her, she should wake up properly in a few hours and maybe be up and about in a few days?"

"Well," the Queen smiled at her, "That's better than the alternatives, and that's the farthest we've managed to wake her up so far."

Arilin and Miss Stone returned with a collection of griffon feathers, a canvas drop-cloth and a fire extinguisher a moment later, although that was probably a little optimistic for dealing with a *magic* fire. Positioning the brazier on the drop-cloth in the middle of the room and about as far from anything potentially flammable as she could get, Carmen admired the first feather for a moment before sighing and striking the lighter the maid had also helpfully provided, kneeling over the brazier in case she had to drop the feather quickly. It was old and dried-out, and caught fire immediately, the edges curling for a moment as the flame touched them. Then something *else* seemed to catch, and the feather erupted in a gout of unearthly green flame a good two feet high, singing her fingers before she could drop it onto the brazier grate. Stone hefted her fire extinguisher menacingly, but Carmen waved her off and they let it burn.

Just the one feather lasted a good two or three minutes, and they added the next one as its magical flame started to gutter out. The maid and Arilin took turns feeding feathers into the brazier, fascinated by the magical flame as Carmen sat down against the wall and let her eyes drift closed. There was... *something* different about the air in the room as the feathers burned and the magic streamed out, something she could almost reach out and touch, shape with her mind like she'd tried to, like she'd dreamed about so many times...

Carmen came to laid out on one of the couches in Beatrice's sitting room with sunlight pouring in the open window. After someone heard her stumbling around as she woke up, an elegant and vaguely terrifying woman in an absolutely pristine, ice-white maid's uniform *appeared* in the room so suddenly she half-thought she was a ghost. Her name was Miss Montrose, and in light of the dubious prospects for her further studies and her invaluable assistance last night, she was there to offer her a job. They had her into a maid's uniform by lunchtime and serving Beatrice tea in bed an hour later. The princess was clearly upset that her new maid was going to be going through her entire collection in search of anything potentially cursed and that her magical studies would be closely and strictly supervised going forward, but she was at least a little mollified that Carmen was scolding her in Royal Elven.

Chapter 20

The Thunder and the Storm

Patricia looked up as Colonel Frost grunted nervously across from her. Following his gaze out the train's window as they pulled into Pine Harbor, she could see why. The sleepy little port town at the mouth of the Great Steel River was crammed with refugees, ramshackle tents sprouting in every piece of open space like mushrooms after a rain. The streets were crowded with a gaunt, travel-worn mass of humanity, people sitting on the sidewalks or shuffling around listlessly. Here and there as the train pulled into the station she could see military policemen or what looked like ordinary soldiers walking about trying to keep order, islands of Royal Army blue in a sea of dirty, desperate people. Then the train braked into the station, Patricia feeling a twinge of anxiety as she noticed the crowd thickening just before it was wiped from sight by the platform walls.

"I don't like this." Her chief of staff remarked, "One bad rumor and this place will burn."

"Why do you suppose they all came in *here?*" She asked, "I guess there's the harbor."

The train ground to a halt and Frost stood, offering her his hand, "I think that's exactly it, milady."

"Thanks, Joseph," she smiled. Taking it, she stood and went on, "Then let's hope it's still open, so we can get them out of here."

They made their way to the doors and stepped out into the station. The platform itself was already starting to fill with men, most of them looking little better than the ones crowding the street outside. A man emerged from the press with a couple of gendarmes in tow, his old-style blue uniform straining to keep his expansive figure in check as he headed towards them. The newcomers saluted as they approached, Patricia noting a single general's star on the man's jacket collar. His nametag read, 'Decker.'

"Milady!" The fortress commander greeted her as she returned the gesture, "Pleased to see you." He smiled apologetically and offered her his hand, "We can use all the help we can get around here."

His handshake was as flaccid as his waistline, and he held on a couple moments too long. After he finally let go Patricia looked around and raised an eyebrow, "I'll say."

The man turned to lead them off the platform, gesturing at the ragged work crews as they went, "We've been able to get *some* use out of the recent... influx." The men were already starting to pull boxcars open and unload supplies, "Even so, milady, I don't want this crowd in town if we get besieged." He chuckled, jowls wobbling a little, "They'll eat us out of here in no time."

"Clearly they're the greatest threat to our food supply," Patricia replied drily. She let it hang for a moment. The man gave her a look, eyes widening, and she smiled blandly and went on, "What's keeping you from moving them along?"

Decker coughed, shook his head and replied, "Well, milady, they keep coming in for one. Also," he went on as something thudded heavily outside, the sound reverberating loudly even inside the station, "Right now the port's closed."

They stepped out into the sunlit street outside as another series of loud booms washed over the city. A line of infantrymen with fixed bayonets and a few gendarmes on horseback were keeping the crowd away from the front of the station and the car the commander had arrived in, but the noise seemed to be doing more to subdue them for the moment. After the last thud finished echoing through the street, Patricia asked, "That sounded like it was outgoing... how long have you been under attack here? We hadn't heard anything when we set off earlier today."

"Well, since this morning, actually, milady." The man huffed, "I've sent up all the proper reports, I assumed you would have been informed."

"We didn't have a telephone on board." Patricia replied matter-of-factly as the man popped open the car door and gestured her inside. Without being prompted, Joseph climbed in after and sat next to her, leaving the disappointed-looked commander to work his way in across from them. After he finished fussily settling himself onto the leather seat, she asked, "What kind of force are we talking about?"

"Destroyers this morning, milady. The big Imperial ones, probably trying to draw the squadron out for a fight." Patricia cocked her head for a moment before she realized he was talking about warships and not cavalry. There were twenty or so destroyers and several larger cruisers based out of the harbor, although the exact numbers escaped her. Decker chuckled, "We chased them off. Last I heard before I came down was they were coming in with heavier stuff."

Their driver cranked the car to life and they pulled out, the gendarmes pushing a hole through the crowd for them and then peeling aside to follow them as they trundled through the streets. Already anxious from the gunfire, the mass of people parted easily and didn't seem to have any particular anger at the sight of their well-fed military governor. Raising an eyebrow, Patricia replied, "What *kind* of heavier stuff?"

The man shrugged, "They said battleships, but it's always battleships when you get the first report. We'll see." The car wobbled slightly on its wheels, and she shot Joseph a nervous look a moment before a long, rumbling crash tore through the air, rattling the car's windows and sending the people crowding the streets into a flurry of motion as they disappeared down alleyways and crammed into doors. There was a loud whinny and equally loud curse outside, and she looked to see one of the gendarmes' horses bolting off down a side street missing its rider. At all this the fortress commander coughed nervously and remarked, "Definitely battleships. We need to get under cover, milady."

"I'll say. I'm assuming you have a bunker?" Joseph weighed in as the car accelerated. Twisting in her seat, Patricia saw the remaining gendarmes break into a canter to keep up, although a couple broke off to assist the fallen rider or galloped off after the lost horse. At least the man seemed to be moving and not out cold or worse from what she could see.

"Of course." Decker huffed as they sped through the streets, the driver taking a couple of turns harder than he needed to. More dull thuds from outgoing gunfire and harsh, ripping crashes from incoming salvos reverberated through the town, and Patricia saw a few windows shatter as a particularly loud blast slammed over. The man slammed on the brakes in front of a hulking, old-looking building that she suspected had housed the fortress headquarters since Steinwitz's days, and they hopped out to be waved inside by a couple of nervous-looking guards standing outside the heavy front doors. The fortress commander hurried up the steps after them, then paused and barked at the guards, "What in the world are you two still doing outside? Get in and lock the door, for God's sake, it's got a slit for a reason!"

Squeezing past them in the narrow entryway, General Decker led them further inside, muttering, "Damn soldiers don't have a lick of common sense in them sometimes." Despite the building's thick stone walls, the interior was reasonably well-lit from a combination of windows that looked like they had been carved out of cannon embrasures and, as they walked deeper, electric lights wired along the ceilings. The whole place was eerily deserted, although Patricia suspected the staff had merely evacuated into whatever bunker was carved out underneath it. Her suspicions were confirmed when the fortress commander pulled open an armor-plated door with a large down arrow stenciled on it and led them down a harshly-lit staircase. The old, worn stonework gleamed under brand-new electrical lighting, the bulbs wrapped in heavy wire cages to protect them from shocks and careless soldiers. Decker remarked proudly, "Just had this modernized, milady. We stripped out the whole old magazine and put in a proper command post for the fortress."

As they emerged from the stairway's lower door the sergeant on duty leapt up behind his desk tucked into a wall niche beside it and called the bunker to attention. Already sweating with condensation from the soldiers packed inside, the walls echoed with scraping shuffles as people climbed to their feet. Decker quickly called out for them to carry on and led them further inside, soldiers sheltering in the hallway pressing themselves against the walls to let them through. They quickly came to a T-intersection and turned, pushing more of the office workers from upstairs out of the way as they went. Rooms opened off the walls to one side of them in what Patricia recognized as an old gunpowder magazine layout, now converted to offices and command posts echoing with artillery jargon as soldiers called out reports. Targets, bearings, ship identifications, rounds remaining. Damage. Turret number three out of action, two killed and five wounded, requesting transport for evacuation. No wonder the walls were sweating. The whole *fortress* was.

Decker finally found the right room in the warren and ushered them inside, closing the door behind them with a sigh of relief. Patricia looked around as he shooed out a couple of junior officers to see the room was completely hung with maps, from small-scale plans of the town and its fortifications to one of the whole lower Great Steel River and the coast going west down to the Ellarian Bay set square in the middle of the room. Stepping up to that one, she saw the fortress staff had been using it to keep track of the situation, and she felt herself grimacing as she looked at it. Stepping up next to her, Joseph saw the look on her face and remarked, "Terrible as usual, milady?"

"When is it ever *not?*" Patricia snapped back, more sharply than she meant to. Looking over at him, she apologized quietly, "Sorry. I've never liked bunkers."

Her chief of staff chuckled, "I don't blame you, milady." As if to make her point the whole room trembled as another Imperial salvo fell, the lights flickering for a moment. Looking over the map himself, he mused, "And this... well, we've got our work cut out for us."

"I'll say!" Decker parked his bulky frame on her other side and went on, "You've arrived just in the nick of time, milady. I hope you know I've got next to nothing for interval troops." He chuckled, "If you'd asked me six months ago we'd be worried about *landings* around here, I'd have called you insane."

"Right... what *do* you have right now, anyways?" Patricia asked.

"For troops, milady?" The man smiled apologetically, "Just my infantry battalion and company of gendarmes, and they're stretched thin as is defending the forts and dealing with the refugees. Plenty of artillerymen, but they're needed at the guns." He pointed out the forts around Pine Harbor itself, the small bay facing east into the estuary just south of where the Great Steel River ran into the Northern Ocean, "We've got the harbor defenses here, mortars and light guns," Decker moved on, tapping the headland closing the bay to the north, "The Old Fort here, which they're not even *bothering* to shoot at." Probably because it was built to fend off ships with *sails*, Patricia thought caustically as he pointed to its replacement closer to town, "And Battery William, which they very much *are*. That's what we heard firing earlier."

"That's, what, six by twelve, in turrets?" Patricia asked, "Do they have high explosive shells?" Both the men looked at her, surprised, and she smiled knowingly, "My shop at the War Ministry *wrote* the Fortress Survey last year, when they weren't golfing."

Joseph recovered quickly and opined, "They should be good for thirty kilometers, more or less."

Their portly host shut his mouth, huffed a little and started back up, "You're correct, milady, although one of those mounts is going to be out of action for a while. We can fire inland, I made sure to lay in a stock of shells." He snorted sourly, "Took them forever to arrive, I think we were the lowest priority for anything."

"What do you have outside of town?" She asked, pointing at the long stretch of coastline sweeping off to the west and the vast, swampy estuary of the Great Steel River to the east as it spread out into the ocean in a broad fan a good fifty kilometers wide. The actual shipping channel and Pine Harbor itself were on the far west of the broad river delta, where through some trick of geology the river had carved out its deepest course into the side of the gently-rising landscape.

Decker shrugged, far too nonchalantly for her taste, "Not much, milady. We've got some observers down the coast and a light battery down in Terenstown, and I've got a few troops guarding bridges and such on the rail line south you came in on." He chuckled, "If the Masks want the swamp they're welcome to it, but I'm worried they'll land further up the coast and cut us off."

Joseph and Patricia snorted in unison, and she shot back, "I wouldn't put anything past them. Can infantry get through the swamp, or cavalry?"

The fortress commander shrugged, "With a lot of difficulty, I suppose. We've gotten reports from locals, people saying they've seen dragoons, spies, whatever. Probably all smugglers taking advantage of the situation." He went on, "They'd need boats, and local guides, and they'd end up facing you all with no real way out once they got through. Good way to die in my opinion. I'm *much* more worried about a landing." He pointed off at the west side of the map, "There's plenty of beaches to choose from, all the way back to the Gulf if they want to get adventurous."

The room rumbled again, as if in agreement. On her other side, Joseph mused, "They've brought an awful lot of ships if they're planning on walking." He tapped a large and menacing enemy icon out at sea on the map, "Is this confirmed, they've got a whole battle squadron out here?"

Decker nodded, his jowls wobbling slightly, "They're the ones engaging Battery William right now. Definitely battleships. And there's been submarine sightings of transports in the last couple days."

Patricia scowled. Watching the Empire operate was like watching a magician on stage and trying to figure out where he was keeping the doves he kept pulling out of his hat. It would have been positively enjoyable if the divisions Slade Anjanou was producing from behind his ears weren't trying to kill them. Tapping the map near the river, she said, "The rest of the corps is covering the coast going west past Terenstown. I'm not putting anything past the Empire... if there's a way to get through that swamp in force, they'll find it. We'll have the Fourteenth screen the coast between Terenstown and Pine Harbor, the Twentieth in the north near the town, the Eighth further south tied into the defenses around Kelsbruck." Which was the throat of the estuary and the first town on the river with a bridge, although that was long-blown now. She went on, "We'll keep the Two-Twenty Fourth in reserve. Can the warships stationed here move upriver if needed?"

Decker hesitated for a moment, then waffled, "I... I think so, milady. You'd have to ask the admiral."

Patricia snorted angrily, "I was wondering why he didn't bother to show up. That could be the difference between whether we can hold this river or not."

Joseph weighed in, "Not to mention he's working for Navy headquarters and not the Army of Drakenburg."

"He still works for the King." Patricia replied, "I'm sure Walter can persuade him. In the meantime it looks like we have another stop he..." Something was hammering faintly overhead. It sounded like a... *machine gun?* Stepping back, she looked between the two men, "Are either of you hearing that?"

Their portly host replied helpfully, "Not at all, milady. Too much time around the big guns, isn't that right, colonel?"

Joseph chuckled, "You're not wrong, sir. I've got nothing."

Jesus Christ. Rolling her eyes, Patricia demanded, "Well, can you go *find* somebody who can tell me why they're shooting a *machine gun* upstairs? Are we being attacked?"

Right on cue the room's side door popped open and a rather nervous-looking captain stuck his head through, "Uh, sir, I'm very sorry to interrupt but you need to know about this."

Decker looked between the man and the two of them, then turned back to him, "Well, come on then."

"They're bombing the port." The captain said.

"You mean shelling?" The fortress commander said, "They've spread the ships all around, I'm not sure what they're hoping to accomplish."

"Uh, no, sir." The man replied, "Aircraft. About a hundred of them if we've counted right."

Joseph furrowed his brow in concern, "Any damage?"

The captain shrugged, "We haven't been able to get the Navy on the phone. We're getting told the whole port's on fire."

"Well, call the Air Corps, have them get some planes up to cover us." Decker told him. The captain retreated, and he turned back to them, "How in the world did the Empire get so many planes together?"

"Probably their carriers." Patricia weighed in, "They had at least one at Diamond Shoals. I know it did a number on the Navy." Decker gave her a look that told her he didn't know what exactly an aircraft carrier *was*, and she sighed and went on, "I want to get a look at this."

With that she turned and walked out of the room, the soldiers sheltering in the hallway outside quickly pressing themselves back against the walls and out of her way as she went. Joseph caught up to her before she got too far, saying, "Are you sure this is wise, milady?"

"No, it's a terrible idea." Patricia replied grimly, "But it's hardly the first time I've done something dangerous to look at something. I'm not asking you to come with."

Her chief of staff laughed, "I'd be remiss if I didn't, milady. This is probably safer than anything we did at Allenby."

"Isn't that true." She replied as they started climbing the stairs, "Now come on." As they emerged upstairs the sound of battle outside built, what sounded like machine guns and a few heavy cannons firing across the city outside. It was a familiar sound for her, but... different somehow. They found the stairs going up as the machine gun on the roof let off another long burst, sounding louder and deeper than anything she was used to. It was probably one of the new heavy models, designed to shoot down aircraft and punch through tanks. They hurried up three flights of stairs to the roof, and a member of the gun crew looked over in surprise as they emerged into the battle practically next to them.

Walking out onto the roof, Patricia looked east towards the harbor and felt her breath catch in her throat. The report hadn't been wrong. If anything, it hadn't been *enough*. Pine Harbor was built on enough of a hill she could see the harbor from the citadel roof, and it looked like the mouth of hell. Stricken ships and what looked like more than a few fuel tanks burned brightly, painting the whole eastern sky black with smoke. And above it all, black dots flitted through the inky plumes like harpies circling the fires of Hell. Imperial warplanes. If she squinted she could make out the red stripes on their wings.

As she watched a few streams of tracers snaked up from the ground nearer the harbor towards the attackers, without much of an effect as far as she could see. Further down the roof another antiaircraft gun emplacement roared to life, sending a long and, given the range, very optimistic burst off towards the enemy. It was close and loud enough she winced and covered her ears, the noise breaking her out of her reverie. After the gunners finally let up and the ringing in her ears subsided a little, she heard Joseph curse beside her, "Are you *God-damn* kidding me?"

For once Patricia didn't have anything to say in reply. Watching the Imperial planes bank off and start trailing away to the north, a story Walter had told her once came to mind unbidden. When he had joined the Army as a young artillery officer, some of his older soldiers had first learned their trade with muzzle-loaders that fired literal cast iron *cannonballs*. War had changed under his feet over the long years he'd spent in service, to the point that some siege guns these days were so long-ranged they had to account for the planet rotating under the shell while it was in flight heading for a target on the other side of the horizon. And, well, now she knew *exactly* what it felt like. She was a *hussar*. She was used to war with a horse and her wits. This was new and different, and she didn't like it *at all*.

She didn't have much of a choice in the matter, though. Hearing the heavy door popping open behind them she turned to see General Decker emerge, red-faced and panting. Shaking his head tiredly, the man looked at her for a second before the apocalyptic pall from the harbor caught his eye, and his mouth slowly opened as he turned to gape at it. Patricia snorted angrily and got his attention back, "Do you have a phone here, assuming the wires are still up?"

"Oh, ah, milady." Decker reluctantly looked back at her, probably the first time he'd been hesitant to look at her all day. The hefty general cleared his throat for a couple seconds, then replied, "Yes, yes, of course we do."

"Good," Patricia replied, "I need to call Walter and tell him to send reinforcements. Whatever the Empire's planning, if it's enough to risk their carriers I doubt my three regiments will last very long."

"Walter, you mentioned him before..." Decker asked as she walked past him, then started incredulously, "Wait, you mean *General Haas*, milady?"

She heard Frost clap him on the shoulder and mutter something as she started down the stairs, and she chuckled despite herself. They'd kept that particular secret so badly at this point she wouldn't be surprised if the Empire started making hay about it.

Chapter 21

The Longest Patrol

The scent of pines filled her nose and the wind tossed Sophia's hair about as they rode along, though it was cooler now that they were getting close to the coast. It had only taken them a week of pedaling, which was a lot better than marching and a lot worse than just taking a train. They could have ridden on the roof or something even if all the boxcars were full. It's not as though Charlie Company hadn't done things ten times worse over the course of the war so far. Sighing at the thought of a peaceful train ride, Sophia pressed on the pedals and pulled out of column to move up, ignoring the twinges of protest from her thighs. She wasn't even *near* tired yet, and the forest roads at least made for a beautiful ride.

Most of the guys gave her appreciative looks as she went by. It wasn't hard to know why, and she hardly blamed them. They'd been issued hot-weather fatigues with shorts along with their new gray service uniforms, and they'd been wearing them since about lunchtime on their first day on the road. The women's cut was... well, it was *significantly* different than the men's. She couldn't say she minded the air on her thighs, or the attention, but it was a little new. She must clean up well. Lieutenant Thorn, however, glanced over to check her out from his position near the front of the platoon and then looked up and called, "Hey, Sophie! You just got back from the front, take a break."

Looking back over at him, she snorted and replied, "Just bored, sir. And ready for this ride to be over."

"Aren't we all," he shot back, leaning into the curve and looking ahead as they went around a turn, the pine forest opening up into a broad landscape of open fields ahead of them. Even this close to the Great Steel River, good roads were a rarity outside of its string of towns. They had learned to be careful trying to take curves on the dirt and gravel they usually found themselves on. "Now stop hogging the point, we're not in comba... wait. What is *that?*"

Sophia followed his gaze to see a smudge of black against the distant sky, much lower and immensely darker than the wispy clouds that had been blowing in from the sea all day. Looking closer, she could see a trail of ugly brown spreading across the horizon over the trees in the distance. It looked to be a ways off, miles probably. Expertly negotiating a pothole, Sophia looked back at her lieutenant and weighed in, "Looks like a fire, sir. Probably a big one, by the looks of it..." She felt something twist in her stomach unpleasantly, and grimaced as she asked, "Aren't we getting close to Pine Harbor?"

"Yeah," he replied, "Which is why I *really* don't like that."

She was about to reply when she heard something over the low, grinding whirr of their wheels in the dirt. A soft *thud*, then another and another, like popcorns the size of wagons in a skillet as big as a football field. Shells falling to earth, big and far away. The forest earlier must have deadened the sound. The thing twisting in her stomach clenched and thrashed, and Sophia looked back at Thorn nervously, "Sir, I'm... hearing artillery up ahead. Heavy and far off."

A murmur started traveling down the platoon as the others noticed it. Thorn grimaced and looked back at her, "That probably explains the smoke."

"Great," Sophia muttered, then replied more loudly, "And here I was hoping we'd get a break and the Empire would just leave us *alone* for once!"

Someone behind them heard her and cheered sarcastically. It sounded like Kelly. Someone else who *definitely* sounded like Edward joined in. Laughing, Thorn shot back, "Maybe they've got a thing for you."

"Hmph." Sophia replied curtly, sticking her nose up at the thought as she pedaled along.

Thorn chuckled and waved her back into line, "Alright, Miss Rose, get back in. No need to rush to give them your autograph."

She swung back into line behind him and they continued on through the fields. Unlike the abandoned and rapidly-overgrowing farms further to the east, here the farmers were still on their land. Here and there they could see men and women working in the rapidly-balding fields with scythes, their movements a little quicker than usual. Most of them seemed to be avoiding looking at the pall of smoke to the north, or at them as they pedaled past. The ones that did looked away quickly, as if they were ashamed. Some of them looked about the right age for the Army. She hated the thought, but with the front line so close, more than a few of them were probably planning on staying right where they were and making whatever accommodations they could with the Empire.

As they got closer to the distant trees Sophia picked a church steeple and then the roofs of a few larger buildings out of the haze covering the northern sky, and she realized the 'forest' up ahead was really more like a little town with the trees and patches of forest intertwined through everything to beautify the place. It looked picturesque up until she picked out the tents and wagons haphazardly packed in under the trees and spread around the town in little groups. Considering that was the alternative, she wasn't sure if she blamed the farmers who were still *farming* quite so much. Soon enough they were passing by refugees pulled off along the side of the road, most of them casting nervous glances off at the battle brewing to the north. Children playing in the late-summer dust waved at them cheerfully as they went by. The adults just looked angry, and hungry. Sophia grit her teeth and pedaled on.

They pulled up in the center of town, in front of the local post office. Swinging himself off his bicycle, Lieutenant Thorn walked inside to find a telephone while the rest of them milled around, stretching tired legs and giving dirty looks to gawking locals. Tony walked up to her, smiled and asked, "How're you holding up, Sophie?"

She chuckled and smiled back, "Been better. Been a lot worse."

"When've you ever been better?" He shot back sarcastically, "This has been a *wonderful* road trip."

Sophia pushed him away playfully, "Maybe for you, hanging out at the back all the time."

Tony pretended to be hurt, "And you never come back to hang out with me!"

Hargrave swung into their conversation, clapping Tony on the back good-naturedly, "That's the wrong approach, my boy, *you* need to be the one chasing after *her*." Tony gave him an aggrieved look and stalked off, and the older man went on, "I still don't know what you see in him."

She snorted and replied, "I've known him forever."

"You didn't answer the question." Hargrave chuckled, "You're not in Jade Falls any more, young lady."

"Well I intend to go back," she pouted.

"*I* intend to go back. *I* have a farm that's currently going to hell." The man shot back, poking her gently in the forehead, "*You* can expand your horizons a little."

Sophia rolled her eyes and brushed his hand away, "I still like him."

They were interrupted by Lieutenant Thorn's familiar whistle as he walked out of the post office. They gathered around and he told them, "I just talked to HQ. Apparently General MacMahon's already in town." He smiled, clearly at the thought of her, then grew serious and went on, "Bad news is Pine Harbor's been hit. That's the harbor we're seeing on fire." A murmur went around the platoon, and he pressed on quickly, "Good news is it was the Imperial Navy, not the Army. They think there's going to be a landing west of here, but we might have to deal with some Masks coming out of the delta at the same time. Nothing we haven't handled before." There were more than a few grim chuckles in the circle as he went on, "The 224th is to continue into town and act as a reserve for the division.

They're asking for reinforcements, but God knows if we'll get them. Miller!" Thorn looked at Third Squad's leader and continued, "Send two men back down the road to take the message to Battalion. They haven't heard from Colonel Espinay since we started off this morning, and he needs to know."

Corporal Miller nodded, "Yes, sir."

Thorn looked around the group, nodded and went on, "Well, we've got our orders. Mount up!"

Climbing back on their bikes, they pedaled out of town and back onto the open road as it twisted gently through the countryside. After a few minutes it slanted off to the right and crested a gentle rise, and Sophia sat up in the saddle to rest her legs as the road sloped downhill. She smiled despite herself as the view opened out in front of her, the Great Steel River gleaming through the pines blanketing the valley below. Beyond it the forest just seemed to roll on forever, and if she squinted into the hazy distance she thought, maybe, she could see the ocean.

She also had a much better view of the fire in the distance. It had looked bad coming in, even with what she now realized was a gentle ridge in the way. Now that she could properly see the *bottom* of it, her stomach clenched at the sight of the ink-black pillar of smoke and the ugly brown haze all around it blotting Pine Harbor itself from sight. That wasn't a normal fire. It was an inferno that was going to burn an ugly scar through that city for years to come. Sighing, Sophia put her head down and rode on, braking a little to stay in column with her friends as they dropped into the valley.

Trees quickly rose around them again, mixed with scrubby clearings and ponds. The place was probably terrifying at night, and it smelled increasingly like rot and worse. From where he had taken Hargrave's advice and come up behind her, Tony commented sarcastically, "Is this the right road?"

The forest was opening up around them again, the road continuing on along an embankment raised above the surrounding swamp as Sophia turned to call over her shoulder, "It's not the Lantern Woods, that's for..." She trailed off as something flashed in the corner of her eye, blinking and squinting as she turned and tried to focus in on it. *Where... there,* she thought as it flashed again, and again, across the scrub and through the sparse trees in the distance. It wasn't just one thing gleaming in the sunlight either, it looked like it was spread across a little bit of the forest. Whatever it was seemed familiar, like she'd seen it before. Sunlight gleaming from distant steel, undulating like the spines of a great beast.

Sophia's heart skipped a couple beats and she felt about a gallon of icewater rush down her back as she remembered *where exactly* she had seen that before. Dragoons on top of Fire Ridge, rank after endless rank of them drawing their swords as they came over that distant rise to crash down onto Prince Adrian's regiment. The afternoon sun had caught their blades the same way, rippling and dancing like a dragon made of light. Shaking her head quickly to get herself back into the present, she raised her voice and shouted, "*Contact!* Dragoons, right, far off in the trees!" Pointing as she rode, she went on, "They've got swords out and they're moving!"

They'd done this on foot more times than she could count. On bicycles was another matter, but they skidded to a halt, picked up their bikes and scrambled down the left side of the embankment in what was probably record time for any jaeger unit in the Royal Army. Lieutenant Thorn found her in seconds, pulling his binoculars out of their case as he asked, "Sophie! Where'd you see them?"

She pointed and he followed her finger as she explained, "They're in among the trees on the far side of the swamp."

After a second she saw his jaw set as he found them, "Those are dragoons alright... but what're they chasing?" He swept left a little and settled on something, "There it is."

"Sir?" She asked, working her rifle's bolt to chamber a round.

"There's another rider out there, a little ways left of the dragoons." Thorn said, holding his hand out for a second to judge the angle before raising his voice, "Platoon! Dragoons on horseback in the far woodline, riding fast right to left! Take care, one friendly on horseback about three fingers left! Range eight hundred! Five rounds independent, commence on my command! Machine guns hold fire!"

Well, *that* was old-fashioned. Just like training back in Jade Falls, and even then they hadn't done platoon firing very often. Her father had thought it was entirely useless, and as Sophia reached to adjust her rifle's sights and realized it was the first time she'd adjusted them in the entire war so far, she thought he was probably dead on accurate. Chuckling at the thought, she slid them to eight hundred, shouldered her rifle, slid up a little to get a sight picture on the distant, flashing swords with her bizarrely high sight picture and waited. A few seconds later Thorn ceremoniously put his binoculars to his eyes and called out, "Open fire!"

Sophia steadied her breathing and squeezed the trigger, her rifle bucking in her hands as it fired, the rest of the platoon joining her in a long, ragged volley. She worked the bolt and fired one, two, three, four more times at the distant, swirling flashes, then flipped on the safety and pushed it forward off her shoulder and onto the soft grass of the embankment. Looking over at the lieutenant, she asked, "Any luck, sir?"

Thorn chuckled, "A little." Raising his voice again, he called out, "Cease fire! Dragoons have scattered and are withdrawing!" Sophia ran her sights back to their normal setting as he went on, "Friendly is continuing north! Miss Rose," he went on a little more quietly given that he was kneeling next to her, "Take your guys and go find whoever that is, then proceed to Pine Harbor. They probably know something General MacMahon would like to know." He raised his voice again, "Second and Third Squads, on me! We're going after those dragoons!"

At this, Sophia shouted, "Hey, First Squad! Top up and get back on your bikes! We're going after that rider!" Her friends quickly made their way over as the rest of the platoon sorted themselves out, Thorn calling for a couple men to stay behind to guard the equipment while the others started fanning out into the marsh. Pulling some loose rounds out of a pocket, Sophia quickly reloaded her rifle's magazine and slung the weapon over her back as she retrieved her bicycle. She swung herself into the saddle, waved for the squad to head out and they were off down the road, quickly leaving the rest of the platoon behind.

Tony quickly caught up with her and asked, "Got any idea where the hell this person's gotten off to?"

"Further this way, I guess." Sophia replied, twisting in her seat to get a look at the squad. They were bunched up way too close together, and she waved for them to open up as she went on curtly, "Now get back in line and spread out, for all we know there's more dragoons out here."

Her, well, she guessed he was her boyfriend now opened his mouth, thought better of whatever he was going to say, and then closed it. He finally replied, "Sure thing, Sophie." Squeezing on his brakes, he dropped back and into line instantly. Hoping he wouldn't sulk later, Sophia snorted and pedaled on. She had much more important things to worry about. Such as, she thought as she scanned the marshy forest around them, where exactly in the world this person would head for and how quickly once they realized they weren't being chased any more. After taking a couple moments to think about it, she figured they would probably slow down, keep heading north through the forest for a while and then turn west towards the road.

Which meant they were going the right way. The forest thickened ahead as the road pitched up and out of the swamp, and she spied what looked like a logging track cutting away from the main road to the right.

Raising a hand to halt the squad, Sophia gestured for them to drop their bikes just inside the wood and squeezed on the brakes herself. A moment later her bike was safely tucked behind a tree's roots, and she unslung her rifle, looked around to make sure the rest of her friends had made it in with her and waved for them to move forward alongside the road. Apparently they were back to being quiet now, she thought with a soft snort.

They padded forward through a deep carpet of pine needles for a few minutes, their footsteps crackling softly in the suddenly-silent woods. Nothing so far... the rider might have doubled back. Or they might not be in far enough. Maybe their rider was skittish, keeping to the deepest forest they could find. There was one thing she could do to help things, though. Holding up a hand to halt the squad, Sophia sank to one knee, the needles tickling the bare skin above her puttee as she sank into the ground. Taking off her cap and setting it down, she rested her rifle's butt against the earth, closed her eyes and *listened*.

She felt her breath, slow and even in her lungs, the elastic of her bra tugging slightly on her skin as her chest rose and fell. She smelled the trees, pine needles and slow-running sap and an unpleasant rotting undertone from the swamp nearby. The wind sifted through the forest, stirring the tops of the trees even though she didn't feel a wisp of it herself. A mosquito buzzed nearby, drawn to her scent. And... *there*. In the distance, off to their left a little, something heavy stamped at the ground. Deer were light on their feet. That was a *horse*. Pointing at it for the squad's benefit, Sophia settled her hat back on her head and waved them forward again. Either her guess had been dead on or, she thought grimly, they had a bigger dragoon problem than they'd thought.

Gunfire popped faintly off to their right as they went along, then again and again. Just rifles, Royal ones. Probably Thorn trying to see if anyone was dumb enough to shoot back at them, but he was making her life more difficult if she was ever going to find this person. Gritting her teeth, she glanced back and waved the squad onwards insistently. They closed up quickly, Hargrave shooing a couple of the others onwards as she turned to stalk forward again, angling a little further off to the left.

The firing died down as they pushed onwards, and after they'd gone a hundred meters or so Sophia saw something dark move through the trees in the distance, even further off to her left. Whoever it was, they were moving quickly, leading their horse through the underbrush. If she didn't hurry she'd lose them. She pumped her fist in the air to signal the squad to hurry and picked up the pace, rushing through the woods after the fleeting figure.

Whoever it was had to fight to get their horse through the underbush, slowing them down enough to let them close. After they'd about halved the distance Sophia saw the figure narrow a little as they turned, glimpsing a pale face as the person looked over their shoulder and froze. Waving for the squad to take cover, Sophia dodged behind a tree that looked sturdy enough to stop bullets and shouted, "*Royal Army!* Put your hands up and walk towards me!"

The figure took a step back, looked around quickly and shouted back, voice unmistakably high and female, "I don't believe you! Show yourself!"

"Fine!" Sophia stepped out of her cover, keeping her rifle up warily, "Do I *look* Imperial to you? Now get over here! And keep your hands up!"

The woman seemed to be... *shaking* as she approached, slowly raising her hands as she came along, awkwardly leading her horse forward with the reins in one of them. Sophia noticed the woman was a few inches shorter than her, with what looked like light hair flowing out over her shoulders from under a broad-brimmed riding hat. The rest of her clothing was excessively practical, a well-worn shirt, dust-caked riding breeches and what looked to have once been a pair of expensive riding boots, now practically worn through. She looked about like they had coming out of the mountains. Her voice cracked a little as she managed, "I... I'm Royal Army. I don't know the password."

"That's fine. Okay, stop right there." Sophia replied curtly as the woman got within a few feet, then turned and looked at where her friends were crouched behind trees and roots nearby, "Hargrave, get her horse. Search the saddlebags. I'll search her, for all we know she's a Pathfinder at this point. Tony, cover us."

Sophia slung her rifle as Hargrave came forward, taking the wild-eyed animal's reins and leading it off. She heard him petting it and cooing calmingly as he went. The woman volunteered helpfully as she stepped forward herself, "I've got a money belt on, it has all my things in it."

"Yeah," Sophia replied as she knelt and started patting the woman down. She tensed and shifted uncomfortably at being touched, obviously uncomfortable, but bore up stoically. Now that Sophia had a good look at her, she didn't seem to be all that much older than herself. She certainly didn't sound it. True to the girl's word, Sophia didn't find anything besides a jackknife in the girl's pocket and a heavy, flat money belt wrapped tightly around her stomach. The girl *shivered* as she pulled up her shirt to undo it, and Sophia asked worriedly, "Are you okay, miss?"

The girl shook her head, "I... I just don't like being touched, I'm sorry. Go ahead."

"Sure..." Pulling the heavy canvas belt off her, damp with the girl's sweat, Sophia unzipped it and looked inside. Money, a *lot* of money actually, a small mirror, some matches and what looked like a box of tinder, some strips of cloth that she guessed were makeshift bandages, and, down at the bottom, a Royal Army identification card. Pulling it out, she squinted in the dim light and read it, then quickly looked up and compared the pictures. The girl looked like she'd been dragged through hell by her ankles since it was taken, but she was definitely the same person. Even so, Sophia asked, "Just to make sure, ma'am, what's your name?"

"Vanessa Gable," the girl started, "Fourteenth Hussars, Ninth Cavalry Division. And I really, *really* need to speak to your commander, immediately."

Just then a machine gun popped to life off to their right, screaming high and shrill in the distance. Imperial. A moment later it was joined by another, and another, as a whole curtain of gunfire unfolded in the distance and lower, deeper Royal guns snarled back. Clearly Lieutenant Thorn had found their dragoons. And just as clearly, they had something more important to do than going to help him. Handing Lieutenant Gable her identification back, Sophia said, "Good, because that's exactly where we're taking you. Now come on." She turned to head back, the lieutenant quickly following her as she snorted, "We're *with* Ninth Division, by the way."

"Really?" The girl asked incredulously, "You don't look like hussars."

Sophia chuckled, "Long story. And you don't either."

The lieutenant actually laughed, a little hysterically, as though an enormous weight had just come off her shoulders. Finally she managed, "Yeah. Long story."

"Good." Sophia shot back, "You can tell us on the way. Now come on."

Chapter 22

Lady and Knight

The light outside was blood-red despite the early hour, and the air smelled like tar even with the windows closed. Turning on the lights as he walked in ahead of her, General Decker started apologetically, "Thank you for coming up, milady." Turning, he half-smiled and went on jokingly, "I was worried about whether I'd ever be able to get you out of there!"

Patricia chuckled, "I thought you'd gone down to the harbor."

Decker patted at the air dismissively, "No, no. Not a lot I could do down there right now even if I wanted to." He gestured her towards a set of chairs in the corner of the room, clearly meant for less formal meetings, "Not to mention the Commodore's taken the fleet out. What's left of it anyways."

Pausing, Patricia looked over at him sharply, "He has? That's news to me."

"Really?" Decker sighed and sat down heavily, his bulk noticeably flattening the armchair's cushions, "I saw them heading out from the roof. I'm surprised they didn't call in."

Unbuckling her sword, she sat down herself and replied, "Not a word downstairs."

"Figures. I'll call down and tell them after we're done here." He gave her a hopeful look, "Heard anything new on your side, milady? They already told me about that battle going on south of here, one of your units, the two-twenty-fourth or some such?"

Patricia grimaced, "They're holding on to the road south to Kelsbruck, although I don't think the Imperials have really tried to hit them yet. Assuming Schraeder's put the spurs in they should be getting support around now." Decker gave her a questioning look and she explained, "He's one of my commanders. Any word on landings up the coast?"

The big general shook his head, "No, no, nothing that I've heard." He cleared his throat and pulled a sheet of paper out of his cuffs, unfolding it as he went on, "I actually asked you up here because I wanted you to take a look at this."

He handed it over, and she raised an eyebrow as she read it, "A proclamation?" It read:

CITIZENS OF PINE HARBOR!

The enemy is advancing! They have already struck from the air and sea, and their army is expected to bring our town under siege in the coming days.

These times demand the utmost fortitude of all soldiers

and civilians alike. We will hold the fortress of Pine Harbor until relieved by the Royal Army. We will fight to the last man, the last bullet, and should the enemy choose not to attack, the last pound of flour.

In so doing we will deny the mouth of the Great Steel River to the enemy's shipping and prevent them from resupplying their armies by sea. This is a monumental task and much is expected of you.

Martial law is in force, effective immediately. All civilians are to register with the garrison authorities.

Do not believe or spread rumors. We will prevail.

By order of Brigadier General Peter Decker, Military Governor.

GOD SAVE THE KING

Finishing the document, she set it down in her lap and leaned back in the chair, "Stirring stuff, but... well..."

"Why now?" Decker chuckled, "I pulled out the old siege proclamation earlier. If I had that pasted up now people would riot."

"That bad, huh? Still." Patricia gave him a level look, "I can't help but think you've got better things to do right now. They're asking after you downstairs."

The fat general shrugged, "Maybe. I'm a fortress commander, milady. I didn't get this job for being quick on my feet." He smiled sadly, "Honestly, I came here to *retire*. My wife found a nice little villa down the coast from here that I've been trying to get ahold of. And now all *this* falls in on my head."

"You didn't want to face it?" She asked.

"No, milady." He shook his head, "Not one bit. Any..." He trailed off as they heard footsteps in the corridor outside, a man's voice sounding like he was protesting something, then a woman's voice in reply. Another woman added something in a familiar, quiet tone, and Patricia felt a dull twinge of recognition in the back of her head as someone knocked on the door, heavy but nervous. She'd heard that kind of knock before many times and done it herself more than a few. A young soldier with important information to give to the general, scared to death about interrupting him in his appointment. Or her, she supposed.

Handing the proclamation back to Decker quickly, Patricia called out, "Come in!"

The soldier outside turned the doorknob cautiously, the old fitting rattling as it turned and the door creaked open. Sophia Rose walked in, wearing a gray uniform jacket with a pair of fatigue shorts barely peeking out beneath the tunic's skirts, an order of dress she was pretty sure was entirely out of regulation and which made an annoying amount of sense for a bicycle soldier. And, she noted with a twinge of jealousy, now that the girl was apparently being *fed* properly she was really filling out. Glancing over at Decker, she could see that Sophia clearly had *his* full attention. The girl was saying, "Milady, I've got someone here...."

Patricia looked back as the other woman followed Sophia in, and the look on her face must have made the poor girl trail off. She must have looked like she'd seen a ghost. Well, Vanessa Gable may as well have been. Her old aide, who she'd sent to her doom back at Fire Ridge, who she'd last heard had been taken prisoner when her platoon was wiped out minutes after she'd arrived at the front, looked at her and smiled nervously. She looked like she'd ridden the whole way back and then crawled through the swamp for good measure. Vanessa was opening her mouth to say something when Patricia leapt out of her chair and threw her arms around her, dirt be damned, and for once she didn't stiffen at her touch. After a few long seconds, Patricia unwrapped herself and demanded, "What happened? I thought you were taken prisoner!" She snorted angrily, "I wrote you a letter you know, I thought it was rather rude you didn't reply."

Vanessa smiled awkwardly, "Ah... I escaped, milady. And, uh, sorry about that."

"Don't be!" Patricia shot back, "Not your fault. Now how did you...?"

The girl shook her head quickly and changed the subject, "It's a really long story, milady. But, um, I know the Empire's not going to try to land up the coast." Patricia's eyes widened as Vanessa pressed on, "I saw a lot of stuff getting across the swamp, and I put it all together talking to Miss Rose here," she nodded politely at a very surprised-looking Sophia before going on, "After she picked me up. Saved me from some dragoons, actually."

Taking a step back, Patricia looked over at Sophia, realizing as she did that she'd only ever talked to the girl from horseback before. She was a tall woman, and Sophia was easily taller and heavier-set than her. No wonder she was doing fine in the infantry. Smiling, she nodded at the girl, "Good job." Sophia turned red, and Patricia turned back to her old aide, "Now what did you see?"

Decker had managed to climb to his feet, and chimed in, "Yes, yes! Please, young lady, what do you have for us?"

Swallowing hard, Vanessa looked between them nervously. Then, uncharacteristically, she took a deep breath and settled herself. Whatever she'd been doing since the battle, she seemed to be immensely more comfortable in her own skin now. Two months ago she would have fallen all over herself trying to blurt it out. Finally, the lieutenant looked up at them and started, "I had to make my way across the swamp to get over here. I thought there wouldn't be many Imperials, that's why I came so far north, but the whole area's *crawling* with them. I had to hide during the day and pick my way across at night." She snorted, "Not easy with a horse."

General Decker cut back in, "We know the swamp's full of Masks, dear, they're attacking out of it right now. How do you know they're not *landing?*"

Vanessa's eyes narrowed in annoyance as she glanced over at him, "I saw their landing craft. Hundreds of them. They've been running them upriver at night and hiding them... all over the place, really." She looked back at her and went on before Decker could wind up again, "The whole swamp's full of signals, milady. Signs, hooded lights at night. You'd never see a thing from the air."

Patricia reached up and pinched the bridge of her nose as she thought. The swamp wasn't just a morass, it was a *river delta.* Just because ships couldn't navigate the small channels didn't mean that shallow-draft landing craft couldn't. And they'd had weeks to infiltrate in their Pathfinders, chart the routes and verify them as their regular troops arrived. Slade Anjanou was a magician, sailing empty assault ships by to threaten a landing up the coast while they'd already quietly unloaded the means to get his army straight through the delta. Not to mention there was nothing the Navy would like to attack quite so much as an Imperial landing operation down the coast. Now the man's covering force was already across and the Cavalry Corps that could have *maybe* given him some trouble was spread out watching a hundred miles of perfectly safe coastline.

The lady general looked at her watch for a second. Her troops were already in combat. That Imperial covering force, if that's what it actually was and not the first wave, was already attacking, probably expanding the bridgehead to give the first wave room to maneuver. If she was in Slade's shoes she would move the first wave across during the night, walk the troops into position and attack properly at dawn. Which meant Vanessa had given them about twelve hours of warning, maybe a little more.

Decker was arguing with the girl, saying that what she was saying was impossible. Something about the enemy ferrying troops out to sea instead. Glaring over at the fat general, she snapped, "It's *not* impossible, Decker. Far from it. They did ten times more at Fire Ridge, and we never saw it coming." Taken aback, the man shut his mouth angrily and she went on, "Miss Gable here just gave us our answer. I need to call headquarters, and then I need to get back to my division. I'd suggest you get that proclamation printed, you're going to be under siege this time tomorrow."

General Decker gave her a long, flat look, then sighed and nodded, "Very well, milady. Your train should be heading back south in about an hour, if you care to take that way out."

"Call the station and make sure they don't leave without us." She told him, then glanced at Vanessa, standing there in ragged, mud-caked civilian clothes, "And... I don't suppose you have a supply room here? She needs a uniform."

"Certainly. First floor on the right as you come down the stairs." Decker replied.

Patricia nodded, "Good." She looked over at Sophia, who seemed to be taking this whole exchange calmly, "Miss Rose, take Lieutenant Gable down to supply, get her a uniform and equipment, and meet me at this building's main entrance, the southern one, at seventeen hundred hours. How many men do you have with you?"

"Just my squad, milady..." Sophia replied.

Patricia cut her off before she could give an exact number, "Good. You'll take the train with us and link back up with your battalion at the next station south. They're falling back to defend there as we speak."

"Will do, milady." Sophia nodded, then looked at her old aide, "Come on, milady, let's go find supply."

It occurred to her suddenly that Vanessa had always been cagey about her family. Now she was apparently volunteering the information. The girl had grown, Patricia thought as she watched the two of them turn and leave. Shaking her head, she turned back to Decker and held out her hand, "General, I think this is where we part ways."

He took it. His hand was as clammy as ever, but at least he squeezed reassuringly and smiled, "I wish I could say it's been a pleasure, milady." He let go and chuckled, "If I'd known there were so many lookers like those two joining the Army just now, I wouldn't have put in my retirement papers."

Patricia laughed and shot back, "What about me, then?"

"According to your chief of staff, you're taken these days." Decker smirked.

"Touché." Patricia snorted and turned to leave, "Anyways, general.

Good luck with the siege."

"Good luck with the war, milady." Decker replied, "I suspect you'll need it more than me."

* * *

Patricia raised an eyebrow at her former aide as the train slowly pulled out of the station and accelerated down the tracks out of Pine Harbor, "How in the world did you get a new uniform, a shower *and* through the mess hall in the time I gave you?"

Vanessa chuckled and glanced over at where Sophia Rose was making faces at some grubby children further down the car. Keen to reduce the number of mouths he'd have to feed in the coming weeks, Decker had packed what he expected to be the last train south with refugees and more than a few had found their way into their car. The infantrymen had at least kept a space clear for them to talk. Finally, the girl replied, "They're... *efficient* when they get the chance to enjoy something."

Patricia laughed, "I'll say! God, she's just like her father."

"You, ah... know Miss Rose, milady?" Vanessa asked, raising her eyebrows questioningly.

"In a sense." Patricia went on, "She was born at the Dragon's Jaw when I was there. I just about fell off my horse when she turned up again and realized who I was looking at. You know her regiment walked off Fire Ridge through the Dragonspines?" The girl shook her head and she went on, "I was there when we pulled them out of the woods, actually. God, they looked like *hell*... which brings me around to how exactly *you* got out of there, Vanessa. Last I heard you'd been captured." Patricia finished, giving her old aide a serious look.

"Well, milady, ah..." Vanessa seemed to collect her thoughts for a moment, then went on, "Most of my girls... the ones that weren't, well..." *Dead* went unspoken as she went on, "They were wounded, some pretty bad. They just put me in with them going back to their aid station to get checked out, and then on the next truck convoy going north." She chuckled nervously, "Well, they stopped in a town after dark to refuel and, uh, they didn't really keep a guard on me so I managed to slip away. They pulled out right afterwards, I don't even think they realized I was gone."

Patricia raised her eyebrows in appreciation, "Good job."

Vanessa went on, "Some locals hid me for a couple days and then helped me get out of town, and I've been working my way west since. The Empire's got rewards up for fugitives but I didn't have too many close calls." She smiled, "Count Gettinger actually put me up on his estate for a week and gave me a horse."

"Old Conrad?" Patricia asked, then snorted, "I can see him doing that. Probably too stubborn to leave."

The girl shook her head, "*I* had to eventually. If I'd had to hear him go off again about how incompetent and useless the Army was I'd have lost my mind. Anyways," she went on, smiling, "Here I am, milady."

"Which brings us to what exactly I'm going to *do* with you." Patricia sighed and looked out the window at the countryside passing by. It was deceptively peaceful, a sunny late-summer afternoon just starting to shade into fall. It didn't look like a war zone, but battlefields rarely did. Maybe the Marchlands front after they'd traded artillery fire across it with the Empire for a year. Turning back to the girl, she went on, "I'd love to take you back as my aide, but I've already got a new one and she's working out."

Vanessa tried and failed to conceal her disappointment, then ventured, "Milady, if I may I'd... prefer not to go back to the regiment."

Patricia smirked, "What, don't want to subject your life and career to Mina Bennett's tender mercies again?"

"Ah... no, milady." Vanessa replied, as bluntly as she'd ever heard her.

"Good, because I wasn't planning on it. I guess I could send you over to the Twentieth, Holly could probably use another girl in her troop to talk to..." Patricia trailed off as she saw Vanessa's eyes shift, and she turned to see their little group of jaegers laughing at some private joke. They noticed her look and quickly quieted down, and Patricia snorted and waved for them to carry on as she turned back to Vanessa, venturing, "Although given that you had to do something crazy to escape from the Empire, maybe the Two Twenty-Fourth would be a better fit. That whole unit would know what you've been through."

Vanessa brightened instantly. *Bingo*, she thought as the girl asked, "Really, milady?"

"Yeah. You should talk to Colonel Espinay sometime, his story's as crazy as yours." She gave Vanessa a serious look, "I'll take care of your horse. I'm assuming you know how to ride a bike?"

"Of course, milady." Vanessa replied.

"Good." Twisting in her seat, Patricia called out, "Miss Rose!"

Sophia hopped up instantly and hurried over, "Yes, milady?"

"Last time I sent this girl down to the line she lasted fifteen minutes before she got herself captured." Vanessa turned red, and Patricia chuckled and went on, "I know you're short on officers, so can you *please* keep her out of trouble? I happen to like this one."

Sophia smiled, "Sure thing, milady."

"Good, because I think we're coming up on our stop." Right on cue, she felt the subtle force as the brakes came on to slow the train into the next station. Standing, she went on, "Now let's go see how much of a mess we're in."

The train squealed to a halt and they stepped out onto the platform, the cool air fouled with the stench of antiseptics as the doors opened. It was crowded with wounded men laid out on the concrete, lancers and infantrymen alike. She heard Vanessa gasp and Sophia mutter a curse behind her as the men on the platform, the ones she'd called there to meet her that weren't laid out flat on the ground, saluted. She played her eyes over them as she returned the gesture. Colonel Schraeder of the 20th Lancers, looking as grim as she'd ever seen him. Colonel Espinay of the 224th Infantry Battalion, a good head shorter than her and incongruously cheerful amid the carnage. And his sergeant major, John Rose, brightening immediately at the sight of his daughter behind her.

Stepping out of the train, she greeted them, "Good to see you, gentlemen..." She looked across the platform with its carpet of bloodied men and hovering medics for effect, then went on grimly, "I'd have told you we're going to get hit by the enemy's main effort tonight, but it looks like they're already pushing."

"Yes, milady." Schraeder spoke first, "They've already got rocket artillery emplaced on this side of the river, and they're using it."

Espinay chuckled, "It's really quite sticky. We've managed to... extricate ourselves and set back up around the station, but we probably need to start retreating after sunset."

Patricia nodded, "Sounds reasonable. By the way, Colonel Espinay..." The main raised his bushy, blonde eyebrows, and she went on, "It's my understanding you're short on officers. If you'll have her, I'll give you Lieutenant Gable here."

"Oho!" The short colonel chortled, nudging his sergeant major, "Certainly! John, we're short in Charlie, aren't we?"

"Yes, Josh needed to move up." John Rose replied, "If we give her his old platoon she'd fit right in, they're already used to Sophia."

Patricia glanced over her shoulder at Vanessa, "Well, there you go. Stay safe out there."

"You too, milady. I'll see you." Vanessa replied as she walked forward, John Rose beckoning for her and his daughter's squad to follow him as he turned and started heading off the platform. The infantry quickly threaded their way past her and through the tangle of wounded men despite their awkward bicycles, hurrying after their sergeant major as he disappeared from view.

Turning back to the two colonels, Patricia gave them her best fake-confident smile and said, "Alright, let's go find someplace where we can figure out how not to lose the war tonight."

Even Schraeder snickered.

Chapter 23
Starting Line

The sky was darkening overhead, the moons strung out across the sky like a string of brilliant pearls, when Sophia heard a door open in the house behind them and then softly shut, footsteps stirring the grass towards them. Turning over onto her back, she saw two dark figures emerge from the shadows of the town under the blood-red sunset, one of them tall and thin, unmistakably Lieutenant Thorn. The other was a good head shorter than him and even more slender, a woman. Lieutenant Gable, their newly-adopted platoon leader. If half the stuff she'd told her on the way up to Pine Harbor had been true, she would have been right at home with them walking off Fire Ridge. She waved, and the two officers adjusted course towards her.

Lieutenant Thorn hopped down into the ditch they had scraped fighting positions out of, followed a moment later by Gable as she gingerly stepped into the long, wet grass lining the bottom. Sophia got the feeling she didn't want to get her feet wet if she didn't have to. Crouching down next to her, Thorn asked, "How's it going, Sophia?"

She shrugged and jerked her chin off over her shoulder at the road heading east out of town, down towards the river, "No dragoons so far, sir."

"I'll take what I can get... the colonel thinks they might wait until morning at this rate." Thorn mused as Lieutenant Gable finally satisfied herself that she wouldn't break her ankle in any unseen gopher holes and knelt on her other side. He changed the subject, "How're the guys?"

Sophia looked past him at where Tony was huddled up further down the trench, his head a dark silhouette against the purpling sky behind the spindly shape of a machine gun. Smiling to herself, she turned back to Thorn and replied, "Good as ever, sir. Sorry we missed the fight earlier."

Thorn snorted, "I'm not going to lie, we could have used you, but..." He glanced over at Gable warmly, "I'm not going to complain. Lady Mac-Mahon told me she was *very* pleased."

Sophia smiled, "Thanks sir. What brings you two out here?"

He chuckled, "I didn't want Vanessa getting lost trying to find you." Gable glared at him half-heartedly, which he ignored, "And I wanted to walk the line anyways. We're..." He trailed off a heavy artillery shell thudded in the distance, one of the heavy fortress guns thrashing at the swamp near the river. They'd been drizzling shells into what they thought was the enemy's lodgment all day, probably annoying them more than anything else. Clearing his throat, he went on, "Anyways, it could get bad tonight."

"I've got you, sir." Sophia looked over at where Gable was kneeling pensively beside her, "You doing alright, milady?"

It occurred to her that Lieutenant Gable wasn't that much older than she was as the girl quickly looked back at her, eyes widening for a moment in the darkness, "Yeah..." She shook her head slowly and snorted, "Last time I took over a platoon things went bad in a hurry."

"Don't worry, milady." Sophia patted her on the thigh reassuringly, "Our luck is as bad as yours."

Gable tried to give her a stern look, "You're not helping."

Thorn was opening his mouth to say something when someone called out from towards the town, "Sir! Sir! We need you back here!"

Thorn looked up, clearly annoyed as he called back, "What's going on?"

A soldier she vaguely recognized rushed up out of the gathering gloom, breathing hard, "We just got a call from the OP... they're seeing enemy troops moving into the open. And they're saying they hear engines."

Their commander raised an eyebrow, then climbed to his feet heavily, "I really hope that isn't what I think it is. Alright, I'll leave you two here." He looked between them, nodded, and hurried off after the man back into town.

Lieutenant Gable watched him leave, then eased herself down into the grass next to her with a visible shiver. "Just my luck," she muttered.

Sophia flipped back over and patted her on the shoulder reassuringly. The girl stiffened for a moment, then relaxed. Easing back up into her scrape, Sophia called out, "Look alive, guys! We might have company here quick."

"Sure thing!" Someone called back cheerily. It sounded like Edward.

Shining faintly in the moonlight, the road ran up a faint rise for a few hundred meters as it ran east away from the town and its train station, then dipped down and out of sight towards the river. The sky beyond it was almost black, stars starting to prick through the darkness as the sunset faded behind them. Then... *there*, she saw it. A tiny figure cresting the rise through the trees lining the road, pedaling hard on a bicycle. A moment later another figure rose into view behind it, hunched low over the handlebars. Pointing, she called out to her companion, "*There*, milady. Looks like the OP coming back in."

Lieutenant Gable fished in her harness for a moment behind her, probably producing her binoculars. A moment later she said, "Looks like it... where do you guys have the field telephone?"

Sophia pointed off down the ditch, "Should be with Sergeant Cross, milady. He's down at the right side of the squad, past Hargrave." She looked over her shoulder to see Gable giving her a nervous look, and she snorted and went on, "Old guy, can't miss him. Sixth man down the ditch from here, he'll show you where Cross is."

Their new lieutenant nodded and moved off down the line, footsteps soft in the long grass. Sophia settled down behind her rifle to wait, watching the two cyclists slowly approach down the road. Thorn was... well, he was comfortable. She'd known him for years, she'd gone through hell with him by now, she trusted him with her life, hell, she'd saved *his* before. Gritting her teeth as the thought of that creepy, long-haired bastard June Anjanou flickered across her mind unbidden, she deliberately turned her mind to Lieutenant Gable. The girl was... well, she was certainly interesting. It was almost like she was quiet and talkative at the same time, not to mention that now she was back at the front her nerves were clearly getting to her. She'd told her what had happened to her last platoon on the ride up to Pine Harbor, and honestly she didn't blame her for it.

Crickets chirped faintly, hidden in the grass. Without the war it would have been a wonderful night, with the cool breeze sifting in from the ocean as the sunset faded. Footsteps sounding like Gable's soft tread swished through the grass behind her as the two cyclists made it back, picking their bikes up to make their way around the trees they had dropped across the road as it ran into the town. A moment later she heard the lieutenant's voice, and the two men replying faintly. Most of it was too faint to make out until Gable replied, her voice high and nervous even with the distance, "Tanks? You're *positive?*"

Sophia felt an icy finger work its way down her back at the words. *Tanks.* Just when they thought it couldn't get worse. When they had been waiting to go to the front back at Wolf Rock, she and Tony had gotten a few hours off and decided to go gawk at the fortress airfield for lack of anything better to do. Their route had taken them past the rail marshalling yard, where the sound of roaring engines and clattering tracks had drawn them to watch something entirely different. They had been loading tanks for transport to the front that day, hulking metal monsters slowly crawling up onto railcars under a shroud of engine smoke, every one of them bristling with weapons and armored to smash through the strongest defenses. She instinctively patted her leftmost ammunition pouch where she still had a clip of armor-piercing ammunition tucked away, for all the good that would do. She'd seen the penetration tables and they weren't confidence-inspiring.

More comforting was the long, spindly shape she could see rising out of the grass as she looked to her left. The 224th had finally managed to reform a weapons company, and they had sent down an antitank squad to help out. Their heavy rifles fired hardened steel bullets the size of her thumb and were large enough they needed a tripod mount like a heavy machine gun. She'd talked to the gunners earlier as they had set up and they seemed pretty confident, but even so... well, they only had *three* of the things across the company's line. God only knew what was coming at them.

Footsteps in the grass behind her broke her out of her thoughts, and Sophia turned over to see Lieutenant Gable approaching, jaw set and worry written over her face. Hoping she'd overheard wrong, she asked, "Ah, milady... did I hear you say something about *tanks?*"

Gable smiled grimly as she knelt next to her, "Yes, I did." Fishing her binoculars out of her harness, she went on, "They said they saw eight or nine of them. They weren't sure, but I am from what they said..." Trailing off, she glanced down at her, "You *do* know what an Imperial tank looks like, right?"

Sophia thought for a moment, "Uh... no."

Lieutenant Gable looked at her blankly for a moment, then sighed heavily, "I'm assuming you've seen a *Royal* tank at some point?"

"Yeah." She replied.

"Okay, so they're about half the size. There's a larger version with a cannon and a smaller one with I *think* an antitank rifle of some kind in the turret." She explained quickly as she raised her binoculars to her eyes, "I saw a few of them on my way out... you've got good eyes, right?"

Sophia raised an eyebrow, "At least Thorn thinks so, milady."

"Can you make anything out up there?" Gable handed her the binoculars with a grimace, "I can barely tell where the ground ends and the sky begins in this soup."

Taking them, Sophia got up onto her knees and peered out at the distant rise. The lieutenant had been right. In the fading twilight the dark-purple sky to the east blended almost perfectly into the murky brown ground. She could barely tell where one ended and the other began. "I'm not having a lot of luck myself," she started as she scanned what she thought was the horizon, "But... huh." She settled the binoculars onto what looked like a *lump* in the distant rise, just a sort of little thing bulging into the dark skyline. Had that been there before? It wasn't like there weren't bushes and trees out there. Mostly to herself, she said, "What *is* that?"

"Got something?" Gable asked behind her, a nervous warble in her voice.

"Maybe..." Sophia moved the binoculars on a little, squinting instinctively as shapes swam out of the darkness at her. Then... *there.* Another little bump in the horizon, just like the first. And, as she watched, a third one peeked up not far from it. Swallowing hard and trying to ignore the icy fingers stroking her heart, she managed, "I've got, I don't know, *things* sticking up over the rise. Just saw one come up. I've seen three so far."

"How large are they?" The lieutenant demanded.

Oh come on, Sophia thought exasperatedly, *would you like me to read their nametags while you're at it?* Still, she bit her lip and gamely guessed at the mil scale in the binoculars. It was seven or eight hundred meters to the rise, and whatever those things were, they were one or two-mil specks along the skyline. One mil was one meter at a kilometer. Doing the math quickly in her head, she ventured, "Three or four feet wide, maybe?"

Lieutenant Gable took a long, deep breath behind her. Sophia was about to ask her what was going on when she finally said, "Those are turrets. They're scoping out the town right now."

Hanging her the binoculars back, Sophia asked, "What's the plan, milady?"

"Same as Thorn told you earlier, I assume. We hit them once and pull back. We've got to keep our distance if we're going to last long." Gable thought for a moment, then went on, "We've got a line to the artillery. I'll see if they can put some flares up so we can at least see what we're shooting at."

Gable started to stand, and Sophia reached out quickly, got a hand around her harness' shoulder-strap and yanked her back down beside her. The lieutenant squawked, but Sophia interrupted her, "Milady, we've got the sunset behind us. They can probably see *us* just fine. Keep down."

"I... good catch, sorry." Gable shook her head and snorted, muttering as she rolled into the ditch and crawled back towards their field telephone, "Come on, Vanessa, get it together. You've got this."

Tony called out to her as the lieutenant passed him, "Did I hear that right, Sophie? Tanks?"

"Yeah, pass it down the line. Three so far, just sticking their turrets out over the hill." Rolling over, she called out to the antitank gunners, "You guys hear that?"

"Yeah!" Someone called back, "We engaging now? I can't see a thing."

"Hold fire, Lieutenant Gable's trying to get us some star shells. She'll call it." Sophia replied.

The man gave her a thumbs-up, and she settled back down behind her rifle to wait. Barely a minute later she heard the lieutenant's voice call out in the darkness, "Platoon! Enemy front, eight hundred meters, tanks on the rise! Stand by for flares, then engage on my command! Be prepared to fall back by squad!"

Well at least she seemed to know what she was doing. Feeling for her sights in the darkness, Sophia clicked them up to what she thought was eight hundred meters and waited, feeling her heart beat faster and faster as she lay there, the long, wet grass slick against her bare thighs. Then... *there*. A cannon's thud in the distance, and a faint flash in the night sky as a flare shell popped high overhead. Moments later a flare blazed to life, washing the battlefield with ghostly, flickering light. For a moment she looked across the distant rise, squinting as she tried to pick out something, anything. And then... *there*. And *there*. And *there*. Her skin *crawled* as she saw the dark dots speckling the distant fields under the rise, blinking in and out of sight as Imperial soldiers rose out of the fields to rush forward and drop back down into concealment. Behind them the tanks' turrets gleamed faintly in the false moonlight like a string of tiny beads fringing the curtain of the hill, light dancing within them as fireflies rose in the distance.

Those are bullets, Sophie, she thought absently as she quickly shoved herself back into her scrape. A moment later something small and angry slapped into the ground nearby, a green tracer snapping overhead a moment later. She heard a window shatter as bullets chewed into the building behind her, then a thud and someone cursing loudly. She had already raised her rifle to her shoulder and flicked of the safety when she heard Gable shouting, "Open fi-"

The rest of her words were blotted out as the platoon opened fire, a wall of noise crashing in on her as Sophia tightened her finger on her own trigger. Her rifle bucked and Tony unrolled a long burst on his machine gun as she worked the bolt, the muzzle flash stabbing at the corner of her eye. More green tracers rose out of the fields in front of them as they fired, the air filling with hissing metal and death. And then something *big* flashed out of the fields, huge green orbs blazing towards them like a unholy meteors. A couple thundered overhead and exploded back in the town, loud enough she could hear it even over the gunfire. A moment later their antitank gun roared in response, a massive violet flare skimming over the fields to whip over one of the distant tanks.

That *really* got the enemy's attention. More of the green meteors whistled in, slapping down all around them and spraying her with dirt. Their gun fired again and again, joined after a moment by the other two antitank guns dug in with the other platoons. A violet tracer that looked about the size of a baseball caromed off one of the tanks' turrets, then another as their gunners found the range. God only knew if they were doing anything. Sophia worked her bolt and fired again and again as the hailstorm thickened overhead and the enemy's infantry pressed closer.

Someone grabbed the back of her harness, and she rolled over to find herself face-to-face with Lieutenant Gable. The girl shouted over the gunfire, "You're first! Get your squad out of here, we'll rally at the train station!"

"Got it!" Sophia shouted back. Gable rolled back into the ditch and crawled for the antitank gun, and she picked up her rifle and scrambled the other direction. Slapping Tony on the back as she reached him, she yelled, "We're falling back! Get back to the train station!"

Tony gave her a thumbs-up, grabbed his machine gun's carry handle and slid back into the ditch. If he followed it past the antitank gun crew it would curve around and he could get back into the shelter of the town's buildings without spending too much time exposed. She crawled on, found Edward and sent him on his way. Then Massey and Montour, the two men vanishing down the ditch behind her as she moved along. Kelly hefted his machine gun and made his way out, and then she found herself lying beside Hargrave. She shouted as she squirmed up next to him, "Time to go, old man!"

"Really?" He looked over at her and raised an eyebrow, "We just got here."

She rolled her eyes, "Take it up with Gable."

"I intend to." He said with mock seriousness, then pushed himself back into the ditch, "After you, young lady."

"Sure, sure," Sophia replied. Quickly slinging her rifle, she rolled into the ditch and scrambled back the way she'd come. Seeing them coming, the antitank gun crew scrambled around their piece and picked it up wholesale by the tripod, a couple men grabbing onto a bar they had slid through the front leg of the mount. Clever system, honestly. They ran off down the ditch with their load, and Sophia had started to hurry after them when something green flared across her vision and an ugly *crack* tore at her ears.

Sophia picked herself back up off the ground where she had found herself and saw the gunners had fallen, the front two kicking at the ditch as they tried to drag their piece forward. The back two were... her mind reeled for a moment at the sight. They were lying in the ditch... all over the ditch, their bodies torn open but still somehow twitching and thrashing spastically. *God-damn it*, she thought helplessly as more of the green meteors slammed in around them, dirt and bits of metal raining down from above.

Then for a moment, just a moment, the storm seemed to clear and she lunged forward instinctively, Hargrave on her heels. Getting her hands around one of the gun's carrying handles, she dug her feet into ground that slipped and skidded and steamed in the cool air and heaved the gun up, Hargrave on her other side. The two remaining crewmen got their feet under them and they ran for it, making it behind a building just as more of those damn meteor-shells crashed in all around them. Something else came in with them, with an eerie scream that sounded nothing at all like an artillery shell and an ear-splitting bang that told her it had pretty much the same amount of explosives in it.

They didn't stick around to find out. The four of them ran back to the train station in silence. One of the gunners, a man Sophia was pretty sure had been in charge of the team, finally spoke to tell them to drop the gun off behind the railway embankment where it could fire down the town's main street running to the east. She and Hargrave left the two men there and went to go find their squad, her head spinning a little as they climbed onto the platform to see Edward hurrying towards them with a bicycle in each hand. His eyes widened as he got a look at them, and he asked, "What happened?"

"The gunners got hit as we came out." Hargrave replied before she could find words, "We helped them back."

"Damn." Edward replied, then shook his head and handed them their bicycles, "I just talked to Sergeant Cross. We're free to head out as soon as we're able... sooner the better, actually."

"Did you?" Sophia replied, looking around the platform. It looked like one of the platoons was already set up around the area, with a constant stream of soldiers trickling in from the front and grabbing bicycles. As she watched another group rushed past her with bikes in hand, got on the road and started pedaling west and out of town, and it occurred to her that the Royal gunfire had almost completely died off. Looking back the way they had come, she made out Lieutenant Gable running back with a rifle in hand, a shape that looked like Sergeant Cross hurrying towards her. And then she saw it, a flickering wave of fire dancing in the sky beyond them, rising over the town's buildings like a demonic aurora.

She jumped off the platform instinctively and flattened herself against its concrete bulk, followed a moment later by her two companions. A few seconds later a ripping, rolling *crash* tore through the town, ear-splittingly loud, worse than any artillery barrage she'd even been through. The earth shook as she huddled against it, and as it died down she shuddered and climbed to her feet to see the entire eastern sky was black with ash and smoke. Flames licked at the unholy pall where they had been fighting just minutes before. "My God..." Hargrave said beside her, "What the *hell* was that?"

Sophia looked over at him incredulously, "I... don't know. Rockets, maybe?"

Edward cut in, "I know I don't want to be around the next time they fire it. Let's get going."

Sophia nodded and hefted her bicycle, "Right. *First squad, first platoon! On me, we're leaving!*"

A minute later they were speeding down the road to the west, with the moons flaming overhead and the road winding along ahead of them clearly in the moonlight. All around them the sound of battle echoed across the plain, thudding artillery and faintly cracking gunfire in the distance. After about twenty minutes of hard pedaling she spotted a light down the road, which quickly resolved into a soldier telling them they had reached Bravo Company's first roadblock and they needed to get off the road and go around. A dirt track took them into and through the position strung out along a forest running across the road, and they eventually got back onto the main road and pedaled onwards.

Sophia finally felt herself relax as they put Bravo's position behind them, until they came over a rise and the landscape spread out all around them. Leaning back in the saddle, she looked up at the moons and the stars spread out overhead until a spark of light off to her left caught her attention. She turned to see green fireflies dancing in the distant valley, far to the southeast but not nearly far enough. Following their path back she saw the moonlight catch at clouds of dust rising from the dry summer fields, as a dozen or more tiny black specks plowed along in a broad, purposeful arrowhead.

Imperial tanks, racing west. Turning, Sophia shouted over her shoulder, "Come on, guys! They're going around, we need to hurry!"

Chapter 24

Open Doors

The top floor of the War Ministry had once been Field Marshall White's lair, a nexus of power where even generals treaded softly as they attended his court. Here careers were made and broken, soldiers were sent to live or die by the division and the fate of the Kingdom hung in the commander's scales. Her father owed his throne to Lawrence White, and he had rewarded his old friend with titles, wealth and near-absolute power over the Royal Army, the greatest fighting force in the world. White had paid him back by leading that army to its greatest disaster since Drakenburg fell to the Faceless King, and shot himself rather than face it. Now the place felt like a tomb, their footsteps echoing through the silent halls.

The last time she had come here, Arilin had been a foolish little princess meddling in her father's affairs while he faced the greatest crisis of his short reign, and she had thought she was helping. Now she was practically the Regent, she had been meddling in the nation's affairs for months, and she was not at *all* sure that she was helping in the slightest. And unlike last time, she thought as she glanced over at Alyssa walking beside her, she had the foresight to have brought a friend with her. The redheaded hussar captain was no Patricia MacMahon, but on the other hand she probably wouldn't need a general to get her in the War Room's front door now.

The guard outside snapped to attention as they approached, "Milady! Coming in?"

"Yes," she replied flatly, then glanced over her shoulder, "Captain Helbrecht is with me."

"Very well," The man smiled, hauling the massive door open for them, "Go along, milady."

That was easy, she thought as she stepped inside, the familiar flood of light from the room's glass wall dazzling her for a second. The murmur of conversation trailed off as she walked in, but there was no pin-drop silence this time. Her arrival had been by no means unexpected, nor should it have been. As her eyes adjusted she made out a few familiar shapes against the bright light of the windows. Where her father had once sat at the head of the great round table, her uncle now stood as she approached, calling out, "Arilin! I confess I wasn't expecting you, I'd say this is hardly a crisis worthy of your attention." He looked her up and down with a too-nonchalant smile, crossing his arms as he went on, "Anyways, isn't school starting soon? I wouldn't want you to be late."

Arilin smiled back humorlessly as she crossed the room and walked around the table, a couple harried-looking majors stepping out of her way as she went, "You should write me a note then. Anyways," she went on as she produced a newspaper from under her arm, throwing it down in front of him dramatically, "*This* seems like something absolutely worth my time, and I'm wondering why you're dealing with it here instead of letting the Labor Ministry figure it out."

Alphonse looked at the newspaper, then back at her with a raised eyebrow, "I'm surprised your mother lets you read the *Star*, dear, there's columns in there dealing with quite... *adult* matters."

On his other side, General Chapman picked it up and examined the front page. Chuckling, he cracked, "Looks like Estelle Villanueva's getting married again. Should be the event of the season, I expect."

The man sitting on his near side, a major general she vaguely recognized, came to her rescue, "Shut up, Chapman." The cavalryman gave him a wounded look, but the man ignored him and turned his gaze on her, "If you're concerned about the general strike, milady, there's nothing at all for you to worry about. I suggest that you run along and let us handle it."

The man's nametag read 'Heinrici,' and he had a face a gargoyle would envy. Now that she had a chance to examine him properly, she pegged him as the commander of the Guards Infantry Division. Given how sour he looked, she expected he was probably cursing his fate being stuck in the capital and pining for the front lines. Giving him an equally sour look back, she demanded, "And what *exactly* are you doing to *handle* it, sir?" She went on, glaring at the three of them, "I'd like to avoid a massacre here, thank you very much."

Heinrici snorted contemptuously, "I can't see why, milady, it's exactly what we need right now."

"Now, now, Oscar," Alphonse cut in apologetically, "A show of force and a few strategic arrests, milady, will get the workers off the streets. We won't do more if they don't force our hand." He pointed at the map spread across the table in front of him, "In any event it's looking like it's confined mostly to the waterfront so far. Honestly, Arilin, this isn't going to last long and you don't need to concern yourself."

Arilin raised an eyebrow, "Then why did you order out the Guards this morning?"

Her uncle chuckled, crossing his arms as he looked down on her, "Purely precautionary, milady."

Turning to look at Alphonse had put Heinrici behind her, and she heard him shuffle his chair back and climb to his feet. Stepping back herself, she turned back to look at him as he unfolded himself to his considerable height, the nametag on his breast pocket coming about level with her eyes. What was it with the Army and freakishly tall generals? Walter was over six feet and he honestly seemed to be one of the shorter ones sometimes. She pushed the thought from her mind as Heinrici spoke, "As my lord said, this is part of the show of force. They won't resist the police when there's soldiers alongside them." He smiled coldly, "I trust we've addressed your concerns, milady?"

Chapman had climbed to his feet himself, and stepped out from behind Alphonse as he added, "This is all very routine, milady. In fact," he added with a smile at Alyssa, who had followed her most of the way around the table, "If you're curious about what exactly we're doing here you should ask your escort. Her regiment specializes in just this sort of thing."

Arilin grimaced slightly, consciously keeping it from turning into a pout. Unfortunately all of what they were saying sounded very reasonable. And maybe it was. Or maybe they just wanted her out of their hair. Crossing her arms, she changed tack, "I don't need to tell you that the Government's situation is very difficult right now. If this escalates into violence it's going to fall."

Alphonse shrugged, "So? I fail to see how that's any of our concern here, milady."

Liar. Snorting, she shot back, "You've been spending an awful lot of time over at the Assembly lately for me to believe that."

Her uncle's face hardened, "Are you suggesting, *young lady*, that I would somehow *benefit* from violence in the streets?"

Arilin glared back at him, "Yes, actually." She went on as he let out his breath with a long, slow hiss, "I'm neither blind nor stupid, uncle. You've been trying to collapse the Government for months now."

"How *dare* you accuse me like that," Alphonse snarled, stepping towards her menacingly, "I have never had *anything* but the Kingdom's best interests at heart at *any* time, *princess.*"

"My lord," Alyssa said quietly, from just over her shoulder. Arilin glanced over to see the hussar had stepped just behind and slightly beside her suddenly, the leather of her sword-belt rustling ever so slightly as she shifted it behind Arilin's back and out of her uncle's sight. And the only reason she'd been able to hear *that* was because the room had gone *absolutely* silent, staff officers frozen in place like a monster had crawled out of a hole in reality at the head of the table. Which was apt now that she thought about it.

Her uncle turned his glare on her escort, but Arilin cut in quickly, "So you don't deny it then."

Alphonse paused as he took a long, slow breath. Finally, slowly, he raised a hand to theatrically rub at his brow for a moment. Chuckling, he looked between the two men and remarked, "Now you see what I have to deal with."

Chapman laughed along, "She is a little spitfire, milord."

General Heinrici gave her uncle a dour look, "Are we done here?"

Alphonse shrugged, "I think so. In any event, princess, your feelings in the matter are entirely irrelevant. Your father was quite clear regarding our mutual... *responsibilities* after your last little intervention." Turning, he sat back down and gestured dismissively, "This is a military matter and you need to keep your nose out of it."

Arilin was sucking in her breath to fire back when she felt a hand on her shoulder and looked over to see Alyssa shake her head slightly. Sighing, she replied with as much dignity as she could muster, "I'd appreciate it, uncle, if you could avoid a massacre regardless."

"Of course," he replied dismissively, tapping the map in front of him with his finger, "Now, *where* exactly did they say they were starting a barricade?"

The two men sat back down and Arilin turned and stormed out, Alyssa hurrying to keep up with her. The door had thudded shut behind them and they were back out into the main hallway when her companion ventured, "That could have gone worse, milady." Arilin stopped suddenly and glanced over at her, her vision blurring as tears started to well up in her eyes. Chuckling softly, Alyssa handed her a handkerchief and went on, "Mind you, if I'd gotten that treatment at your age I'd have lost it on the spot."

Wiping at her eyes, Arilin was about to reply when she heard footsteps ahead of them and a man's voice call out, "Oh my! What's this?" Looking up, she saw a familiar portly shape in the hallway as Colonel Goeben stepped out of a side corridor, almost as if he had been waiting for them to come by. Walking up, he remarked, "A mother hen consoling her lost chick?"

Alyssa started to glare at him, but Arilin cut in quickly, handing her back her handkerchief as she replied, "God, I hope we don't look that bad."

"Oh, certainly not, milady. You're both adorable, and, well, women cry all the time anyways. It can't be helped and I certainly don't blame you for it after that just now." Alyssa opened her mouth, closed it and opened it again as the old staff officer went on, "We could hear you in the other room and, well, I felt terrible for you, dear."

Seeing that Alyssa was still trying to decide whether to be offended or not, Arilin smiled and thanked him, "I appreciate it."

"Oh by the way," Goeben stepped forward and leaned in quickly, his belly practically brushing up against her as she caught way too much of a whiff of tobacco on his breath as he murmured, "It's not just the Guards that are involved. We told the Fortress Corps to mobilize an hour ago."

"Wait, what?" Arilin took a step back in shock.

"What indeed!" Smiling, the colonel turned to Alyssa and went on cheerily, "Now, captain, if I were you I'd take this young lady straight back across the street and put her to bed. She's really had quite the shock. And don't let her protest either, girls her age can't even take yes for an answer." He wagged a finger at the hussar, "You need to be firm with her, you understand?"

Now blushing deeply, Alyssa managed, "Ah... yes, sir!" Seizing Arilin by the hand, she pulled her along after her, "Come on now, milady."

She finally let go of her on the stairs down, and Arilin remarked, "That man is a fine actor."

"I don't think he was acting," Alyssa replied, rubbing the back of her neck pensively as she went down ahead of her, "Still, I can't complain..." She gave her a worried look over her shoulder and went on, "If the Fortress Corps is involved, that could be another division or more going into downtown. They're not messing around."

"Great..." Arilin replied, shaking her head, "I don't suppose *you* have any ideas here?"

"I'm just here to keep you alive, milady." Alyssa shrugged as they emerged into the War Ministry's lobby, "Although... maybe we're looking at this wrong. You're pretty persuasive, can you convince the workers to back off, maybe?

"I don't think they'd want to hear from me..." Arilin trailed off in thought as the duty officer hurried out to open the door for them. Absently giving the man a nod, she stepped out into the morning sunlight, the warm summer air washing over her as she went. After a few steps she smiled and turned to Alyssa, "But I can think of someone they would."

"Oh?" The hussar captain raised an eyebrow, "Who might that be, milady?"

"A friend of mine, actually." Arilin smiled, "In any event, I think it's time I got to school. I wouldn't want to be late."

* * *

Lily gave her a hard, flat look, "I really can't do much here, Arilin."

Arilin shot back, "I think you *really* can, though."

Her friends had apprehended the poor girl as she walked in for the morning and hustled her into a conveniently vacant classroom where Arilin had been waiting. It hadn't done anything for her mood. Surlier than ever, Lily replied, "Oh yeah? *How?*"

"Call your father like you did *last time?*" Arilin demanded, "I don't think he wants to see a massacre any more than I do."

Lily's pale eyes flashed, "You realize, *princess*, he doesn't just command these people? In fact he didn't want them to do it, they went ahead anyways."

"The communists?" Arilin asked. Lily gave her a particularly snide nod, and she plowed onwards, "Well maybe they'd change their tune if they knew they were all going to *die*."

"At this point they think they'll die anyways. They'll roll the dice now instead of waiting to be *murdered*." Lily spat, jabbing a finger at her, "And by the way, they have a chance. People are angry about your draft, and your army isn't as loyal as you think it is."

"If it was actually *my* army, Lily, this wouldn't be so difficult." Arilin stabbed back, "Now how about you stop being difficult for once and give me a hand, considering I'm trying to help *you* out here."

Lily scowled, "Yeah, with the big fat string attached that you're just using us to screw over your uncle."

"Hey!" Liri and Miri, who had been watching them, interjected, "Don't you-"

Arilin waved them into silence, "You seem to be doing alright off of that so far, Lily. Now if your father can't get them off the streets, who do you know that can?"

The girl looked at her with an unreadable expression for a moment, then studied the ceiling pensively, "Nobody that isn't in prison right now." Arilin let it hang before raising an eyebrow, and Lily pressed on quickly, "But maybe someone who is. If you could get him out I'm sure he'd be... ah... grateful."

That was odd. Normally so icily composed, Lily was almost *flustered*. Narrowing her eyes, Arilin demanded, "Who?"

"Ah..." Lily fidgeted for a moment, then blurted out, "Hiram Moore."

"I hope you're joking." Arilin replied flatly.

"Why would I be?" Lily replied, crossing her arms defensively, "They'd listen to him."

"Oh, and how *exactly* would I explain this to my father? Hey, Dad, I just let the guy behind Red December out of prison because the communists will listen to him, because of *course* they will, because he's in charge of the Red Brigades!" Arilin added sarcastically, "And here's the magic beans they gave me."

The girl pleaded, "Trust me, I know it's hard to believe, but he'll get take care of it. He's *not* a bad guy, not at all."

Arilin sighed heavily and shook her head, "I'll do it if he'll follow through."

Lily brightened immediately, "Oh, he will, he will, I'm *sure* you'll like him."

"I doubt it..." Arilin gave Lily a quizzical look for a moment, then chuckled as a whole set of dots connected themselves in her mind. Casually, she asked, "He's your actual father, isn't he?"

Lily's eyes widened as she stepped backwards in shock, "Ah... no, no, of course not... why... why would you think that?"

Arilin smirked, "You're a bad liar, Lily. You don't look anything like Minister Meyer, or his wife for that matter." She went on, "And when I first met you up on the roof, you were up there to look at the Labyrinth, weren't you? He'd be held there."

The girl glared at her, "Go to hell."

"I knew there was something special about you. It's quite romantic, really," Arilin teased her, "A princess in hiding among her enemies, pining for her dear father!" Lily gave her a look that said she was about to slap her, and Arilin backed off, "This will take a couple days, can you keep things from boiling over in the meantime?"

"Yeah, sure." Lily sighed as the bell for classes began to ring, "I'll skip school today."

"I'll go get you excused," Arilin smiled, "Least I can do for someone helping me save the Kingdom."

Chapter 25

The Shattered Battlefield

Artillery rumbled faintly in the distance, a soft, deep grinding that set her teeth on edge. If it was anything to go by there was a huge battle going on around Kelsbruck south of Pine Harbor, more than a hundred kilometers away by now. The Empire couldn't sustain their offensive for long by sneaking landing craft through a swamp, they needed a bridge and they were damn well going to take that town and build one. And between that town and her command post there weren't enough Royal soldiers to fill a decent-sized parade ground, let alone stop the army now pushing west. Sighing, Patricia pinched the bridge of her nose pensively and shook her head. This was either *her* fault, or Walter's, or Kellerman's, but at this point handing out blame was probably pointless. Slade Anjanou had run them out of troops, he had run them out of options, and now he was driving his army through the gap that had inevitably opened up. At this point the real question was what they were going to do about it.

"Milady?" Patricia turned at the voice behind her, and saw one of the soldiers had walked out onto the hunting lodge's porch with a field telephone box in hand. Eschewing the usual practice of finding the grandest manor house possible for her headquarters, Patricia had settled for a cozy lodge backed up against a stretch of forest, with a nice view across the fields to the south and enough room for the staff to work without attracting the attention of every piece of Imperial artillery in ten miles. The girl handed her the telephone, saying, "We've got Army headquarters on the line. Still no luck with Corps."

Oh no, now I don't have a choice about calling Walter, Patricia thought sarcastically. Pretending she wasn't delighted, she took the set and settled into one of the seats scattered around the expansive porch, pulling out the handset and starting as she set it against her head, "Hello? General MacMahon here."

An unfamiliar man's voice answered, "Understood, milady, one second." The voice went on, faintly, as though he was talking to someone else in the room, "Sir, Lady MacMahon's on the line."

"Give it here," she heard Walter say faintly, then a rustle as the man handed the phone over and he answered cheerily, "Patricia! Glad to hear you're still in one piece."

She felt herself blushing as she replied, "Yeah... you too, Walter. How're things going?"

"I've been in much worse, right now I've only got *one* flank in the air." Walter remarked grimly. Clearly lovers' small talk would have to wait, "I've got people here telling me it's a feint and the *real* attack is going to come across the river further south. Considering you're looking right at it, what do you think?"

Leave it to the staff to come up with conspiracy theories instead of be-lieving their lying eyes. Patricia shook her head, cursed herself as an idiot for doing it over a phone line, and replied, "That's probably what Slade wants us to think. I'm looking at tanks and dragoons right now, Walter, and they risked their fleet to get them across. This is their main thrust."

"Are you holding?" He asked, a note of concern making it through the line.

"Depends what you mean by that," She replied, "Good news is the division's intact and on line, but we've had to fall back... God, sixty kilo-meters so far? We were in real trouble last night. Kellerman should be deploying the rest of the corps behind us right now."

"*Should?*" Their location shouldn't have been a surprise to Walter, but she could hear the raised eyebrow on the other end of the line, "When did you hear from him last?"

"This morning?" Patricia replied, "We got a messenger from him around eight, he said he'd deploy the corps on line from Nordsfeld to Darissa, and that we needed to cover him."

"More than I've gotten, we haven't heard from him here since last night. Man's a ghost." Walter added, asking, "So you're around White-wood right now?"

"Our line runs right through it." She answered, leaning back in her seat and letting herself relax a little. Now that she was explaining her situation to someone it sounded a lot less disastrous. She was opening her mouth to go on when something thudded, loud and close. Horse ar-tillery? There was a battery just south of the headquarters. The thought had barely gone through her head when it thudded again, and again, and again, building to a hammering cacophony like a monstrously overgrown machine gun. The artillery usually tried to fire crisp volleys, but this sounded like... independent fire? Feeling an icy finger of unease work its way up her back, Patricia put the handset back to her head and said, "I've gotta go, we're probably being attacked." She chuckled and went on, "Love you, Walter."

"You too," He replied drily, probably mindful he was in a room full of people, "Take care of yourself."

"Will do." Hanging up the phone and standing, Patricia ducked back inside and called out, "Hey! Call the artillery, find out what the *hell* they're shooting at!" She pressed the telephone set back into the opera-tor's hands, "That means you, I want answers *now*, understand?"

The girl set the phone on a nearby table and started working the set immediately. Having heard the commotion, Colonel Frost appeared in the entryway and said, "I heard the firing, do you think...?"

"Wouldn't be the first time something slipped through." As if to make her point, a sharper, faster undertone floated into the hammering gunfire nearby. Patricia scowled, "Get ahold of the reserve, we need them here *now*. In the meantime we need to defend this place. I'll ride out and see if I can get a look at whatever's coming our way."

Frost raised an eyebrow, "Is that wise, milady?"

"No, but it's never stopped me before." Turning to the duty sergeant who had been gawking at them from his table in the entryway, she ordered, "Get me my horse, *now*."

The man swallowed, "She's not saddled, milady, we were-"

"Then get me one that is." Patricia snapped. The man quickly rushed out the door as Frost disappeared back into the lodge, calling for the staff to prepare to defend themselves. Turning to the telephone operator, she asked, "Any luck?"

The girl shook her head, "Nothing so far, milady." Ominously, the hammering artillery outside began petering off as the shrill, faint undertone stepped up in intensity. It didn't quite sound like Imperial machine-gun fire, it was too slow and deeper, like it was coming from a much larger weapon. The implications of *that* made her gut clench up, and she forced the thought aside as the duty sergeant appeared out front with a horse, freshly saddled and ready for the general to go to something irresponsible on.

Walking back outside and down the front steps, Patricia took it, gave the man a nod of approval and swung herself up and onto the saddle. The horse shifted under her uneasily, and she gave it a reassuring pat on the neck and kicked it forward. The lodge was set back in a sort of notch in the forest, on a spur road a couple kilometers south of the main one running east towards Pine Harbor, which turned into a dirt track as soon as it ran off the property going south. The owner had probably paid for the work to improve it in the first place so he could get to his lodge in style and seen little point in continuing the work for the local farmers' benefit. She quickly pulled her horse off to the left and cut through the fields towards the battery's position, angling to get clear of the woods so she could see properly.

Something hissed overhead as she got around the edge of the forest, the landscape unfurling before her as she cleared a little rise to see the battery pulled up a few hundred meters down the gentle slope, one of the ammunition caissons flashing brilliant white as it exploded. The shockwave beat at the grass soundlessly for a second before it hit her, an earsplitting *crack* that left her ears ringing even at the distance, then a popping roar as shells thrown clear of the initial blast detonated like a string of firecrackers lit by a demented god. Men, tiny in the distance, fell and staggered aimlessly through the fog of dust thrown up by the blast as a cannon off at the end of the line stubbornly flashed back.

Patricia had always had good eyes, sharp enough to pick out the little details in terrain and the shapes of enemies lurking in the darkness. As she looked over at the still-fighting gun, she saw it clearly enough to notice the gun shield, a thin sheet of metal designed to protect the crew from shell splinters and spent rifle bullets at long range, *cave* inwards as though it had been smashed with a massive hammer. Ugly, dark flowers of dirt and smoke bloomed all around the piece and its crew a moment later as something larger sparked and exploded, blotting them from view.

Hauling on the reins to get her horse back under control as it shifted dangerously under her, Patricia looked past the wrecked battery, through the haze of smoke and dirt, and saw them. Half a dozen boxy little shapes in the distance, surrounded by coronas of dust as they chewed their way across the dry fields. Imperial tanks, pressing forwards. As she watched one of their cannons flared, ugly black puffs erupting near another cannon as the artillerymen who had started to converge on it fell like wheat. At least their victory hadn't been completely bloodless, though. Beyond the line of advancing tanks a couple more sat motionless in the distance, one billowing ugly, jet-black smoke.

Clearly she needed to have words with Mina, who had swung the Fourteenth around to the south side of the road to stabilize the situation after last night's fighting. The woman had sworn up and down the enemy tanks that had carved their way through the north side of the cuirassiers' line last night were nowhere to be found when she had arrived on scene in the morning. Clearly she hadn't spent much time looking *behind* her, because who would expect to find enemy troops that had broken through earlier exactly where they would logically be. In any event, Patricia thought as something small and angry pocked into the grass nearby, it was time to leave. She could find a new commander for the Valkyrie Knights *after* she survived this.

Wheeling her horse about, Patricia kicked it back towards her headquarters, angling towards a couple of familiar figures on that had appeared on horseback to the side of the lodge. Riding up, she saw dark shapes moving behind the lodge's windows and blue uniforms in the forest to the left as lancers rushed into position in the woodline. Colonel

Frost shouted as she approached, "Milady! What did you see?"

Patricia reined her horse up in front of them, "We just lost a horse artillery battery and I counted six tanks coming at us. They took a couple out before they went down at least." She looked over at the other rider sitting beside Frost, "Holly, are your antitank guns set up?"

Colonel Schrader's daughter, late of the Valkyrie Knights, glanced over at the forest now boiling with blue-jacketed lancers sliding into position and squinted for a moment, then nodded, "Yes, milady. We've got two."

"Good." Patricia replied, "They should start by crossing left to right, make your shots count." Turning back to her chief of staff, she told him, "I hate to say this, Joe, but you probably need to take the advance party and get out of here. Might be worth just going forward to Whitewood."

He nodded, "Sure thing, milady." Wheeling his horse about, he called for the headquarters advance party to fall in on him and get ready to move out. A few moments later some officers ran out the lodge's back door and into the stables for their horses, one of the long-range radio trucks firing up its engine as soldiers began hastily tearing down the its antenna mast. Splitting the headquarters might be too little, too late at this point, but she'd be damned if she let the division be decapitated by one strike.

"Milady, we'd best get to cover." Holly observed, "I think I hear them coming... we've got the horses a ways back, on the road. I'll take yours if you'd like."

"Sure," Patricia replied, swinging herself off her horse, "Where are you going to be set up? I'll send a phone line over."

"Middle of the line, milady." Taking her horse's reins, Holly galloped back onto the road and disappeared into the forest as Patricia called for one of the signalmen to run a line over. No sooner had a couple of girls rushed over stringing out a telephone wire behind them when she picked up a dull, low rumble off over the fields, almost imperceptible over the commotion of soldiers rushing about. They were out of time, and ready or not, the enemy was coming. Patricia cursed to herself and ducked inside. The lodge seemed solidly-built, and hopefully the solid timber walls would stop the automatic cannons those tanks apparently mounted.

Patricia made her way through the detritus of maps and paperwork scattered around the command post to kneel next to the girl from earlier, the one who had brought her the telephone just a few short minutes ago, near one of the front windows. Someone had thrown them open earlier and a breeze wafted in cool summer air from outside, sweeping away the musk that had developed from too many sweating, dirty people cramming into the lodge all at once. If not for the war it would have been a beautiful summer, she thought bleakly.

The girl had set her field telephone box on the floor next to her, and she offered it to her as she noticed her approach. Judging by the wires coming from it, they had strung the line down to Holly's command post outside direct from it. The set buzzed as the girl held it out, probably a communications check, and Patricia gestured for her to answer it herself before she straightened up on her knee and looked out the window. She only had to wait a few seconds for the first dark shape to roll into view around the edge of the forest, a boxy little thing with a skinny cannon protruding from its turret, the long barrel foreshortening as its turret slewed around to pan across the notch in the forest and the little cluster of buildings tucked within. It hesitated over the hunting lodge for a moment, Patricia feeling her breath catch in her throat, before quickly swinging back over the lancers' position in the forest as a thin stream of smoke rose from the turret.

An instant later she heard the sharp crack of the tank's machine gun, and the forest *roared* back as the lancers opened up. Dust spun up around the machine as a hail of gunfire converged on it, its autocannon roaring to life to send shells crashing back into the forest. The antitank rifles spoke, one, two, the armor-piercing rounds sparking as they hammered at the armor. Clearly thinking better of the situation, the driver ground the tank to a halt and started backing up as two more tanks appeared, swinging around the far edge of the forest with their cannons blazing. Someone started firing a machine gun upstairs, and one of those cannons swung onto the lodge and erupted.

Dirt sprayed through the window and Patricia dove for the floor as the tank walked its fire into the lodge, splinters and dust filling the air as the shells tore into the thick wooden walls. Her ears rang from the blasts, the inside of the lodge ringing like a drum. The antitank guns fired again outside, faintly, and the assault stopped as suddenly as it began. Patricia stuck her head back up to see the offending tank backing off quickly, a veil of smoke hanging off its turret. Just as quickly another one pulled out to take its place, lobbing shells into the forest as it angled outside of the remaining two.

Someone was moaning on the other side of the room. More than one person actually. Nobody was *shooting back,* though. Climbing to her feet, Patricia looked down to see the telephone operator still cowering on the floor and kicked her in the ribs, shouting, *"Get up!"* The girl rolled over and looked at her uncomprehendingly, and she went on, "See if you can get some artillery on the line, and then go find someone to direct it, understand?"

The girl nodded and started working the phone, and Patricia ducked across the central hallway and into the den on the far side of the lodge. She almost tripped over a huddle of crouching soldiers as she walked in, two or three of her staff officers huddled around a captain with half a dozen jagged pieces of wood sticking out of his side. A machine-gun set up on a table nearby lolled on its side unattended, the thick timber wall next to it caved in and splintered crazily. The man was alive enough to moan and thrash around and didn't seem to be bleeding too much onto the floor, so she seized the two men that seemed to be fumbling around instead of doing actual first aid by the back of their collars and shouted, "Get back on the gun! He'll be fine!" A window on the far side of the room shattered and a fresh hail of bullets ripped lines into the ceiling, and she added, "And move the gun to the side window, they've got troops in the forest!"

The two men quickly picked up the gun, rushed it over to the other window and began laying down enthusiastic but not particularly accurate-looking bursts into the trees. Stepping to the side of the window herself, Patricia stuck her head out for a moment to see a tiny, dark shape arc out of the forest towards them, and she had the presence of mind to throw herself on the floor a moment before the grenade crashed into the roof, showering them with plaster as the building shook. The machine gun fell silent beside her, and she looked up to see the two men fumbling to reload it as someone screamed upstairs over the ringing in her ears.

Without the machine gun firing she could hear things around her for a moment, the cracking Imperial gunfire mixed with their tanks' hammering autocannons, and the lancers returning fire raggedly from the forest. Her blood ran cold as she realized just *how* raggedly, popping carbine shots distinct among the uneven rattles of the machine guns. That troop had been soaking up fire from those tanks for minutes now, and God only knew if their only proper way to hit back, their antitank guns, were still even functioning. For all she knew she'd ordered them to their deaths. Something sparked and flashed overhead and one of the men fell to the ground next to her, clutching his face as the machine gun crashed to the floor by her feet.

The other man was left standing there stupidly, holding the ammunition belt he had been clumsily fussing with earlier as he had tried to reload the machine gun. He was a private, just some driver she had seen around the headquarters from a few days ago, someone new pulled in to help keep the trucks running, stand guard and run errands. And from his wide eyes and shaking *body* he was as afraid as anyone she had ever seen in her life. A bullet cracked through the window between them as she stood there looking at him, and she knew the only thing keeping him from running for his life was the fact she was standing there.

"Hey." She smiled as she unsnapped her holster and drew her pistol, "Don't worry, I've seen worse. What's your name?"

"M-Moran, milady." He replied, as he realized he had a rifle slung over his back and untangled himself from it, "Really? I think it's pretty bad."

"Nonsense. I don't even think we're outnumbered." As she spoke something new roared outside, a wave of gunfire ripping across the far woods. It sounded... Royal? Patricia stuck her head around the window for a moment to see the forest filled with rushing shapes, smoke and flashing gunfire. A masked soldier stood up and spun around quite clearly, raising his rifle, then crumpled backwards like he'd been poleaxed. The lancers' gunfire strengthened as she watched, one of the antitank rifles hammering out defiantly. Chuckling, she looked back over at the man, "What'd I tell you? Now see to your friend here, I need to go find out what the hell is going on."

Leaving him there, she made her way to the lodge's back exit, noting that the telephone operator she had left in the other room had found one of the officers to talk on the phone and presumably deal with the artillery. The newcomers were so fast they were already most of the way to the end of the forest by the time she made her way out of the lodge and around to the corner of the building to peer out at the battle. Seemingly oblivious to the short, murderous battle going on behind it, one of the tanks had pulled forward a little past the edge of the woods as it hammered away at the lancers, and Patricia saw a bulky projectile whirl out of the forest to land on its back deck. An improvised demolition charge, made out of a bundle of hand grenade heads wired around a central, fully-assembled stick grenade. It detonated with a satisfying crack that she felt even at the distance, leaving an ugly pall of smoke around the tank that built and billowed as the war machine caught fire.

The remaining two tanks were farther away out in the fields and out of reach of even the boldest grenadier, but under a hail of gunfire and with artillery starting to slam down around them they clearly decided they weren't going to win this fight. They both backed up for a ways before slewing around and retreating off to the south, chased by shellfire until they ducked out of sight below a fold in the terrain.

They'd won, somehow. If this amounted to winning. Sighing heavily, Patricia turned and sat down against the lodge's rough wooden wall, pinching the bridge of her nose. One more close call. If she got out of this in one piece, again, somehow, she was getting *real* serious about Walter.

"Holding up, milady?" A familiar voice cut into her thoughts, and she looked up to see John Rose standing over her, smiling wider than she remembered him as being capable of.

"Bad day at the office." She remarked. He gave her a hand up, and she brushed herself off and went on, "Those were your guys just now?"

He chuckled, "Yeah. We heard you'd called over the reserve and thought they'd need some help."

Looking over her shoulder at the two tanks burning merrily out in the field, snapping and popping occasionally as ammunition cooked off in the heat, Patricia turned back to him and snorted, "You were right. We were in some real trouble there... thanks." She went on, "How's Sophia doing?"

"As well as anyone, and better than most." He smiled again, "I put corporal stripes on her a few days ago, you know."

"Oh, really?" Patricia smiled back, "Tell her I'm proud of her."

"Coming from you that'll mean a lot, I know she likes you..." The sergeant major trailed off, looking over her shoulder, and she turned around and followed his gaze as he asked, "Are you seeing that, milady?"

He'd always had sharp eyes. Patricia had to squint for a moment before she saw it, the faint haze of dust rising out of the countryside. The lodge was up on enough of a hill and the terrain dipped enough that they could see the landscape sweep off far to the south, although it was too obscured by faint rises and bands of forest for her to see anything on the ground properly. Dust rose, though, and it didn't lie. And there was a *lot* of it off that ways, like a whole cavalry division was mulching through the dry fields. Which, she supposed, it might very well be. Maybe it was just the cuirassiers having a proper swordfight with some dragoons. Maybe. And maybe Walter would propose the next time he laid eyes on her, but wishful thinking never got anyone anywhere in war. Patricia swore, "*God*-damnit."

"Probably not ours, milady." Rose observed.

"I'll say." Turning, she called out, "*Hey!* Get me a telephone, *now!*" A moment later the girl from earlier appeared, and she said, "Get the cuirassiers on the line. I need to speak to Colonel Morris."

"Sure thing, milady." The girl worked at the phone for a minute, talked to someone at a switchboard, then handed her the handset, "It's ringing."

A silky-voiced man answered, "Hello, Eighth Regiment."

"Is Colonel Morris there? It's General MacMahon, I need to speak to him *immediately*." Patricia replied.

"Ah... no, sorry. Can I take a message, ma'am?" The man said helpfully.

Ma'am? Who the hell in the cuirassiers didn't know she was a duchess? Raising an eyebrow, she shot back, "Is the Chief of Staff there? Who's in charge?"

"Nope, sorry. I'd be happy to find them after I get off the phone with you, ma'am." The man replied.

"And you are...?" Patricia asked.

"Lieutenant Anjanou, ma'am. It's been a while." Slade Anjanou's son replied from one of her regiment's command posts. That little brat was probably sitting on the table, kicking his legs, twirling the handset wire around his finger like a little girl and having the time of his life.

Well, that answered a few questions. Shaking her head, she pinched the bridge of her nose for a moment, then chuckled and replied, "Yeah, it has. How're Aisha and your sisters?"

He chuckled, "Mom's fine, Feb and April *both* have kids now, May's... well, she's May."

"She still beating on you?" Patricia asked.

"No, actually." He went on, "Took me a couple years, but I took your advice and stood up to her finally."

"Good to hear." The poor kid had gotten bullied mercilessly by that evil little witch.

"Oh, while I have you on the line, are you and General Haas really a thing now? Every prisoner we take swears up and down you two are in love." June went on, smirking so broadly she could *hear* it over miles of bad military phone line, "I think you're a cute couple, you know."

"A lady has her secrets." Patricia replied tersely, "Now I'd tell you to take care, but..."

He chuckled, "I understand. See you soon, ma'am."

The line went dead. Sighing, she gave the handset back to the operator wordlessly and pinched her nose again. If she kept at it she was probably going to leave a mark, she thought absently. John Rose considerately waited for a moment, then ventured, "Milady... who was *that?*"

She shook her head, "June Anjanou, Slade's kid. Long story." Looking over at him, Patricia smiled weakly, "And I think we've got bigger problems to deal with now."

Sergeant Rose raised an eyebrow, "Did he always have long hair?"

"Ugh, he used to be *worse*." Patricia rolled her eyes, "I thought he was a *girl* for a while."

Chapter 26

The Emperor's Sword

Chuckling to himself, June hopped off the table and stretched his arms over his head, groaning a little as the stretch worked at his abdomen. He was just letting it go when he heard the door behind him creak open and steady, familiar footsteps tap across the floorboards. He could hear the smile in Colonel Vann's voice as she chided him, "Lieutenant, one of these days I need to have a talk with you about answering people's phones without permission." Turning, he saw that she had raised what he knew was an ice-blonde eyebrow behind her mask, "Someone you know?"

June smiled apologetically, "General MacMahon actually. Long story." He chuckled and went on, "If I'd known you were here I would have put you on."

The commander of the 5th Dragoon Regiment laughed, "Next time, then. Anyways," She went on, looking around the shot-up hotel lobby the 8th Cuirassiers had been using for a headquarters, "I'm wondering what you've gotten out of this place so far."

"Well they didn't want to give it up, for starters." June glanced at the row of bodies they had dragged off to the side along one of the walls, just a row of bulky lumps covered by tablecloths now. One of them was a full colonel, a big man with a gray beard. They had found him sprawled out with pistol in hand as though he had been urging on the defenders. Morris, June was pretty sure his name was. Grimacing, he went on, "Without the tanks it would have been more of a fight."

"I'll say." The colonel's mask shifted as she grimaced. Half the room was smashed to matchsticks from autocannon fire. Walking up to the table he was standing at, one of the few pieces of furniture that hadn't been destroyed, she went on, "Hardly seems fair... is this their map?"

"It is," he replied, pointing out a few units marked on it, "We just went through the south side of the 9th Division's line. It looks like they're screening for the rest of their cavalry corps to deploy behind them. That's another two divisions, maybe more."

Vann's mask shifted slightly as she narrowed her eyebrows beneath it, "Which means I have a decision to make. Do we turn north for a rematch with Lady MacMahon and risk letting those two divisions deploy, or do we keep pushing west to catch them on the march?" She looked over at him and snorted, "Or do we dig in here and wait for support? Even with the tanks, what this is telling me is that we're outnumbered at least six to one right now. If we wait a few hours that will change." She chuckled, "I always try to get my commanders' opinions before this kind of thing. It makes you all feel *valued*."

"Hm." June stroked at his chin, the leather over his mask's steel jaw-plate rough under his fingers. After their failure at Allenby, the idea of crushing Lady MacMahon's too-persistent division once and for all was tempting. And for such a big war, he'd run into Sophia Rose *far* too many times for comfort. All that being said, war was no place for personal grudges. Tapping the cavalry corps assembly areas marked out on the map, June said, "We need to keep pushing west. If we hit that corps before it deploys we can win this battle *today*. Our follow-on forces will mop up MacMahon."

Vann's mask shifted again as she raised an eyebrow, "How do you know they're not already deployed?"

June shook his head, "If they were they'd have known about it here. Everything I've seen is saying they haven't heard from that corps all day, which is telling me they're *disorganized*." Something tingled at the back of his neck, and he gave the colonel a look as he went on, "Wait, ma'am... did you say *commanders?*"

"I *did*, actually." Vann chuckled, reaching into her pocket. Producing a set of captain's bars, she pressed them into his hands, "Your father told me to hang these on you when I got the chance, and I need Marsten to fill a slot over in Third Battalion. You're ready."

June looked at it in a daze, feeling a shock like slow lightning crawl up his spine. It was just a little pin, three bars side-by-side in steel gray. In a minute he'd put it on his collar, walk out and take command of the whole company. A hundred and fifty-odd dragoons all counting on him to keep them alive and bring them victory. Really it wasn't much more complex than just managing his old platoon, and yet it was so much more. Sighing, he nodded and replied, "Will do, ma'am. What do you need from us?"

Vann said, "I like your plan. I like it so much, in fact, that I've already given orders for it. Most of First is already moving." Her mask's jaw-plate tilted annoyingly as she smirked at him, then went on, "Take your company and head northwest until you hit Nordsfeld *there*, then turn and push down the road west. You'll be on the regiment's right wing as we go forward." Pulling out a pencil, she sketched the plan on the map, "You'll be with First Battalion pushing northwest, Second will head directly west, Third will follow and support. Each battalion will have a tank company along with the usual support, so you'll have firepower on hand if you need it. We'll keep the heavy artillery in the middle of the formation until we can feel out the situation a little better. Questions?" June shook his head and she finished, "Good... oh, and June?"

"Ma'am?" He turned to look at her as he hefted his rifle to leave.

Vann's eyes narrowed behind her mask, "You've lost more soldiers out of your platoon so far than some of the *companies*." She went on icily, "Don't think for a minute I don't notice."

June looked back at her levelly, "What would you rather I do, ma'am?"

The colonel snorted, "Just be careful with them. You can't win the war yourself."

"I'll keep that in mind." June replied, a little more curtly than he intended, "Is that it, ma'am?"

"Yes, get going." Vann turned back to the map, dismissing him, "I know Marsten's saying his goodbyes outside."

Turning himself, June slung his rifle over his shoulder and walked out the wrecked front doors, wincing a little as his eyes adjusted to the bright sunlight pouring down outside. Aegis Company, his now, had taken shelter from the sun with their horses under the trees lining the town's main street. Besides the hotel and a few shell scars and bullet holes here and there the town was unscathed, and a few curious locals had emerged to gawk at the Empire's legendary dragoons as they watered their mounts and adjusted their saddles. Compared to the Royal Army's splendid cavalry, June thought wryly, they were probably a singularly unimpressive bunch in drab uniforms on mismatched horses.

June spotted Captain Marsten as he emerged from a group of dragoons and started towards him when someone called out hoarsely, "Hey, young man!" Looking over, he saw one of the local civilians coming towards him out of a doorway, an old man sagging with age and hobbling heavily with a cane. Even so, the man seemed determined, and June paused to let him catch up. As he approached slowly June noticed a young woman step into the doorway behind him and then hesitate, eyes wide with fear as she watched them. The man eventually made his way over and looked him up and down, then chuckled, "Well look at you! You're with the Empire, aren't you, son? I'd know that mask anywhere."

Bemused, June nodded, "Why yes I am."

"Ha! I knew we'd make it back one day." Turning, the man called over his shoulder, "You can come on out Molly, we've got nothing to fear here! We're back in the Empire!"

The girl darted out into the street quickly, avoiding his eyes as she grabbed at the old man's sleeve, stuttering, "I... I'm sorry, sir, he's, well, he's very old and he's not in his right mind..."

The man fended her off with more energy than he had seemed to possess just a minute ago, saying, "Nonsense, girl." Looking back at him, he straightened up and went on, "I fought for Lady Xia once, back... God, I was just a kid, younger than you." He chuckled, "We didn't stand a damn chance, but you lot look a lot better than we did. When you get to the High City, you spit on Steinwitz's grave for me, will you?"

June laughed and clapped him on the shoulder, "Will do, friend." Turning to the girl, he went on, "You take good care of him, understand? I don't know what you're used to here, but we Imperials look after our own."

"Y-, yes, sir," she sputtered as he turned away, pleading with her charge, "Come on now..."

Captain Marsten had been watching the exchange from behind him, horse's reins in hand. As June approached he remarked, "Good to know we've got *some* friends around here." Laughing, he went on, "Anyways, June, they're all yours. Got your new rank with you?"

June produced his bars from a pocket, "As a matter of fact, I do."

"I'll do you one better." Marsten's mask cocked over as he smirked, pulling a major's four-pointed star from one of his own pockets, "Second Battalion needed a new XO. Guess I'm still a 'sir' to you, kid."

June chuckled, "Guess so, sir. I'll see you."

The old commander swung himself up onto his horse and galloped off gallantly. Sagara had appeared with Lucky, and June climbed onto his own mount, patting his horse on the shoulder affectionately as he settled into the saddle. Now or never, he supposed. Taking his old lieutenant's rank off his collar, he pinned his captain's bars on in their place on the black dragoon's tab on his collar. The prongs went through his summer jacket's loose weave easily enough. Pocketing his old rank, he nudged Lucky out into the middle of the road and was turning to address the company when a deep rumble built through the town, and he turned to see trucks rumbling through the crossroads just past the wrecked hotel.

Not any normal trucks, either. These were towing artillery pieces and loaded with ammunition, gunners leaning out to gawk under canvas covers rolled up to catch the breeze. Along with the tanks, the regiment had gotten another artillery battalion for the operation, equipped with the Emperor's latest and most final arguments. The cannons they were towing made their usual horse artillery look like popguns. The colonel had taken to calling her command 'Battlegroup Vann' recently, and looking at the artillery rolling past in a cloud of dust and steel it almost didn't seem pretentious.

Chuckling to himself, June waited until he had a chance of being heard and turned to the company. Raising his voice, he called out, "Aegis! I'd love to make a speech, but we've got our orders and a war to win! Mount up!" The masked dragoons quickly climbed onto their horses, and June waved towards road, "Onto the main road and head west, order of march three-two-one-headquarters! Marin, Rudenko, Vasa, First Sergeant, on me!"

The company quickly fell out onto the road, his new subordinates finding him easily enough despite the cloud of dust lingering over the road from the artillery's passage. Lieutenant Rudenko spoke first, her long red hair shifting across her shoulders as she shook her head, "Good job on the promotion, June." She laughed and corrected herself, "Guess we should call you 'sir' now, though, eh?"

Sergeant Marin cut in, "So what's the plan, sir? We're leaving in an awful hurry."

June chuckled, "Thanks, Catalina." Looking over at his old sergeant, he went on, "We're short on time. Right now we think the enemy's got another two cavalry divisions deploying between Nordsfeld and Darissa. We're aiming to catch the northern one while it's still in march column." Looking over at the somber leader of Third Platoon, he went on, "Jasper, you'll take the right flank. When we break here, get your guys off the road and deploy heading northwest towards Nordsfelt. We should be on the right flank of the regiment, so if you see cavalry to *your* right it's probably enemy."

"Got it." Lieutenant Vasa replied tersely.

"Catalina, you deploy to his left, and keep your eyes out for the rest of the battalion to your left. They should have moved out already. If you need to push forward to get on line with them, go ahead." June looked back to Marin and continued, "First will follow and support, I'll be with you. First Sergeant," The grizzled veteran gave him a skeptical look as June turned to him, the little man riding like he had grown out of the saddle itself. June finished, "Follow us in and get ready for wounded."

The man nodded and peeled away wordlessly. Laughing, Catalina remarked, "Sure thing!" The girl kicked her horse forward, and June overheard her as she shouted to her platoon, "Alright, guys, here we go again! The boss says..." Jasper snorted and nudged his horse into a trot in her wake, leaving June alone with Marin.

His old sergeant grunted, "Looks like you're moving up in the world, sir."

"Missing me already?" June quipped.

"I'm not answering that." Marin shot back.

June chuckled, "Suit yourself." Ahead of them the dragoons were already spilling off the road, Catalina's sword flashing in the sunlight as she enthusiastically directed her troopers to and fro. Jasper had disappeared into his line as usual as it deployed, the dragoons easily spreading out across the fields. They rode on for a mile or so, negotiating ditches and the occasional fence as the company spread out across the dusty fields, the dragoons on the far wings shrinking to tiny figures in the distance. Beyond them June spied dust rising in the distance, and taking a look through his binoculars spied more dragoons pushing west, barely more than dots across the golden fields in the distance.

The fields looked flat from a distance but they had enough folds and dips to hide an army, at least if it was determined about staying behind them. Coming over a rise in the fields, June looked over the shallow depression beyond and snorted to himself as he saw the line of tanks carefully arrayed along the bottom, all four of them pushed just far enough forward to get their spindly autocannons clear of the far lip. As he watched they cranked up their engines one by one, engines belching plumes of black smoke as they growled to life. One commander in particular seemed to be nervously observing the process from his perch in his tank's turret, and June picked him out as the man in charge and nudged Lucky forward in his direction.

"Hey, you!" June called out as he reined Lucky up beside the tank. The engine's dull-edged roar almost swallowed his words as he went on, "Are you in charge here?"

Noticing him, the tank commander untangled himself from his headset and yelled back, "Yeah! Alpha one-five, right? Are you guys pushing up?" June gave him a thumbs-up, and the man nodded and went on, "Okay, we're with you! Callsign's Lance Two!"

June nodded, "Great, I'm Aegis Six! Go ahead and start pushing forward! You'll move up and support when we hit the enemy!" Giving him a thumbs-up back, the commander was settling himself back against the turret ring when June heard a faint *crack* over the rumbling engines and added, "Looks like that's now!"

The tanker nodded and ducked down inside the turret, emerging again a moment later as the war machine lurched forward. Soon all four of them had rattled up and out of the depression and were churning forward across the fields as more gunshots cracked in the distance. June rode Lucky forward in their wake, squinting into the distance. The platoons ahead seemed to be dismounting, dark bunches of horses gathering up and heading back towards him while the dragoons themselves disappeared into the dusty fields.

The gunfire ahead built to an uneven crackle as dirt puffed in the field ahead of him, June frowning as a hammering burst of machine-gun fire rolled back across the fields. Clearly they'd found the enemy, but beyond that the situation was murky. Resisting the urge to ride forward and check things out himself, June pulled out his map and looked it over as the gunfire spread across the line up ahead like cracking wildfire. They had gone a few kilometers already and should be getting close to Nordsfeld, but he had yet to actually *see* the town, which meant... yes, *there* they were. As flat as the terrain *seemed*, they had actually been riding up a slight rise the whole time, crowned by a railway embankment where the line turned south sharply after running east out of the town. Probably why they'd chosen to deploy part of the corps there, actually.

The embankment would make an ideal defensive position, a natural bastion from where a few machine-guns could dominate the terrain around the town. And if he was where he thought he was, he might actually be able to see it. Pulling his binoculars back out, June peered ahead through the rising dust of battle to see... nothing, just a couple dragoons rising out of cover to rush forward far ahead. Some joker over on the left had their sword out and was waving it to urge the troops forward... Catalina, actually. Clearly things weren't *too* dangerous over there then.

Even so, he needed a better vantage point. June scowled for a moment, then chuckled as a bright idea flashed through his head. Giving Lucky a reassuring pat, he shifted in the saddle, got his feet up under him and rocked over them, the horse giving him an incredulous look as he stood up on top of his saddle. Ignoring Lucky's skepticism, June took another look through his binoculars and smiled. *There* was the embankment, a brown line barely visible across the top of the hill, disappearing off to the right where it curved off to the west. A blue-jacketed figure rose out of the fields as he watched and ran back over the embankment, then another and another as smoke started puffing and then rising steadily from it. Royal lancers falling back into cover under his troops' attack, and judging by the amount of dust coming out of the fields and small, angry things whizzing through the air around him it looked like they intended to fight. One of the tanks let loose with its autocannon as he watched, sending a gout of earth and sparking fire stitching across the enemy's positions. As the Royal fire surged in return, June thought it was really quite a bit like poking a hornet's nest.

"Sir, you're going to get yourself killed doing that." June turned to see Sergeant Marin had pulled alongside him on his horse, giving him a quizzical look. Changing the subject, he went on, "See anything?"

June chuckled, "How we win this fight, I think." Dropping back down into the saddle, he went on, "We'll have to move fast, though. There's an embankment up there they're defending, and it curves west into Nordsfeld on the right side of our line." He pointed and went on, "I haven't seen any fire coming from that curve yet. I don't think it's occupied, at least not in force."

"You want us to take it, sir?" Marin asked.

June nodded, "Once you've got it you can enfilade their line to the left and we can look down into Nordsfeld. Now get moving!" Looking around he spotted Sagara nearby, the signalman having followed Marin over. June called out to him, "Sagara! Get over here, I need your radio!"

The man spurred his horse over as Marin shouted for the platoon to follow him and galloped off. Taking the radio's handset as Sagara offered it, June keyed it and said, "Aegis, this is Six, One's pushing right, watch your fire. Lance Two, I need you to direct fire right in support."

"Lance Two, acknowledged. Two-Four, slew right and support by fire." A voice crackled back from what sounded like a battle inside an anvil factory.

"Two-Four, roger." As June watched the rightmost tank rotated its turret right and started hammering autocannon shells into the curve of the embankment.

Another voice sparked over the net, gunfire hammering in the background, "Six, Two!" Catalina, her normally-confident voice cracking, went on, "They're dug in up here, we're not making a lot of progress!"

Great. Now everyone expects me to solve their problems. Scowling, June snapped into the handset, "Seven, are you on the net?"

"This is Seven." The First Sergeant replied calmly.

"Get ahold of Bronze and tell them we need support, *now*." June went on, "Two, you've got first crack with Bronze. Understand?"

Catalina came back, "Yeah."

"Good. Six out." Shaking his head, June handed the handset back to Sagara and spurred Lucky after his old platoon as they galloped past, the signalman kicking his own mount after him. He caught up with the group as they dropped into a shallow depression running along the length of the rise, the battle disappearing from sight momentarily as the angry wasps zipping through the air flew harmlessly high. They galloped along for a minute, angling left under the slope's cover before Marin gave the signal to wheel left and dismount. An instant later the platoon came around and the troopers hopped off their horses. As the dragoons started to fan out on line June tossed Lucky's reins to the girl hanging back with Third Squad's horses and joined them, Sagara hurrying after him a moment later.

"Move! Move!" Marin was shouting, "Spread out, hold fire until we get engaged! We'll hit them while they're looking left!" The embankment loomed back into view as they emerged from the depression and charged through the fields. Marin had done his job well, and June could see the embankment's steep slope straight ahead as it curved away to the west, earth and smoke churning off its top as the tank hammered away at it. Something evil-sounding whistled in and exploded off to their left as they ran. With his feet pounding through the dust and sweat starting to pour down the inside of his mask, June couldn't tell whether it was Royal or Imperial.

Fire and smoke danced atop the embankment and bullets seethed through the air around them. Someone cried out as June launched himself into the ground, the soft dust cushioning his fall as he hit, kicked forward, raised his rifle to his shoulder, his finger tightening on the trigger as the little black bar of the front sight fell onto the smoking crown atop the railroad tracks. Worked the lever and fired again as gunfire erupted all around him, the platoon roaring back as one. Pushing himself back to his feet, he half-turned and waved his troops forward, shouting, *"Come on!"*

They came on alright. One lunge, two lunges, three, four, the embankment looming above them as it curved towards the town, now suddenly visible spreading out before them. As he ran and blinked the sweat from his eyes, his vision suddenly cleared and he saw the streets were dark with soldiers, horses, wagons, the organized chaos of soldiers getting ready to move out. They probably barely even knew they were under attack. The whistling bullets suddenly cut off as they approached, June realizing dully that the enemy didn't dare crawl forward far enough across the berm's flat crest to get a shot on them as the tank's fire scythed across it. As they threw themselves onto the base of the embankment and the first Royal stick grenade clanged off his helmet, he thought idly that they clearly didn't seem inclined to just *give up*, though.

Chuckling at the absurdity of it all, he calmly picked the thing up and threw it back. It exploded just as it cleared the embankment's crest, showering them all with flying gravel. Someone screamed on the other side of the berm as the rest of the dragoons got the idea and a *hail* of Imperial grenades flew up and over the embankment. They erupted with an earth-shattering roar and a volcano of flying earth that blotted out the afternoon sun. Digging his feet into the grassy embankment, June clawed his way up the steep slope and leveled his rifle over the top as a sudden breeze picked up and whipped away the lingering dust of battle.

A dead man stared back at him over the scarred and dented lip of the railroad tracks, sightless eyes caked with dust from where he lay behind an abandoned Royal machine gun. Gritting his teeth, June wormed forward to the tracks themselves, his eyes widening as he caught sight of what lay beyond. It wasn't often you saw that kind of target these days on the battlefield, a solid wall of blue-jacketed lancers crowded together practically shoulder to shoulder behind the embankment to their left. No wonder his troopers were having so much trouble, even with the tanks. Some of them had turned at the explosions, wide eyes clear in pale faces as he leveled his rifle's sights into the middle of the writhing blue mass and pulled the trigger. Again, and again, and again, as machine guns screamed to life around him.

A minute later the first tank's turret appeared over the far embankment, above the motionless windrow of dead carpeting the near side. Leveling its autocannon coldly, it paused for a second before opening fire down towards the town. Following the flaming tracers, June saw densely-packed streets erupt into pure chaos as the shells rained down, men and horses rushing about like ants pouring from a smashed anthill. More tanks quickly joined it, followed moments later by dark helmets and spindly machine-guns as the rest of the company got up onto the embankment.

Gritting his teeth, June rolled over on his back and called out, "*Sagara!* Get up here with the radio!" The man climbed up to him, opened his mouth to say something and froze for a moment as he saw the bodies carpeting the far side of the railroad tracks. Ignoring his reaction, June took the handset out of the man's hand and looked over onto the town coldly as he keyed it, "Any Bronze station, this is Aegis Six. I've got a target for you, highest priority."

"Six, this is Bronze Control." The woman's familiar, silky voice floated back out of the handset, "You always bring me the best presents. What have you got?"

There was a dead man staring at him a foot away, and he *really* wasn't feeling it. June replied flatly, "I've got observation into Nordsfeld. It's full of troops. Cavalry division assembly area."

"*Excellent.* So excellent, in fact, I'm passing this mission to Meteor." That was the heavy artillery battalion that had come in to reinforce their light horse artillery for the attack, the big guns that had rumbled by on the road earlier. Bronze Control was practically licking her lips, "Got co-ordinates for me, or should we just hit the town?"

"Just smash the town, start on the east side and roll west." June said coldly, "I'll adjust if needed."

"Understood." She seemed to have caught his tone, even over the radio, that he wasn't interested in flirting. She went on, "Medium battalion, twelve volleys, two hundred sixteen rounds. Shake and bake. Stand by, shot in... one minute."

"Got it, standing by." Shaking his head, June looked around. Most of the company was up on the embankment now, taking measured potshots at the boiling chaos down below. Searching over the dragoons around him with his eyes, he picked out Sergeant Tarai's familiar, lithe form and called out, "Tarai! Get over here!"

The woman turned and hurried over, asking, "Sir? What's up?"

"Where's Marin?" June demanded.

Tarai's mask moved as she grimaced, and June's heart dropped as she pointed at a couple figures receding back across the field carrying a dark shape between them, "He got hit coming in, I told them to get him back to the aid station."

June snorted angrily, "How bad?"

"Clean through the chest, although he didn't notice for a minute. I was talking to him when he did." She shook her head, "He'll be fine."

June sighed, "Well, you're in charge then." He handed her the radio handset, "There's a fire mission coming in on the town, I need you to spot for the artillery. I'll go... sort out of the company." He gestured off to their right side, "Get a squad to cover our flank. We're wide open out here."

Her reply was cut short by a dull, powerful thud off towards the town, then another and another as the artillery came down like a crashing wave. June looked over to see Nordsfeld disappear under a curtain of smoke, the dirty black pall of explosive shells mixing a moment later with a pure, blinding white shroud of white phosphorous. The barrage went on and on, shells flaying the town open as they rolled slowly across it like the teeth of an immense grinding wheel.

They walked into Nordsfeld about an hour later, although it could easily have been Hell. Pitch-black smoke turned the sun to a bloody disk overhead, the fires burning through the town searing-hot through the openings of his mask. Blood ran through the cobblestones, slippery and tacky at once under his boots. And then there were the screams. The *screams*, rising over the demonic cacophony of detonating ammunition, as shrill and desperate as the cries of the damned. Although, June thought darkly, he wasn't sure the *wounded* were the sinners there.

Many of the abandoned wagons jamming the streets, abandoned with dead or dying horses hitched to them, were military, piled with supplies and ammunition. So too were many of the bodies, Royal cavalrymen sprawled in undignified death across the streets and pinned under dead horses. The rest of the wagons were piled high with smashed belongings, the pathetic few things the refugees that had crowded into the town with its train station and promise of salvation west had managed to carry with them. And the rest of the bodies were civilians. Men, women and innocent children blasted across the streets, the wide-eyed survivors shrinking at their approach.

It was an awful lot of people to kill, June thought, just to spit on a dead man's grave.

Chapter 27

Courage and Cowardice

Sensing an opportunity while the officers figured out what to do next, the cooks had worked their wagon into the forest and brazenly rang the dinner bell to announce that, damn the war, chow was ready and they were serving. It had taken more than a little shouting from Sergeant Cross to keep the whole platoon from abandoning their positions to line up all at once, and judging by the cursing coming out of the rest of the forest they weren't the only hungry soldiers in Charlie Company. The food itself wasn't anything special, thick Army stew with meat and vegetables, thick Army bread about as dense as the potatoes they rounded the flour out with, and thick Army coffee they joked they could use to strip paint. If they had been back training at Jade Falls, people would have complained because they had much better meals waiting at home and usually someone or other could still see their house. After a couple weeks on the march people complained because they were too tired to eat. Now... well, Sophia thought, hot Army food was one of the few luxuries they still had and nobody who had been through the Dragonspines would put mere sleep ahead of it. Clearly the rest of the company agreed with her.

Ahead of her in line, Tony stretched his arms over his head and yawned, mess kit and canteen clanking together as they dangled from his fingers. Smiling, she asked, "Doing alright there, Tony?"

Turning, he grinned back at her, freckles darker than ever on his sunburned face, "Yeah. Just tired. Although these bikes beat the hell out of walking."

"I'll say." She remarked. They must have covered fifty miles from Pine Harbor already, and it had only been a day. On foot they would have been far behind and swallowed up by the steel-masked tide already.

Tony's brow furrowed as the thought crossed her mind. It must have showed on her face, the bloodcurdling monster lurking just out of sight any time any of them talked about anything that didn't have to do with the war or the enemy for a change. They weren't that far from the Serpent River, not really. They weren't that far from *home*. Everybody knew it, and nobody wanted to say it. A note of concern in his voice, he asked, "Are *you* doing alright, Sophie?"

She raised an eyebrow and chuckled, "Me? I'll hold up. Somehow" She gestured at the cooks' wagon with one of the mess kits she was holding, "Come on."

Tony was getting filled up when Sophia heard familiar footsteps in the forest litter behind her and turned to see her father approaching, a pleased look on his craggy face. Seeing her, his look turned into an actual smile, although he raised an eyebrow as his eyes played across the mess tins in her hands, "Helping someone out, Sophie?"

"Ah, yeah." She handed the first one to the cooks to fill, who were smart enough to not object while she was trying to talk to the sergeant major, "Lieutenant Gable asked me to take care of it before she left."

"Really?" Her father shook his head, "Look, I know you're the only other girl and she's latched on to you...."

Sophia shrugged, "It's not a big deal, Dad, I'm happy to help her out."

He gave her a stern look, "It's a big deal to *me*, because Cross should be doing it and he isn't. You're much too young to be babysitting lieutenants, young lady." He held out a hand, "Give it here, I'll deal with this."

"Okay!" Sophia handed the mess tin over quickly and stepped aside so the next man in line could come forward. Tony helpfully handed her own full one back to her with a hunk of bread balanced on top, and she slid her hand into the wire handle and took it from him gingerly, the tin's metal hot enough she could feel the heat radiating off it in the cool air. Seizing the opportunity, she asked, "Do you know what we're doing next, Dad?"

Her father grimaced and gestured for them to follow him a little ways away from the cook wagon, lowering his voice, "I gave the colonel my opinion half an hour ago before I left. And I saw those lancers heading out south just a moment ago, so I think Lady MacMahon agreed." They both gave him quizzical looks, so he explained, "When things are moving as fast as they are right now, Imperials won't even think about dressing their lines. They'll just *go*. I'd bet all of our lives that unit that blew by south of us is *alone*, and we can probably slip the whole division through before they close that gap, especially given that we probably took out the unit that was supposed to do just that earlier."

Her father gave a significant glance at one of the tanks still burning out in the fields, the guttering pillar of smoke visible faintly through the trees. Sophia swallowed heavily. That entire fight had been, well, they were *all* terrifying, but worse than most. At least they knew they could *kill* the damn things now. With luck. They'd been close enough to hear someone screaming as one of the war machines caught fire, white-hot flame pouring from every gap and chink in the armor as its ammunition exploded. Finally she ventured, "So... we're heading south?"

He nodded, "Yeah, I'd say so. Eat fast, once the officers finish talking they're going to want us to move." Her father paused for a moment as he looked between them, then said, "I've gathered you two are a thing now."

Tony *blanched*. Sophia felt herself blushing as she looked around nervously, stammering, "Ah... er..."

Her father chuckled, "I can see I gathered correctly. Don't worry, nobody ratted you two out." He reached out and patted her on the shoulder warmly, "I should be scolding you two right now, but given our Lady General's sterling example and how I met your mother, well... you two take care of each other. I'd like to get you both home."

"What, she wasn't a Black Cloak or something, was she?" Tony ventured, insanely, chuckling as he did it.

Sophia and her father exchanged a very serious look. Finally, she turned back to Tony, glaring at him, "No, of course not! Why would you *ever* think that?"

"Well, I mean..." Her boyfriend saw the way the conversation was going and smiled apologetically, "Never mind, I was joking. Sorry!"

"Your sense of humor needs work, Mister Gravesend." Her father growled, then turned and stalked off.

Tony looked over at her and started, "I... you know what, let's go eat."

"Fine by me," Sophia shrugged. Her parents had been married, and she had been born, at the Dragon's Jaw. Her mother had been a 'local,' someone hired on to do work at the fortress from the surrounding countryside, crawling with Imperials as it was. Rumors were inevitable in a small town like Jade Falls. Her father had told her the story once, in the middle of the night in low tones on the incredibly unlikely chance one of their neighbors was eavesdropping. And, well... she may have been indirectly responsible for saving the fortress as a child in her mother's womb, and she was planning on taking *that* particular story to her grave. Giving Tony a patently fake smile, she gestured back towards where their squad was set up on the perimeter, "Come on, let's go eat before this gets cold."

The rest of the squad had gone up before them and was well into their food by the time they sat down on either side of one of their machine guns. From their spot at the edge of the forest Sophia could see a couple of the burned-out tanks from earlier and, far beyond them, a line of dark specks spread out across the distant fields in the golden, late-afternoon light. The riders were spread out too evenly to be Imperial. It was probably, she thought, the lancers from earlier, Captain Schrader's troop, clearing the way south. Artillery growled off to the west as she looked them over, deeper and more menacing than the usual Imperial field guns, and Sophia pushed down the ugly knot in her stomach and set about filling it with something nutritious.

The wind picked up as she finished eating, shaking the trees and rushing cold across her bare legs. Hearing a match scratch and hiss, Sophia turned to see Hargrave lighting his pipe. The old man gave her a thin smile as he puffed it to life and commented, "It's still light out, Sophie, no need to growl." Exhaling a cloud of smoke with a satisfied look, he watched it quickly whip away and commented, "Probably rain tonight... can't complain, all told."

Edward chimed in from his other side, "You think? It's been great so far."

Hargrave smirked and puffed at his pipe again, "Just watch."

Sophia was opening her mouth to say something when Lieutenant Gable's voice rang out in the darkening forest, "First platoon! Get your mounts and assemble on the road, squad leaders on me!"

Time to go. The plan, delivered by a well-fed but unusually subdued Lady Gable, was exactly as her father had predicted. They were to head south, break through any enemy forces and link back up with Royal troops. Where exactly safety *was* nobody seemed to know, but that was depressingly normal by this point. Just another day in Charlie Company. A few minutes later they were on their bikes and speeding south in the twilight, the darkness gathering twice as fast as low clouds gathered overhead.

Soon it was so murky she could barely see the riders in front of her. Ordinarily they would have gotten out their flashlights, but with artillery still rumbling menacingly off to their right and God knew how many dragoons lurking out there in the darkness nobody so much as suggested it. They closed up a little and pushed on as rain started to mist down, darkening the road's gravel and turning it a shade closer to the dark-gray sky overhead and the light-black fields all around them. They pedaled on regardless. They didn't have a choice.

Cresting a rise she hadn't realized was there, Sophia picked out a light in the inky distance, tiny and flickering in the misting rain but unmistakably blue. One of the lancers probably, left behind to direct traffic with a blue filter over his flashlight as a signal. Hoping there weren't any lost dragoons out there thinking it was one of theirs, Sophia shifted back in the saddle and let gravity help her out a little as they descended towards the light. As she watched another light flickered behind it, and for a moment she thought she was seeing double in the rain. She blinked and wiped her eyes, and a couple more lights sprung to life, white and bobbing around faintly behind the blue one. Somebody doing... something on the road ahead of them. God only knew. Gritting her teeth in the cold, wet night, she pedaled onwards.

Buildings and trees rose out of the murk around them as they approached the blue light, a mass of crazy black shapes against the darkness. The will-o'-the-wisp finally resolved itself into the solid disk of a military flashlight held by a man huddled under a tree against the rain, holding his horse's reins as it stamped nervously at their approach. Holding up a hand to signal the halt, Sophia squeezed her brakes carefully as she approached and swung herself off her bike beside him, hoping she wasn't about to come face to face with a dragoon.

The man's pale face and flat cap told otherwise. Looking up at their approach, the man started, "Hey, I've been waiting for you. Hell of a night for this kind of thing."

"No password?" Sophia raised an eyebrow.

The lancer shook his head and joked, "If you guys are Masks in disguise, I quit."

She chuckled despite the cold. Hearing footsteps behind her, she turned as Lieutenant Gable walked up and asked, "You there, you're traffic control, right?"

"Ah, yes, ma'am." The man pointed down the road behind him, where a few more lights had appeared a little ways off, bobbing in the misting rain. Squinting, Sophia thought she saw people silhouetted down the road through the misting rain, standing around in what looked like a loose circle. The lancer was going on, "Keep going straight through town. We came through about an hour ago, had to clear out a few Masks while we were at it. Nothing too serious, but I'd watch out going forward. Some of them might still be around."

"What's that?" Sophia asked, pointing at the lights down the road.

The man shrugged, "No idea. The Eighth apparently had their headquarters down the street that ways, I heard they found a lot of..." He trailed off for a second, grimaced and continued, "Well, *bodies* in there. Probably locals poking around."

"What do you mean, *poking around?*" Gable demanded, much sharper than her usual soft tone.

The man glanced between them sourly, "Look, I'm just one guy here and I got told to direct traffic. For all I know they're down on their knees praying." He paused for a second, then added, "Ma'am."

The lieutenant said nothing, so Sophia stepped in, "Right, thanks. We'll handle it." She looked over at Gable, "Milady?"

The girl shook her head suddenly, turned and called out, "Platoon! Dismount, weapons ready! We're walking through town!" Looking back at her, Gable said, "Lead on, Miss Rose."

"Sure thing, milady." Holding her bike by the handlebars, Sophia unslung her rifle with her free hand and started walking down the street toward the lights, the platoon spacing themselves out behind her as she went. Her footsteps crunched unnaturally loud in the gravel as though the sifting rain had created a bubble of silence around her. The darkness was comforting, at least. It made her feel a little less naked walking down the middle of a street with no cover towards God only knew what.

The shapes ahead of her gradually resolved from ghostly suggestions between flickering lights to hard silhouettes as she approached. Men carrying lanterns, milling around a couple shapes sprawled in the street. Her pulse quickened and she felt herself draw breath quickly as one of the silhouettes turned and lengthened suddenly, a rifle's wooden stock gleaming in the light where the man had it balanced atop his shoulder lengthwise, holding it by the barrel in an entirely unmilitary style. Playing her eyes carefully across the others in the darkness, she realized they were *all* armed, or at least most of them. Not one was carrying his weapon any way she recognized, not the familiar Royal Army positions and certainly not the Empire's peculiar muzzle-down 'ready' stance. They looked like hunters back home. Civilians.

The shape, no, *shapes* sprawled on the ground between them were depressingly familiar. Bodies. The one in front was a dark and nondescript lump in the street, but beyond it the second one's bright clothing caught at the lantern-light. A woman's dress? Civilians caught in the crossfire? Looking at the men again, Sophia felt her blood run cold and then slowly turn to ice. They hadn't covered the bodies, much less carried them off, and their straight-backed postures said they didn't give the slightest damn about them. Sophia's fingers tightened on her rifle instinctively at the realization.

"You hear that?" One of the men's voices drifted over, silhouette twisting as he looked around into the darkness. Sophia realized his eyes probably weren't properly adapted to the dark. He called out, "Someone out there?"

Sophia kept her mouth shut. After a couple seconds of silence, the men started shining the lanterns around and Lieutenant Gable responded softly, "Royal Army."

Sophia added, "*Don't* shine those at us."

The men ignored her, half-blinding her in the process as they started over. One of them started, "God, you gave us a scare!" It was hard to tell behind all the lanterns being shone at her, but the speaker seemed to be a middle-aged man, maybe a little younger. He was going on, "Good job dealing with the Masks."

"Thanks." Lieutenant Gable said flatly, stepping out from behind her, "Who're they?"

"That?" The man snorted, turning to shine his light on the bodies in the street, "Couple of spies for the Masks. They're dealt with."

The 'spies' crumpled in the street were an old man in a dark suit and a young woman in a colorful floral dress, now streaked with blood. It was hard to tell on the man, but she could clearly see the bullet holes stitched across the girl's dress like ugly black pimples. She counted more than a dozen. Sophia had seen more than enough death, and more than a few times when a bullet clean through the chest hadn't even seemed to faze a man for a while. They'd probably kept shooting until she stopped moving.

Someone lit a match behind her, and she turned to see Hargrave had come forward and was taking full advantage of all the light. Puffing his pipe to life meditatively, he blew a cloud of smoke at the men and asked, quietly, "Why do you think they were spies?"

"They let the bastards in. The Empire just showed up this morning, shot the hell out of the cavalry and moved on." The man gestured back down the street into the darkness. Before she'd been half-blinded by all the lanterns, Sophia had made out a substantial building down that direction that seemed to have had half its frontage blasted in.

Hargrave asked, "How?"

"Don't know, but they were talking to them afterwards. One of the Masks' officers, a real long-haired dandy type-" *June*, Sophia thought tiredly, "He came out of there and these two came right out to talk to him. Thought they were living in the Empire now and they were free and clear. We all knew that old coot was a damn Mask, but we figured he was harmless." The man chuckled, "Well, we were wrong, but it's fixed now."

"So you shot them?" Hargrave asked levelly, puffing at his pipe.

"Yeah, what about it?" The man replied.

He was so blasé it was *eerie*. Sophia's eyes narrowed as she shifted her rifle in her hands, the smooth curve of the trigger-guard sliding under her finger as her hand wrapped around the stock. She was starting to open her mouth to say something, she didn't know what, when Hargrave finished blowing out his cloud of smoke and looked over at her and the lieutenant, "What do you think?" He glanced back at the group of men, "It's late and it's raining, I say we just shoot them now."

"The hell did you say?" Their leader asked, starting to heft his rifle.

Sophia's rifle sights snapped into position square on his head. *"Drop it,"* she growled. The men hesitated, staring at her, so she added, "You heard me."

The man puffed up like a balloon, taking a step towards her as he growled, "I don't know what you're-"

The unmistakable *click-clack* of a pistol being charged stopped him in his tracks, and he looked over at where Lieutenant Gable was standing beside her. Sophia absently noted the shape of her pistol leveled at the man in her peripheral vision as the girl came to life, finally speaking, "What my subordinates are saying is you're all under arrest." She added bluntly, "For murder."

Sophia heard the unmistakable creaking and clicking of a dozen rifles being leveled behind her as the rest of the platoon came up. Looking at the wall of guns disbelievingly, the men slowly set their motley collection of weapons down in the gravel and raised their hands. Their leader was the last to do so, and as he straightened up he protested, "These two were *Masks.* Spies!" He spat, "The hell were we supposed to do, just let them run free?"

Hargrave took another puff at his pipe, "I assume you have police here." The bastard still had his rifle slung. He went on snidely, "And it's not illegal to talk to Masks, you know."

Right on cue, artillery sounded off to their right, close enough she could hear the individual thuds as each gun fired in turn. Another battery sounded a moment later, softer but no less distinct. Heavy and light cannons, pounding away at some unfortunate target even farther to their west. It was as if Emperor Sai had butted in to correct them as to whose country they were standing in. Starting at the sound, the man looked around them quickly and hissed, "Oh, I get it now. We're surrounded and you're planning to surrender, aren't you?" He snapped, "God-damn cowards. I bet you think they'll treat you well if you turn us in. And I thought Fire Ridge was a flu-"

Something darted past her in the darkness and the man's rant cut off with a sickening crunch, then a bone-rattling thud as his poleaxed body slammed backwards to the ground. Drawing his rifle's bloody butt back, Tony viciously kicked the man in the groin as he writhed on the ground once, twice, and was winding up to do it again and probably keep doing it another thirty or forty times when Sophia got a hand on his shoulder. Stepping back, he cursed viciously, *"Bastard.* That'll teach you some *God-damn* respect."

"What's going on here?" Lieutenant Thorn's voice called out, loud and commanding.

"These men confessed to murdering these two here, I've arrested them." Lieutenant Gable reported bluntly.

"Just what we need now, prisoners." The artillery thudded off another salvo for emphasis. Sophia could hear the raised eyebrow in Thorn's voice behind her, "I'm assuming this one resisted? Broke noise discipline, gave our position away?"

There was a short silence before Tony said, "Yeah."

"Very well. Vanessa, have a detachment get the road clear and guard the prisoners until our trucks come by so you can load up. And then get moving, the whole company's stopped here." Thorn ordered, obviously impatient.

"Kind of unfair, sir, them relaxing in the trucks while we're all sweating." Sergeant Cross, who had apparently arrived too, weighed in. At this rate she was expecting General MacMahon to gallop up and weigh in while she was occupied with staring down the rest of the prisoners.

Thorn chuckled unpleasantly, "I said load up, sergeant. I didn't specify *whom*. If you want to drag them that's fine by me."

"Okay." Vanessa said flatly. Turning back to the blanching prisoners, she hefted her pistol and announced, "You are under arrest on suspicion of murder and will be tried by general court-martial at Lady MacMahon's earliest convenience. Now move your victims off my road, we've got a war to fight." Turning, she called out, "Third squad, you're on guard duty! Sergeant, can you handle this while we get moving?"

"Sure thing, milady! Third squad, fix bayonets!" Sergeant Cross called out, more cheerily than the situation really called for. But just like that, they were off again. Sophia swung herself back onto her bicycle's saddle as the men were herded off to the side of the road carrying the bodies between them. More Imperial artillery echoed through the empty streets as she pushed off. In the rain and fog it seemed to be coming from everywhere. The hotel's smashed façade stared at her as she went by, the holes blasted in its face a surreal echo of the bullet holes stitched across that girl's back. Shuddering, Sophia grit her teeth against the worsening rain and pedaled onwards through the night.

They pedaled on for an hour, then another, the rain soaking her down to her soul. They passed a couple forlorn-looking lancers who waved them on mutely, their blue flashlights will-o'-the-wisps for all she could tell until she was practically on top of them. It was miserable work but, she thought bitterly, at least the Imperials were out in it with them. Maybe it had even taken the edge off their usual zeal, although she pushed that thought aside as more artillery volleys rolled through the night. The Empire wasn't quitting, *June Anjanou* wasn't quitting, and she sure as hell wouldn't.

That long-haired bastard showed up a lot more often than he had any right to. She'd seen him, what... four times now, she thought, and heard about him just as often. It could be total coincidence that the 5th Dragoons had just ended up facing them again and again, and he happened to be their most distinctive member. Maybe it was fate messing with her. And maybe she was going insane. It wasn't like he was the only dragoon with long hair, she'd seen plenty of others. None *quite* like him though. Did he ever think about her, in the darkness and the rain when his thoughts wandered, riding through the darkness like that shadow on horseback she was pretty sure she just saw to her right off across the fields. *Shadows*, not more than a stone's throw away and so well-hidden in the night they disappeared when she jerked her head over to look at them squarely.

That was an optical illusion. They were there. Sophia jerked her bike's brakes violently and leapt off as it skidded to a halt, the muscles of her legs feeling like they'd turned to cold jelly as they creaked and buckled beneath her. Her voice cracked as she called out in the darkness, "C-C-Conta..." Someone had noticed her and was skidding to a stop as she plunged into the roadside ditch, the icy water searing her bare thighs as she finally found her voice, "Contact! Right! *Close!*" Almost as an afterthought she added, "Hold fire! They might be ours!"

Men splashed into the ditch all around her, cursing and shouting. Someone she was pretty sure was Kelly leapt in beside her and sent a wave of frigid water crashing over her as he threw himself forward onto the far bank. The evil clack of his machine gun's charging handle sounded clearly through the rain as Gable splashed down on her other side with a determination she wouldn't have expected out of the girl, saying, "Rose! What do you..." She trailed off as the sound of horses whinnying and stamping drifted through the seething darkness, then wet hoofbeats receding into the distance. "Right," she said quietly, then raised her voice, "*Identify yourselves!*"

"*You first!*" A man's voice floated back faintly.

"They're not lancers, milady." Sophia muttered as she tightened her rifle into her shoulder, "And I don't think they've run into ours either."

"Well, let's find out." Hefting her own rifle, Gable called back, "*Royal Army! Two-Twenty Fourth Infantry!*"

A long silence followed. Just as Sophia was opening her mouth to suggest they were dragoons who were in the process of slinking away, a voice called back, *"What's your name, missy?"*

Oh my God, Sophia thought, *are these guys serious?* Glancing over at the lieutenant, she said, "I've got this, milady." She raised her own voice, *"Sophia Rose! That was Lieutenant Gable, she's new!"*

"There's more of you now?" The man called back incredulously.

"Yes!" Sophia snapped, *"Now who the hell are you?"*

"Eighth Cuirassiers!" The voice called back, then added, *"Second squadron! We didn't get hit, we've been looking for survivors!"*

In this weather? Sophia felt her respect for the armor-plated cavalrymen click up a notch before the realization fully hit her, and she let out a breath she hadn't realized she'd been holding. Despite the cold, and the slimy water rushing past up to her armpits where she lay there half-submerged in the ditch, and the dead pain in her legs, despite it all, it felt like a great big warm blanket had suddenly wrapped around her. Looking around at the men murmuring in the darkness, she could tell the rest of her friends felt the same way.

It wasn't their first time. The Rattlesnake Regiment had a way of getting lost. Even so, Sophia thought, you don't really appreciate the Army until you've lost it for a while. They were back in friendly lines. They had survived another battle. Somehow. Of course it was pouring ice-cold rain on them, they were probably miles from shelter and there were still *plenty* of dragoons out there waiting to kill them in the meantime, but these days getting hypothermia in friendly lines was a privilege.

Chapter 28

Dinner with the Help

Mr. Masters' staff had really outdone themselves to put on a spread so impressive on such short notice. From what she could see of her down the table even Becky looked grudgingly pleased. So far they had laid on golden caviar, an excellent and surprisingly rustic lentil soup, fish balls in mustard sauce, and they had just finished the main course of tender braised duck, rutabaga and potatoes mashed together, and peas. Her host clearly had a taste for the Union's food, and it was a bit of an eye-opener given her mother's staunchly southern allegiances on the topic. It was one of the world's many little ironies that the Dominion's own cuisine at the *Orient* had led to the greatest disaster for Stahlberg diplomacy in generations, and its former proprietor fed it to her family practically every day as Queen. And while she wasn't sure she'd enjoy it quite as much as a routine, Arilin didn't mind an occasional change of pace.

The servants disappeared the dishes, and Arilin leaned back in her seat and sighed contentedly, feeling her corset's grip tighten around her body reassuringly. It was a wonderful dinner with, she thought, some very fine company, but it was also only the proverbial first course of the evening's "entertainment." Looking over at Liri and Miri where they were sitting next to her, fidgeting in hussar uniforms, and Lily beyond them wearing an unreadable expression in a borrowed evening gown, she supposed she was probably getting *far* too used to these kind of cloak-and-dagger games. Although, looking across the table at Alyssa's luminescent blush, she clearly wasn't the only one enjoying herself tonight.

"Now, Miss Helbrecht, do you see this here?" Masters was saying, as he produced a gold 20-mark coin from his pocket. Turning to the rest of the table, he smiled, "The rest of you, too, watch this." Her friends quieted down and turned to him as he walked it across his knuckles, bounced it on top of his thumb and flipped it into the air. Catching it, he flexed his wrist and moved his hand around in a little circle, dropping the coin down his sleeve in the process before opening his now-empty hand to show the group, to general gasping and squealing. Looking at his hand theatrically, Masters raised an eyebrow and remarked, "That wasn't supposed to happen. I should have two of these."

Alyssa remarked, smiling, "Did something go wrong?"

"Yes... here, help me out." Closing his fist again, he offered it to her, "Take your dessert fork there, yes, that one," Masters said, shucking something into his hand as everyone else watched Alyssa pick out the correct utensil, "That should do for a magic wand. Now hold it by the tines and tap my fist with the handle."

Giggling, Alyssa did as she was told and gently tapped his fist with the fork's ivory handle, "There you go... I hope it works!"

"Okay, I think it's coming now..." Masters opened his hand, then furrowed his brow perplexedly as he showed them the two ten-mark coins that had appeared, "I seem to have made *change*."

They all laughed, except for Lily giving him a dirty look. Even knowing *exactly* what he was doing, he was still pretty funny. Smiling, Arilin leaned forward and asked, "Need a little help?"

"Yes, actually, milady." Masters said apologetically, "Try the butter-knife." That got them four big, silver five-mark coins. Liri used a nutcracker to produce a twenty-mark *bill*, and Miri, almost beside herself giggling, tapped his hand with a spatula to get the original gold coin back. How exactly he kept the contents of his sleeves straight was beyond her. "Hrm," he grunted, looking at it with a nonplussed expression before exclaiming, "Oh, I know!" Turning back to Alyssa, he offered it to her, "Here, I think you need to do it."

"Me?" Her redheaded companion took it reluctantly, blushing deeply, "I don't know how..."

"Nonsense!" Masters said confidently, closing her fingers around it with both of his hands and slipping the second one in there while he was at it. "Let me try this," he smiled warmly, before bending down to kiss her hand.

Arilin felt her *own* face heating as Alyssa slowly opened her hand to reveal two coins. "Oh... wow!" Her friend exclaimed, giving him an attentive look, "How'd you do that?"

"Magic." He winked at her, disappearing the coins again as he signaled the servants, who had been waiting in the back of the room looking amused, to put on the next course. Chuckling, he went on, "How do you think I got rich in the first place?"

Everyone laughed, even Lily this time. It loosened the tension in her chest a few notches, her corset gripping her warmly as she giggled along with her friends. Giving Masters a look as she calmed down, Arilin remarked, "I sure wouldn't want to play cards with you."

He laughed, "Milady, I'll have you know it's *perfectly normal* for a deck of cards to have five aces." She snorted with mirth, and he paused for a moment as the servants set down their next course, a foreign but very refreshing-looking cucumber salad. She could practically taste the fjords as she took a bite and her host went on apologetically, "I hope this has all been to your liking, milady. If I'd had more time I would have put on something more, well... elaborate."

"Nonsense!" She replied, smiling, "This is wonderful. You should tell your cook he's outdone himself. Not to mention you've been a fine host, I was worried with everything going on, well..."

"Milady, I received some *excellent* news from my daughter this morning." Masters smiled and made a dismissive gesture with his hand, "I'm not letting a little strike ruin my day. Actually," He gave her a look, suddenly serious, "You know her pretty well I think, you might be interested in it yourself."

"Oh?" Trying remember a Miss Masters, for once in her life Arilin drew a complete blank. Confused, she raised her eyebrows questioningly, "I don't *think* I know her?"

Chuckling, he nodded, "Oh, no, you do. Vanessa normally goes by her mother's name, Gable. Less attention that way." *That* explained a few things. Across the table from her, Alyssa made a strangled noise through a mouthful of salad and gave Masters an alarmed look as he went on, "I'd heard, God, two months ago now she'd been taken prisoner, and *nothing* since."

The last time she had seen Vanessa the quiet hussar lieutenant had been tucking her into bed at that inn near Fire Ridge. The girl had left like a ghost in the night, riding for the front lines to rejoin her regiment as the fighting worsened. Patricia had sent her a letter a couple weeks later with what she had managed to piece together about her fate, and it still made her skin crawl thinking about it. Her platoon had been *wiped out* that night, every last girl killed or taken prisoner, their final signal that they were being overrun by Imperial infantry. Vanessa had apparently been subdued, relatively unhurt, in hand-to-hand combat. And since then... well now that she thought about it, she hadn't heard anything herself.

Leaning forward in her seat, Arilin asked, "Well, please, what have you heard? I've been worried about her myself."

"Apparently she escaped." Apparently being slippery ran in the family. Chortling, Masters went on, "She sent me a telegram from Pine Harbor of all places, telling me she'd made it back and was already set up with a new unit, not the Fourteenth, thank God." Realizing his gaffe, he gave Alyssa an apologetic look, "Present company excepted, of course, but she did *not* like it there and, well..."

The hussar captain shook her head, "Given what she went through, I don't blame her at all. I mean..." She trailed off, shaking her head, "I was there, I *gave* her the assignment that night when she walked in, scared as scared could be, because Bennett couldn't be *bothered* to stay up and meet her." Alyssa's voice, normally so confident, cracked as she went on,

"Look, I'm... I'm sorry, I should have done something. *Said* something. She shouldn't have been put in that position, and I knew it was going to go bad *halfway* through talking to her."

"Please, please, dear." Smiling, Masters her hand in his, "No harm done. I'm sure you had as little choice in the matter as she did."

Alyssa gave him an unreadable, wide-eyed look for a second, then blushed deeply and seemed to deflate, looking down at her plate as she replied, "T-thank you. That means a lot."

It hung in the air for a moment as they sat there in silence, far from unpleasant but cold nonetheless. Keeping a reassuring hand on Alyssa's, Masters glanced over at Arilin and changed the subject, "At the risk of being rude, milady..." He glanced around the bizarre group sitting around his table, the hussar officer and her two fake subordinates, the princess, her maid and the obviously-uncomfortable girl glowering in an evening gown, "I'm quite curious as to this scheme you seem to have involved me in."

Leaning forward and steepling her fingers in front of her, Arilin replied, "It's not too different from what you were just doing yourself." She went on, "I need to meet someone tonight without my uncle knowing."

"So you're doing a little sleight of hand?" Masters gave her a sly look, "Can I guess how?"

She smiled back, "Be my guest."

He nodded at Liri and Miri, "Your two friends are much too young for the hussars, even with the war on. And," he nodded again at Lily, "That girl's been fighting her corset all evening and was tripping on her skirts walking in. She's clearly not used to a gown like that." He leaned back in his seat and gave her a level look, "I'd wager you girls are switching outfits before you walk out of here."

"Oh?" Arilin smirked, "Go on."

"Well, I know you three showed up in a carriage with about a dozen cuirassiers in tow. Probably that tail you want to lose. And *you* three," Masters squeezed Alyssa's hand and gestured at the other two hussars, "Walked in right ahead of them, with every excuse given how many troops have been running around here recently. Ladies in cloaks and veils, girls in uniform with their hair tucked up in their hats..." He chuckled, "Those big lugs won't notice a thing. Makes me want to go down myself and play along."

Arilin laughed, "We can use all the help we can get."

He raised an eyebrow, "I hope those two have some heels. You two are *not* short, you know."

"Of course." Arilin leaned over to him conspiratorially, "You know we tried this on the Foot Guards first."

Masters chuckled, "Why am I not surprised?"

* * *

Thoroughly distracted by the master of the house going around personally handing every one of them a big, shiny 20-mark coin in thanks for their 'heroism,' the cuirassiers didn't so much as bat an eye as they walked out past them. The rest of Alyssa's detachment was waiting out front with their horses, the girls looking thoroughly pleased after their own meal in the servants' quarters. As they mounted up and left Mr. Masters' palatial townhouse behind, Arilin remarked, "I wish you could have brought Midnight."

Alyssa, riding beside her, snorted, "That horse is more recognizable than you are, milady. And I'm not sure *I'd* want to have ridden her down here."

"I know, but I like her anyways." Arilin pouted. It was indeed a little strange finding herself in uniform on such a mild-mannered horse, probably one picked out to behave itself no matter what Liri or Miri was doing on it. Alyssa needn't have bothered given her friends were perfectly fine riders themselves, but the woman also barely knew them. Midnight *coiled* with power beneath her, and she'd probably have to whip this thing just to get it to canter.

Not to mention it was her first time back in uniform since... well, her brother's vigil, and her first time in her gray and red *service* uniform since she'd come back from the front. Since she'd last seen Vanessa, really. The heavy jacket with its web of lace, the breeches hugging her thighs, the snug boots and the reassuring weight of her saber on its belt, all of it made her feel like a proper soldier for once instead of a little girl playing way out of her league. And as a soldier she was going to have to see this through, come what may.

The Low City's streets were deserted, their hoofbeats echoing off deserted storefronts as they headed towards the harbor. Normally the streets would be bustling with life, streetcars, carriages and automobiles all crowding for space with pedestrians and riders like themselves forced to slide in between the traffic, but her uncle's curfew order had put an end to all that. She spied one of his posters as they rode by, freshly pasted up that afternoon and shouting, 'CURFEW BY MILITARY ORDER, 8:oo P.M. VIOLATORS SUBJECT TO ARREST. GOD SAVE THE KING.'

Of course it didn't apply to Mr. Masters' ritzy district or anything south of the harbor, but it was still a bit, well, a *lot*, much. The strikers had abandoned their barricades quarter-built hours ago and gone home, and by this point the biggest threat to the peace was probably nervous soldiers and police accidentally shooting at *each other*. And speaking of strikers... Arilin cast an enquiring eye over Lily as the girl rode beside her, silent and stony-faced in the saddle. She certainly rode adequately, but she wore the uniform like she was allergic to it. Which, considering just how many people the Valkyrie Knights had *killed* during Red December, Arilin wasn't entirely sure she blamed her. It occurred to her, given who Lily was and where her sympathies lay, that girl would probably be her enemy for the rest of her life.

Snorting, Arilin looked away and nudged her dopey horse after Alyssa. Her uncle would *definitely* be her enemy for the rest of her life, and she had to take what she could get. She had to take help where she could get it, to whatever extent she could get it, and make it work until she either ran out of crises or ran out of power. Noticing her come up alongside her, the redheaded hussar looked over and asked, "Nervous, milady?" She snorted, "I wouldn't blame you, honestly. *Nothing* about this is normal."

"Last time I was down here someone threw a bomb at me." Arilin replied drily, "I'm not blaming *myself*. Now, aren't we supposed to be meeting someone? We've got to be getting close."

"You're right..." Alyssa furrowed her brow for a moment as she fished in her jacket, then produced a couple of white handkerchiefs. Tucking one into her collar, she handed the other to Arilin, "Here, milady. So our man knows it's us and not any old hussar patrol."

"Smart," Arilin replied as she took it and tucked it into her collar herself. They rode on for a few more minutes as the dark storefronts and dimly-lit apartments above made way for the heavier industrial architecture of the waterfront, silent except for their clattering hoofbeats and the harsh buzz of the streetlights. The alleys between the factories and warehouses were bottomless pits of darkness, as though the arc lamps overhead had cut off reality with a knife. It made her skin crawl. Midnight would have sensed her discomfort and snorted sympathetically, but her current, dumb mount just plodded on morosely, making it twice as worse.

The harbor's dead fish-and-oil reek built as they approached the docks. Arilin was about to turn and ask Alyssa if they had gone too far when she spotted something detach itself from the shadows down the street. The shadow resolved into a nondescript man as it walked forward into the streetlights and gave them a small wave as they approached. Holding up her hand to halt the detachment, Alyssa reined her horse up next to the man and growled, "You're breaking curfew. What's your business?"

The man snorted, "I'm here on orders from the Palace."

"Whose orders?" Alyssa demanded. Arilin snorted at her commitment to the act.

"Your subordinate's there." The man jerked his chin at her, the harsh streetlights catching at his silver-streaked beard, "Hell of a night for a ride, princess."

Arilin chuckled, "I'm not here for my health. You're Sean, I take it?"

He grunted, "Yeah." From what Becky had told her earlier, he worked for Charlotte in some capacity. Their little network was expanding, although he didn't look the slightest bit happy about being part of it. Giving her a hard look, he went on, "You're playing a dangerous game, milady. I'd take Masks over these people any day of the week."

Arilin grimaced, "So would I, but I don't have much of a choice right now."

"Just don't get Miss Charlotte into anything you can't get her out of." The old man let it hang for a second, then went on, "Sikorsky's down at the second dock to the left once you hit the waterfront at the end of the street. He's got a boat and a couple of his men with him, but nothing that should worry you lot."

Alyssa cut in, "Did you see anyone else around, reinforcements or an ambush, maybe?"

Sean chuckled, "I'm an old jaeger, ma'am. They're alone."

"Good to hear." Her redheaded friend tossed him a 20-mark coin for his trouble, the big golden disk catching the light as he caught it. She made as though to wave them on again, then paused and turned back, "How're you getting home tonight? Your excuse from before isn't going to pass with a real patrol."

He chuckled, "I'm not. I'll find a hidey-hole around here, wait until dawn and try not to get robbed for my trouble."

"I've got a better idea." Alyssa smirked, "You're under arrest for breaking curfew with that cockamamie excuse. Spencer, Roberts, escort this *vagrant* back to Regiment. He needs to be interrogated to see if there's any truth at all to his story. And then, you know," She gave the two girls, the smallest, least-imposing ones in the entire group, a look, "He'll over-power both of you and escape when it's safe."

"Sure thing, ma'am!" They both chorused, before setting about ostentatiously menacing Sean with their sabers. He gave Alyssa a pained look, but shuffled off good-naturedly under their watchful eyes.

"Alright." Alyssa said, more to herself than anyone else. Giving Arilin a look, she nodded, "Let's go, milady."

Arilin nudged her horse forward wordlessly, and they quickly emerged onto the waterfront itself. The oil-slicked bay was a flat, black mass under the dark overcast, an almost vertigo-inducing hole in reality. The Labyrinth was lost in the darkness, a small black island rising from a black sea on a black night. Normally Sapphire Bay at night was a whole galaxy of stars, the Northern Fleet and countless civilian ships glowing cheerfully amid the encompassing swath of the Capital and the distant lights of the bay's many islands. Now the remaining half of the fleet was at sea, the Capitol was shuttered under martial law, and the ships and the islands were blacked out by military order. What a difference a few months made.

Sighing, Arilin turned to look down the street. They hadn't gone far when she heard the faint rumble of an engine and smelled acrid smoke over the oil and fish of the harbor. They emerged around the bulk of a naval freighter tied up for some kind of repair and finally spotted their ship, a completely unassuming tugboat idling at its mooring without a single light showing. A shadow moved on the pier, Arilin feeling her heart flutter as a bayonet glinted and a voice called out, "Halt! Who goes there?"

Alyssa reined up her horse and called back, "Friends!"

"Advance one to be recognized!" The voice called back tersely. For communist fighters they seemed to be awfully well-disciplined although, Arilin supposed as she peered into the darkness, Sikorski *was* some kind of petty officer in the Navy. His men were probably all sailors themselves. Alyssa nudged her horse forward towards him, tugging the handkerchief at her collar at give the man a hint. After a moment he got it and Arilin saw the bayonet swing back upright as the man said, "Pass, friend! Although, uh, we don't have room for all of you."

"We're not all going." Alyssa replied tersely, "Come on milady. First Squad, you too. Second, Third, wait until we're properly on our way and then head back to Regiment."

The leading squad dismounted, collecting their carbines from their cavalry scabbards before they handed their horses over to the remaining girls. Climbing down herself, Arilin handed off her horse's reins, took a deep breath to steady herself and walked into the shadows alongside Alyssa. She made out the sentry as her eyes adjusted to the darkness, a tall, scruffy-looking silhouette of a man in what looked like a sailor's uniform, a rifle with an old-fashioned quill bayonet sloped against his shoulder. Noticing her, he chuckled and gave her a workmanlike salute with his rifle, greeting her, "Evening, princess." His eyes shifted, and he nodded at someone who had emerged to her side, "And to you, Miss Moore."

Arilin touched the brim of her cap as she walked by, replying, "That it is, thank you."

Lily added, "Comrade."

Grimacing, Alyssa stepped ahead of them to walk down the short gangplank and step down onto the tug's decking. A voice she recognized as Sikorski's floated out of the wheelhouse in the darkness above as she did, "No asking to come aboard today, miss?"

The hussar chuckled, "It's her father's ship, chief."

"And if he was here that would mean something." Sikorski growled back.

Arilin stepped down after her and asked politely, "Well, do you mind?"

"Not at all, Princess, make yourself at home. Although," The man laughed, "Might not be up to your standards. Come on, the rest of you come along, we need to get going!"

The rest of the girls trooped aboard, followed a moment later by the sentry and another man who emerged out of the shadows further down the dock. Alyssa gestured for the hussars to check the boat for any unwelcome surprises, and after a few seconds of milling around and opening hatches and doors they returned empty-handed. Chuckling at the show of diligence, Sikorski called out for his men to cast off, and a few moments later they were chugging through the still water of the bay.

Toward the Labyrinth. Pushing aside the queasy feeling in her stomach, Arilin climbed the ladder up to the cockpit above the pilothouse to find Sikorski working at the controls. Hearing her coming up, he turned and remarked, "Come to watch, princess? There's a seat over there."

Easing herself down into the canvas sling seat, she replied, "Good to see you again, although I wish we'd met under better circumstances."

He grunted, "Not your fault. Well, probably it was your fault, but I don't blame you."

"So you *do* think they were after me." Arilin replied coyly.

"Probably more like two birds with one stone." Sikorski shot back, "If it makes you feel better, I can't think of anyone I'd rather get murdered alongside."

Arilin laughed, "What about my uncle?"

After a long pause, Sikorski grunted, "You've a fast one, princess." Someone else emerged up the ladder, and he turned and, seeing who it was, nodded respectfully, "Lily. Good to see you, miss."

"You too, Leon." Lily swung herself up onto the decking and found a seat on the other side of the cockpit, "Can't believe we're really doing this."

They both looked at Arilin, then exchanged significant glances. Turning back to the controls, Sikorski replied levelly, "We've got her to thank for it."

"And her father to blame for it." Lily added sourly.

"My father could have had him *hung*." Arilin shot back.

"Life in the Labyrinth." Lily's hair shimmered pale in the darkness as she tossed her head, "Some mercy."

Arilin snorted sarcastically, "It came out to three years, he got off pretty light."

Lily's eyes flashed dangerously, "Three years when you had your-"

"*Stop it*, girls, you're both pretty." Sikorski cut in sternly, "I'm not going to listen to you two catfight all the way there on my ship, now be civil with each other or you'll both regret it."

They looked at him, then at each other, then snorted angrily in perfect unison. Lily seemed to take his threat seriously though, and Arilin wasn't in the mood to twist the knife. They continued on in silence for a while, just the soft thrum of the engine and the lap of the waves, Sikorski adjusting the wheel every now and then to steer clear of some half-visible ship in the darkness. It was brutally late on a day that had been far too long already, and Arilin felt her eyelids drooping as the boat rocked through the darkness.

She jolted awake as the boat bumped into something, opening her eyes to see a light shining into the cockpit from nearby. Holding her hand up to block it out, she made out the outline of a wooden pier beside them and a uniformed figure behind the light. The guard called out, "What are you doing out here? There's no ship scheduled." He added, hefting a carbine in his other hand, "This is a restricted area. Any funny business and I *will* shoot."

"I wouldn't do that if I were you." Sikorski called back snidely, "Princess Arilin's here with me."

"Bullshit." The man snapped back.

"No, it's true." Alyssa cut in from the deck below, "Captain Helbrecht, 14th Hussars. I'm her escort."

"You serious?" The guard asked incredulously, "Come up here, I need to see your papers before you're going *anywhere*." Alyssa dutifully hopped up onto the quay and handed him her identification, and after scrutinizing it for a few long seconds he finally said, "I'm going to have to get the warden. Why in the *world* is the princess out here, ma'am?"

Alyssa replied, "She's considering commuting a sentence and she wants to speak to the man first." The man nodded and started to turn away, but Alyssa stopped him, "Oh, and we're trying to do this *quietly*. The Justice Ministry doesn't know we're here, so if your warden can refrain from making any panicked phone calls back to the mainland before he comes out I'd appreciate it."

The man swallowed hard, his prominent Adam's apple moving noticeably in the flashlight's backsplash. After a moment he managed, "I'll tell him that, ma'am." Retreating to his guard shack at the foot of the quay, Arilin saw him set his flashlight down and pick up a phone, his shadow a garish puppet painted across the far wall as he dialed a number. After a short conversation he stuck his head out and shouted, "You can all come ashore, he's coming shortly!"

The warden showed up just as she was starting to get impatient waiting on the dock, an unassuming older man, rumpled and bleary-eyed from being turned out of bed at the late hour. Looking over their little group, he paled as he picked her out and asked, "M-milady, I'm sorry to have kept you waiting. What can I do for you?"

"I'm thinking about commuting Hiram Moore's sentence. It's political." Arilin explained bluntly, "Can you get him? I need to make talk to him before I make my decision." Lily hissed beside her, and Arilin gave her a look as she went on, "If he doesn't cooperate the only thing he's getting tonight is a family visit."

The warden swallowed visibly, "I'll... get him cleaned up, milady."

"Please don't." Arilin replied tiredly, "It's late, I am quite tired and this is going to be one of *my* prisons one day. I'd like to see the *actual* condition of your inmates."

The man gave her a long look, then hardened. And hardened. And hardened still, until he reminded her of nothing so much as a sharp piece of flint. *There* was the prison warden. Finally, he replied callously, "Very well, milady. Your choice. I'll be back shortly." Stalking back to the guard shack, he made a short phone call, then stalked off into the darkness.

Arilin's eyes quickly readjusted without anyone shining flashlights into them, and she was able to make out the outline of the Labyrinth it-self against the dark, overcast sky. Seeing it up close, standing on its dock for the first time, she couldn't help but feel unimpressed. A squat, dark building hulked behind ugly walls topped with razor wire and punctuated with equally ugly guard towers. Given the place's reputation it deserved a nightmare forest of impaled corpses and a chorus of screaming prisoners. The place was almost *banal*, just an old fortress with a few changes to turn it into a prison, which made it far more unsettling in its own way. Chains rattled off in the darkness, and Arilin swallowed involuntarily. God only knew what went on in the bowels of that place in the dark of the night.

By the look of the man stumbling out of the darkness, manacles scraping across the concrete as he was shoved along roughly by a couple of guards, it was nothing good. He was wearing what had once been a striped prison uniform, now little more than threadbare rags that hung loosely off his skeletal frame. The skin of his face, what of it she could see above his unkempt beard, stretched too-tight across his skull. The man's eyes were two gleaming stars through a curtain of shaggy gray hair, darting across the group uncomprehendingly until they fell on Lily and suddenly widened as he stopped in his tracks. The guards were about to shove him forward again when he suddenly hobbled forward a couple steps, reaching out towards her, mumbling, "L-Lily... no, no, I'm seeing things." He shook his head quickly, "No, this is another trick..."

Arilin heard the familiar *clack* of a saber being broken loose in its scabbard beside her, and suddenly realized that giving Lily a sword had been a mistake. The girl had the blade halfway out of its scabbard and was coiling up to launch herself at the guards when Alyssa seized her. Struggling to break free, Lily screamed, "*You bastards! What the hell have you done to my father!*" A couple of the quicker-thinking girls piled onto her as she shrieked, "*I'll kill you! I'll kill you a-aamngh!*"

Having finally gotten a hand over the thrashing girl's mouth, Alyssa remarked drily, "Maybe you should have let him clean up him up first, milady." Lily gave an outraged squawk, and the hussar captain growled, "That's *quite* enough out of you tonight, missy."

From her other side Leon growled, "Lily, you're *not* helping. Control yourself." At that the girl finally stopped struggling, and he added, "Go ahead, princess."

More than a little unnerved, Arilin shook her head quickly and took a deep breath to steady herself, gesturing for the guards to step back to give them some privacy. Once they were out of easy earshot, she asked, "You're Hiram Moore, correct?"

"Y-yes..." He looked past her at where Lily was being held, "I... I don't understand, why is my daughter here... and you too, Leon... just who are you, miss?"

It occurred to her in the back of her head just how *few* people didn't recognize her on sight. Although it was quite dark out, she thought as she replied, "Princess Arilin Wehrherz. I'm here to make you an offer."

The man looked at her blankly for a couple long seconds, then *shook* himself. Straightening up, he brushed the hair out of his eyes, revealing a string of ugly bruises mottled across the side of his skull-like face. It made his quick, piercing eyes doubly unnerving. Finally, he said, "I'm listening."

"How much do you know about what's going on?" She asked.

Shrugging, he gave the guards a contemptuous look, "I've gathered we're at war. If you need *my* help it's probably going very badly indeed." He snorted, his breath rattling in his throat, "Let me guess, princess. Labor strikes? A workers' uprising? I said it at the time, you know." He chuckled, making a strained sound like he hadn't done it in years, "We're just the *symptom*, not the disease."

Arilin set her jaw and pressed on, "My father's at the front and my uncle has most of the real power in the Capital right now. And he'd like nothing more than having another one of your uprisings to crush to cement his position." Moore looked at her levelly as the continued, "The workers will listen to you. I need you to keep them in the factories and out of the streets, unless and until Alphonse moves against *me*."

Moore raised an eyebrow questioningly, "Where's Prince Adrian in all this?" She looked away quickly, lip quivering, and he backtracked, "I'm... sorry, princess. They don't give us *anything* here."

She sighed and shook her head, "Not your fault. He's... gone."

"I'm sorry for your loss." The man let it hang for a second before he hardened, "However, princess... what's in it for me?" He looked between Leon and Lily significantly, "For *us?*"

"My father tolerates your movement. He might even *sympathize* with it if you weren't constantly talking about overthrowing him. My uncle will not." Arilin replied coldly, "If Alphonse gets into power, Red December will look like a tea party."

"What about you, *Crown Princess?*" Moore's eyes narrowed dangerously as he rattled his manacles for emphasis, "Will you continue your father's *tolerance?*"

Arilin snorted, "I'm not going to pretend I'll ever be your friend. But," She glared back at him, "As Queen the well-being of all of my subjects will be my responsibility. Even those who'd rather see me gone."

The corner of Moore's mouth twitched up in something that might pass for a smile. "Well, there you go." Looking past her at Sikorski, he asked, "What do you think, Leon?"

The chief shrugged, "Boss, she's offering to let you out of here. Don't look a gift horse in the mouth."

Moore snorted, "Good point." Looking over at his daughter, he went on, "What about you, Lily?"

"Urgh, will you all let go of me already?" Lily gave Alyssa a furious look, and the hussar captain motioned for her girls to release her. Brushing herself off theatrically, Lily replied, "Dad, Alphonse is trouble." She glanced at Arilin significantly and went on, "Don't get me wrong, *she's* trouble too, but she's also, uh... really nice and caring and diligent and, uh, I *really* like her and I'd *much* rather have to deal with her."

She sounded like she *couldn't wait.* Arilin gave Lily an incredulous look to see the girl had turned *red. Great,* she thought nervously. No wonder Lily acted so weird around her. Even so, she supposed, she'd rather deal with a hundred of her than Alphonse. *He* wanted her dead, but the way Lily was looking back at her she probably just wanted to force her to *marry* her. Now *that* was a thought....

Moore brought her back to reality as he actually gritted out a laugh, "I never could say no to you, dear. Looks like you've got a deal, princess."

Arilin coughed awkwardly, shook her head to clear it and managed, "Ah... good. Great!" Raising her voice, she called out, "Mister Warden, I'm freeing this man, I have his commutation here!"

The warden stomped back over, giving her a sour look the whole way. Producing the papers from her jacket, she handed them to him and he read them quickly by flashlight, then looked back at her sternly, "I had one of my men call the Justice Ministry just now, you know."

"Oh?" She raised her eyebrows innocently, "What did they tell you?"

After a moment he replied, "That they had a copy of the commutation and were waiting on your final approval."

Arilin smiled, "Then we're in agreement."

"We are." The warden gestured to his men, and they quickly set about unlocking Moore's manacles. Freed herself, Lily rushed to his side and helped him onto the boat, Leon ushering them both into the pilothouse immediately. Arilin and the hussars trooped on board a moment later, and they cast off and headed back to shore in record time.

Sighing, Arilin settled herself onto a locker behind the pilothouse and leaned back against the rough wood, closing her eyes for a moment. *Very rough wood.* She'd be lucky if she didn't splinters in the back of her neck. Someone sat down next to her with an exhausted groan, and she opened her eyes and looked over to see Alyssa doing the exact same thing she'd been doing just a moment ago. Feeling her eyes on her, her redhead-ed friend looked back at her, chuckled, and wrapped an arm around her shoulders.

"Why, what's up?" Arilin asked.

"Milady, I was going to ask you if you were sure about what you're do-ing, but I think we're well past that point by now." Alyssa snorted, "I think at this point I'm just going to have to deal with it." Pausing for a moment, she went on, "By the way, milady, I'm assuming Alphonse knows about this by now. I don't suppose you have a plan to keep him from *re*-arresting our friend as soon as he steps ashore?"

The princess laughed, "Yeah, Charlotte's been leaking the story to ev-ery newspaper in town for hours now. A little curfew isn't going to keep every single one of their reporters from meeting us at the docks."

"That's... a plan, milady." Alyssa shook her head, "Your uncle's going to hit the roof, you know."

"I'll deal with him later." Arilin replied tiredly, "Now... I don't suppose you have some makeup on you? They're going to be taking photos and I feel like I need a touchup."

Alyssa looked at her for a moment, then laughed, "You look fine, mi-lady. But. I never leave home without it, so look at me here."

"I was going to do it myself." Arilin pouted.

"You're a princess." Alyssa scolded her gently, "Now shut up and relax for once in your life, you need to act spoiled and entitled *occasionally*."

Arilin laughed, "I'll work on that."

Chapter 29

Pursuit and Retreat

The storm had passed, and the False Sun's ghostly light painted the countryside like a watercolor in pastels as they ground forward on the muddy road. Even on horseback she felt like she was coated in mud and worse from the night's marching, not to mention soaked to the bone. God knew how the infantry made it on their bicycles. *Welcome to the hussars,* Patricia thought sarcastically, *where you'll spend ninety-nine nights lost in the rain for every swordfight. And those aren't what they're cracked up to be either.*

Riding next to her on his big cuirassier's charger, Colonel Jenssen looked like he was doing even worse than she was. She could hardly blame him. Her old subordinate and ally against Chapman had spent the last afternoon recovering the detritus of his regiment after the Empire had smashed most of it to hell and killed Colonel Morris in the process, and had somehow managed to both find them last night *and* make contact with the Tenth Cavalry Division in Darissa. The man was a miracle worker. Noticing her glance, he looked back at her and grimaced, "You holding up, milady?"

She snorted back, "I've had worse."

"*When?*" He asked incredulously.

"The Marchlands." Patricia replied flatly. And she'd had it easy compared to the infantry in the trenches. Even thinking about it still made her blood run cold, as soaked as she was. The mud had gotten so deep it swallowed horses without a trace, in a featureless moonscape of shell-craters and sloughs of barbed wire, twenty feet deep with dark lumps smashed into their coils.

Eric grunted, taking her out of Hell, "They didn't have *tanks* then."

She chuckled, "I'll give you that." Changing the subject, Patricia gave him a sly look, "By the way, Eric, feel up for a larger command?"

He looked back at her skeptically, "Am I allowed to say no?"

"Nope." She replied cheerfully, "I'm firing Mina as soon as that woman shows me her face. And, well, the 14th is short a squadron, your squadron is short a *regiment* and I trust you over either of her commanders. Both of whom are majors right now anyways, so it's not like you'd leapfrog anyone."

"You want me to take command of the *Valkyrie Knights*." Eric replied incredulously.

"Until I can find a female hussar colonel who is senior to you from outside of the Regiment to take over the job, yes." Patricia snorted, "That's a list of three people, none of whom want the job. Anyways, it's temporary, I won't make you wear pink."

Eric shot back drily, "That's a shame, milady, I think I'd look rather good in it."

"You would, actually..." Patricia trailed off as she noticed a disturbance in the column of riders ahead of her, lancers pulling their horses aside to make way for someone fighting his way through the traffic. A hussar with the blue facings of the Second Regiment on his gray jacket finally emerged from the press of troopers, and she called out to him, "Looking for me, trooper?"

"Ah, yes, milady!" The man, a captain now that she had a better look at him, wheeled his horse about expertly and fell in on her other side as he went on, "General Kellerman sent me to find you. You are to report to him immediately in Darissa."

Patricia shrugged, "Very well then. Care to come along, Eric?"

He chuckled, "Sure thing, milady."

Twisting around in the saddle, she spotted Colonel Frost behind her and shouted, "Joe! Kellerman's turned up in Darissa, I'm going forward to meet him!" Her chief of staff nodded and waved for her to go, and Patricia kicked her horse forward behind the hussar. After a while of pushing through lancers and dodging wagons, Patricia spotted two familiar figures trotting along in a bit of a clearing in the scrum. Smiling, she reined her horse in next to Colonel Schrader and his daughter.

The old colonel, hard as ever despite the soaking she knew he'd gotten, greeted her, "Milady. Good to see you."

Riding ahead, the hussar turned and gave her an annoyed look as she fell back. Ignoring him, she replied to Schrader, "Kellerman's turned up. Want to come with?" Looking over at Holly, she went on, "Good work last night, by the way."

The girl bowed her head graciously, doing her best to not look exhausted, "Thanks, milady."

Patricia looked back at Schrader, who shrugged, "Might as well. Lead on, milady."

Barely concealing a sneer, the hussar captain wheeled his horse back about and shouted, "Get off the road, damnit! Coming through! Move!" Patricia was turning to give Schrader a skeptical look when she saw he had glanced the other way, at Holly. From the look on *her* face he was giving her a very specific look indeed. Holly kicked her horse forward a moment later, drawing her riding crop as the hussar thundered, "I do *not* ha-"

His voice turned into a strangled scream as Holly viciously whipped his horse across its backside, the animal bolting off the road and through the fields as the man desperately clung to his seat. After about fifty meters he came off, landing flat on his back in the field as the lancers roared with laughter. Covered in mud, the man got up and started to chase after his long-gone horse as Colonel Schrader remarked, "*My God*. That man's horse spooked for no reason." He gave her a disapproving look, "I hope that isn't representative of the hussars, milady."

Patricia sighed theatrically, "The Second Regiment's always had lousy horsemanship. Really, there's no excuse for a horse to just bolt like that, completely out of the blue." She added, "You should probably send someone to go get it, there *are* Imperials off that way if it goes far enough."

"Oh, he'll catch it eventually." Eric added from her other side, "*God*, that man is *coated*. What do they grow in that field, shit?"

"Onions, I think." Schrader added wryly, "Anyways, milady. Darissa, and Kellerman."

"Right," she nodded, and kicked her horse down the road. The lancers got out of the way quite happily for their own commanders, and they were soon clear of the regiment and galloping down the road as the town rose around them. Much more polite sentries sporting the red facings of the First Guards Hussars waved them through, some of the men shouting as they recognized her. They didn't have to go far before she started noticing bicycles piled up outside of houses and the occasional tired, dirty infantryman sitting listlessly on a porch, and she realized the 224th had adopted the old expedient of barging into random houses at their destination to dry off and warm up after their ordeal. It could be disconcerting for the local civilians, to be sure, but they rarely had anything to fear from tired, hungry and wary front line-troops. It was the rear-echelon ones with time on their hands they needed to watch out for.

They spotted Colonel Espinay and Sergeant Major Rose on a nicer-looking house's porch, chuckling over steaming coffee with an older couple she pegged as the residents. Waving, the little colonel called out, "Milady! Going somewhere?"

"Yes, actually, trying to find General Kellerman!" She shot back, reining her horse in, "I don't suppose you know where he is?"

Rose asked the householder something quietly, and the older man nodded and spoke up, "Well, yes, actually. Ah, milady, pardon me. Last I saw they were set up in the old reserve barracks, down the street and take a left at the post office." He added helpfully, "They've got a flag up, you can't miss them."

"Thank you, sir." She smiled at the old man, then turned to Espinay, "Care to come along? Saves me the trouble of telling you later when you could get it from the horse's mouth."

The blonde colonel nodded and went to collect his bicycle, pedaling along behind them as they set off again. He looked mildly ridiculous doing it, but she supposed no infantryman would *dare* fall out of line if someone like him was riding along and keeping up. They'd never live it down. At the rate they were going she was half-expecting to run into Mina before they got to the Corps headquarters, but they clattered to a halt in front of a nondescript country Reserve barracks without further interruption. The sentries out front, more hussars from the Winged Knights, saluted and pulled the doors open at their approach, and they stepped into Kellerman's sanctum.

At least she was *expecting* Kellerman's sanctum. She was familiar with the Cavalry Corps staff, and it occurred to her as the orderly sergeant called the building to attention that she didn't recognize *anyone*. In fact, judging by the flag they had posted in the hallway this was the 12th Cavalry Division's headquarters, not Corps. Well, it wasn't unusual at all for generals to stop in at subordinate units. After a minute another captain from the Second Hussars, with a blessedly better attitude this time, appeared and ushered them upstairs to what she gathered was the old commander's office. A captain's lair was a little bit of a downgrade for a three-star general, but, she thought wryly as she stepped inside with her subordinates in tow, they were all having to deal with downgrades these days.

General Kellerman glanced up from his seat behind the desk as they came in, then back down at his papers with affected boredom. Stopping in her tracks, Patricia felt her blood start to chill, then run cold as he leafed through the papers on his desk, reports of little significance, office memos and pieces of administrative. Back when she had been a colonel in charge of the 14th Hussars, just a couple years ago now that she thought about it, he had been *her* commander, the man in charge of the Guards Light Cavalry Brigade, and then the Division itself. At the time the Valkyrie Knights had been a disaster, and she had found herself standing in the old man's office many, *many* times to answer for some real or imagined failure on her girls' account. She knew how Kellerman was when he was angry.

This was *well* beyond that. Her commander was *murderous*. Which given the circumstances she probably should have expected. Swallowing hard, Patricia heard a chair creak and looked over to see the office's other occupant getting up, a slender man wearing a single star on the high collar of his lancer's jacket. General Bormann, Kellerman's chief of staff. Clearing her throat nervously, she remarked, trying to sound casual, "I hope I'm not interrupting something."

"Oh, no, we've been expecting you." Bormann said, with a genuinely unpleasant smile, "Thanks for bringing your subordinates along, by the way. This will make things *considerably* easier."

"You can fill us in later, sir, we'll wait outside." Colonel Schrader interjected. Clearly he'd read the room just as well as she had. Turning on his heel, he physically pushed Eric and Colonel Espinay outside before they could protest, saying before he shut the door behind him, "Out, out, *everyone* out, this is general business and I want no part in it..."

The door's latch thunked shut too-loudly, and Patricia turned back to the two men. They'd gone as far as pulling all the chairs to the side of the room. Clearly they wanted her to stand for this. Which, if she had been a wet-behind-the-ears colonel promoted out of her competence and hung out to dry in the Army's worst cavalry regiment, getting called on the carpet over some sordid scandal perpetrated by some bored rich girl in the ranks, she would have done. That was then and this was now, and she'd been personally shooting at Imperial tanks hours earlier. Sighing, she walked over to the wall, got a chair, planted it in front of Kellerman's desk, and sat down. Ignoring Bormann's scandalized look, she asked, "What *things* are we dealing with?"

Kellerman finally looked up from his papers, asking with deceptive calmness, "Did I give you permission to sit down, MacMahon?"

"I wasn't aware I needed to ask, *Gus*." Crossing her legs, she leaned back in her seat, "Look, I've gotten about an hour of sleep in the last two days-"

Bormann interrupted her sharply, "*Watch your tone, Mac-*"

Patricia interrupted him back, "*Shut up*." Looking back at Kellerman, she went on, "Doesn't this guy have a staff to run or something?"

Kellerman snorted, "Not any more. I'm giving him your division."

"You're firing me?" Patricia chuckled, "At this point I'd almost say he's welcome to it, but I don't want him getting all my guys killed."

"Like you just got half of Fifth Division killed?" Kellerman's eyes narrowed, "I was in Nordsfeld yesterday, and I recall giving you orders to cover our deployment. Not only did you fail utterly, you didn't even *deign* to inform me of the fact. And now you expect to waltz in here like nothing happened?" He shook his head, "I had my men's blood soak through my boots yesterday. You're lucky I don't have you *shot*."

"That's odd." Patricia glared back at him, "I recall trying to contact you about, you know, the fact the Imperials were hitting us with tanks, *all of yesterday*. And *most* of the night before. Radio, telephone, even sent messengers. And I know for a fact Walter hasn't heard from you since the day before." She looked over at his chief of staff, "Maybe you should ask him why you went dark."

"Good commanders find a way. Clearly you weren't trying hard enough, it's not like you didn't know we had an advance party in Nordsfeld." Kellerman grunted, "In any event I'm not interested in your excuses and I am well within my rights to relieve you. This discussion is over."

"No, it's not." Patricia pointed at the phone on his desk, "I'm entitled to an immediate appeal to *your* commander, and by regulation there is *nothing* you can do to delay or impede me. So, *Gus*, do you want to explain to Walter why your losing communications during an enemy breakthrough is somehow *my* fault? Because he's probably not going to be very happy you just lost a division, blew *your* entire mission, and you're trying to hang it on someone he hand-picked for a job."

Her commander gave her a disappointed look, "Someone he's in an inappropriate romantic relationship with. Which I'm sure the King would love to hear about."

"Oh, we're going to the King now?" Patricia rolled her eyes, "God help me I happen to fall for a guy. Y'know His Majesty asks me for advice about his daughter sometimes, right?"

"You may have given him some *unintentionally*." Kellerman smirked, "Those walls weren't as thick as you thought they were."

If she hadn't been so tired she would have turned red. As it was Patricia shook her head and shot back, "Not like I haven't had that idea myself. But in any event, unless you want to have this whole discussion *again* with those two, I suggest we move on to our next moves here."

Bormann snapped, *"How dare you-"*

"Oh, calm down." Kellerman waved at him dismissively, "As angry as I am at *her*, you own a piece of this too." Sighing, he leaned back in his chair, "MacMahon, you make a strong case. For all the wrong reasons, mind you, but I'll give you another shot."

Patricia let out a breath she hadn't known she was holding, then pinched the bridge of her nose. Hard. It made the world stop swimming for a moment. Looking back at her commander, she replied, "Thanks." She glanced at the door, "Should I get my subordinates back in here?"

Kellerman grunted, "Sure. Oh," he said, turning to Bormann, "Go get

Isaac and get him in here, we need to figure this out properly."

Bormann gave him a long, hard look, then looked at the ceiling, sighed, and walked out, leaving the door open. Getting up herself, she stuck her head out into the hallway to see her three colonels waiting outside too-nonchalantly and announced, "Okay, general business is over. Get in here."

The three of them exchanged looks, shrugged, and filed in after her. A couple awkward minutes later another man walked in, tall, dark-haired, in a cuirassier's ash-colored tunic with two stars on his collar. General Rosenburg of the 12th Cavalry Division gave her a long, disdainful look, then turned to Kellerman, "I was under the impression..."

The corps commander snorted and waved dismissively, "Lady Mac-Mahon explained her situation convincingly." He gave Rosenburg a hard look, "Same as you a few times, now that I think of it, Isaac. Now let's get down to business."

Rosenburg grimaced and turned to a map conveniently posted on the wall, saying, "Very well then."

She had been so focused on Kellerman that she had barely noticed it herself earlier. Some conscientious staff officer had carefully marked out the Army of Drakenburg's unit locations for the boss earlier, along with what the intelligence shop had pieced together about the enemy. As tired as she was, looking at it now gave her *vertigo*. Turning her chair from earlier to face it, she sat down to study it properly. It took the edge off what she was looking at.

Two nights ago they had been strung out between Pine Harbor and the end of the defensive line proper north of Kelsbruck where the Great Steel River fanned out into its great delta. They had been thrown back a hundred kilometers since then, most of it in the course of two long, *long* night marches, first straight to the west as they struggled to keep the Imperial thrust contained and then in a dogleg south to Darissa as they slipped between the enemy's spearheads. And through that gap the whole Imperial Army was pouring, like a red tide from a spigot. They had already stabbed south to isolate Kelsbruck and had forced bridgeheads across the river proper south of the city itself. The Imperial Army at work, a sledgehammer behind a cloak of lies and shadows.

Walter of course had accounted for this. A lesser general would have deployed the Army of Drakenburg forward along the Great Steel River and would be beginning the process of watching helplessly as the enemy rolled up his line over the course of the next week or so. Knowing the enemy would break through *somewhere*, Walter had instead deployed the

Royal Army in what was probably the deepest defensive scheme ever used in the history of war. If someone had told her when she was at the Academy, in those sunny days of ten-mile marches and one-day battles, that she would see two field armies lined up a hundred kilometers *behind* two other field armies, she would have laughed in their face. As it was Walter had eight corps with half a million soldiers marching north to meet the enemy head-on. Not to mention that he had another corps in Wolf Rock, another two hundred kilometers west, a strategic reserve in case the Empire pulled a trump card.

That trump card was currently rolling through the smoking ruins of Nordsfeld having shredded the force that was supposed to contain it long enough for proper reinforcements to arrive. Patricia could chart out their route of march already, a raid audacious enough to turn even Walter's defensive scheme on its head. If they turned south now they would evaporate in the Royal tide as it rolled north. But if they pushed west along the coast as it angled southwards into the Ellarian Riviera... she felt an icy finger work up her spine. Four hundred kilometers to Brightangel and the northernmost set of bridges over the Serpent River. Beyond that the Shield Mountains, the Great Pass and Drakenburg, currently defended by about enough gendarmes to *maybe* keep the enemy's saboteurs from blowing up anything really important.

If the Empire seized a bridgehead over the *Serpent*, they didn't need to actually beat the Royal Army. They could *bypass* it and punch straight into the Great Pass, leaving it to wither on the vine while they marched on Drakenburg and descended onto the High City. What had taken the Faceless King centuries, General Anjanou would have finished before Christmas. And, looking around the room, Patricia could see the men had come to the same conclusion. Or at least, if their grimaces were anything to go by, one equally bad.

"Oh, my." Colonel Espinay spoke first. They all looked at him, and the little infantryman gestured at the map, "Looks like we'd best be moving if we're going to get ahead of that."

There was a long, pregnant silence as they all thought about it. Then Kellerman snorted and replied, "That's the spirit. Rosenburg, how soon can your division move out?"

"Immediately." The general replied, "You want me to get ahead of them?"

"Yes. Delay them, and see if you can find what's left of the Fifth while you're at it, we're going to need all the help we can get." Kellerman looked over at her, "MacMahon, how about your division?"

The room was spinning a little and the usual considerations for how quickly her troops could move wouldn't come to mind. How long had they been marching? How long had they been up? Casualties? What about the horses? They had vehicles that needed to be refueled. How long had it been since she'd eaten? If this was training they'd get a rest day. If this was training they wouldn't have even *tried* what they just did. Fortunately, Colonel Schrader came to her rescue, "We'll need six hours to feed the horses and rest."

If this had been in training they would have asked for, and probably gotten, the weekend off after a forced march like that. And possibly some medals. As things stood, though... shaking her head, she finally replied, "That sounds about right."

"Very well." Kellerman replied sharply, "You'll maintain contact with the south side of this Imperial formation and delay them if they decide to cut south. If they keep pushing west, harass them. Tanks need a great deal of fuel and they'll have convoys coming up to them soon. Avoid becoming decisively engaged in any event." He gave them all a stern look, "Now get out of my office, all of you. I need to call General Haas and tell him we'll be fighting the enemy on the Serpent this time next week, and I need his reserve to win it."

Patricia nodded and stood, "Yes, sir. Come on, guys, let's go." She stood, then remembered something and paused for a second. Turning back to Kellerman, she said, "By the way, I've got a court martial I need to take care of. Assuming you're on board with it, your staff lawyer might need to put it together for the King."

The older man raised an eyebrow, "A firing squad candidate?" He snorted, "Haven't had one of those in a while. What happened?"

Patricia shook her head, "We caught some civilians who murdered an old Imperial veteran. Guess the dragoons came through town and he was out shaking their hands. Him *and* his granddaughter."

Kellerman gave her a sour look, "Play up the kid in the judgement, there's graveyards in the Empire full of Royalist civilians." She gave him one of her own back, and he rolled his eyes, "That was before your time, mind you, but it sure as hell wasn't before the King's. Now run along, I'm busy."

Patricia nodded and turned to leave, and her subordinates filed out behind her. They passed Bormann on the stairs and he gave her a vicious look, which she ignored. Stepping outside, they were met by a clatter of hooves and she looked to see Mina Bennett and Colonel Frost reining in their horses. The woman looked like she'd seen a ghost. Frost had probably filled her in on her plans. Leaping off her mount, she started, "Milady-"

Patricia held up a hand to forestall her, "Calm down, I changed my mind." She looked over at Eric, "If we fired everyone who lost a fight with the Empire we wouldn't have an army pretty soon.   Eric, I'm attaching your squadron to the Valkyrie Knights for the time being, try to keep my girls out of trouble."

Shrugging, he nodded, "Ma'am." He nodded again at Mina, "Ma'am."

Mina started opening her mouth again and Patricia went on, "The last time I gave you a subordinate that I liked you got them captured six hours later. *Please* try to beat your record with this one." Turning to the other two and ignoring the hussar's squawks of protest, she went on, "Do either of you two know where I can get some sleep? Or some food? My head hurts right now."

Schrader remarked drily, "You did look like you were dying a little in there."

She rolled her eyes, "I wasn't doing well when I went in and Old Killer-Man didn't help."

They both snickered. Recovering, Espinay volunteered, "You know, milady, that house I was at had a *wonderful* ladies' guest room that we were all too embarrassed to use."

"Works for me." Looking over at Frost, who had wheeled his horse around to join them, she went on, "Joe, we're moving out again in six hours, we're going to hug the south side of this Imperial spearhead and make their lives miserable. Tell the staff to get some rest, they're probably worse off than I am."

Her chief of staff nodded, "Sure thing, milady." Kicking his hose, he disappeared back down the street in a clatter of hooves.

Patricia turned back to Espinay and asked, "I don't suppose those folks do breakfast? I'd kill for some eggs and bacon right now."

"They were actually starting to talk about it when I left, milady." He smiled cheerily, "Come on, the day's looking better already."

Chapter 30

Light and Shadow

The defense attorney, a major she had never seen before in her life, tugged theatrically at his cuffs as he paused. She had seen more than a few hussars in her short time in the Army, but never one with black facings on his dove-gray jacket. Sophia glanced across at the prosecutor while she had the breathing room, and the man looked up from his papers to give her a reassuring smile. As he did it she realized the collar on his cuirassier's jacket was black, something that had completely escaped her earlier. She was absent-mindedly processing the fact that the Legal Corps' branch color was black when the defense attorney finished preening and turned his glare back on her, demanding, "So, Miss Rose, just so we're *perfectly* clear here, you didn't actually see any of the accused shoot any-"

"Objection." The prosecuting officer cut in tiredly, "Asked and answered."

"Sustained." Sophia looked over to see General MacMahon giving the hussar a stern look, "We have a war to fight, Clemens, are you done?"

The man sighed, "Just trying to keep my clients *behind* the firing squad, milady. But, yes, I think the record stands at this point."

Gasps went up among the audience at his words. The Army had taken over Darissa's little courthouse for the court-martial, and the sight of the defendants being herded in, civilians in shackles, had drawn a crowd. Probably intending to make a point about reprisals, General MacMahon had ordered the gawkers let in to the viewing gallery. The murderers themselves barely reacted, staring ashen-faced at their table, except for the young one. *That* guy was looking around nervously, eyes wide as saucers. They all looked completely normal, if she was being honest with herself, people she would pass on the street without a second thought. Then again, so had their victims. War made people crazy. And with the death she'd seen, the men and women she'd killed herself... well, she wasn't sure any of them had the right to judge at this point.

Lady MacMahon was speaking, "Very well. If you're not calling any of your own witnesses, we'll close here." Artillery cracked outside, close enough it had to have landed in the town itself. The war was calling, and she pressed ahead over the crowd's uneasy murmur, "I see no reason to delay judgement."

"Milady, can my witness get off the stand first?" The prosecutor interjected bravely.

General MacMahon looked over at her, then snorted and waved for her to get up, "You're dismissed, Miss Rose." Sophia stood, but she stopped as she made to leave, "By the way," She turned, and the lady general gave her a smile and went on, "Your platoon performed admirably dealing with this. It's not always easy doing the right thing under these circumstances, or even obvious that it should be *done*. There aren't medals for this kind of thing, but there probably should be."

Swallowing hard, Sophia managed, "Thanks, milady."

"Now go win the war." Sighing with relief, Sophia turned and walked out of the courtroom, ignoring the stares and murmurs as she went. She had stepped out through the open door and looked over to see Tony standing there with her rifle when she heard General MacMahon go on, faintly, "I find you all guilty of all charges, and sentence you to be shot to death by musketry at dawn. An appeal-"

She didn't catch the rest of it. People started shouting and the rest of the lady general's words were drowned out. Glancing back inside nervously to reassure herself that she didn't need to stick her bayonet on her rifle and go keep the crowd in their seats, she turned back to Tony and said, "How about we leave?"

Handing her rifle back to her, he gave the courtroom a nervous glace before turning, "Yeah, sounds good." As they walked down the steps he went on, "Are you okay, Sophie? You look like you've seen a ghost."

She probably did. The noontime sun was beating down on the street, turning the cobblestones into an oven, but she felt like Tony had been waiting with a bucket of icewater along with her rifle. Shot at dawn. *Christ.* And Lady MacMahon hadn't even *blinked.* It occurred to her that as nice as the woman was, just like her father, she had killed a *lot* of people. A few civilian murderers were nothing more to her than a distraction from her duties. Two hours' time to go through the formalities of a court-martial when she had better things to do. Shaking her head, Sophia replied, "Yeah, just... where's Hargrave? I thought he was going to wait with you."

"Sergeant Cross came around and grabbed him right after he came out. I think Gable's trying to get us moving and needed to tell him the plan." Tony replied.

"About time..." Sophia trailed off as she noticed a gaggle of girls on the other side of the street eyeing them and giggling, and pushed back a bit of vertigo as she realized they were all their age. They weren't in school uniforms though... was it a Saturday? She couldn't remember which day it was. It simply wasn't important. Tony felt energetic enough to smile and wave, and she pawed at her hair a little and stood up straighter as they walked past. The girls murmured as she noticed them, and she remarked,

"I think they're into you, Tony."

He chuckled, "They're *into* you, Sophie. They're *jealous* of me."

Sophia shook her head as they left the girls behind, "Never understood that myself."

Tony gave her a skeptical look, "I know you got love letters back in school."

She rolled her eyes, "Yeah, they were all weird and creepy." Artillery thudded in the distance, friendly and outbound. "Anyways, you think they'd get to cover or something."

He wouldn't let it go, "With a tall drink of water like you on the loose?" He reached over and squeezed her butt playfully, "They're *thirsty*, Sophie."

She pushed him away, laughing, "Oh, lay off, Tony." They went around a corner to see the rest of the squad sitting by their bicycles on the side of the road, and she gave him a stern look, "Now keep your hands to yourself, there's the guys."

Tony pouted, "Boo."

Hargrave stood as they approached, chuckling, "You two look happy."

Sophia cleared her throat and tried to look serious, "Ah, yes... thanks?"

Tony added shiftily, "Beautiful weather today, you know."

The older man rolled his eyes, "God, I can't leave you two alone. Anyways, the rest of the platoon's already taken off, Lieutenant Gable gave us a separate mission." He produced a map, and they looked over his shoulders as he pointed out, "They took a radio team out to this hill here," He pointed at a hill about ten kilometers northwest of town, on the edge of the thick forest that spread out far to the west and south of Darissa, "The lancers are pushing north right now trying to get back *into* contact with the enemy, our company's been assigned to support them, and they wanted an observation post set up."

More rounds whistled in on the north side of town, in the general direction of the train station. Snorting, Sophia remarked, "Looks like they won't have far to look.

"Right?" Hargrave remarked drily, "Anyways, we're going *here*." He pointed to a small icon a couple kilometers southwest of the original hill, sitting atop an even taller hill within the forest proper, "There's a fire tower here, we should be able to see for miles all around. Gable was worried they either wouldn't be able to see anything from their original hill or the enemy would be there ahead of them, so she wanted us to check it out."

Sophia raised an eyebrow, "Any reason she didn't just take the platoon there instead?"

He shrugged, "It's harder to get to and Cross thought it would be an obvious target, but if it's all we've got it's what we'll have to use." He went on, pointing out the next town to the west, a good twenty kilometers away, "The rest of the company's already moved out for here. If we don't find them there when we pull off the hill we're to keep pushing out to, uh, Highgrove. It's off the map to the west, another thirty kilometers or so I think."

"Alright, looks like we've got a long day ahead of us." Sophia pointed out the road out of town on the map, "We'll take the road west and cut north *there*, hide the bikes and make our way up to the tower. We should be able to signal the rest of the platoon from there, it's not far."

"Just so long as we can do it without getting shot at." Tony added drily.

"That too." Sophia stretched her arms over her head quickly, then announced, "Alright, let's get moving."

Mounting their bicycles they pedaled out of town, just one small detachment in the tide of traffic moving west out of Darissa, horses drawing the many wagons strung out along the road increasingly wide-eyed as the enemy's artillery walked closer and closer. Occasionally it slapped down raggedly across the road itself, never close to them but close enough to scare horses and snarl traffic. Gritting her teeth, Sophia drove her squad on through the jam, a couple times having to walk cross-country to get around some wreck or overturned wagon surrounded by struggling men and jittery horses. The annoying thing wasn't so much that the enemy was obviously trying to shell the road out of town, she thought, it was that they were doing such a bad job at it and *still* creating so much havoc.

Eventually they left the town behind them, the traffic cleared, and they set off properly. The forest quickly closed in overhead, mercifully shielding them from the heat of the sun. Despite the rising road and their heavy loads they made good time, and less than an hour later they pulled off on a dirt road by a helpful sign pointing the way up to the fire tower. Walking their bikes a ways into the forest, they camouflaged them with leaves and brush and set off single-file up the road, Sophia leading with her rifle in hand.

The road wasn't as steep as she had feared and they made good time on foot, walking through the dappled sunlight as artillery slapped and popped off to their right. It reminded her of Fire Ridge, without the inescapable phosphorous reek, the shredded trees and the bodies. *God,* the bodies. Shaking her head to get the image out of it, Sophia thought grimly that at least they weren't *currently* getting shot at, just as she went around a bend and saw figures down the road with a long, dark shapes in their hands.

Sophia dove off the road automatically, and the others didn't need to be told to follow as shots rang out. She was maneuvering her rifle to bear down the road from around the tree she had found herself behind when she realized the gunshots weren't the normal, harsh cracking of Imperial rifles or the powerful booms of Royal ones. They were high-pitched *pops*, and they honestly didn't sound all that dangerous. She suspected she still wouldn't like to be on the receiving end of one of them, though. Before anyone had more of a chance than she did to get a bead on a target she called out, "*Hold fire!* I think they're civilians!'"

Kelly's voice came back from the other side of the road, "You're right! That's a twenty-two if I ever heard one!"

Great. They were being engaged by local idiots with squirrel guns. Pushing herself up behind her tree, Sophia called out, "*Royal Army!* Drop your weapons and come forward with your hands up!"

A high, cracking voice called back faintly, "There aren't any *girls* in the Army!"

Another one added, "Go to hell, Mask!"

Correction. They were being engaged by local *children* with squirrel guns. A couple more gunshots rang out, bullets whistling through the trees harmlessly as she rolled her eyes. This was embarrassing, not to mention someone could get hurt. Rolling her eyes, Sophia called out, "They're kids, guys! Take a few shots over their heads!"

She'd barely gotten the words out when Kelly's machine gun erupted, and kept going, and going, and going until he'd burned off what sounded like about fifty rounds. Over the ringing in her ears she heard him shout, "*That was high on purpose!* I'm giving you the rest of it *dead on* unless you little shits come out *right now!*"

* * *

"Alright, Kelly, you can stop now." The machine-gunner turned and gave her a sour look, but he lowered his belt and stepped back from the two suffering boys. Looking at them sternly, she added, "You two are lucky I kept him from using the buckle end. Now get up and stop crying."

The two children scrambled to their feet, whimpering as they and gingerly felt their newly-bruised bottoms. Kelly hadn't been holding back *at all.* They couldn't have been older than eight or nine, a couple kids with squirrel guns doing their bit for the King. One of them blubbered, "We were just doing what we were told!"

"Oh yeah?" She demanded, "By who?"

The other one explained, "We were up at the watchtower and some Royal soldiers came out of the woods and told us to do it."

The first one added, "They told us to shoot our guns in the air to warn them if anyone came along."

"But we thought you were Masks!" The second one chimed in, "You don't look anything like them!"

"I still think they're Masks." The first one muttered petulantly.

Feeling her hair start to stand on end, Sophia glanced over around at Hargrave and said, "Are you thinking what I'm thinking?" He nodded and motioned for the squad to get into cover, and as her friends darted behind convenient trees and rocks she forced herself to smile, crouched down and tried a different tack with the kids, "Hey, hey, now, you might be able to help us out still. How many of them were there?"

"Three!" The second kid volunteered, "And they were wearing blue uniforms, like you're *supposed* to be wearing. Before we left I heard them talking about a radio."

Sophia tapped her calf, where she had wrapped a long strip of black cloth from the top of her boot up to just below her knee, "Were they wearing puttees like me, or boots?"

The second one, who by now was staring at her bare thighs with something entirely different from intimidation, replied helpfully, "Black, uh, wraps. Just like you." *Old infantry uniforms,* she thought. He added, "Oh, and one of them had a big machine gun."

Smiling again, she picked up both of their guns and handed them to the helpful kid, "Thanks, you've been a real help. Because your *friend* here clearly wants to work for the Emperor I'm putting you in charge of him, understand?" The boy nodded eagerly and she went on, "He's your prisoner now. You march him straight home and then you give him his gun back. And then you go straight home yourself. That's an order, you got it?"

"Yes, ma'am!" He chirped happily, then prodded his by now probably-former friend down the road, "Now move, you! Hands up!"

"I know that isn't loaded." His friend shot back.

"Want me to?" She overheard him say from down the road, "Now no talking, prisoner!"

From where he was lying with his machine gun, Edward sniped, "*Please* tell me you took their ammo."

Sophia looked over at him nervously, "Um... no?"

"Great." She could see him rolling his eyes despite the fact he was facing away from her. His neck muscles gave it away, "That kid's *dead.*"

After a long, pregnant pause, she coughed and changed the subject, "Anyways. We've got what sounds like most of a Pathfinder team up at the fire tower wearing old infantry uniforms." She added, "And they know we're coming."

Kelly replied from his spot on the other side of the squad from Edward, "Well they know we have a machine gun, so they're probably not going to try to fight."

"Right..." She thought for a moment, then went on, "Pathfinders come in four-man teams. If they came out of the woods at the top they probably came in from the north, and if they had horses they'd want to leave someone with them before the woods got thick. Which means we *might* catch them if we circle around the hill and hurry."

"They've probably booby-trapped the tower by now, too." Tony added.

"That too." Hefting her rifle, she called out, "Alright, squad, on me, single file, we're moving!"

They sprang to their feet and ran after her through the forest, churning a path through the deep loam behind her as they worked their way around the hill. She scrambled up and down ravines, vaulted fallen trees, and was about to wade across a burbling spring when she thought better of it and held up a hand for a halt. Tucking herself in behind a tree, she waited for the rest of them to stop thrashing through the brush behind her, closed her eyes and listened for a second.

Sophia heard her heartbeat, water flowing over the rocks, Tony's heavy breathing, distant popping gunfire, trees swaying in the wind and... *there.* Ever so faint in the distant, a horse's unmistakable whinny floated over the water. It stood to reason they'd keep the horses by a stream so they could drink while the team was up on the hill. Motioning for the squad to follow her again, Sophia stood and set off downhill parallel to the stream. She stalked along for a hundred meters, two hundred meters through the trees, her feet sinking into the loam as she scanned through the forest for something, *anything* in the dazzling quilt of sunlight and shadow before her.

Something was off. *Something...* Sophia held up a hand for a halt as she swept her eyes back and forth through the trees. An insect buzzed in her ear, and as the sound receded she realized the forest had gone *silent*. The steady chorus of birds singing in the branches was simply gone. Going to crouch down, she looked down and saw light glimmer a few inches in front of her feet, a thin little line reflecting back at her where the dappled sunlight hit it. A tripwire.

Sophia's breath caught in her throat as her hand clenched automatically into a fist. *Don't just stop, freeze in place.* Shuffling backwards carefully, she looked around, at the ground this time. *There.* And *there.* And *there*, tripwires glimmering in the sunlight further into the woods, attached to ugly little lumps sitting like toads on the tree roots. Imperial grenades. Looking back up, she thought she could make out what had caused the enemy all the bother, a churned-up area in the distance near where the forest dropped down into the streambed. The Pathfinders' horses must have been there not more than a few minutes ago.

She pointed out the tripwires and heard Tony curse softly behind her, then motioned for the squad to back up. Quickly doubling them back, she led them on a wide arc around the Pathfinders' bivouac to the north, casting a careful eye on the ground every few steps. The last thing she wanted was to run into more booby traps, or worse, an ambush. After another couple hundred meters the forest thinned, and she motioned for the squad to get on line and crawl forward to the edge of the trees.

The distant gunfire, which she hadn't been able to pin down in the forest, instantly sharpened off to her right as Sophia pushed her way through the brush at the edge of the forest, and she looked over and tried to get her bearings. They had come quite a ways, off the hill and down into the valley, and were looking out onto what looked like pastureland. Off to her right she could see a forested spur jutting out past their position as it gradually sloped down into the grassy fields to the north. The gunfire seemed to be coming from its upper slopes, some of it at least, deep Royal rifles and machine guns. Imperial weapons seemed to be cracking back from a wide arc around it, some farther away and some closer. Whoever it was, they were hanging on to their position atop the ridge as the enemy gradually felt around their flanks.

Then it hit her, and Sophia felt like an idiot for the second before her blood turned cold. They'd moved a *ways* pursuing the Pathfinders, easily a kilometer as they worked their way to the northeast down off their hill. Towards the rest of the platoon, which was currently in a full-blown firefight with what sounded like a *lot* of dragoons. As she watched light flashed in the trees atop the ridge and debris sprayed skywards, followed seconds later by thudding explosions and the shriek of incoming shells.

A lot of dragoons with artillery in support, it seemed.

Tony spoke up beside her, "I see them." Looking over, she followed his finger as he pointed to see four small dots in the distance, horsemen in blue uniforms milling around halfway across the valley. What exactly they were milling around wasn't entirely clear until she squinted, looked closely, and realized that particular green dot wasn't some unusual plant sticking up out of the grass in front of her. *That* was an Imperial soldier on foot, talking to the Pathfinders. Probably being told there were more Royal troops back the way they'd come.

Might as well confirm their suspicions. Swallowing hard and gripping her rifle, Sophia said, "Alright, guys, crawl forward. Let's get a better look at this." As one they slithered out of the forest into the bright sunlight, Sophia feeling painfully exposed as she pushed herself forward. One meter became ten, twenty, thirty, before they crested an almost imperceptible rise and found themselves looking full-on at the enemy. At that distance their green uniforms blended into the choppy vegetation of the pastures and it was hard to tell how many there were, but one was standing to talk to the Pathfinders. Squinting for a moment, she saw that he didn't have long hair and let out a breath she hadn't known she was holding.

Behind them something crumped loudly, and she rolled over to see the fire tower atop the hill disappearing into the trees as it collapsed. Beside her, Tony remarked, "Told you it was booby-trapped."

Sophia chuckled, "Good call." The conversation out in the field had stopped for a moment at the blast, but a moment later the dragoon officer waved the Pathfinders on and turned back to look at their hard-pressed platoon's position. If Charlie Company was going to do a wide flanking maneuver the commander would go forward to lead the operation himself, or at least keep tabs on its progress. Which meant this was probably their command post. And their reserve was probably around somewhere, now that she thought about it.

Well, their friends needed help and it wasn't like the Imperials were going to surrender. After taking a moment to click her sight forward to the right range, Sophia propped herself up onto her elbows to shoulder her rifle and called out, "Enemy troops front, I think a company headquarters! Range five hundred, independent fire!"

Dropping her sights on to the distant enemy officer, Sophia steadied her breathing for a moment and squeezed the trigger. Her rifle cracked and thudded into her shoulder, and a moment later the whole squad was hammering away. *Just another day in Charlie Company*, she thought wryly as enemy bullets started cracking overhead.

Chapter 31

Shadows in the Fog

Her father's sanctum was his office. Her mother's was her kitchen. The King had spared no expense to give his new queen a culinary lair that any chef in the Kingdom, and most of the ones in the Dominion, would kill for. The fact he had torn out his ex-wife's parlor to do it only made it sweeter to him, she was sure. Given how little as she'd cooked recently, she felt like almost as much of an intruder walking in to use the place.

Almost. Unlike her father, her mother had been quite eager to teach her the craft. And while she was never going to run a five-star restaurant, Princess Arilin was more than capable of cooking brunch for her friends. Whether she *needed* to was another matter entirely, but the maids had other things to do and she needed to do something simple and domestic to settle her mind. Everything had gone far too smoothly since the tugboat had nudged into the dock last night and she had stepped out with Hiram Moore into a dazzling wall of camera flashbulbs.

Arilin had said a few words, he had said a few words, and she had collapsed into a car Alyssa had helpfully arranged, leaving him and Lily to make their own way home. He was a free man now, after all, with no need for babysitting by the Crown. She had expected to be confronted by a furious Alphonse on her arrival home, or to hear about him coming by in the early morning while she slept, but so far she hadn't heard a peep from the man. The morning newspapers she'd seen ran the gamut from the *Sentinel* diplomatically calling her a traitor to the *Star* saying she'd saved the nation, which was pretty normal for the Saturday editions. It left her wondering when the other shoe was going to drop.

Charlotte, who apparently now had the privilege of being able to just turn up at the Palace and waltz into the Residence like she lived there herself, had apparently arrived while she was still in the bath. The *granter* of that privilege, by dint of the fact he knew all the guards, had walked in on her elbow and the two of them had surprised Arilin in her own sitting room just a few minutes ago. She knew why they'd done it, they wanted to hear all about her latest adventure, but she was probably going to have to have words with them at some point about dropping in on the Royal Family without at least calling first. At least her mother was out at some Red Cross function and wouldn't have to know about it.

That said, the least she could do as hostess was make them brunch. Tying on an apron, she popped open the refrigerator and retrieved what she needed for Eggs Royale, trying not to rummage through her mother's meticulous organization too much while she was at it. She was just about to start cracking eggs when someone pushed through the door and she heard Charlotte say, "Milady, are you... oh!" Arilin looked over at her and raised an eyebrow, and her friend explained, flustered, "I... I didn't know you cooked, you don't have to do that for us..."

Chuckling, Arilin turned back to her bowl and cracked the first egg, "Mom taught me, now give me a few minutes here and I'll make something for the three of us."

"Oh, ah..." Charlotte pushed ahead, "If you don't mind, milady, Beatrice just came out..."

"*What.*" Arilin said, looking back over at her quickly. Sure enough, past her and through the door she could see her sister sitting at the table, looking like the short walk from her bed had just about drained the life out of her. Beatrice's *life* hadn't been in danger since her accident with the grimoire, but she'd barely been out of bed since. Smiling, Arilin called out, "*BB!* How are you? Want anything? I'm cooking!"

Beatrice said something quietly to someone off to the side, and a moment later Carmen's voice floated back in Elven, "*The mage-second-princess gratefully agrees!*"

Her sister's maid sounded like she'd been put through the wringer herself, in more ways than one. Arilin shot back, "How about you?"

"*I do not wish to impose upon you...*" The woman trailed off weakly, telling her the exact opposite was the case.

"Nonsense, Carmen," Arilin shot back "Now sit down and be quiet, I want to talk to you anyways."

Arilin heard the maid pull out a chair and half-collapse into it as Charlotte stepped back out of the kitchen. Tom started talking a moment later, then Charlotte, the two of them sounding like they were fussing over Beatrice, whom she suspected was rather enjoying it. Then it sounded like Tom started regaling them with the story of his latest adventure with the regiment, and the two girls started fussing over *him.* Rolling her eyes, Arilin turned back to trying to make sure her hollandaise sauce came out right. If someone didn't get claws into him quick, and if the High City was still standing in a few years, Tom was going to burn a swath through Royal society and probably barely realize what he was up to.

Sensing the commotion Becky appeared a few minutes later, served her guests coffee and tea, took the plates out as she finished them, presumably glowered at Carmen for not taking care of herself, and disappeared as Arilin came out herself. Sitting down to her own plate at the head of the table, Arilin looked out the window for a moment before she picked up her utensils. The High City's promontory had buried its head in the clouds this morning, and the fog was so dense she could barely make out the Royal Plaza below. The plaza itself was deserted, the flagstones shifting eerily as the mist flowed around the Palace. It made her half-think something awful was coiling just out of her sight. Which, if she fully thought about it, it probably was.

Sighing, Arilin forced herself to smile and turned to her guests. The spooky atmosphere didn't seem to have affected them in the slightest. Beatrice had some color in her cheeks, Tom was smiling easily and Charlotte kept shooting him sidelong glances, and Carmen didn't look like she wanted to die. Progress. Arilin turned to her sister first, "Are you alright to be out of bed, BB?"

The younger princess gave her maid a hurt look, "Carmen didn't think so, but I insisted." She yawned and went on, "I *do* need to get out occasionally, you know."

Her maid looked all the way up from her food to the ceiling and shot back, "*May the heavens have mercy, mage-second-princess, you can barely walk.*" Glancing at Arilin sheepishly, she added, "*This is excellent and a high honor,*" She added a compound title she didn't recognize and finished, "*First-princess.*"

Arilin raised an eyebrow, "You can switch gears, you know... also, what did you just call me?"

Carmen sighed, shook her head and dropped the twice-dead language with an obvious effort, "It's... easier to just keep it up, milady, I've been going through so many grimoires lately I've been thinking in Elven." She chuckled and went on, "I was calling you a cooking knight, I had to construct the term just now."

Beatrice giggled, "Sounds about accurate."

"Hush you." Arilin riposted, "How's your research going?"

"Well, I've confirmed the vault isn't going to explode, although given some of the stuff in there I'd advise you find an old mine shaft somewhere and start pouring concrete in after it." She shook her head, "I didn't know any of the Eyes of Teldaros even still existed, and there's *three* of those things in there." Giving her a stern look, she went on, "Your old mages, milady, were either insane, stupid or both."

That sounded about right, from what she'd gathered. By the time their profession became completely obsolete the Kingdom's wizards had gained a truly impressive reputation as madmen and charlatans. Giving Carmen a thin smile, she replied, "I'll keep that in mind. Made any progress on what attacked Beatrice?"

Charlotte gasped, and Arilin looked over to see her two friends' eyes widening. Realizing belatedly that they'd kept *that* particular incident under wraps, she explained, "*Something* came through an old grimoire and almost killed Beatrice." She went on as Tom swallowed visibly, "We're still trying to figure out what it was, but that's why she's been, well... *sick* recently."

Carmen added, "That's a secret, by the way." She answered her original question, "No, although I've *felt* the damn thing a couple times. That book wasn't the only one it had a hook on. Although," The mage chuckled, "It hasn't tried to reel me in yet. I think it went after Beatrice because it could get something *out* of her. That took a lot of energy and it would have needed a good reason."

Beatrice gave her a questioning look, "You think it had to do with the Stigmata?"

The Wehrherz family curse and the reason for their red eyes. Carmen nodded, "Probably." She looked between the two of them and went on, "There is *no* reason that curse should still be functioning in this day and age. Whatever the Faceless King did to Maximilian, it wasn't just incredibly smart, *it generates its own magic*. That should be impossible." She went on, shaking her head, "And because of that you two have a huge amount of magic to drain, at least by modern standards."

Arilin shivered despite the warmth of the room and looked down at the food on her plate, feeling her stomach turn. Her father had told her, afterwards, that the prospect of them actually *getting* the Stigmata hadn't even been on his mind when he decided to legitimate them. Royal children kicked in the womb and were born with red eyes because of some ancient curse, but she and Beatrice had been born to his mistress at the time and had none of that. She'd had green eyes and Beatrice bright blue. And then he signed the papers and the Faceless King had spent the next week hammering red-hot railroad spikes into her eye sockets. Sparks flaming with hate in an endless abyss, and *pain*. So much pain. They'd both cried blood and screamed for a week, when they weren't sedated for mercy's sake.

Shaking herself, she looked up at her sister and asked, "BB... was it like getting the Stigmata?"

Beatrice shook her head slowly, "No, it was *cold*. Almost like the opposite of it. And there was something *there* doing it to me."

"Hm." Taking a drink of tea, Arilin swirled it around in her mouth and thought for a moment. As she did, something that had been scratching at the back of her mind ever since Beatrice's incident pushed itself to the front of her thoughts, and she gave her mage a level look, "Carmen, I don't suppose you know what happened to the Mask of the Faceless King?"

The temperature of the room seemed to drop about ten degrees. If she hadn't known it was all in her head, Arilin would have sworn ice started forming on the windows. After a long pause, Carmen finally replied, "Why... would you be worried about that, milady?"

"Because I know it's loose, and it was powerful enough to *melt* the wards around it." Arilin shot back, "And those were carved into stone."

"That's..." The mage shook her head and sighed, "We've spent the last fifty years looking for it without so much of a whiff of magic. The thing *vanished*."

"Who's *we?*" Arilin asked sarcastically.

Carmen gave her a patronizing look, "Every arcanologist in the world and half the treasure hunters, milady. The consensus is that it had largely discharged by then and was probably destroyed afterwards, not that the Faceless King is out there somewhere lurking in the shadows. I wrote an article on it myself."

Beatrice perked up and was about to say something, but Arilin cut her off, "And yet we're still cursed and something magical went after my sister. Do you have a better explanation?"

"Yes. My theory is that there's a vampire loose in the Capital, probably very old, who woke up recently with enough old artifacts hoarded to power this kind of magic." Arilin gave her a look, and she sighed again, "I realize that sounds only slightly *less* crazy than the Faceless King, milady, but it's much more plausible."

Charlotte gasped again across the table, and Tom reached over and squeezed her hand reassuringly. Pressing on resolutely, Arilin asked, "Humor me and look into it, will you?"

"Sure." Carmen replied tiredly, then added apologetically, "Milady."

Sighing, Arilin returned to her eggs and their cooling hollandaise sauce. Charlotte irrepressibly started asking about her last night's adventure, and she had gotten most of the way through her food and the story when someone knocked on the open door politely. She looked over to see Lieutenant Remarque standing there in her white dress uniform, a document case slung adventurously over her back. Her part-time military aide ventured, "I hope I'm not interrupting, milady, Miss Stone told me you wouldn't mind."

Wiping her mouth with a napkin, Arilin smiled politely and replied, "I was just finishing, Maria. What do you have for me?"

"Just your regular briefing, milady." *Regular* was stretching it, the girl only came over when she had some juicy tidbit to share that hadn't made the newspapers yet. Stepping into the room, Remarque hesitated as she looked over the table festooned with dishes and silverware, "Um..."

Arilin stabbed the last piece of food on her plate with her fork, popped it into her mouth, dropped her fork back onto her plate and gave Carmen a look. The maid stared back at her blankly for a couple seconds before the proverbial light bulb turned on behind her eyes and she coughed awkwardly, stood and set about clearing the dishes. After the maid self-consciously walked out under a precarious pile of china, Maria asked, "Is she... new?"

Chuckling, Arilin replied, "We didn't hire her because she's any good as a maid. Anyways," she went on, "How's the war going?"

Extracting a large-scale map of the New Kingdom from her bag, Maria unfolded it on the table and gestured for them to pay attention. Tom leaned in eagerly, and Charlotte and Beatrice a little more politely, as she started pointing to the map near the Great Steel River, "We're retreating slowly in the east, it looks like the front is *starting* to stabilize south of their bridgehead at Kelsbruck, although that's probably what they want us to think at this point."

Tom jumped in, "Why's that?"

Maria shook her head tiredly, "Maybe we're all jumping at shadows by now, but there's a theory going around the Intelligence staff that they're basically trying to get us to commit most of our forces well to the north trying to hold a line running west from the river. Which they're certainly succeeding at so far." She tapped the Great Steel River further south, around Grenville, "Then they wait until we're committed on *that* line and do what we *thought* their original plan was, which is attack across the river in the south."

Tom looked up at her, "So a pincer attack."

Arilin raised an eyebrow and added, "We've got, what, sixty divisions out there right now? We should be able to hold that line and still secure our flank."

"That river's wide," Tom added, "You can't just get across it easily."

The lieutenant shook her head, "Worst case I've seen so far is they're throwing more than a hundred at us. That's more than enough to punch across as stretched as we're getting."

"That's... a lot." Arilin conceded. It also meant they probably *never* had any kind of advantage over the Empire, even before Fire Ridge. What was infuriating was that they hadn't figured this out *before* the war, but that was water under the bridge by this point.

Tom piped up, derailing her trail of thought before she could get any angrier, "How's Pine Harbor?"

General Decker's siege proclamation had been printed in all the papers yesterday, a rallying cry amidst the political chaos in the High City and the strikes below. He had certainly put his sleepy little port town and its naval fortress on the map. Maria unexpectedly grimaced, "Not well, I'm afraid. They were expecting a siege, not a frontal assault, and they did not have a lot of troops to hold the land defenses. The town fell last night and the garrison appears to have retreated into the coastal fortress."

"That's unfortunate." Arilin said, "I hope they can hold out there, at least. But, Maria, I get the feeling you're holding out on me right now."

Maria nodded, "I'm worried about what's going on up here." She pointed *much* further west, down the coast almost to the Ellarian Riviera, "The papers this morning didn't treat this like it was a big story. Milady, this *is* the crisis right now. Nothing's happening on the main front for another week probably."

Arilin looked up at her and raised an eyebrow, "I'm assuming there's more to this than my vacation spot next summer?" The Royal Family had a villa in the Riviera with a private beach. Before the war her father had been talking about taking the family on a sailing trip there from Sapphire Bay, going up through the Spires, across the Diamond Shoals and down into the Ellarian Bay, which actually sounded kind of amazing now that she thought about it.

Arilin pushed aside her postwar vacation plans as Maria replied, "Milady, the enemy went through the Cavalry Corps yesterday like they weren't even *there*. They've got tanks, a *lot* of them, and they're halfway to the Riviera already."

Arilin's heart fluttered, and she asked quickly, "How's Ninth Division?"

Maria replied, "They're fine, although apparently they got bypassed and had to break out. They're actually *chasing* them right now." She chuckled, "Lady MacMahon's as good at getting out of jams as she is at getting into them, apparently."

Arilin let her breath out, "Good... please, continue."

Tom jumped in worriedly, "How big of a force are we looking at here?"

The lieutenant shrugged, "We identified *one* of their armored divisions on Fire Ridge, a fully-motorized one." Tom gave her a blank look and she explained, "With trucks to move their infantry, haul their supplies and guns and so on. No horses at all." He raised his eyebrows and leaned back in his chair skeptically as she said it. She couldn't blame him, the idea of an army without horses was a little insane. Maria was going on, "We think they've put together a second one by reinforcing one of their cavalry divisions with tanks. That's the one leading this attack. We think the first one is actually following it."

"So two of these armored divisions?" Arilin raised an eyebrow.

Maria nodded, "At least in this group. Most of what they've gotten across, they're pushing south to expand their bridgehead. It's just..." She gave her a serious look, "Milady, this isn't just some cavalry raid. This is the Imperial Army's spearhead, they've clearly got something in mind for it."

The princess snorted, "Distracting us while the rest of their army beats us the old-fashioned way?"

"That's also possible." The intelligence officer smiled thinly, "Or they're trying to get across the Serpent."

Tom stated the obvious, "That would be bad."

"That's an understatement, cadet." Maria tapped Gyrburg on the map, "If they get troops into the mouth of the Great Pass, there go two of our two and a half railways heading east." The third line labored up the Misty Pass, far to the south near the Storm Range, and wound down out of the mountains through the heart of the Fairy Forest and north to Wolf Rock. It wouldn't support an army. She went on, "At that point we'd be lucky to hold them in the Pass itself."

"So what are we doing about it?" Arilin aksed.

"Right now Fifth Corps is deploying north from Wolf Rock. They'll have two divisions on line south of Requinville by tomorrow." The lieutenant went on, "That should stop them."

That brought back memories. Thinking idly that she should write Mrs. Kunst and Charles a letter, Arilin turned her attention back to the map. Requinville was a *vacation spot*, a seaside city of beach resorts and wineries that happened to host the major rail hub connecting the coastal line running east from Brightangel with a transverse line coming up from Wolf Rock. Looking back at the lieutenant, Arilin raised her eyebrows questioningly, "What if they don't?"

Maria sighed and smoothed her uniform's skirt nervously, her hands pulling the white fabric tight across her thighs for a moment. Finally, she said, "That's... most of why I'm here, milady. I think... well, a lot of us think, that the Guards Division needs to start getting ready to deploy."

"I'm guessing you haven't gotten a lot of traction on this?" Arilin remarked drily, "We have to have more troops *somewhere*."

"That's the thing, milady, we *don't*." Maria shot back, "We're *beyond* thin down south right now. And I don't even *know* what the Dominion's doing right now, I don't trust any of the reports we've been getting. Ever since your run-in with their ambassador they've been..." She trailed off and shook her head, "*Too* normal. Just nothing at all threatening, no training exercises or *anything*. I don't like it."

Arilin sighed, "I'll have to ask my father. No guarantees."

The lieutenant raised an eyebrow, "You can't order it yourself, milady?"

She snorted, "I *could* before my run-in with Ambassador Rosenheim. Then Alphonse told Father the pressure was driving me insane, and that *he* needed to be making all the serious decisions. And no, there's *no* way he'll deploy the Guards right now." Arilin shook her head, "Of course Father didn't listen to *me*. I feel like I'm talking to a wall sometimes with him."

Maria narrowed her eyes, "Hm... milady, can I ask you a favor?"

She nodded, and the lieutenant pulled out a seat and sat down at the table. Producing a pen and notebook, she quickly wrote something down and passed it and the pen over to her. Examining it, Arilin read it aloud, "Am concerned enemy armored force moving west of Kelsbruck-Pine Harbor bridgehead intends to seize crossings over the Serpent. Recommend you order..." Arilin wrote something in and went on, "*Second* Guards Infantry Brigade deploy to Gyrburg immediately, prepare to defend bridgeheads on Serpent should Fifth Corps fail to hold enemy vicinity Requinville. Alphonse unwilling due to preoccupation with now-resolved labor unrest."

"Why Second Brigade, milady?" Maria asked.

She nodded at Tom, who smirked, "Because I happen to know the First Regiment is loyal to *me*, and I'll take my odds on the Second." Signing the note with a flourish, she passed it back to her, "Will that get you into the telegraph room?"

Lieutenant Remarque stood, nodding, "Yes, milady. I'll let you know what comes of it."

The woman stood, took her map and departed, leaving the four of them sitting there. Leaning back in her seat, Arilin shook her head, "Am I the only one here wondering when the other shoe is going to drop?"

"It hasn't already?" Beatrice asked, "You seem to be enjoying yourself."

Arilin gave her a look, "Part of that was because *you* were enjoying yourself a little too much earlier."

Beatrice pouted at her, but Tom cut her off, "By the way, milady. In case you need to get ahold of Charlotte, she'll be staying with me for the next few days."

She and Beatrice both gave the two of them *very* inquisitive looks for a second. Charlotte was turning red by the time he gave her a slick smile and explained, "Her mother's never home and she gets lonely in that flat with just her servants."

Charlotte gave him an unexpectedly grateful look, and Arilin felt the dots connect and her blood run cold. Tom was apparently a nerveless liar, and there was *exactly* enough truth in there that someone wouldn't think to ask questions. Charlotte's mother had run off to the High City *ahead of her own daughter*, an act of parental irresponsibility that had left the poor girl in the hands of the Empire for weeks. And now the day after she had to spend the night without her grizzled male servant around she was trying to find somewhere else to stay.

Christ. She'd put the girl in *danger*, from whatever sleazy men her mother was bringing home every night. To be fair Alice seemed like she knew how to fight and she'd been with her, but still. Lady Espinay being a serial adulterer made *so* many things make sense. And of course Charlotte had kept this a complete secret, except apparently from Tom. Not to mention her father was at the front right now. Deciding she was going to have Lady Espinay thrown out of the nobility if it was the last thing she did, Arilin took a sip of tea to cover her reaction and replied teasingly, "So when's the wedding?"

Charlotte somehow turned even redder and Tom winked and held his finger to his lips, "*It's a secret.*"

Beatrice started giggling. Snorting herself, Arilin winked back at him and said, "You two have fun." Stretching her arms over her head, she smiled and asked, "So, what do you all want to do today?"

Someone knocked on the door and Arilin looked over to see Becky standing in the door, her mouth set in a grim line. It looked like the other shoe had dropped. "Milady," she started, walking in unbidden and producing a note, "We just got this from the Assembly."

"Oh?" Arilin turned and took the paper resignedly, unfolded and read it. Then read it again. Then folded it back up, spun it onto the center of the table and leaned back in her chair, closing her eyes and pinching the bridge of her nose like Patricia did. Of course it did absolutely nothing. Maybe it would when she was older. She was about thirty years too young to have to deal with this kind of nonsense. The absolute worst she should have to deal with, in any proper and just world, would be Tom and Lily fighting over her, not being schemed against by mustachioed idiots in the Assembly.

Beatrice, who clearly hadn't learned her lesson from the *first* cursed document she'd read, was reading from it, "Today's minutes... oh my." She coughed slightly and went on, "Motion for vote of no confidence by Count Straaken, Royalist Party, and speech." The same Royalist Party that had crossed the aisle to vote with the Socialists and the Liberals to avoid being seen as disloyal after the attempt on her life. She went on, "Speeches against by Baron Gainsborough, Liberal Party, and Mr. Meyer, Socialist Party. Speech for by Mr. Henriks, Dissenting Union. Speech for by Baron Jager, Conservative Party." The old lion himself. Rumor was he had a nephew who'd been drummed out of the Army recently for cowardice.

She'd already read it herself, but it felt twice as sickening to hear Beatrice say it out loud, "Exceptional speech by... is this serious? It says Prince Alphonse."

Charlotte piped up crossly before she could say anything, "I'd assume so, I don't think the Assembly is in the business of playing jokes on the Palace."

"True... anyways," Beatrice continued, "Vote held, measure passed three hundred fifty-four to one hundred sixty-one." An absolute massacre. Half the Liberals had voted for it. Gainsborough was finished in politics, "Motion to form..." Beatrice trailed off again, shaking her head, "This is crazy."

"Well, let me see it." Charlotte demanded, taking the paper from Beatrice. She finally read, "Motion to form new government by Count Straaken, Prince Alphonse as Prime Minister, portfolios to be determined by governing coalition. Measure passed, four hundred thirty-eight to seventy-six, one abstaining." Probably Gainsborough himself, poor man, watching his entire party betray him. Snorting contemptuously, she spun the paper back onto the table and spat, "Is this even legal?"

Beatrice volunteered before she could muster up the energy to respond, "There's no law against it, as far as I know... Alphonse probably approved it himself, too, as Regent." Now *that* was a thought. She wondered if he'd propped one knee up on a chair to formally ask himself permission to form a government.

"Milady," Tom finally spoke up, quieting Charlotte before she could snap back. Taking a sip of his coffee, he drily set the cup back in his saucer and said, "You should probably call the War Ministry and see if we can get Lieutenant Remarque back here. You may want to add a few lines to that telegram."

Shaking her head to clear it, Arilin sat up and replied, "I think I will." Scooting her chair back, she stood and looked around her little circle of friends, "Unfortunately things are going to get worse before they get better, but," she smiled and went on, feeling herself starting to blush as she said it, "I appreciate all of your support. You're... the best friends I could ever hope for."

Charlotte blushed herself and looked at the table, "It's... the least I can do, milady."

Beatrice shrugged, "I'm your sister."

"Milady," Tom looked her dead in the eyes and said matter-of-factly, "I'd die for you."

Arilin chuckled nervously, "Let's hope it doesn't come to that."

Chapter 32

Burning Dust

The gravel of the vineyard's path crunched under her boots in the ghostly light of the moons and the False Sun. The dawn itself was just starting to spread out across the eastern horizon, reddening the very rim of the dusky sky above the shallow hills they had come through last night and finally, so tired they could barely walk, pulled off the road and found a place to throw themselves down amidst the vines. If there was any consolation at all, it was that the enemy was at least as tired as they were.

They had made their camp on the north side of this particular vineyard, up on the side of the valley overlooking a stylishly-understated house, its stables and a few other buildings that she couldn't quite place but which she was fairly certain had something or other to do with making wine. The whole complex was crawling with wagons and trucks now, lined up along the road or tucked in among the buildings. She could see sleep-deprived soldiers leading equally sleep-deprived horses around down below, trying to get them limbered up for the day's forced march. At this rate it was a miracle they weren't dead. At this rate it was a miracle they *all* weren't dead.

Charlie Company had ridden a hundred kilometers yesterday on top of the firefight they'd had with the dragoons. Edward had done it with his neck and arm bandaged, courtesy of a burst of Imperial machine gun fire as they'd fallen back towards the road. Honestly he was fine, although he did seem to attract bullets somehow. The rest of the platoon had suffered more. A shell had come down between Corporal Miller and one of his guys in Third Squad. Somehow Miller was still alive, at least last she'd heard. From what they'd carried out on a stretcher that was another miracle.

The cooks had pulled their wagon out of the scrum and managed to find a level patch along the path leading up the hill. Next to their little wagon and its potbellied stove Sophia could see a couple familiar figures talking with the cooks, and she smiled despite it all and picked up her pace. Her father noticed her as she approached and cracked a rare smile himself, greeting her, "Sophie! Good to see you!" Glancing at the canteen cups in her hands, he went on, "Who're you getting coffee for?"

Sophia chuckled, "I figured if I waved some coffee under Gable's nose she'd wake up easier." She added, "She was hurting yesterday."

From his other side Lieutenant Thorn added, "I'll say. Poor girl was dead on her feet. I think she's a little more used to having a horse do all the work for her." They all laughed. Looking her up and down, he changed the subject, "How're you doing, Miss Rose?"

Putting her elbows up on the side of the cook wagon, she smiled slyly,

"I'd say I'm at about three-quarters of where I was when we got lost up in the Dragonspines."

Thorn came back, "So you only *kind of* feel like you want to die?"

"I feel like I've been hit by a truck, but I'm still in a good mood about it." Sophia replied cheerfully, "Now is the coffee ready?"

Footsteps crunched unsteadily on the path behind her, and she turned to see Lieutenant Gable wobbling down the path towards them, jacket unbuttoned and hair rumpled. Collapsing onto the cooks' wagon, the girl gave her a bleary look and mumbled, "I was... wondering who went through my stuff..."

Sophia's father gave her a look and observed, "You know... I agree with the coffee plan."

Sophia quickly filled a cup and gave it to the half-dead lieutenant, who stared at it blankly for a couple seconds before she started slowly drinking. While they waited for her to come back to life, Lieutenant Thorn asked her, "You're the duty sergeant right now, aren't you, Miss Rose?"

"Yeah," Sophia replied, "I got it until reveille."

"Alright then," The commander told her, "Go wake all the other platoon and squad leaders up, most of the company's moving out at sunrise and I need to get you all up to speed." She nodded and started to turn away when he added, "Oh, and... get Hargrave too."

Sophia turned back and raised an eyebrow, "Mr. Hargrave... sir?"

Thorn grimaced and replied, glancing at Lieutenant Gable, "Yeah. I'm giving him your third squad, Vanessa, unless you have any issues with it."

Gable looked at him blankly for a moment, then sighed and shook her head. Clearly the coffee was starting to have at least a little bit of an effect. Finally she said, "No, that's fine, Josh. I... needed someone anyways." She looked over at her father, "Any word on Miller?"

Her father set his jaw and shook his head, "He didn't make it. Damn fine man."

Thorn shook his head, and Gable muttered, "I... I'm sorry. If there's anything I can do..."

Her father gave her a hard look for a moment, then sighed, "He's got a wife and a little kid back in Jade Falls. Fiona and Timothy. Get me a letter and I'll make sure they get it." He shook his head again, "Half the damn town's going to hate me when we get back at the rate we're going."

"It's not your fault, Dad." Sophia cut in indignantly.

He shot her a glare hard enough to raise the hair on the back on her neck, "It *is*, though. I recruited most of them." Softening a little, he jerked his chin back up the path, "Now get going, Sophie. You've got your orders."

She quickly retreated and set about waking up the rest of the company's leaders, padding through the rows of trellises and prodding at blanket-clad forms tucked under the vines until they stirred enough to complain. Hargrave leaving, off to Third Squad. Honestly it was overdue, he could probably lead a squad better than she could, he was sharp as a razor and at his age men would respect him. She half suspected he'd lingered in First Squad as long as he had just to back her up. But now with the company in combat again and the black drip of dead and wounded starting back up that was a luxury none of them could afford. Sighing, Sophia finished her circuit by rousting him and telling him the news.

"I'll be sad to leave." Hargrave lit his pipe as they walked back down, blew a smoke ring theatrically and remarked, "But at least I'm not going to have to deal with you whining about my pipe again, young lady."

She pouted equally-theatrically, "I'm telling Lady Gable on you."

The older man chuckled, "I think my daughter's older than her, I'll take my chances."

"What about me?" She pouted harder.

"You, Sophie, are adorable." He gave her a look, "You wrapped me around your little finger *quite* successfully. Now stop pouting, you look ridiculous."

He was right, of course, and she snorted and slid in alongside him where the others had gathered in a circle around a folding table Lieutenant Thorn seemed to have produced from somewhere. Seeing them arrive, he nodded and gestured to a map he had spread out across it, "Alright, that's everyone. Listen up!" He drew his finger across the map, east to west, "We've got another long day ahead of us. We made a hundred kilometers yesterday, but that was a short day. Division thinks we need to push a hundred and *fifty* today to keep up with the Imperials."

Gasps and whistles all around. A *third* of that would have been difficult on foot. Fortunately they had the bicycles, but even so it would be a feat. Sergeant Brockman spoke up from Second Platoon's part of the circle, "Sir, why don't we just *attack* these guys? They'll have to slow down to fight us."

The commander sighed, "Because Twelfth Division spent all day yesterday trying to do that and it did *not* go well." That explained things.

They'd heard artillery fire off to the west during the whole previous day. "They've got an awful lot of tanks for us to just go charging in and expect things to work out." He tapped the western side of the map, "Fortunately, Fifth Corps, good old General Kunst himself, is deploying on line south of Requinsville. They're digging in and they have their own tanks. And, here's the good news, if we make that distance we'll link up with them *tonight*. Or at least the Twelfth will." He smiled and went on, "All goes well and we'll be back at Wolf Rock with our feet up tomorrow night. I'm serious about that, by the way, we're supposed to move there by train to recover."

Uneasy grumbling went around the group at his words. About three months ago they had mustered with the rest of Fifth Corps at Wolf Rock Fortress, taking a train from there into their first battle south of Grenville. The thought of heading back there and having to defend it from the Empire made her feel the morale draining out the bottom of her feet. At this rate they'd be fighting them in Jade Falls before long, God forbid. Thorn paused to let them finish muttering and pushed ahead, "We'll be supporting the Valkyries again today. Second platoon, you'll be in reserve in the center of the column. Third, you're with the hussars' First Squadron. Fourth, you're with their Second Squadron. They'll both be pushing north as we move along to try to get back into contact. First," He looked at Lieutenant Gable, "You've got rearguard duty. There'll be a platoon from the cuirassiers *behind* you, so don't just go shooting at whatever you see."

Gable nodded. Before Thorn could go on the notes of Reveille started drifting up the valley from the camp below. As they died off he chuckled and said what they were all thinking, "Imagine if we'd done *that* on Fire Ridge. Anyways, there's your signal. Move out."

"Deeds alone, sir." Sophia gave Charlie Company's traditional reply, if a bit sarcastically.

Everyone stared at her for a moment before the lightbulbs went off and they joined in, "*Deeds alone.*"

They all scattered, Sophia walking back uphill to where the squad was starting to wake up. Hargrave walked back up with her, collected his equipment, said his goodbyes and went to go find his new squad. She watched him go for a moment, puffing on his pipe as he walked along the hillside, leading his bicycle with his pack slung jauntily over his shoulder. At least he wasn't going far. At least he wasn't *dead*, she thought darkly, then picked up her own bicycle and waved the rest of her friends down the hill. They had work to do.

Soldiers on foot marched at four or five kilometers an hour. They could go faster, but not for very long. With a ten-minute break every hour and breaks on top of that for meals, this made a forty-kilometer march a miserable, all-day affair, soldiers swearing under their packs through a cloud of dust for hours on end. Going above that tended to turn it into an all-evening affair as well. With the bicycles they could triple that quite easily, even with all their equipment. And the cavalry didn't drive their transport wagons like the infantry, a couple horses plodding along with a cart behind the marching footsoldiers. They used four or six horses on the same size of wagon, a soldier riding one of each pair to simplify controlling the team as it trotted along. Compared to marching, they moved at lightning speed.

The sweat was the same though. And the dust, rising in endless clouds from the sunbaked gravel road as thousands of hooves and hundreds of wheels hammered over it. And the endless hours with the sun climbing overhead, the False Sun an angry spark leading it onwards as it slowly broiled them in the saddle. Sophia drank canteen after canteen and still felt herself getting lightheaded as they crunched along through the heart of the New Kingdom's wine country, once host to flocks of wealthy vacationers searching for the ideal bottle.

Now it was hosting a war. Not the kind of grinding, head-on slugging match she'd seen on Fire Ridge, but a sort of swirling skirmish rolling over the plains and hills of the Riviera. Gunfire popped and crackled off to the north every few minutes, punctuated by the rolling thunder of artillery fire. Sometimes Imperial shells whistled in near the road, sending shrapnel hissing overhead and more than once snarling traffic as horses were wounded further ahead in the column. Occasionally they made out their own artillery hammering back in reply, farther up the column or off to the north. A steady stream of wounded hussars and a few infantrymen made their way back to the support column as it thundered along, and the medics got them into the wagons and did what they could for them.

They stuck pretty close to the main column as it snaked along, just keeping far enough back to keep clear of the worst of the dust cloud. The cuirassiers did not. Once in the mid-morning they sent a rider up to make sure the column was still on track, the man quickly appearing in a clatter of hooves and disappearing after making an unsuccessful pass at her and a more determined and equally unsuccessful pass at Lieutenant Gable. They were winding their way through a rare patch of forest and enjoying the merciful shade when she heard Hargrave call from his new squad's place at the rear of their little column, "Rider coming up, one of ours!"

Sophia turned to see a man cantering up the road towards them in the distance. After a couple minutes he closed up on them in a clatter of hooves, the trooper pulling up beside Lieutenant Gable where she was riding behind her, "Milady! Column's still on track?"

"Yep." Gable caught her breath for a second, "They're just up ahead."

"Good, I was getting worried." The man replied, "You're a lot farther up than I expected, we're a couple miles back at this point. I'll tell them we need to close up."

The lady lieutenant replied tersely, "Thanks."

The man wheeled his horse about and galloped back, and they kept on pedaling. The wagons slowed and stopped on the road ahead of them a few minutes later. Seeing it, Gable called for a halt and Sophia swung herself off her bike and walked for a minute, her legs rubbery and un-steady under her. She felt for her canteens. One was empty. The other still had a bit of water and she took a swig, swishing it around and feeling it unstick her gummed-up mouth. Shaking her head, she looked around her squad and asked, "You guys good on water? I'm almost out."

Tony shook his head, "I'm out... don't we have a water can around here somewhere?"

Edward paused mid-drink and offered him the canteen, "Here you go. Even backwashed in it for you."

Her boyfriend rolled his eyes, "I'll go find it." Turning, he called out, "Hey, who's got the water jug!"

That started a general scrum to fill up on water. Sophia was about to go get in line to fill up herself when something, a little feeling tickling in the back of her head, made her pause. Walking by, Kelly looked over at her and asked, narrowing his eyes, "Sophia, do you hear something?"

Not at that rate. "Maybe...?" She replied. It was just gunfire, the same gunfire they'd been hearing for hours now. Sporadic popping gunshots and bursts of machine-gun fire which seemed to float out of the forest from no particular direction, soft and broken up by the trees.

"Here, give me those." Kelly took her canteens from her and quickly walked off towards the rest of the platoon, shushing them, "Sophia hears something, everybody shut up..."

They went dead-silent in an instant. Closing her eyes, Sophia walked a little out into the road and tried to listen. What had made her ears perk up in the first place? It was just... gunfire. The same gunfire she was *far* too used to, rifles and machine guns hammering away in the distance. If her head hadn't been swimming with some brain-melting combination of fatigue, heat and lack of sleep she was sure she'd have figured it out right away. What *was* it? *Something* was wrong, damn it, she thought as a few isolated gunshots rang out and machine guns chattered back at them, *some*-oh God.

This whole time they'd only been properly hearing *one* side of the firefight around them, *their* side. She'd barely been able to make out Imperial gunfire, if she could at all. As it should be, the hussars were keeping the enemy at arms' length and the dragoons didn't seem inclined to push. But this wasn't just an *exchange* of gunfire that she could hear clearly, fire responding to fire, *it was all the same volume.*

God-damn it. Her eyes flying open, Sophia turned to look at Lieutenant Gable and called, "Milady! Someone near here's being overrun!"

Everyone else turned to look at Gable with her. Nervously, the girl asked, "Can you tell who?"

Sophia shook her head. Before she could reply properly, Sergeant Cross cut in, "Milady, let's set up first and *then* figure this out." Gable nodded, and he called out, "First Squad, left side of the road! Third Squad, right side! Second, collect the bicycles and follow me, we'll drop them at the rear of the column and see if we can find some wire for a roadblock while we're at it."

They all scattered, Kelly handing her canteens back as he rushed by to get his machine gun. Stuffing them back into their pouches on her belt, Sophia walked up to Gable and volunteered, "Not really, milady. Although... I'd assume it's the guys behind us." Tony ran by with his machine gun, and she looked over at him, "Tony! Set up to fire down the road, Ed's on your left and Kelly's team left of him."

Tony gave her a thumbs-up and ducked behind a sturdy tree just beside the ditch. Meanwhile, Gable furrowed her brow and nodded, "Yes, I'd... think that's safe. Thanks." Looking around, she noticed they were the only two people still standing in the road, chuckled and said, "Go see to your squad, Miss Rose."

Unslinging her rifle, Sophia nodded, "Will do, milady." Her friends were already set up in position, so there was nothing for her left but to walk their line, quibble with Kelly over his field of fire, tell Montour to either find a more impressive tree to hide behind or start digging, and then realize with a sinking stomach that she had condemned them all to digging in without even realizing it. Sighing, she found a likely spot between Edward and Massey, produced her entrenching tool and set to work.

It didn't take more than a few minutes to scrape out a shallow hole for herself, and then it was just a matter of waiting. A little while later Second Squad returned with coils of barbed wire, headed a little ways down the road and hurriedly strung it across, wiring it to sturdy trees on either side of the road. The road bent off to the north and out of sight through the trees maybe a hundred meters from their position, which meant that any attack coming down the road would probably try to flank their position from the left. Gable called for Second to fall in to the left of Sophia's squad on that account, and came down the line herself a moment later. Crouching down beside her, the lieutenant filled her in, "There's a little bridge up ahead and it's causing a traffic jam, the column's still trying to get across."

Sophia rolled half-over and raised an eyebrow, "Think we could blow it?"

The girl chuckled, "Way ahead of you there. Cross apparently told them to wire it up."

Gable moved off down the line, and there was nothing more to do but wait. And wait. And wait, as gunfire popped faintly in the distance and the hot air under the trees shifted lazily. Her legs ached, and lying down in the shade was an almost unimaginable luxury. Her eyelids drooped, and more than once Sophia had to prop herself up and shake herself to keep from falling asleep. Looking at Edward and Massey to either side of her, she wasn't the only one of them fighting to stay awake. Maybe she'd been wrong. She hadn't heard any gunfire quite like that since, maybe it had just been a coincidence and she'd read too much into it. Maybe the cuirassiers had won their fight. And maybe the enemy was about to come around that bend. Shaking her head again, Sophia settled back behind her rifle and tried to be patient.

Hooves clattering on the road behind them brought her out of her thoughts, and she rolled over to see a gray-uniformed rider on the road. The man called out nervously, "Is this the roadblock? The column's clear, you can get moving now."

She heard Gable climb to her feet and start walking towards the road, calling back, "Yes, thanks! We'll get moving!" Sophia rolled back onto her stomach and looked back down the road as the lieutenant called out, her voice almost drowning out a low growl from down the road, "Second Squad-"

"Milady!" Sophia shouted back, glancing back over her shoulder for a moment, "Some-" The words died in her throat as she looked back at the road and saw an angular shape nose around the corner and jerk to a halt as the driver saw the barbed wire strung across the road and the rider standing there clean in the open, gaping at the Imperial armored car as its turret swung down on him.

Nobody gave the order to fire. They all just pulled the trigger simultaneously, the forest calm disintegrating into screaming chaos. The armored car half-disappeared in a cloud of dust for a second, machine gun flashing back angrily as it lurched backwards, tilting crazily on rapidly-flattening tires. Bullets cracked overhead, slapping into the trees, and then for a moment most of them stopped shooting and she heard Gable shouting, *"Fall back! Move!"*

Climbing to a knee, Sophia fired another shot in the general direction of the armored car and called out, *"First Squad! Fall back!"* Looking over, she locked eyes with Edward and shouted, "Go!"

He picked himself up and ran back through the woods first, Montour flashing through the trees beside him. Then Massey and Kelly, the man picking up his machine gun and darting easily through the trees. She called out for Tony to move, saw him climb to his feet and rushed back alongside him as the others fired past them. Looking over at him, she couldn't help but notice the man lying there lifeless in the middle of the road and the horse collapsing not far beyond him, blood streaming from its flanks. Tearing her gaze away, she dove behind a sturdy-looking tree, turned and fired back down the road.

They did it again, and again, and again, Imperial machine guns hammering away from the road beyond the bend. Small, angry wasps darted through the trees, showering them with splinters and kicked-up earth. Sliding behind a tangle of roots, Sophia looked out to see Massey fall as he ran back behind her, get up, keep running and dive behind the other side of the tangle. Rolling up to one knee, Sophia fired once, twice, then struggled with her bolt for a moment before she realized her rifle was empty.

They were fighting armored cars. She *had* something for that. She'd been carrying that clip of S-bullets since they'd left Wolf Rock, in fact. Reaching down to pop open her leftmost ammo pouch, the one she rarely ever used because it was inconvenient to reach for, she looked over and saw Massey had slumped over against the roots, his curly black hair dug awkwardly into the forest debris filling them. His hand, in fact most of his *arm*, was a shocking, bright red in the shaded sunlight where he must have pawed at his wound.

Forgetting her armor-piercing bullets, Sophia flipped the man back over onto his back, her eyes widening as she saw the little hole clean through his chest and the angry red slick running down his front from it. His eyes stared vacantly at the leaves overhead through a film of dirt and dust. Shot clean through the heart. Dead.

She hadn't known Massey very well, not really. He'd been quiet by nature and he'd been one of Stennis' guys, brought over when he took over the squad after Fire Ridge. She'd never really shaken the feeling that he thought she was a second-rate replacement not worth bringing up his issues with. And now... now the forest was full of bullets and she had four other people to keep alive. She'd figure out how she felt about him later. Gritting her teeth, she felt around his neck for his dog tags, pulled them off over his head, wrapped them around her hand and got back to reloading her rifle. Jamming the S-bullets into the magazine, she slammed the bolt home, fired a shot, got up and fled.

The bridge was only a couple hundred meters down the road, a little wooden span over a narrow but treacherous ravine. By the time they got there the bushes on the far side were boiling with gray uniforms as what looked like a couple hundred cuirassiers settled into position and started firing to cover their retreat. Quickly picking up their bicycles, they pounded across the bridge's planking and tried not to step on any of the wires now running across its structure as they made it across. Sergeant Cross had the presence of mind to station himself on the far side and count them in, and he yelled at her as her squad made it across, "*Rose!* Where's Massey?"

Sophia thrust her hand out at him, the one with his dog tags wrapped around it. As she did it she noticed one of them had a bullet hole clean through it. Cross looked between the tags and her, then set his jaw slowly. Sophia shook her head, "He didn't make it."

The sergeant cursed and jerked his chin at where the rest of her friends were ducking off the road behind her, "Go and get down, they're blowing this bridge in a minute. We'll talk later."

Sophia shook her head to clear it and rushed after the others. Not thirty seconds later she heard Cross shouting that the platoon was across, and someone else shouted to take cover. A moment later the charges went off and the bridge collapsed into the ravine with a splintering crash.

They were pedaling back down the road a few minutes later, climbing out of the forest in silence. The cuirassiers seemed to have taken their comrades' failure as a stain on their honor and insisted on taking over the rear-guard, properly this time. Honestly, she thought as they emerged from the shade and onto the top of a shallow ridge running down to the west, *proper* had nothing to do with it. She was quite certain they'd done their best, as they all had since the start of this war. As Massey had, his bullet-holed dog tags still wrapped around her hand.

Looking off to her right as they descended, Sophia could see dust rising across the entire northern horizon, burning white in the afternoon sun. The Imperial Army, crashing west into the heart of the Kingdom like a steel-masked avalanche. The problem with this whole war, she thought as she pedaled along with her dead friend's last memento in her hand, wasn't that any of them hadn't done their *best*.

It was that their best wasn't good enough.

Chapter 33

Enigma

Armed with a new and longer message after her second meeting with Princess Arilin that morning, Maria Remarque stepped out of the Palace's rear gate and walked across the street to the War Ministry, squinting a little in the bright glare of the late-morning sun. The sentries, under orders not to salute anyone lower than a general officer, ignored her. Dodging the thin stream of staff officers heading out to the cafes in search of an early lunch, she made her way up the steps and into the cool air of the building's lobby. She was studying the directory on the lobby wall when she heard heavy footsteps behind her and a familiar, paternal voice remarked, "Gotten yourself lost, young lady?"

Maria turned to see Colonel Goeben standing there, smiling beatifically despite the fact he was sneaking out himself. Given his waistline he probably wouldn't be back for a while. Plastering on a smile, she replied, "Just looking for the telegraph office, sir."

"Oh?" He slid in beside her and produced a pair of glasses from his breast pocket, "Let's see where it is, I haven't been down there in a while myself. Message from the princess?"

"Hm?" Maria looked over at him quickly, raising an eyebrow, "Yes, actually."

He chuckled, "You don't spend nearly enough time waiting on her, you know... ah, here we go! B34. I assume you have a pass?"

"I'm in Intelligence, I have a clearance." Maria replied defensively, "... and I usually don't have a reason to go over there."

"What, you need an excuse to go play around with girls your age?" Goeben teased her.

Turning back to the directory so he couldn't see her rolling her eyes, she managed, "I'll consider it, sir."

He chuckled, "You should. I was going to ask if you were free for lunch, actually, but this takes priority."

Maria snorted and gave him a sidelong look, "I'm a little young for you, sir."

He smiled back at her innocently, "Purely mentorship, dear. You're doing a terrible job as that girl's aide."

Now that she thought about it, she probably *was*. Whoever heard of a part-time aide? Her boss down in the Intelligence Section, that was who. Sighing, she shook her head, "I don't have much of a choice in the matter, sir. My boss thinks I'm shirking half the time as is."

"Bradley?" Goeben chuffed, "He can pound sand. Tell you what, young lady," He leaned in conspiratorially, giving her way too much of a whiff of tobacco on his breath, "You take care of your message, and then come meet me at the Victory Square Beer Garden if you've got the time. We'll figure out how to fix your problem."

Maria swallowed hard, feeling a chill work its way up her back. Hopefully his proposed solution involved her keeping her clothes on. Even so, she supposed there was a limited amount of sexual harassment that could take place in broad daylight at a beer garden. And he'd presumably be buying. Giving him a fake smile, she replied cheerily, "I'll come if I can make it, sir!"

"Excellent!" Stepping back, Goeben spun on his heel and walked out the door, giving her a nonchalant wave over his shoulder as he went.

Creep. Shivering despite herself, Maria turned and headed for the stairs. She had a long way to go. The War Ministry was built on the northern edge of the High City's promontory, where the ground already had a considerable slope. The southern entrance facing the Palace was actually on the third floor. Descending into a growing stream of increasingly-junior soldiers heading out for lunch, Maria eventually got to the bottom of the building's grand central staircase, checked the signs and headed off towards the secure communications office. Unlike most of the building the architects hadn't provided for natural light, and the shaded lightbulbs in the hallway cast a dim, calming glow that probably never changed. Like a well-lit tomb. It didn't help that whoever worked down here apparently believed in releasing their soldiers for lunch *on time* and the halls were deserted.

A sentry marked the correct door, a big military policeman with a pistol and a scowl. The man looked her up and down as she approached, then raised an eyebrow and demanded, "Purpose? I don't see a badge."

Ma'am? Maria thought sarcastically as she fished her security badge out of a pocket. Her own shop never wore theirs outside of the office. Handing it to him, she replied tersely, "I'm cleared."

He handed it back to her and repeated himself, "Purpose?" She gave him a hard look back and he added grudgingly, "Ma'am."

"Secret and need to know." Maria shot back.

"I'm cleared." He replied flatly.

"The *hallway* isn't." Maria snapped, "Now step aside, *corporal.*"

"I'll buzz you in." The man replied, glaring daggers at her as he pressed a button hidden into the door jamb. The Palace had to have some kind of alternate way to get its messages sent if this was how the communications office ran things. No way would this guy let a maid in. A few awkward seconds later a slot opened in the door at eye level and he said, "Got a visitor. She'll need an escort."

"Purpose?" The woman inside demanded. What *was* it with these people?

"My *purpose* is a state secret and not for discussion through a *door*." Maria announced.

"Hmph." The woman sniffed, then reluctantly pulled the door open. She found herself confronted with a stern-faced captain in a blue service uniform that looked like she'd had it pressed after breakfast. Considering she was supposed to be Arilin's aide, maybe it was time she started doing that herself. The hatchet-faced woman stepped aside and waved her through reluctantly, and Maria stepped inside a moment before she slammed the door back shut.

For the Royal Army's nerve center, the Secure Communications Office didn't look like much. Past the short entryway with its desk for the duty officer she could see a smallish office lit by the same shaded lights as in the corridor outside, albeit a little more brightly. She could see a couple clerks from where she stood, privates working away at what looked like bulky typewriters. Cryptographic teletypes. Beyond them, against the far wall, a large teleprinter chittered away faintly as it spat out a message. As she stood there she heard the familiar whoosh of the War Ministry's pneumatic mail system, and a girl announced, "Priority three for the Admiralty!"

Someone out of her line of sight remarked, "Intelligence again? They're awfully chatty today."

Because we're still looking for that Dominion battle squadron, Maria thought sourly. The duty officer interrupted her ruminations about the naval balance of power between the Kingdom, the Dominion and the Union in the northern seas by handing her a ledger and demanding, "Sign in. Now, *lieutenant*, what's this state secret you need to come in here for?"

The woman had *not* handed her a pen. Producing her own, Maria took her time printing, signing and dating the ledger before handing it back to her. She was opening her mouth to speak when she caught sight of the wall behind the duty desk and, for just a second, *froze*.

Every office in the Army had a row of portraits on the wall. Not just the usual one of King William that you'd find in every civilian shop, office, and many of the homes of patriotic Westerners. No, no, no, that simply would *not* do. The military had moved *far* beyond that. They would put up a picture of every single person in the chain of command, from the overworked captain in charge of the company up to the Field Marshal of the Royal Army and the King above him. Ostensibly this was to make the troops aware of who their leaders were, although she suspected it had a lot more to do with stoking commanders' egos. And right there, squarely between the bespectacled colonel in charge of the Telegraph Regiment and General Heinrici's gargoyle visage at the Guards Corps was one for the commander of the Strategic Signal Brigade, a unit which she had never heard of before in her *life*. General Chapman's face smirked out of it.

She'd spent enough time around Arilin to know she *despised* Chapman. Apparently she'd had a hand in getting him fired and relegated to the War Ministry in the first place. And he was Prince Alphonse's man. The fact that a cavalry officer with, as near as she knew, no relevant experience *whatsoever* and deep ties to someone who was probably trying to usurp the throne was suddenly in charge of a brand-new unit responsible for the Army's vital communications was suspicious, to put it lightly. And now she was staring someone who was probably one of this guy's loyal operatives square in the face, with a communique from Princess Arilin in her pocket that would undermine him. Suddenly an awful lot of things were starting to make sense.

That being said, however, she had to think fast. The woman's eyes narrowed and she was opening her mouth to snap at her again when Maria looked her square in the eyes and lied, "Security audit. You just failed." Forcing herself to chuckle, she went on, wagging her security badge at the reddening woman, "Do you have *any* idea how many of these things are missing right now? For all you and Tweedle Dee out there know I'm a Black Cloak. Anyways," She chuckled, "We'll be back later to inspect your shop properly, make sure it's in order for us."

Maria yanked the door open and fled before the woman could erupt. She could feel the guard's eyes burning into her back as she walked down the hall, and she flexed her knees to run in case she heard the pop of his holster's retaining strap. Making it to the turn in the hallway, she finally let her breath out and shook her head. What in the world had she gotten herself into? Regardless, now she had to get herself *out* of it. Which meant Goeben was getting his date after all.

Victory Square was a good fifteen minutes' brisk walk on the far side of the Palace and some way into downtown proper. Feeling herself wilting in the heat as she walked up to the beer garden, Maria idly thought that with Goeben's waistline he had probably called a taxi, and if her nerves hadn't been completely shot walking out of the War Ministry she would have had the presence of mind to get one herself. Resigning herself to a soggy rest of the day, she stepped through the front gate and quickly spotted the big colonel sitting in the shade outside, working his way through a sizable lunch and an equally sizable beer stein.

He smiled as she walked up, "Lieutenant! I wasn't sure if you were going to make it." He raised an eyebrow as he got a better look at her, "You look like you've seen a ghost."

Maria sighed and shook her head, "I may as well have."

"Well, sit down." He smiled again, raising his hand to flag down a waitress, "Tell me all about it." Hefting his beer stein, he added with a wink, "Although I'd advise you against getting one of these, at your size you'd be drunk on duty."

She snorted, "I'll take that as a compliment."

"It is." Goeben replied drolly, as a waitress in a low-cut dress with a mildly scandalous skirt appeared to take her order. As the girl left he commented, "You know all the waiters got drafted."

She gave him a look, "I don't suppose it's hurting business." He chuckled, and she went on more seriously, "I think we've got a problem. Have you ever heard of the Strategic Signal Brigade?"

Goeben pursed his lips for a moment, then nodded, "Yes, actually. One of Alphonse's pet projects since he got hold of things. Supposed to streamline communications with the front." He shook his head, "Useless headquarters if you ask me."

"You know Chapman's in charge of it?" Maria raised an eyebrow.

"I *do*." Goeben gave her a questioning look, "I'm not sure why that's important though, young lady."

"You *do* know Arilin had him fired from his old job, right, sir?" She asked.

"No, I did *not*." He pursed his lips again, thinking, "And he's been one of Alphonse's hangers-on since they were in the Academy together. Hmm..." He trailed off for a moment, then looked back up at her, "I'm assuming this has to do with your little trip to the telegraph office?"

She nodded, "It would certainly explain why Arilin has had so little luck with her father since." Goeben raised an eyebrow and she explained, "He's been ignoring her telegrams or sending her vague replies. She *thought* it was because he was busy at the front, but..." She trailed off. It seemed absurd, now that she was saying it out loud.

The colonel finished her thought, "You're saying her messages may have been intercepted."

"Alphonse put his friend in charge of a brand-new unit that's in a position to do exactly that." Maria replied quietly, "And they did *not* want to see me when I went down there. I didn't even tell them I had a message, I pretended I was doing an inspection."

Goeben looked around nervously to make sure they hadn't been overheard. Fortunately the beer garden's tables were well-spaced and the other patrons didn't seem to have paused a beat in their conversations. Turning back to her, he pursed his lips and thought for an awkwardly long time. Finally, he asked, "You said you were inspecting them?"

"Yeah, a security audit. I said I'd be back later for a proper inspection." She shrugged helplessly, "It was the only thing I could think of on the spur of the moment."

"You should have gone straight to Bradley, not me." He gave her a look that made her feel like she was about an inch tall, "They're going to check behind you, and if he tells them you were lying then your cover is blown." He furrowed his brow for a second, "They might take a while to do it, though. Let's see if we can get him on the phone from here."

"Uh... we don't need to do that." Maria replied, as she spotted a lanky and far-too-familiar colonel stride in the front gate, sweep his eyes around furiously and settle on her.

She felt herself wilting as Colonel Bradley himself stormed over, slammed his hand down on their table and shouted, "*Maria Erica Remarque!*"

The restaurant went *dead* silent. Before he could go on, Goeben cut in drily, "You might want to keep it down, Vic. We're not in your bunker."

Her boss rolled his eyes, glared around balefully until the other diners returned to their business, sat down and lit into her quietly, "I just got off the phone with General Chapman. He wants to know why in the bleeding hell we're doing security probes on his operation." He went on, "The funny thing is I don't remember ordering one."

"Did you *tell* him that?" Goeben asked.

Bradley rolled his eyes again, "No, of course not. If his people let *Maria* of all people in there they deserve whatever they get."

"I have a clearance." She protested weakly.

"And I shudder every time you walk into the office, *lieutenant*." He growled, "So before you and I go back there and potentially decertify the *Telegraph Office*, I'd appreciate it if you'd tell me exactly what you actually *were* doing down there."

Swallowing hard, she pulled out her notebook, fumbled through the pages until she got to Arilin's note and handed it to him. She started, "I... er, ah..."

Goeben rescued her, "What Miss Remarque is trying to say, but for you terrifying her into incoherence, is that she's concerned Chapman may be interfering with communications between Princess Arilin and her father through his control over the Strategic Signal Brigade. A concern which I must say I share now that I think about it." Taking a long pull of beer, he went on, "I hope you're a Legitimist, by the way."

"If half the gossip my wife tells me is true, it's hard *not* to be." Bradley muttered, glaring at her for a moment, "I let her take on that aide job for a reason." Handing her notebook back to her, he demanded, "So you think we've got a man in the middle attack happening right now?"

Swallowing hard, Maria managed, "Yes. Sir. Arilin telegraphs her father frequently, but ever since Alphonse took over responsibility for the military she's rarely gotten a proper answer back." Bradley's eyes narrowed, and she went on, "Letters too. It's like he's not receiving most of what she sends."

Bradley took a long breath, curling his nose up angrily as he thought. Finally, he replied, "We'll look into it when we get back to the office." The look he was giving her could curdle milk. Unexpectedly, he glanced over at Goeben, then back to her, "Also, you're *not* to go on any more lunch dates with *this* fellow."

"What'd I do?" The fat colonel protested, too-innocently.

"At least ten female lieutenants I know of." Bradley snapped, "And I'd appreciate it if you kept your grubby paws off *mine*."

Goeben shrugged she felt her hair starting to stand on end, "I don't recall any of *them* claiming I did anything improper."

"'She enjoyed it' *isn't a defense*." Her boss growled heroically, like an alpha wolf defending his cub.

"It actually is though." Goeben replied nonchalantly, "Consenting adults and all that. Anyways, Vic, you should order something, the food here's really quite good."

Bradley looked at his watch angrily, then stood, "I'm standing up my wife for lunch as is. Maria, you're coming with me. Did you already order?"

"Ah... yes?" She replied helplessly.

He glared at Goeben, "Stick him with the bill. He deserves it, and he'll eat it, too."

The fat colonel somehow managed to smirk and take another long pull from his stein simultaneously.

* * *

As they walked down the stairs to the War Ministry basement and their date with destiny, Maria looked over at her boss and asked, "Sir, did you *really* have to introduce me as your most useless soldier?"

Bradley gave her a sidelong look and snorted, "Stop pouting. And most of the time you're either out of the office allegedly doing research for your princess or telling me things I found out from other sources *weeks* ago."

"I helped you find that double agent though." Maria replied sourly.

"I hadn't been taking him seriously for months, lieutenant." He went on, his tone just light enough to tell her he wasn't *entirely* serious, "I could probably replace you with an office cat, at least we'd save paper that way and I wouldn't look at your blackboard and wonder if I was having a stroke."

"Hrmph!" Maria stuck her nose in the air and pouted furiously.

Bradley ignored her, "Anyways, look alive, lieutenant. We've got an operation to blow open."

They had posted a new guard since the morning, and the map snapped smartly to attention as they approached. They stopped in front of him and he said, "No entry without authorization, sir." Looking over at her, he added, "Ma'am."

Bradley gave him a tired look, "We're here because you failed an intrusion test this morning. Under General Staff Policy two dash three the Intelligence Section is responsible for physical security and may inspect any shop or workspace at any time for any or no reason, to include overt and covert audits." He leaned forward a little and growled, "I'm the chief spook. Knock knock, open sesame."

Swallowing, the guard hauled the door open for them and they stepped inside. The captain on duty had been replaced with a dour-looking major, who stood as they entered and started, "Sir, good to see-"

"Enough of the pleasantries, you know why I'm here." Maria swung the door closed behind her as Bradley cut the man off. The bolts thudded home heavily and he went on, "I had my subordinate here try to talk her way in earlier, *successfully* I might add, because we've received a number of frankly disturbing reports indicating that confidential communications between Princess Arilin and King William have been compromised and their contents made known to the enemy."

The major's eyes widened as Bradley spoke, and he shook his head, "Oh, no, no, sir, that can't have happened." He smiled, "At least, not out of this office."

Bradley raised an eyebrow, "Why not?"

"We don't handle any of her communications here. Those are all routed to the, uh..." He trailed off, realizing that he was about to say something extraordinarily damning.

"The, uh...?" Bradley repeated theatrically.

The man swallowed and finally said, "The General Telegraph Exchange, sir, same as any other cable for a soldier by a family member." Where they would be opened, read and censored as a matter of course, even without malevolent intent. He added quickly, "Brigade revoked her privileges months ago. Sir."

"Oh? Why's that?" Her boss asked, deceptively calm.

"I think it had something to do with that war scare with the Dominion, sir." The man smiled, "Can't have that girl getting us into any *more* of them, now can we?"

Bradley snorted contemptuously, "We're in for a bumpy ride with her, that's for sure. Lieutenant!"

"Sir?" Maria snapped to attention instinctively.

"I can finish up here. I need you to run back to the office before the soldiers leave for the day and organize a detail for us to take down to the Exchange tomorrow. *That* will be a hell of a job and we'll need an entire crew." Turning, he winked at her out of the major's line of sight, "Now *go*."

The guard outside probably thought it was strange that a lieutenant would break into a *dead sprint* back down the hall as soon as the door thudded shut again. She didn't care, and she didn't stop running until she skidded to a stop on the Palace's roof verandah in front of Arilin, Beatrice and the Queen as they sat down to afternoon tea.

Chapter 34

Battlegroup

A small crowd of vacationers had gathered to watch the gendarme nailing up the martial law proclamation on the boardwalk. From what he could see in the sunset's dying light it looked like pretty standard fare, the city was now under martial law, a curfew would be enforced, don't spread rumors, beaches were closed indefinitely by order of Colonel Such-and-Such, commander of the local Fortress Brigade. God Save the King. The line about the beaches was new, and the crowd seemed to be mostly worked up about it. He supposed he couldn't blame them. Requinsville was a *legendary* resort town, the jewel of the Ellarian Riviera. It wasn't like the Imperial Army was supposed to be anywhere near, and the Black Fleet wasn't exactly going to be harassing swimmers.

Nudging Lucky forward to the edge of the crowd, June shouted over the unhappy grumbling, "Hey! You there! Aren't you guys a little late on this? I heard there were Masks around here."

First Sergeant Kato reined his horse in next to him, already drawing his pistol as he demanded, "Sir, what the *hell* are you doing?"

June gave him a look, "I'm asking this man why it's taken so long to put this town under martial law. There's clearly been some kind of oversight." He raised an eyebrow, "You think we should keep the beaches closed? Might make these folks like us."

Kato shrugged, "Your call sir, I think you're the senior man in town right now." Looking back at the gendarme still fumbling with his nails and ignoring them, he thundered, "*Hey, you!* You've got an officer talking to you, soldier, how about you turn the *hell* around and stand at attention!"

The gendarme just about jumped out of his boots as the crowd suddenly noticed they were there and went *silent*. Spinning around, he braced himself to attention and shouted, "Sir! I apologize, I didn't hear..."

June snorted at the look on the man's face and replied, "I'm sorry for my man here confusing you. You see, he told you to stand at attention when you should *really* be putting your hands up right now. Yep, there you go." Nodding graciously to the wide-eyed crowd, he went on, "Welcome to the Empire! We're opening the beach back up!"

With absolutely perfect timing their tanks roared by just as he finished, drowning out anything the civilians cared to reply. He was just starting to smirk under his mask when a gunshot rang out near the front of the column, high and sharp, then another and another. A dragoon shooting from the saddle. Turning to his sergeant, he said, "Looks like we've found his friends. Can you deal with this guy here?" Kato nodded, and June wheeled Lucky about and back onto the main street going into town.

Something small and angry whistled overhead as he got turned back out onto the street, followed a moment later by the faint crack of a Royal rifle far down the street, where June could already see a few riders coming back leading horses. It looked like First Platoon had already dismounted. A moment later an Imperial machine gun chattered back, then another and another as his dragoons went into action. Waving one of the troopers down as she passed by, he climbed off Lucky and handed her his reins, then turned as another rider clattered up in a cloud of dust. His new friend and partner in running his little battlegroup asked with a familiar husky voice, "*June!* What's going on, do you want us emplaced?"

"Natasha!" Hefting his rifle, June jerked his chin down the street, "Keep your guns pushing forward, we'll need them for assault fire at this point." Noticing Kato marching their new prisoner out of the alley at gunpoint, June turned to him and called out, "First Sergeant! Get the rally point set up around here!"

"Sure thing!" His artillery battery's commander, until quite recently going by Bronze Control in charge of fire direction at the Fifth Horse Artillery Regiment, wheeled her horse about and galloped back down the street to harangue her gunners onward. If there hadn't been a battle happening he would have watched her go. In person she *absolutely* lived up to her voice. As things stood, however, the unholy hammering of a tank's autocannon reminded him that he had a bridge to seize and a battle to win. Hefting his rifle, June rushed down the street towards the fight.

He was *in* the fight, running his company around with a tank platoon and an artillery battery in tow, because the entire offensive was in trouble. Intelligence had figured out, probably through spies hanging around Wolf Rock, that their old enemies at the Royal Fifth Corps were deploying north to defend Requinsville. Pathfinders had filled in the enemy's deployment, reporting regiment after regiment and more than a few tanks unloading along the rail line running south from the town. General Kunst had coldly deployed his troops to tackle them head-on and left them with two options. They could fight his corps head-on, two exhausted armored divisions against three fresh infantry divisions. They would lose. Or they could cut south into the Royal cavalry corps that had been dogging their heels since they got across the Great Steel River, in which case they would win the initial fight and then have Kunst's divisions fall on them like a pile of bricks.

They had chosen the third option. Requinsville itself was being held by a reserve fortress infantry regiment and had excellent roads in, out and around. If they could take the bridges over the river going through the middle of town and avoid getting dragged into an urban fight they could push through quite easily and attack Kunst's troops from *behind*. That was, admittedly, a big *if*. Big enough that when Fifth Regiment had gotten the mission to take the town, Colonel Vann had put together this little battlegroup for him and told him to lead the attack.

The fight was over by the time he arrived, tanks grinding forward cautiously and dragoons starting to get up to stalk forward down either side of the broad main street. A few had adopted the expedient of walking along behind the clearly-bulletproof tanks. The road curved to the left a little where it was strewn with gleaming Imperial shell casings, and June could see what had caused the commotion. About a block farther up were the smoking remains of a couple fighting positions, optimistically sandbagged out into the street. Coils of barbed wire hunched against the storefronts nearby, unused.

Spotting Sergeant Tarai peering out from behind one of their metal monsters, June slid in beside her. She noticed him and volunteered, "Hey sir. Just a couple bunkers, nothing we can't deal with."

"I'm worried about what comes next." June shot back. Up ahead one of his old soldiers got up to run across a side street in front of them. It looked like Carsten actually, the short man toting a machine gun that looked too large for him. A flaming blue tracer whipped across the street just behind him before he'd taken three steps, the air around him filling with cracking death as his careful run turned into a frantic sprint. As Carsten dove into the next street corner's cover, June went on, "Like that." Something flashed down the street in the gathering darkness, and he tucked himself back behind the tank as more blue tracers whipped down the street and cracked disconcertingly off the machine's armor, "*And that!*"

Tarai looked over at him, "You want us to keep pushing or take left, sir?"

The tank they were hiding behind unleashed an *incredibly* long burst from its machine gun back down the street, probably fifty or sixty rounds, then revved its engine dangerously. June shouted over the noise, "*Push! I'll have Second deal with them!*"

"Got it!" Tarai turned and started shouting orders to her troops as he took off running back down the street. Almost immediately the gunfire behind him intensified, machine guns and rifles cracking back at the enemy. A moment later they were all drowned out by the thunder of an autocannon, and he glanced back to see a tank had pulled into the intersection and slewed its turret left, its cannon lighting the whole street as it fired.

Catalina had run forward to meet him, radioman in tow with a wildly-swaying antenna sticking out of his backpack. Pointing to what was now his right, June skidded to a stop and said, "They're getting hit from the flank up ahead. Infantry. Take your platoon, attack on the left and push them back."

The girl, although now that he thought about it she was almost certainly older than him, nodded, "How far do you want us to push?"

"Far enough to secure our left flank. I'm sending Third straight in after First down this street. You need to keep them off us while we push." Catalina was nodding as Natasha rode up on her charger in a clatter of hooves, and June shouted up to the new woman, "Can you loan some guns to Catalina here? She's pushing left and she'll need the support." He pointed back down the street, "Get the rest of your battery moving down the street and ready to support the advance. I think we're about to hit something hard."

A ricocheting blue tracer spiraled down out of the air and smacked off the cobblestones nearby, as though to emphasize things. The two women nodded and rushed off back down the street, leaving him quite alone as they started shouting orders to their troops. It was kind of absurd, honestly. Here his company was in the fight of its life, the war hung in the balance, he was *responsible* for it, and he had time to duck into one of the nice little cafes along the street for a cup of coffee. Although looking at the hastily-abandoned spreads next to him it seemed like this was more of a wine hour.

Or not so abandoned. Looking at the café's storefront, June could see more than a few shapes peering over the windowsills from the darkness within. The patrons had probably all run inside when the tanks went roaring past and the gunfire started up. Just then something buzzed overhead and June jumped as the city's streetlights came on, bathing the street in a cheerful glow. Either it was on a timer or some municipal employee was well and truly off their rocker. Shaking his head, June took a deep breath to steady himself and started off to find Third Platoon.

More gunfire crackled to his right as he set off, Catalina's troops making contact with the enemy. A few Royal rifles and what sounded like a machine gun hammered back, and the gunfight built for a few seconds until a sharp, harsh *bang* drowned everything out, the force of the blast strong enough to push at his face and rattle windows even from his distance. Another one followed, and another, and the gunfire stopped. The artillery had ended the fight before it even really began. And speaking of the artillery, Natasha cheerfully met him coming up the street with what looked like three more of her guns, Third Platoon and his mortar section in tow, still mounted on her horse.

"June!" She greeted him, "What's the plan now?"

He chuckled, "We keep going until we take the bridge." Looking over at where Lieutenant Vasa was hovering a little ways away, he shouted, *"Third, on me! We're moving up!"*

They reached the front line quickly, the enemy's gunfire thickening overhead as they made the first shallow turn to see First Platoon and the tanks lodged in a little ways past the bunkers from earlier, where the street curved a little to head into downtown and straight onto the bridge. The air around them almost *glowed* with the hellish light of a flood of blue tracers coming down the street, and they passed one man, then another coming back on stretchers. The second one looked like Carsten. Up ahead one of the two leading tanks fired a long burst from its autocannon, without the slightest effect on the enemy as far as he could see. In response a blue tracer that looked about the size of a baseball whipped down the street, whacking off the tank's turret and ricocheting into a building nearby. An antitank rifle. Someone screamed.

Meanwhile Second Platoon's gunfire, behind and to his left, had rapidly built up again, uninterrupted by the occasional thunderclaps of their cannons. Clearly the enemy had redoubled their efforts to flank them. More pressing, however, was the situation to their front. Turning, June laid eyes on Vasa and shouted, *"Jasper!* Get your platoon on line to the right and attack!" Looking back forward as the man shouted what sounded like a yes, he realized something and turned back, "I'll get you some tanks!"

Even fighting down a broad street as they were, they was only enough room for two tanks to actually fight at the front. The other two hung back a little, turrets traversed to either side to watch their flanks. With Second pushing forward on their left and the ocean on their right it was a useless gesture. Rushing up to one of them, June hefted his rifle and slammed its steel-plated butt into the side of the turret a couple times. A moment later a little hatch in the back of the turret popped open and a woman stuck her head out, shouting at him, *"There's a call button, you idiot!"* Seeing who he was, she added apologetically, "Sir."

June raised an eyebrow under his mask, "There is?"

"Yeah, it's on the back." She stuck an arm out the hatch and pointed at a general area of the tank's rear.

Walking around the war machine, June saw a little red button set into the back of the tank. Huh. He'd never realized that was what it was for. Apparently the engineers who designed the thing had thought of everything. Sarcastically, he jabbed it once, pointed at the other idling tank and yelled, "This is your section, right?" The woman gave him a thumbs-up and he went on, pointing for emphasis, "I need your section to support Third Platoon right now! They're pushing up on the right!"

"Sure thing sir!" She quickly swung her hatch shut with a clang, and a moment later the tank revved its engine and slewed around to the right to follow Third as they rushed into the next street over. He could already see blue tracers starting to snap by across the side street as the enemy noticed them, but not nearly as many as the ghostly flood coming down the main one. The second tank had to skid to a stop for a moment as the artillerymen pushed one of their cannons down the street in front of it, and June turned to see the other guns unlimbering and a horse team gal-loping back down the street towards safety.

The gunners nosed their cannon into the street, June noticing the gun shield dimpling unsettlingly as Royal rounds slammed into it. They didn't even bother to spread the piece's trails as the loader slammed a round into the breech. The gunner shouted something unintelligible over his shoulder, worked the traverse and elevation wheels and clamped his hand down on the gun's trigger. The cannon roared, the blast beat-ing at his face as the gun rolled backwards amid a clatter of shattering glass. *That* calmed the Westerners down a little. A moment later another gun rolled on line between the tanks and fired, and the enemy's fire died down to a sporadic drizzle. Nodding, June ducked into a storefront's open door, ducked under a window as something small and evil hissed through it, and fetched up alongside Tarai as another cannon fired outside. The walls shook and plaster rained from the roof as the concussion beat at the building.

"Hey!" June shouted over the racket, as another dragoon let off a long machine-gun burst from the next window down. "Get your guys moving! Third's pushing on the right!"

Glancing back over her shoulder, Tarai nodded and shouted to her troops, "*Move up! Let's go!*"

Dragoons quickly started rushing through the side door into the alley, and June emerged to see they had kicked their way into the next build-ing and were rapidly filing in. People started screaming inside as they entered, but no gunshots rang out. Civilians. Sliding over to the edge of the street, June waved to get the attention of the tanks in the street and gestured for them to move up, then carefully stuck his head out around the corner.

The river was *right there*, maybe two or three hundred meters away,

just the next block down the street. The bridge itself was obscured behind a burning barricade made out of cars, a jumble of furniture and hast-
ily-strung concertina wire that gleamed darkly in the firelight, stretched
between two impressive-looking buildings set on either side of the bridge.
Something sparked out of an upper-floor window on the left-hand one
and June ducked back into cover as bullets ripped at the side of his building and punched gravel out of the brick wall in front of him.

Footsteps sounded in the alley and June turned to see his mortar
section sergeant, a man he was still getting to know, emerging from the
doorway with a reel of field telephone wire in hand. Seeing him, the man
approached and said, "Sir! We're setting up in the cross street!"

June nodded, "Good! Set up an OP here and fire in support." A tank
rumbled past as it pushed up the street, and he grabbed the man and
pulled him to the alley corner, pointing down the street, "The bridge is up
there! I want fire on the barricade, on the bridge itself, and on the far side
of the bridge." He added, "And anywhere else that looks helpful. Got it?"

The man nodded, "Will do, sir!" Then he slung the cable reel over his
back alongside his rifle, wrapped his hands around a downspout a little
ways further back down the alley and shot up it towards the roof. June
whistled at the feat and ducked into the door on the far side of the alley,
following his troops. Sure enough, the back room they had broken into
was packed with civilians, now crammed into an even smaller space along
the wall where his dragoons had pushed them aside. Just dark shapes and
pale eyes, barely lit by the pale light filtering in through the door.

Someone caught at his sleeve. A girl, "Please, sir, you have to stop this,
we'll all be-"

A cannon thundered just outside, shaking the building and turning
her plea into a high-pitched scream, loud enough to grate at his bones.
Another woman, probably her mother, tried to shush her, "Dear, *please*,
quiet, quiet, you're safe..."

"No I'm not!" The girl screamed, *"I don't want to die! They're going to
kill us! Please-"*

Sighing, June stepped out of the room wordlessly and left them. It
was the same story in the rest of the building, in the rest of the *block* as
his soldiers pushed forward towards the bridge. People huddling in back
rooms, under tables, crouched in corners. People caught up in something terrifying they barely understood as death filled the air outside and
steel-masked soldiers, the stuff of legends and nightmares in the West,
tramped rudely into their reality. The refugees packing Nordsfeld had at
least had time to flee or hide properly before their assault, and they had

known exactly what they were facing. They had made a decision to be there, knowing the Empire was coming. Here... these were tourists who hadn't even been told they were in danger. The town was full of them. And unless he ended this quickly, a *lot* of them were going to die.

He caught up with the couple of squads with Tarai at the block's last building, a fancy restaurant facing the hulking hotel the Royal Army was now fighting out of. Pushing his way through a throng of crying civilians and angry chefs hiding out in the kitchen, June crouched as he entered the expansive dining room and made his way through the tables to the front wall where his dragoons had tucked themselves into cover around the windows and front door. The place smelled delicious, half-eaten meals still warm on the tables as the street outside hammered with gunfire. Just another little absurdity of the war.

A mortar shell whistled in as June slid in next to the sergeant and thudded into the façade of the hotel above them, sending shattered masonry and dust raining into the street outside. Noticing him, she looked over her shoulder and asked, "What's the plan, sir?"

June jerked his chin towards the street outside said, "We wait for the tanks to close up and we storm across while they cover us. One squad covers, the other moves. I'll lead in."

Tarai nodded and shouted, "First Squad! We're on suppressive fire, on my signal! Second, you're with the boss!" She went on, "Grenadiers, get those doors on the far side down after we open up!"

Crouching there in the darkness, June slung his rifle over his back and meditatively drew his sword. All around him he saw others doing the same thing, locking bayonets to rifles, or drawing and cocking their pistols. Close combat was a very personal business, and there was no reason to begrudge their choices. They'd all find victory or meet their Maker soon enough. The room seemed to quiet for a moment, the battle dying down just enough for him to hear tracks squealing outside and someone across the street shouting, *"Tank! Open-"*

Then all hell broke loose. Autocannons roared outside, first from the right and then the left, barely louder than the hammer of what sounded like dozens of machine guns firing across the street. Tarai shouted something unintelligible and the dragoons smashed the windows out as one and opened fire, bullets stitching madly across the hotel's façade. An antitank rifle barked, the massive firefly of its tracer streaking low and skipping off the cobblestones despite the close range. Grenade launchers thudded behind him, the stubby little shells plopping down squarely in the double doors of the hotel's side entrance and blowing them crazily ajar. And June yanked the restaurant's door open, shouted, *"Follow me!"* and sprinted into the street.

He was across in a heartbeat, feet pounding across the cobblestones as death snapped around him. He vaulted the shattered doors to come face to face with a Royal soldier in an old-style blue uniform, the man staring at him in disbelief as he climbed to his feet from where he had dove for cover from the grenades. June was already slashing. Him, and the man behind him raising his rifle, and the man behind him turning from a machine gun, and the man next to him before he had even dropped the ammunition belt he was holding, three leaping steps to the next team, batting aside a rifle, slashing down on a man's head, across and into another man's chest, stabbing through a Royal soldier's throat, *on and on and on* until the last group at the end of the hall fled around the corner. Pulling out his pistol, June swiveled around it himself and shot them all in the back before they made it twenty feet. Scowling, he tucked his sword under his arm, pulled out a spare magazine and jacked it into his pistol as he turned to look back at the corridor and see how the rest of the squad was faring.

The hallway, fancy marble floors, elaborate wallpaper and gilded fixtures, was *red*. Blood and bodies everywhere, most of them still twitching and gargling as they died amid a litter of weapons and glittering shell casings. Down on the far end a few gunshots rang out from what looked like the lobby, facing onto the street just in front of the bridge. Tarai and the rest of her squad were just coming in as he walked back up to the entryway, his boots squelching in the gore, and her eyes went wide as she saw him. "Sir..." she started, "Ah..."

"We need to keep pushing, sergeant." June said brusquely, "Leave a squad here to secure the building and let's get across that bridge. And send someone to get Vasa's platoon over here, I'm going to push to the west side of the city with him and the tanks once we're across."

"We were just supposed to capture the bridge, sir..." Tarai objected.

"Which won't help at all if we get bogged down in the city west of the river." June snapped, "Now move!"

Tarai fled as autocannons flared and cannons crashed outside. As June walked into the hotel's lobby he could see more dragoons storming into the building across the street. Blue-jacketed men started spilling into the street a minute or two later, hands raised in surrender as the tanks battered their way through the barricade outside. June paced in the lobby for a moment, then decided to do something more productive and sidled into the entryway, cleaning his sword absent-mindedly with his handkerchief as he peered out towards the bridge. Every few seconds a mortar round thudded down on the far side of the river, and a drizzle of eerie blue tracers and invisible little wasps flitted back down the street at them. As he stood there, one slammed into a light outside the main entrance with a blinding flash and a clatter of broken glass.

After a minute the tanks ground up level to the entrance and the artillery started hammering away at the buildings on the far side, the passage of the massive rounds beating at his face as they whipped down the street. The enemy fire had petered away to practically nothing when Tarai reappeared with the squad she had taken in herself, and June looked over at her, "Ready to go?" She nodded and he added, "Alright. We're following the tanks across." June snorted, "If you see any wires on the bridge, *cut them.*"

Tarai chuckled nervously and replied, "Got it."

Ducking into the street, June darted behind the nearest tank and pressed the call button on the back as more dragoons piled in around him. Sure enough, that little hatch opened up again and the same woman stuck her head out, "Hey, you figured it out!"

"Yeah." June shot back brusquely, "Push. Over the bridge, stop of the far side. Once we're across and consolidated your platoon's coming with me to the west side of the city and we're defending there. Got it?"

The woman gave him a thumbs-up and disappeared back into the turret, shutting the hatch with a clang. A moment later the tank's engine revved and they were off, hunkering behind the tank's reassuring steel presence as it ground across the bridge's cobblestones. At one point it had been a scenic little bridge, probably one of Requinsville's architectural showpieces, lined with artistic wrought-iron streetlamps and tasteful statuary. Now the lamps were all shot out, the statues of the long-dead Western luminaries were scarred with gunfire to the point they all looked like smallpox victims, and the bridge was covered with a half-finished spiderweb of wires and littered with abandoned demolition charges. Tarai yelled at her troops as she noticed the explosives, and dragoons started ducking out from behind the tanks to heave the charges into the river as they passed.

Off to his left June could see the town's railroad bridge, still up for now but blocked with what seemed to be an abandoned, lifeless train parked across it. On his right was the ocean, barely a couple hundred meters away, with Requinsville's harbor opening out off to their front and the lighthouse blinking merrily on the end of the harbor's long mole. As he turned his gaze behind them he felt his hair stand on end for a moment as he recognized the low, hulking shape of one of the town's sea forts out past the hotels on the river, before he picked out a thin stream of soldiers emerging from a sally port at its base, pale faces and empty, raised hands shining in the moonlight. Clearly Vasa had found a way to make himself useful.

The enemy fire died off completely as they crossed the bridge, and they made it to the far side without incident. Tarai barked at her soldiers to secure the buildings to either side of the street and the dragoons darted inside instantly, leaving him alone with the tanks. Pushing the call button again, June asked as the hatch opened, "Hey, can I get on your radio?"

"Sure, boss." The tank commander fished around for a moment inside the turret, then handed him a handset, "Push to talk, it's set to the battlegroup net."

June clicked the receiver and it hissed merrily. Holding it to his head, he started, "Aegis Seven, this is Six, over."

Kato's voice floated back after a moment, "This is Seven. You still alive up there?"

June chuckled, "Alive and on Bullseye. Intend to push on to secure Goal. Please pass up."

"Acknowledge Bullseye, pushing to goal." His first sergeant sounded extremely pleased, "Good work sir. Will inform. Be advised heavy sea threat reported inbound."

Battleships? We've really rattled their cage. Feeling his hair stand back on end, June replied grimly, "Acknowledge all." June went on, "Two, this is Six, how're you?"

The net cracked back with the sound of a machine gun firing. A moment later Catalina's voice came back, "We're holding. Three dead, three wounded so far..." She trailed off as someone said something inaudible in the background, then went on, "I think they're done for the night, sir, I'm getting told they're starting to pull out."

"Sounds good, hold what you've got." June tried his next platoon, "Three, Six, good work on that fort."

"Thanks sir." Vasa's voice floated back, "Heard you want us up there pronto. You're at Bullseye?"

"Yeah." June went on, "How long do you need to clean up there?"

After a moment the lieutenant replied, "I'll leave a couple squads here and take the rest up. That alright with you?"

"It'll have to be." June replied. The last thing they wanted to do was leave those forts operational or have what were probably hundreds of prisoners escape and run amok. He went on, "Waiting on you and your tanks here."

Hooves clattered behind him and he turned to see Natasha galloping up, still on horseback. How she wasn't *dead* yet charging around this close to the enemy was completely beyond him, but she had his admiration for sheer bravado at least. Yanking her mount to a halt next to the tank, she called down, "How's the war?"

"Fine." June snorted, "Can you take command of the crossing site? I'm taking a detachment and pushing on to the far side of the city while we've got the momentum here."

"Sure." The woman laughed, "Seems like they're starting to give up. I don't think they expected a fight."

"I doubt they did." He looked back up at her, "Oh, and I'll need that platoon of yours to come with me."

"So you want me to be a glorified crossing guard while you charge off with the *rest* of my guns?" Natasha demanded.

"Look at it this way." June shot back slyly, "I'm letting you play with most of *my* dragoons and still keep half of *your* guns."

The woman shrugged, "Good point. You can have them." Wheeling her horse around dramatically, she galloped back over the bridge and faintly started shouting orders at her gunners. A couple minutes later the artillerymen had reassembled their horse teams, limbered their cannons back up and come over the bridge at a stately trot, followed shortly by the other tanks and Vasa's detachment.

As they sorted themselves out in the street the tank commanders, feeling a little safer now that the battle had died down for the moment, popped out of their hatches like oversized jacks-in-the-box. The commander from earlier weighed in, "Hey, sir, I've got an idea." June looked up from pointing out the route to Vasa, and she went on, "How about you guys ride on the tanks? We'll get there a lot faster."

June thought for a moment, then nodded, "Works for me. You ready to go?" She gave him a thumbs-up, and he called out to the troopers, "Mount up on the tanks! We're heading out!"

They clambered aboard, the tanks revved their engines and they were off, the artillery cantering along behind. Fortunately the designers had seen fit to include handholds on the war machines. The commander popped her turret's top hatch open and emerged into the breeze so he could give her directions as they sped along. The grand hotels and restaurants of downtown quickly gave way to seedier quarters as they moved into the harbor district, the masts of fishing boats sprouting beyond the low buildings to the north. Hard-looking fishermen emerged from taverns to stare at them, quite the contrast from the disappearing tourists on the far side of the city. They glared back, secure in the knowledge that for the time being they were the ones with the guns and the tanks.

Off to the west, over the buildings and through the thicket of masts, June occasionally caught glimpses of another squat concrete shape at the base of the breakwater at the far side of the harbor. The West Fort, however, remained sullenly silent as they rolled along. It was supposed to have a few light guns that could fire into the harbor itself, although June suspected they were leery of firing into the city they were supposed to be protecting. Their problem, not his. June turned back to his map and shouted more directions to the commander over the tank's shrieking tracks. They were close now, as the city's buildings thinned and the road curved south beyond the shoreline. The glowering fort disappeared behind a low hill, and June let out a high of relief he hadn't realized he'd been holding.

They churned across the railroad tracks, startling a gendarme who fled into the night without firing a shot, and pressed onwards. There was a crossroads south of town where the road split, one branch continuing down the coast towards Brightangel and the other heading south along the river. A service station's lights glowed cheerily at the crossing as they came up over a small rise, a well-dressed man and woman standing by an expensive-looking car parked out front staring at them wide-eyed as they rumbled up. June waved at them politely, then tapped the commander's shoulder, "We'll defend here. Get your tanks into position, main threat's to the south."

The woman gave him a thumbs-up, then muttered something into her headset. A moment later the tank's engine quieted to a low growl and the tank rolled gently to a halt as the commander turned and announced, "Alright, your boss says we're here so we're here! Get off my damn tank!"

The dragoons hopped down and the tanks quickly scattered to hide themselves behind the small rise with the artillery as the troopers folded themselves into the fields and rushed forward to take cover behind the more solid-looking and less-explosive parts of the service station. Someone with sense marched the slack-jawed couple inside at gunpoint, and a moment later the station's lights died as they cut the power. Walking back to where his tank was idling, mostly-concealed behind the rise, June called out, "Hey, got your radio handy?" The commander produced her handset and handed it down, and he keyed it, "Aegis Seven, this is Six.

We're at Goal. Any word on the cavalry?"

Kato's voice crackled back, broken from the distance, "..even, they're at my... now and continuing... read?"

"I read they're at your position and continuing at this time." June replied.

"Good read." Kato's voice drifted out of the mic.

June was opening his mouth to reply when the commander whistled and he looked up to see her peering through her binoculars at something in the distance. Having gotten his attention, she said, "Sir, we're about to have a lot of company."

Boosting himself back up onto the tank, June produced his own binoculars and looked down the road to the south. Dust rose ghostly in the moonlight as a squat shape slowly appeared over a distant rise, so large it almost filled the narrow country lane. June looked down for a moment at the tank he was kneeling on, then at the road nearby, just to make sure his eyes weren't deceiving him. That thing was *enormous*, half again as wide as his own tanks and easily twice their height. As he watched another one emerged into view behind it, and another, gray-jacketed Royal infantrymen looking like toys as they walked beside their monstrous war machines. Setting the handset back against his head, June keyed it and said, "Seven, this is Six. Tell them to hurry, we're looking at enemy armor and infantry here."

"...ill do." Kato came back. June thought he could hear the clanking of more tanks' tracks in the background, although it might have been the static.

"Six out." Tossing the handset back to the commander, he asked, "Can you kill those things at this range?"

The woman shook her head, "No way, we'd have to flank and push up."

"Alright, focus on the infantry then. I'll have the artillery take them out." She nodded, and he shouted, "*Contact front on the south road, tanks and infantry! Engage on my command! Artillery, the tanks are yours, ev*eryone else engage the infantry!" Artillerymen gave him thumbs-ups and started slamming rounds into their guns, and the tankers revved their engines to claw forward into firing positions. Hefting his binoculars, June walked forward to crouch by the side of the road, raising his hand to signal his troops to wait as the enemy came closer, into the fields and away from easy cover. Closer, and closer, the long column of marching infantry coming fully into view, the enemy tanks' turrets swiveling as though they sensed something was wrong.

Finally, June dropped his hand and shouted, "*Open fire!*"

The rest of the regiment finally arrived as they were fighting it out with the second, much larger Royal counterattack, the sudden flood of tanks and dragoons scattering the enemy into the night. Finding June peering into the distance atop a disabled and abandoned Royal tank, Colonel Vann reined in her horse and shouted, "Good work! I knew I could count on you!"

Turning, June sat down on the edge of the great machine's top deck, feeling his blood-soaked uniform stick to his body in the cool night. He smiled grimly, "We got it done, ma'am. Got a little lucky, too."

The woman looked at the carnage surrounding them, then snorted, "Luck is what happens when opportunity meets preparation, captain." Her mask's jaw-plate tilted as one side of her mouth curled up, "Now come on. I've got a new mission for you."

Hopping down off the tank, June chuckled tiredly and asked, "Where to now?"

The woman pulled out a map, her mask shifting as she smiled predatorily, "Oh, I think you'll like this..."

Chapter 35

End of the Line

It was pitch dark and starting to rain by the time they pulled into the station, so tired they rode straight past the gendarme trying to direct traffic at the blacked-out platform and jumbled into the wagon staging area. Chaos ensued. Men yelled at them for things, most of which she supposed were valid, and people yelled back. Lieutenant Thorn appeared after far too long to sort things out, using the reserve of strength he seemed to have been issued when they put him in charge of the company, and he eventually resorted to physically grabbing her by the collar and leading her... somewhere. At least he seemed to know where he was going. Chancing a look over her shoulder, Sophia saw Sergeant Cross shepherding the rest of the squad along as they stumbled behind her.

The growing downpour stopped as Thorn dragged her along, replaced with the metallic rattle of rain hitting a metal roof. Looking around blearily, Sophia saw they seemed to be in some kind of open-sided shed, probably built to shelter cargo. Flashlights bobbed in the darkness outside, silhouetting horses and wagons churning about in the rain. He was starting to shout something at her when the long blast of a train's whistle shrieked through the darkness, cutting him off. Eventually it died down and she heard him say, "...rest of the company! You can rest here, understand, but be ready to move! We're loading trains tonight!"

Her vision was swimming and the rest of her squad was already throwing their bikes down and collapsing onto the gravel. Even so, her curiosity got the better of her and she asked shakily, "Where to, sir?"

"Hey, you're alive!" Thorn shouted back sarcastically, "Don't know!" Looking at the ground next to her, he added, "Watch out for Vanessa there before you lay down, by the way."

"Oh?" She looked down to see a vague outline in the darkness she recognized as Lieutenant Gable, sprawled on the ground and dead to the world, "...okay."

Cross added, to everyone in general, "All of you make sure you take your boots off and let your feet air out. Your blood will pool and I'm not losing anyone over this."

"Sure thing, sarge," she replied, but the two of them had already gone. Carefully dropping her bike so as not to hit her lieutenant, Sophia unhooked her pack from it and threw it on the ground for a pillow. Sitting gingerly, she felt every bone, muscle and tendon in her body loosening as the weight came off, and she slowly drew her legs in and started unwrapping her puttees to get at her boots. They had ridden their hundred and fifty kilometers for the day and kept going into the darkness for... she wasn't sure how long, actually. Hours on a dark road, as clouds gathered and blotted out the moons overhead. Eventually the wagons ahead had hung out lanterns to keep them from crashing into them. They had to have made near two hundred. God knew how they hadn't all passed out from exhaustion, or crashed in the darkness making it.

The puttees came off, and Sophia fumbled with her bootlaces in the dark. Eventually they came loose too and she pulled her feet out, gasping as they seemed to expand in the cold air. Her socks... she'd deal with her socks later. Glancing over at her squad, she felt a spike of panic as she counted four silhouettes tiredly pulling their boots off and groaning in the darkness. There should be six, it was seven with her, and then the realization crashed in again. Hargrave was in charge of Third Squad now, in fact from the smell he seemed to be smoking nearby somehow. And Massey's dog tags were in her pocket with a bullet through them. His body was lying in a forest a hundred miles away. *Maybe* the Imperials had found him and would give him a proper burial. And maybe the crows were doing it for them.

God damn it. Shaking her head tiredly to get rid of the thought, Sophia somehow found her flashlight and played it over her guys to make sure they had their boots off and, more importantly, that they actually *were* her guys and not four random soldiers who had followed her into the shed. Tony, Kelly, Edward and James Montour all had their boots off and all of them except Kelly were already asleep. The machine-gunner ribbed her sourly, "Checking up, Sophie?"

"Mostly on Tony," she shot back, "Now shut up and go to sleep."

Kelly snorted philosophically and leaned back into his pack, "Sure thing, boss."

Slinging her rifle across her chest on the off chance someone would try to make off with it while she slept, Sophia set her head against her own pack and blinked.

* * *

She woke up wet and shivering in utter darkness, half-frozen and so sore she couldn't move. After a few heart-wrenching moments her body started responding again, every movement stiff and painful. It was raining harder than ever and most of the lights outside seemed to have disappeared, save for a couple flashlights bobbing faintly in the distance, distorting as her breath fogged in the cold. Twisting around, she felt for her blanket in the darkness and fumbled with the buckles holding it to her harness. First one, then the other came free, and Sophia unfurled the damp wool over herself and rolled up in it, the movement automatic from long practice. It helped a little.

As her shivering died down she leaned back against her pack again, closed her eyes and tried to relax, letting the hammering sound of the rain on the shed's steel roof wash over her. Distant thunder rolled out in the storm, just the thing they needed right now, although... thunder didn't hammer rhythmically like that and she hadn't seen lightning. Artillery, pounding away in the distance. Sophia grit her teeth instinctively at the thought. As far as they'd come the Empire was still ahead of them, pounding at the Kingdom's door.

Someone's boots were crunching on the gravel nearby, someone with a light tread but not a particularly delicate one. In front of them someone *else* was walking like a tiger, heavy footsteps so soft she thought she might be imagining them in the rain. If her father hadn't had a companion on his rounds she never would have heard him. Opening her eyes again, Sophia peered into the darkness in the general direction of the footsteps, shifting her focus around to try to make out silhouettes in the night. Eventually one of the thin steel girders that held the roof up swam out of the murk, and right next to it she saw someone she would recognize even in the faintest silhouette on the darkest night. Her father, making his way around and over his sleeping soldiers as gently as he ever did when trying not to wake her. And behind him Lady MacMahon was doing a rather bad job at following his footsteps.

Seeming to recognize her, the two of them carefully threaded their way over. Sophia shook herself and was starting to sit up when they stopped in front of her, the sergeant major forestalling her with a gentle, "No need to get up, Sophie. Just making the rounds."

"You're in good company tonight, Dad." Sophia replied softly. Lady MacMahon giggled softly as she went on, "Any word when we're getting out of here?"

"Should have been an hour ago." The commanding general shot back, before her father could reply, "But they needed to reconfigure a train for us and the Rail Service seems to be allergic to rain."

Sophia leaned back against her pack and replied, "I don't mind the sleep, milady."

The woman yawned, clearly in spite of herself, "I've been waiting for the train. Maybe I shouldn't be." She gave her father a look in the darkness, "I don't know how he does it."

Her father shrugged, "Practice. Anyways, Sophie," he went on, "God knows when they'll be ready, go back to sleep."

"Don't need to tell me twice. Dad. Milady." Sophia said, closing her eyes, "Night."

The two of them turned and walked off, their footsteps quickly fading into the rain and the distant, unsettling rumble of the artillery. Her blanket was warmer than she remembered from the Dragonspines. God, it must have been cold up there.

* * *

Someone was shaking her shoulder, and Sophia opened her eyes to murky gray light. Twisting around, she saw Sergeant Cross had woken her. He looked like he was on his last legs himself, gaunt and unshaven as he told her, "Get your guys up and ready to go, Rose. We're moving out in a few."

"Sure..." Sophia shook herself and stretched, feeling her muscles shriek in protest. She ignored them and asked, "They finally get the train ready?"

Cross grunted, "God, I hope so. Now get moving."

The man disappeared, and Sophia reluctantly unwrapped herself from her blanket, got her boots and puttees back on and set about getting her guys up. It was raining harder than ever, enough that the railyard outside was shrouded in an almost-impenetrable mist, and every now and then artillery rumbled over the drumming rain. Most of it sounded like the deep booms of their own artillery going out, mixed with the occasional crack of Imperial shells coming in. It was all pretty distant, if a little closer than earlier. But occasionally, every minute or so, through the hissing rain and the other artillery, she made out a low, dull rumble. She'd never heard anything like it, so powerful it almost seemed to be coming out of the *ground* but still incredibly distant. It made her hair stand on end. God only knew what was going on up north.

Her guys got up easily enough, except for Tony. He hadn't had the good sense to get his blanket out in the night and they practically had to strap his gear back onto him and wrap him up in his blanket until he warmed up enough to think straight. He was about finished shivering uncontrollably when Cross came back around and barked, "Alright everyone, listen up! We're loading trains! Get your bikes and follow me, order of march First, Second, Third, Fourth Platoons!"

They had all modified their blankets in some way to make them wearable up in the Dragonspines. Sophia tied hers around herself as a cloak, pulled her poncho over her head, grabbed her bike and ventured out into the downpour with her friends in tow. Even with the waterproof sheet on she could *feel* herself getting soaked underneath as she ground through the wet gravel behind Cross, across a barren freight yard recently churned up by thousands of hooves and hundreds of wagon wheels towards a waiting train. It looked to be about half-freight and half-passenger cars, and she could see smoke curling cheerfully from its engine. Through the sheeting rain she spotted the battalion's cooks as they finished loading their own vehicles, men leading horses and manhandling wagons into some of the freight cars just behind the engine.

After a painfully long walk they finally reached the train and Cross started barking orders. Bicycles and bags into the freight cars that weren't already locked, soldiers into the passenger ones. Get moving. They made it happen in double time and soon Sophia's squad was climbing into one of the carriages ahead of her, boosting themselves up awkwardly into a car made to be boarded from a high platform. Kelly and Edward grabbed her and hauled her aboard, and James signaled them where he'd found some space for them to sit down. Tony was already dead asleep next to him.

They didn't talk as they sat down. It was too early, none of them had eaten, they were soaked to the bone and, judging by the looks on their faces, the guys were as sore as she was. Tough as ever, though, Kelly quickly produced his own folding stove and canteen cup, poured some water, unwrapped a fuel tablet and set it alight. Letting Tony sleep, the other three of them quickly followed his example, and by the time the train lurched into motion they were all enjoying some of the best coffee she had ever had in her life. They had used loose grounds and she had to clench her teeth as she drank it, but that barely even registered given the circumstances.

"So." James ventured, setting his half-finished cup down, "Where do you think we're going?"

They all looked at her. She was the corporal, she was supposed to know. Sophia shrugged, "No idea. Wolf Rock, I guess."

Edward sighed, "Wolf Rock, huh?"

It was a depressing thought. They had left for the front from the old fortress. Now the Empire was knocking at the door. She sighed, "Better than Southbend."

"We'll be back in Jade Falls by next week at this point." Kelly grumbled bitterly.

"God, I hope not." James replied.

That put a damper on the conversation, all the worse for her as she realized just how *awful* the car smelled as they rocked along the tracks. Most of the rest of their platoon, or the part of Second Platoon she could make out occupying the other side of the railcar, hadn't been as enterprising as them about getting up for the day and were slumped over on the benches asleep. Even with the coffee, the atmosphere of a railcar packed with filthy, wet, sleeping men, with all the sounds and smells that involved, made her head spin. And with the pouring rain outside, opening a window was out of the question. Sophia was shaking her head to try to clear it when an idea occurred to her and she asked, "Hey, Kelly. You're done, right?" He looked at her and raised an eyebrow, and she went on, "Can you brew another cup? I'm going on a spy mission."

The man shrugged and wordlessly made another cup, which she poured into a now-empty canteen before she stood and fled. Her eyes stung as she made it the vestibule and got into the car behind them. That one was just as bad, as was, *somehow*, the one behind it. *Men. Eyugh.* The entire gender must have no sense of smell. Or *taste*. The next car was *worse*. On the plus side it was only half-full, of cavalry troopers she didn't recognize. Far and away on the minus side, however, most of them were smoking and they didn't have so much as a window cracked. Trying not to faint, Sophia marched through like she was on a mission and pulled open the end door, stepped into the vestibule, closed it behind her firmly, and took a deep breath of the cool outside air leaking in through the flexible walls. After her head stopped spinning she gently slid the far door open and stepped inside.

Cool, fresh air greeted her as she stepped into the observation car. The plush interior was deserted, the neatly-arranged interior only disturbed by what looked like a few leather saddlebags piled on a table. The *exterior*, the little platform at the very end of the train where passengers could step outside and feel the wind in their hair... was not. A lone figure was leaning against the railing, saber bumping gently against the curve of her hip as she watched the rain-soaked countryside unfurl behind them. Lady General MacMahon.

She looked like she wanted to be left alone. Even so, Sophia had a mission, and nobody had ever been court-martialed for bringing someone coffee. *Yet*, she thought darkly as she took a deep breath, pulled the door open and stepped into the wind. Compared to the train's miasma, the wet, rushing air outside was divine. She felt like she could breathe again.

"Air got to you too, huh?" Lady MacMahon was looking at her tiredly. Probably a little more than just *tiredly*, Sophia realized as she noticed the flask dangling from the woman's fingers. The top was unscrewed, bouncing against her hand on its chain as the train jolted along.

"Yeah. Milady." Putting on a smile, Sophia slid her hot canteen out of its cup and held it out to her, "I, uh, brought you some coffee. Thought you could use it."

The woman turned away from her, leaning back on the railing as she swung the flash between her fingers pensively. Finally she said, "What I could *use*, Miss Rose, is some sleep. It's why I chased everyone out. But that didn't work, so I'm drinking instead."

Feeling like more of an intruder than ever, Sophia swallowed and managed, "I'm sorry, milady."

Lady MacMahon chuckled, "Not your fault, kid. *Mine.*" After a long pause, she gave her a sidelong look, "Your father told me you're doing alright, but from what I saw earlier you sure don't look like it." It took Sophia a moment to realize the lady general was talking about her *unit*, not her personally, as the woman went on, "I've *never* seen troopers laid out like that."

"We're fine, milady. Just tired." Sophia leaned on the railing next to the woman, feeling herself smiling as she glanced over at her, "The Dragonspines were..."

She trailed off, and the lady general said something in reply. She didn't catch it. It wasn't important. Because the train had gone over a slight rise and out in the countryside, through the sheeting rain, barely visible in the mist-shrouded distance, was a *shape*. Sophia blinked, shook her head and looked again. It refused to go away, just a little speck sitting on top of a distant rise, even then starting to fade from sight as the train sped along. Sophia's blood chilled so fast she *shivered* standing there, staring at the oblong little dot with tracks and a turret through a mile of rain.

Seeing the look on her face, Lady MacMahon turned and followed her gaze out into the countryside for a moment. By the time she did the war machine had already disappeared in the shifting storm outside. The woman shook her head as she turned back to her, and Sophia heard her this time as she demanded, "What'd you just see?"

"Tanks, milady." Sophia replied, exhaling slowly, "I'd bet my life on it. They were a ways off in the distance."

The lady general's eyes widened, "*Goddamn it.*" Pinching the bridge of her nose suddenly, she shook her head and fixed her with a burning glare, "Are you serious? I didn't see a thing!"

Sophia stood her ground, "I know what I saw, milady."

Lady MacMahon's opened her mouth angrily to reply, but her words disappeared into a howl of shrieking steam and clashing metal as another train sped by going the opposite direction. For a minute it was impossible to talk as the air whipped around them violently, and Sophia grabbed the rail to keep herself on balance. Looking over at the passing train, she saw a few flatcars piled with familiar little crates whip by, followed by a seemingly-endless string of cars stacked with drab green artillery shells and metal canisters she guessed were for propellant charges. Ammunition for Fifth Corps as they tried to hold back the steel-masked tide.

The train was gone as soon as it had appeared, and she was left standing there with the lady general. The woman was shaking her head again, saying, "I don't even know what to *do* about this. I'll call Kunst when we get to Brightangel, I guess." That answered her question as to where they were going. It made sense now that she thought about it. Wolf Rock sort of sat in a basin surrounded by hills tumbling down out of the Dragonspines, and the countryside around them was flat as a pancake. Seeming to get ahold of herself, Lady MacMahon glared at her again and went on, "Look, you've got good eyes and I appreciate you coming back here with coffee, but I *really* need some sleep right now. Get-"

Something flashed back down the tracks behind them, and the woman fell silent as Sophia turned. She felt her eyes widening as the light down the tracks built, throwing sparks for an instant before *exploding* in a blinding flash so powerful she felt the heat on her face despite the distance and the rain. Opening her eyes again, Sophia gaped at the great, flaming mushroom rising silently in the distance, a white shockwave rippling out all around it. Towards them.

The sound started to hit, the distant chug of Imperial autocannons, the crack and pop of exploding ammunition, and then... Sophia winced as the earth-shattering *crack* of the train exploding punched her in the face. Glass shattered behind her as the train bounced sickeningly on the tracks, and Sophia caught Lady MacMahon as she stumbled and fell against her. Quickly regaining her balance, the woman gave her a horrified look for a second before spinning to look at the portal to Hell now receding down the tracks, then back at her. Then down at the flask still in her hand.

Setting her jaw, General MacMahon threw her engraved, silver-plated flask off the back of the train. Turning back to Sophia, she clapped her on the shoulder and looked her dead in the eyes as she said, "I've changed my mind on the coffee, Miss Rose."

Sophia smiled, "Happy to help, milady."

Chapter 36

Stained Glass

The windows at Saint Valeria's were dull and dark from the pouring rain outside, and the congregation wasn't nearly what it had been the last time she was there. Sunday Mass just wasn't the kind of *social event* that burying a prince was, she supposed. The ceremony had finished and the thin crowd was starting to file out, but Arilin remained seated, feeling unease slowly twisting around in her stomach. Now that she thought about it she was really being *far* too dramatic. At least Becky and Maria were being good sports about it, she thought as she glanced over at them sitting patiently next to her in the Royal pew.

She studied the windows while she waited. Every one of them was a masterpiece in stained glass, telling stories of Christ, the Church and the Kingdom. A dozen saints were represented, Valeria herself twice. There she was rejecting her tribune's order to slaughter a group of Christians who had been uncovered defying one of the endless Imperial edicts against the faith, her sword cast down contemptuously at her feet. And there she was again, taming the griffon they had sent to kill her in the arena, her shoulders streaked with blood dripping from the stumps of her docked ears. Side with the humans, elf, and you'll die like one, the message had been. Considering Lady Valeria was a saint now and had a cathedral named in her honor, Arilin supposed it hadn't exactly landed.

After a few minutes a kindly voice broke her out of her reverie, "A bit bold, milady, wearing red to church?"

She looked over to see Cardinal Grayson smiling down at her from the aisle. Behind him the cathedral was deserted, except for a few congregants who had lingered in search of salvation. Smiling coyly, she replied, "Isn't hypocrisy a sin, father?"

The old cardinal chuckled and brushed a speck of dust from his vestments, "I have dispensation."

"I don't think that's in the Bible." Arilin shot back sarcastically, "Or the Catechism, for that matter."

Grayson shrugged, "You'll have to take it up with the Hierophant, milady. I just work here."

Chuckling, Arilin stood, her companions rising behind her a second later. "Anyways, father," she said, feeling the smile slide off her face at the thought, "I'm here to see my brother and confess my sins. Would you mind taking me to him?"

The man gave her a nod and stepped back to let her out of her pew, gesturing towards the transept, "Unfortunately I'm not Saint Peter, but I'm happy to accompany you to the vaults." Becky and Maria filed out after her, trailing a respectful distance behind as they walked out onto into the cathedral's grand arm. Their footsteps echoed faintly in the gigantic building as they went, the cardinal angling towards a heavy wooden door set into the far wall. Its extravagant carvings and lustrous wood somehow managed to be understated, a feat that could have only been accomplished in the cathedral's radiance.

They paused before it for a moment, and Arilin studied the carvings as the cardinal fished for something in his voluminous robes. She'd been down to the Royal crypt a few times, but she'd never noticed that the door showed the women fleeing from the empty tomb. It was *appropriate*, she thought as she felt her teeth slowly grind together, but at the same time *extraordinarily* tasteless. Prince Adrian would not get the executive treatment. *His* tomb would only lay empty on Judgement Day.

Her eyes burned, and she rubbed at them for a second. It wouldn't do to break down in tears before she so much as got down the stairs. Maybe coming here had been a mistake. No, it was *definitely* a mistake. The cardinal's voice snapped her out of her thoughts before she got any further, "Are those two coming down with us, milady?"

Shaking her head quickly to clear it, she replied, "Yes. They'll make sure we can speak privately. And," she added, "I'll probably want to speak to them afterwards."

"Very well." The old man produced a massive, old-fashioned key from his robes and inserted it into a particularly deep curl of the woodwork that concealed a keyhole. Turning it, the bolt thudded back with a deep, soft thud that belied just how heavy it really was. They must have had an altar boy squirting oil into it every day since they'd installed the thing. Probably not an altar boy, actually, she thought as the cardinal pushed the door open. It wasn't like they didn't have a lay handyman.

They stepped inside, the cardinal flicking a light switch as he went. Dim lights set in what looked like repurposed lamp niches along the top of the walls flared to life, illuminating a staircase leading down, straight away from the door. Saint Valeria's architects had cleverly concealed the entrance to the crypts in one of the great buttresses along the transept walls, and Arilin felt the weight of the cathedral loom overhead as she walked down the smooth, black marble steps. One of the girls pulled the door closed behind them and latched it, and they were alone with the dead.

The gloom brightened as they hit a landing and turned, descending another set of stairs widening to meet a broad archway. Emerging into the vaults themselves, Arilin marveled at the sight, feeling her cares slip away for a second. The Royal Crypt beneath Saint Valeria's was almost as much of a marvel as the great hall above, and few ever laid eyes on it. Marble vaults arched gracefully overhead, golden flowers inlaid into a white background that seemed to gather and radiate the light seeping in from the cathedral above. Saint Valeria's engineers had laid prisms into the great cathedral's floor, bathing the vaults beneath with soft light while the glassy blocks went unnoticed by most of the parishioners.

Her ancestors laid around her, their ostentatious sarcophagi standing out amid the restrained vaulting. A thousand years and more of monarchs, princes and princesses sleeping side-by-side on their plinths, each coffin a story, its occupant's final statement to the world. Arilin glanced over into the vault under the nave as they walked towards the cathedral's central crossing, feeling goosebumps crawl over her skin as she recognized Maximilian's restrained tomb. The elaborate gilding of Queen Angelique's peeked out behind it. Behind it lay the rest of her family, the medieval stonework of the Seyam graves heavy and unsettling as they filed off into the gloom under the nave. She wasn't there to ask *them* for their wisdom, however. Setting her jaw, Arilin turned her gaze back ahead and walked onwards under the vault beneath the cathedral's crossing.

The enormous space was simply *empty*. Even the golden filigree from earlier was gone. A bare, glass-smooth dome rose overhead, converging on a single light at the center of the vault. As dim as it was, the whole ceiling seemed to glow as their footsteps echoed in the emptiness. The final light before Judgement, rendered in stone by mortal hands.

They passed out of the Vault of Souls, and Arilin felt her own return to her body. Shaking her head, she walked onwards with the cardinal as their two escorts unobtrusively fell behind, then stopped a few sarcophagi short of their destination. Prince Adrian's tomb. Her brother's tomb, carved from black-veined marble so fresh she could cut her hand on the edge. It showed him as he would have wanted to be remembered, a stone knight reclining in his armor, sword resting on his chest. He would have fit right in with the Seyams around the corner, or with Maximilian for that matter. A perfect knight, born hundreds of years too late.

Her vision clouded over suddenly. Sobbing despite herself, Arilin felt her knees buckle and reached out to steady herself, her hand coming to rest on the stone Adrian's armored boot. That just made it worse. Cardinal Grayson settled a reassuring hand on her shoulder and let her cry. It wasn't *fair*. None of it, none of it at all. *Adrian* was the Crown Prince, *he* was the one who was going to be King and she just wanted to help him when he needed it. That was all. That was everything. And now he was dead, and the help he needed was for her to step into his shoes and shoulder his burdens. But his shoes were too big and the load he had shouldered so happily was crushing her.

Admittedly he hadn't had Alphonse to deal with. Her uncle had known to keep well enough away while her brother was around. Adrian would have dealt with him in an instant, and never even let on that there was a problem. He'd gone through life just... happy, smiling all the time. She couldn't even *remember* him angry, not at her or anyone, really. The perfect prince. Her brother, and her friend. She missed him. God, did she miss him.

She knew one thing, though. If Adrian was in her shoes, he would *deal* with Alphonse. He would not allow this challenge to her father's authority to go unanswered. He would fight for his throne, with a sword in hand if need be. Anyone who stood between him and his birthright would pay the price. And that was the answer she needed. Gradually she felt the tears stop and the strength return to her knees, and the cardinal stepped back as she straightened up. Wiping her face clean with her handkerchief, she looked over at him and said, "Forgive me, Father, for I have sinned."

Cardinal Grayson smiled, "Always, Princess. God's grace is infinite. What have you done?"

"Disobeyed my father. Willfully." Arilin explained, "After the war scare with the Dominion..." She trailed off for a moment, then set her jaw and went on, "Which I caused, he told me, *very* clearly, that I was to stay entirely out of political and military affairs. Those were supposed to be Alphonse's responsibility. I was to defer to his judgement on those matters and stick to Royal ceremony." Arilin rolled her eyes, "Kissing babies and cutting ribbons, that kind of thing."

"An important role nonetheless, milady." Grayson went on, "I expect he wanted your uncle to take the blame of whatever disasters came along while strengthening your own popularity."

Arilin paused for a second, thinking. She had actually never thought of it that way, and it *did* make a certain amount of sense. A lot of it, actually. After all, why would her father tell her that he didn't trust Alphonse and then turn around and put him in charge? He was the King for a reason. Wheels within wheels. Or maybe he had taken it a step further and *expected* her to rebel. God only knew. Shaking her head quickly, she replied, "Well it struck me as unfair and stupid at the time. He told me himself he doesn't trust the man."

Grayson chuckled, "Milady, *nobody* trusts Alphonse. The man is a snake. I'd refuse him communion if he ever showed his face at Mass."

"Oh?" Arilin perked up, "Anything you can share?"

The old man raised an eyebrow, "Outside of the confessional? I'm running out of fingers to count his mistresses, and not all of them consented in the matter." He scowled, "The man enjoys the company of married ladies so much I'm amazed he hasn't made a pass at your *mother* yet."

Arilin snorted, "He probably thinks he's too good for her."

"I wouldn't be surprised. Anyways, milady, I've already dealt with the small matter of your parents committing adultery with each other." Grayson gave her a stern look, "We're here for you now."

"Right." Arilin bit her thumbnail nervously, then went on, "Anyways, I've been undermining Alphonse every way I can think of for the last couple months. I've recruited... God, dozens of people by now to help me. Hundreds, probably, if you count the ones *they've* brought in. Some of them are risking their lives."

"All of this clearly against your father's orders." The cardinal observed, "That explains all the convenient rumors I keep hearing."

She went on, "Well, I just found out that Alphonse has gotten in between me and my father. Intercepting my telegrams, reading my mail. Probably the other way around too."

"That's treason, milady." Grayson replied coldly, "Do you have proof of his involvement?"

"Just that the guy he hired to run the Strategic Signal Brigade is doing it." Arilin shook her head, "And at this point I'm not so sure he couldn't just brazen it out."

"Scoundrels always have an excuse." The man remarked, hardening, "I know a few myself."

"Anyways, I..." Arilin swallowed, then went on, "I don't have *time* to resolve this properly right now. I need to take action, *now*, to keep the Kingdom safe. To do that I need to forge some documents in my father's name."

"You can't repent for things you haven't done yet, milady." Grayson replied drily.

Arilin rolled her eyes, "Well I've *thought* about it, there's your sin."

"People think about sinful things all the time, milady, it's the *doing* that concerns me." The cardinal looked at the ceiling with a little more than just piety, "If mental adultery is really that bad, God would have turned my entire flock to *salt* by now. Anyways, you've been disobeying your father because you're an arrogant child and you know better. Got anything else I should bring up with the Lord?"

"Um..." Arilin thought for a moment, then blushed deeply, "Uh... I've got a classmate. Well, she was my classmate, I haven't seen her for a while, I think she transferred out..."

The Cardinal of the High City raised a frosty eyebrow, "*Lesbian schoolgirl fantasies?*"

Feeling like she wanted to melt into the ground, Arilin mumbled, "... yes?"

The man shook his head, "Of course. Well," He gave her a stern look, "Regarding your father, you will confess *exactly* what you've been doing to him at your earliest opportunity and not complain about whatever richly-deserved punishment he imposes on you."

Arilin felt herself blanch, but she managed, "Okay."

"*Okay?*" Grayson glared at her, "Children these days."

She coughed quickly and corrected herself, "Yes, Father."

"Very good, child. Now, I want you to go get yourself a rosary. One of the *long* ones." He produced one out of his sleeve for a moment and shook it in front of her face, "And you will pray it, *all of it, out loud*, every day for a *week*. Understand?"

Arilin swallowed, "Yes, Father... that's for my friend, right?"

Grayson rolled his eyes, "No, child, that's for taking the Lord's name in vain during *confession*. When I was your age, Father Malthus beat me for that. More than once." He grimaced, "Not deserved. I swear that man was actually a Dissenter." Seeing the look on her face, he chuckled, "Don't worry about your friend, by admitting it you're doing better than most of the congregation. Anyways," Grayson smiled, "I absolve you of your sins in the name of the Lord."

Arilin managed, "Thank you, Father."

He snorted, "I would tell you to go in peace, but I suspect you're about to walk out of here and do the exact opposite."

The princess shrugged, "Sometimes it's necessary."

"Most of the time it's not." Grayson gestured towards the exit, back across the Vault of Souls, "Anyways, we should be going. You can plot with your friends elsewhere. The people down here deserve their peace and quiet."

Arilin snorted as they turned to walk out, "You don't think they'd enjoy the excitement?"

"I rather think they'd be a little too eager to give you *advice*, milady." Grayson snipped, "Saint Valeria's doesn't have any ghosts right now and I'd like to keep it that way, thank you very much."

Something rattled off in the darkness, and Arilin raised an eyebrow, "Are you sure of that, Cardinal?"

He chuckled, "I'm not saying it doesn't take a continuous effort on my part. Now be silent and think on your penance, child. You talk too much."

They walked out through the Vault of Souls. It didn't have quite the same effect. Maybe she was in a better state of mind, but it just seemed like a spooky, empty dome the second time. The cardinal ushered them back upstairs into the cathedral, deserted now after the service, and shooed them out the front doors. She got the feeling he was about to go back to his chambers, uncork a bottle of wine and administer a few sacraments to himself.

They emerged onto the steps to find the rain had stopped, replaced by a chill wind blowing in off the sea and rushing clouds so low the cathedral's spires were lost in the mist. In a few minutes the whole High City would probably be buried in them. Despite the cold, Arilin pulled her veil off as they walked down to their carriage, wrapping it around her hand meditatively. Such a thin piece of lace, with a thousand tons of meaning woven into it. Modesty, chastity and piety. It didn't seem right to wear such a thing when she was about to go stick a thumb in her uncle's eye and *twist*.

"So, milady..." Maria started, "Are we a go?"

Remembering the cardinal's words, though, Arilin thought about it another way. Really, she wasn't sticking a thumb in her uncle's eye, she was sticking a knife in his back. Or more accurately, deceiving his own subordinates into pulling the rug out from under him. And for it to work, she needed to be as modest as a mouse in church.

Finally, she looked over at her aide and responded, "Yes. Go ahead as soon as we get back." Turning to her maid, she asked, "Becky, isn't Mom doing something this afternoon?"

"Yes, milady." The woman replied as she gestured Arilin and Maria into the carriage ahead of her, then climbed in herself. Settling down and smoothing her skirts, she went on, "She's hosting lunch for the new government in about an hour, then traveling to the Naval Shipyard for the *Griffon's* refloating. Ceremony and reception ball."

"I should go along, I sponsored that ship after all. And I might as well meet the new regime properly." Settling back into her seat and crossing her legs, Arilin smiled predatorily, "Prepare us all ball gowns for this evening, Becky. The only person brooding tonight is going to be my uncle."

Maria pursed her lips for a moment, then observed, "It *will* give me a cover story. I can claim I was being fitted in the meantime." She suddenly giggled, "You think we can dance with all the officers between us?"

Becky interjected drily, "Knowing you two, you won't need my help."

Arilin laughed. It felt good.

Chapter 37

Striking Sparks

They had set up their headquarters in a castle, laid out the war room in the great hall at the center of the keep, wrapped securely in enough stonework to stand off the Faceless King's armies until doomsday. Unfortunately, *Emperor Sai's* armies had weapons well beyond anything that old wizard had ever put in the field. Shellfire rumbled throughout the ancient fortress, loud enough to set his teeth on edge without him even realizing it. Walter could have sworn he felt it coming out of the *floor* like a distant, never-ending earthquake. Which now that he thought about it was probably accurate. God only knew how many tons of explosives were going off every second at the front.

Well, God *knew*, but his supply officer could probably give him a pretty good guess. Resolving to ask him later, Walter stood up from the map table. Staring at it wouldn't make things any better. He had to start making some decisions. Or *not* making decisions. The infuriating thing about being a general was that the days of galloping around the battlefield and waving troops around with a sword were long over. Well, long over for *most* people, he thought with a smile. Patricia still seemed to get results doing it. *He* fought his battles over a map, moving pieces around based on reports that never lined up with each other. Occasionally he'd go forward to look at maps belonging to people closer to the action, who might be getting their information directly from someone in the thick of the fighting. Of course it was still wrong because soldiers in combat can barely tell between their left and their right, let alone whether the enemy's reserves are committed or what their ammunition stockpile looks like. Half the time it was smarter to look at the blank spaces on the map and figure out what *wasn't* happening.

Speaking of reports, he heard the teletype chatter off in its corner, and a moment later an orderly called out, "Attention, gentlemen! Report from Third Army!" Just now swinging into position on First Army's left flank, a hundred miles west of the enemy's crossing-point at Kelsbruck, "Fifteenth Corps is fully engaged south of Ironhome and cannot advance! They estimate ten percent casualties so far! Situation with Seventeenth Corps unclear!"

Ten percent. What a dry way to put it. That was a *regiment* plowed under in the hours since they'd engaged. Not to mention if the army was reporting they couldn't advance that probably meant the divisions were retreating by now. It was the same story everywhere, units simply buckling as Slade Anjanou's avalanche crashed down on them. Gritting his teeth, Walter called back, "Anything on Eighteenth Corps?"

"No, sir!" The man called back. So he had an army that was lying to him about one corps, clueless about the second, and had entirely lost their third. Typical. One of the staff majors walked up beside him and had started fussing with the map markers when he heard the teletype chatter again, and the orderly called out, "Attention! Uh…"

The man trailed off nervously, and Walter snapped at him, "Out with it!"

Visibly swallowing as the room went silent, the orderly went on, "Fifth Corps reports they're surrounded south of Requinsville. Overwhelming enemy armor. Also both rail lines out of Brightangel are down."

Someone groaned. There went half their supply line. Taking a deep breath, Walter tapped his finger on the map for a moment, the sound echoing around the room's medieval stonework. Finally he growled, slowly clenching his fist as he did it, "No, they *aren't*. I know exactly what he's fighting and there's nothing at all *overwhelming* about it." Glaring as the mass of officers cowering over by the operations desk, he went on, "Send Kunst a message, on the radio, that he needs to stop panicking and start fighting. Those words!" He shouted, slamming his hand down on the table for emphasis. The little unit tokens bounced crazily, "And tell him if he doesn't confirm receipt the Empire's the *least* of his worries!"

"Well, I seem to have walked in at a good time." King William re-marked drily from over by the grand double doors. Either the guards had been too nervous to call the room to attention or, more likely, he'd waved them to silence. Granted if they called him out every time he stuck his head in they'd never get any work done. He continued as he walked inside, "Trouble with your old colleague?"

Walter nodded at his liege lord with forced politeness, pulling his monocle out of his pocket and cleaning it deliberately on the corner of his uniform jacket to buy himself some time to calm down. After a moment he screwed it into his bad eye and replied, "Nothing new, my lord. How was your tour?"

"Very good, very good." King William smiled beatifically, "Took me right back to my time in the infantry. Just *great* soldiers. You and I need to visit the front proper sometime, it'll do wonders for morale." It would probably do more harm than good at this rate, but Walter nodded politely as the King looked around at the staff and went on, "You all can get back to work, I don't think I'm *that* rare of a sight around here."

The staff fled back into their work, and the King joined him at the map table as the room's hubbub quickly built back up. Gesturing at the map, Walter said, "I don't think we're in too much trouble for the time being, here at least. I'm more worried about what's happening west of us." He added, "I'm going to have trouble running this army through Southbend."

The King raised an eyebrow, "You think the enemy's waiting on that to play out themselves?"

"Hm." Walter thought for a moment, stroking his goatee, "It's certainly possible. We haven't even seen their second echelon yet, they might decide where to commit based on that."

The King frowned. He couldn't blame him, the idea of another thirty or forty Imperial divisions floating around somewhere waiting on events to play out was terrifying. At least the Intelligence guys had finally given up on the theory it didn't exist. Finally, the man asked, "Do we have anything in the west *behind* Fifth Corps?"

"The Cavalry Corps, what's left of it." Walter shot back as the teletype started chattering again, "I can pull a corps out of Fourth Army if you'd like."

"What about the Storm Range Army?" William IV asked. He really needed to have them move that machine, it was hard to even think while it was hammering away in the background.

Walter replied over the teletype's annoying chatter, "Half of it is in contact at Ironhome right now. There's not a lot of it still *left* in the actual Storm Range, my lord. Not to mention the Dominion."

The teletype stopped, and the King was opening his mouth to say something when the orderly called out, "Attention, gentlemen! Orders from Royal Headquarters, Army of Drakenburg! Wait, wait... what?"

The King looked at him and raised an eyebrow. Walter raised one back and replied, "This sounds interesting." Looking over at the teletype orderly, he shouted, "Bring that over here!"

"Yes, sir!" The man sprang up, clutching a sheet of paper the machine had just spit out, and hurried over.

Taking the sheet, Walter read it. Then read it again. Then looked back at the orderly, just a corporal actually, and asked, "This came in encrypted, right?"

The man nodded eagerly, "Yes, sir, we changed wheel settings this morning on schedule. I can show you the chiphertext if you'd like." Of course he wanted to show him a bunch of gibberish to prove it. He'd probably draw him a full wiring diagram of his machine while he was at it. Signal nerds. He was an *artilleryman* and looking at their math made his head hurt.

Walter was about to tell the man 'no' when the King cut in, "If you could stop keeping in suspense, please?" He handed him the paper and saw the same confusion slowly grow on his face as had probably grown on his own a minute ago. Finally he looked back at him and shrugged, "I mean it makes perfect sense. I'm just a little surprised there's another Royal Headquarters out there. Do you think my evil twin's in charge of it?"

"We probably shouldn't talk about this on the floor, my lord." Walter jerked his chin at one of the hallways leading off the great hall, "Care to take a walk?"

"Certainly." William replied with fake cheer, following him out. Stepping through a heavy doorway just off the hall, Walter led him up a heavy staircase up towards the castle's battlements. Through some trick of acoustics the ancient tower seemed to resonate with the distant, grinding shellfire, so loudly that he could barely hear their footsteps in what should have been dead silence. It was a relief to finally step out on top of the walls, although the King still had to raise his voice over the thunder when he started, "I don't suppose you have any idea what the *hell* is going on right now, General."

Walter turned away from him to look out over the countryside, clasping his hands behind his back. Low clouds shrouded the countryside, speckling his monocle with misting rain as they stood there. If it hadn't been so gloomy he could probably have made out smoke rising from the front. The thought put things in perspective. Finally, Walter looked back at his companion and said, "Whoever's impersonating us wants the Guards Division deployed." Turning back to the countryside, he unclasped his hands and shrugged, "I can't disagree with their judgement."

The King shot back, "Yes, let's strip out the Capital when we're *this* close to another Red December." Walter didn't need to look at him to know he was turning red, "No thanks to my daughter deciding to *appease* these people. She had *Hiram Moore* released, for Christ's sake. Alphonse has been tearing his hair out dealing with her."

"You don't suppose that might have calmed things in Sapphire Bay rather than inflamed them, milord?" Walter asked, still looking out at the countryside. A tiny kernel of unease that had been sitting in the back of his head, mostly forgotten with the war, was starting to force its way forward again. The absolute last thing he needed to deal with now was Royal politics, and yet he was getting an awful feeling that the exact way out of this crisis was tangled up in them.

"Not according to Alphonse it hasn't." William snapped, "He's expecting a revolt any day now. Strikes, weapons stockpiles, talk of revolution in the streets..."

The man trailed off and Walter looked back at him, "And Arilin?"

The King groaned in frustration, "She barely writes!" Turning, he set his hands on the battlements beside him, "I think she's been in a snit ever since I told her to get her nose out of Army business."

"Hm." Walter grunted, "She clearly *cares*, milord."

"That's the problem, she cares *exactly* enough to create disasters." William IV snapped, "I wanted her to keep an eye on Alphonse, not run the realm."

The tickling in the back of his head got more persistent. Glancing over at the King, Walter mused, "You don't suppose this is *her* doing?"

"It seems like the kind of harebrained scheme she'd come up with." The girl's father shot back dismissively.

The artillery hammered louder in the distance as a volley of particularly large shells hammered down. He was an old artilleryman. Even a simple thing like firing a cannon accurately required a book of firing tables, a chart, pins, pencils, protractors. Slide rules if you wanted to do it quickly. Pages and pages of calculations to account for the weather. A whole team of soldiers to do all of this. And any time you moved, you had to do all of it *over again*. It was never-ending work. So was everything in the military, everything complex anyways. Like sending a message over the Royal Army's encrypted radioteletype system. Arilin could fight with a sword, ride a horse and get people to do as she wished, but he doubted she knew anything about code wheel settings. Snorting, Walter remarked, "If this is one of her schemes, milord, she's recruited half the War Ministry for it."

"What do you mean?" The King demanded.

Turning around, Walter leaned back against the battlements, propping an elbow up on the old wall's rough stone. Gesturing at the castle with his other hand, he said, "That message was sent using a strategic cipher machine and today's code settings. I don't think Arilin knows how to operate one of those, or would even know where to *find* one. And if she did they wouldn't let her in, princess or no." He chuckled, "It's not the War Room, the guards won't just wave her through."

William IV gave him an offended look for a moment, then shook his head, "Then it's the communists, or the Empire's broken our codes."

Walter gave him a hard look, "This hurts the Empire and the communists aren't that bold, not these days. Nor do they have the access." He went on coldly, "And your brother wouldn't need to play tricks."

The King drew himself up to his considerable height and set his jaw as he glared down at him, "Then what exactly would you have me do about this, General?"

Walter felt the corner of his mouth twitching up in a half-smile as he replied, "Give that girl a good spanking next time you see her. God knows she deserves one." Giving the man a sly look, he went on as he was opening his mouth angrily to reply, "Don't bother about the message, we need the troops more than Alphonse. In fact I'll have the guys hurry him along, although if I know anything about old Heinrici he's probably got half the division loaded by now."

William opened his mouth, closed it, opened it again, then deflated and shook his head. Finally he leaned on the battlements next to him and groused, "That's an *odd* taste to have, you know."

Walter chuckled, "I don't have the *slightest* idea what you're talking about."

"I *noticed* you stopped smoking." William shot back.

"It's a bachelor's habit, my lord. Anyways," Walter replied as he pushed himself off the battlements and clapped the King on the shoulder, "You mentioned earlier we should visit the front, and I think I know just the corps to drop in on. Care to come along?"

"How could I miss it?" Straightening up himself, William IV went on sourly, "If half of what I heard earlier is true, I'm wondering if I should draw a rifle before we go."

"Just like old times, my lord?" Walter gave the King a sidelong look as he fell in beside him on the way to the door.

"No." The man shook his head as another, particularly loud volley of shells popped in the distance, "Last time *we* had all the big guns."

Chapter 38

The Griffon and the Snake

The High City's gate loomed out of the darkness, the medieval stonework lit by streetlights glowing like fireballs in the fog. It looked like a great mouth opening to swallow them whole. Swallowing hard, Arilin felt her hands shaking and curled them into fists in her lap to hide it. The skintight leather of her gloves protested, and she quickly unclenched her fists and nervously smoothed her skirt instead, silk rustling too-loud in the quiet. Perceptive as ever, her mother gave her a sympathetic look from her seat across the passenger cabin and asked gently, "Nervous, my dear?"

Arilin tried to take a deep breath to sigh. Getting ready for the ball earlier Becky had laced her up tighter than she'd ever been before, and it didn't really work. Shaking her head in frustration, Arilin shot back, more sharply than she meant to, "How could I *not* be?"

Her mother gave her a kind smile, "I don't blame you, dear." Laughing softly, she added, "I'd be lying if I told you I wasn't myself."

"You're doing a good job hiding it." Arilin replied, settling back into the seat's padding and shaking her head, "And, Mom, by the way... thanks."

The Queen raised a perfectly-shaped eyebrow, "What for, Arilin?"

"For *believing me!*" Arilin replied, her voice cracking. Damn. Pulling out her handkerchief, she dabbed at her eyes. She'd cried enough already today, and she was *not* going to another function with destroyed makeup. Sternly getting ahold of herself, she looked back up at her mother and went on, "I... well, I was worried you wouldn't."

Her mother laughed again, "You should give me more credit than that, dear. Frankly I'd been getting worried myself, you just confirmed my suspicions."

"About having your mail read?" Arilin asked.

The car started to turn to head around the promontory and down towards the Low City, but the driver straightened out early, sending them off through an unfamiliar district of the Middle City. All to plan. Her mother grimaced slightly, "You understand, Arilin, that court ladies are professional gossips. I've been hearing things lately that could only have come out of my private letters to your father." She gave Arilin a hard look that she'd never seen before, like she was *evaluating* her, "I hate to think that Alphonse would go that far, but it's hardly the first time I've been wrong about someone. He wouldn't have put that *cretin* Chapman in charge of the mail otherwise."

Arilin giggled, "I see you share my opinion there."

The Queen rolled her eyes, "His wife is *insufferable*. That being said, she *is* the third wheel in her own marriage, so I can't blame her too much."

Arilin chortled, her corset's grip keeping her from giving the jibe the scandalized laugh it really deserved. After a shocked moment Tom joined in from where he was sitting beside her, and then Alyssa from her perch across from him. The redheaded captain somehow managed to laugh properly despite her own tightly-cinched ball gown. Maybe there was a trick to it. Arilin was resolving to ask her later when the woman looked over at Tom and teased, "First time carrying a girl's sword for her, Cadet Strathclyde?"

Tom shifted the two swords he had corralled between his knees, an infantryman's long, stabbing blade and a shorter, curved hussar's saber. She could tell he was smiling coolly as he replied, "Yes, actually. Ma'am."

"It's a high honor." Alyssa replied playfully, dress rustling softly as she leaned forward in her seat, "Princess Arilin can't fight in that dress of hers, *you're* completely responsible for her safety, you know." Arilin felt herself redden as she realized Alyssa was intentionally giving Tom a pretty good look down her bodice as she went on, "Tonight's going to be *dangerous*, are you ready for it?"

It clearly had the intended effect. Flustered, Tom replied, "Y-yes. Ah, ma'am."

Alyssa chuckled as she sat back upright, "I think you'll do just fine."

Her mother gave the woman a reproachful look, "Now he's blushing. You shouldn't tease men like that, they'll remember forever." The redheaded hussar petulantly blew a strand of hair off her face, and the Queen rolled her eyes and turned back to her, "And speaking of men, Arilin, I expect Masters will be a perfect gentleman but I *am* more than a little worried this is going to create a scandal regardless."

Arilin smiled and teased her back, "Worried it'll look bad if you run off for a couple weeks touring factories across the Kingdom with a dashing, single industrialist?" Her mother rolled her eyes again, but Arilin went on reassuringly, "I wouldn't be too worried about it, Mom. *You're* going to be the third wheel on this trip." Giving Alyssa a significant look, she chuckled and went on, "And if you play your cards right, Alyssa, everyone in the Kingdom will know by the time you get back."

 Now it was Alyssa's turn to blush. She stammered back, "I-I don't appreciate you just, just..."

Arilin rolled her own eyes, "Condemning you to an existence as a trophy wife to a man who's, let's see," she ticked off on her gloved fingers,

"Handsome, charming, intelligent, young, healthy," she started on her other hand, "Adventurous, extremely interesting, kind of exotic, *fabulously* wealthy, oh, and by the way he's crazy about you. He's been bothering me ever since you two met." She gave the woman a level look, "I'll just have to ask you to bear it for the sake of the Kingdom."

Laughing, her mother weighed in, "Sometimes men make you offers you can't really refuse."

Alyssa complained, "He's got a daughter who's *my* age, for God's sake."

"Yeah, and Vanessa's great, you'll really like her." Arilin shot back, "Mom, I'm out of fingers, can you help me out?"

Her mother smiled and extended her thumb gamely. Defeated, Alyssa pouted and turned to look out the window, pointedly ignoring the two of them. Chuckling, her mother stowed her finger and turned back to look at her, suddenly growing serious as she said, "You're welcome to come along, Arilin. Honestly I'm wondering if I shouldn't give you the choice."

Arilin shook her head, "I can't, Mom. I just *can't*. You can leave, BB can leave, but if I flee the Capital..."

The Queen shook her head, "I know, I know. Alphonse will declare himself King inside the week." She went on, "Dear, you're my *daughter*. I can't help but worry, same as with your father."

"I know, Mom." Arilin replied, feeling herself smile, "Thanks." A moment later the car turned, the driver gently applying the brakes to slow them to a stop. Glancing out the window, Arilin saw the high, evenly-spaced lights of a train station out the window, the glossy bulk of an overnight passenger train looming over the platform. A man's dark shape loomed suddenly in front of the window, quickly pulling the car's heavy door open. Cool evening air flowed inside instantly, heavy with the hiss of an idling locomotive and the clatter of people milling about on the platform.

Her mother swung herself outside, nodded to the guardsman who had opened the door, and set her eyes on a familiar shape hurrying towards them in the darkness. She was so used to seeing men in uniforms it was a little strange to see one wearing a *suit*. Mr. Masters arrived as Alyssa swung herself out, and he smiled as he saw her. Her redheaded friend smiled back, clearly hoping the darkness would conceal just how red her *face* was. It didn't. Turning his attention back to her mother, Masters gave her a short bow, and the two women curtsied graciously.

Alyssa had rather boldly given him her hand, and he was in the process of kissing it when Arilin impulsively climbed out of the car and called out, "Mom!"

"Dear?" Her mother turned.

Arilin rushed forward and hugged her, "I love you, Mom."

Wrapping her arms around her, her mother squeezed her back, "You too, Arilin." She trembled a little as she held her. Even so, she rubbed her head lovingly, "You take care of yourself, light. Like I always tell your father, the Kingdom isn't worth your life. You remember that, understand?"

Arilin nodded, "Yes, Mom, I will."

After a while she pulled away reluctantly, and turned to see Beatrice smirking up at her, having alighted from the following car with the servants. Her sister teased, "Aww, you're adorable."

"Shut up, BB." Arilin stepped forward and hugged the girl, "I love you too. Take care of Mom for me, okay?"

Beatrice hugged her back, just as tightly as her mother had, and muttered, "Put Alphonse in a box if you have to, Arilin, it worked just fine for Dad."

She chuckled, "I'll keep that in mind." Finally pulling away, she gave her mother and her sister a smile she didn't feel and called out, "Love you, I'll see you soon!"

They waved and were gone in an instant, Masters quickly ushering them onto the platform and out of her sight as a cloud of servants closed around them. Farther down the train she could see a mismatched segment, clearly Masters' private cars specially attached for the journey. As a wealthy industrialist his comings and goings would elicit little comment, nor would his taking a couple of lady friends along with him, their identities shrouded in the night. They'd be in the Sea Provinces by sunrise, Alphonse none the wiser. And if her uncle decided to make a play that was hopefully far enough to take them out of his minions' easy reach.

Sighing heavily, Arilin swung herself back into the car. The same guardsman swung the door shut behind her and disappeared back to their tail car, and she settled herself back against the seat's smooth leather and shook her head slowly. Just as she was worrying that she'd made a terrible mistake a warm, strong hand enveloped her own, and she looked over to see Tom had reached over. He smiled back at her and remarked, "Come on, milady. Let's go show your uncle who runs this town."

"Thanks," she managed, nervously brushing a loose strand of hair off her neck with her free hand.

Tom let go politely as the car started rolling forward, and she looked over at him in surprise. He didn't strike her as the kind of guy to back off like that. *Unless....* Reading her mind, he remarked, "You're out of my league, milady. Charlotte's jealous enough as is, you know I'm going to hear about this later."

Arilin chuckled, "I see she's stolen a march on me."

"Smart girl knows her enemies." Tom said, annoyingly nonchalant, "As for me, well, I know my *limits*."

"So," Arilin asked, smiling, "Who do you suppose is *in* my league?"

Tom thought for a minute, working his fingers over the swords in his lap. Finally he snorted and looked back at her, "He'd sure as hell have to be a better *schemer* than you." Furrowing his eyebrows, he thought for a moment before adding, "But he'd have to keep a low profile. You'd feel inadequate otherwise and get angry."

Arilin winced. Clearly having a girlfriend had done something to Tom's diplomatic touch with other women. And she had a sinking feeling that he was dead on target. Still, she fired back doggedly, "So you think I need someone to be the power behind my throne?"

He smiled back, unfazed, "I don't think you need that, milady. I think you *want* it."

"Hmph." Feeling herself reddening, Arilin joked, "I wonder if Lord Sai's single, it'd fix the war. God knows we could use it at this point."

Tom laughed.

* * *

The car bumped along for a while in the darkness, their driver taking a circuitous route to avoid any bomb-throwing anarchists Alphonse may have hired out for the night. Ironically this meant driving through the middle of the Tidewater district. Lookouts slouching on street corners straightened up and waved as they rolled past, and Arilin smiled politely and waved back. It was a bad day, she thought, when she could trust the communists more than she could her own uncle, but the Western Kingdom had been having a few bad months now and she had to take what she could get.

Eventually the lights of the naval dockyards emerged ahead of them as they drove onto the waterfront itself, a line of dim stars curving off to her left along the shoreline with a brilliant jewel set square in the middle.

They had lit up the *Griffon* for the ball like it was peacetime, Imperial submarines be damned. If they were close enough to start taking shots at the dockyard the Navy probably thought they had much bigger problems than just giving them an easy target.

Just as they started heading into the Naval Yard proper the driver unexpectedly braked to a halt. Arilin leaned over, looking out the windshield to see a barrier bar stretching across the road and silhouettes with rifles standing by. Clearly the Navy had decided to invest in security after she'd almost been murdered on their property. Putting the car's parking brake on, their driver climbed out and walked forward to speak to the man who seemed to be in charge of the checkpoint. After a few words the guards visibly stiffened, and Arilin couldn't help but giggle as they rushed around to pull the barrier aside and wave them through. She heard a man faintly calling the guards to attention as their driver swung himself back into the car, and she waved graciously as they pulled through.

They drove along the waterfront for a good mile, past dozens of docked warships. The casualties of the Diamond Shoals. A month ago most of them had sported mangled battle scars, and more than a few had been sitting uncomfortably low in the water. Now they were starting to look shipshape again, none more so than the mighty *Griffon* as they turned onto her pier. The sheer *size* of the thing always took her breath away, just under nine hundred feet of steel and guns sheathed in a coat of sea-blue paint so fresh she could smell it from the curb as she alighted. It was almost as long as the Palace. Telling herself not to touch any of the metalwork, Arilin gave Tom a smile as he came around the car, still adjusting her sword where it sat behind his own on his belt.

"Not sitting quite right?" She asked.

Deciding to leave it be, he smiled back at her and quipped, "No, I'll probably be fussing with it all night." He offered her his right elbow, "There's a metaphor in there somewhere."

She slid her left arm around his, and replied as they started off, "I suppose there is, now that I think of it."

"By the way, milady," he started. She glanced at him to see that he was looking back at her, more than a little red-faced, "Ah... I like your dress. Red suits you."

Arilin felt her smile widening, and she stepped a little closer to him as they went along, "I thought I'd have to fight with Mom over it, but she went right along. Thanks," She gave him another look, "And you don't look so bad yourself, Tom."

Her date, probably the lowest-ranking soldier in the Royal Army to own one of its brilliant white gala dress uniforms, inflated at her words, "Thanks, milady!"

"Don't spoil him too much, milady, he'll get a big head." Becky said, sweeping up in a rich purple ball gown from where she had followed them in the rear car. Glancing over at her own companion, she chuckled and remarked, "Looks like we'll have our hands full with these two tonight."

"I'll say." Maria arrived, the lieutenant a little awkward in a gorgeous golden dress. Arilin got the sense she'd probably never been corseted *quite* that tightly before, or had to walk much in heels when she couldn't see her feet. Catching her breath, her aide managed to joke, "But which one do you think we need to watch?"

"It's Tom we need to worry about." Becky winked at her, "Arilin's just going to sit there and scowl at her uncle all night."

Arilin rolled her eyes back, "Oh, come on. Let's go already."

There was an honor guard of sailors waiting for them at the gang-plank, and the petty officer in charge called for them to present arms as they approached. Long, old-fashioned rifles with long, old-fashioned bayonets snapped vertical, and Arilin resolved Tom's dilemma by return-ing their salute with her own free hand. Turning, the man announced them, "Princess Arilin and the young Lord Strathclyde!" The murmur of conversation from the ship above stopped instantly. Hesitating for a mo-ment, he turned back and asked, "Ah, milady... I'm sorry to ask, but I was told the Queen would be attending?"

Arilin smiled and lied, "Beatrice has been ill recently, she stayed back to care for her." The man sighed with relief, and she asked, "Has Alphonse arrived yet?"

He nodded, "Yes, milady. He just went up, actually."

"Thank you, chief." She nodded back politely, then glanced over at Tom, "Ready to meet our Prime Minister?"

He chuckled as they started up the long gangplank, "You say that like I might have to fight him."

"Last time I went to a party with him you would have." Arilin replied quietly. She felt him swallow nervously in reply, and they emerged at the top of the gangplank a moment later. Spotting an older man with a naval Captain's elaborate stripes on his sleeves working his way towards them, Arilin called out, "Captain Ramsay! Permission to come aboard, sir?"

Arriving, the ship's commander bowed and replied graciously, "You're our sponsor, you're as much a part of the crew as I am, milady."

"I'll take that as a yes." Arilin replied, stepping onto the *Griffon's* quarterdeck. Her heels bit into the teak decking reassuringly. Now stained dark for camouflage in the inky Northern Ocean, it was a vertigo-inducing void under the bright lights they'd set up for the ball. Looking back at the man, she asked, "I trust I'm not any more than fashionably late?"

"A princess cannot be late, milady," He winked at her, "But I actually thought you weren't showing up at all."

Between her dress and the corset shrugging was out of the question, so Arilin cocked her head instead, "We took a detour. Can't be too careful these days."

"Certainly." The man grimaced for a moment, then gestured at the tables set up around the quarterdeck. Arilin spotted a much-too-familiar man in a dazzling blue cuirassier's gala uniform dripping with gold lace, tall enough to stand head and shoulders above the knot of admirers he had gathered towards the fore-end of the deck. Alphonse gave her a calculatedly short glare and went back to holding court, deliberately ignoring her. Arilin felt her skin crawl as she realized the captain was still talking, "...the service out, milady. I can show you to your seat if you'd like."

"When's the dancing, sir?" Tom asked adventurously.

Captain Ramsay chuckled, "I can see why you'd be interested in that, young man. Just as soon as dinner's over."

"Is Alphonse speaking?" Arilin cut back into the conversation, "If he is I'd like to say a few words myself afterwards. As Crown Princess."

"Certainly, milady. In fact I need to go tell him to get on with it, now that you're here. If you'll excuse me..." The captain turned on his heel, calling for one of the sailors to take them to their seats. Becky and Maria peeled off, and a minute later she and Tom had a prime table in front of the *Griffon's* rearmost gun turret, cannons big enough to swallow her whole looming against the dark sky overhead. Unfazed by the dramatic backdrop, Tom pulled her chair out for her before sitting down himself. The commander sat down on her other side shortly afterwards, as she heard the knot of officers and ladies around Alphonse start dispersing behind her.

Feeling her uncle's glare on the back of her head as she sat there, Arilin determinedly ignored it. After a few long moments the angry pressure went away, and Arilin looked over to see Alphonse stalking past their table to disappear around the side of the turret. His heavy footsteps creaked on what sounded like a wooden staircase and thudded across the turret's solid top before he emerged atop the mount, his uniform's golden knotwork gleaming under the harsh lights. Prince Alphonse's voice boomed across the deck, easily audible despite the fact the Navy seemed to have neglected to install a sound system, "Ladies and Gentlemen! We are gathered here today to mark the mighty *Griffon's* return to the Northern Fleet! *Without Equal!*"

The ship's officers shouted its Elven motto back, and Alphonse went on, "I am honored to be able to speak to you today on such a momentous occasion. Today marks nothing less than the turning point of this war." That was a little bold. Leaning back, Arilin shared a look with Tom as her uncle warmed to the audience, pausing for a moment before going on gravely, "It pains me that I have to speak of *turning points* at all, gentlemen. No war this nation embarks upon should ever *require* a turning point. And yet, unfortunately, this one does."

Alphonse thundered on, "In the East, our invincible Royal Army *retreats*," he sneered at the word, "Yes, retreats, from an *inferior* enemy. Our mighty Navy was brought low by base deception, perpetrated by *scum* at the Diamond Shoals. My nation is fighting for its life against the *Empire of Masks*," he said, voice dripping with scorn, "And I feel as though I have to ask myself, *why?*"

On her other side, the *Griffon's* captain leaned over and murmured to her, "About forty battleships worth of base deception I recall."

Arilin stifled a giggle as her uncle continued, warming to his speech, "Because of the weakness of men!" The audience murmured uneasily as he went on, "Gentlemen, when His Majesty, my brother, asked me to return to my nation's service in its hour of need, I was *shocked* at what I found. *Socialists* in the government. *Defeatists* in every hall of power. An Army in disarray, afraid of an enemy our ancestors *crushed* beneath their heels." He continued, brushing away a fake tear, "My nephew slain on the battlefield, and my brother having to resort to putting my dear young niece forward as the face of the Crown."

"This humiliation ends now!" Prince Alphonse thundered, "Weak men no longer run this Kingdom! As your new Prime Minister, and as the senior Royal in the High City, I swear to you this, my friends. I will not rest until our nation is restored to its former glory, and the Masks once again *tremble* before us!" He looked around dramatically, "How fitting is it then that I am speaking here today, at the resurrection of the mighty *Griffon?*" Her uncle clenched his fist dramatically, shouting from atop the mighty battlecruiser's turret, "*You* are the tip of my spear. *You* are my enemies' waking nightmare. *Your* cannons are my *final* argument."

God in heaven. Alphonse wasn't speaking like he'd taken her place, he was acting like he'd taken her *father's*. It was amazing what a grandstand with cannons did to a man. He was still going on, "Gentlemen, my charge to you today is simple. Bring the *Griffon* to life and sink its claws into the enemy! God bless the Navy! God preserve the Kingdom! *God be with us!*"

Raising her glass, Arilin shouted back, "God save the King!"

Leaping to his feet beside her, Tom raised his own glass and cried, "God save Crown Princess Arilin!"

Alphonse looked down at them with unbridled *hate* as his audience leapt to their feet to echo them. Mostly for her father, but she heard a few voices raised in her support as well. Turning, he stalked off his stage before they were even finished chanting, emerging around the side of the turret with a murderous look in his eyes. Gritting her teeth, she deliberately remained seated as he stalked over. Looming over her, Alphonse growled, "Just when I thought you couldn't get any more *irresponsible*, Arilin. What are you doing here?"

Swiveling herself over in her seat to face him, Arilin raised an eyebrow and asked, "How so, Uncle?"

"It's *dangerous*, for one." He snapped, "And for two I don't recall you being *invited*. Are you drinking? For God's sake."

Crossing her legs under her dress, Arilin shot back, "Clearly not so dangerous my mother couldn't come. Or *you* for that matter. And," She swirled the wine in her glass appreciatively, "I don't recall you being the temperance type, Alphonse."

Alphonse rounded on Ramsay, who had stood at his approach, "Is this how you run your ship?"

The man opened his mouth, hesitated, and Arilin cut back in, "Leave him out of this, Alphonse. If God saving my father offends you, you need to take that up with *him*."

Ignoring her, Alphonse repeated himself, "Is *this* how you run *your* ship, *Captain Ramsay?*"

Ramsay took a deep breath and deliberately let his hand fall on his sword's hilt. Squaring up to Prince Alphonse, the *Griffon's* commander replied deliberately, "Princess Arilin will always be welcome here, my lord. And it's King William's ship, not mine."

Arilin looked to her other side to see Tom had discreetly maneuvered his sword around to be able to draw it easily. Alphonse was going on, "Are you just tolerate her doing whatever she pleases, then?"

"So far she's showed up for dinner and toasted the King." Ramsay rolled his eyes, "Quite the juvenile delinquent. Are you drunk, milord?"

"I'll remember your attitude, *captain*." Alphonse huffed, then glanced over at her dismissively, "That dress makes you look old, princess."

Her uncle spun on his heel and stormed off, all the way to and down the gangplank as they watched in awkward silence. As he finally disappeared Arilin quipped, "If I was ten years older I'd be insulted."

Ramsay chuckled nervously, "It is a bit bold, milady. I'd never let my daughter wear that."

"Red suits me, captain." Swirling her wine around again, Arilin smiled innocently and asked, "I don't suppose you have some juice around here? I don't understand how you adults drink this stuff, it tastes like *battery acid*."

The captain smiled graciously, "I'll ask the steward, milady. It's an acquired taste... oh, you wanted to say a few words, didn't you?"

Arilin chuckled, "That speech would be a hard act to follow. How about I just dance with all of your officers instead?" She glanced over at Tom slyly, "My date's got a jealous girlfriend, you see, I can't just spend all night in his arms."

Tom sighed theatrically, knowing full well he was going to have a gaggle of adoring women petting him later, "I guess I'll just have to spread my attentions out tonight. It's only polite, you know." He gave her a look, "And I don't think you're exactly in need of defense right now, milady."

"Maybe on the ride home." She gave the ship's commander a look, "I don't suppose we could borrow a boat later? I'd like to get home tonight without getting any bombs thrown at me."

The man chuckled nervously, "I'll have one standing by."

Chapter 39

Line of March

Patricia jerked awake in darkness as thunder crashed, rain beating on the room's windows and the wind howling outside. Somewhere a loose shutter slapped loudly in the storm. For a heart-stopping instant she didn't know where she was or how she'd gotten there. The last thing she remembered clearly... a blinding flash, an ugly red fireball like an evil eye staring into her soul, the air itself distorting as the shockwave caught up to them. Breaking glass over the explosion's earth-shattering roar. Sophia Rose had caught her, she had decided to give up drinking on the job, and the girl had poured her a very large cup of coffee.

That coffee had kept her going long enough for their train to pull into Brightangel and for her to find where Colonel Frost had stuffed the division's command post into one of the town's hotels. Breakfast had kept her going long enough to figure out how to defend the town and give the regiments some orders. And then... nothing. The last thing she remembered was seeing Mina Bennett out the door and watching her gallop off into the rain. The hotel had a parlor off the entryway, she had sat down to rest her feet for a moment, and... she must have passed out. She could just see Frost telling their clerks to bundle her upstairs and put her to bed. Feeling around under the covers gingerly, Patricia discovered that whoever had done it had undressed her. Well, that was embarrassing.

Shaking her head, Patricia got up and fumbled around in the darkness for the lights. Eventually she found the switch and the room blazed to life. She whistled at the sight. They'd given her quite the suite. Richly-carved hardwood and overstuffed brocades, crystal glass and gilding. Someone had folded her uniform and left it on a chair, then set her saber and pistol with their tangle of carrying straps on top of them. From the looks of things it had all been cleaned. Quite the room service, really. She hadn't stayed at a place like this since, well, the last vacation she'd taken before the war. It was nice being rich, she thought, chuckling as she turned and stepped into the bathroom.

The shower's hot water took her cares away for a minute. She hadn't had a proper shower since... well, she'd had one at Lorenvale, three days ago. It seemed like much longer, although now that she thought about it the fact she had been in *Lorenvale* three days ago was probably the reason. If they were fighting the Dominion that would have been a year's campaign. If they were fighting the Dominion they would have been going the *other direction*. If, if, if. They were dealing with the Empire of Masks, and it was like fighting lightning. Pitch darkness and then, bam, you're flat on your back with your hair on end, wondering what just happened, and they're already miles past you.

Shaking her head, Patricia pushed the thought from her mind and set about actually cleaning herself up. Maybe it wasn't the time in the saddle that mattered, it was the *mileage*. She sure felt like she had a year's worth of grime built up on her body from the ride. She'd probably been staining the sheets, she realized sheepishly. Finally finishing up, she reluctantly turned off the tap and stepped out of the shower. The white hotel towels still came away a little grimy after she was finished drying herself, but there was nothing to be done for it. While rank had its privileges, she was not about to go soak in a bath while there was a *battle* on.

Patricia dressed, sliding her feet reluctantly back into her boots and strapping her weapons back on. Her saber's cold weight bumped against her thigh as she opened the door and stepped into the hall, realizing as she did that she didn't even know which *floor* she was on. After a disorienting moment she saw a sign for elevators and made her way over, boots sinking into the hallway's plush carpet. The car arrived with a cheerful ding, and she pulled the iron grating aside, stepped in and punched the button for the lobby. It swung back shut automatically, and the elevator lurched and slowly started to descend. Patricia smiled despite herself. If things worked out she wouldn't mind keeping the headquarters there for a while, they *had* come an awful long way and they needed the rest after all.

The elevator rattled to a stop with a cheerful ding. Patricia pulled the grating aside and stepped out into the lobby's cool air, the marble floor glass-smooth underfoot. Thunder rolled again outside, duller than before, laid over a gentle hubbub of conversation. It didn't sound like the staff at work, there were too many people talking at once, and too quietly. It sounded like they were... *socializing?* The hotel had a bar, she recalled, but still. The enemy could attack at any minute. *Maybe it's civilians, there's still a few in town*, she thought as she turned on her heel and strode towards the hotel's restaurant.

Half of her staff looked up from their drinks as she appeared, the conversation dying like it had been cut with a knife. After a long, pregnant pause, *Colonel Frost* raised his beer stein from his spot at the bar and announced, "Milady! Good to see you up!" Her chief of staff continued unflappably, "Care to join us?"

Patricia raised an eyebrow, "Did we win the war while I was out?"

"No, but the scouts haven't seen a mask since we got here." Joseph smiled, crinkling the corners of his impressive mustache, "I didn't see any reason to sit around staring at an empty map."

Sighing, Patricia surrendered, "Might as well."

The staff *cheered*. Was she really that much of a taskmaster? Maybe she wasn't really all that different from Walter. Shaking her head, Patricia wound her way over to the bar, the man sitting next to Frost hopping off his stool to give her room. She glanced at him, then raised her eyebrows despite herself as she gave him a more thorough looking-over. Tall, blonde and rakish Navy lieutenants weren't her style, but this guy probably had women walking into light poles wherever he went. He smiled gallantly, "Milady. Colonel Frost has been telling me all about you."

She smiled and shot the older man a glance as she sat down, "I hope he used discretion."

The sailor smiled back as he leaned against the bar on her other side, "Of course."

Chuckling, Patricia asked, "So what's the Navy doing here, lieutenant..." She found the nametag on the man's chest, "Strickner?"

"Felix, milady." The man's smile got wider. Yep. He was good at it. He went on dreamily, "I took my squadron in from the storm. Little destroyers, you know."

"I do, actually." Crushing Lieutenant Strickner's hopes and dreams, Patricia swiveled all the way back around to look at Joseph, "So, no, really, how are things going around here?"

The man shot a smug look at Strickner where he was standing behind her and replied, "I wasn't kidding, milady. The cavalry's been out for hours with nothing to report." He gestured for the bartender, "You still drinking these days, milady? A little bird told me you quit."

"Just during the day." Patricia chuckled, "Considering I just got up, I'd take a Bloody Mary." She gave the bartender a look, "And don't go putting a bunch of weird stuff in it. I want a drink, not appetizers."

The man shrugged and wordlessly set to work. Joseph took a pull of his beer and remarked, "Not up for a crab claw, milady?"

"Not in a drink, eyugh." She shook her head. Thunder crashed outside, and she jumped a little. She felt sorry for the hussars out in the storm, although, she thought wryly, if they were anything like her when she was younger they had found a roof to do their picket duty under by now. Looking for an enemy who had yet to show up. Hm. Patricia mused, "It doesn't make sense." Joseph looked over quizzically, and she explained, "The Empire. This is the fastest way over the Serpent. Why didn't they follow us?"

"They seem to be dealing with Fifth Corps." Joseph replied, "Last we heard from Kunst was he was pulling back towards Wolf Rock." He snorted, "He *insisted* he was breaking out, you know. Thinks he's surrounded."

A blinding white flash and black smoke in the rain, the blast punching her backwards from half a mile away. Coming back to reality, Patricia gave him a look, "I wouldn't put it past them at this point."

The man grunted, "At least we're being reinforced. Royal Headquarters and the War Ministry were yelling at each other all morning over deploying the Guards Division."

She raised an eyebrow, "They don't want to let them go?"

He shook his head, "*Absolutely* not. They're screaming about how we're five minutes from another Red December." The man snorted, "Haas didn't buy a word of it."

"Good." The bartender deposited her drink in front of her, garnished with a simple celery stalk. Given the sour look on his face he'd been looking forward to showing off. Taking a sip, she gave the man an approving look and a nod, and he softened and went to find a glass to polish. Turning back to Frost, Patricia thought for a moment and went on, "It begs the question, though, of what the Empire's up to. They didn't come this far just to kill a couple divisions, and they haven't pushed on us."

"Your guess is as good as mine, milady." Frost smiled, raising his stein, "Cheers."

"Long live the King." Patricia smiled back, clinking her glass against it. Taking another sip, she let the smoothly-acidic drink swirl across her tongue for a moment before swallowing and looking back at her companion, "So what's your guess, then?"

The big man shrugged, "I think they've already done what they set out to do. Half the rail lines heading east are cut and General Haas is worrying about *this* instead of whatever's in front of him."

Patricia grimaced, "That doesn't seem like their style." She thought for a moment, then groaned, "I'm going to have to look at a map to figure this out."

Frost chuckled and stood, "After you, milady."

Collecting her glass, Patricia made her way out of the bar and across the hall to the ballroom the staff had turned into a command center. Compared to the houses they'd been operating out of lately it was magnificent, tables laid out neatly by section, a big map set up in the middle of the room, the officer on duty talking quietly to someone on the phone at his desk. Someone scrambled to their feet behind her as they entered, a familiar voice calling out, "Attention! Commanding general!"

Patricia turned to see Sophia Rose and another soldier standing to attention beside the door, a gangly young man with a big scar on his forehead. She recognized him vaguely from the trial. After the jihad the thought of five murderers in front of a firing squad wasn't even worth a grimace. Smiling instead, she nodded, "Carry on, you two."

The two soldiers, apparently their runners for the night, sat down smartly. The cuirassier on duty turned back to his phone call, and Patricia and Colonel Frost walked up to the map. The situation looked about the same as it had when the staff had laid it out that morning. Fifth Corps was starting to draw back into a compact block north of Belmont, the crossroads town where they had boarded trains earlier. Enemy icons were all over the map. They poured south out of Requinsville, where someone had helpfully put down some siege artillery markers for the heavy batteries that had been standing off the Navy all day, enveloping the friendly block on both sides and sweeping off to the southwest. Some were laid out disconcertingly across the rail lines heading east from their position at Brightangel. One was so far south it was *beyond* Belmont.

After a minute of staring wordlessly at the map, Patricia observed, "I don't know about you, Joe, but it looks to me like they're still maneuvering."

The man raised an eyebrow, "Wolf Rock, maybe? They'd cut every rail line that way."

She replied dismissively, "They'd never take it. Unless... hm." Feeling peevish, she set her drink down squarely on Lorenvale off to the east and thought for a moment. The Imperials didn't seem to want to get across the Serpent or they would have pushed on them at Brightangel, so they were going after rail lines. Cut enough of those and the Army of Drakenburg would die on the vine. Wolf Rock was out of the question, they'd never beat Fifth Corps back to it and even if they did it was still full of troops. Unless... Patricia felt her heart skip a beat as it hit her. They were *insane.* Those masks they were wearing must have scrambled their brains.

"Milady?" Frost was giving her a worried look.

Patricia shook her head and motioned for him to move over. He obligingly stepped aside, and she settled herself squarely beneath the line of the Serpent River on the map, tracing it with her eyes. There they were in the north at Brightangel just before the river emptied into the gulf, the rail lines leading east from it cut and useless. Swinging her eyes south, Patricia felt her eyes narrowing as she studied the Serpent's course, twisting down out of the mountains to emerge from the Fairy Forest at a little town named Jade Falls. Just to the north was the only other railhead across the Serpent. Southbend.

Patricia stretched her fingers across the map, judging distances. It was a hundred and fifty miles from Southbend to Wolf Rock, a little farther to Belmont. About the same to Brightangel, as the crow flew. The enemy's spearhead had cut the line from Belmont to Brightangel, what... she looked at her watch. It was past midnight. Eighteen hours ago. At their tireless rate of march they were probably *halfway there* already. Giving Frost a worried look, she asked, "Joe, what do we have in Southbend right now?"

Normally so unflappable, he gave her a worried look back. Finally he said, "Maybe a... company of gendarmes?"

Feeling her stomach sinking, Patricia asked, "How long do you think they'll hold up one of those battlegroups we've been fighting? A dragoon regiment, tanks, artillery?"

"About ten minutes." Frost replied grimly.

"Get the staff back in here." Patricia growled, "*Now.*"

* * *

"Milady, it *can't be done.*" Her Rail Service liaison gestured angrily at the map, "With the lines down we're backed up all the way to Gyrburg. The yard here's so full I can't even turn trains around!"

"*Find a way!*" Patricia shouted at him, "And if *you* can't, find someone in the Rail Service who has the authority to not *lose the war!*" Rounding on the unfortunate duty officer, she demanded, "Have you gotten ahold of Heinrici yet?"

"Just got his chief of staff." The man replied, deflating with relief.

"Give him here." Patricia held her hand out and the captain deposited the telephone's handset into it. Swinging it up to her ear, she started, "It's General MacMahon. Is Heinrici there? It's urgent."

A voice warbled out of the line, "Urgent enough for him to hang up on Prince Alphonse?"

"*Yes.*" Patricia replied flatly, "If you guys don't get troops in Southbend by this afternoon we're probably going to have to take it *back* from the Empire."

"Really? It's that bad?" Heinrici's chief of staff asked, an edge of incredulity in his voice. She knew the guy, vaguely. He was a weasel who'd been promoted out of his competence and who was in the process of blowing a sure thing, namely getting a star after serving as a chief of staff in the *Guards*.

"*Yes*. Now when are you moving out?" Patricia demanded.

After a too-long pause, the man ventured, "We... haven't started loading trains yet, Alphonse hasn't released us." Hearing her inhale to explode at him, the man rushed on, "This changes things! Thanks! Uh, I'll need to call you back!"

The line went dead. For a moment Patricia held the handset out and looked at it, fighting the urge to fling it across the room. She felt her eye *twitching*. The entire room fell silent as people held their breath. Finally, with a force of will she handed it back to the duty officer like a dead and particularly smelly fish, and sighed heavily. It almost but not quite covered the sound of the rest of the room exhaling.

Collapsing into a chair someone had conveniently pulled up to the map table for her, Patricia closed her eyes and pinched the bridge of her nose. Hard. It did nothing. Really it wasn't even her problem, it wasn't her sector, she'd blown the whistle and it was her higher-ups' issue to deal with now, if they needed anything from her they would ask. And anyone with a brainstem knew that was pure and utter nonsense because her superiors all had their *pants* around their ankles and were pointing fingers at each other over who'd left the bathroom door unlocked instead of doing anything about it. Think. Think. *Think!* There had to be something she could do.

A smooth voice intruded on her despair, "Milady, have you considered the river?"

She looked up to see that flashy naval officer, Strickner, smirking at her gallantly. Truth be told it *was* a good idea, at least with the rail network the way it was. Good enough that he probably should have volunteered it an hour ago. She narrowed her eyes as she looked back up at him, "You're the expert. Should we be?"

"I think it's the only option left at this point." He gestured at the map, "With a fast passage we could have troops in Southbend tomorrow afternoon."

"*We?*" She raised an eyebrow, "Are you volunteering your squadron?"

He smiled back annoyingly, "Of course."

Leaning back in her chair, she set her elbows on the armrests and steepled her fingers, thinking. Finally she shook her head and asked, "Can your ships even make it that far upriver?"

The man shrugged, "We've got a six-foot draft. There's ferries and barges running up and down the Serpent all the time, it's got to be at least that deep."

"That's a big assumption." Patricia narrowed her eyes, "You'd need a pilot. Which means we'll need to hunt one up at this Godforsaken hour. Should I also assume you even know where to find one?"

"It shouldn't be too hard, milady." Strickner replied nonchalantly.

"It's one in the morning, lieutenant. Easy things get hard at this hour..." Someone was yelling off to her side, sharp voice cutting through the staff's hubbub. She looked over to see Sophia Rose physically pushing her friend towards them, hectoring him as they went. She gave the girl a look and snorted, "You're nothing but helpful today, Miss Rose. Got something I should know about?"

The girl glared at her companion, "Tell her, Edward."

Edward swallowed hard, his prominent Adam's Apple bobbing up and down, before he ventured nervously, "Ah... milady. I'm, uh, actually a river pilot. Licensed last year, just finished my apprenticeship. I've got my card here..."

He fumbled out a battered-looking wallet and pulled a card out of it. Strickner took it and read it for a moment before asking incredulously, "What the hell are you doing in the *Army?*"

The gangly riverboat pilot-turned-infantryman glared at Sophia, "Her father *recruited* me." He rolled his eyes, "Said it'd be a fun change of pace."

Patricia looked at him for a moment, then laughed, "I can just *see* him doing that." Quickly growing serious, she fixed the man with her gaze and went on, "Lieutenant Strickner here has a squadron with a six-foot draft. Can that even make it upriver right now?"

Now that he was dealing with a professional question Edward seemed to be calming down. Thinking for a moment, he nodded, "With all the rain we've had recently, yeah." Swallowing again, he added, "Milady."

"We need your unit there tomorrow afternoon." Patricia replied bluntly.

Edward glanced at Strickner, "How fast can you go, sir?"

"Twenty-eight knots. Thirty if needed." The lieutenant replied.

The river pilot whistled, "Might have to run some barges off the river, but I've always wanted to set a record."

"Good." Patricia said, then stood, "*Joe!* Get me Colonel Espinay! The rest of you look lively, you've got two hours to get the Two-Twenty Fourth ready to fight and out of here!"

Chapter 40

Eye of the Storm

They marched to the docks in silence, tramping footsteps lost in the howling wind and pouring rain. Lightning rent the sky apart, blinding light slicing through the darkness and catching them frozen mid-step before the night crashed back down with a hammer-blow of thunder. Sophia shuddered despite herself, the motion shaking a waterfall of droplets from the inside of her soaking poncho. They couldn't have found a worse night for this. There hadn't *been* a worse night than this, not all year. It was all she could do to keep putting one foot in front of the other, her harness bearing down on her every step with its load of brass, lead and steel.

It was like they were going up Fire Ridge again. Their bicycles were left behind, piled up next to their packs in the hussars' supply dump. On the way out the Valkyrie Knights had given them as much ammunition as they could carry, and then some. Between her belt pouches and cavalry bandolier Sophia had no less than two hundred rounds just for herself, and two rolled machine-gun belts bumped against her hip with every step. They had been stingier on the grenades this time, though. She only had four, their long handles brushing her thighs as she walked. The back of her belt, heavy with the food in her haversack, full canteens, and that same blanket rolled around the sections of her spear, struggled to balance the sheer weight of metal up front. And she had it easy. James and Tony were struggling along behind her carrying an ammunition crate between them.

Lightning flashed again, and she saw buildings opening in front of them and a forest of masts beyond, fishing boats bouncing at their berths in the storm-whipped waves. The leading companies were already making the turn onto the waterfront like a great rain-soaked millipede, soldiers wincing and hunkering into the wind as they left the shelter of the buildings. Sophia winced herself as she stepped around the corner and into the storm's full force. These clouds had last seen land over the North Pole, and she felt every last inch of icy water they had swept over on the way in her *soul*. Hoping the slushy feeling on her face was just her imagination and not sleet, Sophia leaned into the wind and kept walking towards a particularly bright set of lights alongside a distant pier.

After a few too-long minutes of struggling into the wind, dark shapes loomed under the lights and then resolved into the long, lean silhouettes of destroyers. The sailors had helpfully used their searchlights to mark their position in the freezing darkness, and they swung the beams down onto the pier as they approached. It was a long concrete affair, with a crane swaying dangerously overhead in the darkness. Before the war it had probably handled cargo ships. Now it had four warships heaving uneasily in the surf alongside. Just a look at the spindly, bucking gangplanks leading up into the darkness was enough for Sophia to swallow uneasily.

"Battalion!" Sophia heard her father, *somehow*, over the howling wind as the lead company stepped onto the pier ahead, *"Eyes right!"*

Officers saluted. Soldiers smartened up their step and looked over at the pair of figures standing at the base of the pier. One tall and one short. Colonel Espinay and General MacMahon. Lieutenant Gable saluted as they got close to the turn, and the Lady General moved her cloak aside and tossed a long, curved object to the woman, shouting over the wind, "Vanessa! You'll need this!"

Her lieutenant caught the hussar's saber out of the air, drew it and saluted with it smartly, calling back, "Thanks, milady!"

Sophia called out as they marched past, "We'll keep her safe, milady!"

"You do that!" General MacMahon called back, and then they were past. Despite the cold and the weight on her shoulders, Sophia felt her back straighten a little as they marched onto the pier. It wasn't the first time they'd had someone important come down to see them off on a mission, and it probably wouldn't be the last, but Patricia MacMahon was *her* general. Thinking for a second, she chuckled. She couldn't even remember the name of the old Eighth Infantry Division's commander, and they'd gone up Fire Ridge on his orders. It wasn't like he'd led them. That was the difference.

Up ahead, Lieutenant Thorn was shouting, "Charlie Company! Forward to the left, file onto the transport!" He added helpfully, "Careful on the gangplank!"

There were no formalities going up, just a few grim steps across the pitching ramp until her feet thudded down onto solid wood decking. Sailors in dark raincoats shouted and pointed for them to head to the ship's stern and sit down. Even in the darkness she could tell the destroyer was tiny, and most of the space that *was* there was taken up by weapons, funnels and command platforms. The crew had at least mercifully put up an awning over the stern to keep the worst of the rain off, and as she went to sit down she realized a couple of stubby boxes protruding from the rear fighting platform were steaming in the damp. The ship's designers may not have anticipated hauling infantry, but they *had* designed it to prowl the Northern Ocean in winter and included a few strategically-placed steam heaters to keep sentries from freezing to death.

Sophia plopped herself down right beside one with her back against the rear superstructure, worked her blanket free from its straps behind her back, and wrapped it around herself under her poncho. Noticing her choice spot, the rest of her squad flopped down around her, then the rest of the platoon. Hargrave gave her a wink as he worked his way into her exact spot against the heater on the other side of the quarterdeck. The sailors started yelling for the rest of the company to get up into the superstructure or go below decks, and soon enough she heard the gangway coming up and cries as the men took in lines.

Sophia jerked out of her stupor as the ship's horn let out two long blasts. Water churned beneath her, the deck thrumming as the destroyer quickly backed away from the pier. Whoever was steering, clearly an old hand at rapid maneuvering, spun the ship end-for-end disconcertingly quickly, and she made out engine bells faintly below. A moment later the churning water turned to streaming froth behind them and they accelerated away from the dock. Behind them another destroyer was already turning about, and she could see a third one starting to back away behind it.

The full force of the wind hit her in the face as they turned upriver, the canvas straining and snapping overhead worryingly in the storm. Beside her, Tony had worked his own blanket loose and was shifting around awkwardly trying to wrap it around himself. She hadn't been wrong about the sleet earlier. His eyebrows were crusted with slush. Noticing her look, Tony gave her a half-smile, "I've had worse. Last night actually."

Sophia snorted and leaned back against the bulkhead, settling her rifle's butt between her knees with its barrel resting under her arm as she shot back, "That was all your fault, you know."

"Should have checked me properly, corporal." Tony cracked suggestively.

Sitting on his other side, Kelly worked an arm out of his poncho and slapped him in the back of his head, "What, she has to tuck you in now?" Tony gave him a hurt look as she laughed, "I don't know what you see in this guy, Sophie. Next thing you know he'll need his boots tied."

She shrugged, "I've known him forever, I guess."

"Hey!" Tony squawked, glaring at the machine-gunner, "Lay off her."

"I wasn't talking about *her*." Kelly batted back.

James turned and chimed in from where he was sitting against the heater's front, "Yeah, Tony, he was making fun of *you*."

"Oh, come on!" Her boyfriend complained, "What have I ever done to deserve that?"

There was pause. A very long pause. Finally someone from *Second Squad* asked, "Wait, do you really want us to tell you?" Being charitable she could think of ten or twenty reasons, and those were just the ones since they'd joined the Army. The guy went on as she tried to keep from laughing, "Who wants to go first?"

"Go to hell!" Tony replied angrily, then gave her a hurt look as she snorted with mirth, "Sophie, you too, really?"

"Alright, alright, enough of that!" Sergeant Cross barked, yelling over the rushing water from further astern, "Save it for the Masks, Gravesend. The rest of you, you're all idiots too so don't go thinking you're all special. Now shut up and try to get some sleep, we're going to be here for a while."

Giving her a final hurt look, Tony wrapped his blanket tighter around himself and curled up away from her. Sighing heavily, she closed her eyes for a moment, then looked out across the water as the platoon settled down around her. The three other destroyers were strung out in a line behind them, curving away from the dim lights marking the Brightangel harbor. As she watched the ships' searchlights went out one-by-one, leaving only a few dim running lights floating in the storm's murk. Just a few little red and green balls flickering in the sheeting rain and spraying water as they accelerated into the main channel. And now that she thought about it, this was a bit much for the Navy in wartime. Out in the open ocean they'd probably run completely dark.

The ship bucked a storm-driven swell, sending spray crashing onto the canvas overhead as it smashed down disconcertingly. People shook themselves and edged away from the precarious rope railings, and she backed herself further into her corner and dug her heels into the deck. Closing her eyes, she tried to relax. The ship bucked again, and again, icy wind and spray whipping against her face each time. Someone groaned and vomited noisily. The ship's horn blasted out again, something clacking noisily overhead as it did. Probably a searchlight. After a while it all blended together.

Sophia opened her eyes to dull gray light. Shaking her head, she tried to wipe at her eyes. After a confusing moment of fighting her blanket and poncho she managed to get an arm free and wiped the icy grit out of the corners of her eyes. After a few blinks to free up what seemed to be a layer of congealed mucous she got her eyes open. The Serpent had closed in around them. Off to her right a town was rolling by, red-brick houses with dark slate roofs gleaming darkly in the rain. A ferry emerged into her line of sight and blocked out her view of the town as she watched, looming alarmingly close as it chugged downstream.

Shaking her head, Sophia sat up and looked around properly. The rest of the platoon was out cold, a few men snoring loudly. One of them was Tony, still curled up angrily away from her. The crew seemed to have come around during the night and, probably worried about soldiers and equipment rolling under the flimsy lifelines and falling overboard if they swerved, strung up cargo netting around the ship's stern. A hand grenade dangled nonchalantly in the web of ropes. Instinctively patting herself down to make sure she still had all of *hers*, she breathed a sigh of relief as she felt all four handles, then heaved herself up and started to pick her way over, her muscles twinging as they stretched in the cold.

Fortunately the grenade was stuck pretty well and Sophia retrieved it without too much of a problem. Cold rain and rushing wind beat at her face as she left the cover of the awning, and she shivered and quickly stepped back into the cover's meager sanctuary. Then her stomach growled loudly. If she'd had the spare blood flow for it she would have blushed. As it was she carefully made her way back to her old seat, pawing at her haversack as she went. Eventually the flap came open and she fished out one of the Royal Army's infamous assault rations. Dodgy meat spread and crackers she wouldn't have fed to dogs. At least it had coffee and a fuel tablet to cook it with. Plopping herself down, Sophia sighed and set about wiggling all the different bits of her mess kit out of her harness.

Somehow she actually managed to keep her coffee in its cup and on her field stove as the destroyer slewed through an alarming series of turns, dodging a tug and a string of barges disturbingly close on their right side. She could have thrown a canteen and nailed the boat's captain square between his wide eyes as he flew past. Then they shot past the ferry that had been trying to pass the barge on their *left*, close enough she could have jumped across and punched the captain in the face personally. Somehow the other destroyers managed to thread the needle behind them, the huge ships slipping through the tiny gap like so many bulls through a chute.

The next few minutes passed mercifully steadily, and she was able to eat and get a start on her coffee without danger of being thrown overboard by any more maneuvering. Although given how the mechanically separated pork product tasted she could have used the excuse to throw it overboard. Deciding that any more sleep was well and truly out of the question, Sophia picked up her coffee cup and her rifle and stepped back out into the elements, bracing her feet on the decking as the destroyer slewed into another turn. At least this one seemed to be around a bend in the river and not traffic.

She hadn't realized earlier just how *small* the ship was. It was a wonder the company could even fit onboard. Making her way forward along the railing, she could see men sleeping above her on the fighting platform at the rear of the superstructure, clustered around a naval cannon on its pedestal. The crew had been hard at work with awnings and cargo nets there as well, and Sophia reached up and carefully pushed a machine gun back onto the platform as she walked past. Wouldn't want to lose that. The ship's funnels were hot enough to feel on her face as she walked by to see that more infantrymen were sprawled out along the ship's bow, so she changed course and pulled herself up a steep naval staircase ahead of the funnels. She had a soldier to check on.

The destroyer's pilothouse, a little glassed-in structure with its back to the forward funnel, was much too small to be dignified as a 'bridge.' Alarmingly, nobody seemed to be inside. The wheel spun of its own accord to slew them into another turn around the river ahead, and Sophia felt her stomach start to flutter before she heard a familiar, cheerful voice call down from above, "Miss Rose! How are the troops?"

Sophia looked up to see Colonel Espinay peering down at her from atop the pilothouse, the little man looking faintly ridiculous in a big Army greatcoat. It was the first time she'd seen anyone in the unit *wearing* one actually, he had probably brought his own when he took command. Smiling, she called back up, "Nobody's gone overboard yet!" She produced the hand grenade, "Saved this though, sir!"

He laughed, "You can find those anywhere, they grow on trees nowadays!" The colonel gestured at a metal ladder set against the back of the pilothouse, next to the door, "Come on up! The captain won't mind..." Trailing off, he looked over his shoulder, "You won't mind, will you? Good, good!" He quickly looked back at her, "He doesn't mind. Come up!"

Chuckling, Sophia pulled herself up the ladder and into the wind and rain rushing through the destroyer's upper steering position. The view took her breath away. Green countryside and trees gleamed all around them, spreading out beyond the Serpent's dark, rain-beaten ribbon. Out on the riverbank she spied a couple kids in bright raincoats, running down the riverbank after them. They must have been quite the sight. Turning from his perch out on the wing platform, Edward called out happily, "Sophie! How are you?"

He looked weatherbeaten and half-frozen, but he was grinning. Sophia smiled back, "That's what I wanted to ask you!" She snorted, "Although I shouldn't have bothered, you look fine."

The tall man at the wheel cut in, letting the wind carry his words back towards them as he made a minute adjustment to their course, "Your friend is a first-class river pilot, Miss Rose. At least so far." He was wearing a long pea-coat with shoulder boards, blonde hair poking out beneath his rakishly crushed-down service cap. An officer, and not just any officer.

'Lieutenant' Strickner, the captain and their little flotilla's commander. He added wryly, "He's certainly done a better job than my last two helms-men. You mind if I kidnap him, sir?"

Sophia opened her mouth to reply, then hesitated as she realized he'd been talking to Colonel Espinay. The short man snorted, "I'll think about it." After a while he smiled slyly and added, "Tell you what, if we *win* this battle he's all yours. I owe you that much."

"Deal." There went another one of her guys. And *Edward* too. With him gone it'd be just her, Tony and Kelly left from the original squad that had marched out of Jade Falls a lifetime ago. Sophia's heart sank as Strickner turned and barked over his shoulder at a sailor standing on the far side of the platform, "Run up a signal. Prepare full shore parties for immediate action, landing on my command."

Immediate action? As the man ducked past her onto a catwalk going back to the ship's spindly mast and started pulling flags out of a locker set against its base, she looked back at Colonel Espinay and asked nervously, "Should I start getting the guys up, sir?"

The little man nodded, "Yes... we're actually quite close, aren't we?"

"That would be wise, we've got, what, an hour left?" Strickner weighed in.

Edward replied, "A little less than that at this rate." He chuckled, "Only beating the record by four hours or so. I'll need to stop by the Association when we get there and make sure this gets in the logbook."

"Speaking of, we haven't seen these Imperials of yours yet." The ship's captain weighed in as he slewed them around another bend in the river, expertly swinging close outside of a ferry running upstream with them. The landscape opened up ahead, familiar rolling hills shrouded with scraps of cloud, dark swathes of freshly-harvested fields lining the val-leys, trees growing like patchy moss out of the landscape. Picturesque tree-lined roads in the distance, dotted with traffic. Sophia narrowed her eyes, half-listening as he went on, "...think we're on a fools' errand. Not like I'm complaining, mind you."

"Do you have binoculars?" Sophia asked, then added, "Sir?"

She saw Lieutenant Strickner turn to look at her curiously out of the corner of her eye. Finally he asked, "Why? See something?"

Behind her, Colonel Espinay laughed, "She's got the best eyes in the battalion, Felix. If she thinks she saw something, it's probably out there." She heard him fishing in his greatcoat, "Here, take mine."

She reached her arm behind her to take them without taking her eyes off the road. Raising them to her eyes, she blinked, rubbed at her eyes and looked again, hoping what she'd seen had been a trick of the rain. Civilians. Hussars. Anything but exactly what it looked like, a long line of riders strung out evenly along the distant road. Even with the binoculars she could barely make them out, couldn't see the color of their uniforms or whether they were on the usual mess of mismatched horses. She didn't need to. This deep in friendly country, even hussars would be trotting along knee to knee. Swallowing hard, she announced, "Dragoons on the road, I see... ten or so. They're spread out."

"Bellamy, take the helm." Strickner growled. Edward rushed over to relieve him at the wheel as he fished out his own binoculars and stepped beside her. After a long moment of looking he asked, "You're sure? They could be ours."

"Even when they're being *shot at* our guys don't spread out that much, sir." Sophia replied. The dragoons were disappearing behind a little hill in the distance, and she swept her binoculars past it, trying to pick the road up again. Then something, *something*, told her to sweep them back onto the hill itself. Strickner was saying something back to her. She didn't catch it. She *couldn't*, not with her blood turning to ice and her hair standing on end.

"Miss Rose, are you alright?" Colonel Espinay must have noticed.

"*God-damn it.*" She said, to no-one in particular, as she stared back at the horse and rider emerging atop the distant hill, little more than a tiny speck in her binoculars, "Damn it, damn it, damn it." A speck that had ridden out of the mist shrouding the valley and up onto the hill where she could see it better. A speck with long hair whipping in the breeze as the wind caught at it, June Anjanou staring straight into her soul through his own pair of binoculars. "It's *him*, and he's looking *right at us.*"

"Anjanou? You're sure?" The colonel asked nervously. She nodded, and he started, "Felix..."

"Well, looks like I was wrong." Lowering his binoculars, the destroyer's captain stepped over to a small box mounted on one of the side consoles marked 'General Alarm,' popped it open and flipped the large red switch inside. A moment later Sophia winced as a painfully-loud alarm crashed through the ship, Lieutenant Strickner's voice booming out of the ship's loudspeakers a moment later, "*Battle stations, battle stations, all hands man your battle stations. This is not a drill. I repeat, this is not a drill.*" She looked over to see he had retrieved a microphone from the console and was speaking into it, "*Prepare for shore bombardment and close action off the port side. Embarked infantry, clear the gun plat-*

forms immediately." Turning, Strickner shouted at his signalman over the clanging alarm, "Signal the others! Action port, follow my fire! And then run up the battle flag!"

The man sprang back into action, and Sophia turned to hand the colonel his binoculars back. Clapping her on the shoulder as he took them, he nodded and said, "Good work, corporal. Now see to your men."

"Will do, sir," Sophia replied as she spun herself into the ladder and slid down, almost knocking over a couple of sailors rushing into the pilot-house as she landed. Those she had left, at least. She set her jaw as she walked back towards the stern, dodging sailors rushing to their stations and infantrymen trying to get out of the way. They were *minutes* from Southbend. If things went well enough, she could make the walk easily and sleep in her own bed tonight. Back in Jade Falls. Home felt close enough to touch. Close enough to *hurt* when she thought about it.

But June Anjanou, that long-haired bastard, was standing in her way. And, she thought as something large and angry whistled overhead and cracked into the far bank, he'd brought all of his friends and they were in no mood to give up and go home themselves. Having finally managed to get ahold of the dragon's tail, God help them, they were about to face its claws.

Chapter 41

Jackboots

The morning breeze floated through the classroom's open windows and picked at the pages of her book, brisk enough that Arilin had to slide her thumb it over to keep her place. It smelled like the sea. Glancing out the window, she couldn't help but smile a little. The weekend's clouds had blown off overnight and the High City was soaking in sunlight. The trees lining the Royal Academy Middle School's great courtyard gleamed in the light, leaves startlingly green and still dripping from the storm. It was hard to believe anything bad could happen on a day like this.

Her mother had even sent her a telegram that morning, informing her that she and Beatrice had arrived safely in Zilverdam off the overnight train and Alyssa was already warming up to their host. If the total lack of news about their departure in the morning papers was anything to go by, her plan had worked perfectly. Now it was just her and Alphonse staring at each other across the High City. She'd made her moves. Now it was his turn, and if he had a brain he'd stand down. Knowing him it was a lot more likely he'd *double* down.

"What's bothering you *now*, Arilin?" She looked over to see Charlotte glaring down at her good-naturedly. Barely. The girl only came up to her collarbone when she was standing. Pouting, her friend tossed her long, blonde hair and went on, "I don't lend you *my* boyfriend for the night to see you scowling like you want to kill someone the next morning."

Arilin looked at her for a moment, then snorted, "It's not Tom's fault, if that makes you feel better."

Charlotte raised an eyebrow, "So what is it then?"

Arilin shrugged, "Worrying that Uncle Alphonse is going to try to murder me?"

The eyebrow stayed raised, "I'm assuming you've figured out a way to tell your *father* about all of this?"

She blinked. She knew she'd been forgetting something. After a long second Arilin chuckled and gave her friend a sheepish look, "No, I actually haven't figured out *how* yet. I guess I could send Maria to tell him in person." The princess raised her own eyebrow, "How about *yours?*"

Sighing, Charlotte turned around and perched herself on Arilin's desk. Her legs swung freely underneath. Finally, she said, "Yeah, I sent him a letter." She shook her head, "Haven't heard back yet."

Arilin scowled wordlessly and looked back out the window. There wasn't much to say to something like that, and it was too nice of a day to be thinking about adultery. Or usurpation for that matter. Looking back to Charlotte, she told her as much, "This is depressing." She smiled, "How about we go bother the twins after school? We haven't been over to their place for a while."

Charlotte gave her a proprietary smile back, "Only if I get to bring Tom."

"Don't hold on to him too tight." Arilin gave her a calculating look, "He might bolt."

More students had filtered into the classroom while they were talking. Her somehow-rival was about to push herself off her desk and give her a cocky response when the door burst open and the subject of their rivalry rushed in. Arilin felt the smile fade off her face as she noticed Tom was white as a sheet. Liriel and Miriel were at his heels and they somehow looked *worse*. Quickly picking her out, the three of them hurried over, Tom shouldering a couple of students out of the way in his haste. Feeling her stomach clench into a solid knot, Arilin pushed her chair back and stood, demanding, "What's going on?"

"Cuirassiers." Tom replied bluntly. Her blood ran cold as he went on, "We heard hooves, looked out the window and saw, what..."

"Twenty or thirty, must have been, riding around our side of the school." Miriel volunteered.

Liriel added helpfully, "We stuck our heads out to look, they had more horses sitting out front. With guys holding them."

"Which means they're already in the school." Tom finished, so quickly he was stumbling over his words, "Probably one platoon in front and one in back, get guys in the stairs and exits, search bottom to top-"

"Are they armed? Armored?" Arilin cut him off. She had picked up her backpack from its place by her desk instinctively as he stood. Feeling foolish, she deliberately set it back down as her friend got his thoughts back together. She needed a bookbag weighing her down right now like she needed a hole in her head.

Tom finally replied, "They're in full dress with full arms." He'd explained the Guards' uniform orders to her at one point. Only the Guards Corps maintained an entirely separate set of combat equipment for the explicit purpose of maintaining color-coordination while fighting an actual battle in their dress uniforms. Although considering the Valkyrie Knights had gone into action in their pinks during Red December, maybe it wasn't as far-fetched as it sounded. Seeming to get ahold of himself, he added, "I saw *machine guns*, milady."

Gritting her teeth, Arilin glanced between her friends, "They're here for me. Any ideas on how to get out of here?"

"You could hide," Charlotte suggested, "There's plenty of spots, it'd take them hours to find you..."

"By which time Alphonse will the High City locked down. He's probably got more troops on the way right now. Milady," Tom gave her a serious look, "It isn't just you that needs to get out of here. I need to warn my regiment."

Arilin gave him a look, "You sound like you've got a plan."

"That hat that got stuck on the clocktower at the start of term?" Tom gave her a half-smile, "That was me."

"I'd been wondering who did that." She replied, thinking. The Royal Academy Middle School was crusted with elegant neo-Gothic stonework, ledges and gargoyles. Even coming down from the fourth floor probably wouldn't be too difficult, "You want to climb down?"

He nodded quickly, "I know we can, milady. Once we're in the courtyard we can break out a basement window and get into the steam tunnels, and we're home free."

"Alright," Arilin nodded, feeling her heart quickening at the thought. Hearing the commotion, other students had started to gather around and whisper uneasily. Looking around, Arilin announced, "Very soon there are going to be cuirassiers coming through here looking for me. It's probably my uncle trying to kidnap me to use as a bargaining chip against my father. He wants the throne for himself." The whispers turned into an alarmed buzz. Arilin went on grimly, "I'm not expecting any of you to resist, but if any of you assist them, well... I will consider it to be high treason."

"You can count on us, milady!" One of her classmates, a girl she vaguely knew, called out.

One of the boys added, "Yeah! Snitches get stitches."

"Thanks." Arilin replied, then looked at her blonde friend, "Charlotte, want to earn your future queen's eternal gratitude?"

The girl smirked, "Just so long as you keep my boyfriend alive, milady."

"Do a good enough job convincing them you're me and he's yours forever." Arilin looked over to Liriel, "Can you two help her out?"

The two girls nodded. Miriel had wound her way back to the door to keep a lookout, and she yanked her head back into the classroom and called out, "Milady, they just came up the stairs! Hurry!"

Tom already had the farthest-back window open and was levering himself out. Swallowing hard, Arilin gave Miri a wordless nod, turned

and rushed after him. The view, normally so cozy during class, was vertigo-inducing when she stuck her head out into it and looked down. It
was a *long* drop. Shaking her head to clear it, she got her hands on the
sill and then one leg, then the other over, absently realizing as she did it
that she was probably giving Tom a world-class look up her skirt. Which
given that he was risking his life for her was about the smallest reward she
could give him.

Arilin's feet found a ledge as she lowered herself down, and someone
swung the window briskly shut overhead. At least there wasn't any wind.
Looking over to see Tom already lowering himself down over some decorative stonework further down, Arilin started picking her way after him.
She'd barely found a handhold and shifted herself out from under the
window when she heard Liriel cry out overhead, "Milady, they're coming!
Run!"

A moment later Charlotte gave an extremely princess-like shriek and
ran out of the classroom, to muffled shouts out in the hall. Arilin was
lowering herself over Tom's piece of stonework when the sound of the
cuirassiers' pounding jackboots drifted down as they gave chase. Looking
down to see Tom had slid down to a ledge below and was already dropping down to the next one, Arilin wrapped her body around a ridge in the
stonework and let herself skid down, thankful for the Royal Academy's
stubborn insistence on gloves for its female students for the first time in
her life. Tom had been forced to do it barehanded.

She dropped down next to him on his next perch level with the third-
floor windows and he gave her a surprised look, murmuring, "You're a
natural, milady. Want to come along next term?"

She was opening her mouth to reply when someone started shouting
above them, voice dull through the classroom's windows. A cuirassier
berating her class, and probably an officer at that. Putsch in progress or
not, no trooper would dare speak like that to a class with a dozen heirs
to titles in it. In fact she was pretty sure a *dragoon* would have been a lot
more polite. He was threatening to shoot anyone who moved when she
finally shook her head and whispered, "Let's just get out of here."

Nodding grimly, Tom quickly dropped down to the next level. It
hadn't been immediately obvious at first, but the building tapered slightly as it rose from the ground. It probably wasn't more than a foot or so
on each floor, but that little medieval architectural flourish turned what
would have been a terrifying descent into an easy scramble down the wall's
stonework. Soon they made it down to the second floor and stepped out
onto the shallowly-angled roof over the courtyard verandah. In happier
times, students would gather under its shade to eat or study in the fresh

air. Tom quickly headed towards what seemed to be a specific spot on the roof, then laid down and lowered himself over it, seeming to feel for and find something to hold on to while he slid down. Before he disappeared he explained, with his head sticking up over the ledge, "It's too far to jump, but there's a support here. Just grab on and slide down."

Doing as he'd done, Arilin felt with her feet and quickly found a stone column. Digging her feet into it, she carefully lowered herself down before letting go with one hand. For one heart-stopping moment she felt her hand swing free before it wrapped around the pillar and found a ridge. Then she did the same thing with her other hand and slid down until she felt her feet hit the column's base. Peeking around the pillar, she felt absolutely naked as she looked across the verandah and the school's cavernous indoor cafeteria beyond, deserted in the early morning. Tom was already hissing at her to get down, and she dropped down from the railing and then lowered herself down into the courtyard proper.

Arilin was about to let go with her fingers and drop down when Tom simply grabbed her around the waist and lowered her the last foot or so. She'd expected a terrifying drop. In better circumstances she would have blushed, but as it was she only managed to give him an awkward smile, "Uh... thanks."

Jackboots pounded faintly, far overhead, and she heard Charlotte scream quite clearly, "*Unhand me, you beasts! This is treason! You'll all-*" Her friend's voice cut off suddenly, probably one of the cuirassiers getting a hand over her mouth. It sounded like she was on the *roof.*

"Come on, milady." Tom muttered, already working at one of the low windows looking into the half-basement. He had gotten it open, kicked the screen in and disappeared inside by the time she hurried over. She quickly slid in behind him, finding herself squarely in the middle of the school's kitchen. He was already making shushing motions at the couple of cooks who had come in early to start things for lunch. At the sight of her their alarmed attitude changed immediately. Arilin smiled and waved as cheerfully as she could manage as he started to close up the window behind them.

As he was getting it shut she heard a man shouting, faint and far above them, "*You idiots! Are you-*" He inserted a couple of particularly vile oaths, "*-blind? This isn't her!*"

Tom cut off another particularly choice curse as he pulled the window shut, then turned around and quipped, "Someone's trying to overthrow the monarchy. You guys have any knives handy?"

"Is it Prince Alphonse or the communists?" The particularly

shady-looking cook they had landed next to asked.

Resolving to look into whether the Royal Academy was vetting its staff properly, Arilin clarified helpfully, "Alphonse."

"'Oh, damn, sorry." The woman yanked open a drawer, rifled through it for a moment and produced a foot-long carving knife with a proper sheath, a rarity in the kitchen. She offered it to Tom, "Keep it, some idiot thought we'd use this for field days. You want anything milady?"

Feeling the small of her back, Arilin shook her head, "I'm fine, thank you."

Tom asked, "We need to get to the steam tunnels, do you have access in here?"

Their new communist friend nodded, "Yeah..." She trailed off as heavy footsteps clattered dully in the hallway outside the kitchen, a man shouting to start searching as she motioned for them to follow her towards a set of swinging doors set in the side wall, "Quick, this way."

They ran for it, bursting through an instant before she heard the door to the far hallway pop open and almost bowling over a gaggle of confused bakers who had heard the commotion. The smell of baking bread filled her nostrils, which would have been almost intoxicating but for the doors swinging back and forth behind them on their sprung hinges. On their far side gruff man's voice, probably a cuirassier sergeant, was ordering, "Search everywhere that could hide the princess or her boyfriend! Closets, pantries, cupboards, kettles!" He went on, "Third Squad, you've got the bakery."

One of the older bakers, clearly a senior man in the shop, set his jaw, then gave her a nod and looked around at his fellows. Murmuring, they all crowded around between the three of them and the door before the foreman burst through it and into the kitchen, shouting, "What kind of half-cocked raid is this? The hell are you doing looking for princesses in my bakery? Yeah, you, sergeant, I'm talking to you! Answer me!"

Not waiting for them to follow her, the cook grabbed them both and hustled them along. Arilin could feel the woman's hand trembling even through her stout grip on her upper arm. Behind them the cuirassier sergeant snapped back, "She's to go into protective custody immediately. Orders from the War Ministry. Now stand aside!"

Hurrying around the ovens, they reached a door on the far side of the room marked 'Steam Access.' Shockingly hot air roiled out as the cook popped the door open, wordlessly motioning for them to go in. Arilin could make out what looked like a landing inside with what looked like a spiral staircase at the far end, beside a thick bundle of pipes running up from a void below. The men were still arguing in the next room as she stepped in after Tom, the baker shooting back, "Oh that's a likely story! I did twenty years in the Navy, smart guy. *Who the hell-*"

The heavy door swung shut, turning the shouting match into muffled noise and leaving her and Tom alone in the scalding darkness. She was just about to ask if he had a light when he flipped what looked like a rectangular military flashlight on. Quickly toggling it over to its red lens, he reached out to take her hand, murmuring, "*Come on*, they're not going to stall for long."

Arilin gave it to him and let him pull her down the spiral staircase, every step on the clanking iron spine-chillingly loud over the hum of the steam pipes beside them. Water shone in the flashlight's bloody light as they reached the bottom, and she stepped down into a puddle in the middle of the tunnel's rough concrete floor. Steam pipes hummed malevolently just inches away, and Tom added, "Watch yourself, milady. Those pipes *will* burn you. Badly."

"Okay," Arilin replied nervously, trying to edge away from them. Whoever had designed the steam tunnels hadn't particularly cared about the well-being of anyone unfortunate enough to actually have to *use* them. They had barely two feet of space. Still holding her hand, Tom pulled her along behind him quickly, hurrying her under a bundle of pipes splitting off overhead and past another, larger staircase leading up. It probably went to a larger steam room on the far side of the hall from the kitchens. They kept going the same direction, far enough that they had to have gotten out from under the school and heading to... where, exactly? Finally, she asked, "Tom, where does this take us?"

Still pulling her along, he replied, "The west campus steam plant." They passed another tunnel branching off to the right with a set of subsidiary steam lines, and the passageway widened slightly to accommodate the thicker upstream bundles as they kept going straight. Tom explained, "That tunnel leads to the gym, there's another one going to the stables that branches off of it."

Something unintelligible echoed down the tunnel over the roar of the steam in the pipes. Glancing behind her, Arilin felt her heart freeze as she saw a tiny, white light dancing in the sea of darkness back down the passageway. Feeling her hand tighten around Tom's, she turned back to him and said, "*Hurry!* They're behind us!"

A man screamed in pain far behind them, and Tom replied grimly, "Looks like they found the steam pipes. Come on!"

He pulled her into a run, hugging the far side of the tunnel away from the scalding-hot piping. It was easy enough for them to hurry along, two slender teenagers in their school uniforms. Judging by the faint cursing and screaming behind them, the hulking cuirassiers with their armor and weapons were having a *considerably* harder time of it. They passed another branch tunnel with a particularly thick bundle of pipes running into it, the new pipes awkwardly routed in underneath the old ones where they ran through the main tunnel. Realizing those pipes heated the new pool the Academy had finished near the middle school a couple years ago, Arilin exclaimed, "Oh, I know where we're going. We'll come out near the main stables."

Tom glanced back at her over his shoulder, "Think they've got horses ready to go?"

"We can ride bareback need be." Arilin replied, "No way we're getting out of here on foot."

Her escort wordlessly went back to hurrying her along, as the corridor bent slightly to the right and she lost sight of the light behind them. As it did she was able to make out a dim light in front of them, which quickly resolved into a brick archway leading into a large, sweltering-hot chamber housing a roaring boiler that looked like it had been ripped out of a destroyer's engine room. Now that she thought about it, the Navy's suppliers probably put their expertise to use in the heating sector on the side. A couple men in grubby coveralls gaped at them as they emerged, one of them recovering quickly to shout, "Hey! What're you two doing? That's dangerous!"

"We know, thanks!" Tom shot back sarcastically, as they darted around the men and up a stairway at the back of the room. Emerging into a hallway above, he looked back at her and asked, "Which way did you say the stables are?"

Now it was her turn to pull him along, "This way!" Rushing past another startled workman, they emerged from the maintenance building's side door to see the Royal Academy's grand stables spread out in front of them. A gaggle of what looked like college students dressed for riding were leading their horses back in as they watched. Wordlessly, the two of them broke into a sprint towards them, Arilin looking over her shoulder towards the middle school as she ran. Fortunately the massive new pool, bloated eyesore that it was, blocked her view. Telling herself that she couldn't hear galloping hooves anyways, Arilin sprinted off after Tom. *God*, was he quick when he got going.

"I need two horses!" She heard him shout ahead of her, "We're running from kidnappers, and that's Princess Arilin with me!" The riders quickly looked at him, looked at her running along behind him, and two of them gamely handed him their reins as he arrived. Tom was climbing aboard his horse as she ran up, and he threw her the other set of reins, "Here you go, milady!"

Catching them, she leapt up into the saddle and settled herself exactly as he kicked his foot down into his far stirrup. None too soon, as she wheeled her horse around to see a wave of blue jackets, silvered breastplates and massive horses loping along at a canter emerge around the side of the pool. One helmeted head, then another, then all of them snapped over towards them as the wave adjusted course, and steel flared in the morning sunlight as the lead rider drew his sword. Looking over at Tom, she kicked her horse and shouted, "*Go!*"

The horse gathered itself and launched forward under her, sparks flying from the cobblestones as it accelerated. After it settled into a steady gallop she looked over her shoulder to see Tom a little ways behind her with a workmanlike if not particularly elegant seat on his mount, and behind him the wave of cuirassiers cresting around the side of the maintenance building and roiling behind them. Most of them had their swords out. All the better, she supposed. It was one less hand on their reins and on those big horses there was no way they'd even catch Tom, let alone her.

Settling into her saddle, Arilin looked back to her front as she angled onto the campus' main promenade leading out to the street, and felt her breath catch at the sight. On the other hand, they probably didn't *need* to catch them if they could herd them into the platoon of cuirassiers strung out across the main gate ahead of them. God in Heaven, how much of the regiment had they *sent?* Even as she watched a couple of the troopers ahead noticed them and turned, shouting something to their fellows as they kicked their horses forward. Waving for Tom to follow her, Arilin dodged her horse onto a side street, almost bowling over a few college students heading to classes.

Another massive building loomed ahead of them, the Royal Academy's main library with its own grand plaza fronting onto it. University Square, with a handful of lost-looking cuirassiers milling around the plinth of Charles IV's equestrian statue at its center and the street running straight to the palace fronting on its far side without a gate in sight. Yanking her horse to the right to hug the near edge of the square, Arilin kicked it again as it dug into the cobblestones and surged forward. The cuirassiers in the square spotted her, wheeling their ponderous steeds around to head them off. Big men on big horses. Big, strong, *slow* horses. Arilin felt her heart leap into her throat as she saw them surge forward, too slow to cut her off. From here it would be a straight shot to the palace, and Tom... her heart clenched up in her throat as she glanced over her shoulder to see him just making the turn, several lengths behind her.

Tom was kicking his horse forward after her gamely, hand reaching down to the knife on his belt. He'd have to take his chances against their swords, *unless*... Arilin glanced forward quickly and her heart fluttered back to life as she saw it. Every single cuirassier in the square was kicking their horses to head them off to the right of the statue, their leader already pointing his sword at Tom and shouting orders, unintelligible over the crashing hooves and rushing wind. As a couple troopers started to angle after him, Arilin prayed someone had taught Tom the hand signals she'd learned with the Army, waved her left hand and then pointed it straight away from her body.

She didn't need to look behind her to know he'd gotten the message. Half the cuirassiers pulled on their reins to start to rein their mounts completely around as Tom juked left, the heavy horses coming about like a squadron of sailing yachts tacking and slowly starting to thunder after him as he took the long way around the square. The look on the lead cuirassier's face as she passed him said it all. Waving over her shoulder insolently as she darted out of the square, Arilin steered into the street and kicked her horse down the middle of the road towards the Palace, traffic be damned. Glancing over her shoulder, she saw Tom galloping across the street, burning the cobblestones towards the Foot Guards' barracks. Another glance a few seconds later revealed the street filled with cuirassiers, the sheer mass of cavalrymen battering civilian traffic aside. Pulled by spooking horses, a carriage careened just ahead of the building charge. Arilin winced as the one of the wheels slammed up onto the curb, sending the driver tumbling into the street. His body disappeared under the cavalry's steel-tipped hooves as she tore her gaze away and kicked her horse forward again.

It was less than a mile to the Palace, ninety-odd endless seconds of pounding hooves, wide-eyed drivers staring at her and the avalanche following her as they struggled with their teams, slamming her heels into her horse's ribs again and again. It got the message, dug deep and sped up somehow, spittle flying from its mouth as it pressed itself to its limits. The Palace loomed before her, and she juked her horse around one last time as she cleared the last building and galloped across the front promenade towards the open corner gate. The sentries on duty unshouldered their carbines as she thundered up to the gate, but just stood there gaping at her as she reined her horse to a stop and wheeled around. They were teenaged girls in pink jackets, because, as she suddenly remembered, the

Guards were shorthanded with the deployment and the Fourteenth Hussars' training squadron was filling in.

On the plus side that did make her their superior officer. They snapped out of their stupor as Arilin screamed, *"Shut the gate!"* The first cuirassiers emerged around the corner as the heavy ironwork bars slammed into position, and she added, "They've been chasing me! *Open fire!"*

The girls looked at her, then at the oncoming tide of steel and horseflesh. A pistol shot rang out, the bullet splattering off the gate's bars and kicking up a fan of dust between the two of them, and they raised their carbines as one and started firing into the mass of cuirassiers outside as Arilin wheeled her horse about and kicked it towards the Royal Plaza and the Palace's main entrance. More gunfire rang out behind her, pistols firing rapidly, and the heavy carbine shots stopped. Arilin looked over her shoulder to see the two girls crumpled on the flagstones and a cuirassier already atop the wall, about to jump down and open the gates.

A gunshot rang out, high overhead, and the man collapsed backwards into the mob of enemy troopers beyond. The sharpshooter fired again and again as Arilin cleared the corner of the Palace, almost running into a hussar lieutenant riding towards the commotion. Arilin pulled her horse up again, and the woman demanded, "Milady! What's going on?"

"My uncle's throwing a coup!" Arilin yelled back, "Half the Second Cuirassiers chased me here from the Academy, and they just shot two of your guards!" She added, "I sent someone to the Foot Guards' barracks, they should be sending help soon."

The woman nodded, trotting closer, "Good, milady." Arilin followed her gaze to see the Palace's massive main gate sliding shut under the shoulders of several Valkyrie Knights. Even at the distance she could hear the massive *clang* as it slammed home and locked. The woman was adding, "We should be able to hold out until they arrive, they're not getting through the walls any time..."

Through the gate's heavy steel bars, down at the far side of the High City's grand central avenue where it narrowed into a more normal collection of urban streets, team after team of horses was trotting across the street, towing small, dark objects behind them. As they watched the teams paused, men jumping out to disconnect them before they rode back into the side streets' cover just as quickly as they had come, leaving their burdens spaced evenly across the broad avenue. Burdens whose crews were spinning them around, spreading their steel legs, sledgehammers working as they wedged recoil spades into the cobblestones. The muzzles of the Second Cuirassiers' horse artillery bearing down on the

Palace's main gate.

"Milady!" The lieutenant shouted, "We need to-"

Arilin was already off her horse and running for one of the Palace's side doors, shouting over her shoulder, "What're you waiting for? Come on!"

The woman had just dodged in behind her when the first shell slammed into the Palace's gates.

Chapter 42

Bell of Doom

Southbend loomed around them, and the sky was screaming. Up in her perch in the destroyer's mast, Sophia winced as another wave of shells howled in out of the dark clouds overhead. A thudding drumroll erupted behind her, something cracking loud over it as she hunkered into her jacket instinctively. Something fast and angry slammed into the mast below her a moment later. She looked down nervously, half-expecting the mast to start toppling over as she clung to it uselessly. Just an ugly smudge on the paintwork a few feet down from her. Looking further back on their ship, she sighed with relief as she saw it was still in one piece, soldiers in their gray uniforms huddled on the side away from the shelling and black-jacketed sailors doggedly ramming another round into the ship's rear cannon.

The sigh caught in her throat as the next ship in line plowed into view from the cloud of spray that had erupted across the Serpent behind them, black smoke boiling from its side as it veered out of the column. Twisting back around, she called down, "Sir! They've hit the ship behind us!"

Down on the bridge, Lieutenant Strickner turned and looked up at her, "Are they still in line?"

"No!" She looked over her shoulder to make sure, to see the ship trailing a pall of smoke like a comet as it swung further out of line to her right. She felt her eyes widen as something sparked white in the twisted wreckage that had been its forward gun platform. The soldiers packing its deck crowded backwards as blinding flames erupted in front of them, fifty feet high and building as the stricken ship careened towards the bank. Someone jumped overboard. Shivering, she swung back and yelled, "They're going in!"

Down below her Strickner looked down and set his jaw, hard enough she could see the muscles bulging at its corners as he ground his teeth together. After a long moment his jaw relaxed and he looked back up, "Any idea how they're still spotting fire, Miss Rose?"

Sophia looked around quickly. She'd seen the exact same view any number of times before coming back into Southbend on the ferry. Even aside from her father dragging her along on business trips, every summer they'd take a nighttime ferry ride to look at the lantern trees as they came to life all along the river. Her, him, her *mother*... and just like that she had a lump in her throat. She was home, but... but. So was the Empire. And she couldn't look for their observers if she was crying. Gritting her teeth, she wiped her eyes and looked out over the city. Low buildings lined the waterfront, docks and fishing skiffs in the rain. Off in the distance to her left she could see a thick plume of smoke rising, black mixed with flaring white. Phosphorous. As she watched a green tracer flared out of the smoke, then another. And that way was... she looked down at the bridge, shouting, "Regiment's getting hit, I see tracers and smoke that way!" She added, "I don't see any spotters, but they could be anywhere!"

"Well, that's a problem!" Colonel Espinay called back up cheerily from his perch beside Strickner, "Keep looking, Miss Rose!"

Sophia looked back upriver as the ship slewed around the last curve to the left, the bend to the south that had given the city its name. The wind and rain beat at her face as the ship surged under her, and she tightened her grip on the mast as it heeled over in the turn and swung her out over the water alarmingly. She'd been able to see the far side of the road bridge as they had run in and it had looked alright, but her breath caught in her throat as the near side emerged into view around the bend. No wonder she hadn't seen any traffic on it. Where it had once butted up against the eastern bank from a concrete piling set in the river, the bridge's eastern span slumped into the water in a mass of shattered, twisted steel. Dirty smoke still lingered over the river as they approached, and she looked over to see a handful of blue-jacketed gendarmes over by the bridge's old entrance holding back an angry-looking crowd with fixed bayonets as they swung into the center of the river and passed under the still-intact center span.

Swallowing hard, Sophia looked farther up ahead to make out the massive rail bridge arching proudly across the Serpent above the river mist. *That* one was still intact. She could make out a few dark dots hurrying back and forth atop them, which... wasn't right. If they were just civilians fleeing or soldiers going towards the fighting they'd at least be going the *same way*. Raising her borrowed binoculars to her eyes, Sophia swept them across the bridge for a second. The dark dots resolved into soldiers in dark blue uniforms piling heavy-looking boxes around the bridge supports. As she watched a man ran down the near bridge from one of the piles of boxes, trailing a wire reel behind him. Engineers rigging it to blow.

Sophia swung her binoculars down and left, towards the ferry station, and felt her heart jump into her throat. The docks were packed with civilians, men, women and children jamming onto the ferries standing-room only. One of the old paddle-wheelers started backing away from the dock as she watched, a man jumping after it and grabbing for the railing. He bounced off, fell, grabbed again desperately and latched onto the deck, feet kicking inches over the churning water. The passengers had gotten hold of his jacket and were pulling him back aboard when she pulled the binoculars away and shouted down, "Ferry dock's full of civilians, sir!

We'll never get through there!"

"I noticed, Miss Rose, thanks for the update!" Strickner let his own binoculars drop on their strap around his neck. He was opening his mouth to speak again when another freight-train of shells screamed in, something *furious* screaming past close enough to touch. Geysers erupted all around them, showering them all with water. Their captain calmly lifted his cap off, brushed the water out of his rakishly-long blonde hair and looked over at Edward, "Mister Bellamy, you're the local expert. I need an alternate landing zone." He added, "Preferably one where we're not going to be *sitting ducks.*"

Her friend nodded, "We'll come alongside the cargo pier. It's in line with the river, we won't even need to stop." He pointed, "It's past the passenger ferries, up there!"

Sophia brought her binoculars back up and looked past the ferry docks, instinctively leaning over as she tried to see around a ferry pulling in. After a moment it cleared and a long concrete dock emerged into view beyond it, one she remembered barges usually came alongside for loading. It was empty, just a stretch of weather-beaten concrete studded with cranes sandwiched between the railyard and the river. She called down, "It's clear, sir!"

"You'd better get down from there and see to your men, Miss Rose!" Strickner yelled back, "And try not to get Mister Bellamy killed while you're at it, he's got a bright future in the Navy!"

"Yes, sir!" Sophia slid down the ladder, handed the colonel his binoculars back, turned and called out over her shoulder, "Come on, Ed!"

"Coming, Sophie!" Edward hurried after her as she made her way astern along the superstructure, dodging past burning-hot funnels and through half the ship's light gun emplacements. The crew manning the heavy stern cannon had the breech open and were tiredly swabbing it out as they dropped down onto its platform and rushed through the knot of sailors. The gun chief cursed after them, Sophia ignoring it as she spotted where her squad had taken cover under the right side of the rear gun platform and hopped down.

Tony looked up at her arrival, "Sophie! What's up?"

Before she replied she glanced off the ship's stern. The stricken destroyer from earlier had run hard up onto the riverbank, smashing into one of the buildings along the waterfront and setting it afire. The water around it was full of soldiers and blue-jacketed crewmen wading ashore, a few still leaping overboard as the inferno engulfing its bow flared brighter. As she watched something flashed and the fire disappeared for a second in a shower of smoking debris. The cracking thud of the shell cooking off reached them a moment later and snapped her out of her reverie, and she shook her head quickly and replied, "Sorry. We're landing in a couple minutes, get ready."

"We're already *ready*, Sophia." Kelly replied. A little snidely, although he seemed to be right given that they'd all packed up their cumbersome ponchos and blankets. He went on, "The question I've got is where we're landing. And *how*."

Sophia rolled her eyes and shot back, "Then listen up, wise guy. We're coming in at the cargo docks and we're be unloading to the left side of the ship." She pointed across the deck as a crewman ran by and began quickly taking down the lifelines, "We think there's enemy artillery observers in town, so we need to move *fast*. The pier runs along the river so we're probably not even going to stop. As soon as we come alongside and slow down enough to get off, you jump, got it?"

Looking around, she noticed her little talk had an attracted an audience. Namely the entire platoon. Hargrave was opening his mouth to ask her something when Lieutenant Gable's voice floated over the scrum, "I was actually about to say all of that, but it seems Miss Rose beat me here." They all turned to look at her, and she smiled nervously and patted the saber hanging at her side as though to reassure herself before she went on, "We'll secure the eastern approach to the rail bridge. The rest of the company will be forward of us defending at the rail station. If need be we'll come up and support them." Glancing back at the destroyers slicing through the water behind them, she went on, "Once Alpha and Bravo are ashore they'll attack east towards what I understand is this unit's old garrison."

"And Delta, ma'am?" Sergeant Cross cut in. What was left of it anyways, wading ashore from their burning ship.

An uneasy murmur quieted down as Lieutenant Gable said, "They'll take the north side of town. The colonel said he'd send a runner over to find them and get them straightened out."

"Charlie Company." Someone said sarcastically.

Someone else shot back, "Deeds alone."

"Oh, come on! We're back home!" Sergeant Cross called out, "Once we've chased out the Empire we're all going to the Figurehead, and milady Gable's paying for it!"

That got a cheer out of them, as their lady lieutenant smiled shyly and scraped at the deck plating with a booted toe. As the noise died down

Sophia heard something new murmur over the thrum of the ship, the crashing water beneath them and the thrum of the rain on the canvas cover overhead, and she looked around quickly to find its source. It certainly *sounded* like someone cheering, but softly. Thinking it was one of the other platoons, Sophia looked around to see one of the ferries heading towards the far bank on the ship's right, and she whipped around as she realized exactly what the noise was.

The ferry terminal appeared around the edge of the ship's superstructure, and Sophia was tall enough on her tiptoes to make out the crowd thronging the piers cheering and waving hats and handkerchiefs as they steamed by. After the Empire's attack their sudden appearance must have seemed like a deliverance from Heaven. Someone up front rang the ship's bell jauntily. Soldiers started waving back. Then the too-familiar scream of Imperial shells floated over the racket, and Sophia flattened herself against the superstructure as she yelled, "*Incomi-*"

A deafening crack cut her off as the ship staggered, something slamming into her back as she felt her feet leave the deck. Shaking herself, she rolled over on top of someone and looked up from her new position hanging in the lifelines. Tony had kept his feet somehow and helpfully gave her a hand up, but her words caught in her throat as she started to thank him. A dark mass was caught in the railing around the gun platform overhead. More than one, navy-blue lumps gargling and twitching as blood ran down the bowed-out bulkhead. Something black caught at her peripheral vision, and she twisted around to see another ragged *shape* spinning into the water nearby. *Jesus Christ.*

"Take cover!" Sergeant Cross called out, a little redundantly, "Everyone all right? We lose anyone? Squads, report!"

Kelly shot back sarcastically, "*They're* not!"

"Shut up, Kelly," she retorted as Tony pulled her to her feet. A quick glance revealed Edward and James were as good as ever, and she yelled, "First is good!"

"Seven out of seven in Second." Mr. Hargrave reported, steady as ever.

Cameron, who had taken over Third Squad a few days ago, quipped, "We're up."

"G-good." Lieutenant Gable said, a little shakily. The ship banked to the left noticeably, and she pushed her way through the scrum to step out onto the fantail and look out towards the docks ahead. Looking past her, Sophia noticed the civilians on the docks had dissipated into a mob fleeing back towards the city, leaving the ferry docks strewn with luggage. Looking back towards them, Gable called out, "Looks like the dock is coming up, get out here and get ready!"

No sooner had she said it than she heard Lieutenant Thorn shout from up ahead, "*Charlie Company!* We're coming alongside in thirty seconds! Prepare to dismount!"

Lieutenant Gable shooed them out onto the fantail as the ship rushed towards the bank. Trying not to look too hard at the blood running down the superstructure, Sophia craned her neck out to get a glimpse of the cargo pier looming ahead of them. The long, low slab of concrete was scarred from the gunwales of a thousand barges and piled with abandoned cargo where it butted into the Southbend railyard, fresh-cut logs from upriver oozing sap and piles of coal and gravel glistening darkly in the rain. Just when she thought they were going to plow straight into the pier the ship slewed back alarmingly, water churning to a froth beneath them as the engines roared into reverse.

Sophia crouched on the deck, bracing a hand against the deck plating as the ship swung towards the dock. For a moment it seemed to hang, suspended in space as it slowed. Then something *crunched* up towards the bow, the whole ship lurching uneasily for a couple long seconds as it straightened out against the dock with a long, screaming shriek of steel grinding against concrete. The ship would probably be scarred for the rest of its life. She was just climbing to her feet when Lieutenant Gable called out, "*We're here! Go!*"

Sophia got a running start off the fantail and jumped. Her boots bit rough concrete as she hit, she took a couple long steps as she fought to keep her balance and she was off, unslinging her rifle as she glanced behind herself. Gray-jacketed soldiers were pouring off the ship like water off a horse's back, a couple overbalancing as they landed and falling heavily. They got back up and kept running. As she cleared the cranes and looked back ahead, angling towards a solid-looking pile of crates under a tarp, she heard the ship's engines slam back into drive as it ground its way painfully away from the pier. She looked back again as she skidded into cover to see the destroyer accelerating away from the dock and the next one already angling in, Colonel Espinay strolling along the now-deserted pier nonchalantly. He looked like a *tourist*. The man was insane.

Someone ran up behind her, footsteps uneven from carrying a heavy weight in one arm. Shifting around, Sophia looked over her other shoulder to see Tony running up with one of their machine guns, the rest of the squad close and Lieutenant Gable hurrying along close behind him. James clambered up on top of the crates adventurously and sprawled out on top, and Sophia pushed herself out around the edge of the pile herself and looked out. Nothing. Well, a lot more than nothing, but she didn't see anyone wearing a *mask*. The warehouses surrounding the cargo yard sweated in the rain, and off to her right she could see an eerily-familiar long rooftop peeking over the trains packed into the Southbend railyard. The very train station they'd set off from a lifetime ago, its rain-slicked metal roof gleaming through the cold mist.

A whistle rang out over the pounding boots and shouting all around her, and Sophia heard Lieutenant Thorn shout from a ways off, "Charlie Company! Move out!"

A moment later Gable called out from behind her, "First platoon! Head for the bridge, platoon column!"

Something crashed and shrieked off towards the river as Sophia started to stand, and she looked over to see the next destroyer grinding against the dock right where they'd unloaded earlier. Soldiers were already spilling off it and sprinting across the concrete apron towards them. Looking farther over, she could see the last destroyer had pulled in short and was unloading well down the pier from them. Even at the distance she could make out her father unshouldering his rifle and waving the troops forward. She was raising her own arm to wave her own squad along when she heard another whistle shrieking overhead.

Sophia threw herself down as deafening hammer-blows rained down across the pier, the air overhead seething for an instant with sharp death. Something angry skipped off the concrete in front of her face as the explosions died down and were replaced with a furious, shrieking roar, something glowing sun-bright off towards the river. She looked over to see the infantry coming off the nearer ship doggedly picking themselves up, most of them anyways, hellishly backlit by the towering inferno engulfing their destroyer. The ship's whole superstructure was shrouded in blinding white fog, *glowing* demonically as cannon propellant ignited in the hail of hot steel and burning phosphorous.

God-damn it. Springing to her feet, Sophia shouted, "Come on! Follow me!"

There wasn't any pretense of getting into a pretty formation to march out. They just ran for it. Sophia looked over her shoulder after a few steps to see the rest of her squad sprinting along after her, Gable behind them and the rest of the platoon heaving themselves up to run along behind her. More shells screamed in as she darted deeper into the piles of cargo on the apron, something exploding dully behind her in the wake of their ear-splitting blasts. She kept running and didn't look back until she'd vaulted up onto the long concrete pylon of the cargo station on the near side of the railyard.

What she saw made her wish she hadn't. Even in outline through a cloud of burning smoke, she could see the stricken destroyer was heeled halfway over already, a burning figure jumping into the water desperately as she watched. Half a dozen gray-jacketed shapes were sprawled on the pier near it like shrapnel thrown from a bomb, some of them slowly thrashing around. The others lay too-still. Reaching down to give Lieutenant Gable a hand up onto the platform, Sophia grimaced and turned to look at the bridge as she pulled the girl up. It loomed over the railyard, steel arches reaching over the Serpent's dark water to the mist-shrouded far bank. The engineers were still hurrying around, seemingly unconcerned by the shelling. Getting to her feet beside her, the lieutenant said, "Thanks, Rose." She pointed towards the bridge and went on, "Think you can lead us in there?"

"Will do, milady." Turning, Sophia called over her shoulder, "Follow me, guys! We're going through the railyard, watch out in case they're moving cars!"

Pushing his machine gun up onto the platform before he clambered up heavily himself, Tony shot back, "Sure, can you slow down a *little?* Some of us are carrying stuff."

"Sure, sure, come on." Sophia replied, hopping down on the far side of the platform and hurrying into the railyard. It was packed with trains, probably from the bridge closures. At least most of them seemed to be empty. Open boxcars and vacant passenger carriages dripped in the pattering rain as she made her way through the throng, clambering over end-connectors and empty flatcars. She could hear the rest of the platoon making their way along behind her, up and over and across.

Most, but not all. Pulling a door open and stepping up into a passenger carriage, Sophia jumped down from the other side to find herself face-to-face with a flatcar piled high with tarped-up cargo. An orange warning sign tied to its side dripped in the rain, warning, 'DANGER: EXPLOSIVE CARGO.' Looking from side to side she could see a dozen more of those flatbeds linked together in the train, and more boxcars with the same warning signs further along. Steam curled from a locomotive far off to her left, idling under an overhead water tank. A railway worker in greasy coveralls looked up in surprise from inspecting a flatcar's wheels as she jumped down.

Someone hopped down behind her. Edward, she realized as he remarked, "Well, this is bad."

"No kidding." She replied. Looking over at the worker, she shouted, "Hey! You guys need to get out of here!"

The man raised his eyebrows in surprise, "Can't, missy. We got stopped after we crossed the bridge, said there were Masks further up on the tracks." He jerked his head at the bridge, "And then they closed it behind us. We're stuck."

Lieutenant Gable jumped down behind her and replied, "We'll see if we can get the bridge open for you. Just get ready to move out, if this train goes up you'll take out half the railyard." She turned to her and pointed towards the train's tail, not far off to their right, "We're close. Get moving, Miss Rose."

Sophia nodded and turned, then hesitated for a moment. *Something* wasn't right, with all the artillery fire they'd been taking there had to be Imperials nearby. Which meant... she reached down to her belt, drew her bayonet and locked it to her rifle. Looking back at the lady lieutenant, Sophia hefted her weapon and said, "Just in case, milady."

"Good idea," Gable replied as Sophia turned and hurried off, calling out behind her, "Platoon! Fix bayonets!"

Sophia carefully pulled herself up and over a coupling between two flatcars loaded with artillery shells. Big ones. Between the gaps in the next, somewhat less-explosive looking train, she could see the broad expanse of the rail line proper, no less than three tracks running east through the heart of Southbend. Humble apartments lined the far side, for rent by anyone who could sleep through a couple dozen trains going by every night. Some of the residents had crowded out onto balconies, gawking at the war that had erupted on their doorstep.

Sophia turned and headed to the right between the trains towards the bridge, gravel crunching under her feet as she rushed along. More shells whistled in out over the river and exploded dully in the water, and the distant gunfire behind her, off by Regiment, built again suddenly. It sounded like they were making a final push on the defenders. Hoping the rest of the battalion got up there in time, Sophia reached the end of the last train and peered around the edge of its jauntily-painted caboose. The bridge was *right there*, maybe two hundred meters away. A few gen-darmes stood guard by its entrance, clutching carbines nervously as the engineers scurried about behind them with what looked like hundreds of pounds of explosives. Good thing they'd made it. The military police looked like they were about ready to run for it the moment they saw a mask.

Emerging into the open, Sophia waved for the others to follow her and hurried towards the bridge. Off in the river she could see the destroy-ers maneuvering about slowly as more shells whistled in, drenching what looked like Strickner's ship with spray as they slapped down across the river. She wondered for a moment why he hadn't withdrawn his squadron yet, but at least he seemed to be drawing fire for them. With that happy thought in mind she glanced behind herself to make sure her squad had spread out properly behind her, and seeing the platoon had mostly emerged from the cover of the trains she hefted her rifle and broke into a run.

One of the gendarmes looked over at them and turned to shout something inaudible back towards the bridge. A heavyset man who had been standing on the bridge's entry ramp watching the engineers at work turned to see them with a surprised look on his face, unslung his carbine and walked towards them, raising his free hand as he called out, "Hey! Who are you guys?" He gestured for them to get back, "You can't be up here, they're rigging the bridge to blow right now."

Sophia slowed, and Lieutenant Gable came up next to her, calling back, "We're with the two-twenty fourth, we're here to make sure that doesn't happen!" She went on as they walked up to him, "What's the situation here, sergeant? I'm sure you saw us disembarking just now, we've got less than no idea what's going on beyond that you're clearly under attack." She snorted, "Although we know by who, I guess."

Sophia added wryly, "Fifth Dragoon Regiment. Don't ask us how we know, long story."

The man shrugged, "God, ma'am, I know about as much as you do. I'm just on duty with the bridge detail, I haven't heard *anything.*" He jerked his chin over his shoulder, "These guys showed up about an hour ago, right after I started hearing gunfire off by the barracks. Told me to close the bridge down, so that's what I did."

Behind them Sergeant Cross had started ordering the other squads into position on either side of the bridge. Mr. Hargrave ran by with his men at his heels as Lieutenant Gable raised an eyebrow and replied, "And the Rail Service was just okay with this?" Her lieutenant jerked a thumb over her shoulder, "You've got a train loaded with explosives in the yard right now and we're getting *shelled.* I need this bridge open and that train out of here *now,* or we'll be defending a *crater* pretty soon."

The sergeant shrugged and looked over his own shoulder nervously, "You'll have to take it up with their captain, ma'am." He added, "And just so you know, that guy means *business.* I've just been trying to stay out of his way."

Sophia followed the man's glance to see the officer in question turning to look at them, a tall man with black hair and dark eyes in an old-style blue uniform. She could see the scowl on his face even from the distance. Gesturing to one of the other engineers to follow him, he turned and stalked in their direction. Lieutenant Gable saluted as the man approached and started, "Sir! We're your reinforcements!"

"I can see that." He ignored it, snapping at them as he arrived, "Now go find someone to fight, we've got this bridge under control."

Her lieutenant stood her ground, "There's a train loaded with explosives in the yard right now, sir. We need to get it back across the bridge before it gets hit and goes up."

Sophia studied the captain and the soldier coming up behind him as he rolled his eyes, "And if it gets hit *on* the bridge, missy?" White patches on his throat, with a captain's three pips and the infantry's crossed rifles on either side. The new uniform's shoulder-boards sure uncrowded the collar, she thought idly, until it hit her. Why... why *exactly* were the infantry rigging a bridge to blow? The officers were still arguing, Gable crossing her arms angrily as she riposted. She glanced over at the soldier behind him, another dark-haired infantryman. As she watched the man unslung his rifle and spun it in his hands instinctively, *expertly*, pointing its muzzle down at the bridge's decking with its butt positioned to come right up and into his shoulder.

Just like a dragoon. Time slowed to a crawl, her heartbeat thundering in her ears as she looked over at the captain, then at the other blue-jacketed infantrymen further down the bridge, now setting down their demolition charges and turning to face them warily. As though they were a threat. Another one unslung his rifle, spinning it muzzle-down, and Sophia tore her gaze away and locked eyes with the soldier across from her. His eyes were a dark, flinty gray, and they only narrowed as she slowly lowered her rifle, setting its butt under her arm as she pointed her bayonet just barely off to his left. She flexed her legs slightly as she interrupted the officers, "Milady, these guys are Pathfinders."

"Oh." Lieutenant Gable replied, quite conversationally, "That *does* explain-"

Sophia lunged as the man in front of her snapped his rifle up, finger tightening on the trigger. Her bayonet smashed his rifle aside as he fired, heat searing her face as her ears rang like a bell. She lunged forward again, circling her rifle under his and stabbing as he swung his buttstock down, parrying her thrust aside. He raised his weapon as she lunged again, starting to swing his buttstock towards her head.

Too slow. He'd barely started moving forward when Sophia speared her shoulder into his midsection, lifting him clean off the ground with the force of the impact. He kept hold of his rifle as he flew backwards, caught his feet on the grating and rolled backwards. He was uncoiling back upright when he saw her coming again, flinty eyes finally widening just a little as she stabbed again, rifle coming up to parry her assault.

Too slow. Her bayonet caught him under the chin and he went limp, rifle knocking weakly into hers from its own momentum. It was still falling from his nerveless fingers when Sophia snapped her foot forward and into his chest, kicking him off her weapon and onto the tracks. Blood sprayed onto the bridge's decking, gleaming brilliant red on the dull gray steel.

Something was hammering over the ringing in her ears. A machine gun roaring, nearby, on and on as its gunner unloaded it towards the enemy. She looked down the bridge, the Pathfinders in their captured Royal Army uniforms ducking into the cover of support struts and flattening themselves to the decking as sparks danced from the steel all around them. And then she looked the other way to see Tony sprawled out by the bridge's entrance, casings gleaming in the mist as they spit from the side of his erupting weapon.

Lieutenant Gable was standing dazedly beside him, blood dripping bright red from her drawn saber. The Pathfinder 'captain' was crumpled at her feet. Running over, Sophia half-picked her up and shoved her into the cover of one of the bridge's trusses as angry little wasps started catching at her hair. An instant after she ducked into cover another machine gun hammered to life behind her, and she looked back to see Kelly had flopped himself down a couple struts back and was hosing the far side of the bridge with fire.

Sophia felt the lieutenant shake herself where she had pinned her between the girder and her body, and the girl looked up to meet her eyes, saying, "You can let me go, Miss Rose, I'm... I'm fine."

Something clanged off the truss, inches from both of their heads, and Sophia shot back, "I'm not sure I *want* to, milady. Think you can get the others to support us?" Turning, she waved to get her friends' attention and gestured for them to move up as she shouted over the gunfire, "*Push forward! Let's go!*"

Kelly grimly picked himself and his gun up and rushed past them as Tony fired another long burst. She felt Gable was saying something back to her, but it was lost between her ringing ears and the hammering gunfire. Sophia let her go regardless and the lieutenant darted back off the bridge, shouting something she couldn't make out. Turning, Sophia ducked around the girder and ran to the next one down. Kelly had thrown himself prone behind it, pushing just enough of his body out of the steel plate's cover to get behind his machine gun. Big, heavy bullets snapped by as she made her way up. They certainly *sounded* scarier than the Empire's fast little rounds, she thought as she stepped over Kelly and flattened herself against the truss.

"Sophie!" She looked down to see Kelly had rolled onto his back to look up at her, "Got a belt? I'm low."

"Sure." Sophia felt for her second bandolier with its belted ammunition and yanked one of the pouches open, the thin cloth fabric ripping under her fingers. Fishing the heavy ammunition belt out, she knelt beside Kelly as he rolled back onto the gun and fired another long burst, hot brass pelting her abdomen and burning her bare thighs as she reached out over the screaming, smoking weapon. The receiver was already hot to the touch. She was supposed to do this from the other side, but if she tried that she'd *die*. After a moment of fumbling she managed to stuff the belt into the gun's underslung feed box and hand Kelly the guide tab as he finished his first belt, the gun's bolt thunking forward on an empty chamber. He deftly worked it through the feed port, racked the charging handle back and kept firing.

Tony's gun erupted from the other side of the bridge, and she looked over to see Edward helping him reload his own weapon. Feeling a twinge of nervousness for James, she looked around quickly to see a familiar gray-jacketed form crawling forward between the center pair of railroad tracks, bullets sparking all around him. The idiot. Kelly was rolling up to his knees underneath her, and Sophia darted out into the crackling air over the tracks to dash forward to the next truss. After a couple heart-stopping seconds she skidded back into cover, almost bashing her shin on a heavy-looking box someone had tucked into the cup of the heavy steel I-beam.

A box marked, 'EXPLOSIVE: 10 KG TNT' with a stylized blast and a skull and crossbones, with a thick copper wire plugged into it. Throwing her rifle over her shoulder on its sling, Sophia yanked the command wire free, grabbed the rope handles conveniently set into the bomb, heaved and threw it into the river before her blood even had *time* to chill. Quickly wrapping the wire around her hands, she set a foot against the beam and hauled on it with every ounce of strength she could muster, feeling it pop and jerk in her hands as it tore free of demolition charges further down the bridge. She was re-wrapping it to pull again when Kelly threw himself down beside her again, giving her a quizzical look as he settled behind his gun, "What're you doing?"

"Trying to make sure this damn bridge doesn't explode." Sophia shot back, as she hauled on the wire again. It went slack in her hands and she staggered backwards, almost falling. Untangling herself, she grimly unslung her rifle and was about to lean around the beam to fire when something *clanged* into the girder's far side and the air over the tracks filled with cracking death.

Kelly squeezed a long burst back and reported coldly, "I'm seeing two machine guns, maybe more down there." He added, "You know what the rest of the platoon's up to? We're not winning this fight ourselves."

The roar of a machine gun off to her right answered his question. Sophia looked over to see the weapon beating up a cloud of mist behind a sturdy-looking riverside tree farther down the bank. Probably Cameron's squad. She thought she saw Sergeant Cross rushing between the trees, pointing to direct fire. Leaning out to take a shot herself, she replied, "*Helping!*"

Lights danced in the rain beyond her rifle's sights as she pulled the trigger, and she quickly ducked back behind the girder as another cloud of bullets thundered over the bridge. Underneath her, Kelly shouted back, "*Not enough!*"

Sophia hated to admit it, but she had a sinking feeling he was right. Even as far upstream as they were at Southbend, the Serpent was still a quarter-mile wide and they'd barely made it a hundred feet. All the Pathfinders down the bridge had to do was sit tight behind the protection of the girders and stand them off until their reinforcements broke through, and knowing the Empire they'd *absolutely* brought enough ammunition to do it. In both directions if the gendarmes on the other bank had gotten wise by now. Not to mention she'd gotten a good look at the bridge coming in. Their whole platoon was probably outnumbered, with the surprise of their attack wearing off fast against the Empire's hardest soldiers.

She was searching for something encouraging to say back when the bridge shuddered underneath her, a cracking blast beating at her ears a moment later. Her heart climbed into her throat for an instant as she thought flashed through her mind that the demolition charges had gone off, before the bridge seemed to stabilize under her feet. Swiveling herself out into the suddenly-clear air, she saw a pall of ugly black smoke hanging over the far side of the bridge, a blue-jacketed figure staggering into the open as she watched. Before she could drop her sights onto him he vanished in a cloud of smoke and flaming sparks, something big shrieking through the air nearby. Shrapnel.

Artillery. But they didn't... *no.* Sophia ducked back behind the safety of the girder as another round exploded further down the bridge, then looked out into the river. Strickner's destroyer was cutting a lazy arc across the water towards them, figures working behind the forward gun's shield as they slammed another round into the piece. An instant later the cannon puffed and another round cracked into the Pathfinders. And another, and another, time-fuzed shells bursting inside the web of trusses with virtuoso precision. Probably noticing her look even from the distance, Strickner took a hand off the ship's wheel to wave his cap gallantly.

Sophia rolled her eyes and turned back to her squad. The enemy fire had disappeared, and she peered around the side of the girder cautiously. The smoke clouding the far side of the bridge was slowly clearing, revealing a deck littered with bodies in blue uniforms. The spindly shape of a machine gun lolled on its bipod in front of a torn shape that had once been its gunner. She was opening her mouth to say something when light caught her eye, and she looked up to see a burning red star shining through the girders overhead. An enemy flare. Red for failure? Shaking her head, she called out, "You guys alright?"

Kelly replied curtly from underneath her, "Yep. Now move your legs so I don't burn you."

Sophia looked down to see he had broken his gun open and swung its receiver aside to pull the barrel out. The hot steel steamed in the drizzling rain as he slid his hand into an insulated mitten to pull it out and set it aside gingerly. Stepping back a little, she went on, "How about the rest of you?"

James groaned and waved from his hiding spot between the rails farther back along the bridge, "Still alive. Somehow. Don't know how."

Edward chimed in, "I'm okay!"

Tony added tiredly, shaking his head behind his machine gun, "Still here, Sophie."

Shaking her head, Sophia said, "Ugh, yeah... now come on, let's deal with these bo-" Something very familiar, *too* familiar, *much too familiar*, whistled overhead and she threw herself flat on the bridge's steel decking. It was redundant, but she shouted anyways, *"Get down!"*

The rounds came in short. *Way* short. At least they knew who'd been spotting the enemy fire, Sophia thought as she saw shells flash back in the railyard. A couple landed around the munitions train, dirty smoke puffing and rising among the cars for a long moment. Just long enough for her to let her breath out and start pushing herself up before she noticed the spark shooting up out of the massed cars. Just one little spark, a fiery little ember tumbling up into the sky. A burning little speck at the distance but probably the size of her *arm*. Followed by more and more, a shower of sparks building to a volcano of flame erupting from the far side of the railyard and rushing towards them town its carrier train, shells exploding with a roar like the Apocalypse barreling towards them. Dropping back onto the bridge's cold, wet steel, Sophia shut her eyes, clamped her hands over her ears and prayed.

Something hammered into her chest and she felt herself floating in midair for an instant before she was grabbed and *slammed* back into the bridge's plating, smashing the breath from her lungs as the bridge bucked and gyrated under her. Her ears rang. She tasted blood. Shaking her head, Sophia looked up from the swaying planking to see an enormous, black cloud had blotted out her view of the town beyond. A black cloud speckled with hard, sharp, and very large flecks raining towards them. Most of a railcar whistled by maybe twenty feet away and plunged into the river. Splintered wood and jagged metal rained from the sky, crashing off the truss overhead and slamming into the bridge decking like so many bombs. James shook himself and managed to get up far enough to dive into the safety of the trussing moments before an eight-foot piece of railroad steel shrieked down into the exact spot he'd been laying.

After a while, a long while, it stopped. Even the Imperial guns stopped shelling, probably out of respect more than anything else. Feeling something wet running down her lips, Sophia wiped at it and realized her nose was bleeding. Wiping at it in what was probably a vain attempt to staunch the flow, Sophia crawled to her feet and looked around. Her guys were still seemed to be okay, somehow. The rest of the platoon... she peered into the stinking fog that had suddenly enveloped them. *There*, a shape walking up the bridge towards them. One she knew well, saber still in hand despite how unsteadily she was moving.

"Miss Rose! First Squad! You guys alright?" Lieutenant Gable called out as she walked out of the smoke.

"Yeah, we're fine!" Sophia shook her head, feeling the beginnings of an ear-splitting headache, "Well, we can fight at least. How's everyone else?"

The lieutenant shook her head, "I was with Second, we got under the embankment before that thing went off." Hargrave's squad. She went on, "I don't know about Third, I came here first."

The gendarme sergeant from earlier staggered dazedly out of the smoke behind her, and Gable called out, "Hey, sergeant! Can you get your guys together and mop up the far side?"

"Can't your guys...?" The man asked, trailing off.

Lieutenant Gable shook her head, "No, we need to get set up to defend around here... the Empire's still coming. They're coming, we need to get ready." She looked at her, "Rose, get your guys and follow me. We're going to go *find* Third, and then we're going to figure out how the *bleeding hell* we can hold on here."

Sophia swallowed hard. Hargrave and his guys had been on the far side of the bridge from the explosion. Third Squad, with Sergeant Cross... they'd been much closer to the railyard. But there was nothing to be done for it. Nodding, Sophia hefted her rifle, "After you, milady." Turning, she looked between her squad, her guys... her friends, as she said, "Come on, guys, let's go."

"Day's just getting started." Kelly muttered darkly as he climbed to his feet.

Chapter 43

Battering Ram

The Long Ballroom was one of the marvels of the Western Kingdom and a monument to the Wehrherz monarchy's prestige. At two hundred meters long and five stories tall it was large enough to fit an airship with room to spare, the grand vault roofed over with skylights and strung with gilded chandeliers. It was the perfect counterpart to the Royal Library across the plaza in the East Wing, a declaration of the Royal Family's elegance and sophistication. They could invite everyone who was anyone in the Capital to a ball and not have to worry about a single jostled dancer or stepped-on foot. And they *did*, routinely, at least before the war had intervened. Princess Arilin had spent many a wonderful evening spinning across its marble floor.

She was turning to look back at the hussar lieutenant following on her heels when something flashed through the floor-to-ceiling windows, silhouetting the girl in dirty orange for an instant. Something crashed overhead, thick glass shattering like gunfire as ugly metal fragments and razor-edged crystal shards rained down around them. Finding herself on the floor, Arilin pushed herself up on her elbows to see a chandelier smash to the floor in the middle of the ballroom, lightbulbs exploding in a shower of sparkling glass. Dust billowed from the far wall where something that looked suspiciously like a bent piece of the Palace's front gate had stuck thirty feet off the ground.

Shaking herself, Arilin sprang to her feet and turned to see her companion climbing to her feet behind her. Or trying to, anyways. An ugly red stain was running down one of her legs, the blood shockingly bright against the silky white fabric of her riding breeches. Reaching down as gunfire crackled outside, Arilin grabbed the girl's arm and pulled it around her shoulders as she got her feet under her, saying, "I've got you, come on, let's go."

"You... you shouldn't, milady." The lieutenant gritted, trying to pull away from her. Gunfire crackled outside for emphasis, something snapping through the air nearby and knocking a tiny spray of debris out of the far wall, "Just go-"

"Shut up!" Arilin shouted, wrapping an arm around the girl's body and pulling her back into her, "That's an order, now move!"

The pink-jacketed lieutenant had the sense to shut her mouth, lean on her and hurry along. She whimpered in pain and clutched at Arilin for support every time she tried to take a step with her wounded leg, but she stayed upright as the princess pulled her along. After an excruciating moment they got into a rhythm and sped up, hobbling down the endless room as gunfire cracked outside. Glass shattered and more bullets snapped through the air, high and random. At least it didn't look like they were shooting at *them specifically*. *Yet*, Arilin though as she pulled the girl along at a shambling run, her weight bearing down on her shoulders like a sack of bricks. She'd seen soldiers training to evacuate the wounded before, men carrying other men on their shoulders and *running*. God knew how they did it.

They had gotten maybe halfway when something cracked behind them, impossibly loud. More glass shattered and ugly smoke filled the ballroom behind them as the lieutenant fell on top of her, pinning her to the floor. The marble shuddered beneath her as something large and heavy smashed to the floor nearby. Tasting blood, Arilin shook her head and thrashed out from under the lieutenant, then got her feet under her and pulled the girl back upright, put her arm around her shoulders and *ran*.

Another one of those unholy sledgehammers slammed into the building behind them as they went, almost knocking them to the floor again. Then another, and another, as Arilin realized what was happening. There had been a Valkyrie Knight on the roof of this wing of the Palace shooting down at the cuirassiers trying to force their way through the corner gate. Her pink jacket had probably stood out clearly, silhouetted against the roofline and a perfect target for the artillery out in the plaza. And with the roof swept the cuirassiers wouldn't be far behind.

The ballroom's entryway loomed in front of them, a massive archway thirty feet high with the doors braced open, still maybe fifty meters away. The lieutenant was moaning in agony as Arilin dragged her along, heavier on her shoulders than ever, one bad step away from driving her to the floor as she wobbled under the girl's weight. Something pink peeped around the doorway up ahead and Arilin screamed, *"Hey! Help me!"*

The pink sliver disappeared for a moment, then reappeared, a girl's blonde hair catching the morning sunlight as she stuck her head around the corner. Arilin was close enough to see her eyes widen. A moment later she darted out from behind the doorway, slinging her carbine over her back as she ran towards them, yelling, "Milady!" As she skidded to a stop in front of them Arilin got a look at her collar and realized she was just a private, probably a brand new recruit. Wide-eyed, she went on, "Do you-"

"Get her other arm!" Arilin ordered, and the girl sprang into action and wrapped the lieutenant's other arm around her shoulders. Half-dragging her, they ran for the doorway as another shell shrieked through the air outside and slammed into the Palace's massive front doors, the ones leading directly into the Throne Room from the plaza outside. Shattered glass poured from the walls as stinking smoke blotted out the sunlight outside.

A moment later they stumbled through the doorway, another hussar darting out of her shelter behind the massive stone frame to grab the lieutenant as Arilin's legs buckled and she collapsed to the floor heavily, head spinning. Someone grabbed her by the back of her collar and ignominiously dragged her into the entryway on her stomach before she could think to try to get up. A gunshot hammered nearby, loud enough to set her ears ringing, then another and another as her rescuer finally let go. She flipped over onto her back to see a hussar leaning around the far side of the doorway with her rifle braced on the frame, a brass shell casing sparkling in the light as she worked her carbine's bolt.

Her lieutenant had ended up on the far side of the doorway, with a couple girls frantically working over her leg with what looked like long, thin belts. Tourniquets. Arilin felt her stomach turn as she saw the smeared trail of blood along the glossy marble floor, shocking red even in the dim light. Her stockings suddenly felt clammy and her hand came back bloody as she felt at them, the woman's blood almost glowing against her glove's white leather. She'd never realized it could be that *bright*.

Arilin's head was swimming and her breath catching in her throat when one of the girls working on the lieutenant called over to her, "*Milady!*" A bullet cracked through the doorway and the hussars hiding behind the doorframe flinched back into cover nervously. She was going on, "*-sword?*"

Shaking herself, Arilin sat up and called back, "*What?*"

As she yelled back the pink-jacketed hussar on the far side of the door swiveled back around it and fired again, her carbine's blast drowning out her words. She was going to try again when a girl on the far side, the blonde one who had run out to rescue her, picked up a long, thin object with a tangle of straps attached to it from the floor nearby and threw it over. Arilin reached out and grabbed it out of the air, fingers closing on a flat steel scabbard. A hussar lieutenant's saber with rayskin grips and a brass-plated knucklebow. As she held the weapon it occurred to her, dimly, that with their lieutenant wounded she was now the senior officer present.

That thought broke her out of her stupor. Scrambling to her feet, Arilin buckled the sword belt around her hips, the cool steel of its scabbard pressing into her skirt and laying heavily against her thigh. She looked around at the hussars as bullets snapped through the doorway, more of them this time. One skipped off the floor and ricocheted into the entryway's far wall with a crack, raising a puff of plaster. The other hussar by the lieutenant, the one that hadn't thrown her the sword, yelped and scrambled backwards at the sight.

Four girls, all privates. The horrifying thought crossed her mind that she probably had the most combat experience of the group on top of having the most rank. *God in heaven*, she was going to have to take charge. She looked around again. Two... no, three for the lieutenant. They had a long way up to go. One would be enough to cover their rear. Taking a deep breath, Princess Arilin ordered, "Everyone! Listen!" The hussars all looked at her, eyes widening in surprise as she went on, "The First Guards are coming, we just need to hold out. You three, pick her up." Arilin pointed at the stricken lieutenant, then looked at the girl on her side of the door, "You, cover them as they get across and follow up the rear. We'll head up to the Residence and hold out there." They were still staring at her. Gritting her teeth, Arilin shouted, "*Are you deaf? Move!*"

Another bullet snapped through the doorway. The noise seemed to knock them out of *their* stupor, and the blonde hussar stood and called out, "Get the doors closed first, they'll give us some cover!"

Clearly knowing what she was doing, the girl on the far side of the doors stomped on a foot latch, set her booted foot against the massive oak door and *pushed*. The door, thirty feet tall and a good six inches thick, barely budged for a moment. It must have weighed a ton. Then, ever so slowly, it shifted. It was like watching an avalanche, the door gaining speed until it slammed closed across the archway with a crack like an artillery shell. The girl on her side had taken her cue, and the door on the near side crashed closed a moment later, leaving them in silence.

Then something splintered out of the door and cracked somewhere back in the West Hall. Then another something. Thick as it was, the door wasn't bulletproof. After a few bullets cracked through the cuirassiers outside stopped shooting, and Arilin breathed a sigh of relief and waved for the girls to come over. They obediently picked up the wounded lieutenant as Arilin turned and yanked open the door to the servants' stairway tucked away on the outer side of the Long Ballroom's entryway. Gesturing for them to go ahead of her, she said, "Get up to the top floor! We can get into the Residence from there."

"Assuming they're not waiting for us when we get there, milady." The blonde hussar commented. Arilin thought she vaguely recognized her, probably from some High City ball or function, as she looked at the girl Arilin had told to cover them, "Hey, take my place, I'll watch the rear." The other girl opened her mouth to protest, but she cut her off, "You can't hit the broad side of a stable and we both know it."

"Ugh, *okay*." The girl relented, slinging her carbine and grabbing the lieutenant's legs, "Damnit, Relena, you owe me."

She'd heard that name somewhere before. Arilin looked at her name tag. Strath-*wait*. Strathclyde. Then back up at her face. Honey-blonde hair and matching eyes with rakishly-slanted eyebrows that gave her a dashing look. God in heaven, she was Tom's *sister*. The older one, the one his parents spoiled. Relena Strathclyde gave her a look, "What's wrong, milady?"

Arilin shook her head, "Nothing, let's go." Ducking into the stairwell after the other three girls and their burden, she turned and added, "Just surprised to see you here. Your brother's heading to his regiment to get them moving."

Slamming the door shut behind them, Relena threw the backup deadbolt to lock it behind them and turned to look at her, "I know you two are friends, was he with you earlier?"

The servants' stairway was spacious but plain compared to the ballroom's splendor, lit by arched windows set into the exterior wall. Fortunately they had curtains drawn to keep the public from spying on the Palace staff coming and going, which would do just fine to keep any patrols outside from spotting them. The other three girls were already at the first landing and Arilin hurried up after them, saying, "Yes, he... actually helped me escape." Turning on the landing, she chuckled and added, "If your father comes through today I'll see about upgrading your title."

Unslinging her carbine, Relena ran up after her, turning to keep an eye on the entry door as they climbed. The three girls ahead of them quickly slowed under the lieutenant's weight, and Arilin grabbed one of her legs and pitched in as they hit the third landing. She looked up nervously as they went. Two landings per floor, and they needed to get to the fifth floor... she swallowed hard. Without anyone shooting at them to pin them down the cuirassiers would be free to push forward across the Long Ballroom. They were probably at the outer door already.

"Hear that, milady?" Relena asked as they climbed.

"No...?" Arilin trailed off.

The hussar replied grimly, "Exactly. Nobody's shooting." Right on cue something thudded dully below them. Giving the rest of them a look, Relena went on quietly, "That's the outer door, hurry up and keep quiet. Hopefully they won't hear us."

Arilin nodded and kept climbing, hauling her portion of the lieutenant's dead weight up the stairs. The woman groaned softly as they carried her, kicking and thrashing a little every few steps. Four flights up. Five. *Six.* Arilin felt her heart starting to drop back into her chest as they reached the bottom of the seventh flight when the door below them *thudded*, the noise loud as a gunshot in the quiet stairwell. They all froze instinctively. The door rattled as though whoever was on the other side was working the crash-bar, confused as to why it wasn't opening like it should. Glancing around at the others, Arilin whispered, "Keep going. *Quiet.*"

That got them going again, creeping up the stairs as quietly as they could. Their footsteps on the marble steps sounded like gunfire anyways. Arilin's heart thundered in her ears as the rattling stopped at the door far below, and someone faintly called out, "It's locked!"

A deeper, gruffer voice yelled back, "Shoot it open then, damn it! Stand back, I'll do it myself!"

"Move!" Arilin cried out, as a gunshot hammered out far below them. Then another, and another, as they desperately hauled the lieutenant's dead weight up the stairs. The door below thudded violently, once, twice, as the cuirassier kicked it viciously. Relena paused as they made the next landing, leaning out over the stairway with her carbine aimed down at the entryway far below. Arilin heard the click as she thumbed off her weapon's safety.

The door below finally gave way with a splintering crash as the cuirassier kicked it a third time, his jackboots hammering far below them as he lunged into the stairwell. Relena pulled the trigger, her weapon's blast half-deafening Arilin in the confined space as she fired. She heard the hussar's footsteps behind them as she rushed to catch up, then another deafening gunshot. And another, and another, as they got the lieutenant up that flight of stairs. They'd turned the corner when bullets started coming *up*. Ducking back from the railing, Relena yelled, "Hug the wall!"

Jackboots pounded, echoing over the ringing in her ears and the pounding of her heart. Something small and angry cracked off the stone overhead, showering them with fragments, and the girl on the lieutenant's other leg shrieked and made to drop her. Reaching out, Arilin snatched her collar and physically pulled her up after her, which was enough to keep her *carrying* the poor woman. Relena's carbine barked again as they turned onto the final landing and stared up at the door to the servants' quarters, standing there so cheerily lit by the morning sun. With her breath rasping in her throat and her limbs shaking with fatigue, it might as well have been in Drakenburg.

She'd faced dragoons before. Just a few more steps. Gritting her teeth, Arilin ordered, "Go! We can't stop now!" Glancing behind her, she yelled at Relena, "Go past us, get the door open!"

The hussar leapt past them, bullets snapping at her heels. Looking up after her, Arilin saw her start to work the latch from behind the door, then think better of it and step behind the cover of the wall before awkwardly reaching over and turning it from behind cover. Getting the door open a couple inches, Relena called out, "Friendlies coming out! We've got Princess Arilin with us!" More gunfire snapped beneath them, and she added, "And we're being chased!"

A familiar voice called out from beyond the door as they made it to the final landing, "What're you waiting for, get in here!"

Relena kicked the door open the rest of the way and held it open for the rest of them to carry the lieutenant in. They half-collapsed inside, to a horrified look from Becky as they set the lieutenant down and gasped for air. Arilin managed to glance behind herself to see Relena backing through the door with her carbine raised. A moment later the heavy wooden slab thudded shut and the girl slammed the locking bolt closed. Looking back to her maid, Arilin's eyes widened as she saw the pistol in the woman's hand.

Ignoring her, Becky knelt by the stricken lieutenant and probed at her wound with her free hand, the hussar's blood staining her white glove a brilliant, unsettling red as she peeled her breeches back and felt at the jagged gash down the woman's thigh. Something white glistened deep inside the mass of rent flesh, and Arilin felt her stomach heave as she looked away. After a moment her maid said, "She's lost a lot of blood and she's unconscious, but I should be able to patch her up... you really carried her all the way up here?"

"Yes, ma'am." Relena replied bluntly, "But we need to keep moving, if they start shooting through that door we're done for."

Right on cue they heard jackboots faintly in the stairwell outside. Grabbing the lieutenant under her arms, Becky dragged her brusquely to the side and out of the entryway, ordering, "You three, help me with her. Milady, you can take a rest."

Still gasping for air, Arilin nodded her thanks, then jumped as Relena fired her carbine behind them. Spinning around, she saw the girl leaning around the corner to the entry door, pushing her bolt forward for another shot. Someone cried out in pain and men cursed vilely outside as she fired again, then turned and rushed after her, the bolt of her carbine still pulled back as she felt at her ammunition pouches. Shaking herself back into action, Arilin turned herself and hurried after the others as they made the turn into the western servants' hall, footsteps clattering on the fine hardwood of the floor. Rounds clicked into a carbine's magazine behind her and Relena slammed her weapon's bolt home with a solid, metallic thunk, the stripper clip jingling faintly as it hit the ground and she asked, "How're you holding up, milady?"

Arilin shook her head and gave her what was probably a pretty bleak look, "Alright, I guess."

"There's the spirit. I think we've got this, milady." Gunfire hammered around the corner behind them and the hussar added, "We should hurry, though."

With four people carrying the lieutenant they were able to move at close to a run through the western hall, and as they emerged into the splendid central entry hall Becky started pulling the others towards the Residence's main entry stairs. Which had a magnificent view over the plaza to the south. Where the cuirassiers' artillery was currently parked. Arilin called towards them, "They've got guns in the plaza! Take the private stairs!"

Slowing, Becky looked back towards them quizzically, "Milady, you think...?"

"*Yes!*" Arilin shouted, more gunfire hammering dully behind them as she pointed across the entryway towards the servants' hall on the far side, "We'll go up through my rooms!"

Her maid gamely gestured towards the eastern hall, and they hurried across the entry hall's checkered hardwood toward its broad entryway. No doors to slam shut behind them. Thinking that she needed to get her father to improve Palace security, Arilin followed Becky and the others into the servants' hall with Relena on her heels. They had barely made it inside when a deafening blast shook the Palace behind them, and Arilin turned to see smoke billowing down at the far end of the hall. Explosives, powerful enough to smash the sturdy fire door clean off its hinges.

Shivering, Arilin darted ahead of the others and got the door to Becky's quarters open. Becky and the three hussars quickly maneuvered their burden inside and Arilin ducked in after them, Relena quickly swinging the door shut behind them and locking it. Glancing back at her, she asked, "Where to from here, milady? This is... wow, this is just for servants?"

They had emerged into a large sitting room, with a wide bay window overlooking the Palace's private gardens in its northern court. The War Ministry stood facing them nonchalantly. She was surprised there weren't snipers on its roof already. Becky chuckled, "*Just* a servant's room. God, milady, how do the maids in *your* place live?" It took Arilin a moment for her to realize she'd been talking to *Relena*. Who also happened to be a noblewoman. Her maid added, "Now come on, they won't be far behind us."

"Downstairs, two to a room." Relena muttered. Which Arilin supposed wasn't really that far off, there *were* two bedrooms in the servants' apartment. Although she suspected the Strathclyde servants didn't quite have as much space. Shaking her head, she followed Becky and the others around a corner as the maid pulled open a door that looked like it led into a broom closet.

It actually opened into a narrow staircase leading up. Setting her jaw, Becky said, "We'll have to do this with two of us, let me get her shoulders. Milady, we might get some blood on your clothes."

"No problem." Arilin replied cheerfully as the maid got her hands under the lieutenant's shoulders and started hauling her up the staircase, a hussar supporting her legs as they went. The rest of them crowded in behind them, Relena gently shutting the door after herself. As she did Arilin thought she heard heavy boots drumming out in the hallway.

After a few moments struggling up the staircase in the darkness, Arilin heard Becky work a knob above her and gently push a door open. God knew how she'd managed to get the doorknob and keep hold of the lieutenant. It didn't get any brighter as they emerged into a room that smelled of silk and perfume, their shoulders brushing against delicate fabric hanging in the murk. "Here, get her for me, I'll get the door," Becky said.

The hussars worked their way up and took the wounded lieutenant from her, and Becky gently cracked another door. Light from her bedroom window flooded inside as she opened it, revealing that they had emerged inside of her walk-in closet, hung with everything a modern princess might need for any occasion from peasant-chic gardening dresses to elaborate court gowns. The lieutenant had left an ugly spattering of blood on her carpet. Relena whistled appreciatively behind her. As Becky hurried out and quickly whipped the drapes shut over the window, Arilin volunteered, "You can put her on my bed."

"Use the table in the other room, I have to work on her." Her maid ordered. The hussars obediently carried their stricken commander through the doorway into her private parlor and set her down on the table inside. The woman didn't even moan or twitch, just laid there deathly-still, her blood seeping onto the dark hardwood and puddling beneath her. Noticing her, Becky gave her a hard look, "You'd best get out of here, milady, you've got the guards to attend to."

Gunfire crackled and something thudded faintly, somewhere out in the High City. Arilin hesitated, "And the other maids?"

Becky gave her a look, "Right now it's just me and Carmen, everyone else left with the Queen and Beatrice last night." She shook her head, "And Carmen's got... well, you're going to want to see it. It's something *else*. Now get going, milady."

Turning, Arilin looked around at the hussars, "Come with me, we'll set up at the main door." She snorted, "We keep those servants' stairs secret for a reason."

They stepped aside as she strode over to her suite's main door and pulled it open. Morning sunlight was flooding down through the Residence's skylights, lighting the central hall so brightly it was almost blinding after her room's curtained gloom. The air smelled of fresh-cut flowers from the gardens with an undercurrent of old wood and well-cleaned woolen carpets. It looked like home. It smelled like home. It *was* her home, and if the Foot Guards didn't hurry up she was probably going to die there in a few minutes.

Carmen had clearly been pacing nervously in the hallway when they emerged, and she jumped at the sound. Looking over at her with eyes wide, the bookish arcanologist put a hand to her chest and demanded, "Milady! What's happening? We've heard, and seen... well..." Her eyes widened as she looked down at her leg, "Are you hurt?"

Arilin shook her head, "It's not mine." She explained, "Alphonse's goons from the Second Cuirassiers are trying to kidnap me. I hope." She gave her a bleak look, "It might be murder. I barely got out of school ahead of them." She looked around, "Where are the guards? There should be a few up here."

"They're barricading the front door." Carmen replied matter-of-factly. Now that her ears had stopped ringing Arilin could make out female voices drifting down the hall. Something heavy fell to the floor and someone cursed loudly. Carmen had dropped her hand when Arilin looked back to her, and her eyes almost skipped over the jewel hanging around the maid's neck on a chain like flaming silver. *Almost*. Then she couldn't look away. It was like a baleful eye, a blood-red ruby the size of her thumb with a black slit like a cat's eye shot through it. Light sparked and danced in the endless darkness within.

Closing her eyes with a force of will, Arilin shook herself and looked back up at Carmen's face, avoiding that unholy *thing* she was wearing. Feeling a cold knife dragging its way up her spine, she demanded, "What in the name of *God* are you *wearing?*"

"Oh, this?" Carmen picked up the ancient jewel on its mithril chain and examined it lovingly for a moment, "One of your Eyes of Teldaros, milady." She smirked, "Those griffon feathers had more magic in them than I thought, it's actually starting to spark. I can't even *imagine* how it looked originally..."

"Just... put that thing back in the vault after this." Arilin replied, "That thing scares me."

"Ah... yes, milady." The mage replied disappointedly, "As you wish."

More gunfire crackled outside, and another distant boom rolled over the High City. Then another, and another. It sounded like a building battle out in the streets. Shaking her head, Arilin turned and headed for the main entrance with the others. They found four hussars hastily barricading the entryway with furniture that looked like it had come out of the private library. At least it was solid stuff... although probably not solid enough to stop bullets, she thought. Arilin called out as they turned the corner, "Good thing I wasn't planning on using *that* door!"

The girls jumped and spun around. More privates. God in Heaven, what had happened to their leaders? Although now that she thought about it, the less she knew about that the better. Behind her, Relena added, "There's more stairs you know."

One of the girls was opening her mouth to reply when heavy boots thrummed outside. "Get back!" Arilin cried, and the hussars scattered out of the entryway. Pointing across the hall at the library doors, she ordered, "Get to cover! *Get ready!*"

Pink-jacketed hussars rushed across the hall and dove into the cover of the heavy doorframes, unslinging carbines as they went. Behind her, she heard Relena flick off her safety as she braced her own weapon against the corner of the wall. Another girl did the same, a little farther back. Arilin felt her saber's hilt, the checkered steel and rough rayskin of its grip reassuring under her hand. For a long moment everything was quiet, silent, still, just the crackle of gunfire in the distance and her own heartbeat. She took a deep breath, held it for a moment, and let it out.

Bang! Bang! Bang! The enemy pounded on her front door. It sounded like someone using a rifle butt, the steel buttplate punching dents into the door's thick wood. A man's voice floated through from the far side, "*Open up! In the name of the King!*"

Behind her, Relena called back sarcastically, "No soliciting!"

Arilin giggled nervously. The cuirassier on the far side was unamused, "*Lay down your weapons and hand over Princess Arilin! This is your only warning!*"

Relena changed tack, "She's not here!"

Faintly, as though the cuirassier on the far side had turned and was talking to someone back down the stairs, she heard, "Blow the door."

"Milady." Relena grabbed her by the back of her collar and yanked her back into cover, then shouted, "*Open fire!*"

Carbines hammered, the Valkyrie Knights unloading their weapons into the door. A moment later something hit Arilin, *hard*, smashing her to the ground. Her ears rang as stinking smoke blotted out her vision. Shaking herself, she tried to move and realized that someone had fallen on top of her. Groaning, Relena rolled off of her and climbed to her feet, extending a hand to help her up. Arilin was just getting her own unsteady feet beneath her when she heard a shout, a building, rising battle cry that seemed to shake the Palace to its roots. Men's deep voices, screaming for blood and victory. Someone shouted over it, "*Forward! Attack!*"

Jackboots hammered on the stairs. A couple carbines fired. Jackboots hammered across the barricade's splintered wood. Someone started firing a pistol nearby. Jackboots hammered across the entryway, thunderous even on the deep carpet. Beside her, Relena drew her saber. Gritting her teeth, Arilin grasped her weapon's hilt and pulled it free as hulking shapes loomed in the smoke and demonic light flared behind them. Over the ringing in her ears, over the gunfire and the battle cries, someone was screaming in Elven she didn't understand.

The first enemy cuirassier plunged out of the smoke, fixed his eyes on the two of them as he raised his sword, and then turned his head to look over her shoulder, unholy red light reflecting in his widening eyes. Then something like a spike, a blade of light burning hellish red, slammed through his armored chest and poleaxed him backwards. Another emerged and was smashed backwards, then another, and another, the mage-bolts disintegrating into showers of bloody sparks an instant after they struck home.

Then another shape, a particularly big man, loomed out of the smoke, swinging his sword down as the demonic light flared again. Bloody, burning sparks flashed in a blinding shower as he cut the bolt out of the air, then again, and again, as more shapes loomed in the smoke behind him. Behind her, Carmen gave a bloodcurdling, animal scream and collapsed to the ground, and the magical furnace-light behind them died to the ruddy glow of the still-dancing sparks. Working his sword in his hand as he gave Arilin a murderous glare, General Chapman snarled, "You'll die for this, *bitch*."

Princess Arilin raised her sword and met his eyes, "*You first.*"

Chapter 44

The Valkyrie's Lance

Stinking ash rained from the sky, so thick their boots left prints on the ground as they staggered along beneath their burdens. His weight on her shoulders almost enough to drive her to her knees, Sergeant Cross had stopped groaning with every step she took. Now he just twitched, threatening to work his way off her back as she reeled from step to step, one leg to the other. They had done what they could for him, bandaged his side where something jagged had ripped it open. Scooped his organs back into the hole where they had threatened to spill out. Third Squad had been caught in the explosion with him. The ones they had managed to *find*, the ones who hadn't been buried in debris outright, had gotten it worse.

Looking up from the gray-coated grass in front of her boots, Sophia gasped, "Milady... how much farther?"

Almost lost in the dust and smoke ahead of her, Lieutenant Gable turned around and called back, "I don't know... it can't be much farther." Gasping, Sophia hiked Cross further up on her shoulders and was about to reply when she went on, "There! I see it, it's right ahead!"

Looking up again, Sophia could barely make out the corner of a sturdy brick building, half-smashed in from the blast. Somehow it hadn't been completely demolished. Even so, she could see that the Southbend train station was an absolute shambles as she dragged herself closer. Every window was blown out, and it looked like part of the roof had collapsed onto the tracks. Shapes appeared in the murk covering the platform and a voice called out, "Hey! Who-" Another artillery shell cracked off in the railyard, drowning them out for a moment, "-over here, we've got wounded coming in!"

More shapes swam out of the choking fog, jumping down off the platform and rushing over towards them. Medics with Red Cross armbands, a captain she vaguely recognized as the battalion's doctor and Major Matheson, angry as ever. Someone unfolded a stretcher, and two medics got hold of Cross' arms and legs and helped Sophia lay him down on it. She almost collapsed as his weight came off her shoulders. Looking over her shoulder wearily, she saw that the rest of her guys weren't in any better shape. Except for Kelly, who noticed her and gave her a grim thumbs-up. She couldn't say she was surprised, the man was built like a trash can. He'd carried the heaviest wounded man over his shoulder, holding his legs with one arm and his machine gun by its carrying handle with the other.

Sighing, Sophia shook her head and straightened up. The medics were fussing with Cross on the stretcher, feeling his neck, prodding the blood-soaked bandages around his abdomen. Checking his pulse, checking their work. They glanced at each other worriedly, and one of them curled up his fingers and viciously dragged his knuckles down the man's collarbone. Cross didn't even twitch. Looking up at her concernedly as his companion tried it again even harder, one of the medics asked, "Was he... conscious earlier? Responding at all?"

The other man looked up and called out, "Doc! Come over here!"

As the doctor looked up from inspecting another man's mangled leg and started making his way over, Sophia responded, "Yeah, he was groaning half the way over, every step I took..." She felt her heart chill, "Why... why do you ask?"

"Because he doesn't have a God-damn pulse." The medic shot back bluntly.

Sophia felt her eyes widening, "That can't be right, he was still moving a minute ago." She narrowed them with a force of will, "Check him again."

The doctor arrived as the medic was about to respond, volunteering, "Here, I'll do it, both of you calm down." Stooping, the man pressed his fingers into Cross' throat. Seconds dragged by. Finally, he pulled the man's mouth open with a finger, felt inside. Felt his nose, trying to feel his breath. Cross' eyes were open, staring aimlessly at the sky. Shaking his head, the doctor reached out and closed them, announcing coldly, "He's dead. Find a blanket to cover him and put him out back once we've finished with the others." He grimaced, "The two that aren't *expectant* anyways. We don't have a hell of a lot to work with here." He looked over at her coldly as he stood, "Nothing you could have done, corporal."

She was staring at him blankly. She'd known Sergeant Cross for... the whole war, and years before it. He'd been a friend of her father's, one of the gang of sergeants that ran Charlie Company, always there, haranguing the officers, checking on her friends like a mother hen. Shepherding them along for the whole war so far, up and down Fire Ridge, across the Dragonspines and half the New Kingdom. And now he was gone, just like that. He hadn't even said anything to her, or anyone else for that matter. For him it must have been just a flash, and pain, and darkness. Her vision blurred, and she finally shook her head and said, "I... I'm sorry."

"Nothing to be sorry about." Clapping her on the shoulder, the man spun her around brusquely and pushed her towards where Lieutenant Gable and Major Matheson were talking, saying, "Now go pry the XO off your lieutenant and get your guys some coffee, we have a tureen that survived the explosion."

God-damn it to Hell. Shaking her head slowly, Sophia replied, "Yes...

sir. Will do." Looking over her shoulder, she called out, "Come on, guys! We need to get going."

Her voice shook the others out of their own private stupors, and they straggled after her as she walked over to the two officers. Matheson was saying, "...company's pushed out on the north side of the railyard. How are you set up?"

Lady Gable replied, "I've got a squad down by the bridge with..." She clearly did some counting in her head, "Four machine guns now." Hargrave's men had cleaned up Third Squad's weapons and ammunition, "They're not going anywhere. And I've got these guys."

"Good, you're staying here then." Matheson snorted, "We need a reserve."

Her lieutenant raised an eyebrow, "That's confidence-inspiring."

"*Isn't it.*" The major smirked, "Now go get some coffee and settle down, it's going to be a long day and you look bad already." He shot a glance over Sophia's shoulder at the doctor, "I heard you just now, you know. Don't you have patients to treat?"

Behind her, the man snorted and turned back to the wounded. Sophia followed Lieutenant Gable as she walked back to the half-ruined station and climbed the short flight of stairs up to the platform, now strewn with broken glass and bits of stonework knocked loose by the explosion. There were already a dozen wounded soldiers lined up along the wall, men she recognized from the other companies. Fortunately, the medics had set up the aid station on the near side of the tracks to the railyard. The far side was a jagged mass of broken girders from the roof coming down. They quickly located the coffee pot, a big silver can sitting on one end of a table someone had pulled out onto the platform.

Jenny Musgrave was occupying the other end with her typewriter and a sourer look than usual. Corporal Musgrave now, if the shoulder-boards on her skirted uniform were anything to go by. She raised an eyebrow, "You look like you've had a rough morning. Help yourselves." She went on, deadpan, "Unfortunately no snacks yet, I haven't had the chance to go out and forage. Check back after the battle."

Sophia shook her head, "Thanks... we lost some guys just now."

The woman gave her what was, by her standards, an extremely sympathetic look. Which meant her eyes narrowed a little, "Sorry to hear."

"Yeah, thanks." Sophia looked back at her friends, "Well, what're we waiting for?"

Tony already had his canteen cup half-full. Behind him, Edward looked between her and Lady Gable and winked, "You two." Sophia rolled her eyes and he snorted.

Eventually she got her coffee and sat down against the wall with the others, rifle between her legs. They drank silently. There wasn't much to say, really, and the occasional artillery shell cooking off out in the railyard made conversation difficult anyways. Gunfire crackled in the distance off by their regimental barracks, interspersed with the occasional cracking shell and the loud popping of their mortars firing from somewhere nearby. Closing her eyes, Sophia listened to the battle as it washed around her. She almost didn't want to, but it was second nature at this point.

Fighting off to the east, towards Regiment on the outskirts of town, enemy rifles almost as loud as their own. The other companies must be in close combat with the dragoons. As she listened the roar of an autocannon bellowed above the chorus of gunfire as an Imperial tank made itself known. Artillery shells still cooking off in the burning railyard, sending shrapnel plinking down in the wreckage on the far side of the building. Nothing off to the northeast, where the rest of Charlie Company should have set up to block the streets past the railyard... or was there?

Over the roaring fire and pounding shells, off past the inferno, Sophia could hear distant banging. For a moment she thought it was just rifle rounds cooking off in the fire, she'd been hearing those for a while now, but... no. Those were much too close, and they sounded different. This was actual gunfire. *Imperial* gunfire, high and sharp. Occasionally a deeper Royal rifle or machine gun would snap back at the enemy, but by the sound of it they were losing badly. Lady Gable had sat down next to her, and Sophia gave her a nervous look, "Milady, I think Delta's getting overrun right now. North of us, where they went in."

The lieutenant gave her a quizzical look back, "I can't hear anything, are you sure?"

Tony cut in from her other side, "If she hears it, it's happening." He added, "You want us in position, Sophie?"

"Yeah, get ready while we figure out where." Sophia looked over at her lieutenant, "Where do you want us, milady?"

Gable got to her feet, dusting herself off and arranging her saber at her side deliberately. Looking down at her, she smiled, "Let's figure that out."

"Sure thing." Shaking herself, Sophia hauled herself to her feet and looked down at her guys, "You all come too."

Tony groaned theatrically, but they all got up and followed along as Sophia walked down the platform after Lady Gable. The pall of dust around the railyard was starting to clear under the drizzling rain, and they could see the twisted wreckage of the packed trains through the jagged holes the station's windows had once filled. Flames were still reaching into the sky from the center of the railyard, red-hot, fifty feet tall and billowing inky black smoke. Sophia remembered that she'd seen more than a few cars hauling coal, oil and gasoline out in the yard, on top of the ammunition train. The railyard would probably burn for days at this rate.

The warehouses were closer, a couple rows of drab buildings lining the east side of the railyard, running perpendicular to the station and about level with it. The nearer ones were half-crumpled from the blast, debris strewing the concrete lane between them. Right of them was the town proper, low-rises with shops and cheap apartments in what she recalled was a workers' neighborhood, so close to the railyard and the ferry terminal that the smoke and noise outweighed the convenience. As they watched, two gray-jacketed soldiers ran out of an alley trailing a reel of communications wire behind them, turned and headed for the station down the road running alongside the tracks.

"Well, I don't think they're going to try coming through the railyard, and the river's covered by the ships." Gable observed, pointing on either side of the right-hand row of warehouses, "I'm not sure what the rest of the company's covering, but I don't see them in those two lanes."

"They're probably pushed out, covering the main road." Edward weighed in.

"How far out?" Gable asked.

He shrugged, "Could be on the far side of the railyard. It curves towards the river farther down to run by the ferry terminal."

Sophia thought for a moment, then said, "We don't need to make this complicated. One gun down each lane. Milady?"

Lieutenant Gable nodded, "Works for me."

"Alright." Sophia looked around at her guys, "Kelly, you've got the right-hand lane. You should be able to set up behind the steps at the far end of the platform. Tony, take the left-hand one between the warehouses. Find a table to set your gun up on, these walls will stop bullets." She looked at her two riflemen, "Ed, James, think you two can put together some bundle charges?"

Edward nodded, "I count fourteen between us. If we use four extra cans per we'll have some left over for personal use." He glanced at the communications team, just then running up onto the platform with their wire, "We'll mug those guys for wire."

"Good." Sophia pulled three grenades off her belt and handed them to him, leaving one hanging at her side. The two men promptly turned and started making menacing faces at the poor wiremen, and Sophia turned to look at her lieutenant, "Looks like we're set up, milady."

Gable nodded politely, "Excellent. Thank you, corporal."

That left her... completely unoccupied. Sighing, Sophia instinctively patted her spear where she'd slung it across her back in its carrier, and it occurred to her that the command post could use a flag. God only knew where the battalion colors were, probably up front with the main attack over by Regiment. Unslinging it, she popped it open and pulled the spearhead and the four pieces of its shaft out, unrolled the flag she had wrapped around the topmost segment and started putting it together. It had been designed to pack down with pins and locking collars securing the pieces together tightly, and she quickly got it assembled, pulled the scabbard off the lethal spearhead and hefted it experimentally. Faint patterns glimmered across the blade's steel in the dull light, ghosts of an engraved design that had long since faded with sharpening. Even with the flag on it was beautifully light and well-balanced, a hundred times better than a bayoneted rifle. Sophia let herself have a satisfied half-smile as she swung it around experimentally, then turned to go find her guys.

Ed and James had managed to bully the wire party out of enough field telephone wire to put together their demolition charges with, and the put-upon signalmen had escaped to plug in a field telephone on Jennifer's desk by the coffee pot. Lady Gable was just starting to talk to Lieutenant Thorn when Major Matheson kicked her off and started talking on it himself, and the girl slunk off with a sour look on her face. Snorting, Sophia walked over to her own boyfriend's table, thankful that she didn't have to appropriate time on a military telephone to talk to *him*. A handy potted plant stood beside his table, and Sophia planted her spear there by its buttspike for safekeeping as she arrived.

Tony had pulled up a chair so he could slay the enemy with maximum comfort, and had popped open his machine gun's field tray and was drizzling oil into its feed mechanism. Looking over as she walked up, he scowled, "Got any more ammo? If the Masks come up here I don't want to fumble with a new belt."

"Yeah, sure." Sophia took off her cloth bandolier with its one remaining belt and handed it over, "You doing alright, Tony?"

"What do you think?" Tony snapped, "I knew *all* those guys, I carry Jake all the way up here on my shoulders and the medics take one look at him and says there's nothing they can do." Very deliberately, he popped the bandolier open, unreeled the ammunition belt inside and threaded it into the one already spilling out of his gun's hopper, "*God-damn* medics, don't give a damn about us. *God-damn* Masks. I don't know what the *hell* I was thinking joining the Army."

Sophia snorted, "I know *exactly* what you were thinking, Tony."

He gave her a look, then snorted and turned back to his gun. After a long moment, he looked back at her and asked, "Sophie... when this is over, you want to go back home together?"

"I'm not planning on leaving Jade Falls, but," Sophia smiled, "I don't think that's what you're asking."

Setting the belt of rounds down on the weapon's feed tray, Tony flipped the feed cover down, tapped it to lock it into place and racked the action back, saying, "You know what I meant."

"I did." Reaching out, Sophia set her hand over his where it was resting on the machine gun's wooden buttstock. Looking back at him, she nodded, "And yeah, I think I'd like that. Sounds cozy, right?"

Tony cracked a smile, "Yeah, it does."

Edward cleared his throat loudly behind them, "I've got those bombs ready, by the way, just making sure I'm not interrupting anything here." The both gave him a dirty look, and he walked up and set the heavy charges on the table beside the gun. He had taken the cylindrical heads off four grenades for each of them and wired them tightly around a central grenade with its throwing handle and igniter still attached, the whole assembly forming a flat X-shape. He added snidely, "They kill tanks *and* romantic atmospheres."

"Go to hell, Ed." Tony growled.

He snipped back, "If I go with you two, do you think the ferryman will take us through the Tunnel of Love?"

Sophia snickered, "I don't know, do you *want* to feel lonely?"

Edward sighed theatrically, "You're much too cruel. Tony, I'd think twice with this one."

"*Go to hell, Ed.*" Tony ground out through gritted teeth.

Edward was opening his mouth to say something even snappier when Sophia cut in, "Alright, alright, get along, you two." Turning on her heel, she walked away before they started back up again. She was just thinking, *Men*, when a green spark caught her eye, rising over the rooftops through the windows to her left. A harsh, Imperial crack popped in the distance a second later. Then another, and then the air filled with hammering gunfire as what sounded like a couple platoons opened up on each other.

Sophia flattened herself against the wall instinctively for a moment, then peeked out around the nearest window as the firefight built. Green and blue tracers were sparking to the right side of the warehouses, over the town's tile roofs. As she took a moment to look, however, Sophia felt her eyes narrowing. Some of the Imperial rounds were flying *right*, not streaking overhead towards her. Which meant Charlie Company wasn't being hit head-on, someone was pushing from their left. Which meant they *weren't* covering the edge of the railyard and the warehouses, or at least they weren't going to be able to very well. And if the sinking feeling in the pit of her stomach was anything to go by, that was probably deliberate and a certain long-haired bastard she knew was involved.

"*Contact!*" Kelly shouted from his position down at the end of the platform, "Just saw a dragoon run across the street, left to right! Two more now!"

Unslinging her rifle, Sophia rushed over, calling out, "How far!"

Kelly didn't look up from his position behind the gun as she arrived, "They're down at the end, it's a ways. Maybe five, six hundred. Damn, there's another one."

Lieutenant Gable arrived, holding her sword steady as she ran, "Well, what are you waiting for? Open fire!"

"Yes, ma'am." Kelly said, deadpan, as he squeezed the trigger and his machine gun hammered to life.

Looking over at Gable, Sophia said, "Milady, we need to-" An Imperial bullet smacked into concrete nearby, "-get to cover."

The girl nodded quickly and scrambled back into the protection of the station wall, while Sophia ducked behind the concrete stairs and watched Kelly work. Down at the end of the street she saw a dark shape run across the street. Kelly fired a short burst after it, dust rising at its heels as it disappeared into a warehouse. Just as the echoing gunfire died down she heard Tony call, "Guys, we've got a problem!"

Getting up, Sophia ran back down the tracks until she was level with Tony and heaved herself up onto the platform. Lieutenant Gable had made it ahead of her, and even from behind she looked like she had seen a ghost. Crawling up to Tony's position, Sophia got up on one knee beside him and looked across his table, out the window and down the lane between the warehouses.

A boxy green shape had nosed out into the far end of the street and was slowly trundling towards them, navigating its way through the larger piles of debris that had been blasted into the lane by the explosion. The smaller ones it crushed beneath its tracks. An Imperial tank. As they watched another one nosed out behind it, angling towards the other side of the lane to cover its companion. Tony remarked nervously, "You know, the cannons on those things will go straight through this wall."

"Do you have a better idea?" Lieutenant Gable asked, then said doubtfully, "We can see if the company can get their antitank rifles down here."

Standing up beside the window and out of view, Sophia picked up one of the bundle charges Edward had left on the table and replied, "We've got these."

Gable objected, "We can't let those things get all the way up here."

She was right, of course. For a moment Sophia felt like she was floating outside of her own body, looking down at herself holding the demolition charge. So this was what it felt like, knowing you were about to die and there was nothing you could do about it. Finally, she set her jaw and said, "We won't. I'll go to them."

The lieutenant gave her an alarmed look, her eyes narrowing, "If we're attacking, we're all going."

"I guarantee you they've got a platoon down there at least covering those things, milady." Sophia shot back, "I can get in and out quick. If we all go we'll get bogged down and killed."

"You're sure?" Gable asked worriedly.

Sophia nodded, and was opening her mouth to reply when Tony cut in, "You're not going without me, Sophie." She looked at him, to see that he had set his own jaw determinedly as he glared back at her, "You're just *not*. I don't care. And anyways," He tried to chuckle as he picked up the other demolition charge, "You throw like a girl."

Sophia snorted and handed him her charge, "Alright then. I'll clear the way."

She looked up to see Major Matheson approaching. He remarked, "Judging by the gunfire, I'd say we have company. What's going on?"

Kelly fired off another short burst down at the end of the platform, probably more to remind the enemy that he was there than anything else. Given how enthusiastic he usually was, it didn't seem like he had a whole lot to shoot at. Lady Gable gave a nervous glance down the platform, then turned back to the battalion's executive officer, "We've got tanks coming at us and these two idiots want to go out and blow them up."

Tony added, "I really wouldn't stand in front of this window, by the way. Sir." Looking around nervously, he slid his chair back, pulled the machine gun off the table and set it on the floor, then carefully sidled out of view of the enemy tanks out in the lane.

Major Matheson peeked out anyways, then turned to them and grimaced, "Yeah, that's a problem." He looked between them, "You've got a plan?"

"Yep." Sophia reached over and yanked her spear out of the pot, hefting it experimentally, "Guns attract attention. We move fast, I clear the way, he throws. Simple."

Tony swallowed hard, then hefted the two demolition charges and said, "In and out, sir."

Matheson sighed and shook his head, "I wish I could tell you no right now. Charlie's getting hit hard, they're not going to be able to stop this." He chuckled grimly, "We'll have to distract them, you know. You've got someone else for this machine gun, Gable?"

The lady lieutenant nodded, "Yes, sir."

"Alright then." The major looked between them and nodded, "You'd better get going. We'll start hitting those tanks as soon as you get across the street, keep their attention focused on us."

Sophia peeked out herself. The tanks had moved about a hundred meters closer, pushing their way cautiously forward. They would have to get through one warehouse completely, and then maybe cross a street and get into the second one to get at the tanks. Most likely the infantry would be ahead of them, clearing the way forward through the warehouses. Unslinging her rifle and working her cavalry bandolier loose, Sophia set them against the wall and replied, "For you, sir. You might need it." Running her spear down her hands, she quickly unpicked the knots holding Charlie Company's colors to her spear, and handed the worn, bullet-torn flag to Lady Gable, "Milady."

"Stay alive, corporal." Lieutenant Gable said as she took it, "Your father scares me."

Sophia laughed, "He scares me!" She looked over at Tony, who by now had turned white as a sheet, and added, "And his sister will hex me if he gets killed. We'll be fine." Turning, she ran for the platform's central entrance, calling over her shoulder, "Come on, Tony! Let's go!"

Fortunately the central stairs faced the intact row of warehouses. She rushed down them spear in hand, hearing Tony clattering down behind her. The blast earlier had blown the warehouse's street door loose, and she eased it open and ducked through. The air inside was dark and still, choked with dust thrown up from the explosion. Through the murk she could make out crates and big, heavy-looking sacks piled up ahead with professional care, dense ranks of goods hulking in the darkness running down the warehouse lengthwise. Tony ducked in after her, and she murmured, "Come on, follow me. And keep quiet, they might be in here with us already."

Bent forward instinctively, Sophia hurried forward with Tony close behind her. At least he had enough sense to keep far enough back that he wasn't in danger from her spear's buttspike. They had just gotten into the first row when the machine gun hammered to life behind them, bullets cracking past unsettlingly out in the street. Sophia sped up, eyes searching through the choking murk, ears pricked for enemy footsteps as she hurried along, turning left as an aisle opened up between the rows and moving closer to the tanks' side of the building. Autocannons roared back as she did, heavy shells smashing into the station's masonry walls. It sounded *close*, they had to have almost moved up to the end of the warehouse they were in.

Sophia's heart rose as their machine gun chattered back determinedly, and she broke into a run as she turned into the next row of piled goods, the pea-soup murk lightening as they moved closer to the blown-out windows at the far end of the warehouse. She angled left again as she emerged, another burst of autocannon fire hammering out as they passed into the aisle. By the looks of things there were three separate sets of rows of goods stacked up for shipment, and after the next one they would emerge at the rear wall. The second tank opened fire with what sounded like a machine gun, very close, probably in the lane between the warehouses themselves, almost drowning out the sound of voices in the next aisle as she paused at its end.

Sophia flattened herself to a crate and motioned for Tony to do the same. The first tank hammered out another long burst with its autocannon as he silently pressed himself against the crate beside her. She slid her last grenade from its place at her belt, whispering, "They're down there, I hear them. Follow me when I go."

Tony had tucked the two demolition charges through his belt, but he had a spare grenade of his own. Pulling it out, he said, "I'll put this down the other side when you throw, it'll distract them."

"Good thinking." She cracked off the safety cap on her grenade and worked the igniter cord through the fingers of her left hand, the little porcelain ball gripped tightly against her spear's shaft. Taking a deep breath, she counted down, "Three, two, one... *go*."

Sophia yanked the igniter, the grenade hissing evilly in her hand as the fuse lit. Stepping around the corner, she whipped it down the pathway as hard as she could and ducked back into cover, bumping into Tony as he did the same thing. She was pretty sure she'd seen silhouettes in the gloom, about halfway down. One of the tanks fired again as she and Tony pressed themselves against the crates, but she faintly heard someone shout, "*Grenade! Get do-*"

The warehouse flashed and hammered, once, twice, like a giant had used its corrugated roof for a drum. Sophia was already around the corner, *sprinting*, spearhead flaming through the darkness. Someone was screaming in the murk in front of her, someone else shouting as shrapnel gritted beneath her feet and she came out of the smoke like a steel-tipped comet. A bayonet burned in the gloom as a dragoon lunged at her, and she rammed her spear through the man's throat before he could even uncoil. Another gleamed behind it as she pushed forward, Sophia choking up on her spear to rip it free with brute force and snap it forward again, poleaxing the second dragoon in mid-parry.

The brutal arc of an Imperial sword flashed in front of her, a dragoon screaming a battle cry as she jerked her spear free, spun the weapon around her head and *swung*. Her spear hit the man like a razor-edged sledgehammer, battering his sword aside. He toppled as she twisted to pull her spearhead back under control, his head falling backwards disconcertingly as she turned back to her front and dug in her feet. The warehouse's rear doors swam out of the murk in front of her, big cargo doors and a smaller man-sized one on the left side, all of them blown crazily askew by the explosion. And dragoons, two of them, raising their rifles.

Sophia was faster. Sprinting forward, she slammed her spear through the first one's chest, and ran over him, hammering him down as the second one fired, the bullet snapping by as she pulled her spear free with her momentum and leapt forward, swinging the blade overhead like an eight-foot hammer. It went clean through his head and halfway through his rifle's stock, coming free as she snapped it back up. Tony's feet pounded beside her as he sprinted for the side door, demolition charge already in hand, a dragoon appearing in the crack of the loading doors and raising a rifle at him. *Wrong target.* Sophia lunged forward again, spear snapping forward like a viper to catch the woman in the side of her head under her helmet.

Sophia burst into daylight as Tony slammed through his own door, looking over to see him practically face to face with the tanks. He had a demolition charge in each hand and strings trailing from his *mouth* as he threw them both at once. One of the tanks, the closer one, had a hatch on the side of its turret open, a masked soldier leaning halfway out of it with a pistol in hand. Firing. Firing at Tony, the back of his uniform punching out, blood spraying once, twice, three, four times from her best friend's back. Her love turned to look at her one last time, eyes wide with fear as he staggered and fell and the world exploded.

Concrete bit into her back as the blast slammed her backwards. Feeling an icy hand ripping her heart out of her chest, Sophia leapt to her feet. The tanks were pillars of white-hot fire, shredded and hammering like drums as their ammunition cooked off. Tony was... Tony was... she couldn't even see him, in the pall of smoke and dust from the charges. Where was... where was... she needed to leave, she couldn't stay, it was dangerous, where had he-

"Miss Rose." June Anjanou said it quite conversationally, "You're starting to piss me off."

She looked over to see him drawing his sword.

Chapter 45

Bloody Hands

Chapman roared and leapt at her, his sword flashing blood-red in the demonic light as it descended. He wasn't as tall as her brother had been, but he was built like a Dominion fighting bull and his blade came down like a splitting maul, impossible to block, too heavy even to parry aside. Backing up slightly, Arilin whipped her saber around in a short, circular chop and beat his massive weapon aside. Lunging back at him, she slashed at his face and he pulled his sword back to smash her cut aside with his sword inverted, his weapon's point starting to trace a brutal circle around his hips as he continued the motion around his head.

Arilin leapt backwards as his vicious, reaping blow shrieked towards her horizontally, his sword's tip flashing by an inch from her eyes. Her feet touched the carpet again, digging in as Chapman seemed to coil into himself, sword-arm pulling back as his legs flexed and his point came back online. Shapes boiled out of the smoke behind him, more cuirassiers and Relena rolling back to her feet from where she had fallen to avoid his slash. Half of an Elven word she didn't understand echoed through her mind, and the bloody red mage-light exploded around them again as Chapman lunged.

Sparks flashed as she turned his thrust aside, and she dodged aside as he raised his sword and slashed down at her again. Temporarily out of reach, her opponent glanced aside, towards the hellfire glow burning back down the Residence's broad central hallway. It looked like a wall of burning red light had stretched itself across the hallway, silhouetting Relena's slender figure and the three or four hulking cuirassiers who had followed Chapman after her. Golden Elven filigree danced in its unworldly glow, and off to the side Arilin saw Carmen had pushed herself back up onto her knees. Even facing away from her, the mage's glowing eyes and the gem at her breast turned the smoke and dust pouring through the hall into an unholy corona.

"Kill the girl and the witch." Chapman ordered coldly, then turned back to her, "This one's *mine*."

Arilin saw Relena raise her saber to defend herself, and then Chapman was upon her. His first backhand slash forced her to leap backwards again. Stars exploded in her vision as the far wall slammed into her kidneys and he lunged forward, stabbing at her abdomen as he tried to pin her to the wall like a skewered butterfly. Raising her hilt, she forced his sword aside again, dodging aside and slashing at him as his weapon's point embedded itself in the wooden paneling.

Chapman turned aside contemptuously as he yanked his sword free, and her saber clattered harmlessly off his steel breastplate. Smirking as she backpedaled out of his reach again, he worked his weapon in his hand and growled, "You're a quick one, aren't you."

He was huge. Tall, with almost her brother's dueling hall-crossing reach. Armored. Incredibly strong. And for a man of his age, remarkably quick on his feet. She didn't have *anything* on him, not really. Maybe a little speed and agility, against a man with a good foot of reach on her and the strength to crush her into paste. Cold fear prickled in Arilin's heart as she met his eyes again, flat, dark, glazed a hateful red from the mage-light. The corners wrinkled with something akin to glee as he strode towards her, lips skinning back from his teeth in a murderer's smile.

Arilin grit her teeth and was shooting back, "Fast en-" when Chapman's screamed a battle cry and cut her off. He lunged at her, sword coming straight down in another vicious blow. She beat it to the side, then had to parry again desperately as he disengaged his sword under her own and lunged again, thrusting at her abdomen. Dodging aside and snapping her own blade over his, Arilin turned his thrust aside and stepped back in outside of him, slashing at his exposed arm.

The cuirassier beat her saber aside with his basket-hilt and marched forward, sword hissing as it snapped through the air like a striking snake. Off to her side she heard Relena scream something and someone started firing a pistol out in the hall as Chapman came at her again, face under his helmet's steel brow-plate contorted with hate, demonic in the bloody mage-light. Now retreating the other way across the hall, Arilin saw the open doorway behind her out of the corner of her eye as she parried another murderous blow, and she leapt backwards through it into one of their sitting rooms. The same one the ministers had come to harass her mother in, that night the war started so long ago.

Chapman slashed at her again as she retreated inside, his sword taking a gouge out of the doorframe and sticking as he overshot her. Seeing her chance, Arilin lunged, cutting at his exposed wrist as he tried to yank it free. Instead of retreating Chapman bulled forward, sending her saber skittering off his helmet as he charged into the room after her. His sword-blade fell behind him as she retreated farther into the room, Chapman leaping forward again with another vicious overhand cut.

Too close to retreat, too powerful to block, and if she fell backwards to duck under she'd die before she got back up. But her brother had taught her one move, just in case she absolutely needed to block a power-blow. Gritting her teeth, Arilin set her free hand against the back of her sword and *braced*. Sparks flew as her saber rang and pain shot through her hands, his blow powerful enough to send her staggering backwards. She had just gotten her feet back under herself and was bringing her sword back online when she looked up to see Chapman's deranged eyes inches from her own, his left hand a vicious blur as it snapped forward and slammed closed around her throat.

Arilin felt her feet come off the floor, kicking helplessly as Chapman roared his victory and charged forward, his fingers tightening around her throat like steel pincers. Something hit her in the back, *incredibly* hard, so hard it would have driven the breath from her lungs if she'd been able to breathe. Wood splintered and glass shattered as he smashed her clean through the glass-paneled doors onto the balcony, all the better to kill her in full view of the entire High City. As the color drained out of her world, Arilin saw Chapman in grayscale, drawing his sword back dramatically to finish her off. As he did, she got her left hand around behind her back, under the jacket of her now-bloody school uniform.

Arilin's sword-arm moved like it was stuck in molasses, but it still moved as he stabbed, somehow pushing Chapman's blade aside one last time. Through the darkness clouding down, Arilin saw Chapman's eyes widen as her left hand came free with the knife Becky had given her so long ago gripped in her fist, stabbing it into, through his free arm. Cutting, the sharp little blade going down his forearm like his thick uniform wasn't even there, something hot soaking her own arm as it hit something and hung up, the smooth, lacquered handle slipping from her fingers.

Something hit her in the back again, *hard*, and Arilin gasped. *Gasped*, air flowing into her lungs as her vision cleared. She was flat on her back on the balcony's smooth tiles, with what felt like broken glass digging into her back, and a man was crying out in pain nearby. Shaking herself, Arilin looked to see Chapman had staggered backwards, blood spraying sickeningly from his whole left forearm to where her knife's handle stuck out of his elbow. Noticing her moving, he hefted his sword and screamed, *"You'll pay for this!"*

Arilin rolled to her feet and gave him a cold look. She was about to reply when she heard something, far off and far below. It sounded like... cheering? Shouting, and gunfire. It sounded like the cuirassiers from earlier, before they had burst through her front door, but so much larger and so much farther away. Arilin glanced over, across the plaza and down the grand boulevard, and her eyes widened.

The massive street was *sparking* as the morning sun caught the bayonets of the avalanche of gray-jacketed infantry pouring down it, men roaring as they charged. Carbines popped weakly from the palace as they came on, sending a few soldiers toppling into the street. The others shouted louder and sped up. A soldier in red and black was running at their head, the regiment's colors in one hand and a sword in the other.

Tom, coming to rescue her with the whole First Guards Infantry Regiment at his back.

Feeling herself smirking ever so slightly, Arilin turned back to Chapman and replied coldly, "No, I won't."

Gargling what should have been a battle cry, the cuirassier general lurched at her, bringing his sword down at her head. Slashing up against him, Princess Arilin batted the weak blow aside, spun her saber around her head on its own momentum and hopped a little to get the angle right as her blade came around. Glass crunched underfoot as she came back down lightly. Across from her, almost close enough to touch, Chapman gave her one last furious look as he toppled. His head came off as he hit the ground.

Shivering, Arilin stood there looking at her enemy for a long moment, as his body twitched and his blood pooled on the tiles. It wasn't like she hadn't seen death before, or horrible wounds. Or blood, so bright it almost glowed in the sunlight. And it wasn't like she hadn't fought, she'd left a saber stuck through a dragoon's chest near Fire Ridge. But this... she'd never *killed* before. Not a person.

Shouting from inside brought her back to her senses, and she looked up to see Relena stepping out onto the balcony, wobbling on her feet unsteadily. The hussar's pink jacket and white breeches were spattered with blood, but the sword in her hand was still clean. "Milady!" She called, then looked down at the body crumpled at Arilin's feet, "You... you really?"

"Yeah, I... I..." The words wouldn't come out. Looking down at herself, Arilin saw her own sword, the blade gouged and nicked and the bottom third smeared with blood, already congealing into an ugly stain laced across the bright metal. It had been a perfect cut. She had *made* a perfect cut. Arilin felt herself fish for her handkerchief instinctively to clean it, and then she felt her bile rise.

Relena helpfully grabbed her from behind to keep her from collapsing outright as she vomited, then straightened her up, put her free arm around her shoulders and half-dragged her back inside. Becky appeared in the hall doorway as they got back into the sitting room, and the sight of her almost made Arilin's stomach heave again. The maid's shining-white uniform was *covered* with blood, most of it brilliant, arterial red. She had slung Carmen over her shoulder and was steading her with one arm. In the other she held a blood-drenched infantry sword. Arilin recognized it as one from her own collection in her room.

The mage's lips were still moving, and Becky's shocking appearance was made even worse by the hellish, magical light from the shield down the hall. Somehow it was still intact. She could dimly hear men shouting out in the hall, on the far side of the barrier. Becky gave them both a strained smile and gritted, "Good to see you, milady. Now-" She paused, groaning as she adjusted the mage heavily over her shoulders, "We need to get out of here, I don't think Carmen can keep this up."

Arilin shook herself and Relena let her go. Grimly pulling out her handkerchief and wiping the film of gore off her sword, she sheathed the weapon as she stepped out into the hallway and looked down the hall away from the entryway, towards her parents' chambers. "Let's get to my father's office," she announced, "We can barricade the door, and I think it might be armored. Help's on the way, we can hold out."

"Okay, milady." Becky replied. Arilin glanced over at her for a moment, but her eyes widened as she saw what had spread across the hallway *behind* her. The wall of hellish, red light that had stretched across the hallway was somehow boiling and cracking at the same time, cuirassiers on the far side half-lit shadows as they beat and stabbed at it with their swords. Something flashed dimly and a muffled gunshot rang out as another large crack appeared in the barrier. Her maid had followed her eyes, and she added nervously, "And let's hurry."

They ran down the hall as fast as they could, Relena rushing ahead of them to pull the door to her father's office open. The barrier made an unholy *ripping* sound as they dragged it down the hall behind them, Arilin getting her arms around Becky and pushing her down the hall as she struggled to pull Carmen against an invisible force that seemed to drag back at her. Or almost-invisible, anyways. The air around them sparked and crackled as they went, magic arcing around their bodies like searing-hot electricity.

Finally they stumbled into her father's office, pulled in by Relena with a desperate effort. The girl slammed the door shut behind them, locked it, and started dragging furniture in front of it to make a barricade. Arilin swept her father's desk clean with a clatter of expensive pens and desk ornaments, and Becky rolled the mage off her shoulders and onto it. Carmen's eyes and that evil jewel around her neck were *glowing* a terrifying red, a mage-light that flickered, sputtered and went out as they watched, leaving just an empty, old gem and the girl's eyes, lolling crazily in their sockets and welling blood.

The energy swirling around them like static before lightning flashed and disappeared utterly, and for a moment Arilin knew what it was that had driven so many of the old mages insane. The magic was gone, disappeared into the great nothingness of the world, with no way to bring it back. Just dusty books and Elven trinkets that had once held unimaginable power. But she could ponder the existential wrongness of living in a mundane age later. Shaking herself, Arilin looked over at her companions and asked, "Are you two alright?"

Relena had just finished pulling a particularly sturdy-looking couch in front of the door, and she glanced back at her, "Yeah... yes, milady. Your maid saved my skin."

Arilin looked over at Becky, who was slowly shaking herself and standing up. She'd had a pistol on her earlier... that must have been the gunfire she'd heard. Becky must have come out of her room firing and then attacked with sword in hand as Relena had faced down those two cuirassiers. From the looks of things it hadn't been a particularly easy fight, either. Her maid looked over at her, gave her a reassuring smile turned disconcerting with the amount of blood she had smeared over her face, and suggested, "Milady, we should get behind the desk. I don't think they'll be able to kick that door down but they might start shooting through it."

Arilin looked at her for a moment, then nodded, "Sounds good." She glanced over at the hussar, "You too, Relena."

They quickly rushed around the desk, picking up Carmen and setting her on the floor with them as they huddled down behind its reassuring bulk in the shadowy room, lit only by the light filtering in through the heavy curtains. Heavy jackboots thudded in the hallway, somehow loud even in the deep carpet. Someone rattled the doorknob and a voice called faintly outside, "It's locked!"

Another man yelled back, "We don't have time! Check the others, they can't have gone far!" The cuirassier cursed vilely and added, "This operation's going straight to hell. You, yeah, you, get your squad out on the balcony and set up a defensive position." Gunfire crackled down below and he added, "We might have to hold this place. Go!"

Boots thudded out in the hall and then, faintly, out onto the balcony. Someone swore faintly as they saw Chapman. A couple carbines barked and a hailstorm of bullets snapped back at them, drumming on the Residence's façade. Windows shattered as a man screamed hoarsely outside, and Becky quietly pulled her and Relena back under the desk and pushed them down onto the floor. They lay there, shivering and holding each other, as the battle swept over and into the Palace.

The storm of gunfire rattled the ground floor, flowed eerily up the stairwells and raged just below them for long minutes, punctuated by the occasional crack of a hand grenade or the shouts of a rush with bayonets. Gradually the hammering gunfire moved closer as the Guards Infantry drove the cuirassiers back into the entry hall, then up and around the stairs to the Residence's entryway. The infantry's battle-cry shook the Palace as they made one last rush, a couple carbines barking back at them ineffectually. Jackboots hammered on the carpet outside one last time, then the heavy thud of bodies as the infantry's rifles spoke.

A man's voice boomed outside, gruff and hoarse from shouting, "*Search the Residence, top to bottom!*" Arilin felt the hand gripping her heart ease as she recognized his voice. Colonel Strathclyde went on, "I want this area and Princess Arilin secured! She can't have gone far!"

Becky chuckled and murmured, "Looks like our rescuers are here." Pushing herself off of them, she smiled, "I'll handle this, just make sure they can see your hands when we come out. People get jumpy after gun-fights." She glanced at her hussar friend and went on, "Relena, help me with that couch you dragged across the door, please."

"Sure." The young Lady Strathclyde chirped.

Standing, her maid shouted, "We've got Princess Arilin in here! She's safe! We're coming out, give us a minute to get the door open, we barri-caded it!"

Relena added, "I'm in here too, Dad! I'm safe! Somehow!"

There was a commotion outside in the hallway and a moment later Colonel Strathclyde's voice floated back, dull through the heavy door but clearly delighted, "*Relena!* Come on, come out then, you men stand back. Go sweep the rest of this place for the enemy or something."

Becky and Relena quickly pulled the couch away from the door and her maid slowly pulled it open, saying, "Okay, we're co-"

"*Dad!*" Relena shoved past and launched herself into her father's arms outside, "Are you okay? *Tom!* What happened to your arm? Are *you* okay? Have the medics looked at you... no, of course not, they haven't because you're too stubborn for your own damn good, hey, *you*, yeah, you, medic, come with me, we're going to go look at this *bullet hole* my brother has!"

Becky gave her a look and shrugged, "Or we can do it this way."

Tom protested weakly outside and Relena cut him off, her voice re-ceding down the hall as she dragged him along, "You're already a hero, dummy, now shut up and come along, you can get Arilin to kiss you later."

Smiling slightly, Colonel Strathclyde stepped inside, straightening his jacket. He was a little mussed and seemed to have lost his hat in the fight-ing, but otherwise her rescuer looked as solid as ever. Giving her a short bow, he announced, "Milady, it's good to see you safe." Straightening up, he went on, "My regiment is at your service."

Taking a deep breath, Arilin shook her head and looked at the floor for a second. She wasn't shaking any more, and beyond the acid taste in the back of her mouth her stomach had settled. Setting her jaw, she looked back up at him and ordered, "Send a detachment across the street and secure the War Ministry. I'll establish my command post there." She snorted and went on, "I need to contact my father. Secure cable, no games this time."

Colonel Strathclyde's bushy eyebrows had risen in surprise as she spoke. Gathering himself, he nodded and replied, "Of course, milady. We'll get right to it." Lifting one of them back up, he went on, "And... Prince Alphonse?"

"Contact the guards on duty and have them close the High City gates." Arilin narrowed her eyes and spat, "Then send a column down to the Assembly and arrest him and the rest of his ministers. If they flee, we'll tear the city apart until we find them."

Strathclyde blinked once, slowly, then said, "These are powerful men, milady..." He trailed off, then gave her a wry smile, "Would you take a suggestion from an old soldier who's dealt with an awful lot of guilty people?"

Arilin opened her mouth to snap back at him, then closed it. Taking a deep breath, she replied, "What would you have me do, colonel?"

Reaching out, Colonel Strathclyde set a hand on her shoulder reassuringly and said, "Nothing." The old infantryman went on, "If they're guilty, milady, they'll flee and they'll be out of power. If they're innocent, or if they're good liars..." His graying moustache twitched up as he gave her a half-smile, "They'll come to you."

Sighing heavily, Arilin reached up and took his hand, then shook her head, "No, you're right." She smiled, "Thanks."

Beside her, Becky audibly exhaled. Arilin looked over and she chuckled, "I don't think we'll have many problems during your reign, milady."

"Well," Princess Arilin smiled wryly, "I'll need to make it to my coronation first."

Chapter 46
Victory and Defeat

Sophia's blood froze as she met June Anjanou's eyes, golden and gleaming behind his mask in the light of Tony's funeral pyre. The fire *screamed* as the tanks burned with flame pouring from every hatch and gap opened in their warping armor, brighter than the sun and raking the ground with hellish shadows. Her enemy's sword gleamed like an arc of pure fire, like some magical weapon from bygone days, as he drew it and brought it around, angling the blade down at his side as he paced slowly to her left. Trying to put the fire at his back, she realized. Trying to blind her, like this was some duel from the old days, a Valkyrie Knight and a Black Knight squaring off atop the walls of Drakenburg.

Masked shapes moved behind him and June raised his free hand to stop them. His dragoons paused, looking to him. Still pacing to get between Sophia and the fire, never taking his eyes off her, June's voice was deathly calm as he ordered, "Keep pushing. This one's mine."

"You're sure, boss?" One of them said, a woman. Ignoring her, June dropped his free hand to set it on the end of his sword's long grip, rotate it around to the level of his waist and snap the blade up to point straight at Sophia's eyes. The woman said something else, lost in the blood hammering in Sophia's ears as her fingers tightened on her spear's shaft, the grain of the wood ever so slightly rough in her hand. Dragoons rushed past, behind him. Behind *her*, she realized vaguely, though even glancing to look would have been her death.

Exhaling and then breathing in slowly, Sophia settled her weight and shifted her spear around, grasping it with her left hand and bringing its butt-end up beside her head, her right arm extended and pointing the gleaming blade straight at Anjanou's face. At his eyes, not the permanent leer of his steel war-mask, or at least what she could see of them with the fire behind him tearing at her eyes. Feeling sweat running down her face as his silhouette seared into her vision, Sophia paced to her right, her enemy shuffling with her to keep the fire to his back.

Sophia felt a twinge of despair as her vision blurred, spikes of pain shooting into her skull. June's stance was like a steel shield, impossible to break, death waiting for her in every line of attack. His eyes followed her, golden orbs in a sea of pitch-black shadow and a halo of blinding white flame, looking through her, into her *soul*, watching. Waiting, even for the slightest bit of weakness. A blink, a glance away, and he'd be upon her. And she would waver in seconds. So the only way out was through, *now*. Inhaling, Sophia flexed her back foot against the concrete, feeling rain-slickened grit and debris shift slightly under her boot's rubber sole as she bore down onto it. Time seemed to stand still for a long instant, June's sword shifting ever so slightly in its well of shadow as something like burning electricity sparked down her neck, through her back and into her legs.

Screaming, Sophia lunged at June, her spear flashing straight for his face. For his mask's right eye-hole, with every ounce of power that she'd ever had in her body behind it. Sparks burned against hellfire and her weapon bucked in her hands as the silhouette of June's helmet traced its way across the sea of flame before her eyes. She'd *hit hi-*, her thought cut off as his sword burned above her, June already inside of her spearhead and cutting down at her open right side.

Freed from his helmet, June's long, black hair streamed out behind him as he leapt at her. Twisting aside, Sophia yanked her spear back, scything it at June's legs from behind as she dodged. Her spear bucked in her hands again as he smashed it back down, pivoted to follow her and lunged again, sword screaming back up for her ribs. She leapt backwards, feeling the blade's wind as it passed inches from her face.

Yanking her spear back in midair, Sophia flexed her legs and snapped it forward again as she touched back down. June was ahead of her, some-how, shifting his sword overhead and hammering her weapon aside. Her spearhead bounced back to her right as Sophia recoiled frantically, pull-ing her spearhead back as she opened the distance just enough for her to pivot and whip her spearhead into another slash at June's legs.

Where his legs *should have* been, anyways. Sophia's eyes widened as June loomed before her again, *way* too close, still ahead of her somehow as he slapped her spear back. Splinters flew as his blade carved a gouge into the end of her spear's shaft down to where her blade's tang was set in-side it. She reeled back again, stabbing frantically as she retreated, once, twice, June battering her weapon aside as he charged. His sword hissed like a viper as he struck again and again, sparks flying as her spear bucked in her hands, the hard golden eyes behind the mask closer and closer with every strike.

Sophia's eyes widened as June caught one of the flanges of her spear-head with his blade and threw it aside, his legs flexing as he raised his sword to leap forward one last time. She desperately dodged aside, yank-ing her spear back through her hands and lashing out with its buttspike. Something cracked and her weapon bucked in her hands as she struck, her heart leaping in her chest as she thought, *I got hi-*

The back half of her spear's shaft seemed to hang in midair, slowly spinning under its own momentum behind June's shoulder. Her weap-on was suddenly, *wrongly*, light in her hands as she lost her balance and staggered backwards. Sophia glanced at the ground, taking her eyes off her enemy for an instant as she caught herself, then looked back up as she started bringing what was left of her spear around.

June's mask filled her world, inches from her face. Darkness closed around his flaming golden eyes as Sophia felt her feet come off the ground. The impact came first as she felt herself tumbling helplessly in an empty void, catching, slamming down again, bouncing nervelessly like a rag doll until she finally rolled to a stop. Then the pain, a trickle at first that turned into an avalanche, consuming her for an instant as she gasped for air, her vision clearing patchily as she struggled. She gasped again as she cast her fogged eyes around, her breath not quite catching. Where... *there* he was, maybe fifteen feet away, giving her an unreadable look as he raised his sword overhead and slashed the blade down through the air. Something bright and red slicked off of it, pattering onto the wet concrete and disappearing.

Almost of its own accord, her right hand closed around her spear's shaft. Not now... no, she wasn't beaten yet. *Not yet. Not God-damn yet.* She owed that much to Tony's family, to tell them how she'd failed their son. And she wasn't going to leave her mother and father, not at this *long-haired bastard's* hands. Gritting her teeth, Sophia kicked her feet out and rolled to her feet, broken spear in hand. Locking eyes with June again, she drew breath, got half a lungful and felt blood coating her mouth as she exhaled. In her *nose*, dripping down her face. *What in hell-*

"*Stop.*" June said, voice flat and all the more terrifying for it. He was pacing again, looking over at her levelly.

Sophia spat iron-tasting blood, "*Why sh-*" It welled up and choked her for a second, and she coughed weakly. Tried to, anyways. Gasping again, she got a breath that felt like half air and half liquid and tried again, "*Why.*"

The long-haired bastard snapped back, "Because you've been run through." Against her better instincts, Sophia pawed at her chest with her free hand, still keeping her eyes locked on him. Felt the right side of her chest under her breasts, where a stabbing pain had resolved out of the general mass of agony coursing through her body. Felt something hot and wet, and finally looked down her hand come back shockingly red as she pulled it away. Blood. Her blood.

No wonder she couldn't breathe. Sophia looked back at June, still pacing, sizing her up. There was no way she could beat him like this, not with a hole in her chest. She'd be lucky to get back to the medics... she had to run, *now*, while she still could. Gasping another quarter of a breath, she turned and flexed her legs.

"*Stop.*" He said it again, an *order* this time.

Sophia didn't know what made her do it, couldn't tell. Orders were meant to be obeyed, maybe. But his voice froze her in her tracks. Rounding back on him, she tried to growl through a mouthful of blood, *"I'm not sur..."* She spat, heaved for air again and finished weakly, *"Surrendering."*

"I don't care." June snarled back, "Now drop your spear and get on your *knees* before I change my mind about saving your life."

For a long moment Sophia stared at him. June just looked back at her levelly, fishing in a pocket with his free hand. Stopping pacing, he produced a blackened handkerchief and started to wipe his sword clean, her blood beading up and disappearing into what she realized was a horrifyingly bloodstained cloth. For an instant she felt like she was drifting, drowning, the rain turning to ice on her skin. She was *freezing*, It hadn't been that cold earlier, why was it... she looked down at her spear-arm. She was shaking like a leaf, and she didn't know which way was up any more.

Sophia's knees buckled and her spear clattered to the ground. Footsteps approached and a booted foot kicked it away. She was reaching after it instinctively when something bright and hard descended in front of her face and settled under her chin, its edge a cold, sharp line against her throat. Looking up, Sophia followed June's sword back up to his arm, then his face as he stood over her. She could only meet the golden eyes behind the mask for an instant.

"Your harness." He ordered, "Take it off."

"Y... yes," Sophia felt herself fumbling with her belt, the stiff leather uncooperative under her freezing fingers. She'd done it a thousand times, why wouldn't it come undone?

The cold line at her throat disappeared, and Sophia looked up to see June running his sword back into its scabbard as he walked around behind her. She started to twist around, but he set a hand against the back of her head and turned her back to face forwards, muttering, "You're not going to be able to do any of this for me, are you."

June's grip was firm, with a just a hint of neck-snapping strength underneath it. He knelt painfully across the back of her calves, straddling her from behind and pinning her to the ground, and Sophia moaned in pain as he brushed her numb hands away from her belt, protesting, "That hurts..."

"That's your problem, Miss Rose." June shot back. Quickly uncoupling her harness, he stripped it off her shoulders and threw it aside, then added dangerously, "And while we're talking, *I'm an officer.*"

Sophia fought for air while he reached around from behind her and worked his hands down her chest, unbuttoning her jacket in a few swift motions. Eyes widening, she protested, "*What...*" June snarled behind her, and she gasped again and added, "*...sir?*"

"You're quick." He remarked, then added as he yanked up her jacket and undershirt from behind to expose her bare back, "You need two chest seals. One front, one back. Just calm down and try to breathe... Christ, I got you *good*, didn't I?"

"Easy for you..." Sophia managed to take another quarter of a breath while June popped what sounded like one of the pouches of his harness open behind her, pulled something out and tore it open, "...to say, sir..." He stuck something down against her back that felt like plastic and she heard tape stripping behind her, "...you're not the one..." She gasped a couple times as he taped whatever it was onto her back, "...who's been *stabbed*."

"That look on your face when I did it *was* something else." *Long-haired bastard*, Sophia thought, biting her tongue. Snorting, June ripped something that sounded like cloth behind her and remarked snidely, "What, you're not going to call me a long-haired bastard? I know you're thinking it."

Seizing her arms with a grip like a steel vise, June pinioned them painfully behind her back and started wrapping something around her wrists. Yelping in pain, Sophia bit her lip for a moment before retorting, "I'm brave, sir..." She gasped again, only feeling something sucking horribly on the *front* of her chest as he finished tying a knot she'd probably have had trouble unpicking on a good day, and finished, "...not *stupid*."

God, she even sounded submissive to *herself*. Chuckling behind her, June's weight came off her calves as he replied, "Good girl. Now lean back so I can get this second one on you." Long-haired bastard. He was shifting around to crouch in front of her, and she obediently leaned back and supported her weight with her bound hands on the cold, wet concrete as June brushed her jacket aside and pulled up her undershirt. Hesitating for a moment, he gave her a look that was almost apologetic before he pulled it the rest of the way up past her breasts, wadded up her shirt's hem and set it on top of her cleavage.

Sophia bit back a yelp as she realized he was trying to keep it from falling back down over her wound as he worked. He'd stuck another piece of plastic onto her ribs, right under the sturdy elastic strip of her bra, and was starting to tape it down when she saw something move over his shoulder. Shifting her head a little, she saw another dragoon approaching from behind him, in the direction of the train station. A woman with dark hair sticking out from under her helmet. Much shorter than June's, she thought snidely. Long-haired bastard prettyboy. The woman's mask shifted as her eyebrows went up, and she exclaimed, "Christ, sir... you took her *alive?*" Her mask settled as her eyes narrowed, "It's a damn slaughterhouse in there, and most of it's *her* doing."

"I did the same to her unit once, sergeant." June replied coldly, starting to tape the chest seal down onto her ribs. It was already easier to breathe. He went on, "You were upstairs at the time, I recall." Sophia was already freezing, but she shivered at the memory... what of it she could remember anyways. Darkness and blazing moonlight through the windows, twitching lumps on the floor. June's sword burning like cold fire, and her bayonet spinning away uselessly in the darkness. And then she'd awoken under a table the next morning with a nasty headache. Her old enemy was going on, asking as he finished taping down her chest seal, "Who'd we lose?"

"Most of Third Squad." The woman spat, then went on nervously, "And that's not even the worst part, sir. That damn station's got three or four machine guns covering it, without the tanks we'll need the rest of the company to take the place."

Sophia tried to breathe in again, and her right lung actually felt like it *caught* and filled. The pounding in her ears she hadn't even noticed earlier died away, and as it did she realized there was a *hell* of a battle going on up towards the station. It sounded like... yeah, the woman was right. Three or four Royal machine guns, and as many Imperial ones spitting back at them from inside the warehouse. Hargrave's squad must have moved up to help out. After a long moment, June set his jaw and cursed, "*God-damn it.*" He turned to look over his shoulder at his sergeant, "You're sure, Tarai?"

"Not unless you can pull another miracle out of your hat." Sergeant Tarai replied, then added nervously, "By the way, sir, you're bleeding."

June pressed a hand to the side of his head for a moment. The right side, where her first thrust had taken his helmet off. His hand came back bloodier than before, and he snorted and gave Sophia a look, golden eyes narrowing behind his mask, "Good work, Miss Rose. I'm actually *impressed.*" Furious too, although she didn't get the sense it was really at *her.* Reaching out, he mercifully flipped her shirt back down over her chest and stood, growling, "Get up. I've got a *plan* for you."

Get up? How in the world was she supposed to... well, she'd been standing a minute ago and now she could breathe again. Kind of. Maybe she could get up. Pushing herself forward onto her knees, Sophia shakily got one leg under herself and pushed. Her legs shook like jelly and with her hands tied awkwardly behind her back she overbalanced and stumbled forward as she rose, straight into June's chest. Of course he caught her like it was nothing. Long-haired bastard.

"Sir?" Tarai was saying behind him.

Still holding her, June replied, "I'll give the order to cease fire. When I do, have the platoon gather up the wounded and pull back to the rest of the company."

"And the Royals, sir?" The sergeant asked.

June chuckled and patted Sophia on the shoulder, "That's what she's for." Sophia heard Tarai turn and hurry off towards the warehouse, and a moment later June spun her around and wrapped a powerful arm around both of hers from behind. It was viciously effective as a control hold and, she realized, would let him hide *behind* her almost perfectly. She groaned in pain as he pinioned her arms, which he ignored as he said, "Alright, Miss Rose, we're taking a walk."

He shifted behind her, and her spear clattered on the pavement. She looked over to see him working the toe of his boot under it to kick it up into his free hand effortlessly, and she protested, "What are you..."

Sophia felt June shift behind her again as he looked at her spearhead for a very long moment. Finally, he murmured, "Well, that explains it."

"Sir...?" She asked.

His grip on her arms tightened as he pushed her forward, towards the left-hand corner of the warehouse, saying, "Shut up and walk, corporal."

Long-haired bastard. Giving an iron-tasting sigh, Sophia replied meekly, "Yes, sir," and forced her legs to move. She was still shaking, but she could sort-of breathe, and June was holding her up as much as he was pushing her forward. Gradually they made their way up to the corner of the warehouse, where they'd be staring straight into Kelly's machine gun if they stepped out into the open.

June shifted behind her and a moment later she jumped as he blew his officer's whistle, deafeningly loud in her ears. Or tried to, anyways. His arm tightened around hers, yanking her back as soon as she moved. Her ears rang as he blew a long series of short blasts, and the world spun a little as she felt a wave of nausea pass over her. She probably would have fallen if he hadn't held her up. Finally, mercifully, he stopped, and as the ringing in her ears died down she felt him shift behind her again and her spearhead snake out past her, around the corner.

June waved it up and down a few times, and eventually the loud, deep Royal gunfire up ahead died away. Sophia's heart would have sank if her chest hadn't already been a mass of pain, and she swallowed a mouthful of blood and fought to keep from vomiting as he shoved her into the open. She glanced up for a second at the train station, not really that far away. Her vision was too blurry to see properly, but she could *feel* her friends' eyes on her. Someone was shouting up ahead, and she hung her head and tried to put one foot in front of the other.

Another wave of nausea washed over her, and Sophia stumbled as her stomach heaved. June yanked her back upright, muttering in her ear, "Keep it together Rose, just keep walking, you've got this..."

He sounded... strangely encouraging. Like he wasn't going to let her collapse on him. Not like she'd given him a reason not to be, ever since he'd stabbed her she'd done nothing but meekly submit to his orders. Sophia tried to reply, but her mouth was full of blood and acid. She spit it out and kept walking, one wobbly step at a time. June's grip on her arms somehow got even tighter, practically carrying her at spots as her head spun and her knees threatened to buckle, and every time it did he'd murmur something encouraging in her ear and she'd find her feet again. Eventually she felt the light change and brighten as they made it past the front of the warehouse, into the street in front of the station itself.

Familiar voices floated ahead of her, and Sophia looked up to see two shapes approaching through the haze in front of her eyes. She blinked hard and shook her head, and her vision cleared for a moment to see Lieutenant Gable and Major Matheson approaching from the station's main entrance. Gable looked like she'd seen a ghost as she met her eyes. Just then, she felt her legs give way as June bent and set her down on the cobblestones, the rain-slickened pebbles icy under her bare knees. She hadn't realized just how much he'd been holding her up. It was all she could do to keep her body upright as she knelt there and not collapse in the street. A moment later her spear clattered to the ground in front of her.

The officers were talking, June saying medical terms she vaguely remembered but couldn't grasp. Gable was replying, "...another one with her, what happened to him?"

There was long moment before June finally replied, "Dead."

Tony. Tony was dead, and it was her God-damn fault. He'd only joined the army because of *her.* He'd wanted to come along on this stupid suicide mission, he'd done something stupid and heroic to impress *her,* and it had worked. And now he'd be going back to Beth and his parents in a *shoebox,* and it was all her damn fault. How would she face them? How could she face *anyone?* Her father? Her eyes burned, and she realized she was crying.

Someone was working at her bound hands, and suddenly her wrists came free. A moment later something clattered behind her and she was pulled over backwards onto rough canvas. A stretcher. The medics must have come down. Sophia felt her body lurch and sway as they picked it up and hurried it into the station, then set her down harder than they really needed to. A lot of people were talking over her, some of them pretty familiar, but Sophia closed her eyes and just tried to breathe.

The medics fussed over her for a long while, stripping her jacket and undershirt off and pricking something painfully into the injured side of her chest, and something else into her shoulder. Whatever that was made it much easier for her to breathe, and the pain slowly dulled. They stuck something else into her arm and rolled her onto her right side, which also made it easier to breathe. A wool blanket settled across her, damp but still warm. Something scraped nearby and they left her alone for a moment, and Sophia opened her eyes blearily to see they had stuck an IV in her arm and set the jar of blood on top of Jenny's table from earlier. The clerk noticed her and gave her a reassuring smile.

She was about to closer her eyes again when, through the legs of the woman's chair, Sophia saw a jet of black smoke rising in the distance, off towards the bridge. As she watched it grew closer and closer, resolving into a boxy, familiar-looking locomotive, wrapped up in armor plating. It almost looked like the old *Bad News Express*... no, that was it exactly, it was another one of the same kind of armored train, coming in fast, brakes shrieking for a moment as the engineer slammed them on. Soldiers in smart gray uniforms were riding on the footplate and already visible in the open doors of the carriages.

The train screeched to a halt at the platform and for a moment her head rang with the sound of jackboots, sergeants barking orders, someone demanding to know where the enemy was. Lady Gable shouting directions back, and then in an instant their reinforcements were gone with a roaring battle cry still lingering in the air. Sophia closed her eyes and felt the world slip away.

They rolled her back onto her back at some point and hoisted her up onto what was probably the table. Someone stabbed her painfully in her injured side and Sophia woke up enough to give the doctor a dirty look as he worked on her. Then one of the medics jabbed her with more of what was probably morphine. She was giving him a nasty look when she realized someone was petting her hair and holding onto her free hand, just like her father had done for her when she was younger and she'd had a nightmare and needed comforting to get back to sleep.

Sophia looked up to see her father smiling down at her. "Dad?" She managed, "I…"

He chuckled, "Just relax, Sophie. You're going to be fine." He added, "You and Tony saved us all out there, you know."

Sophia shook her head, "Dad, he…"

"I know, I know." Her father smiled sadly, as darkness closed in around her vision, "We all lose friends. He'll be missed. I'm just happy I've still got you…" Her vision clouded over, and she didn't catch the rest of what he said.

She awoke to gentle rocking, and the rattle of steel wheels on rails. Opening her eyes, Sophia found herself still on her stretcher, lashed down across a row of train seats like a particularly bulky package with the countryside going by out the window. The rest of the car was filled with wounded soldiers, most of them worse-off than her. They had strapped her to her stretcher for good measure, but she was eventually able to flag down an overworked nurse and ask her where they were taking her.

The woman smiled and looked at the tag on her stretcher, "Looks like you're going to the Central Military Hospital in the High City. They've got a pulmonary unit there that's got some space."

Sighing, Sophia thanked the woman and closed her eyes. At least it sounded peaceful.

Epilogue 1

Two Paths Connected

The Central Military Hospital reminded her of a barracks, seemingly-endless galleries filled with hospital beds and their occupants. It probably had been one at some point, now that she thought about it. The only thing unmilitary about it was ironically the soldiers themselves. Not one of them had the same wounds, or would really ever recover quite the same way. They all seemed happy enough to see her, though, men sitting up in bed, smiling and calling out as she approached with her little entourage. Even in the High City, she supposed, a Royal visit was a special occasion.

At least they had the windows open and a cool, late-summer breeze was blowing through, so the place didn't stink of iodine and body fluids. Turning from one last smile and wave, Arilin stepped through the door the hospital's director was holding open for her back into the lobby. Already inside, Becky gave her a smile as she emerged, "You seem happy, milady."

Arilin glanced over at her, feeling her eyebrows go up in surprise, "Really?" She furrowed her brow and thought for a moment, "Well, I..." She sighed, "I think I needed to get out of the Palace. And this place puts it all in perspective."

Her maid chuckled, "I suppose it does, milady."

Shutting the door behind him, the director commented cluelessly, "I confess I *was* surprised to see you here, milady, with your father back in town. And usually we get more notice for this kind of thing." He smiled and joked, "I don't suppose you two had a fight?"

Arilin smiled back and lied through her teeth, "Oh, no, of course not!" Alphonse had fled alright, straight to her father to protest his innocence. And there she'd been this morning with bruises still on her *throat* from Alphonse's most loyal henchman and her father finally *deigned* to walk in and tell her the man hadn't had a thing to do with it and Chapman had been running his own little cabal of traitors. Oh, and also he wasn't pleased in the *slightest* with how she'd connived to get her mother out of town in another man's company, despite the fact the only thing the papers even *cared* about was Mr. Masters' whirlwind romance with Alyssa. There had been screaming. A lot of it, apparently loud enough to hear clearly through his office door. And, well... with the way it had turned out she was happy to have an excuse to stand for a while. Still lying, she went on, "He's just very busy with everything that's been going on, I figured I'd get out from underfoot."

The man smiled, believing everything she'd said, "Oh, I expect he is." He chuckled, "And I know how my girls like to disappear sometimes myself. Now, milady," He went on, "Where would you like to go next?"

She smiled, "I don't suppose you have some more serious cases around? Those men seemed happy for the visit, but I don't really think they *needed* it."

"Oh, certainly, milady!" The man looked around nervously, clearly trying to think of a ward he could take them with soldiers wounded badly enough to be suitably pathetic but not so badly mangled they would upset a princess like her. The burn ward was out of the question. So were the disfigurements, soldiers missing too many limbs... finally he had a good idea, looked back at her and smiled, "We've had a lot of pulmonary cases lately, I'm sure they'd love a visit." He explained, "Lungs, milady."

Arilin nodded gratefully, as though she'd needed the explanation, "Oh, I expect they would! Lead on." Three lies in as many minutes. She'd need to go confess her sins again at this rate.

The director ushered them into an elevator off the side of the lobby, large enough to take a patient on a gurney and a team of medics alongside. The operator, a Medical Corps girl in a sharp white dress uniform, stood to attention as they strode in and wordlessly slid the safety grating closed behind them. Looking at her, the director said, "Third floor, please. Pulmonary."

"Yes, sir." The girl replied, punching the button. Giving Arilin a nod, she went on, "Milady."

The elevator ground its way up, rattling a little alarmingly. Arilin wondered idly what it was like fully loaded as it creaked past the second floor and finally alighted on the third with a loud clank, the whole process probably taking longer than it would have to climb the stairs. She politely kept her thoughts on the matter off her face as the operator pulled the door open for them and the director ushered them out. Walking them down to another large, heavy door marked, 'PULMONARY WARD,' the man pulled it open, smiling, "Here you go, milady."

The air within smelled of disinfectant with an unpleasant, sour undercurrent. Not blood. Serum. The patients stirred as they entered, but nobody called out. Arilin heard a chair creak as it rolled back nearby, and looked over to see the duty nurse pushing herself back from her desk by the door to stand as they entered. The woman's eyes widened as she glanced between her and the director, and Arilin smiled reassuringly before she could get too nervous, saying, "Just here to see the patients. Anyone in particular you think I should see?"

Swallowing hard, the woman visibly took hold of herself and nodded, "Y-yes, milady. We've got a few I think would benefit from seeing you."

"Oh?" Arilin raised her eyebrows questioningly, then gestured for the woman to go ahead, "Please."

The woman led them around to a few patients, men wrapped with bandages and hissing through chest tubes. Judging by the shape of their chests beneath the bandages, it was a miracle some of them had survived. Most of them weren't very talkative, but Arilin held some hands and said some kind words as the nurse conducted her and her little group around the ward. She had just straightened up from her tenth patient, a man who had taken a machine-gun burst through the chest and somehow not only survived but was in good enough spirits to joke with her that he only needed one lung anyways, when the nurse cleared her throat nervously and ventured, "There's also another patient I, ah... I think you'd like to see, milady."

"Her?" The wounded man chimed in hoarsely, "Yeah, she's been having a rough time."

Her? Arilin raised an eyebrow, "You've got a girl in here somewhere?"

The nurse nodded, "Yes, milady. Here, come on."

The woman turned and led her a few rows farther down. A breeze stirred through the open windows as they stopped at the foot of the girl's bed, sweeping away the odor of iodine and pus for a moment with the earthy smell of late-summer greenery and the faintest hint of flowers from the hospital gardens below. She was sleeping, long, red-brown hair framing a strong-featured face and spilling across the pillow, snaking down to disappear under the sheets where she had pulled them up under the generous curve of her breasts. A chest tube hissed as she breathed in and out slowly, and an IV dripped into a catheter stuck into the girl's left hand where she had laid it out across her stomach. To Arilin, she looked... exhausted, more than anything else. Like sleep was a relief.

Arilin was opening her mouth to suggest they let her rest when she felt the girl's eyes on her. She hadn't even *stirred*, just woken instantly to fix her with a hard-edged glare, brilliant blue eyes narrowing for a just moment as Arilin met her gaze. Then they widened in shock. The girl's chest tube sputtered disconcertingly as she tried to clear her throat, finally managing weakly, "...m-milady."

Asleep with her eyes closed, the girl had just been pretty. Looking into them now, well... Arilin thought, with a twinge of annoyance, that she'd found a real rival. Keeping it off her face, she smiled, "Just visiting. What's your story, Miss...?"

"Rose." The duty nurse volunteered. Arilin glanced over at her, and she picked up the clipboard hanging from the foot of the girl's hospital bed and went on, "Sophia. Corporal, Twenty-Fourth Infantry Regiment."

Sophia Rose, 24th Infantry Regiment... Arilin felt her own eyes widening as she looked back at the girl. A corporal. She'd been promoted since Adrian had met her. Twice, and mentioned her in his letters each time. The first time he'd been rather skeptical about this girl in the infantry, apparently there because her father was some kind of senior sergeant in the regiment. The second time he had noted approvingly that she was in charge of her whole squad and seemed to be handling it rather well. Her eyes burned suddenly at the thought of her brother, and Arilin blinked quickly and smiled to hide it, "Good to finally meet you, Miss Rose." She explained, "My brother wrote me about you a couple times, you know."

Miss Rose blushed prettily. After a long moment she looked down and sighed, "I... I'm sorry about him, milady."

"Nothing to apologize for, Miss Rose." Arilin replied, "I blame the Empire myself."

The girl looked at the blanket for a long moment, set her jaw, and looked back up at her, "You don't understand, milady. We were *there*, up on Fire Ridge." She went on, as Arilin felt the floor disappear under her feet, "I wish we could have done more. I wish we'd *known*, we never would have let your brother through. It was... it just happened so fast." Giving her a nervous look, Miss Rose shook her head, "God, what am I saying? I'm sorry, milady."

Arilin inhaled sharply as she crashed back into her body. Setting her jaw, she strode over and knelt at the girl's bedside. Sophia Rose swallowed nervously as she looked back at her from only a couple feet away. Pulling back the girl's blanket a little, Arilin found her free hand and wrapped her hands around it, demanding, "What happened? Please... tell me, nobody's been able to."

After another long moment, Sophia met her eyes and squeezed her hands back reassuringly, her grip shockingly strong. And then she pushed herself up a little on her pillow, took a deep breath and told her. Arilin was crying by the time she was a quarter through. Sophia had lost *friends* on that Godforsaken battlefield atop Fire Ridge, and that was before the cavalry even showed up. They'd thought, after that brutal struggle that had left far too many infantrymen dead, they had finally broken through and the way was clear for her brother's regiment to ride. Her brother had dismounted himself to help the infantry clear away the wire, and the cuirassiers had poured through and charged into what should have been an easy fight. Just a few Imperial guns and whatever reserves the enemy could scrape together. Adrian had jumped his horse over Sophia where she sheltered in the last, captured Imperial trench, and after a minute of thundering hooves his regiment had disappeared through some sparse forest beyond the trench lines. There had been some distant shooting, but everyone thought the charge was going well.

Sophia paused for a moment, sighed heavily and gave her a sympathetic look, "Are you sure you want to hear this, milady?"

Arilin wiped her eyes. The hard linoleum floor was beginning to hurt her knees, and, still holding the girl's hand, she pushed herself up and sat on the edge of her bed. At least the mattress was mercifully soft. Looking back at Sophia, she grit her teeth and nodded, "Yes. Tell me."

"Have you ever heard of June Anjanou, milady?" Sophia asked.

Arilin raised her eyebrows in surprise, "Yes, actually, he's rather... scary, I understand."

"Well there he was, up on his horse on top of a hill we could see out in the distance. Guy's got hair down to his waist, and it was blowing in the wind." Sophia grimaced and went on, "He had his sword out, and he waved it and charged down towards us and out of sight. He probably only had twenty guys with him... honestly, milady, I thought he was done for."

"What happened then?" Arilin asked.

Sophia sighed again, "Well, milady, a couple minutes later the rest of his damn *regiment* came over that hill." Arilin felt her eyes widening as the girl went on, "I've never seen so many dragoons in my life, before or since." Sophia shook her head, "First time I've ever seen Imperial colors out, too... God, there were a lot of them. And, well... milady..."

The girl had trailed off. An icy rock sinking in her stomach, Arilin murmured, "What... what then?"

After a too-long pause she went on, quietly, "Your brother's regiment..." Sophia looked up, her eyes deep sapphire pools as she finished, "It broke, milady."

Arilin's eyes narrowed as she snapped back at her, "That *can't* be."

"Can and was, milady." Sophia shot back bluntly. After a moment she shook her head, "There must have been a couple hundred cuirassiers that fell back just in front of us alone. One of their officers was trying to rally them, and, well... the dragoons were through the trees by that point."

"What do you mean?" Arilin demanded.

"They got machine-gunned." Sophia's own eyes narrowed as she met her gaze, suddenly hard and sharp enough to send a chill up her spine, "We spent the next hour having a firefight with the dragoons *through* them. What was left of them, anyways."

Someone gasped behind her. Shaking her head, Arilin glared back into the girl's now-terrifying eyes, "And Adrian?"

Sophia shook her head, "I don't know what happened. But afterwards, well, June came out and tried to get us to surrender. He told us... told *me* that he'd seen him die."

Arilin felt her eyes narrow further, "You think he killed him?"

"No." Sophia replied without hesitating. Arilin felt her eyebrows go up in surprise as she went on, "He would have said it if he had, and honestly, milady, June would have taken him prisoner. It's just how he is."

Arilin snorted suddenly, about the closest she could come to a laugh as the thought occurred to her, "You sound like you know the guy."

Sophia chuckled, her chest tube sputtering disconcertingly as she did, "I guess I do by now, milady. I keep running into him."

Raising an eyebrow, she asked, "Really?" Arilin changed the subject, "How'd you get hurt? You don't seem... well, as bad off as most of the guys here, honestly."

The girl shook her head, "We were, well..." She trailed off, biting her lip for a moment as she obviously skipped over a story she didn't care to tell, "He ran me through."

"Wait, *June* did?" Arilin came back incredulously, "I've heard, I mean..."

"He's good?" Sophia gave her another hard look, "Milady, he's *incredible*. I was using my spear and I barely had a chance. Scratched him once, that's it."

"How'd you..." The girl blushed and looked away suddenly, as though she was ashamed. *He would have taken him prisoner, it's just how he is.* That explained how she knew *that* with such certainty. It was bad enough to lose a fight, but Sophia probably owed June her *life* on top of it. No wonder she was ashamed, he'd probably humiliated her. Arilin changed tack quickly, "Your spear, you said?"

Sophia looked back at her and brightened instantly, "Oh, yes, milady! It's, uh," With an IV in one hand, Arilin holding the other, and a tube snaking out the right side of her chest, the girl was well and truly pinned in place. Glancing at the floor, she went on, "It's under the bed, if you want to see."

"Sure! Uh..." Arilin let go of her, leaned over and fished under the bed. Feeling a wooden shaft, her fingers closed around it and she retrieved a bundle of wooden shaft segments tied to a spearhead with its own scabbard. The segments didn't seem long enough to make a full shaft, and looking at one of them she could see why. Someone had cut through it at an angle, so cleanly she couldn't even feel splinters as she ran her thumb along the break. Clearly the work of an amazing swordsman.

And that blade... furrowing her brow slightly, Arilin separated it from the shaft pieces, grasped it by its long tang and carefully pulled the scabbard free. The blade, gouged and nicked with recent use but still gleaming and razor-sharp, was broad, almost like part of a sword, and flared at the base like a shallow 'Y'. Looking closely she could see shades of faint designs in the steel. It must have been sharpened without much care to preserve the inscriptions... the inscriptions. She felt her eyes widen as she realized she'd seen something like this before once, with the silvered inlays intact. She was just working through the implications when Sophia's voice broke her out of her reverie, "Milady...?"

Arilin looked over to see Sophia giving her a quizzical look. Nodding at the spearhead, she asked the girl, "Adrian mentioned you'd won the battalion's bayonet tournament... who taught you how to fight?"

"My father, milady..." Sophia went on questioningly, "Why do you ask?"

Arilin ignored the question, "Did he teach you anything else, any *lore?*"

The girl shook her head, "He just said it was a bunch of nonsense and I didn't need to learn it."

"This is a Hunter's spear." Arilin explained, "Which, well, if you're as good at fighting as you seem to be, and if you landed a hit on June Anjanou you're clearly *very* good, explains why."

Sophia gave her a confused look, "You mean, like... werewolves and vampires?"

Arilin nodded, "Yes." If Carmen was at all correct she had a vampire problem. She certainly had a problem with *mortal* enemies. Making a decision, she stood suddenly and looked down at this mysterious girl, "Miss Rose, I have an offer for you. I don't suppose you know how to clean?"

She chuckled nervously and replied, "PFC stands for Professional Floor Cleaner, milady."

Arilin laughed, "Better than the last girl I recruited." Turning, she looked at her escort for the day, "Becky, what do you think?"

Rebecca nodded, "She'll fit right in, milady." She gave her a look, "You know you owe me for Carmen."

"So I do." Arilin turned back to Sophia where she lay beneath her and went on, "As I'm sure you've heard, some people tried to murder me last week. I'm in the market for servants who *really* know how to fight." She smiled, "How'd you like to become a Royal maid, Miss Rose?"

Sophia blinked, thought for a moment, then laughed and looked back up at her, "That doesn't seem like a question I get to say no to, milady."

Her smile broadened, "It's not. I'll talk to the War Ministry and have you transferred properly. Don't worry, we pay *very* well." Turning again, she looked at the nurse, "How long until Miss Rose is discharged?"

The woman looked at her clipboard, "Should be another week in bed, then the tube comes out and she'll be fit for light duty. She's got a couple broken ribs, so probably another month until she's fully healed."

"Very well then." Turning back to Sophia, Arilin nodded, "Miss Rose, I'll be seeing you next week."

Sophia smiled, brought up her free hand and saluted from her hospital bed, "I'll work on my curtsey, milady."

Epilogue 2
Darkness and Abyss

The penthouse elevator stopped with a quiet chime and a barely perceptible bump. The guard at his front door was already at attention at the door opened, and the man saluted as he emerged. A plainclothes officer from the High City Police, still as loyal to him as ever. Prince Alphonse gave him a nod, and the guard helpfully dropped his salute and pulled the door open for him. Before he stepped inside, Alphonse asked, "Is anyone else in? Maids?"

The man shook his head, "No, my lord." He smiled slightly, "Unless you'd like to arrange for one."

"No need." Alphonse went on coldly, "I want my privacy this evening. No visitors."

"Of course, my lord." The man nodded, swinging the door shut smoothly behind him as he stepped through. Throwing the deadbolt behind himself, Adrian turned and strode through the penthouse entryway, emerging into the suite's palatial parlor. The staff had helpfully left the lights on for him, and the room gleamed with gilding and rich wood. His boots sank into the plush carpet underfoot as he strode over to the windows lining the wall and yanked the curtains open.

The High City's lights unfolded before him, rolling out across the great promontory into the distance. The Royal Sapphire Hotel was located convenient to the Assembly in the east of the city, and what it lacked in views of Sapphire Bay it made up for as the best overlook out onto the High City itself. Off to his left he could see the grand spires of Saint Valeria's Cathedral rising high above the surrounding buildings, themselves bowing at a respectful distance around its plaza's protective glacis. Looking straight ahead he could see the bell towers of the Royal Academy rising at the edge of the city through his own ghostly reflection in the glass.

Alphonse saw the muscle at the corners of his jaw clench slowly as he looked at it. That idiot Chapman had somehow, *somehow*, managed to screw up the simplest operation in the world. And he'd done it *twice*. March some soldiers into the Royal Academy and take one little girl out in handcuffs, and stand down a few slightly-older girls guarding the Palace. *His* Palace, the imposing building blazing off to his right, hulking above the distant rooflines. With binoculars he could probably make out the *little girl* with *his* birthright enjoying the night air out on *his* balcony.

He'd planned to leave her alive after his brother abdicated, let the man go quietly into exile with his whore of a wife and his worthless family... but that wasn't possible any more. If his idiot brother could start his reign with his finger on a trigger, there was no reason *he* couldn't. He'd been too clever by half, his plan had blown up in his face, and only the fact that

William was as dumb as he was trusting had saved him. Apparently he'd even *grounded* the girl after she'd called him out on it. The man wasn't just a moron, he was a genuine romantic, and he didn't seem to realize the fact he'd *murdered their father in cold blood* might have damaged their relationship.

Something dark moved in the glass between Alphonse and the Palace, two blood-red lights slowly brightening in the reflection overlaid on top of the Residence. They looked like sharp, angular eyes, glowing like portals into Hell. He was used to this, he should have been used to this, but Alphonse's skin crawled as cold air washed over his face. His... *associate* let him stew for a few long moments as he fought to keep from shivering. Then a few more. Finally, Alphonse took a long, shallow breath and turned, snapping, "Do you *have* something for me, or are you just here to gloat?"

It stared back at him from where it floated in midair across the room, just high enough to look down on him. The burning eyes in the jet-black mask were somehow ice-cold as they bored into his own, and through them into his *soul*. After another long moment the lower plate of the mask, where it would go over the jaw of a person insane enough to put it on, tilted slightly as the *thing* smiled contemptuously. Gritting his teeth, Alphonse turned back to the window and gestured at the Palace angrily, "I've lost very little from this, you know, and gained a *great deal*." He snorted, "My brother's eating out of the palm of my hand, and he's the one I need to worry about. That *girl* is just an annoyance." He glanced back over at it and remarked, "You're welcome to have her afterwards, by the way."

"Very generous of you." It had a voice like steel ribbons, cold, smooth and razor-edged. It seemed to have gotten... *stronger* since last time they spoke. It wasn't whispering any more. He'd hated that. He hated a *lot* of things about it. It went on, the voice instantly breaking him out of his thoughts, "You're so quick to give away things you don't own, *prince*."

"I'll own her soon enough." Alphonse snorted, "Her and her sister. The one you're *really* interested in."

"That girl is something special." It replied, "I owe her much already."

Alphonse snorted, "You do seem... *healthier*."

"Very much so." Alphonse felt his skin crawl as the room chilled further, his breath steaming in front of his face. The lights flickered, and as he turned he saw something like shadows *congealing* underneath the mask. Shadows veined with hellish fire as they knit together into something like the outline of a person, the demonic mask dropping about a foot to settle onto its head. The outline sharpened and filled out, its waist tightening into a disconcerting hourglass shape as it developed shapely hips and a generous bust. He finally shivered involuntarily as the *thing's* arms and legs coiled into existence, long and perfect and made of the abyss. It approached, now looking up at him as it padded silently across the carpet. Its voice had risen by an octave as it said, "Enough to do *this*."

"I... I can see that." He managed nervously. The room was ice-cold, but he was somehow sweating.

Setting an inky hand against his chest, it slowly ran it up the front of his uniform jacket, trailing its fingertips across the standing collar that protected his throat to catch his chin. It touch was like silk and burning ice, and its flaming eyes bored into his own, flaying his mind away and laying his soul bare to its... to *her* gaze. Her mask tilted as she smiled again, predatorily, like a cat playing with its food, "You're pleased, my prince?"

Swallowing heavily, Alphonse stammered, "I... well, yes, but..."

"You thought I was a man?" The Faceless Queen laughed, her voice like steel bells, "How insulting, Prince Alphonse! I was born an *elf*."

"I didn't mean..." He managed.

"Of course you didn't, my prince." Those lovely, demonic, flaming eyes of hers narrowed in a smile as her fingers slid into the flap of his collar, "But you need some *female* companionship right now."

Alphonse gasped for air, his world swimming as she unhooked his collar and slowly started working her way down his cuirassier's tunic, her fingers like fire against his chest, "I... I mean..."

"It's *yes*." Her burning eyes flashed dangerously behind her mask. Her unholy gaze was a knife through his skull, "Yes, *my Queen*."

Trembling, Alphonse surrendered, "Yes, my Queen."

Postscript

The circumstances of this book's creation were at the same time much more and much less intensive than those of *The Maiden's War*. I wrote the vast majority of *Valkyrie Knight* while going to law school from 2019 to 2022, and my personal life during this time was honestly quite boring. I attended class regularly, read legal textbooks by the foot, and eventually took and passed the bar. The world outside, however, has darkened considerably from the comfortable days of the last decade. We've seen most of the Four Horsemen in the last few years, and if you're reading this any time close to its publication in December 2022 you deserve congratulations for making it through the multiplying crises of our age. If you're reading this well *after* its publication, we either made it through and you deserve a chuckle at my expense, or I'm pleased that my work has survived into the post-apocalypse.

In these trying times escapist entertainment is almost a requirement to keep your sanity, and my decision early on to avoid real-world political messages gets better by the day. This book is *not* an elaborate political analogy, even on a subtle level. Nothing raises my own hackles quite like some crude reference or clumsy exchange ripping me out of a fictional world as the writer lets me know exactly what they think about the Current Thing in the Current Year, and unfortunately modern entertainment is rife with this kind of behavior by creators. I have fans across the entire political spectrum, including parts of the it I vehemently disagree with, and you can rest assured that, no, I have not taken any shots at you here. The Five Moons is its own world with its own fictional concerns.

I wrote this book surrounded by friends, and had the opportunity to watch some of them grow and develop as creators in turn. My good friend and fellow US Army veteran Michael Rose published his own book, *The Farvithia Chronicle*, earlier this year. It's a wonderful high fantasy story reminiscent of the old *Shining Force* games (which we both loved) and well worth a look. My artist, Bekarys Zhabagin, is better at his craft than ever, and he did incredible work bringing my characters to life for this new project. My only complaint is that he's – very justifiably – charging more for commissions these days. At this rate I'll be bidding against art galleries to get him for my next book!

Thanks for reading *Valkyrie Knight!* I hope you'll join me again as Sophia, Arilin and June's adventures continue!